Wild Mountain Thyme

Rosamunde Pilcher

1

FRIDAY

Once, before the bypass had been built, the main road ran through the heart of the village, a constant stream of heavy traffic that threatened to rattle the heart out of the gracious Queen Anne houses and the small shops with their bulging windows. Woodbridge had been, not such a long time ago, simply a place you drove through in order to reach some other place.

But since the opening of the bypass, things had changed. For the better, said the residents. For the worse, said the shopkeepers and the garage proprietors and the man who had run the lorry-drivers' restaurant.

Now, the people of Woodbridge could go shopping and cross the road without taking their lives into their hands or having their pet dogs securely leashed. At weekends, children with brown velvet caps jammed down over their eyebrows, and mounted on a variety of shaggy steeds, trotted off to their local pony club meets, and already there had been a positive flowering of open-air events, garden parties and charity fêtes. The lorry-drivers' café became an expensive delicatessen, a ramshackle tobacconist sold out to a precious young man who dabbled in antiques, and the Vicar had begun to plan a festival for next summer, in order to celebrate the tricentenary of his small, perpendicular church.

Woodbridge had come into its own again.

The clock on the church tower was pointing to ten minutes to twelve on a chill February morning when a big shabby Volvo turned the corner by the saddlers, and came slowly down the main street between the wide cobbled pavements. The young man at the wheel saw the whole long empty curve of it, his eye undeflected by thundering streams of traffic. He saw the charming irregularity of houses and bow-fronted shops, the beckoning perspective, and a distant glimpse of willow-fringed meadows. Far above, in a wintry sky full of sailing clouds, a plane droned in towards Heathrow. Otherwise it was very quiet, and there seemed to be scarcely anybody about.

He passed a pub, newly painted and with tubs of bay trees at either side of the door; a hairdresser, Carole Coiffures; the wine merchant with his bow-fronted bottle-glass window, and an antique shop stuffed with over-priced relics of better days.

He came to the house. He drew the car in to the pavement's edge and switched off the engine. The sound of the plane died, thrumming, into the morning quiet. A dog barked, a bird sang hopefully from a tree, as though deluded that the thin sunshine meant that spring had come. He got out of the car, slammed the door shut, and stood looking up at the flat, symmetrical face of the house, with its fanlighted door and pleasing proportions. Flush on the pavement it stood, a flight of stone steps leading up to the front door and tall sash windows discreetly veiled in filmy curtains.

It was, he thought, *a house that had never given anything away*.

He went up the steps and rang the doorbell. The surround of the bell was brass and brightly polished, as was the lion's-head knocker. The door was painted yellow, new and bright-looking, without a sun blister or a scratch upon it. In the lea of the house, out of the sun, it was cold. He shivered inside his thick donkey jacket and rang the bell again. Almost at once there were footsteps, and the next instant the yellow front door opened for him.

A girl stood there, looking rather cross, as though she had been interrupted, disturbed by the bell, and wanted to be put out for as little time as possible. She had long, milk-fair hair, and she wore a tee shirt bulging with puppy fat, an apron, knee stockings and a pair of scarlet leather clogs.

"Yes?"

He smiled and said, "Good morning," and her impatience instantly melted into quite a different expression. She had realised that it wasn't the man about the coal, or someone collecting for the Red Cross, but a tall and personable young man, long-legged in his well-scrubbed jeans, and bearded like a Viking. "I wondered if Mrs Archer was in?"

"I'm so sorry." She looked quite sorry, too. "But I'm afraid not. She is gone to London today. To shop."

She was, he reckoned, about eighteen, and from her accent, some sort of Scandinavian. Swedish, probably.

He said, with what he hoped was engaging ruefulness, "Isn't that just my luck? I should have phoned or something, but I thought I'd take the chance of catching her at home."

"Are you a friend of Mrs Archer's?"

"Well, I used to know the family, some years ago. But we've been . . . well, sort of out of touch. I was passing, on my way up to London from the West Country. I thought it would be nice to come and say hello. Just an idea I had. It doesn't matter."

He began, diffidently, to back away. As he had hoped, the girl delayed him.

"When she comes back, I could tell her that you have been here. She will be back in time for tea."

At that moment, with splendid timing, the church clock began to chime for midday.

He said, "It's only twelve o'clock now. I can scarcely hang around till then. Never mind, I'll maybe be down this way again some time." He looked up and down the street. "There used to be a little café here . . ."

"Not any more. It is a delicatessen now."

"Well, perhaps I can get a sandwich in the pub. It seems a long time since breakfast." He smiled down at her from his great height. "Goodbye, then. It's been nice meeting you." He turned as though to leave. He could feel her hesitation, her decision, as though he had directed them himself. She said, "I could . . ."

With one foot already on the upper step, he turned back.

"What could you do?"

"Are you really an old friend of the family?" She longed to be put out of her doubt.

"Yes, I really am. But I have no way of proving it to you."

"I mean, I was just going to get the lunch for myself and the baby. I could get it for you, too."

He looked reproachful, and she began to blush. "Now, that's very foolhardy of you. I'm sure you've been warned, time and time again, about strange men coming to the door."

She looked distressed. She obviously had. "It is just that, if you are a friend of Mrs Archer's, Mrs Archer would want me to ask you in." She was lonely and probably bored. All au pair girls seemed to be lonely and bored. It was an occupational hazard.

He said, "You mustn't get yourself into trouble."

Despite herself, she began to smile. "I don't think I will."

"Supposing I steal the silver? Or start trying to make violent love to you?"

For some strange reason this possibility did not alarm her in the least. Rather, she seemed to regard it as a joke, and so to be reassured. She even gave a small, conspiratorial giggle. "If you do, I shall scream and the whole village will come to my rescue. Everybody knows what everybody does in Woodbridge. Everybody talks all the time. Chat, chat. Nobody has a secret." She stepped back, opening the yellow door wide. The long, pretty hallway was invitingly revealed.

He hesitated for just long enough to make it seem genuine and then shrugged, said, "All right," and followed her over the threshold, wearing the expression of a man who has been finally, reluctantly, persuaded. She closed the door. He looked down into her face. "But you may have to take the consequences."

She laughed again, excited by the little adventure. She said, in hostess-like tones, "Would you like to take off your coat?"

He did so, and she hung it up for him.

"If you would like to come to the kitchen, perhaps you would like a glass of beer?"

"Well, thank you."

She led the way, down the passage that led to the back of the house, to the modern kitchen, built out into the south-facing garden and flooded now with pale sunlight. Everything shone with cleanliness and order: bright surfaces, a gleaming cooker, stainless steel and polished teak. The floor was blue and white tiles, which looked Portuguese. There were plants along the window-sill, and a table at the window was laid for lunch. He saw the high chair, the bright plastic table mat, the small spoons, the Beatrix Potter mug.

He said, "You've got a baby to look after."

She was at the fridge, getting him a can of beer. "Yes." She closed the fridge door and went to take a pewter mug from a hook on the scrubbed pine dresser. "He's Mrs Archer's grandchild."

"What's he called?"

"Thomas. He's called Tom."

"Where's he now?"

"In his cot, having his morning rest. In a moment, I'll go up and get him, because he'll be ready for his lunch."

"How old is he?"

"Two." She handed him the can and the mug, and he opened the can and poured it carefully, without a head.

"I suppose he's staying here, is he? I mean, his parents are away, or something."

"No, he lives here." Her smiling, dimpled face took on an expression of woe. "It's very sad. His mother is dead." She frowned. "It is funny that you do not know that."

"I told you I've been out of touch since I last saw the Archers. I had no idea. I *am* sorry."

"She was killed in a plane crash. She was coming home from a holiday in Yugoslavia. She was their only child."

"So they look after the grandchild?"

"Yes."

He took a mouthful of beer, cool and delicious. "What about the father?"

The girl had turned her rounded back on him, was stooping to investigate something in an oven. A fragrant smell filled the kitchen, and his mouth watered. He had not realised how hungry he was.

She said, "They were separated. I don't know anything about him." She closed the oven and straightened up. She gave him another searching look. "I thought you would have known about that, too."

"No. I don't know about anything. I was out of this country for a bit. I was in Spain and I was in America."

"Yes. I see." She looked at the clock. "If I leave you, will you be all right? I have to go up and get Thomas."

"If you're sure you can trust me not to help myself to

the spoons." He was teasing her, and she cheered up and smiled again. "I don't think you'll do that." She was wholesome, creamy as a tumbler of milk.

He said, "What's your name?"

"Helga."

"Are you Swedish?"

"Yes."

"They're lucky, the Archers. I mean, having someone like you."

"I'm lucky, too. It is a good job, and they are very kind. Some girls get terrible places. I could tell you some stories."

"Do you go to classes in the afternoons?"

"Yes. English and history."

"Your English sounds perfect to me."

"I am doing literature. Jane Austen."

She looked so pleased with herself that he laughed. He said, "Run along, Helga, and get that baby. I'm starving, even if he isn't." For some reason she blushed again, and then went away and left him alone in the shining, sunny kitchen.

He waited. Heard her go upstairs, her footsteps cross the floor of the room above. He heard her voice, speaking quietly; curtains being drawn back. He laid down his beer and went, soft-footed, rubber-soled, back down the hall and opened the door at the bottom of the staircase. He went in. There were the chintzes, the grand piano, the orderly bookshelves, the unassuming watercolours. A fire had been laid in the Adam grate, but was, as yet, unlit. Even so, the room was warm with central heating and heavy with the scent of hyacinths.

Its neatness, its order, its air of well-bred, well-moneyed smugness, enraged him, as it always had. He longed for muddled knitting, strewn newspapers, a dog or a cat on some familiar cushion. But there was nothing. Only the slow ticking of the clock on the mantelpiece bore witness to any sort of activity.

He began to prowl around. The grand piano was a repository of photographs. Mr Archer in a top hat, proudly displaying some minor order bestowed upon him by the Queen at Buckingham Palace; his moustache like a toothbrush, his morning coat strained across his spreading stomach. Mrs Archer as a misty girl, dressed for her wedding. The baby, propped up on a fur rug. And Jeannette.

He picked up the stylised portrait and stood, looking down at it. Pretty, as she had always been pretty. Sexy even, in her extraordinary, fastidious way. He remembered her legs, which were sensational, and the shape of her well-manicured hands. But nothing much else. Not her voice, not her smile.

He had married her because the Archers hadn't wanted their daughter to be the mother of an illegitimate baby. When the disastrous news had been broken to them that their precious only child had been having an affair with, actually living with, that dreadful Oliver Dobbs, their tidy little world had fallen apart. Mrs Archer had taken to her bed with a *crise de nerfs*, but Mr Archer, harking back to his brief years as a soldier, had straightened his tie and his back and taken Oliver out to lunch at his London club.

Oliver, unimpressed and not a little amused, had recorded the subsequent discussion with the detachment of a totally impartial observer. Even at the time it had seemed as unreal as a scene from an old-fashioned play.

Only daughter, Mr Archer had said, plunging in at the deep end. Always had great plans for her. No question of recriminations, hindsight never did a man any good, was obvious to him that Oliver came from a good family, and he knew for a fact that Oliver had been to a well-known school, so was there any reason that he had to work in a fish-and-chip shop?

Oliver said that yes, there was a reason. The reason

was that he was a writer, and the fish-and-chip shop job was the sort of undemanding occupation he needed to keep himself alive in order to be able to write.

Mr Archer cleared his throat again and began to talk about Oliver's parents, and Oliver told Mr Archer that his parents, who lived in Dorset, were not only penniless, but unforgiving. Living on an army pension, they had denied themselves everything in order to be able to scrape up enough money to send Oliver to that exclusive school. When he had finally walked out of it at the age of seventeen, they had tried, in a broken-hearted sort of way, to persuade him to follow some sensible, conventional course. To join the army, the navy, perhaps. To become a chartered accountant, a banker, a lawyer. But he could only be a writer, because by then he already was a writer. Defeated at last, they washed their hands of their son, cutting him off without the proverbial shilling, and remaining sulkily and stubbornly incommunicado.

This obviously disposed of Oliver's parents. Mr Archer tried another tack. Did Oliver love Jeannette? Would he make her a good husband?

Oliver said that he didn't think he would make her a good husband, because he was so terribly poor.

Mr Archer then cleared his throat for the third and last time and came to the point. If Oliver agreed to marry Jeannette and provide the baby with a legitimate father, then he, Mr Archer, would see to it that . . . er . . . financially, the young couple would be all right.

Oliver asked, how all right? And Mr Archer elucidated, his eyes steadily holding Oliver's across the table, but his anxious hands shifting his wineglass, straightening a fork, crumbling a roll. By the time he was done, his place setting was in chaos, but Oliver realised that he was on to a good thing.

Living in Jeannette's flat in London, with a steady income coming in each month to his bank account, he could give up the job in the fish-and-chip shop and get down to finishing his play. He already had a book under his belt, but that was still with an agent, and the play was something else, something that he had to get down, before it ate his soul out like some ghastly cancer. That was how it was with writing. He was never happy unless he was living two lives. A real life with women and food and drinking in pubs with friends; and the other life, teeming with his own people, who were more vital and sympathetic than anyone he ever met in the normal course of events. And certainly, he thought, more interesting than the Archers.

Over the lunch table, the two men had come to an agreement. Later, it was consolidated by lawyers' letters and drafts and signatures. Oliver and Jeannette were duly married in a registry office, and this seemed to be all that mattered to the Archers. The alliance lasted no more than a few months. Even before the child was born, Jeannette had gone back to her parents. Boredom she could stand, she said, and loneliness too, but abuse and physical violence were more than she was prepared to endure.

Oliver scarcely noticed her going. He stayed in her flat and peacefully, without any sort of interruption, finished the play. When it was done, he left the flat, locked the door and posted Jeannette the key. He took himself off to Spain. He was in Spain when the baby was born, and still there when he read, in some week-old paper, of his wife's death in the Yugoslavian air disaster. By then Jeannette had become a person who had happened to Oliver a long time ago, and he discovered that the tragedy aroused little emotion in him. She belonged to the past.

Besides, by then he was well into his second novel. So he thought about Jeannette for perhaps five minutes and then plunged thankfully back into the company of the infinitely more compelling characters who were now going about their business within the confines of his own head.

When Helga came downstairs again, he was back in the kitchen sitting on the window seat, with his back to the sun, and enjoying his beer. The door opened, and she appeared, carrying the child in her arms. He was larger than Oliver had imagined, dressed in red overalls with a bib and a white sweater. His hair was a sort of reddish gold, like new pennies, but Oliver couldn't see his face, which was buried in Helga's delectable neck.

Helga smiled at Oliver over Thomas's shoulder.

"He's shy. I have told him that there is a visitor, and he doesn't want to look at you." She bent her head to say to the little boy, "Look, you silly. He is a nice man. He has come to have lunch with us."

The child made a mooing, negative sound and buried his face still deeper. Helga laughed and brought him over to his high chair and inserted him into it, so that at last he had to let go of her. He and Oliver looked at each other. The child had blue eyes and seemed sturdy. Oliver didn't know much about children. Nothing, in fact. He said, "Hi."

"Say hello, Thomas," Helga prompted. She added, "He does not like to talk."

Thomas stared at the stranger. One-half of his face was red from being pressed into a pillow. He smelled of soap. Helga clipped a plastic bib around his neck, but he didn't take his eyes off Oliver.

Helga went to the stove to collect their meal. From the oven she took a shepherd's pie, a dish of Brussels sprouts. She put a little into a round dish, mashed it up with a fork and set it down on the tray of Thomas's high chair. "Now, eat it up," and she put his spoon into his hand.

"Does he feed himself?" asked Oliver.

"Of course. He's two now, not a baby any more. Are

you, Thomas? Show the man how you can eat up your dinner." Thomas responded by laying down his spoon. His blue eyes fixed, unwinking, on Oliver, and Oliver began to feel self-conscious.

"Here," he said. He set down his glass of beer, and reaching over, took up the spoon, filled it with squashed meat and potato, and steered it towards Thomas's mouth. Thomas's mouth opened, and it all disappeared. Thomas, munching, continued to stare. Oliver gave him back the spoon. Thomas finished his mouthful and then smiled. A good deal of the smile was shepherd's pie, but there was, as well, the glimpse of an engaging double row of small pearly teeth.

Helga, putting down Oliver's plate in front of him, caught sight of the smile.

"There now, he has made a friend." She brought another plate and sat herself at the head of the table, so that she could help Thomas. "He's a very friendly little boy."

"What does he do all day?"

"He plays, and he sleeps, and in the afternoons he goes for a walk in his push-chair. Usually Mrs Archer takes him, but today I will take him."

"Does he look at books and things?"

"Yes, he likes picture books, but sometimes he tears them."

"Does he have toys?"

"He likes little cars and blocks. He doesn't like teddies or rabbits or things like that. I don't think he likes the feel of fur. You know what I mean?"

Oliver began to eat the shepherd's pie, which was very hot and delicious. He said, "Do you know a lot about babies?"

"At home in Sweden I have younger brothers and sisters."

"Are you fond of Thomas?"

"Yes, he is nice." She made a face at the child. "You are nice, aren't you, Thomas? And he doesn't cry all the time like some children do."

"It must be rather . . . dull for him, being brought up by his grandparents."

"He is too little to know whether it is dull or not."

"But it'll be dull when he's older."

"A child on his own is always sad. But there are other children in the village. He will make friends."

"And you? Have you made friends?"

"There is another au pair girl. We go to classes together."

"Haven't you got a boyfriend?"

She dimpled. "My boyfriend is at home in Sweden."

"He must miss you."

"We write to each other. And it is only for six months. At the end of six months, I shall go back to Sweden."

"What will happen to Thomas then?"

"I expect Mrs Archer will get another au pair girl. Would you like some more shepherd's pie?"

The meal progressed. For dessert there was fruit or yoghurt or cheese. Thomas ate yoghurt. Oliver peeled an orange. Helga, at the stove, made coffee.

She said to Oliver, "Do you live in London?"

"Yes, I've got a basement flat just off the Fulham Road."

"Is that where you are going now?"

"Yes. I've been in Bristol for a week."

"On holiday?"

"Who'd go to Bristol for a holiday in February? No, I have a play being put on at the Fortune Theatre there. I went down to do a small rewrite. The actors complained they couldn't get their tongues round some of my lines."

"A writer?" She turned wide-eyed. "You write *plays*? And get them *performed*? You must be very good."

"I like to think so." He filled his mouth with sections

of orange. Their taste, and the bitter tang of the peel, reminded him of Spain. "But it's what other people think that really matters. The critics, and the people who pay to come to the theatre."

"What is the play called?"

"*Bent Penny*. And don't ask me what it's about, because I haven't got time to tell you."

"My boyfriend writes. He writes articles on psychology for the university journal."

"I'm sure they're fascinating."

"But it isn't the same as writing plays."

"No. Not quite the same."

Thomas had finished his yoghurt. Helga wiped his face and took off his bib and lifted him out of his high chair. He came to stand by Oliver, balancing himself by placing his hands on Oliver's knee. Through the worn denim, Oliver could feel their warmth, the grip of the little fingers. Thomas gazed up at Oliver and smiled again, a grin with dimples and that row of little teeth. He put up a hand to touch Oliver's beard, and Oliver stooped so that he could reach it. Thomas laughed. Oliver picked him up and held him on his knee. He felt solid and warm.

Helga seemed gratified by all these friendly advances. "Now he has made friends. If I got a book, you could show him the pictures while I put the plates in the dishwasher. Then I have to take him for a walk."

Oliver had already decided that it was time to leave, but he said, "All right", so Helga went to find a book, and he and Thomas were left alone.

Thomas was fascinated by his beard. Oliver hoisted him up so that he stood on Oliver's knee and their eyes were on a level. Thomas tugged his beard. Oliver yelped. Thomas laughed. He tried to tug it again, but Oliver caught his hand and held it in his own. "That hurts, you brute." Thomas stared into his eyes. Oliver said softly, "Do you know who I am?" and Thomas laughed again, as though the question were a great joke.

Helga came back with the book and laid it on the table, a large and brightly coloured book with farm animals on the shiny cover. Oliver opened it at random and Thomas sat down again on his knee, leaning forward on the table, to peer at the pictures. As Helga went about her work putting plates away and scrubbing out the dish that had contained the shepherd's pie, Oliver turned the pages, and said the names of the animals, and pointed to the farmhouse and the gate and the tree and the haystack. And they came to a picture of a dog, and Thomas barked. And then to a picture of a cow, and he made mooing sounds. It was all very companionable.

Then Helga said it was time for Thomas to come upstairs and be dressed in his outdoor clothes, so she gathered him up and bore him away. Oliver sat and waited for them to come down again. He looked at the immaculate kitchen, and out into the immaculate garden, and he thought of Helga leaving and the next au pair girl coming, and the pattern repeating itself until Thomas was eight years old, and of an age to be sent to some well-established and probably useless prep school. He thought of his son, slotted, labelled, trapped on the conveyor belt of a conventional education, expected to make the right friends, play the accepted games, and never question the tyranny of meaningless tradition.

Oliver had escaped. At seventeen he had cut and run, but only because he had had the twin weapons of his writing and his own single-minded, rebellious determination to go his own way.

But how would Thomas fare?

The question made him feel uncomfortable, and he rejected it as being hypothetical. It was none of Oliver's business what school Thomas went to, and it didn't matter anyway. He lit another cigarette, and idly opened Thomas's picture book again, lifting the front cover. He saw on the white fly sheet, written in Mrs Archer's neat black-inked script,

Thomas Archer
For his Second Birthday
From Granny.

And all at once it did matter. A sort of rage rose within Oliver, so that if Jeannette's mother had been standing nearby, he would have attacked her; with words that only he knew how to use; with his fists if necessary.

He is not Thomas Archer, you sanctimonious bitch. He is Thomas Dobbs. He is my son.

When Helga came downstairs, carrying Thomas dressed in a sort of ski-suit and a woollen hat with a bobble on it, Oliver was already waiting for her in the hall. He had put on his coat, and he said, "I have to go now, I have to get back to London."

"Yes, of course."

"It was very kind of you to give me lunch."

"I will tell Mrs Archer that you were here."

He began to grin. "Yes. Do that."

"But . . . I don't know your name. To tell her, I mean."

"Just say Oliver Dobbs."

"All right, Mr Dobbs." She hesitated, standing at the bottom of the stairs, and then said, "I have to get the pram and my coat from the cloakroom. Will you hold Thomas for a moment?"

"Of course."

He lifted the child out of her arms, hoisting him up against one shoulder.

"I won't be long, Thomas," Helga assured him, and she turned and went down the passage beneath the staircase, and disappeared through a half-glassed door.

A pretty, trusting, stupid little girl. He hoped they

would not be too hard on her. *You can be as long as you like, my darling*. Carrying his son he went down the hall, let himself out through the yellow front door, went down the steps and got into his waiting car.

Helga heard the car go down the street, but she did not realise it was Oliver's. When she returned with the push-chair, there was no sign of either the man or the child.

"Mr Dobbs?"

He had left the front door open, and the house was invaded by the bitter cold of the afternoon.

"Thomas?"

But outside was only the empty pavement, the silent street.

2

FRIDAY

The most exhausting thing in the world, Victoria Bradshaw decided, was not having enough to do. It was infinitely more exhausting than having far too much to do, and today was a classic example.

February was a bad time for selling clothes. She supposed it was a bad time, really, for selling anything. Christmas was forgotten, and the January sales just a gruesome memory. The morning had started hopefully, with thin sunshine and a light icing of frost, but by early afternoon it had clouded over, and now it was so cold and wet that people with any sense at all were staying at home by fires or in centrally heated flats, doing crosswords or baking cakes or watching television. The weather gave them no encouragement to plan wardrobes for the spring.

The clock edged around to five o'clock. Outside, the bleak afternoon was darkening swiftly into night. The curved shop window had SALLY SHARMAN written across it. From the inside of the shop this presented itself backwards, like writing seen in a mirror, and beyond these hieroglyphics Beauchamp Place was curtained in rain. Passers-by, umbrellaed and gusted by wind, struggled with parcels. A stream of traffic waited for the Brompton Road lights to change. A figure, camouflaged by rainproof clothing, ran up the steps from the street and burst through the glass-panelled door like a person escaping, letting in a gust of cold air before the door was hastily slammed shut again.

It was Sally, in her black raincoat and her huge red fox hat. She said, "God, what a day," furled her umbrella, took off her gloves and began to unbutton her coat.

"How did it go?" Victoria asked.

Sally had spent the afternoon in the company of a young designer who had decided to go into the wholesale trade.

"Not bad," she said, draping her coat over the umbrella stand to drip. "Not bad at all. Lots of new ideas, good colours. Rather mature clothes. I was surprised, I thought his being so young, it would have been all jeans and workmen's shirts, but not at all."

She pulled off her hat, shook it free of raindrops, and finally emerged as her usual, lanky, elegant self. Narrow trousers tucked into tall boots, and a string-like sweater that on anyone else would have looked like an old floorcloth, but on Sally was sensational.

She had started life as a model and had never lost her beanpole shape or the ugly, jutting, photogenic bones of her face. From being a model, she had gravitated to the editorial pages of a fashion magazine, and from there, using her accumulated know-how, her many connections, and a natural flair for business, had opened her own shop. She was nearly forty, divorced, hard-headed, but far more tenderhearted than she liked anybody to suspect. Victoria had worked for her for nearly two years and was very fond of her.

Now, she yawned. "I really hate business lunches. I always feel hung over by the middle of the afternoon, and somehow that throws me for the rest of the day."

She reached into her immense handbag and took out cigarettes and an evening paper, which she tossed down on to the glass counter. "What's been happening here?"

"Practically nothing. I sold the beige overdress, and

some female came in and dithered for half an hour over the paisley coat, and then she went out again and said she'd think it over. She was put off by the mink collar. She says she's a wildlife supporter."

"Tell her we'll take it off and put on plastic fur instead." Sally went through the curtained doorway into the small office at the back of the shop, sat at her desk and began to open the mail.

She said, "You know, Victoria, I've been thinking, this would be a terribly good time for you to take a couple of weeks off. Things'll start livening up soon, and then I shan't be able to let you go. Besides, you haven't had a holiday since goodness knows when. The only thing is, February isn't very exciting anywhere. Perhaps you could go and ski, or stay with your mother in Sotogrande. What's Sotogrande like in February?"

"Windy and wet, I should think."

Sally looked up. "You don't want to take two weeks off in February," she announced resignedly. "I can tell by your voice." Victoria did not contradict her. Sally sighed. "If I had a mother who had a gorgeous house in Sotogrande, I'd stay with her every month of the year if I could. Besides, you look as though you need a holiday. All skinny and pale. It makes me feel guilty having you around, as though I worked you too hard." She opened another envelope. "I thought we'd paid that electricity bill. I'm sure we paid it. It must be the computer's fault. It must have gone mad. Computers do, you know."

To Victoria's relief the question of her suddenly taking a holiday at the end of February was, for the moment, forgotten. She picked up the newspaper that Sally had tossed down, and for lack of anything better to do, leafed idly through it, her eye skimming the usual disasters, both great and small. There were floods in Essex, a new conflagration threatened in Africa. A middle-aged earl was marrying his third wife, and in Bristol rehearsals were under way at the Fortune Theatre for Oliver Dobbs's new play, *Bent Penny*.

There was no reason why she should have noticed this little scrap of news. It was tucked in at the end of the last column on the entertainments page. There was no headline. No photograph. Just Oliver's name, which leapt out at her, like a shout of recognition, from the small print.

". . . it's a final demand. What a nerve, sending a final demand. I know I wrote a cheque last month." Victoria said nothing, and Sally looked at her. "Victoria . . .? What are you staring at?"

"Nothing. Just this bit in the paper about a man I used to know."

"I hope he's not being sent to jail."

"No, he writes plays. Have you ever heard of Oliver Dobbs?"

"Yes, of course. He writes for television. I saw one of his short plays the other night. And he did the script for that marvellous documentary on Seville. What's he been doing to get himself in the news?"

"He's got a new production coming off in Bristol."

"What's he like?" Sally asked idly, half her mind still on the iniquities of the London Electricity Board.

"Attractive."

This caught Sally's attention. She was all in favour of attractive men. "Did he attract you?"

"I was eighteen and impressionable."

"Weren't we all, darling, in the dim days of our youth. Not that that applies to you. You're still a blooming child, you fortunate creature." Suddenly she lost interest in Oliver Dobbs, in the final demand, in the day, which had already gone on far too long. She leaned back and yawned. "To hell with it. Let's shut up shop and go home. Thank the Lord for weekends. All at once the prospect of nothing to do for two days is total paradise.

I shall spend this evening sitting in a hot bath and watching television."

"I thought you'd be going out."

Sally's private life was both complicated and lively. She had a string of men friends, none of whom seemed to be aware of the others' existence. Like an adroit juggler, Sally kept them all on the go, and avoided the embarrassment of inadvertently muddling their names by calling them all "darling".

"No, thank God. How about you?"

"I'm meant to be going out to have a drink with some friends of my mother's. I don't suppose it will be very thrilling."

"Oh, well," said Sally, "you never know. Life is full of surprises."

One of the good things about working in Beauchamp Place was that it was within walking distance of Pendleton Mews. The flat in Pendleton Mews belonged to Victoria's mother, but it was Victoria who lived there. Most of the time she enjoyed the walk. Down shortcuts and narrow back roads, it only took half an hour and provided a little pleasant exercise and fresh air at the beginning and the end of the day.

But this evening it was so cold and wet that the prospect of a trudge through icy wind and rain was almost more than she could bear; so, breaking her own rule about never taking taxis, she succumbed, without much resistance, to temptation, walked up to the Brompton Road and finally flagged down a cab.

Because of one-way streets and snarled-up traffic, it took perhaps ten minutes longer to reach the Mews than if she had made the journey on foot, and cost so much that she simply handed the driver a pound note and let him count out the meagre change. He had set her down at the arch that divided the Mews from the road, so there was still a little way to go, across the puddles and the shining wet cobbles before she reached at last the haven of her own blue front door. She opened the door with her latchkey, reached inside and switched on the light; climbed the steep, narrow stairs, carpeted in worn beige Wilton, and emerged at the top directly into the small sitting-room.

She shed umbrella and basket and went to draw the chintz curtains against the night. The room at once became enclosed and safe. She lit the gas fire and went through to the tiny kitchen to put on the kettle for a cup of coffee; switched on the television and then switched it off again, put a Rossini overture on the record player, went into her bedroom to take off raincoat and boots.

The kettle, competing with Rossini, whistled for attention. She made a mug of instant coffee, went back to the fireside, pulled her basket towards her and took out Sally's evening paper. She turned to the item about Oliver Dobbs and the new play in Bristol.

I was eighteen and impressionable, she had said to Sally, but she knew now that she had also been lonely and vulnerable, a ripe fruit, trembling on its stalk, waiting to fall.

And Oliver, of all men, had been standing at the foot of the tree, waiting to catch her.

Eighteen, and in her first year at art school. Knowing nobody, intensely shy and unsure of herself, she had been both flattered and apprehensive when an older girl, perhaps taking pity on Victoria, had flung a vague invitation to a party in her direction.

"Goodness knows what it'll be like, but I was told I could ask anybody I wanted. You're meant to bring a bottle of something, but I don't suppose it matters if you come empty handed. Anyway, it's a good way to meet people. Look, I'll write down the address. The man's called Sebastian, but that doesn't matter. Just turn up if you feel like it. Any time; that doesn't matter either."

Victoria had never had such an invitation in her life.

She decided that she wouldn't go. And then decided that she would. And then got cold feet. And finally put on a pair of clean jeans, stole a bottle of her mother's best claret, and went.

She ended up in a top-floor flat in West Kensington, clutching her bottle of claret and knowing nobody. Before she had been there two minutes somebody said "How immensely kind," and removed the bottle of claret, but nobody else said a single word to her. The room was filled with smoke, intense men in beads, and girls with grey faces and long seaweed-like hair. There was even a grubby baby or two. There was nothing to eat and – once she had parted with the claret – nothing recognisable to drink. She could not find the girl who had suggested that she come and was too shy to join any of the tight, conversational groups gathered on floor, cushions or the single sagging sofa that had curly wire springs protruding from between arm and seat. She was, as well, too diffident to go and get her coat and leave. The air was filled with the sweet and insidious smell of marijuana, and she was standing in the bay window, lost in nerve-racking fantasies of a possible police raid, when suddenly somebody said, "I don't know you, do I?"

Startled, Victoria swung round, so clumsily that she almost knocked the drink out of his hand.

"Oh, I am sorry . . ."

"It doesn't matter. It hasn't spilled. At least," he added, generously, "not very much."

He smiled as though this were a joke, and she smiled back, grateful for any friendly overture. Grateful too that out of such woebegone company the only man who had spoken to her was neither dirty, sweaty, nor drunk. On the contrary, he was perfectly presentable. Even attractive. Very tall, very slender with reddish hair that reached to the collar of his sweater, and an immensely distinguished beard.

He said, "You haven't got a drink."

"No."

"Don't you want one?"

She said no again, because she didn't and also because if she said that she did, he might go away to get her one and never come back again.

He seemed amused. "Don't you like it?"

Victoria looked at his glass. "I don't exactly know what it is."

"I don't suppose anybody does. But this tastes like . . ." He took a mouthful thoughtfully, like a professional taster, rolling it round his mouth, finally swallowing it, ". . . red ink and aniseed balls."

"What's it going to do to the inside of your stomach?"

"We'll worry about that in the morning." He looked down at her, a frown of concentration furrowing his brow. "I *don't* know you, do I?"

"No. I don't suppose you do. I'm Victoria Bradshaw." Even saying her own name made her feel embarrassed, but he did not seem to think that there was anything embarrassing about it.

"And what do you do with yourself?"

"I've just started at art college."

"That explains how you got to this little do. Are you enjoying it?"

She looked around, "Not very much."

"I actually meant art college, but if you're not enjoying this very much, why don't you go home?"

"I thought it wouldn't be very polite."

He laughed at that. "You know, in this sort of company, politeness doesn't count all that much."

"I've only been here for ten minutes."

"And I've only been here for five." He finished his drink, tipping back his remarkable head and pouring the remains of the noxious tumbler down the back of his throat as easily as if it had been a cold and tasty beer. Then he set the glass down on the window ledge and said, "Come on. We're leaving." And he put a hand under her elbow and steered her expertly towards the door, and without making the vaguest of excuses or even saying goodbye, they left.

At the top of the dingy staircase, she turned to face him.

"I didn't mean that."

"What didn't you mean?"

"I mean that I didn't want *you* to leave. I wanted *me* to leave."

"How do you know I didn't want to leave?"

"But it was a party!"

"I left those sort of parties behind light years ago. Come on, hurry up, let's get out into the fresh air."

On the pavement, in the soft dusk of a late summer's night, she stopped again. She said, "I'm all right now."

"And what is that supposed to mean?"

"I can get a taxi, and go home."

He began to smile. "Are you frightened?"

Victoria became embarrassed all over again. "No, of course not."

"Then what are you running away from?"

"I'm not running away from anything. I simply . . ."

"Want to go home?"

"Yes."

"Well you can't."

"Why not?"

"Because we're going to go and find a spaghetti house or something, and we're going to buy a proper bottle of wine, and you are going to tell me the story of your life."

An empty taxi hove into view, and he hailed it. It stopped, and he bundled her in. After he gave the taxi driver directions, they drove in silence for about five minutes, and then the taxi stopped and he bundled her out again. He paid off the taxi and led her across the pavement into a small and unpretentious restaurant, with a few tables crowded around the walls and the air thick with cigarette smoke and the good smells of cooking food. They were given a table in the corner without enough room for his long legs, but somehow he arranged them so that his feet didn't trip the passing waiters, and he ordered a bottle of wine and asked for a menu, and then he lit a cigarette and turned to her and said, "Now."

"Now what?"

"Now tell me. The story of your life."

She found herself smiling. "I don't even know who you are. I don't know what your name is."

"It's Oliver Dobbs." He went on, quite kindly, "You have to tell me everything, because I'm a writer. A real honest-to-God published writer, with an agent and an enormous overdraft, and a compulsion for listening. Do you know, nobody listens enough. People fall over themselves trying to tell other people things, and nobody ever listens. Did you know that?"

Victoria thought of her parents. "Yes, I suppose I do."

"You see? You suppose. You're not sure. Nobody's ever sure of anything. They should listen more. How old are you?"

"Eighteen."

"I thought you were less when I saw you. You looked about fifteen standing there in the window of that crummy joint. I was about to ring the welfare and tell them that a tiny junior minor was out on the streets at night."

The wine came, uncorked, a litre bottle dumped on to the table. He picked it up and filled their glasses. He said, "Where do you live?"

"Pendleton Mews."

"Where's that?"

She told him and he whistled. "How very smart. A real Knightsbridge girl. I didn't realise they went to art college. You must be immensely rich."

"Of course I'm not rich."

"Then why do you live in Pendleton Mews?"

"Because it's my mother's house, only she's living in Spain just now, so I use it."

"Curiouser and curiouser. Why is Mrs Bradshaw living in Spain?"

"She's not Mrs Bradshaw, she's Mrs Paley. My parents divorced six months ago. My mother married again, to this man called Henry Paley, and he has a house in Sotogrande because he likes playing golf all the time." She decided to get it all over in a single burst. "And my father has gone to live with some cousin who owns a mouldering estate in Southern Ireland. He's threatening to breed polo ponies, but he's always been a man of great ideas but little action, so I don't suppose he will."

"And little Victoria is left to live in London."

"Victoria is eighteen."

"Yes, I know, old and experienced. Do you live alone?"

"Yes."

"Aren't you lonely?"

"I'd rather be alone than live with people who dislike each other."

He made a face. "Parents are hell, aren't they? My parents are hell, too, but they've never done anything so definite as divorcing each other. They just moulder on in darkest Dorset, and everything – their reduced circumstances, the cost of a bottle of gin, the fact that the hens aren't laying – is blamed on either me or the government."

Victoria said, "I like my parents. It was just that they'd stopped liking each other."

"Have you got brothers or sisters?"

"No. Just me."

"No one to take care of you?"

"I take very good care of myself."

He looked disbelieving. "*I* shall take care of you," he announced, magnificently.

After that evening Victoria did not see Oliver Dobbs again for two weeks, and by that time she knew that she was never going to see him again. And then it was a Friday evening, and she was so miserable that she compulsively spring-cleaned the flat, which did not need it, and then decided to wash her hair.

It was while she was kneeling by the bath with her head under the shower that she heard the bell ring. She wrapped herself up in a towel and went to open the door, and it was Oliver. Victoria was so pleased to see him that she burst into tears, and he came in and shut the door and took her in his arms, then and there, at the foot of the stairs, and dried her face with the end of the towel. After this they went upstairs, and he produced a bottle of wine out of his jacket pocket, and she found some glasses, and they sat by the gas fire and drank wine together. And when they had finished the wine, she went into her bedroom to get dressed, and to comb out her long, fair, damp tresses, and Oliver sat on the end of the bed and watched her. And then he took her out for dinner. There were no apologies, no excuses for his two weeks' silence. He had been in Birmingham, he told her, and that was all. It never occurred to Victoria to ask him what he had been doing there.

And this proved to be the pattern of their relationship. He came and went, in and out of her life, unpredictable, and yet strangely constant. Each time he came back, she never knew where he had been. Perhaps Ibiza, or perhaps he had met some man who owned a cottage in Wales. He was not only unpredictable, he was strangely secretive. He never spoke about his work, and she did not even know where he lived, except that it was a basement flat in some street off the Fulham Road. He was moody, too, and once or twice she had seen a terrifying flash of uncontrollable temper, but this all seemed to be an acceptable part of the fact that he was a writer and a true artist. And there was another side to the coin. He was funny and loving and immensely good company. It was like having the kindest sort of older brother who was, at the same time, irresistibly attractive.

When they were not together, she told herself that he was working. She imagined him at his typewriter, writing and rewriting, destroying, starting again, never achieving his own goals of perfection. Sometimes, he had a little money to spend on her. At others, none at all, and then Victoria would provide the food and cook it for him in the Mews flat, and she would buy him a bottle of wine and the small cigars that she knew he loved.

There came a bad period when he went through a slough of despondency. Nothing would go right and nothing seemed to be selling, and it was then that he took the night job in a little café, piling dirty dishes into the automatic washer. After that things began to get better again, and he sold a play to Independent Television, but he still went on washing dishes in order to be able to earn enough money to pay his rent.

Victoria had no other men friends, and did not want them. For some reason, she never imagined Oliver with other women. There was no occasion for jealousy. What she had of Oliver was not much, but it was enough.

The first she heard of Jeannette Archer was when Oliver told her that he was going to be married.

It was early summer, and the windows of Victoria's flat were open to the Mews. Below, Mrs Tingley from number fourteen was bedding out geraniums in her decorative tubs, and the man who lived two doors down was cleaning his car. Pigeons cooed from rooftops, and the distant hum of traffic was deadened by trees in full leaf. They sat on the window-seat, and Victoria was sewing a button on to Oliver's jacket. It hadn't fallen off, but it was going to, and she had offered to sew it on before it did. She had found a needle and thread and put a knot in the thread and pushed the needle into the worn corduroy when Oliver said, "What would you say if I told you I was going to be married?"

Victoria pushed the needle right into her thumb. The pain was minute but excruciating. She pulled the needle carefully out and watched the red bead of blood swell and grow. Oliver said, "Suck it, quickly, or it'll drip all over my coat," and when she didn't, he took her wrist and thrust her thumb into his mouth. Their eyes met. He said, "Don't look at me like that."

Victoria looked at her thumb. It throbbed as though some person had hit it with a hammer. She said, "I don't know any other way to look."

"Well say something then. Don't just stare at me like a lunatic."

"I don't know what I'm meant to say."

"You could wish me luck."

"I didn't know . . . that you . . . I mean, I didn't know that you were . . ." She was trying, even at this ghastly juncture, to be rational, polite, tactful. But Oliver scorned such euphemisms and interrupted brutally.

"You mean, you never realised that there was anybody else? And that, if you like it, is a line straight from an out-of-date novel. The kind my mother reads."

"Who is she?"

"She's called Jeannette Archer. She's twenty-four, a nicely brought-up girl with a nice flat and a nice little car, and a good job, and we've been living together for the past four months."

"I thought you lived in Fulham."

"I do sometimes, but I haven't just lately."

She said, "Do you love her?" because she simply had to know.

"Victoria, she's going to have a child. Her parents want me to marry her so that the baby will have a father. It seems to matter to them very much."

"I thought you didn't pay regard to parents."

"I don't if they're like mine, complaining and unsuccessful. But these particular parents happen to have a lot of money. I need money. I need money to buy the time to write."

She knew that she would cry. Her thumb still ached. Her eyes were filling with tears, and so that he shouldn't see them, she dropped her head and started to try to sew on the button, but the tears brimmed over and rolled down her cheeks and fell, great drops on the corduroy of his coat. He saw them and said, "Don't cry." And he put a hand under her chin and lifted her streaming face.

Victoria said, "I love you."

He leaned forward and kissed her cheek. "But you," he told her, "don't happen to be having a baby."

The clock on the mantelpiece astonished her by chiming, with silvery notes, seven o'clock. Victoria looked at it, disbelieving, and then at her wristwatch. Seven o'clock. The Rossini had finished long ago, the dregs in her coffee mug were stone cold, outside it was still raining, and in half an hour she was due at a party in Campden Hill.

She was assailed by the usual small panic of one who has lost all trace of time, and all thoughts of Oliver Dobbs were, for the moment, forgotten. Victoria sprang to her feet and did a number of things in quick succession. Took the coffee mug back into the kitchen, turned on a bath, went into her room to open her wardrobe and take out various garments, none of which seemed suitable. She took off some clothes and searched for stockings. She thought about ringing up for a taxi. She thought about calling Mrs Fairburn and pleading a headache, and then thought better of it, because the

Fairburns were friends of her mother's, the invitation was a long-standing one, and Victoria had a horror of causing offence. She went into the steaming bathroom and turned off the taps and splashed in some bath oil. The steam became scented. She disposed of her long hair in a bathcap, slathered cold cream on her face and wiped it all off again with a tissue. She climbed into the scalding water.

Fifteen minutes later she was out once more and dressed. A black silk turtleneck with a peasant-embroidered smock on top of it. Black stockings, black shoes with very high heels. She blackened her thick lashes with mascara, clipped on earrings, sprayed on some scent.

Now, a coat. She drew back the curtains and opened the window and leaned out to gauge the weather. It was very dark and still windy, but the rain, for the moment, seemed to have ceased. Below, the Mews was quiet. Cobbles shone like fish-scales, black puddles reflected the light from the old-fashioned street lamps. A car was turning in from the street, under the archway. It nosed down the Mews like a prowling cat. Victoria withdrew her head, closed the window and the curtains. She took an old fur coat from the back of the door, bundled herself into its familiar comfort, checked for her keys and wallet, turned off the gas fire and all the upstairs lights, and started downstairs.

She had taken one step when the doorbell rang.

She said, "Damn." It was probably Mrs Tingley come to borrow milk. She was always running out of milk. And she would want to stand and talk. Victoria ran to the foot of the stairs and flung open the door.

On the far side of the Mews, beneath a lamp, the prowling car was parked. A big old Volvo estate car. But of its driver there was no sign. Puzzled, she hesitated, and was about to go and investigate, when, from the dark shadows at the side of the door, a figure moved soundlessly forward, causing Victoria nearly to jump out of her skin. He said her name, and it was as though she had been taken, very swiftly, down twenty-three storeys in a very fast lift. The wind blew a scrap of newspaper the length of the Mews. She could hear the beating of her own heart.

"I didn't know if you'd still be living here."

She thought, these things don't happen. Not to ordinary people. They only happen in books.

"I thought you might have moved. I was sure you'd have moved."

She shook her head.

He said, "It's been a long time."

Victoria's mouth was dry. She said, "Yes."

Oliver Dobbs. She searched for some change in him but could find none. His hair was the same, his beard, his light eyes, his deep and gentle voice. He even wore the same sort of clothes, shabby and casual garments that on his tall, lean frame did not look shabby at all but somehow contrived and distinctive.

He said, "You look as though you're just going out."

"Yes, I am. I'm late as it is. But . . ." She stepped back. ". . . You'd better come in, out of the cold."

"Is that all right?"

"Yes." But she said again, "I have to go out," as if her going out were some sort of an escape hatch from a possibly impossible situation. She turned to lead the way back upstairs. He began to follow her and then hesitated. He said, "I've left my cigarettes in the car."

He plunged back into the outdoors. Halfway up the stairs Victoria waited. He returned in a moment, closed the door behind him. She went up, turning on the light at the head of the stairs, and was going to stand with her back to the unlit gas fire.

Oliver followed her, his eyes alert, instantly scanning the pretty room, the pale walls, the chintzes, patterned with spring flowers. The pine corner-cupboard that Victoria had found in a junk shop and stripped herself, her pictures, her books.

He smiled, satisfied. "You haven't changed anything. It's exactly the way I remembered. How marvellous to find something that hasn't changed." His eyes came back to her face. "I thought you'd have gone. I thought you'd have married some guy and moved. I was so certain that the door would be opened by a complete stranger. And there you were. Like a miracle."

Victoria found that she could think of absolutely nothing to say. She thought, I have been struck speechless. Searching for words, she found herself looking around the room. Beneath the bookcase was the cupboard where she kept a meagre collection of bottles. She said, "Would you like a drink?"

"Yes, I'd like one very much."

She laid down her bag and went to crouch by the cupboard. There was sherry, half a bottle of wine, a nearly empty bottle of whisky. She took out the whisky bottle. "There isn't much, I'm afraid."

"That's marvellous." He came to take the bottle from her. "I'll do it." He disappeared into the kitchen, at home in her flat as if he had walked out only yesterday. She heard the chink of glass, the running of the tap.

"Do you want one?" he called.

"No, thank you."

He emerged from the kitchen with the drink in his hand. "Where's this party you're going to?"

"Campden Hill. Some friends of my mother's."

"Is it going on for long?"

"I don't suppose so."

"Will you come back for dinner?"

Victoria almost laughed at this, because this was Oliver Dobbs, apparently inviting her to have dinner with him in her own flat.

"I imagine I will."

"Then you go to your party, and I'll wait here." He saw the expression on her face and added quickly, "It's important. I want to talk to you. And I want to have time to talk to you."

It sounded sinister, as though someone was after him, like the police, or some Soho heavy with a switch knife.

"There's nothing wrong, is there?"

"How anxious you look! No, there's nothing wrong." He added, in a practical fashion, "Have you got any food in the house?"

"There's some soup. Some bacon and eggs. I could make a salad. Or, if you wanted, we could go out. There's a Greek restaurant around the corner, it's just started up . . ."

"No, we can't go out." He sounded so definite that Victoria began to be apprehensive all over again. He went on, "I didn't want to tell you right away until I knew what the form was with you. The thing is, there's someone else in the car. There are two of us."

"Two of you?" She imagined a girlfriend, a drunken crony, even a dog.

In answer Oliver laid down his glass and disappeared once more down the stairs. She heard the door open and his footsteps crossing the Mews. She went to the head of the stairs and waited for him to return. He had left the door open, and when he reappeared he closed this behind him, carefully with his foot. The reason that he did this was that his arms were otherwise occupied with the weight of a large, mercifully sleeping, baby boy.

3

FRIDAY

It was a quarter past seven, at the end of a gruelling day, before John Dunbeath finally turned his car into the relative quiet of Cadogan Place, down the narrow lane between tightly parked cars, and edged it into a meagre gap not too far from his own front door. He killed the engine, turned off the lights, and reached into the back seat for his bulging briefcase and his raincoat. He got out of the car and locked up.

He had left his office, and commenced the daily ordeal of the journey home, in lashing rain, but now, half an hour or so later, it seemed to be easing up a little. Dark and still windy, the sky, bronzed with the reflected glow of the city lights, seemed to be full of ominous, racing clouds. After ten hours spent in an overheated atmosphere, the night air smelled fresh and invigorating. Walking slowly down the pavement, his briefcase slapping against his leg, he took one or two deep and conscious lungfuls, and was refreshed by the cold wind.

With his keyring in his hand, he went up the steps to the front door. It was black, with a brass handle and a letter box that the porter polished every morning. The tall old London house had been turned, some time ago, into flats, and the lobby and staircase, although carpeted and neatly kept, always smelled stale and stuffy, unaired and claustrophobic with central heating. This odour greeted him now, as it greeted him every evening. He shut the door with the seat of his trousers, collected his mail from its pigeonhole and began to climb the stairs.

He lived on the second floor, in an apartment that had been cunningly contrived from the main bedrooms of the original house. It was a furnished flat, found for him by a colleague when John had left New York and come to work in London at the European headquarters of the Warburg Investment Corporation, and he had arrived at Heathrow off the plane from Kennedy and taken instant possession. Now, six months later, it had become familiar. Not a home, but familiar. A place for a man alone to live.

He let himself in, turned on the lights and saw on the hall table his message from Mrs Robbins, the daily lady whom the porter had recommended should come in each morning to clean the flat. John had only seen her once, at the very beginning, when he had given her a key and told her more or less what he wanted her to do. Mrs Robbins had made it clear that this was quite unnecessary. She was a stately person, portentously hatted and wearing her respectability like armour. At the end of the encounter he was fully aware that he had not been interviewing her, but that Mrs Robbins had been judging him. However, it seemed that he had passed muster, and she duly took him on, along with one or two other privileged persons who also lived in the house. Since then, he had never set eyes on her, but they corresponded by means of notes that they left for each other, and he paid her, weekly, in the same fashion.

He dropped his briefcase, slung his raincoat on to a chair, picked up Mrs Robbins's letter, and along with the rest of his mail took it into the sitting room. Here all was beige and brown and totally impersonal. Another person's pictures hung upon the wall; another person's books filled the shelves which flanked the fireplace, and he had no wish for it to be any different.

Sometimes, for no particular reason, the emptiness of his personal life, the need for welcome, for love, would overwhelm him, breaking down the careful barriers which he had painfully built. On these occasions, he could not stop the memories flooding back. Like coming home to the shining brilliance of the New York apartment, with its white floors and its white rugs, and a sort of perfection which Lisa had achieved with her eye for colour, her passion for detail and her total disregard for her husband's bank balance. And, inevitably, Lisa would be there, waiting for him – for these memories belonged to the beginning of their marriage – so beautiful that she took your breath away, wearing something gauzy by de la Renta, and smelling unbearably exotic. And she would kiss him, and put a martini into his hand, and be glad to see him.

But most times, like this evening, he was grateful for quiet, for peace; for time to read his mail, to have a drink, to reassemble himself after the day's work. He went around the room turning on lights; he switched on the electric fire which instantly became a pile of rustic logs, flickering in the pseudo firebasket. He drew the brown velvet curtains and poured himself a Scotch, and then read the message from Mrs Robbins.

Her notes were always brief and abbreviated, rendering them as important-sounding as cables.

> Laundry missing pair sox and 2 hankchfs. Miss Mansell called says will you ring her this evng.

He leafed through the rest of his mail. A bank statement, a company report, a couple of invitations, an airmail letter from his mother. Putting these aside for later perusal, he sat on the arm of the sofa, reached for the telephone and dialled a number.

She came on almost at once, sounding breathless as she always did, as though perpetually in a tearing hurry.

"Hello?"

"Tania."

"Darling. I thought you'd never call."

"Sorry, I'm only just back. Just picked up your message now."

"Oh, poor sweet, you must be exhausted. Listen, something maddening's cropped up, so I can't make this evening. The thing is, I'm going down to the country *now*. Mary Colville rang up this morning, and there's some dance going on, and some girl's got flu, and she's desperate about her numbers, and I simply had to say I'd go. I tried to say no, and explain about this evening, but then she said would *you* come down tomorrow, for the weekend."

She stopped, not because she hadn't got plenty more to say, but because she had run out of breath. John found himself smiling. Her spates of words, her breathlessness, her confused social arrangements were all part of the charm that she held for him, mostly because she was so diametrically different from his ex-wife. Tania had, perpetually, to be organised, and was so scatty that the thought of organising John never entered her pretty feather-head.

He looked at his watch. He said, "If you're going to be at some dinner party in the country this evening, aren't you running things a little fine?"

"Oh, darling, yes, I'm going to be desperately late, but that's not what you're meant to say at all. You're meant to be desperately disappointed."

"Of course I'm disappointed."

"And you will come down to the country tomorrow?"

"Tania, I can't. I just heard today. I have to go to the Middle East. I'm flying out tomorrow morning."

"Oh, I can't bear it. How long are you going for?"

"Just a few days. A week at the outside. It depends on how things go."

"Will you call me when you get back?"

"Yes, sure."

"I rang Imogen Fairburn and told her I couldn't make it this evening, so she understands, and she says she's looking forward to seeing you even if I can't be there too. Oh, darling, isn't everything grim? Are you furious?"

"Furious," he assured her, mildly.

"But you do understand, don't you?"

"I understand completely, and you thank Mary for her invitation and explain why I can't make it."

"Yes, I will, of course I will, and . . ."

Another of her characteristics was that she could never finish a phone call. He interrupted firmly.

"Look, Tania, you have an appointment this evening. Get off the line and finish your packing and get moving. With luck, you'll arrive at the Colvilles no more than two hours late."

"Oh, darling, I do adore you."

"I'll call you."

"You do that." She made kissing sounds. "'Bye." She hung up. He put the receiver back on the hook and sat looking at it, wondering why he couldn't feel disappointed when a charming and engaging female stood him up for a more exciting invitation. He mulled over this problem for a moment or two, and finally decided that it didn't matter anyway. So he dialled Annabel's and cancelled the table he had ordered for this evening and then he finished his drink and went to have a shower.

Just as he was on the point of leaving for the Fairburns' a call came through from his vice-president, who had had, on his journey home in the company Cadillac, one or two important thoughts about John's projected trip to Bahrain. Discussing these, getting them collated and noted, had taken a good fifteen minutes, so that by the time John finally arrived at the house in Campden Hill, he was nearly three-quarters of an hour late.

The party was obviously in full swing. The street outside was jammed with cars. It took him another frustrating five minutes to find a scrap of space in which to park his own – and light and a steady hum of conversation emanated from beyond the tall, curtained first-floor windows. When he rang the bell the door was opened almost immediately by a man (hired for the occasion?) in a white coat, who said, "Good evening," and directed John up the stairs.

It was a pleasant and familiar house, expensively decorated, thickly carpeted, smelling like an extravagant hothouse. As John ascended, the sound of voices swelled to a massive volume. Through the open door that led into Imogen's drawing-room, he could discern an anonymous crush of people, some drinking, some smoking, some munching canapés, and all intent on talking their heads off. A couple was sitting at the head of the stairs. John smiled and excused himself as he stepped around them, and the girl said, "We're just having a tiny breath of air," as though she felt she must apologise for being there.

By the open door was a table set up as a bar, with another hired waiter in attendance.

"Good evening, sir. What'll it be?"

"Scotch and soda, please."

"With ice, sir, naturally."

John grinned. The "naturally" meant that the barman had recognised him for the American that he was. He said, "Naturally," and took the drink. "How am I going to find Mrs Fairburn?"

"I'm afraid you'll just have to go and look for her, sir. Like a needle in a ruddy haystack, I'd say."

John agreed with him, took a spine-stiffening slug of whisky and plunged.

It wasn't as bad as it might have been. He was recognised, greeted, almost at once, drawn into a group, offered a smoked salmon roll, a cigar, a racing tip. "Absolute certainty, old boy, three-thirty at Doncaster tomorrow." A girl he knew slightly came and kissed him and, he suspected, left lipstick on his cheek. A tall young man with an old man's balding head swam forward and said, "You're John Dunbeath, aren't you? Name's Crumleigh. Used to know your predecessor. And how are things in the banking world?"

He was nursing his drink, but a waiter nipped up and refilled his glass when he wasn't looking. Somebody trod on his shoe. A very young man wearing a brigade tie materialised at his elbow, trailing a protesting female by the arm. She was perhaps seventeen years old, and her hair looked like dandelion floss. ". . . This girl wants to meet you. Been eyeing you across the room."

"Oh, Nigel, you are *awful*."

Mercifully, he spied his hostess. He excused himself, and edged, with some difficulty, across the room to her side. "Imogen."

"John! Darling!"

She was immensely pretty. Grey-haired, blue-eyed, her skin smooth as a young girl's, her manner unashamedly provocative.

He kissed her politely, because she was obviously expecting to be kissed, with that flower-face turned up to his.

"This certainly is a party."

"So gorgeous to see you. But Tania couldn't come. She telephoned, something about having to go down to the country. So terribly disappointing. I was so looking forward to seeing you *both*. Never mind, you came and that's all that matters. Have you had a word with Reggie? He's longing to have a long, boring chat with you about the stock market or something." A couple hovered, waiting to say goodbye. "Don't go away," Imogen told John out of the corner of her mouth, and then turned from him, all smiles. "Darling. Do you really have to go? Such a sadness. Heavenly to see you. So glad you enjoyed it . . ." She came back to John. "Look, as Tania hasn't come, and you're on your own, there's a girl that perhaps you could go and chat up. She's pretty as paint, so I'm not letting you in for anything gruesome, but I don't think she knows many people. I mean, I asked her because her mother's one of our greatest friends, but somehow she seems a little out of her depth. Be an angel, and be sweet to her."

John, whose party manners had been rigorously drilled into him by his American mother (Imogen knew this, otherwise she would never have appealed to him for help) said that he would be delighted. But where was the girl?

Imogen, who was not tall, stood on tiptoes, and searched with her eyes. "There. Over in the corner." Her little feminine hand closed over his wrist like a vice. "I'll take you over and introduce you."

Which she proceeded to do, shouldering her way across the stifling room without once releasing her grip on him. John tagged along, willy-nilly, feeling like a bulky liner in the tow of a tug. They emerged at last, and it seemed to be a quiet corner of the room, perhaps because it was furthest from the door and the bar, but all at once there was room to stand, or move your elbows or even sit.

"Victoria."

She was perched on the arm of a chair, talking to an elderly man who was obviously going on to some other party, for he was wearing a dinner suit and a black tie. When Imogen said her name, she stood up, but whether this was out of politeness to Imogen, or to escape from her companion, it was impossible to say.

"Victoria, I do hope I'm not interrupting something absolutely riveting, but I do want you to meet John, because his girlfriend hasn't been able to come tonight, and I want you to be terribly kind to him." John, embarrassed both for himself and the girl, continued to smile politely. "He's an American, and he's one of my most favourite people . . ."

With a clearing of the throat, and a small, imperceptible gesture of farewell, the elderly man in the dinner suit also stood up and eased himself away.

". . . and John" – the grip on his wrist had not lessened. Perhaps the bloodstream to his hand had already seized up and in a moment his fingers would start falling off – "this is Victoria. And her mother is one of my best friends, and when Reggie and I were in Spain last year, we went and stayed with her. At Sotogrande. In the most heavenly house you've ever seen. So now you've got *lots* to talk about."

She let go of his wrist at last. It was like being freed from handcuffs.

He said, "Hello, Victoria."

She said, "Hello."

Imogen had chosen the wrong words. She was not pretty as paint. But she had a scrubbed, immaculate look to her that reminded him, with some nostalgia, of the American girls he had known in his youth. Her hair was pale and silky, straight and long, cut cunningly to frame her face. Her eyes were blue, her face neatly boned, her head supported by a long neck and narrow shoulders. She had an unremarkable nose, disarmingly freckled, and a remarkable mouth. A sweet and expressive mouth with a dimple at one corner.

It was an out-of-doors sort of face. The sort of face one expected to encounter at the tiller of a sailboat or at the top of some hair-raising ski-slope; not at a London cocktail party.

"Did Imogen say Sotogrande?"

"Yes."

"How long has your mother lived out there?"

"About three years. Have you ever been to Sotogrande?"

"No, but I have friends who golf, and they get out there whenever they can."

"My stepfather plays golf every day. That's why he chose to go and live there. Their house is right on the fairway. He steps out of the garden gate and he's playing the tenth hole. It's as easy as that."

"Do you play golf?"

"No. But there are other things to do. You can swim. Play tennis. Ride, if you want to."

"What do you do?"

"Well, I don't very often go out, but when I do I play tennis mostly."

"Does your mother come back to this country?"

"Yes. Two or three times a year. She dashes round from one art gallery to another, sees about six plays, buys some clothes, and then goes back again."

He smiled at this, and she smiled back. There came a small pause. The subject of Sotogrande seemed to have exhausted itself. Her eyes moved over his shoulder, and then quickly, as though she did not wish to appear ill-mannered, back to his face again. He wondered if she was expecting somebody.

He said, "Do you know many people here?"

"No, not really. Not anybody really." She added, "I'm sorry your girlfriend couldn't come."

"Like Imogen said, she had to go down to the country."

"Yes." She stooped to take a handful of nuts out of a dish that had been placed on a low coffee-table. She began to eat them, putting them into her mouth one at a time. "Did Imogen say you were American?"

"Yes, I think she did."

"You don't sound like an American."

"How do I sound?"

"Sort of halfway between. Mid-Atlantic. Alistair Cooke-type American."

He was impressed. "You have a sharp ear. I have an American mother and a British father. I'm sorry . . . a Scottish father."

"So you're really British?"

"I have a dual passport. I was born in the States."

"Whereabouts?"

"Colorado."

"Do your parents live there?"

"They have a ranch in southwest Colorado."

"I can't imagine where that is."

"North of New Mexico. West of the Rockies. East of the San Juans."

"I'd have to have an atlas. But it sounds very spectacular."

"It is spectacular."

"Were you riding a horse before you could walk?"

"Just about."

She said, "I can imagine it," and he had a strange feeling that she probably could. "When did you leave Colorado?"

He told her. "At eleven years old I was sent East to school. And then I came over to this country and I went to Wellington, because that's where my father had been. And after that I went to Cambridge."

"You really do have a dual nationality, don't you? What happened after Cambridge?"

"I went back to New York for a spell, and now I'm back in London. I've been here since the summer."

"Do you work for an American firm?"

"An investment bank."

"Do you get back to Colorado?"

"Sure, whenever I can. Only I haven't been for some time, because things have been pretty busy over here."

"Do you like being in London?"

"Yes, I like it very much." Her expression was very thoughtful. He smiled. "Why, don't you?"

"Yes. But just because I know it so well, I mean I can't imagine, really, living anywhere else."

There came, for some reason, another lull. Once more her eyes strayed, only this time it was to the gold watch strapped to her slender wrist. Having a pretty girl look at her watch while he was chatting her up was an unfamiliar experience for John Dunbeath. He expected to be irritated, but instead found himself mildly amused, although the joke was against himself.

"Are you expecting someone?" he asked her.

"No."

He thought that her face had a private look about it; composed, polite, but private. He wondered if she was always like this, or if their lines of communication were being cut by the murderous impossibility of cocktail party conversation. In order to keep this going, she had asked him a number of friendly questions, but there was no knowing whether she had listened to half of his polite replies. They had talked banalities and found out nothing about each other. Perhaps she wanted it this way. He could not decide whether she was totally disinterested or simply shy. Now, she had started glancing around the crowded room once more as though desperate for a means of escape, and he began to wonder why she had come in the first place. Suddenly exasperated, and ready to cast formalities aside, he was about to ask her this, but she forestalled him by announcing, without preamble, that she ought to be going. ". . . It's getting late, and I seem to have been here for ages." At once she seemed to realise that this remark was perhaps not much of a compliment to him. "I am sorry, I didn't mean it that way. I didn't mean that I seem to have been *here* for ages, I meant that I seem to have been at the party for ages. I . . . I've very much enjoyed meeting you, but I shouldn't be too late." John said nothing. She smiled brightly, hopefully. "I ought to get home."

"Where's home?"

"Pendleton Mews."

"That's very close to where I live. I'm Cadogan Place."

"Oh, how nice." Now she was beginning to sound desperate. "It's so quiet, isn't it?"

"Yes, it's very quiet."

Stealthily, she set down her glass, and hitched the strap of her bag up on to her shoulder. "Well, then, I'll say goodbye . . ."

But all at once he was consumed with an unfamiliar and healthy annoyance, and told himself that he was damned if he was going to be palmed off like this. Anyway, with his Scotch finished and no Tania to attend to, the party had gone sour for him. Tomorrow and the long flight to Bahrain loomed on the edge of his mind. He still had to pack, check his papers, leave messages for Mrs Robbins.

He said, "I'm going too."

"But you've only just arrived."

He finished his drink and laid down the empty tumbler. "I'll take you home."

"You don't need to take me home."

"I know I don't need to, but I may as well."

"I can get a taxi."

"Why get a taxi, when we're going in the same direction?"

"There's really no need . . ."

He was becoming bored by the tedious argument. "No problem. I don't want to be late either. I have a plane to catch in the early morning."

"To America?"

"No, to the Middle East."

"What are you going to do there?"

He put a hand under her elbow in order to propel her in the direction of the door. "Talk," he told her.

Imogen was torn between astonishment that he had hit it off so swiftly with her dearest friend's daughter, and a certain peevishness that he had stayed at her party for such a short time.

"But, John darling, you've only just come."

"It's a great party, but I'm headed for the Middle East tomorrow; an early flight, and . . ."

"But tomorrow's *Saturday*. It's too cruel having to fly off on a Saturday. I suppose that's what happens if you're a budding tycoon. But I wish you could stay a little longer."

"I wish I could too, but I really must go."

"Well, it's been divine, and sweet of you to come. Have you talked to Reggie? No, I don't suppose you have, but I'll tell him what's happening, and you must come for dinner when you get home again. Goodbye, Victoria. Heaven to see you. I'll write and tell your mother you're looking fabulously well."

On the landing he said, "Have you got a coat?"

"Yes. It's downstairs."

They went down. On a chair in the hall was a mound of coats. She dug from this an unfashionable fur, probably inherited and much worn. John helped her into it. The man in the starched white coat opened the door for them, and they emerged into the windy darkness and walked together up the pavement to where he had parked his car.

Waiting at the end of Church Street for the lights to change, John became aware of pangs of hunger. He had eaten a sandwich for lunch and nothing since. The clock on his dashboard told him that it was nearly nine o'clock. The lights changed, and they moved out and into the stream of traffic that poured east towards Kensington Gore.

He thought about eating dinner. He glanced at the girl

beside him. Her closeness, her reserve, was a challenge. It intrigued him, and against all reason he found himself wanting to break it down, to find out what went on behind that private face. It was like being confronted by a high wall, a notice saying No Trespassers, and imagining that beyond lay the promise of enchanting gardens and inviting tree-shaded walks. He saw her profile, outlined against the lights, her chin deep in the fur collar of the coat. He thought, *well, why not?*

He said, "Do you want to come and have dinner with me someplace?"

"Oh . . ." She turned towards him. "How kind."

"I have to eat, and if you'd like to join me . . ."

"I do appreciate it, but if you don't mind, I really should get back. I mean, I'm having dinner at home. I arranged to have dinner at home."

It was the second time she had used the word "home", and it disconcerted him, with its implication of close relatives. He wondered who waited for her. A sister, a lover, or even a husband. Anything was possible.

"That's all right. I just thought if you weren't doing anything."

"Really so kind of you, but I can't . . ."

A long silence fell between them, broken only by her giving him directions as to how to get most easily to Pendleton Mews. When they reached the archway that separated the Mews from the street, she said, "You can put me down here. I can walk the rest."

But by now he was feeling stubborn. If she would not have dinner with him, at least he would drive her to her door. He turned the car into the narrow angle beneath the arch and let it idle its way down between the garages and the painted front doors and the tubs that would soon be bright with spring flowers. The rain had stopped, but the cobbles were still damp and shone, like some country street, in the lamplight.

"Which number?" he asked.

"It's right at the very end. I'm afraid there's scarcely room to turn. You'll have to back out."

"That's all right."

"It's this one."

The lights were on. They shone from upstairs windows and through the small pane of glass at the top of the blue front door. She peered anxiously upwards as though expecting a window to be flung open and a face to appear, announcing bad news.

But nothing happened. She got out of the car, and John got out too, not because he wanted to be invited in, but because he had been meticulously brought up, and good manners insisted that a girl should not be simply dumped on her doorstep, but that her latchkey should be located, her door politely opened, her safety and well-being assured.

She had found her key. She had opened her door. She was, obviously, anxious to get away and up the stairs.

"Thank you so much for bringing me back. Really kind of you, and you didn't need to bother . . ."

She stopped. From upstairs there came the unmistakable wail of a furious child. The sound rooted them to where they stood. They stared at each other, the girl looking as astonished as John felt. The wails continued, rising in volume and fury. He expected some sort of an explanation, but none came. In the hard light from the staircase, her face was, all at once, very pale. She said in a strained sort of way, "Good night."

It was a dismissal. He thought, *damn you*. He said, "Good night, Victoria."

"Have a good time in Bahrain."

To hell with Bahrain. "I will."

"And thank you for bringing me home."

The blue front door was closed in his face. The light beyond was turned off. He looked up at the windows, secret behind the drawn curtains. He thought, and to hell with you too.

Getting back into his car he reversed at top speed down the length of the Mews and into the street, missing the side of the archway by inches. There he sat for a moment or two endeavouring to recover his natural good humour.

A baby. Whose baby? Probably her baby. There was no reason why she shouldn't have a baby. Just because she looked such a child herself, there was no reason why she shouldn't have a husband or a lover. A girl with a baby.

He thought, *I must tell Tania that. It'll make her laugh. You couldn't come to Imogen's party, so I went by myself and got hooked up with a girl who had to go home to her baby.*

As his annoyance abated, so did his hunger, and their going left him feeling flat. He decided to skip dinner and instead go back to his flat and make a sandwich. His car moved forward, and deliberately, his thoughts moved with it, ahead to the following day, to the early start, the drive to Heathrow, the long flight to Bahrain.

4

FRIDAY

Oliver was on the sofa, holding the child standing up on his knees. As Victoria came up the stairs the first thing she saw was the back of Oliver's head and the round, red, tear-drenched face of his son. He, surprised by her sudden appearance, stopped crying for an instant, and then, realising that it was no person he knew, at once started up again.

Oliver jigged him hopefully up and down, but it did no good. Victoria dropped her bag and came around to stand in front of them, unbuttoning her coat.

"How long has he been awake?"

"About ten minutes." The child roared furiously, and Oliver had to raise his voice in order to make his voice heard.

"What's wrong with him?"

"I imagine he's hungry." He got to his feet, heaving his burden with him. The little boy wore dungarees and a wrinkled white sweater. His hair was copper-gold, the curls at the nape of his neck tangled and damp. The only information Victoria had managed to elicit from Oliver before she had left for the Fairburns' was that the child was his son, and with that she had had to be content. She had left them together, the baby sound asleep on the sofa and Oliver peacefully downing his whisky and water.

But now . . . She gazed with sinking apprehension. She knew nothing about babies. She had scarcely held a baby in her life. What did they eat? What did they want when they wept so heartbreakingly?

She said, "What's he called?"

"Tom." Oliver jigged him again, tried to turn him around in his arms. "Hey, Tom. Say hello to Victoria."

Tom took another look at Victoria and then let them know, lustily, what he thought of her. She took off her coat and dropped it on to a chair. "How old is he?"

"Two."

"If he's hungry, we should give him something to eat."

"That makes sense."

He was being no use at all. Victoria left him and went into the kitchen to search for suitable food for a baby. She stared into the cupboard at racks of spices, Marmite, flour, mustard, lentils, stock cubes.

What was he doing, back in her flat, back in her life, after three years of silence? What was he doing with the child? Where was its mother?

Jam, sugar, porridge oats. A packet bought, the last time she had been in London, by Victoria's mother, for the purpose of making some special sort of biscuit.

"Will he eat porridge?" she called,

Oliver did not reply, because over the yells of his son he did not hear the question; so Victoria went to the open door and repeated it.

"Yes, I suppose so. I suppose he'll eat anything, really."

Feeling near exasperation, she went back to the kitchen, put on a pan of water, poured in some oats, found a bowl, a spoon, a jug of milk. When it had started to cook, she turned down the heat and went back into the sitting-room and saw that already it had been taken over by Oliver, it was no longer hers. It was filled with Oliver, with his possessions, his empty glass, his cigarette stubs, his child. The child's coat lay on the floor, the sofa cushions were crushed and flattened, the air rang with the little boy's misery and frustration.

She could bear it no longer. "Here," she said and took Thomas firmly in her arms. Tears poured down his cheeks. She said to Oliver, "You make sure the porridge doesn't burn," and she bore Tom into the bathroom and set him down on the floor.

Steeling herself to cope with steaming nappies, she unbuttoned his dungarees and found that he wasn't wearing nappies at all, and was, miraculously, dry. There was, obviously, no pot in this childless establishment, but with a certain amount of contriving she persuaded him to use the grown-up lavatory. For some reason this mild accomplishment stopped his tears. She said, "What a good boy," and he looked up at her, still tear-drenched, and disarmed her with a sudden grin. Then he found her sponge and began to chew it, and she was so thankful that he had stopped crying that she let him. She buttoned up his clothes and washed his face and hands. Then she led him back into the kitchen.

"He's been to the loo," she told Oliver.

Oliver had poured himself another whisky, thus finishing Victoria's bottle. He had his glass in one hand and a wooden spoon in the other, with which he stirred the porridge. He said, "I think this sort of looks ready."

It was. Victoria put some into a bowl, poured milk over it, sat at the kitchen table with Tom on her knee, and let him get on with it, which he did. After the first mouthful, she hastily reached for a tea towel and wrapped it around his neck. In a moment the bowl was empty and Thomas apparently ready for more.

Oliver eased himself away from the cooker. "I'm going out for a moment."

Victoria was filled with alarm, and suspicion that if he went he would never come back and she would be left with the child. She said, "You can't."

"Why not?"

"You can't leave me alone with him. He doesn't know who I am."

"He doesn't know who I am either, but he seems quite happy. Eating himself to a standstill." He laid the palms of his hands flat on the table and stooped to kiss her. It was three years since this had happened, but the after-effects were alarmingly familiar. A melting sensation, a sudden sinking of the stomach. Sitting there with his child heavy on her knee, she thought, oh, no. "I shall be gone about five minutes. I want to buy cigarettes and a bottle of wine."

"You'll come back?"

"How suspicious you are. Yes, I'll come back. You're not going to get rid of me as easily as that."

He was, in fact, away for fifteen minutes. By the time he returned, the sitting-room was once more neat, cushions plumped up, coats put away, the ashtrays emptied. He found Victoria at the kitchen sink, wearing an apron and washing a lettuce. "Where's Thomas?"

She did not turn around. "I put him into my bed. He isn't crying. I think he'll go to sleep again."

Oliver decided that the back of her head looked implacable. He put down the brown grocery bag containing the bottles and went to turn her to face him.

"Are you angry?" he asked.

"No. Just wary."

"I can explain."

"You'll have to." She turned back to the sink and the lettuce.

He said, "I'm not explaining if you won't listen properly. Leave that and come and sit down."

"I thought you wanted to eat. It's getting terribly late."

"It doesn't matter what time it is. We've all the time in the world. Come on. Come and sit down."

He had bought wine and another bottle of whisky. While Victoria untied her apron and hung it up, he found ice cubes and poured two drinks. She had gone back to the sitting-room, and he joined her there and found her settled on a low stool with her back to the fire. She did not smile at him. He handed her the glass and raised his own.

"Reunions?" he suggested as a toast.

"All right." Reunions sounded harmless enough. The glass was cold to her fingers. She took a mouthful and felt better. More able to deal with what he was about to tell her.

Oliver sat on the edge of the sofa and faced her. There were artistic patches in the knees of his jeans, and his suede boots were worn and stained. Victoria found herself wondering on what he chose to spend the fruits of his considerable success. Whisky, perhaps. Or a house in a more salubrious part of London than the Fulham back street where he had lived before. She thought of the big Volvo parked in the Mews outside. She saw the gold watch on his long, narrow wrist.

He said again, "We have to talk."

"You talk."

"I thought you'd be married."

"You said that before. When I opened the door."

"But you're not."

"No."

"Why not?"

"I never met anybody I wanted to marry. Or perhaps I never met anybody who wanted to marry me."

"Did you go on with your painting?"

"No, I threw that up after a year. I wasn't good enough. I had a little talent, but not enough. There's nothing more discouraging than having just a little talent."

"So what do you do now?"

"I have a job. In a dress shop in Beauchamp Place."

"That doesn't sound very demanding."

She shrugged. "It's all right." They were not meant to be talking about Victoria, they were meant to be talking about Oliver. "Oliver . . ."

But he did not want her questions, perhaps because he had not yet made up his mind what the answers would be. He quickly interrupted her. "How was the party?"

She knew that this was a red herring. She looked at him, and he met her gaze with watchful innocence. She thought, what does it matter? Like he says, we have all the time in the world. Sooner or later he's going to have to tell me. She said, "The usual. Lots of people. Lots of drink. Everybody talking and nobody saying anything."

"Who brought you home?"

She was surprised that he was sufficiently interested to want to know this, and then remembered that Oliver had always been interested in people, whether he knew them or not; whether he even liked them. He would sit in buses and listen to other people's conversations. He would talk to strangers in bars, to waiters in restaurants. Everything that happened to him was filed away in the retentive storehouse of his memory, mulled over and digested, only to reappear at some later date in something he was writing, a scrap of dialogue or a situation.

She said, "An American."

He was instantly intrigued. "What sort of an American?"

"Just an American."

"I mean bald-headed, middle-aged, hung about with cameras? Earnest? Sincere? Come along now, you must have noticed."

Of course Victoria had noticed. He had been tall, not as tall as Oliver, but more heavily built, with wide shoulders and a flat stomach. He looked as though he played furious squash in his spare time, or jogged round the park in the early mornings, wearing sneakers and a tracksuit. She remembered dark eyes, and hair almost black. Crisp, wiry hair, the sort that has to be closely cut or it gets out of hand. His had been expertly barbered, probably by Mr Trumper or one of the more exclusive London establishments, so that it lay on his well-shaped head like a smooth pelt.

She remembered the strong features, the tan, and the marvellous white American teeth. Why did Americans all seem to have such beautiful teeth?

She said, "No, he wasn't any of those things."

"What was his name?"

"John. John something. I don't think Mrs Fairburn's very good at introductions."

"You mean he didn't tell you himself? He can't have been a true-blooded American. Americans always tell you who they are and what they do, before you've even decided whether you want to meet them or not. 'Hi!'" He put on a perfect New York accent. "'John Hackenbacker, Consolidated Aloominum. Glad to have you know me.'"

Victoria found herself smiling, and this made her feel ashamed, as though she must stand up for the young man who had brought her home in his sleek Alfa-Romeo. "He wasn't a bit like that. And he's flying to Bahrain tomorrow," she added as though this were a point in the American's favour.

"Ah! An oil man."

She was becoming tired of his teasing. "Oliver, I have no idea."

"You seem to have made remarkably little contact. What the hell did you talk about?" An idea occurred to him, and he grinned. "I know, you talked about me."

"I most certainly didn't talk about you. But I think it's about time you started talking about you. And about Thomas."

"What about Tom?"

"Oh, Oliver, don't fence."

He laughed at her exasperation. "I'm not being kind, am I? And you're simply bursting to know. All right, here it is. I've stolen him."

It was so much worse than she had imagined that Victoria had to take a long, deep breath. When that was safely over, she was calm enough to ask, "Who did you steal him from?"

"Mrs Archer. Jeannette's mother. My erstwhile mother-in-law. You probably didn't know, but Jeannette was killed in an air crash in Yugoslavia, just a little while after Tom was born. Her parents have looked after him ever since."

"Did you go and see him?"

"No. Never went near him. Never set eyes on him. Today was the first time I ever saw him."

"And what happened today?"

He had finished his drink. He got up and went into the kitchen to pour himself another. She heard the clink of the bottle, the ice going into the glass, the tap being turned on and off. Then he returned and resumed his seat, leaning back on the deep cushions of the sofa, with his long legs stretched out in front of him.

"I've been in Bristol all week. I've got a play coming off at the Fortune Theatre, it's in rehearsal now, but I had to do some work with the producer, rewrite some of the third act. Driving back to London this morning, I was thinking about the play. I wasn't really paying attention to the road, and suddenly I realised I was on the A30, and there was a signpost to Woodbridge, and that's where the Archers live. And I thought, why not? And I turned the car and went to call. As simple as that. A whim, you might say. The hand of fate stretching out its grubby paw."

"Did you see Mrs Archer?"

"No. Mrs Archer was in London, buying sheets at Harrods or something. But there was a choice au pair girl called Helga who needed little encouragement to invite me in for lunch."

"Did she know you were Tom's father?"

"No."

"So what happened?"

"She sat me down at the kitchen table and went upstairs to fetch Tom. And then we had lunch. Good healthy fare. Everything was good and healthy, and so clean it looked as though it had been through a steriliser. The whole house is one enormous steriliser. There isn't a dog or a cat or a readable book in the place. The chairs look as though no one ever sat in them. The garden's full of horrible flower-beds, like a cemetery, and the paths look as if they've been drawn with a ruler. I'd forgotten its utter soullessness."

"But it's Tom's home."

"It stifled me. It's going to stifle him. He had a picture book with his name written in the front. 'Thomas Archer. From Granny.' And somehow that finished me, because he's not Thomas Archer, he's Thomas Dodds. So then the girl went to get his beastly perambulator, to take him out for a walk, and I picked him up and carried him out of the house and put him in the car and drove him away."

"But didn't Thomas *mind*?"

"He didn't seem to. Seemed quite pleased, in fact. We stopped off somewhere and spent the afternoon in a little park. He played on the swings and in the sandpit, and a dog came up and talked to him. And then it began to rain, so I bought him some biscuits and we got back into the car again and came back to London. I took him to my flat."

"I don't know where your flat is."

"Still in Fulham. Same place. You've never been there I know, but you see, it isn't really a living place, it's a working place. It's a basement and grotty as hell, and I have an arrangement with a large West Indian lady who lives on the first floor, and she's meant to come and clean it up once a week, but it never seems to look any better. Anyway, I took Tom there, and he obligingly fell asleep on my bed, and then I rang the Archers."

He came out quite casually with this. Moral cowardice was something from which Oliver had never suffered, but Victoria felt quite weak at the thought.

"Oh, *Oliver*."

"No reason why I shouldn't. After all, he's my child."

"But she must have been out of her mind with worry."

"I told the au pair girl my name. Mrs Archer knew he was with me."

"But . . ."

"You know something? You sound the way Jeannette's mother sounded. As though I had nothing but evil intentions. As though I were going to harm the child, bash his brains out on a brick wall, or something."

"I don't think that at all. It's just that I can't help but be sorry for her."

"Well don't be."

"She'll want him back."

"Yes, of course she wants him back, but I've told her that for the time being I'm keeping him myself."

"Can you do that? Legally, I mean? Won't she get the police, or lawyers, or even high court judges?"

"She's threatened all those things. Litigation, ward of court, in the space of ten minutes she threw everything at my head. But you see, she can't do anything. Nobody can do anything. He's my child. I'm his father. I'm neither a criminal nor otherwise unfit to take care of him."

"But that's just the point. You can't take care of him."

"All that's required of me is to provide a home for Tom with resources and facilities for taking care of him."

"In a basement in Fulham?"

There was a long silence while Oliver, with slow deliberation, stubbed out his cigarette. "That," he told her at last, "is why I am here."

So, it was out. The cards were on the table. This was why he had come to her.

She said, "At least you're being honest."

Oliver looked indignant. "I'm always honest."

"You want me to look after Tom?"

"We can look after him together. You wouldn't want me to take him back to that mouldy flat, would you?"

"I can't look after him."

"Why not?"

"I'm working. I have a job. There isn't any room for a child here."

He said, in a false voice, "And what would the neighbours say?"

"It's nothing to do with the neighbours."

"You can tell them I'm your cousin from Australia. You can say that Tom is my Aborigine offspring."

"Oh, Oliver, stop joking. This is nothing to joke about. You've stolen that child of yours. Why he isn't howling his head off with misery and fright is beyond my comprehension. Mrs Archer is obviously distraught, we're going to have the police on the doorstep at any moment, and all you do is make what you think are funny remarks."

His face closed up. "If you feel like that about it, I'll take the child and go."

"Oh, Oliver, it's not that. It's that you have to be sensible."

"All right, I'll be sensible. Look, I've got on my most sensible expression." Victoria refused even to smile at him. "Oh, come along. Don't be angry. I wouldn't have come if I'd thought it would make you angry."

"I don't know why you did come."

"Because I thought of you as being exactly the right sort of person who'd help me. I thought of you, and

I thought of telephoning first, but then I imagined some stranger – or worse, some stiff-necked husband – answering the call. And then what was I going to say? This is Oliver Dobbs, the well-known author and playwright, speaking. I have a baby I'd like your wife to look after. Wouldn't that have gone down a treat?"

"What would you have done if I hadn't been here?"

"I don't know. I'd have thought of something. But I wouldn't have taken Tom back to the Archers."

"You may have to. You can't take care of him . . ."

Oliver interrupted her, as though she had never started to speak. "Look, I have a plan. Like I said, the Archers haven't got a leg to stand on, but still there's the chance that they'll try to make trouble. I think we should get out of London. Go away for a little. There's this play of mine coming off in Bristol, but as far as that's concerned I've done all I can do. The first night's on Monday, and after that it's at the mercy of the critics and the general public. So let's go away. You and me and Tom. Let's just take off. We'll go to Wales or the north of Scotland, or down to Cornwall and watch the spring coming. We'll . . ."

Victoria gazed at him in total disbelief. She was shocked, outraged, indignant. Did he imagine – did he really imagine – that she had so little pride? Had he never truly known how much he had hurt her? Three years ago Oliver Dobbs had walked out of her life, shattering everything, and leaving her alone to put the pieces together as best she might. But now he had decided that he needed her once more, simply to look after his child. And so here he sat, already making plans, trying to seduce her with words, believing that it was only a matter of time before he wore down her resistance.

". . . no tourists, empty roads. We won't even have to book in at hotels, they'll all be longing for business, desperate to have us . . ." He went on, hatching plans, leading Victoria on to images of blue seas and fields of yellow daffodils; of carefree escape, and winding country lanes. And she listened, marvelling at his selfishness. He had helped himself to his son. He wanted, for the time being, to keep his son. He needed someone to take care of his son. And so, Victoria. It was as simple as an elementary mathematical formula.

He stopped at last. His face was alight with enthusiasm, as though he could not envisage any objection to this delightful project. After a little, Victoria said, because she really wanted to know, "Out of interest, what made you think of me?"

"I suppose because you're the sort of person that you are."

"You mean, stupid?"

"No, not stupid."

"Forgiving, then?"

"You could never be unforgiving. You wouldn't know how. Besides, it was a good time we had together. It wasn't a bad time. And you're pleased to see me again. You have to be, otherwise you'd never have let me into your house."

"Oliver, some bruises don't necessarily show."

"What's that supposed to mean?"

"For my sins, I loved you. You knew that."

"But you see," he reminded her carefully, "I didn't love anybody. And you knew that."

"Except yourself."

"Perhaps. And what I was trying to do."

"I don't want to be hurt again. I'm not going to be hurt again."

A smile touched his mouth. "You sound very determined."

"I'm not coming with you."

He did not reply, but his eyes, pale and unblinking, never left her face. Outside, the wind rattled a window-pane. A car started up. A girl's voice called some person's name. Perhaps she was going to a party. From far off came the distant hum of London traffic.

He said, "You can't spend the rest of your life avoiding being hurt. If you do that, then you turn your back on any sort of relationship."

"Just say that I don't want to be hurt by you. You're too good at it."

"Is that the only reason that you won't come with us?"

"I think it's enough of a reason, but there are other things as well. Practical considerations. For one thing, I have a job . . ."

"Selling clothes to idiotic females. Ring up and make some excuse. Say your grandmother's died. Say you've suddenly had a baby . . . now that would be nearly true! Send in your resignation. I'm a rich man now. I'll take care of you."

"You've said that before. A long time ago. But you didn't."

"What a prodigious memory you have."

"Some things really can't be forgotten." From the mantelpiece her little clock chimed. It was eleven o'clock. Victoria stood up and put her empty glass beside the clock, and as she did so, she saw his reflection, watching her through the looking glass which hung on the wall behind it.

He said, "Are you afraid? Is that what it is?"

"Yes."

"Of me, or of yourself?"

"Both of us." She turned from the mirror. "Let's go and have some supper."

It was nearly midnight by the time they finished the makeshift meal, and Victoria was suddenly so tired that she had not even the energy to collect the plates and the empty glasses and wash them up. Oliver was pouring the last of the wine into his glass and reaching for another cigarette, apparently settled for the night, but Victoria stood up, pushing back her chair, and said, "I'm going to bed."

He looked mildly surprised. "That's very unsocial of you."

"I can't help it if it's unsocial. If I don't go to bed I'll fall asleep on my feet."

"What do you want me to do?"

"I don't want you to do anything."

"I mean," he spoke patiently, as though she were being immensely unreasonable, "do you want me to go back to Fulham? Do you want me to spend the night in my car? Do you want me to wake Thomas up and bear him off into the night, never to darken your door again? You only have to say."

"You can't take Thomas. He's sleeping."

"Then I'll go back to Fulham and leave him here with you."

"You can't do that either. He might wake up in the middle of the night and be frightened."

"In that case I'll stay here." He assumed the expression of a man prepared to be accommodating, at whatever cost to himself. "Where would you like me to sleep? On the sofa? On top of some chest of drawers? On the floor outside your bedroom door, like an old dog, or a faithful slave?"

She refused to rise to his teasing. "There's a divan in the dressing-room," she told him. "The room's full of suitcases and my mother's London clothes, but the bed's longer than the sofa. I'll go and make it up . . ."

She left him, with his cigarette and his glass of wine and the chaos of unwashed dishes. In the tiny slip of a dressing-room, she found blankets and a pillow. She removed dress boxes and a pile of clothes from the divan and made it up with clean sheets. The room smelled stuffy and rather mothbally (her mother's fur coat?) so she opened the window wide, and the curtains stirred in the cold damp air which blew in from the darkness beyond.

From the kitchen now came sounds as if Oliver had decided to stack the supper plates, or possibly wash them. Victoria was surprised, because domesticity had never been his strong suit, but she was touched as well, and tired as she was, knew an impulse to go and help him. But if she went to help him, they would only start talking again. And if they started talking, then Oliver would start, all over again, trying to persuade her to go away with him and Thomas. So she left him to it, and went into her bedroom. Here, only a small lamp burned on the dressing-table. On one side of the double bed, Thomas slumbered, one arm outflung, his mouth plugged by his thumb. She had taken off everything except his vest and pants, and folded clothes lay on a chair, his small shoes and socks on the floor beneath it. She stooped to lift him out of the bed. His weight was warm and soft in her arms. She carried him to the bathroom and somehow persuaded him to use the lavatory again. He scarcely woke: his head lolled, his thumb stayed determinedly in his mouth. She put him back into the bed, and he sighed contentedly and slept once more. She prayed that he would sleep until morning.

She straightened up, and listened. It seemed that Oliver had decided that he had had enough of the supper dishes, and he had returned to the living-room, where he had started telephoning. Only Oliver would start telephoning at midnight. Victoria undressed, brushed her hair, put on her nightdress and cautiously slipped into the other side of the bed. Tom never stirred. She lay on her back and stared at the ceiling, and then closed her eyes, waiting for sleep. But sleep would not come. Her brain whirled with images of Oliver, with memories, with a sort of throbbing excitement which maddened her because it was the last thing in the world that she wanted to feel. Finally, in desperation, she opened her eyes again, and reached for a book, intending to read herself to calmness and so to unconsciousness.

From the next room, the telephoning stopped, and the television was switched on. But most of the programmes had finished by now anyway, and eventually Oliver apparently decided to call it a day. She heard him moving about, switching off lights. She heard him go to the bathroom. She laid down her book. His footsteps crossed the little landing, and stopped outside her door. The handle turned. The door opened. His tall figure appeared, silhouetted against the bright light beyond.

He said, "Not asleep?"

"Not yet," said Victoria.

They spoke softly, so as not to disturb the sleeping child. Oliver, leaving the door open, crossed the floor and came to sit on the edge of the bed.

"Just a guy. Nothing important."

"I made up the bed for you."

"I know. I saw."

But he made no move to go. "What will you do tomorrow?" she asked him. "With Thomas?"

He smiled. He said, "I'll decide tomorrow." He touched her book. "What are you reading?"

It was a paperback. Victoria held it up for him to see the front cover. She said, "It's one of those books that you read over and over again. About once a year, I take it out, and it's like being with an old friend."

Oliver read the title aloud. "*The Eagle Years.*"

"Have you read it?"

"Perhaps."

"It's by this man called Roddy Dunbeath and it's all about being a little boy in Scotland between the wars. I mean, it's sort of autobiography. And he and his brothers were brought up in this beautiful house called Benchoile."

Oliver had laid his hand over her wrist. His palm was warm, his fingers strong, but the caress very gentle.

"It was in Sutherland, somewhere. With mountains all around and their own private loch. And he had a falcon that used to come and take food out of his mouth . . ."

His hand began to move up her bare arm, pressing the flesh beneath his touch, as though he were massaging life back into some limb which had been paralysed for years.

". . . and a pet duck and a dog called Bertie that liked eating apples."

"I like eating apples," said Oliver. He lifted a long strand of hair away from her neck and laid it on the pillow. She could feel the solid, throbbing beat of her own heart. Her skin, where he had touched her, felt as though it were standing on tiptoe. She went on talking, desperately, trying to control these alarming physical manifestations with the sound of her own voice.

". . . and there was a place with a waterfall, where they used to go for picnics. And there was a stream running across the beach, and the hills were filled with deer. He says that the waterfall was the heart of Benchoile . . ."

Oliver leaned down and kissed her mouth and the flow of words was mercifully stopped. She knew that he hadn't been listening anyway. Now, he drew aside the blankets which covered her, and slid his arms beneath her back, and his lips moved away from her mouth and across her cheek and into the warm hollow of her neck.

"Oliver." She said his name, but her voice made no sound. His going had left her frozen, but now the weight and the warmth of his body warmed her own, melting resolution, and stirring to life long-forgotten instincts. She thought, *oh, no,* and laid her hands against his shoulders and tried to push him away, but he was a thousand times stronger than Victoria and the puny resistance was pathetic, pointless as trying to topple some immense tree.

"Oliver. No."

She might not have spoken aloud. He simply continued his gentle love-making, and after a little, her hands, as though of their own volition, slid away from his shoulders, under his jacket, around his back. He smelled clean, of clothes dried in the open air. She felt the thin cotton of his shirt, the ribcage, the hard muscles beneath his skin. She heard him say, "You've stopped pretending."

The last shred of common sense made her say, "But Oliver, Thomas . . ."

She sensed his amusement, his silent laughter. He drew away from her and stood up, towering over her. "That can easily be arranged," he told her, and he stooped and lifted her up into his arms as easily and lightly as he had carried his son. She felt weightless, dizzy, as the walls of her bedroom spun and slid away and he bore her through the open door, across the bright landing, and into the airy darkness of the little dressing-room. It still smelled of camphor, and the bed on which he placed her was hard and narrow, but the curtains stirred in the soft wind, and the starched linen of the pillow lay cool beneath her neck.

She said, looking up into the shadowed blur that was his face, "I never meant this to happen."

"I did," said Oliver, and she knew that she should be angry, but by then it was too late. Because by then she wanted it to happen anyway.

Much later – she knew it was much later, because she had heard the clock in the sitting-room strike two with its silvery chimes – Oliver hoisted himself up on to one elbow and leaned over Victoria in order to grope for his jacket and take his cigarettes and lighter from the pocket. The flame illuminated the tiny room for a second, and there came the gentle darkness again and the glow of the cigarette tip.

She lay in the curve of his arm, her head pillowed on his naked shoulder.

He said, "Do you want to make plans?"

"What sort of plans?"

"Plans for what we're going to do. You and me and Thomas."

"Am I coming with you?"

"Yes."

"Have I said I'm coming with you?"

He laughed. He kissed her. "Yes," he said.

"I don't want to be hurt again."

"You mustn't be so afraid. There's nothing to be afraid of, just the prospect of a holiday, an escape. Lots of laughter. Lots of love."

Victoria did not reply. There was nothing to say, and her thoughts were so confused that there was nothing much to think, either. She only knew that for the first time since he had left her, she felt safe again, and at peace. And she only knew that tomorrow, or perhaps the next day, she was going away with Oliver. Once more, she was committed. For better or for worse, but maybe it would work this time. Maybe he had changed. Things would be different. And perhaps, if he felt so strongly about Thomas, he would feel strongly about other things. Permanent things. Like loving one person and staying with her for ever. But whatever happened, the die had been cast. Victoria had passed the point of no return.

She sighed deeply, but the sigh was prompted by confusion rather than unhappiness. "Where shall we go?" she asked Oliver.

"Anywhere you like. Is there an ashtray in this benighted cupboard of a room?"

Victoria reached out and groped for the one she knew lay on the bedside table, and handed it to him.

He went on, "What was the name of that place you were babbling about, when you were so patently anxious not to be made love to? The place in the book, *The Eagle Years?*"

"Benchoile."

"Would you like to go there?"

"We can't."

"Why not?"

"It's not a hotel. We don't know the people who live there."

"I do, my darling innocent."

"What do you mean?"

"I know Roddy Dunbeath. I met him about two years ago. Sat next to him at one of those dismal television award dinners. He was there on account of his last book, and I was there because I was given some piddling little statue for a television script I wrote about Seville. Anyway, there we were, surrounded by moronic starlets and shark-like agents, and thankful for each other's company. By the end of the evening we were friends for life, and he gave me a standing invitation to visit him at Benchoile whenever the spirit moved me. So far I haven't taken it up, but if you want to go there, there's no reason on earth why we shouldn't."

"Do you really mean that?"

"Of course I do."

"Are you certain it wasn't just one of those things people say at the end of a good evening and then forget about, or even regret for the rest of their lives?"

"Not at all. He meant it. Even gave me his card in a rather old-fashioned way. I can find out the telephone number and ring him up."

"Will he remember you?"

"Of course he'll remember me. And I shall tell him that I and my wife and my child want to come and spend a few days with him."

"It sounds like an awful lot of people. And I'm *not* your wife."

"Then I shall say my mistress and my child. He'll jump at that. He's rather Rabelaisian. You'll love him. He's very fat, and extremely, politely drunk. At least, he was by the end of that dinner. But Roddy Dunbeath, drunk, is ten times more charming than most men are stone cold sober."

"It'll take us a long time to drive to Sutherland."

"We'll take it in stages. Anyway, we have a long time."

He stubbed out his cigarette, and leaned over Victoria once more, in order to put the ashtray on the floor. She found that she was smiling into the darkness. She said, "You know, I think I'd rather go to Benchoile than anywhere else in the world."

"It's better than that. You're going to Benchoile with me."

"And Thomas."

"You're going to Benchoile with me and Thomas."

"I can't think of anything more perfect."

Oliver gently placed his hand on her stomach; slowly, he slid it up her body, over her ribcage, to cup one small, naked breast. "I can," he told her.

5

SUNDAY

In the middle of February, the cold weather arrived. Christmas had been sunny and the New Year mild and still, and the weeks of winter crept past, with some rain and a little frost and nothing much else. "We're going to be lucky," said people who knew no better, but the shepherds and the hill-farmers were wiser. They eyed the skies and smelled the wind and knew that the worst was still to come. The winter was simply waiting. Biding its time.

The real frosts started at the beginning of the month. Then came the sleet, swiftly turning to snow, and then the storms. "Straight from the Urals," said Roddy Dunbeath, as the bitter wind whined in over the sea. The sea turned grey and angry, sullen as the colour of wet slate, and creaming breakers flooded in over the Creagan sands, depositing a long tidemark of undigested rubbish. Old fish boxes, ragged nets, knotted twine, plastic detergent bottles, rubber tyres, even a disfigured shoe or two.

Inland, the hills were cloaked in white, their summits lost in the dark, racing sky. Snow blew from the open fields and piled in steep drifts, choking the narrow roads. Sheep, heavy in their winter wool, could survive, but the cattle searched for shelter in the angles of the drystone dikes, and the farmers tractored fodder to them twice a day.

Accustomed to, and expecting, cruel winters, the local people accepted all this hardship with stoical calm. The smaller hill crofts and isolated cottages were cut off entirely, but walls were thick and peat stacks high, and there was always plenty of oatmeal, and foodstuff for the stock. Life continued. The scarlet post-van made its daily round of the glens, and sturdy housewives, wearing rubber boots and three cardigans, emerged from doorways to feed hens and hang out lines of washing in the freezing wind.

Now, it was Sunday.

The Lord's my Shepherd, I'll not want.
He makes me down to lie
In pastures green . . .

The pipes in the church were faintly warm, but the draughts excruciating. The congregation, thinned to a mere handful by the weather, bravely raised their voices in the last hymn of the morning service, but their efforts were almost drowned by the fury of the wind outside.

Jock Dunbeath, standing alone in the Benchoile pew, held his hymnbook in mittened hands but did not look at it, partly because he had sung this hymn all his life and knew the words by heart and partly because, by some oversight, he had left his reading spectacles at home.

Ellen had fussed over him. "You must indeed be mad thinking you'll get to the kirk today. The roads are blocked. Would you not stop off at Davey's and get him to drive you?"

"Davey has enough to do."

"Then why not sit by the fire and listen to the nice man on the wireless? Would that not do as well for once?"

But he was stubborn, immovable, and she finally

sighed and tossed her eyes to heaven and gave in. "But don't be blaming me if you die in a drift on your way."

She sounded quite excited at the thought of such a happening. Disaster was the spice of life to Ellen, and she was always the first to say "I told you so." Irritated by her, in a hurry to get away, he forgot his spectacles, and was then too pig-headed to go back for them. However, his determination was vindicated, and, in the old Land-Rover, grinding in bottom gear down the four miles of the glen, he had managed to make it safely and had come to church. Chilled as he was, and blind as a bat without his glasses, he was glad that he had made the effort.

All his life, unless prevented by illness, war, or some other act of God, he had come to church on Sunday mornings. As a child because he had had to; as a soldier because he needed to; as a grown man because he was the laird of Benchoile and it was important to be involved, to uphold the established traditions, to set a good example. And now, in his old age, he came for comfort and reassurance. The old church, the words of the service, the tunes of the hymns, were some of the very few things in his life that hadn't changed. Perhaps, at the end of the day, the only thing.

Goodness and mercy all my days,
Shall surely follow me,
And in God's house for ever more
My dwelling place shall be.

He closed his hymnbook, bowed his head for the blessing, collected his driving gloves and his old tweed cap from the seat beside him, buttoned up his overcoat, wound himself up in his scarf, started up the aisle.

"Morning, sir." It was a friendly sort of church. People came out with conversation in their ordinary voices –

none of those pious whispers as though there were a body dying in the next room. "Terrible weather. Good morning, Colonel Dunbeath, and how are the roads up with you? . . . Well, Jock, and you're a fine one, making the trip to the kirk on a day like this."

That was the minister himself, coming up at Jock from behind. Jock turned. The minister, the Reverend Christie, was a well-set-up man with a pair of shoulders like a rugby player, but still Jock topped him by half a head.

He said, "I thought you'd be a bit thin on the ground this morning. Glad I made the effort."

"I imagined you all cut off up at Benchoile."

"The telephone's dead. There must be a line down somewhere. But I managed the road in the Land-Rover."

"It's a bitter day. Why don't you come into the Manse for a glass of sherry before you start back?"

His eyes were kind. He was a good man, with a homely and hospitable wife. For a moment Jock let himself imagine the living-room at the Manse. The chair, which would be drawn up for him by an enormous fire, the air fragrant with the smell of roasting Sunday mutton. The Christies had always done themselves very well. He thought of the dark, sweet, warming sherry, the comfortable presence of Mrs Christie, and for a small instant was tempted.

But, "No," he said, "I think I'd better get back before the weather worsens. Ellen will be expecting me. And I would not want the constable to find me frozen in a snowdrift with the smell of alcohol on my breath."

"Ah, well, that's understandable." The minister's kindly countenance and robust manner masked his concern. He had been shocked this morning to see Jock sitting solitary in his pew. Most of the congregation, for some reason, gathered themselves at the back of his church, and the laird, isolated like some outcast, had stuck out like a sore thumb.

He looked old. It was the first time that Mr Christie had seen him looking really old. Too thin, too tall, his tweed hanging loose on the lanky frame, the fingers of his hands swollen and red with the cold. The collar of his shirt was loose on his neck, and there had been a hesitancy in his actions, fumbling for his hymnbook, for the pound note that was his weekly contribution to the offertory plate.

Jock Dunbeath of Benchoile. How old was he? Sixty-eight, sixty-nine? Not old for nowadays. Not old for hereabouts, where the menfolk seemed to go on well into their eighties, sprightly and active, digging their gardens and keeping a few hens, and making small tottery excursions to the village inn for their evening dram. But last September Jock had suffered a slight heart attack, and since then, thought Mr Christie, he seemed to have gone visibly downhill. And yet, what could one do to help? If he had been one of the country folk, Mr Christie would have gone visiting, taken a batch of his wife's scones, perhaps offered to cut a stack of kindling; but Jock was not country folk. He was Lieutenant-Colonel John Rathbone Dunbeath, late of the Cameron Highlanders, the laird of Benchoile and a Justice of the Peace. He was proud, but he was not poor. He was old and lonely, but he was not poor. On the contrary, he was a well-respected landowner with a large house and a farm in hand, twelve thousand or so acres of hill, a thousand or more sheep, some arable land, some stalking, some fishing. In all respects, an enviable property. If the big house was rambling and shabby, and the laird's shirt had a frayed collar, it was not because he was poor. It was because his wife was dead, he was childless, and old Ellen Tarbat, housekeeper to Jock and his brother Roddy, was getting beyond it.

And somewhere, some time, before the eyes of them all, the old man seemed to have given up.

Mr Christie searched for some remark that would keep

their conversation going. "And how is the family?" was a useful starter on most occasions, but not this one, because Jock didn't have a family. Only Roddy. Oh well, thought the minister, any port in a storm.

"And how is your brother keeping?"

Jock responded with a gleam of humour. "You make him sound like a box of herring. I think he's all right. We don't see that much of each other. Keep to ourselves, you know. Roddy in his house and me in mine." He cleared his throat. "Sunday lunch. We have Sunday lunch together. It's companionable."

Mr Christie wondered what they talked about. He had never known two brothers so different, one so reserved and the other so outgoing. Roddy was a writer, an artist, a raconteur. The books that he had written, some almost twenty years or so ago, were all still in print, and the paperback editions could always be found on station bookstalls and in the racks of the most unlikely country shops. *A classic* said the blurb on the back covers, under the photograph of Roddy that had been taken thirty years ago. *A breath of the outdoors. Roddy Dunbeath knows his Scotland and presents it, with native perception, within the pages of this book.*

Roddy did not come to church unless it was Christmas or Easter or somebody's funeral, but whether this was due to his inner convictions or his inherent idleness, the minister did not know. Roddy did not even appear very often in the village. Jess Guthrie, the shepherd's wife, did his shopping for him. "And how is Mr Roddy, Jess?" the grocer would inquire, fitting the two bottles of Dewars down the side of the carton of groceries, and Jess would avert her eyes from the bottles and reply, "Oh, he's not so bad," which could have meant anything.

"Is he working on anything just now?" Mr Christie asked.

"He mentioned something about an article for the *Scottish Field*. I . . . I never really know," Jock ran a diffident hand down the back of his head, smoothing down the thinning grey hair. "He never talks much about his work."

A lesser man might have been discouraged, but Mr Christie pressed on, and asked after the third Dunbeath brother.

"And what news of Charlie?"

"I had a letter at Christmas. He and Susan were skiing. At Aspen. That's in Colorado, you know," he added in his mannerly way, as though Mr Christie mightn't.

"Was John with them?"

There was a small pause. Jock put back his head. His eyes, pale and watering a little in the cold, fixed on some distant, unfocused spot beyond the minister's head.

"John doesn't work in New York any longer. Got sent to the London branch of his bank. Works there now. Been working there for six months or more."

"But that's splendid."

The church was nearly empty now. They began to tread, side by side, up the aisle towards the main door.

"Yes. Good thing for John. Step up the ladder. Clever boy. Suppose he'll be president before we know where we are. I mean president of the bank, not president of the United States of America . . ."

But Mr Christie was not to be diverted by this mild joke. "I didn't mean that, Jock. I meant that if he's living in London, it shouldn't be too hard for him to get up to Sutherland and spend a few days with you and Roddy."

Jock stopped dead and turned. His eyes narrowed. He was suddenly alert, fierce as an old eagle.

Mr Christie was a little taken aback by that piercing glance. "Just an idea. It seems to me that you need a bit of young company." And someone to keep an eye on you, as well, he thought, but he did not say this aloud. "It must be ten years since John was last here."

"Yes. Ten years." They moved on, slow-paced. "He

was eighteen." The old man appeared to be debating with himself. The minister waited tactfully, and was rewarded. "Wrote to him the other day. Suggested he come up in the summer. He was never interested in the grouse, but I could give him a bit of fishing."

"I'm sure he needs no such bait to lure him north."

"Haven't had an answer yet."

"Give him time. He'll be a busy man."

"Yes. The only thing is, these days I'm not quite sure how much time I have to give." Jock smiled, that rare wry smile that warmed the chill from his features and never failed to disarm. "But then, it comes to all of us. You of all men know that."

They let themselves out of the church, and the wind caught the minister's robes and sent the black skirts ballooning. From the porch, he watched Jock Dunbeath clamber painfully up into the old Land-Rover and set off on his uncertain journey home. Despite himself he sighed, heavy-hearted. He had tried. But, at the end of the day, what could anybody do?

No more snow had fallen and Jock was glad of this. He trundled through the quiet, shuttered village and over the bridge and turned inland where the road sign pointed to Benchoile and Loch Muie. The road was narrow and single-tracked, with passing places marked by black and white painted posts, but there was no other traffic of any sort. The Sabbath, even in weather like this, cast its gloom over the countryside. Beset by icy draughts, hunched over the wheel, with his scarf up to his ears and his tweed cap pulled down over his beak of a nose, Jock Dunbeath let the Land-Rover take its own way home, like a reliable horse, up the tracks in the snow that they had made themselves that morning.

He thought about what the minister had said. He was right, of course. A good man. Concerned and trying not to show it. But he was right.

You need a bit of young company.

He remembered Benchoile in the old days when he, and his friends, and his brothers' friends, had all filled the house. He remembered the hall overflowing with fishing boots and creels, tea on the lawn beneath the silver birches, and in August the sunlit purple hills echoing to the crack of guns. He remembered house parties for the Northern Meetings Hunt Ball in Inverness, and girls coming downstairs in long, pretty dresses, and the old station wagon driving off to collect guests off the train at Creagan Halt.

But those days, like everything else, were gone. For the brothers, youth had gone. Roddy had never married; Charlie had found himself a wife, and a sweet one too, but she was an American girl, and he had gone back with her to the States, and made a life for himself as a cattleman, ranching his father-in-law's spread in southwest Colorado. And although Jock had married, he and Lucy had never had the children they so ardently wanted. They had been so happy together that even this cruel trick of fate could not mar their content. But when she had died, five years ago, he had realised that he had never before known the true meaning of loneliness.

You need a bit of young company.

Funny, the minister bringing John's name up like that, just days after Jock had written him the letter. Almost as though he had known about it. As a child, John had visited Benchoile regularly, in the company of his parents, and then, as he grew older, alone with his father. He had been a quiet, serious little boy, intelligent beyond his years, and with a searching curiosity that manifested itself in a long stream of endless questions. But even in those days, Roddy had been his favourite uncle, and the two of them would go off for hours on end, to search for shells, or watch the birds, or stand, on still summer evenings, casting their trout rods over the deep brown pools of the river. In all respects, a likeable and satisfactory boy, but still, Jock had never been able to get close to him. The main reason for this was that John did not share with Jock his abiding passion for shooting. John would blissfully lure and catch and slay a fish, and very soon became accomplished at the sport, but he refused to go up the hill with a gun, and if he stalked a deer, would carry nothing more deadly than his camera.

And so the letter had not been an easy one to write. For John had not been to Benchoile for ten years, and this gap of time had left a yawning void that Jock had found almost impossible to bridge with words. Not, he assured himself quickly, that he didn't like the boy. He remembered John Dunbeath at eighteen as a composed, reserved young man with disturbingly mature attitudes and opinions. Jock respected these, but he found his coolness and his polite self-confidence a little disconcerting. And since then they had somehow lost touch. So much had happened, Lucy had died and the empty years had slipped away. Charlie had written, of course, giving news. John had gone to Cambridge, played squash and rackets for the university, and left with an honours degree in economics. He had then returned to New York and there joined the Warburg Investment Corporation, a position that he achieved entirely on his own merits and without any assistance from his influential American connections. For some time he had been at the Harvard Business School, and in due course, inevitably, he had married. Charlie was too loyal a father to spell out the details of this misalliance to Jock, but gradually, reading between the lines of his brother's letters, Jock realised that all was not well with the young couple. So he was distressed, but not surprised, when the news came through that the marriage had broken up, divorce proceedings were being taken, and legal settlements made. The only good thing about it was that there were no children.

The divorce, painfully, was finally accomplished, and John's career, apparently untouched by the traumas of his personal life, continued to go from strength to strength. The appointment in London was the latest in a succession of steady promotions. Banking was a world about which Jock Dunbeath knew nothing, and this was another reason why he felt so totally out of touch with his American nephew.

> Dear John,
>
> Your father tells me that you are now back in this country and working in London.

It wouldn't have been so hard if he had felt that he had anything in common with the young man. Some shared interest that would have provided him with a starting point.

> If you are able to get a little time off perhaps you would think about making the journey north and spending a few days at Benchoile.

He had never been much of a letter writer and it had taken him nearly half a day to finally compose this one, and even then the finished result did not satisfy him. But he signed it, and wrote the address on the envelope and stuck down the flap. It would have been so much easier, he thought wistfully, if only John had shown some interest in the grouse.

These reflections had brought him halfway home. The narrow, rutted, snow-filled road took a turn and the length of Loch Muie slid into view, grey as iron beneath the lowering sky. There was a light on in Davey Guthrie's farmhouse, and away at the end of the loch stood Benchoile itself, sheltered by the stand of pines which stood silhouetted, black as ink, against the snow-covered slopes of the hill.

Built of grey stone, long and low, turreted and gabled, it faced south, across a wide sloping lawn, to the loch. Too big, draughty and unheatable, shabby and constantly in need of repair, it was, nevertheless, his home, and the only place, in all his life, that he had ever really wanted to be.

Ten minutes later, he was there. Up the slope and through the gates, over the rattle of the cattle grid, and down the short tunnel of wild rhododendrons. In front of the house the drive opened up into a wide gravel sweep. At the far end of this was an ornate stone arch which attached the house, by one corner, to the old stable block where Jock's brother Roddy lived. Beyond the arch was a spacious cobbled yard, and at the far end of this were the garages, which were originally built to house carriages and shooting brakes but now contained Jock's old Daimler and the aged green MG into which Roddy squeezed his bulk when the spirit moved him to make some excursion into the outside world.

Alongside these two ill-assorted vehicles, in a thick gloom occasioned by the dreariness of the day, Jock Dunbeath finally homed the Land-Rover, pulled on the brake, and killed the engine. He took the folded wad of Sunday newspapers off the seat beside him, got out of the car, slammed the door shut, and went out into the yard. Snow lay thick on the cobbles. The light was on in Roddy's sitting-room. Cautiously, anxious not to slip or fall, he made his way across the yard to Roddy's front door, and let himself in.

Although it was often referred to as a flat, Roddy's house was, in fact, a two-storey dwelling, converted out of the old stables at the end of the war, when Roddy had come back to Benchoile to live. Roddy, fired by enthusiasm, had architected the conversion himself. The bedrooms and bathrooms were downstairs, the kitchen and the living-room upstairs, and access to these rooms was by an open teak stair, like a ship's ladder.

Jock stood at the foot of this and called, "Roddy!"

Roddy's footsteps creaked across the floorboards over Jock's head. In a moment his brother's bulk appeared, and Roddy peered down at him over the rail of the stairhead.

"Oh, it's you," said Roddy, as though it might be anybody else.

"Brought the papers."

"Come on up. What a bloody awful day."

Jock mounted the stairs, and came out at the top in the living-room where Roddy spent his days. It was a marvellous room, light and large, the ceiling gabled to the shape of the roof, and one wall taken up by an enormous picture window. This had been designed to frame a view over the loch to the mountains, which, in fine weather, took the breath away. But this morning what could be seen was enough to chill the soul. Snow and grey water, running before the wind and capped in white; the hills on the far shore were lost in murk.

It was a man's room, and yet a room of taste and even beauty; lined with books and cluttered with a number of objects which, though worth little, were visually pleasing. A carved overmantel; a blue-and-white jar filled with pampas grasses; a dangling mobile of paper fishes, probably Japanese. The floorboards had been sanded and polished and sparsely scattered with rugs. Elderly armchairs and a sofa sagged invitingly. In the cavern of a fireplace (which had had to be specially constructed at the time of the conversion, and had proved to be the most costly item of all) a couple of birch logs sizzled on a bed of peat. The room had an extraordinary and quite unique smell about it. Compounded of cigar smoke, and peat smoke too, and the sharp aroma of linseed oil.

Roddy's old Labrador, Barney, lay supine on the

hearthrug. At Jock's appearance, he raised his grizzled nose, and then yawned and went back to sleep again.

Roddy said, "Have you been to the kirk?"

"Yes." Jock began to unbutton his overcoat with frozen fingers.

"Did you know the telephone's dead? There must be a line down somewhere." Roddy gave his brother a long, measuring look. "You appear to be blue with cold. Have a drink." He moved ponderously towards the table where he kept his bottles and glasses. He had already, Jock noticed, provided himself with a large, dark whisky. Jock did not ever drink in the middle of the day. It was one of his rules. But somehow today, ever since the minister had mentioned that glass of sherry, he had been thinking about it.

"Have you got some sherry?"

"Only the pale kind. Dry as a bone."

"That'll do very nicely."

He took off his coat and went to stand in front of the fire. Roddy's mantelpiece was always littered with undusted bits and pieces. Curling photographs, old pipes, a mug of pheasant quills, and out-of-date invitations, probably unanswered. There was today, however, a sparkling new card propped against the clock, impressively copper-plated, gold-edged and marvellously pretentious.

"What's this? Looks like a royal command."

"Nothing so splendid. A dinner at the Dorchester. Television awards. Best documentary of the year. God knows why I've been invited. I thought I'd been crossed off all the lists. Actually, apart from the tedium of the after-dinner speeches, I used to quite enjoy those occasions. Met a lot of new young writers, new faces. Interesting to talk to."

"Are you going to this one?"

"I'm getting too elderly to travel the length of the country for a free hangover." He had laid down his whisky, located the sherry, found a suitable glass, poured his brother's drink. Now he retrieved a smouldering, half-smoked cigar from an ashtray, picked up the two glasses and came back to the fireside. "If it were to take place somewhere civilised, like Inverness, I might deign to add tone to what will otherwise be a vulgar brawl. As it is . . ." He raised his glass. "Slainte, old boy."

Jock grinned. "Slainte."

Roddy was nine years Jock's junior. When they were young, Roddy had been the handsome one of the three brothers, the dallying charmer who had broken more hearts than could be decently counted, and who never lost his own. Women adored him. Men were never quite so sure. He was too good-looking, too clever, too talented at all the sorts of things that it was not considered manly to be talented at. He drew and he wrote and he played the piano. He could even sing.

On shoots he always seemed to get the prettiest girl of the party into his butt, and quite often forgot that the object of the exercise was to slay grouse. No sound, no blast would come from his butt, while the grouse sailed serenely over him in coveys, and at the end of the drive he would be found deep in conversation with his companion, his gun unfired, and his dog whining and frustrated at his feet.

Naturally brilliant, he had skimmed through his schooldays without apparently doing a stroke of work, and had gone on to Oxford in a blaze of glory. Trends were started by Roddy Dunbeath and fashions set. Where others sported tweed, he favoured corduroy, and soon everybody was wearing corduroy. He was president of the OUDS and a renowned debater. Nobody was safe from his wit, which was usually gentle, but could be barbed.

When the war broke out, Jock was already a regular soldier with the Camerons. Roddy, impelled by a deep patriotism which he had always kept to himself, joined up the day that war was declared. He signed on, to everybody's surprise, with the Royal Marines, on account of, he said, they had such a pretty uniform; but in no time at all, he was training to be a Commando, struggling up precipitous cliffs on the end of a rope and hurling himself from training planes with tightly closed eyes and his hand clenched around the ripcord of his parachute.

When it was all over and the country was at peace again, it seemed to Jock Dunbeath that everyone who wasn't married rushed to rectify the situation. There was a veritable epidemic of matrimony, and Jock himself had fallen prey to it. But not Roddy. Roddy picked up his life where he had left it in 1939 and went on from there. He made himself a home at Benchoile and started to write. *The Eagle Years* came out first, and then *The Wind in the Pines*, and then *Red Fox*. Fame embraced him. He went on lecture tours, he made after-dinner speeches, he appeared on television.

By now he was putting on weight. While Jock stayed thin and spare, Roddy became stout. Gradually his girth spread, his chin doubled, his handsome features were lost in heavy jowls. And yet, he was as attractive as ever, and when the gossip columns in the daily papers ran out of tidbits about the nobility, they would print blurred photographs of Roddy Dunbeath (*The Eagle Years*) dining with Mrs So-and-So, who was, as everybody knew, a champion of wildlife.

But youth had gone, lost somewhere over the years, and at last even his mild fame began to slip away. No longer fêted in London, he returned, as he had always returned, to Benchoile. He occupied himself in writing short articles, the scripts for television nature films, even small items for the local newspapers. Nothing changed him, he was still the same Roddy, charming and witty, the engaging raconteur. Still willing to squeeze his bulk into his velvet jacket and drive himself for miles down dark country roads to make up the numbers at some remote dinner party. And, even more astonishing – somehow getting himself home again in the small hours of the morning, half-asleep and awash with whisky.

For he was drinking too much. Not uncontrollably nor offensively, but still he seldom seemed to have a glass out of his hand. He began to slow down. He, who had always been physically indolent, was now becoming chronically idle. He could scarcely make the effort to get himself into Creagan. His life had become encapsulated at Benchoile.

"What are the roads like?" he asked now.

"Passable. You wouldn't have got far in the MG."

"No intention of going anywhere." He took the cigar from his mouth and aimed it at the fireplace. It made a tiny flame. He stooped to lift more logs from the great basket that stood by the hearth, and toss them into the grey ashes of the peat. Dust rose in a cloud. The fresh logs flickered and caught fire. There was a small explosion, and one or two sparks flew out on to the aged hearthrug. The smell of burning wood filled Jock's nostrils. Roddy trod out the sparks with the sole of his brogue.

"You should have a fireguard," said Jock.

"Can't stand the look of the things. Besides, they keep all the heat in." He gazed thoughtfully down at his fireplace. "Thought I might get one of those chain curtains. Saw one advertised the other day, but now I can't remember where I saw it." He had finished his drink. He began to drift back towards the bottles on the table. Jock said, "You've hardly time for another. It's past one o'clock already."

Roddy looked at his watch. "Well, bless my soul, so it is. It's a wonder Ellen hasn't yet given us her weekly screech. I suppose you couldn't persuade her to use the old gong. She could bring it out into the stable yard and ring it there. It would be so much more in keeping if I could be summoned to Sunday lunch in the big house by the dignified rumble of a gong. Gracious living and all that. We mustn't let ourselves go, Jock. We must keep up appearances even if there is no person to appreciate our efforts. Think of those old empire builders, dining in the jungle in their starched shirts and black ties. There's backbone for you."

The glass of sherry had freed Jock's inhibitions a little. "This morning the minister told me that we need some young company at Benchoile," he told Roddy.

"Well, what a pretty thought." Roddy hesitated over the whisky bottle, thought better of it, and poured himself a small sherry instead. "Handsome lads and pretty lasses. What happened to all those young relations of Lucy's? The house used to be running with her nephews and nieces. They were all over the place. Like mice."

"They've grown up. Married. That's what happened to them."

"Let's stage a grand reunion and get them all back again. We'll put a notice in the personal column of the *Times*. 'The Dunbeaths of Benchoile require young company. All applications will be given consideration.' We might get some rather amusing replies."

Jock thought of the letter that he had written to John. He had not told Roddy about that letter. Cautiously, he had made up his mind that when a reply came from John, and not before, he would take Roddy into his confidence.

But now, he found that resolution wavering. He and Roddy saw so little of each other, and it was seldom that they found themselves on such easy and companionable terms as they were at this moment. If he brought the business of John up now, then they could discuss it over Sunday lunch. After all, some time, it all had to be thrashed out. He finished his sherry. He squared his shoulders. He said, "Roddy . . ."

But was interrupted by a banging on the door downstairs, and then a blast of icy air as it was opened. A voice, shrill and cracked, rose from the foot of the stairs.

"It's past one o'clock. Did you know that?"

Roddy looked resigned. "Yes, Ellen, we did."

"Have you got the colonel with you?"

"Yes, he's here."

"I saw the Land-Rover in the garage, but he's not been near the big house. You'd better both come over now, or the bird'll be ruined." Ellen had never been one for much formality.

Jock laid down his empty glass and went to collect his coat. "We're coming now, Ellen," he told her. "We're coming right away."

6

MONDAY

The fact that the telephone lines were down and the phone not working was of small concern to Roddy Dunbeath. Where others tried six or seven times in a morning to make outside calls, jigged the receiver in empty exasperation, and finally trod out into the snow to the nearest functioning call-box, Roddy remained unperturbed. There was no person with whom he wished to get in touch, and he actively enjoyed the sensation of being undisturbed and unreachable.

And so, when the phone on his desk suddenly began to ring at half past eleven on Monday morning, he was at first startled out of his skin and then irritated.

During the night the wind had died, having first blown all the clouds out of the sky, and the morning had dawned, late and clear and still. The sky was a pale, arctic blue. The sun, rising over the foot of the loch, turned the snow-clad countryside first pink, and then a dazzling white. The lawn in front of the house was patterned with the random tracks of rabbits and hares. A deer had been there, too, feeding off the young shrubs that Jock had planted at the back end of the year and tree shadows lay like long, smoky blue bruises. As the sun climbed over the rim of the hills, the sky deepened in blue, and this was reflected in the waters of the loch. Frost glittered, and the icy air was so still that when Roddy opened his window to throw out a handful of crusts for his birds, he could hear the baa-ing of the sheep which grazed on the slopes at the far side of the water.

It was not a day for much activity. But, with a certain resolution, and a deadline hanging over his head, Roddy had managed to finish the first draft of his article for the *Scottish Field*. With this behind him, he succumbed once more to idleness and was sitting at his window with a cigar and his binoculars at the ready. He had seen greylags feeding on the worn stubble of the arable fields beyond the pines. Sometimes, in hard weather like this, they would settle in the thousands.

The telephone rang. He said, aloud, "Oh, bloody hell," and at the sound of his voice Barney raised his head from the hearthrug. Thump thump went his tail. "It's all right, old boy, it's not your fault." He laid down his binoculars, got up, and went, reluctantly, to answer it.

"Roddy Dunbeath."

There came strange peeping sounds. For a moment Roddy felt hopeful that the tiresome instrument was still out of order, but then the peeping sounds stopped and a voice came on, and hope died.

"Is that Benchoile?"

"The Stable House, yes. Roddy Dunbeath here."

"Roddy. This is Oliver Dobbs."

After a little, Roddy said, "Who?"

"Oliver Dobbs." It was a pleasant voice, young, deep, vaguely familiar. Roddy dug about, without noticeable success, in his unreliable memory.

"I'm not with you, old boy."

"We met at a dinner in London a couple of years ago. Sat next to each other . . ."

Recollection dawned. Of course, Oliver Dobbs. Clever young man. A writer. Won some prize. They'd had a great crack together. "But of course." He reached behind him for a chair, settled himself for conversation. "My dear boy, how splendid to hear you. Where are you calling from?"

"The Lake District."

"What are you doing in the Lake District?"

"I'm taking a few days off. I'm driving up to Scotland."

"You're going to come here, of course."

"Well, that's what I'm calling about. I tried to ring you yesterday, but they said the phone lines were down. When we met, you issued an invitation to come and see you at Benchoile, and I'm afraid I'm taking it up."

"Nothing to be afraid of. I couldn't be more pleased."

"We thought perhaps we might be able to come and stay for a couple of days."

"Of course you must come." The prospect of a couple of days in the company of that lively and intelligent young man was quite stimulating. But, "Who's we?" asked Roddy.

"Well, there's the rub," said Oliver Dobbs. "We're a sort of family. Victoria and me and Thomas. He's only two, but he's quite undemanding and very well-behaved. Would there be room for us all, because if not Victoria says we can go to a pub if there's such a thing nearby."

"Never heard such rubbish." Roddy was quite indignant. Benchoile hospitality had always been legendary. True, during the last five years, since Lucy died, the entries in the battered leather-bound visitors' book, which lived on the hall table in the big house, were few and far between, but that didn't mean that there wasn't still the warmest of welcomes for any person who wished to come and stay. "Of course you must come here. When will you arrive?"

"Perhaps about Thursday? We thought we'd drive up the west coast. Victoria's never been to the Highlands."

"Come by Strome Ferry and Achnasheen." Roddy knew the Scottish highways like the back of his hand. "And then down Strath Oykel to Lairg. You've never seen such country in your life."

"Have you got snow up there?"

"We've had a lot, but the good weather's back again. By the time you get here, the road should be clear."

"And you're sure you don't mind us coming?"

"Absolutely delighted. We'll expect you Thursday about lunchtime. And stay," he added with the expansiveness of a potential host who has no intention of being involved in the tedious necessities of airing sheets or dusting bedrooms or cooking meals, "stay as long as you like."

The telephone call, coming out of the blue as it had, left Roddy in a pleasurable state of mild excitement. After he had replaced the receiver, he sat for a little, finishing his cigar, and anticipating, with the satisfaction of a boy, the forthcoming visit.

He loved young people. Trapped in the spreading bulk and the balding head of approaching old age, he still thought of himself as young. Inside, he still felt young. He remembered with pleasure the instant rapport that had sprung up between himself and Oliver Dobbs. How they had sat through that dinner, serious-faced and boiling with suppressed laughter at the endless, cliché-ridden speeches.

At one point, Oliver had made some remark, thrown from the corner of his mouth, about the chest measurements of the lady across the table from them, and Roddy had thought, *You remind me of me*. Perhaps that was it. Oliver was his alter ego, the young man Roddy had once been. Or perhaps the young man he would like to have been, if circumstances had been different, if he had been born to a different way of life, if there had been no war.

The pleasure had to be shared. Not only that, Ellen

Tarbat had to be told. She would put on a face, shake her head, accept the tidings in martyred resignation. This was customary and meant nothing. Ellen always put on a face, shook her head and looked martyred, even if one happened to be the bearer of delightful news.

Roddy stubbed out his cigar, and without bothering to put on a coat, got up out of his chair and started down the stairs. His dog followed him. They went out into the cold morning air together, crossed the icy cobbles of the stable yard, and let themselves in through the back door of the big house.

The passages that lay beyond were stone-floored, cold, and seemingly endless. Doors gave off to coalsheds, woodsheds, laundries, storerooms, cellars, pantries. He came at last through a green-baize-covered door, and emerged into the big hall of the old house. Here, the temperature rose by a few degrees. Sun poured in through long windows and the glassed inner front door. It sent long beams, dancing with dust motes, down the Turkey-rugged staircase and quenched the fire, which smouldered in the immense grate, to a bed of dusty ashes. Roddy stopped to replenish this from the basket of peats which stood alongside and then went in search of his brother.

He found Jock, inevitably, in the library, sitting at the unfashionable roll-top desk, which had belonged to their father, and dealing with the endless accounts and paperwork related to the management of the farm.

Since Lucy had died, the drawing-room had, by wordless consent, been closed and shut away, and this was now the apartment in which Jock spent his days. It was one of Roddy's favourite rooms, shabby and worn, the walls lined with books, the old leather-covered chairs sagging and comfortable as old friends. Today this room too was filled with the pale sunlight of the winter's day. Another fire burned in the hearth, and Jock's two golden Labradors lay drugged in the warmth.

As Roddy opened the door, Jock looked up, over the spectacles which habitually slid to the end of his long beak of a nose. Roddy said, "Good morning."

"Hello." He took off the spectacles, leaning back in his chair. "And what might you be wanting?"

Roddy came in and shut the door. He said, "I am the bearer of pleasing news." Jock sat politely, waiting to be pleased. "You might even say, I was some sort of a fairy godmother, granting all your wishes."

Jock still waited. Roddy smiled and let his weight cautiously down into the armchair nearest the fire. After his trek across the yard and down the arctic passages of Benchoile, his feet felt cold, so he toed off his slippers and wriggled his stockinged feet in the warmth. There was a hole in one of his socks. He would have to get Ellen to mend it.

He said, "You know, yesterday, you said that the minister at Creagan said that what we needed at Benchoile was some young company. Well, we're going to get it."

"Who are we going to get?"

"A delightful and bright young man called Oliver Dobbs and what he pleases to call his 'sort of family'."

"And who is Oliver Dobbs?"

"If you weren't such an old reactionary, you'd have heard of him. A very clever young man with a string of literary successes to his name."

"Oh," said Jock. "One of those."

"You'll like him." That was the extraordinary thing, Jock probably would. Roddy had called his brother a reactionary, but Jock was nothing of the kind. Jock was a liberal, through and through. Beneath his chilling, eagle-proud appearance lay concealed the real man, gentle, tolerant, well-mannered. Jock had never disliked a man on sight. Jock had always been willing and ready, in his reserved and diffident way, to see the other man's point of view.

"And what," asked Jock mildly, "does the 'sort of family' consist of?"

"I'm not quite sure, but whatever it is, we may well have to keep it from Ellen."

"When are they coming?"

"Thursday. Lunchtime."

"Where are they going to sleep?"

"I thought over here, in the big house. There's more space."

"You'll have to tell Ellen."

"I am steeling myself to do that very thing."

Jock sent him a long amused look, and Roddy grinned. Jock leaned back in his chair and rubbed his eyes with the gesture of a man who had been up all night. He said, "What time is it?" and looked at his watch. Roddy, who was longing for a drink, said it was twelve o'clock, but Jock didn't notice the hint, or if he did he took no account of it, but said instead, "I'm going out for a walk."

Roddy suppressed his disappointment. He would go back to his own house and pour himself a drink there. He said, "It's a beautiful morning."

"Yes," said Jock. He looked out of the window. "Beautiful. Benchoile at its most beautiful."

They talked for a little and then Roddy departed, with conscious courage, kitchenwards, in search of Ellen. Jock got up from his desk, and with the dogs at his heel, went out of the room and across the hall to the gunroom. He took down a shooting jacket, shucked off his slippers, climbed into a pair of green rubber boots. He took down his cap, pulled it down over his nose. A muffler to wind round his neck. He found knitted mittens in the pocket of the jacket and pulled them on. His fingers protruded from the open ends, swollen and purple as beef sausages.

He found his stick, a long shepherd's crook. He let himself thankfully out of the house. The cold air hit him, the piercing chill of it biting deep into his lungs.

For days he had been feeling unwell. He put it down to tiredness and the bitter weather, but all at once, in the meagre warmth of the February sun, he felt a little better. Perhaps he should get out and about more, but one needed good reason to make the required effort.

Tramping over the creaking snow towards the loch, he thought of the young people whom Roddy had invited to stay, and he was not dismayed, as many men of his age would have been, by the prospect. He loved young people as much as his brother, but somehow he had always been shy with them, had never been much good with them. He knew that his manner, and his upright, soldierly appearance, were off-putting, but what could you do about the way you looked? Perhaps, if he had had children of his own, it would have been different. With children of your own, there would be no necessity to break down the barriers of shyness.

People to stay. They would have to get the rooms ready, light fires, perhaps open the old nursery. He had forgotten to ask Roddy the age of the child who was coming to stay. A pity there would be no fishing, but the boat was laid up anyway, and the boathouse locked for the winter.

His mind strayed back to other house parties, other children. He and his brothers when they were small, their friends, and then Lucy's numerous young nephews and nieces. Rabbit's friends and relations he had called them. He smiled to himself. Rabbit's friends and relations.

He had reached the edge of the loch. It stretched before him, edged with ice from which the winter-pale rushes grew in straggling clumps. A pair of peewits flew overhead, and he raised his head to watch their passing. The sun in his eyes was blinding, and he put up a hand as shade from the dazzle. His dogs nuzzled into the snow, scenting exciting smells. They inspected the ice, in small nervous darts, but were not brave, or perhaps foolhardy, enough to venture out on to the shining surface.

It was indeed a beautiful day. He turned back to look at the house. It lay, a little above him, across the snow-covered slope; familiar, loved, secure. Sunlight glinted on windows, smoke issued from chimneys, rising straight up in the still air. There was a smell of moss, of peat, and the resin of the spruces. Behind the house, the hills rose to meet the blue sky. His hills. Benchoile hills. He felt immensely content.

Well, the young company was coming. They would be here on Thursday. There would be laughter, voices, footsteps on the stairs. Benchoile was waiting for them.

He turned away from the house and set out once more upon his walk, his stick in his hand, his dogs at his heel, his spirit untroubled.

When he did not put in an appearance for his midday meal, Ellen became worried. She went to the front door to look for him, but saw only the single line of footprints that led to the edge of the loch. He had been late many times before, but now her Highland instincts were dark and foreboding. She went to find Roddy. He rang Davey Guthrie and in a moment Davey appeared in his van and the two men set out together to look for Jock.

It was not a difficult search, for the prints of him and his dogs lay clear in the snow. They found the three of them in the lea of a drystone dike. Jock lay quietly, his face serene and turned up to the sun. The dogs were whining and anxious, but it was instantly clear that their master would never know anxiety again.

7

TUESDAY

Thomas Dodds, wearing new red rubber boots, squatted at the water's edge, fascinated by this strange new phenomenon that had suddenly come into his life, and staring at it with the mesmerised, unblinking gaze of some old seafarer. It was all bigger and brighter and wetter than anything he had ever before encountered in his short life, and there were, as well, the added diversions of the little choppy waves, so sunlit and cheerful, the screaming of the sea birds which wheeled in the cold air over his head, and the occasional passing boat. Every now and then he dug up a handful of gritty sand and threw it into the sea.

Behind him, a few yards off, Victoria sat on the shingly beach and watched him. She wore thick, corduroy trousers and three sweaters, two of them her own and one borrowed from Oliver, and she sat huddled, with her knees pulled up and her arms wrapped around them for warmth. It was, indeed, extremely cold. But then, at ten o'clock on a February morning in the north of Scotland – well, nearly the north of Scotland – it would have been surprising if it had been anything else.

It wasn't even a proper beach, just a narrow strip of shingle between the wall of the hotel garden and the water. It smelled fishy and tarry, and was littered with scraps of debris from the boats that plied up and down the long sea loch on their way to and from the fishing grounds. There were bits of string, an old fish-head or two, and a damp furry object, which on investigation proved to be a rotting doormat.

"The back of beyond," Oliver had said yesterday evening as the Volvo topped the pass and began the long gradual descent to the sea, but Victoria thought that the isolation was beautiful. They were now much further north than they had intended to come, and so far west that if you took another step, you fell into the sea; but the views, the sheer size and grandeur of the country, the colours, and the brilliance of the sparkling air had made the long drive more than worthwhile.

Yesterday morning they had woken to a Lake District streaming in rain, but as they drove up into Scotland a wind had sprung up from the west, and the clouds had been blown away. All yesterday afternoon, and this morning again, the sky was clear, the air piercing cold. Snow-covered peaks of distant hills glittered like glass, and the waters of the sea loch were a dark indigo blue.

The loch, Victoria had discovered, was called Loch Morag. The little village, with its tiny shops and fleet of fishing boats tied up at the sea wall, was also called Loch Morag, and the hotel was the Loch Morag Hotel. (Oliver said that he expected the manager was called Mr Lochmorag and his wife, Mrs Lochmorag.) Built for the sole purpose of catering to fishermen – both freshwater and sea fishing, the brochure boasted, was on their doorstep – it was large and ugly, constructed of some strange stone the colour of liver, and much crenellated, towered and turreted. Indoors, it was furnished with worn Turkey carpets and uninspired wallpaper the colour of porridge, but there were peat fires burning in the public rooms and the people were very kind.

"Would the wee boy like high tea?" had asked the comfortable lady in the mauve dress who appeared, in this quiet season, to have taken on the duties not only of head waitress and barmaid, but receptionist as well. "Maybe a boiled egg, or a wee bit oatcake?" Thomas stared at her, unhelpfully. "Or a jeely. Would you like a jeely, pet?"

In the end they had settled for a boiled egg and an apple, and the kind lady (Mrs Lochmorag?) brought it up to his bedroom on a tray, and sat with Thomas while Victoria had a bath. When she emerged from the bathroom, she found Mrs Lochmorag playing with Thomas and the pink-and-white calico pig that they had bought him in London before they left, along with a wardrobe of clothes, a toothbrush and a pot. Victoria had wanted to buy an endearing teddy bear, but Oliver informed her that Thomas did not like fur, and chose the pig himself.

The pig was called Piglet. He wore blue trousers and red braces. His eyes were black and beady and Thomas approved of him.

"You've got a lovely wee boy, Mrs Dobbs. And what age is he?"

"He's two."

"We've made friends, but, mind, he hasn't said a word to me."

"He . . . he doesn't talk very much."

"Oh, he should be talking by now." She heaved Thomas on to her knee. "What a lazy wee boy, not saying a word. You can say Mummy, now, can't you? Are you not going to say Mummy? Are you not going to tell me the name of your pig?" She took Piglet and jigged him up and down, making him dance. Thomas smiled.

"He's called Piglet," Victoria told her.

"That's a bonny name. Why does Thomas not say Piglet?"

But he did not say Piglet. He did not indeed say anything very much. But this in no way detracted from his charm. In fact, it added to it, because he was such a cheerful and undemanding child that four days of his company had been nothing but pleasure. In the car, during the long drive north, he sat on Victoria's knee, hugging his new toy and gazing out of the window at passing lorries, fields, towns; obviously enjoying all the new and strange sights, but seeing no reason to comment upon them. When they stopped for meals or to stretch their legs, Thomas joined them, eating bacon and eggs or drinking milk or munching the slices of apple that Oliver peeled and cut up for him. When he became tired or bored, he plugged his mouth with his thumb, settled himself with endearing confidence in Victoria's arms, and either slept or sang to himself, with eyes drooping and dark lashes silky against his round red cheeks.

"I wonder why he doesn't talk more?" she had said to Oliver once, when Thomas was safely asleep on her lap and could not overhear the discussion.

"Probably because nobody's ever talked to him. Probably they were all too busy sterilising the house and manicuring the garden, and boiling his toys."

Victoria did not agree with Oliver. No child, so well-adjusted and content, could have been neglected in the smallest way. Indeed, his behaviour and his sunny disposition gave every indication that he had spent his short life enveloped in affection.

She said as much and instantly aroused Oliver's ire. "If they were so marvellous with him, then how come he doesn't seem to be missing them? He can't have been particularly fond of them if he hasn't asked for them once."

"He hasn't asked for anything," Victoria pointed out. "And most likely his being so confident and unafraid is all to do with the way he's been brought up. Nobody's ever been unkind to him, so he doesn't expect unkindness. That's why he's being so good with us."

"Balls," said Oliver shortly. He could not stand a single good word being said on the Archers' behalf.

Victoria knew he was being unreasonable. "If Thomas howled for his grandparents all the time, and complained, and wet his pants and generally behaved like most children would under the same circumstances, I suppose you'd have blamed that on the Archers, too."

"You're talking in hypothetical circles."

"I'm not." But she didn't know what a hypothetical circle was, and so couldn't argue further. Instead, she lapsed into silence. *But we must ring up Mrs Archer*, she thought. Or write to her or something. Oliver must let her know that Thomas is all right. Some time.

It was, perhaps, their only quarrel. Otherwise, the entire undertaking, which could have been, and even deserved to be, disastrous, was proving an unqualified success. Nothing had gone wrong. Everything had proved simple, easy, delightful. The winter roads were fast and empty; the scenery, the open skies, the stunning countryside, all contributed to their pleasure.

In the Lake District it had rained, but they had put on waterproofs and walked for miles, with Thomas, cheerful as ever, atop his father's shoulders. There had been fires burning pleasantly in their bedrooms at the little lakeside hotel, and boats moored at the jetty that lay at the end of the garden, and in the evening a kindly chambermaid had watched over Thomas while Oliver and Victoria dined by candlelight on grilled trout and rare beef-steaks that had never seen the inside of a deep-freeze.

That night, lying in the soft darkness, in feather-bedded warmth, in Oliver's arms, she had watched the curtains stirring at the open window and felt the cool damp air on her cheeks. From the quiet darkness beyond the window came the sounds of water and the creak of the boats tied up at the jetty, and there had come a distrust of such perfect content. Surely, she told herself, it could not go on. Surely something would happen that would spoil it all.

But her apprehension was unfounded. Nothing happened. The next day was even better, with the road pouring north to Scotland and the sun coming out as they crossed the border. By the afternoon, the great peaks of the Western Highlands lay ahead of them, iced in snow, and at the foot of Glencoe they stopped at a pub for tea and ate homemade scones dripping with butter. And after that the countryside grew more and more magnificent, and Oliver told Victoria that it was called Lochaber, and he began to sing "The Road to the Isles".

"Sure by *Tummel* and Loch *Rannoch* and Loch*aber* we will go . . ."

Today Loch Morag. Tomorrow, or perhaps the next day, Benchoile. Victoria had lost all sense of time. She had lost all sense of anything. Watching Thomas, she hugged herself more tightly and rested her chin on her knees. Happiness, she decided, should be tangible. A thing you could take hold of and put somewhere safe, like a box with a lid or a bottle with a stopper. And then, later, some time when you were miserable, you could take it out and look at it and feel it and smell it, and you would be happy again.

Thomas was tiring of throwing sand into the sea. He straightened up on his small legs and looked about him. He spied Victoria, sitting there, where he had left her. He grinned, and began to stump unsteadily towards her up the littered little beach.

Watching him filled her heart with an almost unbearable tenderness. She thought, *If I can feel like this about Thomas, after only four days, how does Mrs Archer feel, not even knowing where he is*?

It didn't bear thinking about. Basely, cowardly, she pushed the idea to the back of her mind and opened her arms to Thomas. He reached her and she hugged him. The wind blew her long hair across his cheek, and tickled. He began to laugh.

While Victoria and Thomas sat on the beach and waited for him, Oliver was telephoning. The previous night had been the first performance of *Bent Penny* at Bristol, and he couldn't wait to hear what the critics had said in the morning papers.

He was not exactly on tenterhooks, because he knew that the play was good – his best, in fact. But there were always elements and reactions that were apt to take one unawares. He wanted to know how the show had gone, how the audience had responded, and whether Jennifer Clay, the new little actress getting her first big chance, had justified the faith that the producer and Oliver had put in her.

He was on the telephone to Bristol for nearly an hour, listening while the ecstatic reviews were read aloud to him along six hundred miles of humming wires. The critics from the *Sunday Times* and the *Observer*, he was told, were coming down to see the play at the end of the week. Jennifer Clay was on the brink of being swept to stardom, and there had already come interested noises from a couple of important West End managements.

"In fact, Oliver, I think we've got a hit on our hands."

Oliver was gratified, but he had watched the show in rehearsal, and he was not particularly surprised. The Bristol call finally finished, he rang his agent, and all the good news was confirmed. As well, there had been feelers from New York about his play *A Man in the Dark*, which had done so well in Edinburgh a summer ago.

"Would you be interested?" the agent asked.

"What do you mean, 'interested'?"

"Would you be prepared to go to New York if you have to?"

Oliver loved New York. It was one of his favourite

places. "I'd be prepared to go even if I didn't have to."

"How long are you going to be away?"

"Couple of weeks."

"Can I get in touch with you?"

"After Thursday, I'll be at Benchoile, in Sutherland. Staying with a guy called Roddy Dunbeath."

"*Eagle Years* Dunbeath?"

"The very man."

"What's the phone number?"

Oliver reached for his leather diary, thumbed through it. "Creagan two three seven."

"OK, I've got it. If I have any fresh news I'll call you."

"You do that."

"Good luck then, Oliver. And congratulations." His agent rang off. After a little, as though reluctant to put an end to such a momentous conversation, Oliver replaced his own receiver, and sat looking at it for a moment or two, while slowly, relief flooded through him. It was over. *Bent Penny* was launched, like a child sent out into the world. A child conceived with passion, brought to life with the most agonising birth pains, nursed and coaxed to maturity, and bludgeoned into shape, it was, at last, no longer Oliver's responsibility.

All over. He thought of the production, the rehearsals, the personality problems, the temperaments, the tears. The chaos, the panics, the rewriting, the total despair.

I think we've got a hit on our hands.

It would make him, probably, a lot of money. It might even make him rich. But this was of small account compared to the easement of his spirit, and the sense of freedom that existed now that it was all behind him.

And ahead . . .? He reached for a cigarette. There was something waiting for him, but he wasn't sure what. He only knew that the subconscious edge of his imagination, the part that did all the work, was already filling with people. People living in a certain place, a certain style. Voices had conversations. The dialogues had a form and a balance all their own, and the words, and the faces of the individuals who spoke them, swam up, as they always did, out of his prodigious memory.

These first stirrings of life made everyday existence, for Oliver, as intense and dramatic as it is for most men when they fall in love. This, for him, was the best part of writing. It was the same as the anticipation of waiting in a darkened theatre for the curtain to go up on the first act. You didn't know what was going to happen, but you knew that it would be marvellous and tremendously exciting and better – much better – than anything you had ever seen before.

He got up off the bed and went to the window and flung it open to the icy morning air. Gulls wheeled and screamed over the funnel of a weather-beaten fishing boat as she butted her way, against the western wind, out to the open sea.

On the far side of the dark blue water the hills were frosted in white, and below him was the hotel garden and the scrap of a beach. He looked down upon Victoria and his son Thomas. They did not know he was watching. As he observed them, Tom grew tired of his game of throwing sand into the water, and turned and made his way up the beach to Victoria's side. She opened her arms to him and drew him close, and her long fair hair blew all over his red and chubby face.

The combination of this delightful scene and his own euphoric frame of mind filled Oliver with an unfamiliar content. He knew that it was ephemeral; it might last a day or even an hour or two. But all at once it seemed that the world was a brighter and a more hopeful place;

that the smallest incident could take on immense significance; that affection would turn to love, and love – that humdrum word – to passion.

He closed the window and went downstairs to tell them his good news.

8

THURSDAY

Miss Ridgeway, that impeccable private secretary of undetermined years, was already at her desk when, at a quarter to nine in the morning, John Dunbeath emerged from the lift on to the ninth floor of the new Regency House Building and the opulent, elegant offices of the Warburg Investment Corporation.

She looked up as he came through the door, her expression, as always, polite, pleasant, and impassive.

"Good morning, Mr Dunbeath."

"Hi."

He had never before had a secretary whom he did not call by her Christian name, and sometimes the formality of "Miss Ridgeway" stuck in his throat. They had, after all, worked together for some months. It would have been so much easier to call her Mary or Daphne or whatever her name was, but the truth of the matter was that he hadn't even found this out, and there was something so strictly formal about her manner that he had never plucked up the courage to ask.

Sometimes, watching her as she sat there, with one shapely leg crossed over the other, taking down his letters in her faultless shorthand, he pondered on her private life. Did she care for an aged mother and take an interest in good works? Did she go to concerts at the Albert Hall and spend her holidays in Florence? Or did she, like a secretary in some film, remove her spectacles and shake loose her mouse-pale hair, receive lovers and indulge in scenes of unbridled passion?

He knew that he would never know.

She said, "How was the trip?"

"OK. But the plane was late getting in yesterday evening. We got held up in Rome."

Her eyes moved over his dark suit, his black tie. She said, "You got the cable all right? The one from your father?"

"Yes. Thanks for that."

"It came on Tuesday morning. I thought you'd want to know. I sent a copy through to Bahrain right away. The original is on your desk with some personal mail . . ." John moved through to his own office, and Miss Ridgeway rose from her chair and followed him ". . . and yesterday's *Times* that the announcement was in. I thought you'd like to see it."

She thought of everything. He said, "Thank you," again and opened his briefcase and took out the report, and twelve pages of foolscap, covered with his own neat writing, that he had composed in the aeroplane during the flight back to London.

"You'd better get one of the typists on to this right away. The vice-president will want to see it as soon as possible. And when Mr Rogerson gets in, tell him to give me a buzz." He glanced at his desk. "And this morning's *Wall Street Journal*?"

"I have it, Mr Dunbeath."

"And the *Financial Times* as well. I didn't have time to pick one up." She started out of the office, but he called her back. "Hang on a moment." She returned and he dealt out more papers. "I want the file on this. And if you can, find me some information on a Texas company called Albright; they've been drilling in Libya. And this has to be telexed through to Sheikh Mustapha Said, and this . . . and this . . ."

After a little, "Is that all?" asked Miss Ridgeway.

"For the moment." He grinned. "Except that I'd appreciate a large cup of black coffee."

Miss Ridgeway smiled understandingly, becoming quite human. He wished that she would smile more. "I'll get it," she said, and left him, closing the door, without a sound, behind her.

He sat at his gleaming desk and debated for a moment as to what he should do first. His In-tray was piled high, letters neatly clipped to their relevant files, and, he knew, arranged in their order of priority, with the most urgent documents on the top. The three personal letters had been placed in the middle of his blotter. The blotting paper was, as it was every day, new, and pristine white. There was also the copy of yesterday's *Times*.

He reached for the green telephone to make an internal call.

"Mr Gardner, please."

He tucked the receiver under his chin and opened the newspaper to the back page.

"John Dunbeath here. Is he in yet?"

"Yes, he's in, Mr Dunbeath, but he's not in the office right now. Shall I get him to call you?"

"Yes, do that." He replaced the receiver.

DUNBEATH. Suddenly, on February 16th at Benchoile in Sutherland, Lt.-Col. John Rathbone Dunbeath, DSO, JP, late Cameron Highlanders, in his 68th year. Funeral Service in the Parish Church, Creagan, 10.30 a.m. Thursday February 19th.

He remembered the old boy, tall and lean, every inch a retired soldier; his pale glare and his prow of a nose; his long legs striding easily up the hill through knee-high heather; his passion for fishing, for shooting grouse, for his land. They had never been close, but there was still an empty sense of loss, as there must be when a man, bound close by family and blood, dies.

He laid down the paper and took his father's cable

from the envelope in which Miss Ridgeway had protectively placed it. He read what he had already read, in Bahrain, two days previously: YOUR UNCLE JOCK DIED RESULT OF A HEART ATTACK BENCHOILE MONDAY 16TH FEBRUARY STOP FUNERAL CREAGAN 10.30 THURSDAY MORNING 19TH FEBRUARY STOP WOULD BE GRATEFUL IF YOU COULD REPRESENT YOUR MOTHER AND MYSELF STOP FATHER

He had sent cables from Bahrain. To his parents in Colorado, explaining why he would not be able to comply with his father's request. To Benchoile, to Roddy, he had sent sympathy and more explanations, and before he left Bahrain, he had found the time to write Roddy a letter of condolence, which he had posted by first-class mail on his arrival at Heathrow.

The other two letters waited for his attention, one envelope handwritten, the other typed. He picked up the first and began to open it, and then stopped, his attention caught by the writing. An old-fashioned pen nib, black ink, the capitals strongly defined. He looked at the postmark and saw "CREAGAN". The date was the tenth of February.

He felt his stomach contract. *A ghost going over your grave* his father used to say when John was a small boy and scared by the unknown. *That's what it is. A ghost going over your grave.*

He slit the envelope and took out the letter. His suspicions were confirmed. It was from Jock Dunbeath.

Benchoile,
Creagan,
Sutherland,
Wednesday, 9th February.

Dear John,

Your Father tells me that you are now back in this country and working in London. I do not know your address, so I am sending this to your office.

It seems a long time since you stayed with us. I looked it up in the visitors' book and it seems to be ten years. I realise that you are a very busy man, but if you are able to get a little time off, perhaps you would think about making the journey north and spending a few days at Benchoile. It is possible to fly to Inverness or to catch a train from Euston in which case either I or Roddy would come to Inverness to meet you. There are trains to Creagan, but they are few and far between and involve several hours' delay. We have had a mild winter, but I think cold weather is on the way. Better now than in the Spring when late frosts play havoc with the young grouse.

Let me know what you think and when it might be convenient for you to visit us. We look forward to seeing you again.

With best wishes,

Affectionately,
Jock

The arrival, out of the blue, of this extraordinary invitation; the coincidence of timing, the fact that it had been written only days before Jock's fatal heart attack, were intensely disturbing. John sat back in his chair and read the letter through again, consciously searching for some inner meaning between the carefully penned and characteristically stilted lines. He could find none.

It seems to be ten years.

It was ten years. He remembered himself at eighteen with Wellington behind him and all the joys of Cambridge ahead, spending part of the summer holidays with his father at Benchoile. But he had never gone back.

Now, it struck him that perhaps he should feel guilty about this lapse. But too much had happened to him. Too much had been going on. He had been at Cambridge, then in New York, and then at Harvard, spending all his vacations in Colorado, either at his father's ranch, or else skiing at Aspen. And then Lisa had come into his life, and after that all his spare energy had been spent in simply keeping up with her. Keeping her happy, keeping her amused, keeping her in the high style which she was convinced was her due. Being married to Lisa meant the end of vacations in Colorado. She was bored by the ranch and too fragile to ski. But she adored the sun, so they went to the West Indies, to Antigua, the Bahamas, where John missed the mountains and tried to work off his physical needs in scuba diving or sailing.

And after the divorce, he had buried himself so deeply in his work that somehow there didn't even seem to be time to get out of the city. It was his president in New York who had finally read the riot act, and had him posted to London. Not only was it a promotion, he told John, but it would make a vital and necessary change of pace. London was quieter than New York, the rat race not so frantic, the ambience generally more easy-going.

"You'll be able to get north and see Jock and Roddy," his father had said over the telephone when John had called to give him the news, but somehow with one thing and another John had never got around to doing this. Now, it struck him that he should feel guilty about this lapse. But the truth was that Benchoile, though undoubtedly beautiful, held no irresistible lure for John. Having been brought up in the heart of the Rockies, he had found the hills and glens of Sutherland peaceful, but somehow tame. There was fishing, of course, but fishing in Colorado, in the tributaries of the mighty Uncompahgre, which ran through his father's spread, was unsurpassable. Benchoile had a farm, but again, that seemed small compared to the endless ranges of the ranch, and the grouse shooting, with its rules and shibboleths, its traditions of butt and beat, had left the young John totally cold.

Even as a boy, he had rebelled against slaughtering wildlife, and had never gone hunting, for mule deer or elk, with the other men, and there seemed no reason, just because he was staying in Scotland and it was expected of him, to give up the habits and convictions of a lifetime. Finally, and this was the most important reason of all, he had never thought that his Uncle Jock liked him very much. "He's just reserved. He's shy," John's father had assured him, but still, try as he could, John had never been able to work up a rapport with his father's eldest brother. Conversations between the two of them, he remembered, had never done more than creak painfully along, like wagon wheels in need of a good greasing.

He sighed, and laid the letter down, and picked up the last envelope. This time he slit it open without inspecting it first, and with his mind still brooding over the letter from Jock, he unfolded the single sheet of paper. He saw the old-fashioned letterhead, the date.

McKenzie, Loith & Dudgeon, Solicitors,
Writers to The Signet,
18 Trade Lane,
Inverness.
Tuesday, 17th February

John Dunbeath, Esq.,
Warburg Investment Corporation,
Regency House,
London.

Dear Mr Dunbeath,

John Rathbone Dunbeath Deceased

I have to inform you that under the terms of the Will of your Uncle, John Rathbone

Dunbeath, you have been bequeathed the Benchoile Estate in Sutherland.

I suggest that you take an early opportunity to come north and see me in order to make practical arrangements for the management and future of the property.

I shall be happy to see you at any time.

Yours sincerely,
Robert McKenzie

When Miss Ridgeway came back into the room, bearing his black coffee in a fine white Wedgwood cup, she found John sitting motionless at his desk, an elbow on his blotter, the bottom half of his face covered by his hand.

She said, "Here's your coffee," and he looked up at her, and the expression in his dark eyes was so sombre that she was moved to ask if he was all right, if anything had happened.

He did not reply at once. And then he sat back in his chair, letting his hand fall to his lap, and said that yes, something had happened. But after a long pause, during which he showed no signs of wishing to elucidate this remark, she laid the cup and saucer beside him, and left him alone, closing the door between them with her usual tactful care.

9

THURSDAY

As they drove east, up and away from the mild-mannered sea lochs of the west of Scotland, leaving the farms and villages and the smell of sea-wrack behind them, the countryside changed character with dizzying abruptness, and the empty road wound upwards into a wilderness of desolate moorland, apparently uninhabited except for a few stray sheep and the occasional hovering bird of prey.

The day was cold and overcast, the wind from the east. Grey billows of cloud moved slowly across the sky, but every now and then there came a break in the gloom, a ragged scrap of pale blue appeared, and a gleam of thin wintry sunshine, but this only seemed to accentuate the loneliness rather than do anything to alleviate it.

The undulating land stretched in all directions, as far as the eye could see, patchworked in winter-pale grasses and great tracts of dark heather. Sometimes this was broken by a gaping peat-pit or the sombre black of bog. Then scraps of snow began to appear, like the white spots of a piebald horse, and lay where they had been trapped in corries and ditches and in the lea of low drystone dikes. As the gradient steepened, the snow grew thicker, and at the head of the moor – the roof-ridge, as it were, of the country – it was all about them, a blanket of white six inches deep or more, and the road was ice-rutted and treacherous beneath the wheels of the Volvo.

It was like finding oneself in the Arctic, or on the moon. Certainly in some place that one had never even remotely imagined visiting. But then, just as abruptly, the wild and desolate moor was behind them. They had crossed the watershed, and, imperceptibly, the road began to slope downhill once more. There were rivers and waterfalls and stands of larch and fir. First appeared isolated cottages, and then hill farms and then villages. Presently they were running alongside an immense inland loch, and there was the great rampart of a hydroelectric dam and beyond this a little town. The main street ran by the water's edge, and there was a hotel and a number of small boats pulled up on the shingle. A signpost pointed to Creagan.

Victoria became excited. "We're nearly there." She leaned forward and took from the cubbyhole on the dashboard the Ordnance Survey map that Oliver had bought. With Thomas's dubious help, she opened it out. One corner spread out over the driving wheel, and Oliver flipped it back. "Watch it, you'll blind me."

"It's only about another six miles to Creagan."

Thomas, using Piglet as a weapon, struck the map a blow and knocked it from Victoria's hands and on to the floor.

Oliver said, "Put it away before he tears it to pieces." He yawned and shifted in his seat. It had been a hard morning's drive.

Victoria rescued the map and folded it up and replaced it. The road ahead of them wound steadily downhill, between steep banks of bracken and copses of silver birch. A small river kept them company, chuckling and sparkling on its way in a series of little pools and waterfalls. The sun, obligingly, came out from behind a cloud; they turned a final corner, and ahead, glinting and silvery, lay the sea.

She said, "It's really amazing. You leave one coast behind you, and you drive up and over the moor and through the snow, and then you come to another sea. Look, Thomas, there's the sea."

Thomas looked, but was unimpressed. He was getting tired of driving. He was getting tired of sitting on Victoria's knee. He put his thumb in his mouth and flung himself backwards, striking her a resounding blow on the chest with the back of his bullet-hard head.

His father snapped, "Oh, for God's sake, sit still."

"He has sat still," Victoria was moved to point out in Thomas's defence. "He's been a very good boy. He's just getting bored. Do you suppose there's a beach at Creagan? I mean a proper sandy one. We haven't found a proper sandy beach yet. All the ones on the west seemed to be covered in stones. If there was one I could take him."

"We'll ask Roddy."

Victoria thought about this. Then she said, "I *do* hope he isn't going to mind us all turning up like this. I hope it isn't going to be difficult." She had never quite got rid of this apprehension.

"You've already said that a dozen times, at regular intervals. Stop being so anxious."

"I can't help feeling that you cornered Roddy. Perhaps he didn't have time to think up an excuse."

"He was delighted. Jumped at the chance of a little lively company."

"He knows you, but he doesn't know Tom and me."

"In that case, you'll both have to be on your best behaviour. If I know Roddy, he won't care if you've got two heads and a tail. He'll just say how do you do, very nicely, and then, I hope and believe, will hand me an enormous gin and tonic."

Creagan, when they reached it, proved a surprise. Victoria had expected the usual small Highland township with its single narrow main street, flanked by rows of plain stone houses built flush on the pavement. But Creagan had a wide, tree-lined street, with deep cobbled pavements on either side. The houses, which stood back from the road and were separated from it by quite large gardens, were all detached and remarkably attractive, with the simple proportions and elegant embellishments associated with the best period of Scottish domestic architecture.

In the middle of the town the main street opened up into a wide square, and in the centre of this, sitting on a sward of grass, rather as though it had been set carefully down in the middle of a green carpet, rose the granite walls and slate-capped tower of a large and beautiful church.

Victoria said, "But it's lovely! It's like a French town."

Oliver, however, had noticed something else. "It's empty."

She looked again, and saw that this was true. A stillness brooded over Creagan, like the pious gloom of a Sabbath. Worse, for there was not even the cheerful clangour of bells. As well, there seemed to be scarcely anybody about, and only a few other cars. And . . . "All the shops are shuttered," said Victoria. "They're closed and all the blinds have been pulled down. Perhaps it's early closing."

She rolled down the window on her side of the car to let the icy air blow in on her face. Thomas tried to put his head out, and she pulled him back on to her knee. She smelled the salt of the sea and the tang of sea-wrack. Overhead a gull began to scream from a rooftop.

"There's a shop open," said Oliver.

It was a small newsagent, with plastic toys in the window and a rack of coloured postcards at the door. Victoria rolled up the window again, for the blast of cold air was bitter. "We can go and buy postcards there."

"What do you want postcards for?"

"To send to people." She hesitated. Ever since that morning by Loch Morag, her conscience had been constantly troubled by the nagging awareness of Mrs Archer's anxiety and distress for Thomas. The opportunity to confide in Oliver had not, so far, presented itself, but now . . . She took a deep breath and went on with the bold determination of one intent upon striking while the iron is hot, "We can send one to Thomas's grandmother."

Oliver said nothing.

Victoria took no notice of this lack of response. "Just a line. To let her know he's safe and sound."

Oliver still said nothing. This was not a good sign. "Surely it couldn't do any harm." She could hear the pleading note in her own voice, and despised herself for it. "A postcard, or a letter or *something*."

"How you do bang on."

"I'd like to send her a postcard."

"We're not sending her a bloody thing."

She could not believe that he could be so blinkered. "But why be like that? I've been thinking . . ."

"Well, stop thinking. If you can come to no conclusion more intelligent than that one, then simply make your mind a blank."

"But . . ."

"The whole point of coming away was to get away from the Archers. If I'd wanted them on my doorstep, hounding me with lawyer's letters and private detectives, I'd have stayed in London."

"But if she *knew* where he was . . ."

"Oh, shut up."

It was not so much what he said as the tone of voice that he used to say it. A silence grew between them. After a little, Victoria turned her head and looked at him. His profile was stony, his lower lip jutted, his eyes narrowed and staring straight at the road ahead. They had left the town behind them, and the car was picking up speed when they turned a corner and came all at once upon the signpost, pointing inland, to Benchoile and Loch Muie. Oliver was caught unawares. He braked abruptly, and swung the car around with a screech of tyres. They started up the single-track road, heading for the hills.

Unseeing, Victoria gazed ahead. She knew that Oliver was wrong, which was perhaps one of the reasons that he was being so stubborn. But Victoria could be stubborn, too. She said, "You've already told me that she hasn't got a leg to stand on, legally. That she can't do anything to get Thomas back. He's your child, and your responsibility."

Again, Oliver said nothing.

"So if you're so certain of yourself, there can be no reason not to let her know that he's all right."

He still was silent, and Victoria played her final card. "Well, you may not intend telling Mrs Archer that Thomas is safe and well, but there's nothing to stop me writing to her."

Oliver spoke at last. "If you do," he said quietly, "if you so much as pick up a telephone, I promise you, I'll batter you black and blue."

He sounded as though he actually meant it. Victoria looked at him in astonishment, searching for some sign to put her mind at rest, to convince herself that this was simply Oliver, using words as his strongest weapon. But she found no reassurance. The coldness of his anger was devastating, and she found herself trembling as though he had already struck her. His stony features blurred as her eyes filled with sudden, ridiculous tears. She looked away, quickly, so that he should not notice them, and later, surreptitiously, wiped them away.

So it was, with the sourness of the quarrel between them, and Victoria struggling not to cry, that they came to Benchoile.

* * *

Jock Dunbeath's funeral had been a big and important affair, as befitted a man of his position. The church was full and later the graveyard, crowded with sombrely clad men, from all walks of life, who had come – some many miles and from all directions – to pay their respects to an old and much-liked friend.

But the wake that followed was small. Only a few close colleagues made the journey to Benchoile, there to gather about the blazing fire in the library and to partake of Ellen's homemade shortbread, washed down with a dram or two of the best malt whisky.

One of these was Robert McKenzie, not only the family lawyer, but as well a lifetime friend of Jock Dunbeath. Robert had been Jock's best man when Jock married Lucy, and Jock was godfather to Robert's eldest boy. Robert had driven up that morning from Inverness, appeared in the church wearing his long black overcoat that made him look like one of the undertakers, and afterwards had acted as pallbearer.

Now, with his duties behind him, and a drink in his hand, he had become once more his usual brisk and businesslike self. In the middle of the proceedings, he drew Roddy aside.

"Roddy, if it's possible, I'd like a word with you some time."

Roddy sent him a keen glance, but the other man's long face was set in its usual professional lines, and gave nothing away. Roddy sighed. He had been expecting something like this, but scarcely so soon.

"Any time, old boy. What do you want me to do, nip down to Inverness? Beginning of next week, maybe?"

"Later, perhaps that would be a good idea. But I'd rather have a moment or two now. I mean, when this is over. It won't take more than five minutes."

"But of course. Stay and have a bit of lunch. It won't be more than soup and cheese, but you're more than welcome."

"No, I won't do that. I have to get back. I've a meeting at three o'clock. But if I could just stay on after the others have gone?"

"Absolutely. No trouble at all . . ." Roddy's eyes wandered away from the lawyer. He spied an empty glass in somebody's hand. "My dear fellow, another dram for the road . . ."

It was not a gloomy gathering. Indeed, there were nothing but happy memories to recall, and soon there were smiles and even laughter. When the guests finally took themselves off, driving away in Range Rovers, or estate cars, or battered farm vans, Roddy stood outside the open front door of Benchoile and saw them on their way, feeling a little as though he were saying goodbye to the guns at the end of an enjoyable day's shoot.

The simile pleased him because it was so exactly the way that Jock would have liked it. The last car made its way down through the rhododendrons, over the cattle grid, and out of sight around the corner. Only Robert McKenzie's old Rover remained.

Roddy went back indoors. Robert waited for him, standing in front of the mantelpiece, with his back to the fire.

"That went very well, Roddy."

"Thank God it didn't rain. Nothing worse than a funeral in a downpour." He had had only two whiskies. Robert still had a bit in his glass, so Roddy poured himself another small one. "What was it you wanted to talk to me about?"

"Benchoile," said Robert.

"Yes, I imagined it was that."

"I don't know if Jock told you what he intended doing with the place?"

"No. We never discussed it. There never seemed to be any pressing need to discuss it." Roddy considered this. "As things have turned out, perhaps we should have."

"He never said anything about young John?"

"You mean Charlie's boy? Never a word. Why?"

"He's left Benchoile to John."

Roddy was in the act of pouring water into his tumbler. A little of it spilled on to the tray. He looked up. Across the room his eyes met Robert's. Slowly he laid down the water jug. He said, "Good God."

"You had no idea?"

"No idea at all."

"I know Jock meant to talk it over with you. Had every intention of doing so, in fact. Perhaps the opportunity never came up."

"We didn't see all that much of each other, you know. More or less lived in the same house, but didn't see that much of each other. Didn't really talk . . ." Roddy's voice trailed off. He was confused, confounded.

Robert said gently, "Do you mind?"

"Mind?" Roddy's blue eyes widened in astonishment. "Mind? Of course I don't mind. Benchoile was never mine, the way it was Jock's. I know nothing about the farm; I have nothing to do with the house or the garden; I was never particularly interested in the stalking or the grouse. I simply roost in her. I'm the lodger."

"Then you didn't expect you'd be taking over?" Robert was considerably relieved. One could never imagine Roddy Dunbeath being disagreeable about anything, but he might well have been disappointed. Now, it appeared, he was not even that.

"To tell you the truth, old boy, I never even thought of it. Never thought of Jock dying. He always seemed such a tough old thing, walking the hill, and bringing the sheep down with Davey Guthrie, and even working in the garden."

"But," Robert reminded him, "he had had a heart attack."

"A very mild one. Nothing to worry about, the doctor said. He seemed to be all right. Never complained. But then, of course, Jock was never a man to complain . . ." Once more the sentence drifted to silence. Even for Roddy Dunbeath, thought the lawyer, his thought processes seemed more than usually vague.

"But Roddy, since Jock died, surely you must have wondered what was going to happen to Benchoile?"

"To tell you the truth, old boy, I haven't had much time for wondering. Hell of a lot to organise, you know, when something like this happens. I've been waking up in a cold sweat in the middle of the night, trying to remember what it is I've forgotten to do."

"But . . ."

Roddy began to smile. "And of course, half the time I haven't forgotten it at all."

It was impossible. Robert abandoned Roddy's future, and brought the discussion sharply back into line.

"About John, then. I've written to him, but I haven't yet had a reply to my letter."

"He's been in Bahrain. I had a cable from him. That's why he wasn't here this morning."

"I've invited him to come up and see me. The future of the property will have to be discussed."

"Yes, I suppose it will." Roddy thought about this. He said, with some conviction, "He won't want to live here."

"What makes you so certain?"

"Just that I can't imagine he would have the smallest interest in the place."

"Jock didn't seem to think that."

"It was hard to know, sometimes, exactly what Jock was thinking. I never thought he particularly liked Charlie's boy. They were always so intensely polite to each other. It's not a good sign, you know, when people are too polite. Besides, John Dunbeath has a career of his own. He's a clever, cool, successful young man, wheeling and dealing and making a lot of money. Not that he needs to make a lot of money, because he's always had it through his mother. And that's another thing, he's an American."

"Half American." Robert permitted himself a smile. "And I'd have thought you'd be the last man in the world to hold that against him."

"I don't hold it against him. I have nothing against John Dunbeath. I mean that. He was an exceptional boy and extremely intelligent. But I don't see him as the laird of Benchoile. What would he do with himself? He's only twenty-eight." The more Roddy thought about it, the more preposterous the idea became. "I shouldn't think he knows one end of a sheep from the other."

"It doesn't take much intelligence to learn."

"But why *John*?" The two men looked at each other glumly. Roddy sighed. "I know why, of course. Because Jock had no children and I had no children and there wasn't anybody else."

"What do you think will happen?"

"I suppose he'll sell it. It seems a pity, but for the life of me, I can't think what else he'd do with the place."

"Let it? Come here for holidays?"

"A weekend cottage with fourteen bedrooms?"

"Well then, keep the farm in hand and sell the house?"

"He'd never get rid of the house unless he let the shooting and the stalking rights go with it, and Davey Guthrie needs that land for his sheep."

"If he does sell Benchoile, what will you do?"

"That's the sixty-four-thousand dollar question, isn't it? But I've lived here, on and off, all my life, and perhaps that's too long for any man to stay in one place. I shall move away. I shall move abroad. Somewhere distant." Robert had visions of Roddy in Ibiza, wearing a panama hat. "Like Creagan," he finished, and Robert laughed.

"Well, I'm glad you know," he said, and finished his drink and set down the empty glass. "And I hope, between us all, we'll be able to sort it all out. I . . . I expect John will want to come here sooner or later. To Benchoile, I mean. Will that be all right?"

"Right as rain, old boy. Any time. Tell him to give me a ring."

They moved towards the door.

"I'll be in touch."

"You do that. And Robert, thank you for today. And for everything."

"I'll miss Jock."

"We all will."

He drove away, headed for Inverness and his three o'clock meeting, a busy man with much to think about. Roddy watched the Rover disappear, and then he was all alone, and he knew that now it was really over. And successfully over, which was so surprising. No small mishaps had occurred, and the funeral had passed in an orderly and soldierly fashion, just as if Jock had organised it himself, and not his singularly disorganised brother. Roddy drew a long sigh, part relief and part sadness. He looked up at the sky, hearing the chatter of greylags high above the clouds, but they stayed out of sight. A thin wind moved up the glen from the sea, and the slate-grey surface of the water shivered beneath its touch.

Jock was dead and Benchoile now belonged to young John. So perhaps this day was not only the end of the beginning, but also, if John decided to sell it all, the beginning of the end. The idea would take some getting used to, but in Roddy's book, there was only one way to tackle such gargantuan problems, and that was as slowly as possible, a single step at a time. This meant no anticipation and no precipitate action. Life would move quietly on.

He looked at his watch. It was now half past twelve. His thoughts moved ahead to the remainder of the day, and he suddenly remembered the approaching car, and the young family coming to spend a few days at Benchoile. Oliver Dobbs and some female or other and their child. It occurred to Roddy that Oliver was the sort of man who would always have some female or other in tow.

They would be arriving at any moment, and the prospect lifted his spirits. The day was a sad one, but, thought Roddy, where God closes a window, he opens a door. What this old saw had to do with Oliver Dobbs, he couldn't be sure, but it helped one to realise that there could be no time for useless grieving, and Roddy found this comforting.

Thinking of comfort brought him sharply back to an awareness of the physical agony that he had endured all morning.

It was to do with his kilt. He had not worn this garment for two years or more, but for the laird's funeral, it had seemed appropriate to put it on. Accordingly, this morning he had taken it, reeking of camphor, from the cupboard, only to discover that he had put on so much weight that the kilt would scarcely go round him, and after struggling with it for five minutes or more, he had been forced to take himself over to the big house and enlist the aid of Ellen Tarbat.

He found her in the kitchen, dressed in the inky black that she kept for funerals, and with her gloomiest hat – and none of Ellen's hats were very cheerful – already skewered to her head by an immense jet-headed hatpin. Ellen's tears for Jock had been shed privately, decently, behind the closed door of her bedroom at the top of the house. Now, dry-eyed and tight-lipped, she was engaged in polishing the best tumblers before setting them out on the damask-covered table in the library. When Roddy appeared, clutching his kilt about him like a bath-towel, she said, "I told you so," as he had known she would, but she laid down the tea towel and came manfully to his aid, heaving her puny weight on the leather straps of the kilt, like a tiny groom trying to tighten the girth of some enormous, overfed horse.

Finally, by brute force, the pin of the buckle went into the last hole of the leather strap.

"There," said Ellen triumphantly. She was quite red in the face, and a few stray white hairs had escaped from her bun.

Roddy held his breath. Now, he let it out cautiously. The kilt tightened across his belly like a pair of tightly laced stays, but the straps, miraculously, held.

"You've done it," he told her.

Ellen tidied her hair. "If you were to ask me, I'd say it was about time you went on a diet. Or else you'll need to take your kilt into Inverness and get the man to let it out. Otherwise you'll be giving yourself a seizure, and it's yourself we'll be burying next."

Infuriated, Roddy strode from the kitchen. The kilt straps had held, somehow, all morning, but now, gratefully, he realised he need suffer no longer, and accordingly he made his way back to the Stable House, took off his finery and climbed into the most comfortable clothes he owned.

He was just shrugging himself into his old tweed jacket when he heard the approaching car. From his bedroom window, he saw the dark blue Volvo approach up the drive between the rhododendrons and come to a halt at the edge of the grass in front of the house. Roddy gave a cursory glance in the mirror, smoothed down his ruffled hair with his hand, and went out of the room. His old dog Barney hauled himself to his feet and followed. He had spent the morning shut up and alone, and was not going to risk being left behind again. The two of them emerged from the stable yard just as Oliver climbed out from behind the driving wheel of the car. He saw Roddy and slammed the car door shut behind him. Roddy went towards him, feet crunching over the gravel, his hand outstretched in welcome.

"Oliver!"

Oliver smiled. He looked just the same, Roddy thought, with some satisfaction. He did not like people to change. At the television dinner Oliver had worn a velvet jacket and a flamboyant tie. He was now in faded corduroys and a huge Norwegian sweater, but otherwise he seemed just the same. Same coppery hair, same beard, same smile.

Oliver came towards him, and they met in the middle of the gravel. The very sight of him, tall and young and handsome, gave Roddy new heart.

"Hello, Roddy."

They shook hands, Roddy taking Oliver's hand in both his own, so pleased was he to see him.

"My dear fellow, how are you? How splendid you were able to make it. And right on time, too. Did you have any trouble finding us?"

"No trouble at all. We bought an Ordnance Survey map in Fort William and simply followed the red lines." He looked about him, at the house, the slope of the lawn, the grey waters of the loch, the hills beyond. "What a fantastic place."

"Yes, it's lovely, isn't it?" Side by side they regarded the view. "Not much of a day to see it on, though. I'll have to arrange some better weather for you."

"We don't mind about the weather. However cold it is, all Victoria seems to want to do is sit on beaches." This reminded Oliver of the other occupants of his car. He seemed to be about to do something about them, but Roddy stopped him.

"Look . . . just a minute, old boy. I think we should have a word first." Oliver looked at him. Roddy scratched the back of his neck, searching for the right words. "The thing is . . ." But there seemed no way of getting around it, so he brought it straight out. "My brother died at the beginning of the week. Jock Dunbeath. His funeral was this morning. In Creagan."

Oliver was horrified. He stared at Roddy, taking this in, and then he said, "Oh, God," and there was everything in his voice: distress and sympathy and a sort of agonised embarrassment.

"My dear fellow, please don't feel badly about it. I wanted to tell you right away, so that you'd understand the situation."

"We came through Creagan. We saw all the shutters down, but we didn't know the reason."

"Well, you know how it is. People like to pay their respects in this part of the world, specially when it's a man like Jock."

"I'm so dreadfully sorry. But, when did this happen?"

"Monday. About midday. Just about this time. He was out with the dogs and he had a heart attack. We found him in the lea of one of the dikes."

"And you couldn't get in touch with me and tell us not to come, because you didn't know where I was. What a ghastly situation for you."

"No, I didn't know where you were, but even if I had, I wouldn't have got in touch with you. I've been looking forward to seeing you, and I should have been most disappointed if you hadn't come."

"We can't possibly stay."

"Of course you can stay. My brother is dead, but the funeral is over, and life must go on. The only thing is, I'd originally planned that you should sleep in the big house. But it struck me that without Jock there, it might be a little depressing for you, so if you don't mind rather close quarters, you'll be staying in the Stable House with me. Ellen, Jock's housekeeper, and Jess Guthrie from the farm have made up the beds and lit the fires, so everything's ready for you."

"Are you sure you wouldn't rather we just took ourselves off again?"

"My dear boy, it would make me miserable. I've been

looking forward to a little young company. Don't get nearly enough of it these days . . ."

He glanced across at the car, and saw that the girl, perhaps tiring of sitting there while the two men talked, had got out of it, and now she and the little boy were making their way, hand-in-hand, down the slope of the grass towards the water's edge. She was dressed more or less as Oliver was dressed, in trousers and a thick sweater. She had tied a red-and-white cotton scarf around her head, and the red of the scarf was the same as the little boy's dungarees. In such a setting, they made a charming picture, investing the grey, brooding scene with colour and a certain innocence.

"Come and meet them," said Oliver, and they began to walk slowly back towards the car.

"Just one thing more," said Roddy. "I'm taking it for granted that you're not married to this girl?"

"No, I'm not." Oliver's expression was amused. "Do you mind?"

The inference that Roddy Dunbeath's attitudes might well be out of date and out of touch made Roddy feel mildly indignant. "Heavens, no. I don't mind in the very least. Anyway, it's nothing to do with me, it's your affair entirely. There is just one point, though. It would be much better if the people who work at Benchoile believe you to be married. It sounds old-fashioned, I know, but people are old-fashioned up here, and I wouldn't want to offend them. I'm sure you understand."

"Yes, of course."

"Ellen, the housekeeper, would probably have a heart attack and pass out on me if she knew the wicked truth, and God knows what would happen to Benchoile if that happened. She's been here for ever, longer than most people can remember. She arrived in the first instance, fresh from some remote Highland croft, to look after my younger brother, and she's remained, immovable as a rock, ever since. You'll meet her, but don't expect a devoted, smiling, gentle old dear. Ellen is as tough as old boots and can be twice as unpleasant! So you see, it's quite important not to offend her."

"Yes, of course."

"Mr and Mrs Dobbs, then?"

"Mr and Mrs Dobbs," Oliver agreed.

Victoria, with Thomas's fat hand held firmly in her own, stood by the reedy margins of Loch Muie and struggled with a terrible conviction that she had come to a place where she had no business to be.

It is better to travel hopefully than to arrive. Arrival, it seemed, had brought nothing but a sense of desolation and disappointment. This was Benchoile. But the Benchoile that Victoria had imagined was the Benchoile seen through the eyes of the ten-year-old boy that Roddy Dunbeath had been. *The Eagle Years* was a saga of summertime, of blue skies and long golden evenings and hills purple with heather. An idyll that bore no relation to this windswept and foreboding scene. It seemed to Victoria unrecognisable. Where was the little rowing boat? Where was the waterfall where Roddy and his brothers had picnicked? Where the children, running barefoot?

The answer was simple. Gone for ever. Shut away between the covers of a book.

This now, was Benchoile. So much sky, so much space, so quiet. Only the sough of the wind in pine branches and the lap of grey water on the shingle. The size and the silence of the hills was unnerving. They enclosed the glen, rose sheer from the opposite shore of the loch. Victoria's eyes followed their slope, upwards, past great bastions of rock and scree, over swelling shoulders dark with heather, to distant summits veiled in the scudding grey sky. Their very size, their watchfulness, had an obliterating effect. She felt shrunk, dwarfed, insignificant as an ant. Incapable of dealing with anything, least of all the sudden deterioration of her relationship with Oliver.

She tried to call it a silly quarrel, but knew that it was more than that, a breach both bitter and unexpected. That it had blown up at all was Victoria's own fault. She should have kept quiet about sending the stupid postcard to Mrs Archer. But at the time it had seemed important, an issue worth fighting for. And now everything was spoiled, and not a word had either of them spoken since Oliver's last violent outburst. And perhaps that was Victoria's fault too. She should have stood up for herself, given threat for threat, and, if necessary, threatened blow for blow. Proved to Oliver that she had a will of her own instead of sitting mesmerised like a rabbit, and with her eyes so full of tears she couldn't even see the road ahead.

She felt overwhelmed. By the quarrel, by Benchoile, by a physical tiredness that made her ache, by the uncomfortable feeling that she had mislaid her own identity. Who am I? What am I doing in this outlandish place? How did I ever get here?

"Victoria." She had not heard them approaching across the grass, and Oliver's voice startled her. "Victoria, this is Roddy Dunbeath."

She turned to face a man huge and shabby as a much-loved teddy bear. His clothes looked as though they had been thrown at him, his sparse grey hair blew in the wind, his features were lost in fat. But he was smiling at her. His blue eyes were warm with friendliness. Before them, Victoria's depression, her first fearful impressions of Benchoile, abated a little.

She said, "Hello." They shook hands. He looked down at Thomas. "And who's this?"

"This is Tom." She stooped and lifted him up to her shoulder. Tom's cheeks were intensely red, and he had mud on his mouth where he had been tasting pebbles.

"Hello, Tom. How old are you?"

"He's two," Oliver told him, "and you'll be delighted to hear that he scarcely ever utters a word."

Roddy considered this. "Well, he appears to be quite healthy, so I don't suppose you've got anything to worry about." He looked back at Victoria. "I'm afraid Benchoile isn't at its best today. There's too much cloud about."

There was an old black Labrador at his heels. Thomas caught sight of him, and wriggled, wanting to be put down so that he could go and pat the dog. Victoria set him back on his feet, and he and the dog looked at each other. Then Thomas touched the soft, grizzled muzzle.

"What is he called?" asked Victoria.

"Barney. He's very old. Almost as old as I am."

"I thought you'd probably have a dog."

"Victoria," Oliver explained, "is one of your fans, Roddy." He sounded quite cheerful and ordinary again, and Victoria wondered if the quarrel that had blown up that morning was, for the time being, forgotten.

"How splendid," said Roddy. "Nothing I like better than having a fan about the place."

Victoria smiled. "I was looking for the waterfall."

"Even on a fine day you can't see it from here. It's hidden behind an outcrop. There's a little bay. Perhaps if the weather clears and I can find the key to the boathouse, we'll get over one day and you can see it for yourself." A gust of wind, with a cutting edge like a knife, keened down upon them. Victoria shivered and Roddy was galvanised into hostly action. "Now, come along, we'll all get pneumonia standing here. Let's get your cases out of the car and get you all settled in."

Again, it was like nothing that Victoria had imagined. For Roddy led them, not into the big house, but through the archway into the stable yard, and so on to what was obviously his own little house. The bedrooms were on the ground floor. "This is for you and Oliver," said

Roddy, going ahead of them like a well-trained hotel porter. "And there's a dressing-room off it, where I thought you could put the child; and here's the bathroom. It's all pretty cramped I'm afraid, but I hope you'll be comfortable."

"I think it's perfect." She set Tom down on the bed, and looked about her. There was a window facing out over the water, and a deep window-sill, upon which stood a little jug of snowdrops. She wondered if it was Roddy who had put them there.

"It's a funny sort of house," he told her. "The living-room and the kitchen are upstairs, but I like it that way. Now, when you've unpacked and made yourselves comfortable, come up and we'll have a drink and something to eat. Does Thomas like soup?"

"He likes anything."

Roddy looked suitably amazed. "What an accommodating child," he remarked, and went off and left her.

Victoria sat on the edge of the bed, and lifted Thomas on to her knee and began to divest him of his little jacket. And all the time her eyes went around the room, loving it because it was so right, whitewashed and simply furnished, and yet containing all that any person could possibly need. It even had a fireplace, built across one corner of the room, in which a stack of peats was smouldering, and there was a basket containing more peat alongside the hearth, so that one could replenish it oneself, keep it going all night if need be. She thought of going to sleep by firelight, and it seemed, all at once, the most romantic thing in the world. Perhaps, she told herself cautiously, perhaps after all, everything was going to be all right.

Oliver appeared behind her, bearing the last of the suitcases. He put this down and shut the door behind him.

"Oliver . . ."

But, abruptly, he interrupted her. "Something ghastly's happened. Roddy's brother died at the beginning of the week. That was his funeral in Creagan this morning. I mean, that's why all the blinds were down."

Victoria stared at him, over the top of Thomas's head, in horrified disbelief. "But why didn't he let us know?"

"He couldn't. He didn't know where we were. And anyway, he swears he wanted us to come."

"He's just saying that."

"No, I don't think he is. In a way, I think we're probably the best thing that could happen to him. You know, give him something to think about. Anyway, we're here now. We can't go away again."

"But . . ."

"And there's another thing. We're Mr and Mrs Dobbs like in the hotel register. Apparently, there's a string of old retainers who'll all give notice if they know the terrible truth." He began nosing around, opening cupboards and doors, like a great, long cat making itself at home. "What a fantastic setup. Is this where Thomas is sleeping?"

"Yes. Oliver, perhaps we should only stay one night."

"What do you mean? Don't you like it here?"

"I love it, but . . ."

He came to drop a kiss on her open, protesting mouth, and Victoria was silenced. The quarrel still lay between them. She wondered if the kiss was meant as an apology, or whether she was going to have to be the first to say she was sorry. But before she was able to make up her mind about this, one way or the other, he had kissed her again, patted Thomas on the head, and left them. She heard him running upstairs, heard his voice mingling with Roddy's. She sighed, and lifted Thomas off the bed and took him to the bathroom.

It was midnight and very dark. Roddy Dunbeath, steeped in brandy, had taken a torch and whistled up his dog, and gone the rounds of the big house, to make sure, he explained to Oliver, that the doors and windows were all securely closed, and that old Ellen, up in her attic bedroom, was safe for the night.

Oliver wondered, safe from what? They had been introduced, formally, to Ellen during the course of the evening, and she had seemed to him not only older than God but just as formidable. Victoria had long since gone to bed. Thomas was sleeping. Oliver lit the cigar that Roddy had given him and took it out of doors.

The silence that greeted him was immense. The wind had dropped and there was scarcely a sound. His footsteps crunched as he went across the gravel, and then fell silent when he reached the grass. He could feel its cold dampness through the soles of his shoes. He reached the loch and began to walk along the edge of the water. The air was icy. His light clothes – the velvet jacket and the silk shirt – were no protection, and the cold washed over his body like a freezing shower. He revelled in the shock of it and felt refreshed and stimulated.

His eyes grew accustomed to the darkness. Slowly, the massive presence of the surrounding hills began to take shape. He saw the translucent shimmer of the loch. From the trees behind the house, an owl hooted. He came to the little jetty. Now, his footsteps sounded hollow on the wooden planking. At the end, he stopped, and threw the butt of the cigar into the water. It sizzled and then was dark.

The voices were there. The old woman. *It's not the way your father would have done it*. She had been living in his head for months, but she was Ellen Tarbat. And yet she was not Ellen from Sutherland. She was called Kate and she came from Yorkshire. *Your father didn't do things that way, not that way at all*. She was embittered, she was worn, she was indestructible. *He was always a man to pay his way. And proud. When I buried him, I did it with ham. Mrs Hackworth buried her man, but she's that mean, she did it with nobbut buns.*

She was Kate, but she was Ellen too. This was the way it happened. Past and present, fantasy and reality, all spun together like a steel rope, so that he did not know where one ended and the other began. And this thing inside him would begin to grow, like some tumour, until it took over altogether, and he would become possessed by it, and by the people who fought to get out of the inside of his head; to get down on paper.

And for weeks, perhaps months, he would exist in a shambling vacuum, incapable of anything except the most basic and essential of bodily functions; like sleeping, and ambling around the corner to the pub, and buying cigarettes.

The anticipation of this state filled him with trembling excitement. Despite the cold, he found that the palms of his hands were sweaty. He turned and looked back at the dim bulk of the house. A light burned in the attic, and he imagined old Ellen pottering about, putting her teeth into a tumbler, saying her prayers, getting into bed. He saw her, lying, staring at the ceiling, her nose sticking up over the edge of the sheet, waiting for the fitful sleep of old age.

There were other lights. From Roddy's sitting-room, from behind drawn curtains. From the bedroom below it where Victoria slept.

He made his way, slowly, back to the house,

She was asleep, but she woke when he came in and switched on the light by their bed. He sat beside her, and she turned on the pillow and yawned, and saw who it was and said his name. She wore a nightdress of thin white lawn, edged with lace, and her pale hair spread on the pillow like strands of primrose-coloured silk.

He pulled off his tie and undid the top button of his shirt, and she said, "Where have you been?"

"Out."

"What time is it?"

He kicked off his shoes. "Late." He leaned across and took her head between his hands. Slowly, he began to kiss her.

He slept at last, but Victoria lay awake in his arms for an hour or more. The curtains were drawn back and the cold night air flowed in through the open window. In the hearth the peat fire burned steadily, and its flicker and glow were reflected in patterns of light on the low, white ceiling. The quarrel of the morning had been dissolved in love. Victoria was reassured. She lay there in the tranquil knowledge – as calming as a sedative – that nothing this perfect could possibly go wrong.

10

FRIDAY

She was suddenly, intensely, wide awake, disoriented, with no idea where she was meant to be. She saw the wide window, and beyond it, the sky – pale, pristine, cloudless. The outline of the hills was sharp as glass, the topmost peaks touched by the first rays of the rising sun. Benchoile. Benchoile, possibly at its best. It looked as if it were going to be a beautiful day. Perhaps she could take Thomas to the beach.

Thomas. Thomas's grandmother. Mrs Archer. Today she was going to write to Mrs Archer.

Just like that, while she slept, her mind, perhaps realising that Victoria was capable of dithering about this problem indefinitely, had apparently made itself up. The letter would be written this morning, posted at the earliest opportunity. She would find out the address by going to the post office in Creagan and asking for the relevant telephone directory. Woodbridge was in Hampshire. It was only a small place. There would not be many Archers living in such a small place.

The form of the letter began to frame itself: *I am writing to let you know that Thomas is well and very happy.*

And Thomas's father? Beside her Oliver slumbered soundlessly, his head turned away from her, his long arm stretched outside the covers, the palm of his hand turned up, the fingers curled and relaxed. Victoria raised herself on her elbow and looked down at his untroubled face. He seemed, in that moment, defenceless and vulnerable. He loved her. Love and fear could not share the same bed. She was not afraid of Oliver.

And anyway – cautiously she lay back on her pillows – Oliver need never know. *Oliver did not want me to write to you,* she would put, *so perhaps it would be better if you do not acknowledge this letter or try to get in touch.*

She could not think why this harmless deception had not occurred to her before. Mrs Archer would understand. All she would want was reassurance about her missing grandson. And Victoria would promise, at the end of the letter, to write again, to keep in touch. It would seem that it was going to be quite a correspondence.

From the next room, from beyond the closed door, came sounds of Thomas stirring. A strange sound, "Meh, meh, meh," disturbed the morning quiet. Thomas, singing. She imagined him sucking his thumb, thumping Piglet against the wall by his bed. After a little the singing stopped, there were scuffling sounds, the door opened and Thomas appeared.

Victoria pretended to be asleep, lay with her eyes closed. Thomas climbed up on to the bed and lay on top of her, forcing her eyelids open with a stubby thumb. She saw his face, only inches from her own, the blue eyes alarmingly close, his nose nearly touching her own.

She had not yet written to his grandmother, but today she was going to, and the knowledge freed Victoria of guilt and filled her with tenderness towards Thomas. She put her arms around him and hugged him, and he laid his cheek on hers and thoughtfully kicked her in the stomach. After a little, when it became obvious that he was not going to be still for a moment longer, she got out of bed. Oliver still slept, undisturbed. She took Thomas into his room and dressed him, and then dressed herself.

They left Oliver sleeping, and hand-in-hand climbed the stairs to forage for breakfast.

The domestic arrangements at Benchoile appeared to be fluid – the two establishments, the big house and the Stable House running, as it were, in harness. Yesterday they had lunched on soup and cheese in Roddy's cheerful, littered living-room, eating off a table drawn up to the window, the meal as informal as a picnic. Dinner, on the other hand, was a quite different affair, served in the immense dining-room of the big house. By some unspoken agreement, they had all changed for this occasion. Oliver had put on his velvet jacket, and Roddy wore a straining doublet made of tartan, with a cummerbund filling the gap between his shirt and the dark trousers, which would no longer do up around his waist. A fire had burned in the grate, there were candles in the silver candlesticks, and tall, dim portraits of varied Dunbeaths looked down upon them from the panelled walls. Victoria had wondered which was Jock, but didn't like to ask. There was something vaguely unnerving about the empty chair at the head of the table. She felt as though they were all intruding, as though they had walked into another man's house, without permission, and at any moment the owner was going to walk in and find them there.

But she, apparently, was the only one of them troubled by this uneasy guilt. Oliver and Roddy talked incessantly, of their world of writers, publishers, producers, about which Victoria knew nothing. The conversation flowed, well-oiled by an abundance of wine. And even the old woman, Ellen, had seemed to see nothing amiss in such good spirits on the very night of the laird's funeral. To and fro she trod in her worn-down shoes, her best apron over her black dress, handing the heavy ashets through the hatch that led to the kitchen, and taking away the used plates. Victoria had made signs that she would like to help, but Roddy had stopped her. "Jess Guthrie's in the kitchen, giving Ellen a hand. She'll be mortally offended if you so much as rise from your chair," he had told Victoria when Ellen was out of earshot, and so she sat, against all her better instincts, and let herself be waited on with the others.

At one point during the course of the meal Ellen had taken herself off for ten minutes or more. When she returned with the coffee tray, she had announced, without preamble, that the wee boy was sleeping like an angel, and Victoria realised that she had made the journey down the long stone passages and across the stable yard, to check on Thomas, and was touched.

"I was just going to look at him myself," she told Ellen, but Ellen's mouth had bunched up, as though Victoria had said something indecent. "And why should you be getting up from your dinner, when there's me here to see to the child?" Victoria felt reprimanded.

Now, the following morning, she struggled with the inconsistencies of another person's kitchen, but, by the lengthy expedient of opening one door after another, she ran to earth eggs, bread, a jug of milk. Thomas was no help at all, and always seemed to be under her feet. She found suitable plates and mugs, knives and forks. Some butter and a jar of instant coffee. She laid the small plastic-topped table, sat Thomas up on a chair, tied a tea towel around his neck, took the top off his egg. He settled down, silently, to demolish it.

Victoria made herself a cup of coffee and pulled up a chair to face him. She said, "Would you like to go to the beach today?"

Thomas stopped eating and looked at her, the egg yolk running down his chin. She wiped it away. As she did this the door that led into the house from the stable yard opened and shut. Footsteps came slowly up the stairs. The next moment Ellen appeared at the open kitchen door.

"Good morning," said Victoria.

"Yes, and you're up and about already. You're an early starter, Mrs Dobbs."

"Thomas woke me."

"I came over to see if you'd like me to give him his breakfast, but I see you've already seen to that yourself."

Her manner was disconcerting, because you could never tell by her voice whether you were doing the right thing or not. And it was no help looking at her face, because her expression was one of constant disapproval, the faded eyes cold and beady and her mouth pursed as though someone had run a string around it and then pulled it tight. Her hair was thin and white, dragged back from her temples and screwed into a tight little bun. Beneath it her scalp gleamed pinkly. Her figure seemed to have shrunk with age, so that all her clothes – her ageless and seemly clothes – appeared to be a size too big. Only her hands were large and capable, red with scrubbing, the joints swollen and twisted like old tree roots. She stood with these folded across her stomach, over the flowered apron, and looked as though, in her long life, she had never once stopped working. Victoria wondered how old she was.

She said, tentatively, "Perhaps you'd like a cup of coffee?"

"I never touch the stuff. It doesn't agree with me at all."

"A cup of tea, then?"

"No, no. I've had my tea."

"Well, why don't you sit down? Take the weight off your feet?"

For a moment, she thought that even this mild overture of friendliness was going to be rejected, but Ellen, perhaps seduced by Tom's unblinking stare, reached for a chair, and settled herself at the head of the table.

"Eat up your egg, then," she said to Thomas, and then to Victoria, "He's a beautiful child." Her Highland voice turned this into, "He's a peautiful chilt."

"Are you fond of children?"

"Oh, yes, and there used to be so many of them at Benchoile, all over the place." She had come, it was obvious, to see Thomas and have a gossip. Victoria waited, and inevitably the old voice rambled on. "I came here to look after Charlie when he was a baby. Charlie was the youngest of the boys. I looked after the others as well, but I had Charlie all to myself. Charlie's in America now, you know. He married an American lady." Casually, as though they could not help themselves, her hands went out to spread Thomas's toast with butter, to cut the toast into fingers for him.

Victoria said, "I feel so badly, us arriving to stay so soon after . . . I mean, we didn't know, you see . . ."

She stopped, lost in confusion and wishing that she had never started, but Ellen was quite unperturbed.

"You mean, the laird dying so suddenly like that, and the funeral only yesterday?"

"Well, yes."

"It was a beautiful funeral. All the grand people were there."

"I'm sure."

"Mind, he was a lonely man. He had no children of his own, you see. It was a great sorrow to Mrs Jock that she was never able to have any babies. 'There you are Ellen,' she used to say, 'and there's the empty nursery upstairs, waiting for the babies, and it doesn't look as though there's going to be a single one.' And, indeed, there wasn't."

She put another finger of toast into Thomas's hand.

"What happened to her?"

"She died. Five years ago or more. She died. She was

a beautiful lady. Always laughing." She told Thomas, "Yes, yes, you are eating a splendid breakfast."

"Didn't your baby . . . didn't Charlie ever have any children?"

"Oh, yes, Charlie had a boy, and what a bright little lad he was. They used to come over for the summers, all three of them, and what good times those were. Picnics up the hill or on the beach at Creagan. 'I've too much to do in the house to come for picnics,' I used to tell him, but John would say, 'But Ellen, you must come too, it'll not be a proper picnic without you.'"

"He was called John."

"Yes, he was named for the colonel."

"You must have missed him when he had to go back to America."

"Oh, the place seemed empty after they had gone. Like a tomb."

Victoria, watching Ellen, suddenly liked her very much. She stopped feeling intimidated or even shy. She said, "I knew a little bit about Benchoile before I got here yesterday, because I'd read all Roddy's books."

"Those were the best times of all, when the boys were young. Before that war."

"He must have been a funny little boy with all his strange pets."

Ellen clicked her tongue and held up her hands in horror at the memory. "I sometimes thought he'd be the death of me. Just a wee devil. He looked like an angel, mind, but you never knew what Roddy would be up to next. And when it came to washing his clothes, as likely as not the pockets would be filled with mealy worms."

Victoria laughed. "That reminds me," she said, "I wonder if there's somewhere I could do some washing. We've been travelling for four days and I haven't been able to wash anything, and soon we're all going to run out of clothes."

"You can put them in the washing machine."

"If I brought it all over to the big house after breakfast, perhaps you could show me where the washing machine is, and how to use it."

"Now, you don't worry about that. I'll see to the washing. You don't want to spend your holiday doing washing. And . . ." she added, with cunning innocence, ". . . if you should want to be away on a wee outing with your husband, I could keep an eye on the child for you."

She was obviously longing to get her hands on Thomas, to get him to herself. Victoria thought of the letter she was going to write. "I ought to do some shopping, in that case. We seem to have run out of toothpaste, and Oliver's bound to want cigarettes. If I took our car to Creagan this morning, would you really look after Thomas for me? He doesn't like shopping very much."

"And why should he like shopping? It's a dull occupation for a little man." She leaned forward, nodding her head at Thomas as though already they had some sort of a conspiracy going between them. "You'll stay with Ellen, won't you, pet? You'll help Ellen with the washing?"

Thomas stared at the small brown wrinkled face bobbing up and down so close to his own. Victoria watched for his reaction to this in some anxiety. It would be embarrassing if he screamed and hurt Ellen's feelings. But Thomas and Ellen recognised each other. They were years apart in age, but they both belonged to the same world. Thomas had finished his breakfast. He got off his chair and rescued Piglet from the floor by the refrigerator and took him to show Ellen.

She took the pig and bounced him up and down on the table as though he were dancing.

Kitty Birdy had a pig
She could do an Irish jig

saing Ellen in her cracked old voice. Thomas smiled. He laid his hand on her knee, and her own gnarled hand came down to close on the fat fingers.

It was amazing how simple, how straightforward, things became as soon as you had reached a decision. Problems ironed themselves out, difficulties dissolved. Ellen bore Thomas and the washing away, thus relieving Victoria, in a single stroke, of two of her most pressing commitments. Roddy and Oliver, probably sleeping off the brandy they had consumed the evening before, had still not appeared. Victoria, in search of writing paper, went into Roddy's living-room and found the curtains still undrawn and the atmosphere thick with stale cigar smoke. She drew the curtains and opened the windows and emptied the ashtrays into the remains of last night's fire.

In the letter rack on Roddy's littered desk, she found writing paper both plain and headed. She hesitated for a moment, debating which to use. If she used the plain paper, and wrote no address, then Mrs Archer would still not know where to find them. But surely this smacked a little of secrecy, as though she and Oliver really had something to hide.

Besides, the headed paper, thickly embossed, had a certain opulence about it, which would in itself be reassuring. "BENCHOILE, CREAGAN, SUTHERLAND." She imagined Mrs Archer being impressed by the very simplicity of this. So she took a sheet of the headed paper, and found an envelope lined with dark blue tissue. She found, in a tarnished silver mug, a ball-point pen. It was as though some person had arranged it all, ready for her, making it even easier.

Dear Mrs Archer,

I am writing to let you know that Thomas is well and very happy. Ever since we left

London, he has been very good, hardly cried at all, and has never woken up at nights. He is eating well, too.

She paused, chewing the pen, debating whether she should tell Mrs Archer that not once had Thomas asked for his grandmother. She finally decided that this would not be tactful.

As you can see we are now in Scotland and the sun is shining, so maybe we will be able to take Thomas to the beach.

She paused again, and then went on to the final and most tricky bit of all.

Oliver does not know I am writing to you. We did discuss it, but he was very against the idea. So perhaps it would be better if you do not acknowledge this letter or try to get in touch. I will write again later and let you know how Thomas is.

With best wishes,

Yours sincerely,

Victoria . . . Victoria what? She was not Victoria Dobbs and she no longer felt like Victoria Bradshaw. In the end she wrote just her Christian name and left it at that. She put the letter into its envelope and put the envelope into her cardigan pocket. Downstairs, she crept into the bedroom and collected her handbag with her money in the wallet. Oliver hadn't moved. She let herself out again, and got into the Volvo, and drove herself to Creagan.

Roddy Dunbeath, wearing a large blue-and-white striped apron which made him look like a successful pork butcher, stood at the counter in his little kitchen, chopped vegetables for the lunchtime pot of soup, and tried, at the same time, to disregard the fact that he was suffering from a hangover. At twelve o'clock he was going to pour himself a sustaining, medicinal horse's neck, but it was only now a quarter to twelve, and so he was filling in the time – and so managing to resist jumping the gun – with a little soothing culinary activity. He liked cooking. Was, in fact, an excellent chef, and it made it all the more enjoyable having a little house party to cook for besides himself.

The house party in question, whether by private arrangement, or by chance, was happily living up to Benchoile traditions, and had taken itself off. By the time Roddy had prised himself out of bed this morning, the girl Victoria and the child had disappeared. Roddy was thankful for this. He had a horror of visitors hanging about and looking bored, and he needed peace and quiet in which to attend to his small domestic duties.

But he went through to the big house to make a few polite inquiries, and was told by Ellen that Victoria had taken the Volvo and gone to Creagan. The little boy was with Ellen, helping her to hang washing on the line, and playing with the basket full of pegs.

Oliver, when he finally put in an appearance, seemed unperturbed by all this independent activity on the part of his family. In fact, thought Roddy, if anything he appeared relieved to be shed of them for an hour or two. Together, he and Roddy had eaten an enormous breakfast, and together had hatched a plan to drive, that afternoon, up to Wick. There, a friend of Roddy's, tiring of the rat race in the south, and the endless commuting, had started a small printing business, specialising in limited editions of beautifully hand-bound books. Roddy, interested in anything that smacked of genuine craftsmanship, had been meaning for some time to go and see the presses working, and to be shown around the bindery, and Oliver, when the idea was put to him, was equally enthusiastic.

"What about Victoria?" Roddy asked.

"Oh, she'll probably want to do something with Thomas."

The telephone call to Wick was made, and the visit arranged. Whereupon Oliver, after a bit of restless prowling, admitted that he wanted to do some work, so Roddy lent him a scribbling pad and sent him off to the library in the big house, where, with a bit of luck, Oliver would spend the morning undisturbed.

In the meantime Roddy, left to himself, had lit a roaring fire, written a couple of letters, and was now making soup. The air was filled with the crisp, sharp smell of celery, sunlight streamed through the window, Vivaldi burbled from his transistor. The telephone started to ring.

Roddy swore, and went on cutting celery, as though the telephone would somehow answer itself. But of course it didn't, so he laid down the knife and wiped his hands on a tea towel and went through to the living-room.

"Roddy Dunbeath."

"Roddy, it's John Dunbeath."

Roddy sat down. Luckily there was a chair behind him. He could not have been more astonished. "I thought you were in Bahrain."

"No, I got back yesterday morning. Roddy, I'm so dreadfully sorry about Jock. And that I couldn't make the funeral."

"My dear boy, we quite understood. Good of you to send the cable. Where are you calling from? London? You sound as though you're in the next room."

"No, I'm not in London. I'm in Inverness."

"*Inverness?*" Roddy's thought processes, blunted by last night's cognac, were not working in what you would call top gear. "How you do get around. When did you get to Inverness?"

"I caught the Highlander last night. I was here this morning. I've spent the morning with Robert McKenzie. He said it would be OK if I rang you . . . if I came to Benchoile."

"But of course. How *splendid*. Stay for a few days. Stay for the weekend. When can we expect you?"

"Well, this afternoon some time. I'm hiring a car. Would it be all right if I came this afternoon?"

"Marvellous . . ." Roddy started to say, and then remembered the complications. He struck his forehead with the heel of his hand, a theatrical gesture of recall, totally wasted when there was no person to observe it. "Oh, damn, except that I won't be here. I've arranged to go up to Wick. I've got a chap staying and we're going to go there and look at a printing press. But that doesn't matter. We'll be back some time, and Ellen'll be here."

"How is Ellen?"

"Indestructible. Puts us all in the shade. I'll tell her you're coming. I'll tell her to expect you."

"I hope I'm not putting you out."

Roddy remembered that John had always been an intensely well-mannered person. "Not putting us out at all." He added, because there seemed no point in not doing so, "Besides, it's your house now. You don't have to ask yourself to stay."

There was a tiny silence. Then, "Yes," said John and he sounded thoughtful. "Yes. That's one of the things I want to talk to you about. There's an awful lot to discuss."

"We'll have a good old chinwag after dinner," Roddy promised him. "Anyway, see you later. I'm really looking forward to it. It's been too long, John."

"Yeah," said John, suddenly sounding very American. "I guess it's been too long."

* * *

Victoria returned ten minutes or so later, just as Roddy had finished the soup, tidied the kitchen, and poured himself the longed-for brandy and ginger ale. He was sitting by the window, watching a flock of black-and-white shelduck which had settled down to feed by the edge of the loch, when he heard the sound of the returning car. A moment or so later the downstairs front door opened and shut.

He called, "Victoria!"

"Hello."

"I'm up here. All on my own. Come and join me."

Obediently, she came running up the stairs, and saw him at the far end of the room, sitting in solitary state, with only Barney for company.

"Where is everybody?" she asked, coming over to join him.

"Oliver's in the big house closeted in the library and working. And Thomas is still with Ellen."

"Perhaps I should go and get him."

"Don't be ridiculous. He's perfectly all right. Sit down. Have a drink."

"No, I don't want a drink." But she sat beside him, pulling off her scarf. He thought, all at once, how pretty she was. Yesterday, when he had first seen her, he had not thought her pretty at all. She had seemed to him both shy and colourless; dull, even. At dinner she had scarcely said a word, and Roddy had been hard put to understand what Oliver saw in her. But this morning, she was a different person. Shining eyes, pink cheeks, a mouth all smiles. Now, Roddy found himself wondering why Oliver didn't marry the girl. Perhaps it had something to do with her background. How old was she? Where had he met her? How long had they been together? She looked ridiculously youthful to be the mother of a two-year-old boy, but then young people these days seemed to plunge into relationships when they were scarcely out of school, committing themselves to domesticity in a manner that the young Roddy would have found intensely frustrating. She had, he noticed, beautiful teeth.

He said, "You're looking very bright eyed and bushy tailed. Something good must have happened in Creagan."

"It's just that it's such a beautiful morning. You can see for miles, and everything's all sparkly and bright. I didn't mean to be so long. I only went to buy some toothpaste and cigarettes and things, but Ellen said she didn't mind looking after Thomas, and Creagan is so pretty, I just stayed there and looked around, and I went into the church, and into that house they call The Deanery, but it's a craft shop now."

Her enthusiasm was endearing. "Did you buy anything?"

"No, but I might go back and buy something. They've got beautiful Shetland sweaters. And then I went and looked at the beach. I can't wait to take Thomas. You'd have thought it would be cold, but it wasn't. The sun was quite warm."

"I'm glad you had a good morning."

"Yes." She met his eyes, and some of the brightness went out of her face. "I somehow didn't get the chance to say anything last night, but . . . Well, Oliver told me about your brother, and I was so sorry. I just feel so awful about us all being here."

"You mustn't feel awful. You're good for me."

"It's just something else for you to worry about. I've been feeling guilty all morning because I should have been helping you or Ellen, instead of simply abandoning Thomas."

"Do you good to get away from Thomas for an hour or so."

"Well, as a matter of fact, it was rather nice." They smiled, in complete understanding. "Did you say that Oliver was working?"

"That's what he said."

Victoria made a little face. "I didn't realise that he wanted to work."

"Probably wants to get some idea down on paper before it goes out of his head." He remembered the projected trip to Wick that afternoon and told her about it. "We'll take you with us if you like, but Oliver thought you'd want to do something with Tom."

"I'd rather stay here."

"In that case, you can do something for me. There's a young man arriving some time during the afternoon. He's going to stay for a day or two. So if we're not back, perhaps you could look after him, pour the tea, generally make him feel welcome."

"Yes, of course. But where's he going to sleep? We seem to have filled your house."

"He's going into the big house. I've already had a word with Ellen and she's alight with excitement; linen sheets on the bed, everything scoured and polished."

"I'd have thought she already had enough to do without more visitors arriving."

"Ah, but you see, this young man is Ellen's precious baby. In fact, he's my nephew John Dunbeath."

Victoria stared at Roddy in astonishment. "John Dunbeath? You mean your brother Charlie's boy? Ellen told me about him this morning at breakfast. But I thought he was in America."

"No, he's not. In fact, he's just telephoned me from Inverness."

"Ellen must be over the moon."

"She is. Not just because he's coming to stay, but because John is the new laird of Benchoile. My brother Jock has left Benchoile to John."

Victoria was confused. "But I thought you were the new laird."

"Heaven forbid."

She smiled. "But you'd be such a wonderful laird."

"You're very kind, but I'd be a useless one. I'm too old, too set in my evil ways. Better a new young broom to sweep us all clean. When I told Ellen the news a gleam came into her beady eye, but whether it was a tear or a glitter of triumph I wouldn't be able to say."

"Don't be horrid about her. I like her."

"I like her too, but one day she'll drive me into a nuthouse." He sighed and looked down at his empty glass. "Are you *sure* you wouldn't like a drink?"

"Quite sure."

"In that case, be a good girl and go and run Oliver and that little boy of yours to earth, and tell them lunch will be ready in about ten minutes." He heaved himself off the window seat and went to throw more logs on to his dying fire. As usual they sparked violently, and as usual Roddy tramped the glowing embers to death on his long-suffering hearthrug.

Victoria went to do as he had asked. At the top of the stairs, she paused.

"Where did you say I'd find Oliver?"

"In the library."

She left him, clattering down the open treads like an eager child. Alone, Roddy sighed again. He debated, and finally succumbed. He poured himself another drink, and took it through to the kitchen where he inspected his fragrant soup.

Victoria put her head around the door. "Oliver."

He was not writing. He sat at the desk in the window, with his arms hanging loose and his legs outstretched, but he was not actually writing.

"Oliver."

He turned his head. It took a second or two for him to recognise her. Then his blank eyes came to life. He smiled, as though she had just woken him up. He put up a hand to rub the back of his neck.

"Hi."

"It's lunchtime."

She closed the door behind her. He held out a long arm and she went over to him, and he drew her close, burying his face in her thick sweater; nuzzling, like a child, into its warmth. Memories of last night filled her with sweetness. She laid her chin on the top of his head, and looked down at the desk and sheets of paper, covered with scribbles and doodles and Oliver's narrow, tight writing.

She said again, "It's time for lunch."

"It can't be. I've only been here five minutes."

"Roddy says you've been here since breakfast."

"Where did you get to?"

"Creagan."

"What were you doing there?"

"Shopping." He put her away from him, and looked up into her face. Coolly, Victoria met his eyes, and repeated herself. "Shopping. I bought you cigarettes, I thought you'd soon be running out."

"Marvellous girl."

"And there's someone else coming to stay; arriving this afternoon."

"Who's that?"

"John Dunbeath. Roddy's nephew." She put on a spurious Highland accent. "The new young laird of Benchoile."

"Good God," said Oliver. "It's like living in a novel by Walter Scott."

She laughed. "Do you want some lunch?"

"Yes." He pushed the scribbling pad away from him, and stiffly stood up. He stretched and yawned. "But I want a drink first."

"Roddy's longing for someone to have a drink with him."

"Are you coming too?"

"I'll find Thomas first." They moved towards the door. "Ellen's had him all morning."

"Bully for Ellen," said Oliver.

John Dunbeath, driving the hired Ford, came through Eventon, and the road swung east. To his right lay the Cromarty Firth beneath the cloudless winter sky; blue as the Mediterranean and in all the extravagance of a flood tide. Beyond it, the peaceful hills of the Black Isle drew a skyline sharp as a razor in the clear, glittering light. Rich farmland swept down to the edge of the water, sheep grazed on the upper slopes, and scarlet tractors, minimised to toys by the distance, were out ploughing the rich dark earth.

The dazzling brightness of the day came as an unexpected bonus. John had left London cloaked in grey rain, and boarded the Highlander in a state of unrelieved exhaustion. Weary from forty-eight hours of ceaseless activity, suffering from jet lag, and still in a mild state of shock occasioned by Jock Dunbeath's unthought-of bequest, he had drunk two enormous whiskies, and fallen into a sleep so deep that the sleeping-car attendant had had to come and shake him awake, and inform him that the train had actually arrived at Inverness Station five minutes before.

Now, on his way to Benchoile, and with nothing but necessarily unhappy news to impart to all who lived there, he could not get rid of the feeling that he was going on holiday.

Part of this was due to association of ideas. The further he got from London and the closer to Benchoile, the clearer and more vivid became the memories. He knew this road. The fact that he had not driven it for ten years did not seem to matter at all. He felt that it could have been yesterday, and the only thing amiss was the fact that his father was not beside him, cheerful with anticipation, and anxious for John not to miss a single familiar landmark.

The road forked. He left the Cromarty Firth behind

him and climbed up and over Struie and down to the further magnificence of the Dornoch Firth. He saw the wooded slopes on the distant shore, and behind these the snow-capped ramparts of the hills of Sutherland. Far to the east lay the open sea, still and blue as a day in summer. He rolled down the window of the car and caught the smells, damp and evocative, of moss and peat, and the sharp tang of the sea-wrack washed up on the shoreline far below him. The road sloped away, and the Ford idled its way down the smoothly cambered curves.

Forty minutes later, he was through Creagan. He began to slow down in anticipation of the turning to Benchoile. He came upon it and left the main road, and now all was familiar in quite a different way. For he was back on Benchoile land. Here was the path that he had taken one grey day with his father and Davey Guthrie, that led over the distant summit of the hill and down into the desolate glen of Loch Feosaig. There they had fished, and late in the evening, Jock had driven around by the road to collect them and bring them home.

Below him purled the river, and he passed the spot where he had once stood for two hours or more, fighting a salmon. The first line of grouse butts swung into view; the Guthries' farmhouse. The trodden garden was cheerfully bannered with washing, and the tethered sheepdogs raged at the passing car.

He rounded the final bend of the road. Before him lay the long sweep of Loch Muie, and at the end of it, slumbering, solitary in the late afternoon sunshine, the old grey house.

This was the worst of all, but his heart was hardened and his mind made up. *I shall sell it*, he had told Robert McKenzie this morning, because, from the moment he had read the lawyer's letter, he had known that there was nothing else that he could possibly do.

Whether she had been watching for the car or not,

John had no idea, but Ellen Tarbat appeared almost instantly. He had only time to open the boot of the Ford and take out his suitcase before she was there, coming out of the front door, down the steps towards him. A little tottery about the legs, smaller than he remembered her, strands of white hair escaping from her bun, her red, knotted old hands flung wide in welcome.

"Well, well, and you are here. And what a delight to see you again after all these years."

He laid down his suitcase and went to embrace her. He had to bend almost double to receive her kiss and her frailness, her lack of substance, was unnerving. He felt that he should urge her indoors before she was caught up by a breath of wind and blown away. And yet she had pounced on his suitcase and had started to try to lug it indoors before he could stop her, and he had to forcibly wrest it from her grasp before she would let it go.

"What do you think you're doing? I'll carry that."

"Well, let's get in, away from the cold."

She led the way back up the steps and into the house, and he followed her and she closed the big doors carefully behind her. He walked into the big hall and was assailed by a smell made up of peat smoke and pipe smoke and floor polish and leather. Blindfolded, or drunk, or dying, he would have known by that smell that he was back at Benchoile.

"And did you have a good journey? What a surprise when Roddy told me this morning that you were coming. I thought you were away with all those Arabs."

"Where's Roddy?"

"He and Mr Dobbs have gone to Wick. But he'll be back this evening."

"Is he all right?"

"He seems to be bearing up very well. It was a terrible thing your uncle dying, and such a shock to us all . . ." She had begun to lead the way upstairs, very slowly, one hand on the banister. ". . . But I had a premonition. When he did not come in for his lunch, I was certain that something had happened. As, indeed, it had."

"Perhaps it was a good way for him to go."

"Yes, yes, you are right. Out on a walk, with his dogs. Enjoying himself. But it is a terrible thing for the folk who are left behind."

She had reached the turn of the stair. She paused, to sigh, to draw fresh breath for the next flight. John shifted his suitcase from one hand to the other. They went on up.

"And now you have come to Benchoile. We wondered, Jess and I, what would happen with the colonel dying so suddenly, but it didn't seem very fitting to start inquiring. So when Roddy came to tell me this morning, you can imagine my delight. 'Why,' I said to him, 'that is the right person for Benchoile. Charlie's boy! There was never anybody like Charlie.'"

He did not want to continue this line of conversation. He changed the subject firmly. "And how about yourself, Ellen? How have you been keeping?"

"I am not getting any younger, but I manage to keep busy."

Knowing the size of the house, he wondered how she would manage to do anything else. They had now, at last, reached the landing. John wondered where he was sleeping. He had a ghastly suspicion that Ellen might have put him in his uncle's bedroom; it was just the sort of horror she would be capable of springing on him, and he was thankful when she led him towards the best spare bedroom where, before, his father had stayed. She opened the door to a flood of sunlight and a gust of cold, fresh air. "Oh," said Ellen, and went to close the windows, and John, following her into the room, saw the high, wide beds with their white starched cotton covers, the dressing-table with the curly framed mirror, the velvet-covered chaise longue. Even the blast of fresh air could not dispel the smell of polish and carbolic. Ellen, it was obvious, had been busy.

"You won't find anything changed." Having closed the windows Ellen pottered about, straightening a starched linen mat, opening the immense wardrobe to check on coat hangers, and letting out a wave of camphor. John laid down his suitcase on the luggage rack at the foot of one of the beds, and went to the window. The sun was beginning to slip out of the sky and a rosy flush stained the hilltops. The mown grass of the lawn spread as far as a shrubbery, and beyond this to a copse of silver birch, and as he stood there, two figures appeared through these trees, making their way slowly towards the house. A girl, and a little boy. Behind them, looking more exhausted than they, an old black Labrador. "And the bathroom's just through that door. I've put clean towels out, and . . ."

"Ellen. Who's that?"

Ellen joined him at the window, peering with her old eyes.

"That is Mrs Dobbs and her little boy Thomas. The family is staying with Roddy."

They had emerged from the trees and were now out in the open. The child, tagging behind his mother, suddenly spied the water, and began to make for the loch's edge. The girl hesitated, and then resignedly followed him.

"I thought that you and she could have tea together in the library, and Thomas can have his tea with me." She went on, tempting him, "There's a batch of scones in the oven and heather honey on the tray." When John neither spoke, nor turned from the window, Ellen was a little put out. After all, she had opened the heather honey especially for him. "I've put towels on the rail, so that you can wash your hands," she reminded him, with some asperity.

"Yes. Sure." He sounded abstracted. Ellen left him.

He heard her slow descent of the staircase. The girl and the child seemed to be having a small argument. Finally, she stooped and picked him up and started to carry him up towards the house.

John left the window and went out of the room and downstairs, and out of the front door. They saw him at once, and the girl, perhaps startled by his sudden appearance, stood still. He crossed the gravel and started down the slope of the lawn. He could not tell the exact moment of her recognition. He only knew that he had recognised her instantly, as soon as she appeared through the trees.

She wore jeans and a brilliant green sweater with suede patches on the shoulders. Her face, and the child's face, so close, observed his approach. The two pairs of wide blue eyes were ridiculously alike. There were freckles on her nose that had not been there before.

Mrs Dobbs. With, doubtless, the child who had been making such a hullaballoo the night John drove her home. Mrs Dobbs.

He said, "Hello, Victoria."

She said, "Hello."

Now, there were four of them around the dinner table, and the empty chair at its head was no longer empty.

Victoria wore a caftan of soft blue wool, the neck and the edges of the sleeves threaded with gold. She had, for the evening, put up her hair, but the arrangement seemed to John Dunbeath to have been ineptly contrived. It trailed one or two pale strands of hair, and served, instead of making her look sophisticated, only to enhance her air of extreme youth. The exposed back of her long neck seemed, all at once, as vulnerable as a child's. Her eyes were darkened, her beautiful mouth very pale. The shut-away, secret expression was still there. For some reason, this pleased John. It came with some satisfaction to realise that if he had not been able to break down the barrier, then neither had Oliver Dobbs.

"They're not married," Roddy had told him over a drink before dinner, when they were waiting for the Dobbses to appear. "Don't ask me why. She seems a charming little thing."

Charming, and reserved. Perhaps in bed, in love, those defences came down. His eyes moved from Victoria to Oliver, and he was annoyed to discover that from these pretty images his instincts shied like a nervous horse. Firmly, he brought his attention back to what Roddy was saying.

". . . the great thing is to keep investing capital in the land. Not only money, but resources and time. The aim is to make one good blade of grass grow where nothing grew before; to keep up employment for the local people; to stop the endless drift of the country population to the big cities."

This was Roddy Dunbeath, revealing a totally unexpected side to his character. Victoria, helping herself to an orange from the bowl in the middle of the table, wondered how many people had heard him expound thus on a subject that was obviously close to his heart. For he spoke with the authority of a man who had lived in Scotland all his life, who recognised its problems, and was prepared to argue to the hilt against any easy solution that he believed to be inadequate or impractical. People seemed to lie at the root of it all. Everything came back to people. Without people there could be no sort of community. Without communities there could be no sort of future, no sort of life.

"How about forestry?" asked John Dunbeath.

"It depends how you go about it. James Dochart, who farms Glen Tolsta, planted a stretch of hill with woodland, maybe four hundred acres . . ."

She began to peel the orange. He had been at Benchoile

for about five hours. She had had five hours in which to get over the shock of his sudden appearance, but she still felt bewildered. That the young American she had met in London, and John Dunbeath, nephew to Roddy and only son of Ellen's beloved Charlie, should be one and the same person, still seemed impossible, unacceptable.

He sat now, at the end of the softly candle-lit table, relaxed and attentive, his eyes on Roddy, his expression sombre. He wore a dark suit and a very white shirt. His hand, on the table, slowly turned his glass of port. The candlelight gleamed on the heavy gold of his signet ring.

". . . but he did it in a way that meant those four hundred acres still support some cows and four hundred sheep and his lambing has improved. But forestry, the way the state goes about it, is no answer to the hill farmer's problem. A solid mass of sitka spruce, and you're left with a three per cent return on capital and another shepherd out of a job."

Mrs Dobbs. She wondered if Roddy had told him that she wasn't married to Oliver, or whether he had guessed this for himself. Either way, he seemed to take it for granted that Thomas was her child. She told herself that this was a good thing. She and Oliver had come beyond justifications and explanations. This was the way she wanted it to be. She had wanted to belong to somebody, to be needed, and now she belonged to Oliver and she was needed by Tom. She began to break the orange into segments. Juice dripped over her fingers, and on to the delicately trellised Meissen plate.

"How about the tourist industry?" John was asking. "Highlands and Islands."

"Tourism is very tempting, very nice, but it's also dangerous. There is nothing more dismal than a community depending on tourists. You can convert holiday cottages, you can build log-cabins, you can even open your house to summer visitors, but given one bad summer and the wet and the cold frighten the ordinary family man away. All right, if he's a fisherman or a hill walker or a bird-watcher, he probably won't object to a bit of rain. But a woman with three children, trapped in a small cottage for a long, wet fortnight, is going to insist on being taken to Torremolinos next summer. No, any population must have jobs for men, and it's their jobs that are being lost."

Oliver sighed. He had had two glasses of port and he was becoming sleepy. He listened to the conversation, not because it was of much interest to him, but because he found himself fascinated by John Dunbeath. The epitome, one would have thought, of the quiet, well-bred, Down-Easter, with his Brooks Brothers shirt, and elusive mid-Atlantic accent. As he talked, Oliver observed him covertly. What made him tick? What were the motivations behind that polite, reserved facade? And what – most intriguing of all – did he think about Victoria?

That they had already met in London, he knew. Victoria herself had told him this evening, while Oliver soaked in a bath, and she brushed her hair, and they talked through the open door.

"So extraordinary," she had said, in her lightest and most casual of voices. He knew that voice. It was Victoria's keep-out sign, and always aroused his avid curiosity. "He was the man who brought me home from the party that evening. Do you remember? When Tom was crying."

"You mean John Hackenbacker of Consolidated Aloominum? Well, I never did. How extraordinary." This was fascinating. He mulled it over, squeezing spongefuls of peat-brown water over his chest. "What did he say when he saw you again?"

"Nothing really. We had tea together."

"I thought he was flying off to Bahrain."

"He was. He's flown back again."

"What a little bird of passage he is. What does he do when he's not flying hither and yon?"

"I think he's in banking."

"Well, why isn't he in London, where he should be, cashing people's cheques?"

"Oliver, he's not that sort of a banker. And he's got a few days' leave to try and sort out his uncle's estate."

"And how does he feel about being the new young laird of Benchoile?"

"I didn't ask him." She sounded cool. He knew he was annoying her, and went on with his teasing.

"Perhaps he fancies himself in a kilt. Americans always adore dressing themselves up."

"That's a stupid generalisation."

There was now a definite edge to her voice. She was, Oliver realised, sticking up for the new arrival. He got out of the bath and wrapped a towel around himself and came through to the bedroom. Victoria's anxious blue eyes met his through her mirror.

"That's a very long word for you to use."

"Well, he's not that sort of an American at all."

"What sort of an American is he?"

"Oh, I don't know." She laid down her comb and picked up her mascara brush. "I don't know anything about him."

"I do," Oliver told her. "I went and talked to Ellen while she was bathing Tom. Get on the right side of her and she's a mine of the most delicious morsels of gossip. It seems that John Dunbeath's father married a veritable heiress. And now he's been landed with Benchoile. To him who has shall be given. He's obviously been walking about with a silver spoon sticking out of his mouth since the day he was born." Still wrapped in the bath-towel, he began to prowl around the bedroom, leaving wet foot-marks on the carpet.

She said, "What are you looking for?"
"Cigarettes."

To he who has shall be given. Roddy had given Oliver a cigar. He leaned back in his chair, and through its smoke, through narrowed eyes, he watched John Dunbeath. He saw the dark eyes, the heavy, tanned features, the closely cut pelt of black hair. He looked, Oliver decided, like a tremendously wealthy young Arab, who had just climbed out of his djellaba and into a Western suit. The malice of the simile pleased him. He smiled. John looked up at that moment and saw Oliver smiling at him, but although there was no antagonism in his face, he did not smile back.

"What about the oil?"

"The oil, the oil." Roddy sounded like Henry Irving intoning "The bells, the bells!"

"Do you reckon it belongs to Scotland?"

"The nationalists think so."

"How about the private millions that British and American companies have invested before the oil could be discovered? If it hadn't been for that, the oil would still be under the North Sea, and nobody would know about it."

"They say this is what happened in the Middle East . . ."

Their voices faded to a soft murmur. Their words became indistinguishable. The other voices moved in, the real voices. Now the girl was there, sullen and pushy.

And where do you think you're going?

I'm going to London. I'm going to get a job.

What's wrong with Penistone? What's wrong with getting a job in Huddersfield?

Oh, Mum, not that sort of a job. I'm going to be a model.

A model. Tarting up and down some street with no knickers on, more like.

It's my life.

And where are you going to live?

I'll find somewhere. I've got friends.

You move in with that Ben Lowry, and I'm finished with you. I tell you straight, I'm finished . . .

". . . soon there won't be any real craftsmen left. And I mean real ones, not the weirdos who come from God knows where and set themselves up in windswept sheds to print silk scarves that no one in their right minds would ever buy. Or to weave tweed that looks like dishcloths. I'm talking about the traditional craftsmen. Kiltmakers and silversmiths, being seduced away by the big money to be earned in the rigs and the refineries. Now, take this man we went to see today. He's got a good business going. He started with two men, and now he's employing ten, and half of them are under twenty."

"What about his markets?"

"This is it. He'd already contacted his market outlets before he came north." Roddy turned to Oliver. "Who was that publisher he worked for before – when he was in London? He told us the name, but I can't remember it."

"Umm?" Oliver was dragged back into the conversation. "Sorry, I wasn't really paying attention. The publisher? Hackett and Hansom, wasn't it?"

"Yes, that's it, Hackett and Hansom. You see . . ."

But then Roddy stopped, suddenly aware that he had been holding forth for far too long. He turned to Victoria to apologise, but at this instant, to her obvious horror, she lost herself in an enormous yawn. Everybody laughed, and she was covered in confusion.

"I'm not really bored, I'm just sleepy."

"And no wonder. We're behaving abominably. I am sorry. We should have saved it for later."

"It's all right."

But the damage was done. Victoria's yawn had broken

up and ended the discussion. The candles were burning down and the fire was nearly out, and Roddy looked at his watch and realised that it was half past ten. "Good heavens, is that the time?" He put on an impeccable Edinburgh accent. "How it flies, Mrs Wishart, when you're enjoying yourself."

Victoria smiled. "It's the fresh air," she said, "that makes you sleepy. Not the lateness of the hour."

Oliver said, "We're not used to it." He leaned back in his chair and stretched.

"What are you going to do tomorrow?" Roddy asked. "What are we all going to do tomorrow? You can choose, Victoria. What would you like to do? It's going to be a good day, if we can rely on the weather forecast. How about the waterfall? Shall we take a picnic over to the waterfall? Or has anybody got a better suggestion?"

Nobody had. Pleased with his notion, Roddy enlarged on the plan. "We'll take the boat across if I can find the key to the boathouse. Thomas would like a boat trip, wouldn't he? And Ellen will pack us a nosebag. And when we get over there we'll light a fire to keep us warm."

This seemed to meet with everybody's approval, and on this note, the evening began to come to an end. Oliver finished his port, stubbed out his cigar, and stood up.

"Perhaps," he said, mildly, "I should take Victoria off to bed."

This suggestion was made to the company in general, but as he said it, he looked at John. John's face remained impassive. Victoria pushed back her chair, and he got to his feet and came around the table to hold it for her.

She said, "Good night, Roddy," and came to kiss him.

"Good night."

"Good night, John." She did not kiss John. Oliver went to open the door for her. As she went through it he turned back to the dusky room, and said with his most charming smile, "See you in the morning."

"See you," said John.

The door closed. Roddy threw more peat on the fire, stirred it to life. Then he and John drew chairs up to its warmth and resumed their discussion.

11

SATURDAY

The weather forecasters had been only partially correct. The sun indeed was shining, but intermittent clouds blew across its face, driven by a western wind, and the very air had a liquidity about it, so that hills, water, sky, all looked as though they had been painted by a huge sodden brush.

The house and the garden were sheltered by the curve of the hills, and only the smallest of breezes had shaken the trees as they waited to embark themselves and an immense amount of equipment into the old fishing boat, but they had no sooner moved forty yards or so from the shore, when the true force of the wind made itself felt. The surface of the beer-brown water was flurried and driven with quite large waves, foam-crested and splashing over the gunwales. The occupants of the boat huddled into the various waterproof garments that had been gleaned from the Benchoile gunroom and handed around at the start of the voyage. Victoria wore an olive drab oilskin with enormous toggle-fastened poacher's pockets, and Thomas had been wrapped in a shooting jacket of immense antiquity, lavishly stained with the blood of some long-defunct bird or hare. This garment restricted him considerably, and Victoria was thankful for this, because it made the task of holding him still less difficult, his one idea apparently being to cast himself bodily overboard.

John Dunbeath, without any spoken agreement, had taken the oars. They were long and heavy, and the sound of creaking rowlocks, the faint piping of the wind, and the splash of breaking waves against the side of the boat were the only sounds. He wore a black oilskin that had once belonged to his Uncle Jock, and a pair of green shooting boots, but his head was bare, and his face wet with spray. He rowed expertly, powerfully, the swing of his body driving the prow of the baulky old boat through the water. Once or twice he shipped his oars in order to look over his shoulder and judge how far the wind and the run of the water were carrying them off course, and to get his bearings. He looked very much at home, at ease. But then he had done this thing, and come this way, many times before.

Amidships, on the centre thwart, sat Roddy and Oliver. Roddy with his back to Victoria, and with his dog Barney secure between his knees; Oliver astride the thwart, leaning back with his elbows propped on the gunwale. Both men had their eyes on the approaching shore, Roddy scanning the hillside through his binoculars. From where she sat, Victoria could see only the outline of Oliver's forehead and chin. He had turned up the collar of his jacket, and his long legs, straddled in their faded jeans, ended in a pair of aged sneakers. The wind caught his hair and blew it back from his face, and the skin, fine-drawn over his cheekbones, was burnt russet with the wind.

In the bottom of the boat, pools of water, inevitably, slopped. Every now and then, when he thought about it, Roddy would lower his binoculars on their leather strap and bail absent-mindedly, dipping the water up with an old tin bowl and emptying it overboard. It didn't seem to make much difference. Anyway, the picnic baskets, the box of kindling, the bundles of tarpaulins and rugs had all been stowed with care, out of reach of the puddles.

There seemed to be enough food to feed an army, and various vacuum flasks and bottles had a special basket to themselves, with divisions, so that they did not bang together and break.

Roddy, having finished with a little bit of bailing, took up his binoculars again, and began to cover the hill.

"What are you looking for?" Oliver asked.

"Deer. It's amazing how hard they are to see on a hill face. Last week when we had the snow you could pick them out from the house, but there don't seem to be any about today."

"Where will they be?"

"Over the hill probably."

"Do you get a lot here?"

"Sometimes as many as five hundred. Deer and does. In cold weather they come down and eat the fodder we put out for the cattle. In the summer they bring their young down, after dark, to graze in the pastures and drink from the loch. You can drive up the old cattle road from the foot of the loch. Keep the headlights of the car turned off, and you take them unawares. Then turn the lights on to them, and it's a beautiful sight."

"Do you shoot them?" Oliver asked.

"No. Our neighbour over the hill has the stalking rights. Jock let them to him. However, the deepfreeze at Benchoile is full of haunches of venison. You should get Ellen busy on it before you take yourselves off again. It can be dry and tough, but Ellen's a way with venison. It's delicious." He lifted the leather strap over his head and handed the binoculars to Oliver. "Here, you have a look, see if you can spot anything with your young eyes."

Now, in the magical way that such things come about, the other shore, their destination, drew nearer and began to reveal its secrets. No longer was it a landscape blurred by distance, but a place of rocky outcrops, emerald green swards, white pebble beaches. Bracken, dense as fur, coated the lower slopes of the hill. Higher up, this gave way to heather and the occasional lonely Scots pine. The distant skyline was edged by the uneven outline of a drystone dike, the march wall between Benchoile land and the neighbouring property. In places this dike had broken, leaving a gap like a missing tooth.

But there was still no sign of the waterfall. Holding Thomas in the circle of her arms, Victoria leaned forward, meaning to ask Roddy about this, but at that moment the boat swept past a great promontory of rock, and the little bay was revealed before them.

She saw the white shingle beach, and purling down the hillside, the burn, tumbling and twisting through heather and bracken, until, twenty feet or so above the beach, it leapt out over a ledge of granite and spouted down into the pool at its base. White as a mare's tail, dancing in the sunlight, fringed with rushes and moss and fern, it lived up to all Victoria's expectations.

Roddy turned to smile at her face of open-mouthed delight.

"There you are," he told her. "Isn't that what you came all this way to see?"

Thomas, as excited as she was, lurched forward and escaped from her hold. Before she could catch him, he had stumbled, lost his balance, and fallen forward against his father's knee.

"Look!" It was one of his few words. He banged Oliver's leg with his fist. "Look!"

But Oliver was still engrossed with Roddy's binoculars, and either did not notice Thomas, or else paid no attention. Thomas said, "Look," again, but in the throes of trying to get his father to listen to him, he slipped and fell, bumping his head on the thwart and finishing up in the bottom of the boat, sitting in three inches of icy water.

He began, not unnaturally, to cry, and the first wail

was out before Victoria, scrambling forward, could rescue him. As she picked him up, and lifted him back into her arms, she looked up and saw the expression on John Dunbeath's face. He was not looking at her, he was looking at Oliver. He was looking as though, quite happily, he could have punched Oliver on the nose.

The keel ground up on to the shingle. John shipped his oars and climbed overboard, and heaved the prow of the boat up on to the dry beach. One by one they alighted. Thomas was carried to safety by Roddy, Oliver took the forward painter and tied it up to a large, concrete-embedded spike, which was, perhaps, for this very purpose. Victoria handed out picnic baskets and the rugs to John, and finally, herself jumped ashore. The shingle of the beach crunched beneath the soles of her shoes. The sound of the waterfall filled her ears.

There seemed to be a strict protocol for Benchoile picnics. Roddy and Barney led the way up the beach, and the others followed, a straggling, laden procession. Between the waterfall pool and the tumbledown walls of the ruined croft was a sward of grass, and here they set up camp. There was a traditional fireplace, a ring of blackened stones and charred wood bearing witness to previous picnics, and it was very sheltered, although high above, the clouds still raced. The midday sun blinked in and out, but when it shone, it shed a real warmth, and the dark waters of the loch took on the blue of the sky and danced with sun pennies.

The group shed their bulky waterproofs. Thomas set off by himself to explore the beach. John Dunbeath took up a stick and began to scrape together the ashes in the fireplace. From the drinks basket Roddy took two bottles of wine, and stood them at the edge of the pool, to cool. Oliver lit a cigarette. Roddy, his wine safely dealt with, stopped to watch a pair of birds, twittering and anxious, circling a rock ledge at the edge of the waterfall.

"What are they?" asked Victoria.

"Dippers. Water ouzels. It's early for them to be nesting." He began to climb the steep bank in order to investigate this. Oliver, with the binoculars still dangling around his neck, watched for a moment, and then followed him. John was already searching for kindling for the fire, gathering handfuls of dry grass and charred heather stalks. Victoria was about to offer her help, when she spied Thomas, heading for the loch and the pretty waves. She ran after him, jumping down on to the beach, and catching him up, just in time, into her arms.

"Thomas!" She held him close and laughed into his neck. "You can't go into the water."

She tickled him and he chuckled, and then arched his back protesting and frustrated. "Wet!" he shouted into her face.

"You're wet already. Come along, we'll find something else to do."

She turned and carried him back up the beach, to where the pool overflowed to a shallow stream that ran over the pebbles to the loch. Beside this she set Thomas, and stooping, picked up a handful of stones, and began to throw them, one by one, into the water. Thomas was diverted by the little splashes they made. After a while he squatted down on his haunches and began to throw pebbles for himself. Victoria left him and went back to the picnic place, and removed the plastic mug from the top of a vacuum flask. She took this back to Thomas.

"Look." She sat beside him and filled the mug with stones. When it was full, she poured them out into a heap. "Look, it's a castle." She gave him the mug. "You do it."

Carefully, one at a time, with starfish hands, Thomas filled the mug. The occupation absorbed him. His fingers, red with cold, were clumsy, his perseverance touching.

Watching him, filled with the tenderness that was by now becoming familiar, Victoria wondered about maternal instincts. Was one meant to have them, if one didn't have a child of one's own? Perhaps, if Thomas had not been such an engaging person, she would never have experienced this basic, unreasonable surge of protective affection. But there it was. Like a child in some sentimental old film, he seemed to have found his way into her heart, made himself snug and was there to stay.

The whole situation was odd to say the least of it. When he had first told Victoria about stealing Thomas from the Archers, Victoria, although shocked at Oliver, had also been moved. That Oliver Dobbs, of all people, should be so aware of his own parenthood as to take this extraordinary step was somehow a marvellous thing.

And to begin with, he had seemed both amused and involved; buying Thomas a toy, carrying him around on his shoulders, even playing with him in the evenings before Victoria put him to bed. But, like a child quickly bored by a new diversion, his interest seemed to have waned, and now he took little notice of Thomas.

The incident in the boat was typical of his attitude. Against all Victoria's better instincts, it was becoming impossible not to suspect that Oliver's impulsive removal of his son had not been prompted by fatherly pride and a real sense of responsibility, but that in his own oblique way he was simply getting back at his parents-in-law. The taking of Thomas from them sprang more from reasons of spite than reasons of love.

It really didn't bear thinking about. Not just because of the slur this cast upon Oliver's motivations and so upon his character, but because it rendered Thomas's future – and indirectly her own – miserably precarious.

Thomas banged her with his fist and said, "Look." Victoria looked, and saw the tumbled pile of pebbles and his beaming, grubby face, and she pulled him up on to her knee and hugged him.

She said, "I love you. Do you know that?" and he laughed as though she had made some tremendous joke. His laughter eased everything. It would all be all right. She loved Thomas and she loved Oliver, and Oliver loved Victoria, and obviously – in his own undemonstrative way – loved Thomas as well. With so much loving around the place, surely nothing could destroy the family that they had become.

Behind her, she heard the crunch of footsteps coming down the beach towards them. She turned and saw John Dunbeath. Beyond him, the fire now blazed, plumed with blue smoke. The other two men had disappeared. She searched for them, and saw their distant figures, more than halfway up towards the march wall, and still climbing.

John said, "I guess we won't get our lunch for another hour. They've gone up to search for the deer."

He reached her side, and stood a moment, looking out across the water, to the distant sunlit blur of the house, half-hidden in the trees. From here it looked infinitely desirable, like a house in a dream. Smoke rose from a chimney, a white curtain blew, like a flag, from an open window.

Victoria said, "It doesn't matter. About lunch, I mean. If Thomas gets hungry we can always feed him something to stave off his pangs till the others get back."

He sat beside them, leaning back with his elbows in the shingle. "You're not hungry, are you?" he asked Thomas.

Thomas said nothing. After a bit, he clambered off Victoria's knee and went back to his game with the plastic cup.

Victoria said, "Don't you want to go and look for deer too?"

"Not today. Anyway I've seen them before. And

that's quite a climb. I didn't realise Oliver would be so energetic and interested in wildlife."

There was no hint of criticism in his voice, but even so Victoria sprang to Oliver's defence. "He's interested in everything. New experiences, new sights, new people."

"I know it. Last night after you'd gone to bed, Roddy finally got round to telling me that he's another writer. It was funny, because when I was introduced to him, I thought 'Oliver Dobbs, I know that name,' but the associations eluded me. And then when Roddy told me, the penny dropped. I've read a couple of his books, and I saw one of his plays on television. He's a very clever man."

Victoria's heart warmed towards him. "Yes, he is clever. He's just had a new play put on in Bristol. It's called *Bent Penny*. The first night was on Monday, and his agent says he's got a hit on his hands. It's probably going to the West End, just as soon as they can find a theatre."

"That's great."

She went on extolling Oliver, as though praise of him could in some way obliterate the memory of the fleeting expression she had caught on John Dunbeath's face when Thomas fell in the boat. "He hasn't always been successful. I mean, it's a notoriously difficult business to get started in, but he never wanted to do anything else, and I don't think he ever got discouraged or lost faith in himself. His parents practically disowned him because he didn't want to go into the army, or be a lawyer, or do anything like that. So, at the beginning, he really didn't have any security at all."

"How long ago was that?"

"I suppose from the moment he left school."

"How long have you known him?"

Victoria leaned forward and picked up a handful of pebbles. So close to the water's edge they were wet and shining and cold to the touch. "About three years."

"Was he successful then?"

"No. He used to take dreadful, undemanding jobs, just to earn enough money to buy the groceries and pay the rent. You know, like barrowing bricks and mending roads and washing dishes in a fish-and-chip shop. And then a publisher began to take interest in him, and he got a play on television. And since then things have just snowballed, and he's never looked back. He and Roddy met through television. I expect Roddy told you. That's why we came to Benchoile. I read *The Eagle Years* when I was at school, and I've reread it at regular intervals ever since. When Oliver told me he knew Roddy and we were coming here to stay, I could hardly believe it was true."

"Has it lived up to its expectations?"

"Yes. Once you get used to it not being summer all the time."

John laughed. "It certainly isn't that." She thought he looked much younger when he laughed.

The sun had, for the last moment or so, been hidden behind a cloud, but now it came racing out again, and its brightness and warmth were so welcome that Victoria lay back on the beach, and turned her face up to the sky.

She said, "The only thing that spoiled coming here was being told about your uncle dying. I felt we should have turned right round and gone away again, but Roddy wouldn't hear of it."

"It's probably the best thing in the world that could have happened. A bit of company for him."

"Ellen told me you used to come here when you were a little boy. I mean, when you weren't in Colorado."

"Yes. I used to come with my father."

"Did you love it?"

"Yes. But it was never home. Colorado and the ranch were my real home."

"What did you do when you used to come here? Did you slay deer and grouse and do manly things like that?"

"I used to fish. But I don't like shooting. I never have. It made life a little difficult."

"Why?" It was hard to imagine life for John Dunbeath ever being difficult.

"I suppose because I was the odd-man-out. Everybody else did it. Even my father. My Uncle Jock didn't understand it at all." He grinned. "Sometimes I thought he didn't even like me very much."

"Oh, I'm sure he liked you. He wouldn't have left Benchoile to you if he hadn't liked you."

"He left it to me," John told her flatly, "because there wasn't anybody else."

"Did you guess he was going to leave it to you?"

"It never entered my head. That probably sounds crazy to you, but it's true. I got back from Bahrain and found this lawyer's letter waiting for me on my desk." He leaned forward to pick up a handful of pebbles and started to pitch them, with deadly accuracy, at a lichened rock which jutted from the edge of the loch. He said, "There was another letter as well, from Jock. I guess he wrote it just a couple of days before he died. It's a funny feeling getting a letter from a person who's already dead."

"Are . . . are you going to come and live here?"

"I couldn't, even if I wanted to."

"Because of your job?"

"Yes. That and other reasons. I'm based in London just now, but I may be sent back to New York at the drop of a hat. I have commitments. I have my family."

"Your family?" She was taken by surprise. But, on consideration, why should she be so surprised? She had met John in London, at a party, as a single man, but that did not mean that he had not left a wife and children behind him in the States. Businessmen all over the world were forced to lead such lives. There was nothing unusual about such a situation. She imagined his wife: pretty and chic as all young American women seemed to be, with a space-age kitchen and a station wagon in which to fetch the children from school.

He said, "By family, I mean my mother and father."

"Oh," Victoria laughed, feeling foolish. "I thought you meant you were married."

With immense care, he pitched the last stone. It hit the rock and fell into the water with a miniature splash. He turned to look at her. He said, "I was married. Not any more."

"I'm sorry." There didn't seem to be anything else to say.

"That's all right." He smiled reassuringly and she said, "I didn't know."

"Why should you know?"

"No reason. It's just that people have been talking about you, telling me about you. Roddy and Ellen, I mean. But nobody said anything about your being married."

"It only lasted a couple of years, and they never met her anyway." He leaned back on his elbows and looked out across the loch towards the hills and the old house. He said, "I wanted to bring her to Benchoile. Before we were married I used to tell her about it, and she seemed quite enthusiastic. She'd never been to Scotland and she had all sorts of romantic imaginings about it. You know, skirling pipes and swirling mists and Bonnie Prince Charlie draped in tartan. But after we married . . . I don't know. There never seemed to be time to do anything."

"Was . . . the divorce why you came to live in London?"

"One of the reasons. You know, a clean break, all the rest of it."

"Did you have children?"

"No. Just as well, the way things turned out."

She knew then that she had been wrong about John. Meeting him for the first time, he had impressed her as being self-contained, self-reliant, and totally cool. Now she realised that beneath that smooth veneer was a person just like anybody else: vulnerable, capable of being hurt, probably lonely. She remembered that he had been meant to have a girlfriend with him that evening, but for some reason she had let him down. And so he had asked Victoria to have dinner with him, and Victoria had refused. Thinking of this, she now felt, in some obscure way, as though she had let him down.

She said, "My parents got divorced. When I was eighteen. You'd have thought I'd have been old enough by then to cope with the situation. But it does something to your life. Nothing's ever quite the same again. Security is lost for ever." She smiled. "Now, that's something that Benchoile has got and to spare. Security oozes out of the walls. I suppose it's something to do with the people who've lived in the house, and the way people live there now, as though nothing has changed in a hundred years."

"That's right. It certainly hasn't altered in my lifetime. It even smells the same."

She said, "What will happen to it now?"

He did not answer at once. And then he told her, "I shall sell it."

Victoria stared at him. His dark eyes, unblinking, met hers, and beneath their steady regard, she slowly realised that he meant what he said.

"But, John, you *can't*."

"What else can I do?"

"Keep it on."

"I'm not a farmer. I'm not a sportsman. I'm not even a true-blooded Scot. I'm an American banker. What could I do with a place like Benchoile?"

"Couldn't you run it . . .?"

"From Wall Street?"

"Put a manager in."

"Who?"

She cast about for some person, and came up, inevitably, with, "Roddy?"

"If I'm a banker, then Roddy is a writer, a dilettante. He's never been anything else. Jock, on the other hand, was the strong pillar of the family and an exceptional man. He didn't just stride around Benchoile with a dog at his heels and a string of instructions. He worked. He went up the hill with Davey Guthrie and brought the sheep down. He helped with the lambing and the dipping. He went to the market in Lairg. As well, it was Jock who kept an eye on the forestry, took care of the garden, mowed the grass."

"Isn't there a gardener?"

"There's a pensioner who cycles up from Creagan three days a week, but keeping the kitchen garden in vegetables and the house in logs seems to take up most of his time."

But Victoria was still unconvinced. "Roddy seems to know so *much* about everything. Last night . . ."

"He knows a lot, because he's lived here all his life, but what he can actually *do* is another matter altogether. I'm afraid that without Jock, supporting him and giving him a shove every now and then, Roddy is in mortal danger of simply sinking into the ground."

"You could give him a chance."

John looked regretful, but he shook his head. "This is a big property. There's twelve thousand acres of hill to be farmed, fences to be kept up, a thousand or more sheep to be reared. There's cattle involved, and crops, and expensive machinery. All that adds up to a lot of money."

"You mean you don't want to risk losing money?"

He grinned. "No banker wants to risk that. But in

fact, it isn't that. I could probably afford to lose a bit; but no property is worth holding on to, unless it's a viable proposition and capable, at least, of washing its own face."

Victoria turned away from him, sitting up with her arms wrapped around her knees, looking back across the water to the old house. She thought of the warmth of that house, of its hospitality, of the people who lived there. She did not think of it as a viable proposition.

She said, "What about Ellen?"

"Ellen is one of the problems. Ellen and the Guthries."

"Do they know you're going to sell Benchoile?"

"Not yet."

"Does Roddy?"

"I told him last night.'

"What did he say?"

"He wasn't surprised. He said he hadn't expected me to do anything else. And then he poured himself the biggest cognac you've ever seen and changed the subject."

"And what do you suppose will happen to Roddy?"

"I don't know," said John, and for the first time he sounded miserable. She turned her head over her shoulder, and once more their eyes met. His own were bleak and sombre, and she was moved to sympathy for him in his dilemma.

She said, impulsively, "He drinks too much. Roddy, I mean."

"I know it."

"I love him."

"I love him, too. I love them all. That's why it's so ghastly."

She felt impelled to try to cheer him. "Perhaps something will turn up."

"Who are you, Mr Micawber? No, I'm going to sell it. Because I have to. Robert McKenzie, he's the lawyer in Inverness, he's fixing an advertisement for me. It'll go into all the big national newspapers around the middle of the week. Desirable Highland Sporting Property For Sale. So you see, I can't go back now, I can't change my mind."

"I wish I could make you."

"You can't, so don't let's talk about it any more." Thomas was getting bored with his game. He was also getting hungry. He had dropped his plastic mug, and now he came to climb on to Victoria's knee. John looked at his watch. He said, "It's nearly one o'clock. I think you and I and Thomas should go and find something to eat . . ."

They got slowly to their feet. Victoria brushed shingle from the seat of her jeans. She said, "What about the others?" and turned to look up the hill, and saw Oliver and Roddy already on their way down, moving a great deal faster than they had on the way up.

"They're feeling hungry, too, and thirsty as well, no doubt," said John. "Come along . . ." he stooped and hoisted Thomas up into his arms, and led the way back to where his fire smouldered, ". . . let's see what Ellen's put in the picnic baskets."

Perhaps because of the picnic – which had been so successful – and the memories of former happy parties that this had evoked, the conversation that night at dinner did not concern the literary world of London, nor the problems of the future of Scotland, but became instead a feast of reminiscence.

Roddy, sated with fresh air, flushed by wine and good food, and relentlessly prompted by his nephew John, was in his element, carried along on an unstoppable flood of anecdotes that reached far back into the past.

Around the polished, candle-lit table, old retainers, eccentric relations, domineering dowagers, most of them long since defunct, came back to life. There was the story of the Christmas house party when the tree caught fire;

the grouse shoot at which a universally disliked young cousin peppered the guest of honour with shot and was sent home in disgrace; the long-forgotten winter when the blizzards cut the house off for a month or more, and its occupants were reduced to boiling snow to make the porridge and playing endless charades to keep themselves amused.

There were the sagas of the overturned boat; the sheriff's Bentley, which, inadvertently left with its handbrake off, had finished up in the bottom of the loch; and the gentlewoman of reduced circumstances, who had come to stay for a weekend, and remained firmly installed in the best guest room two years later.

It took a long time to run out of stories, and even when he did, Roddy remained inexhaustible. Just as Victoria was about to suggest that perhaps it was time to retire to bed (it was now past midnight) he pushed back his chair, and led them all purposefully away from the table and across the hall to the deserted, dust-sheeted drawing-room. There stood the grand piano, draped in an old sheet. Roddy turned this back, pulled up a stool to the keyboard, and started to play.

The room was piercingly cold. The curtains had long since been taken down, and the windows shuttered, and the old melodies echoed like cymbals against the empty walls. High above, descendent from the centre of the lavishly decorated ceiling, a crystal chandelier of immense proportions sparkled like a cluster of icicles, and scattered facets of coloured light were reflected in the bars of the brass fender that stood before the white marble fireplace. Roddy sang songs from before the war. Noël Coward at his most sentimental, and Cole Porter.

> I get no kick from champagne,
> Mere alcohol doesn't thrill me at all,
> So tell me, why should it be true . . .

The rest of the party grouped themselves about him. Oliver, his dramatic senses stirred by the turn that the evening had so unexpectedly taken, leaned against the piano and smoked a cigar, watching Roddy as though he could not bear to miss a single nuance of the other man's expression.

John had crossed to the fireplace, and stood before it, with his hands in his pockets and his shoulders propped against the mantelpiece. Victoria had found a chair in the middle of the room, draped in faded blue gingham, and had perched herself on one of its arms. From where she sat, Roddy had his back to her, but above him, flanking a centrally hung mirror, were two tall portraits, which she knew, without being told, were of Jock Dunbeath and his wife Lucy.

With her ears full of the nostalgic tinkling music, she looked from one to the other. Jock had been painted in the full dress kilt of his regiment, but Lucy wore a tartan skirt and a bracken-brown sweater. She had brown eyes and laughter on her mouth, and Victoria wondered if it was she who had decorated this room, and chosen the pale carpet with its swags of roses, or whether she had inherited it from her mother-in-law, and liked it just the way it was. And then she found herself wondering if Jock and Lucy knew that Benchoile was going to be sold. Whether they were sad about it, or angry, or understood John's dilemma. Looking at Lucy, Victoria decided that she probably understood. But Jock . . . Jock's face above the high collar, the golden epaulettes, was carved into an expression of suitable blankness. The eyes were deep-set and very pale. They would reveal nothing.

She realised that she was slowly freezing. She had put on, that evening, for some reason, a most unsuitable dress, sleeveless and far too light for a winter evening in Scotland. It was the sort of dress meant to be worn with suntanned arms and bare sandals, and in it she knew that she looked thin and colourless and cold.

> You're the cream in my coffee,
> You're the milk in my tea . . .

Victoria shivered, and rubbed her arms with her hands, trying to warm herself. From across the room, John Dunbeath's voice came quietly, "Are you cold?" and she realised that he had been watching her, and this made her self-conscious. She put her hands back in her lap and nodded, but made a secret face to let him know that she did not want to disturb Roddy.

He took his hands out of his pockets and left the fireplace and came over to her side, on the way gathering up a dustsheet, revealing the French rosewood chair that it had been protecting. He folded the dustsheet like a shawl, and bundled it around her shoulders, so that she was swathed in folds of soft, old cotton, very comforting to the touch.

He did not go back to the fireplace, but settled himself on the other arm of her chair, with his arm lying along its back. His nearness was somehow as comforting as the dustsheet that he had wrapped around her, and after a little she did not feel cold any more.

Roddy stopped at last for breath, and to refresh himself from the glass that stood on top of the piano. "I think that's probably enough," he told them all. But John said, "You can't stop yet. You haven't played 'Will Ye Go, Lassie, Go.'"

Over his shoulder Roddy frowned at his nephew. "When did you ever hear me play that old song?"

"I suppose when I was about five years old. But my father used to sing it, too."

Roddy smiled. "What a sentimental guy you are, to be sure," he told him, but he turned back to the piano, and the old Scottish tune, in the three-four time of a slow waltz, filled the empty, haunted room.

O the summer time is coming
And the trees are sweetly blooming
And the wild mountain thyme
Grows around the blooming heather.
Will ye go, lassie, go?

I will build my love a tower
Near yon pure crystal fountain
And on it I will pile
All the flowers of the mountain.
Will ye go, lassie, go?

If my true love, she were gone,
I would surely find another,
Where wild mountain thyme
Grows around the blooming heather.
Will ye go, lassie, go?

12

SUNDAY

It was ten o'clock on the morning of the Sabbath. Once more the wind had come round to the northeast, swirling in from the sea, clean and bitterly cold. Overcast with high sailing clouds, the sky glimpsed through, blue as a robin's egg, only occasionally. It was hard to believe that only yesterday they had been picnicking at the waterfall, sitting in the sunshine with pleasant anticipatory thoughts of the approaching spring.

John Dunbeath sat by the fire in the Guthries' kitchen and drank a cup of tea. The kitchen was snug as a nest. A fire burned redly in the stove, and thick walls and tightly closed windows defied the blustering wind. The air was filled with the smell of burning peat, overlaid by the fragrance of simmering broth, and the table in the centre of the room was already laid for the Guthries' midday dinner.

Jess was going to church. At the sideboard, she took up her hat, and, sagging slightly at the knees, in order to see her reflection in the mirror, put it on. Watching her, and then looking back at Davey, John decided that of all the Benchoile people, the Guthries had changed the least. Jess was still slim, still pretty, with only a trace of grey in her springy fair hair, and Davey looked, if anything, even younger than John remembered him, with his bright blue eyes and tufty, sandy eyebrows.

"Now," Jess picked up her gloves and pulled them on. "I must get away. You'll have to excuse me, but I promised I'd pick up Ellen Tarbat and give her a lift to the kirk." She glanced at the portentous clock in the middle of the mantelpiece. "And if you two are going to be up the hill and home again in time for your dinner, you'd better not be sitting here all day, drinking your tea."

She departed. A moment later there came a great crashing of gears and the revving of a hard-worked engine, and Davey's small grey van bounced down the bumpy path in front of the house and disappeared in the direction of Benchoile.

"She's a terrible driver," Davey observed mildly. He finished his mug of tea, set it down on the table and stood up. "But she's right. We should go." He went through to the little lobby and took down his waterproof jacket from the peg by the door, collected his deerstalker, his crook, his spyglass. The two golden Labradors, who had been lying, apparently asleep, by the fireside, now sprang into feverish action, scenting walks. They barged to and fro, nuzzling Davey's knees, tails going like pistons. They were, Jess had told John, Jock Dunbeath's dogs.

"Poor creatures, they were with him when he died. And afterwards they wandered about Benchoile like a pair of lost spirits. There was some talk of putting the old one down. She's nearly nine years old now. But we couldn't abide the idea. The colonel had been so fond of her, and she's a great lass to the gun. So they both came to live with us. Mind, we've never had a dog in the house. Davey would never have a dog in the house. But these two had never been in a kennel in their lives, and so he had to relent. They could have stayed at Benchoile, I suppose, but Mr Roddy has his own dog, and Ellen has enough to do without caring for a couple of great babies like these two."

Now Davey opened the farmhouse door, and the two Labradors escaped into the windswept, scrubby garden, racing like puppies around the blowing grass beneath the washing-line. At their appearance, Davey's sheep-dogs, shut up in their pen, began dementedly to bark, racing to and fro in the netted run. "Shut your mouths, you silly bitches," Davey told them good-naturedly, but they went on barking, and could still be heard long after the two men and the two dogs had gone through the gate in the wall at the back of the house, and started the long walk up through the heather.

It took them over an hour to reach the march fence that separated the northern boundary of Benchoile from the desolate Glen Feosaig which lay beyond. A long, steady climb, taken at Davey Guthrie's unhurried pace, pausing only to point out some landmark, to scan the hill for deer, to watch the soaring, hovering flight of a kestrel. The dogs were kept well to heel, but even so, every now and then a pair of grouse would explode from the heather at their feet, and go wheeling away, their flight lying close to the slope of the hill; "go-back, go-back," they called.

It was immense country. Slowly, Benchoile sank below them, the loch a long ribbon of pewter grey, the house and trees concealed by the swelling contours of the land. To the north the summits were still snow-clad, and snow lay in deep corries as yet untouched by the low winter sun. As they climbed, Creagan itself came into view, reduced by distance to a cluster of grey houses, a strip of green that was the golf course, the tiny spire of the church. Beyond was the sea, the horizon blanketed in cloud.

"Yes, yes," observed Davey, "it is a dreich sort of a day."

At the crest of the hill there was not even heather underfoot; only pits of peat starred with strange mosses and lichens. The ground was boggy. Black water oozed up around their feet as they trod upwards, and the hoofprints and droppings of deer were everywhere. When they came at last to the straggling dike, the wind pounced on them from the north. It filled ears, nostrils, lungs; whistled through stormproof clothing and brought tears to John's eyes. He leaned against the wall and looked down into Feosaig. The loch at its foot lay black and deep, and there was no evidence of human habitation. Only the sheep and the kestrels, and showing white against the distant hill, a pair of gulls, working their way inland.

"Are those our sheep?" John asked, raising his voice against the wind.

"Yes, yes," Davey nodded, and then turned and sat himself down, out of the wind, with his back to the wall. After a little John joined him. "But that's not Benchoile land."

"And this is not Feosaig land, either, but we have many Feosaig sheep grazing with ours."

"What happens, do you have a roundup?"

"We start to gather them in, around the end of this month. We bring them down to the sheepfolds in the fields by the farmhouse."

"When do the ewes start lambing?"

"About the sixteenth of April."

"Will it still be as cold as this?"

"It may well be colder. Some big storms can blow in April, and they can leave the hills as white as mid-winter."

"That can't make your job any easier."

"Indeed, it does not. I have seen myself digging ewes, heavy with lamb, out of the ditches and drifts. Sometimes a mother will desert her lamb, and then there's nothing for it but to take it back to the farmhouse and hand-rear it with a bottle. Jess is a great one with the sickly lambs."

"Yes, I'm sure she is, but that doesn't solve the

problem of how you're going to cope with all this on your own. Roddy's told me how much my uncle did at the lambing. You're going to need another man, probably two, to help you during the next six weeks."

"Yes, that is indeed a problem," Davey agreed, not looking in the least perturbed. He felt in his pocket and came out with a paper bag. From this he extracted two large bread-and-butter sandwiches. He gave one to John and began to eat the other himself, munching at each mouthful like a ruminating cow. "But I have spoken to Archie Tulloch and he says that this year he will give me a hand."

"Who's he?"

"Archie is a crofter. He farms a few acres down the road to Creagan. But he is an old man – seventy years or more – and he won't be able to carry on with the crofting much longer. He has no son. A month or so before your uncle died, he spoke to me about Archie's croft. He had the idea that he would buy the place from Archie, and take it in with Benchoile. We can always use more land or the arable, and he has a fine cattle pasture down by the river."

"Would Archie be agreeable?"

"Yes, yes. He has a sister in Creagan. He has talked for some time of going to live with her."

"So we'd have more land and another house."

"Your uncle thought we would maybe take on another man, and put him to live in the croft. Your uncle was a fine man, but after that first heart attack he had begun to realise that, like the rest of us, he was not immortal."

He took another mouthful of bread and munched some more. A movement on the side of the hill caught the attention of his blue eyes. He laid down his half-eaten sandwich, drove his crook into the ground, and took out his spyglass. Using his crook and the thumb of his left hand as a steadier, he put the glass to his eye.

There was a long silence, broken only by the buffet of the wind.

"A hare," said Davey. "Just a wee hare." He put the spyglass back in his pocket, and reached for the crust of the sandwich. But the old Labrador had already wolfed it. "You are indeed a greedy bitch," he told her.

John leaned back against the wall. Awkward stones dug into his back. His body was warm from the hard exercise, and his face cold. Ahead of them a gap had appeared between the racing clouds. A gleam of sunshine broke across the gloom, and lay like a shaft of gold across the dark waters of Loch Muie. The bracken on the hill turned russet. It was very beautiful, and he realised in that instant, with some shock, that the land, for almost as far as he could see, belonged to him. This was Benchoile. And this . . . he took up a handful of black peaty soil, crumbling it between his fingers.

He was assailed by a sensation of timelessness. This was the way things had stayed for decades; tomorrow they would be no different, nor in the weeks, nor the months that lay in the future. Action, of any kind, had all at once become distasteful, and this took him unawares, because apathy was a mood he had never suffered from. He had made his reputation, achieved a considerable personal success in his job, simply by means of swift and shrewd decision, immediate action, and a confidence in his own convictions that left no room for moral shilly-shallying.

He had arranged this morning's expedition with the sole intention of getting Davey on his own, and letting fall the information, as tactfully as possible, that by the middle of next week Benchoile would officially be up for sale. And yet now he found himself discussing its future policies with Davey, as though he had every intention of digging himself in for the rest of his life.

He was procrastinating. But did that matter so much? Was today, this morning, this moment, the right time to bring to an end everything that Davey Guthrie had worked for? Perhaps, he told himself, knowing that he was ducking the issue, it would be better to hold a sort of board meeting in the dining-room at Benchoile, thus protecting himself from the human element of the problem by erecting a shield of businesslike formality. He would get Ellen Tarbat around the table, and Jess as well, and Roddy, to lend a little moral support. Better still, he would ask Robert McKenzie, the lawyer, to come from Inverness and take the chair at this meeting. Then he could be given the job of breaking the bad news to them all at one fell swoop.

The sun went in. It was cold and dark again, but the silence between the two men remained companionable and totally unstrained. It occurred to John that the true Highlander like Davey Guthrie had much in common with the ranch hands who worked for his father in Colorado. Proud, independent, knowing that they were as good as any man – and probably better – they found no need to assert themselves, and so were the most straightforward of beings to deal with.

He knew that he must be straightforward with Davey. He said, breaking the silence, "How long have you been at Benchoile, Davey?"

"Nearly twenty years."

"How old are you?"

"Forty-four."

"You don't look it."

"It's the clean living that keeps a man healthy," Davey told him, without a smile. "And the good air. Do you not find working in London and New York and such big cities that the air is very oppressive? Even if Jess and I have a day's shopping in Inverness, I cannot wait to get home and breathe the clean air of Benchoile."

"I suppose if you have a job in a place, you don't think too much about what you're breathing." He added, "Anyway, if I get to feel too stifled, I usually head back to Colorado. There, the air is so rarefied that the first gasp is as intoxicating as a jigger of Scotch."

"Yes, yes, that ranch must be a fine place. And a great size, too."

"In fact, not as big as Benchoile. About six thousand acres, but of course we carry more stock. Six hundred acres of that is irrigated hay meadow, the rest is known as open-range grazing."

"And what breed of cattle do you rear?"

"No particular breed. They vary from fine Hereford and Black Angus, all the way down to what's known in the west as Running Gear. If the snows have been heavy, and the high meadows are well irrigated and we don't have a killing frost in the late spring, we can graze a thousand head."

Davey ruminated on this, chewing on a blade of grass, and gazing peacefully ahead of him. After a little, he said, "There was a farmer from Ross-shire, and he went to the bull-sales in Perth, and there he met one of those big cattlemen from Texas. And they got talking. And the Texan asked the farmer how much land he owned. And the farmer told him, 'Two thousand acres.'"

At this point John realised that Davey was not continuing their dissertation on farming, but telling a joke. Anxious not to miss the punch line, or worse, to laugh at the wrong moment, he listened with sharpened attention.

"And then the farmer asked the Texan how much land he owned. And the Texan said to the farmer, 'You would not understand. You could not comprehend, if I told you how much of Texas I own. But I'll tell you this. If I got into my car and drove all day around my boundary fence, I still should not have circled my property.' And the farmer thought a little while, and then he said to the Texan, 'I had a car like that, once upon a time. I got rid of it.'"

There came a long pause. Davey continued to gaze

ahead. John stayed straight-faced as long as he could, and then the grin, unstoppable, crept up his face. Davey turned his head and looked at him. His blue eyes held a certain gleam, but otherwise he was as dour as ever.

"Yes, yes," he said, in his gentle Sutherland voice. "I thought that you would enchoy that. It is a very good choke."

Ellen Tarbat, dressed in her good Sunday black, pulled her hat down over her ears and pierced it to her bun with a formidable hatpin. It was a decent hat, only two years old, and trimmed with a buckle. There was nothing like a buckle for lending a bit of dignity to a hat.

She looked at the kitchen clock. It was a quarter past ten, and Ellen was going to church. She was giving them a cold lunch today instead of the usual roast. She had peeled the potatoes, and made a jam tart, and the dining-room table was ready and laid. Now, she was ready for Jess to pick her up. Davey was not coming to church with them, because he and John Dunbeath had gone up the hill to look at the sheep. Ellen did not approve of such goings-on on the Sabbath and had said as much to John, but he had pointed out that he had not all the time in the world, and would soon have to go back to London. Ellen could not imagine why he should want to get back to London. She herself had never been to London, but her niece Anne had taken a trip a couple of years ago, and what she had told Ellen about it had left Ellen in no great hurry to follow her example.

Her hat settled, she picked up her coat. She had brought all her things downstairs earlier in the morning so as to save a trip up all those flights of stairs to her attic bedroom. Climbing stairs was one of the things that tired her. She hated being tired. She hated the way her heart thumped when she was tired. Sometimes she hated being old.

She put on her coat and buttoned it up, and adjusted the

lapel where she had pinned her best Cairngorm brooch. She took up her bulging handbag, her black gloves. From the front of the house, the telephone rang.

She stood still, waiting, trying to remember who was in the house and who out of it. Mrs Dobbs had taken the little boy out for a walk. John was with Davey. The telephone continued to ring, and Ellen sighed and laid down her bag and gloves and went to answer it. Out of the kitchen, across the hall, into the library. The telephone stood on the colonel's desk. Ellen picked up the receiver.

"Yes?"

There came a series of clickings and buzzings, distasteful to her ear. The telephone was another thing she hated. "Yes?" she said again, beginning to sound testy.

A final click, and a man's voice. "Is that Benchoile?"

"This is Benchoile."

"I want to speak to Oliver Dobbs."

"He's not here," said Ellen, instantly. Jess Guthrie would be at the door at any moment, and she did not want to keep her waiting.

But the caller was not so easily put off.

"Is there no way you can get hold of him? It's very important indeed."

The word *important* caught her attention.

It was splendid when important people came to stay and important things happened. It gave a body something to talk about that wasn't simply the price of lambs or the weather.

"He . . . he'll maybe be over at the Stable House."

"Could you go and get him?"

"It may take a moment or two."

"I'll hold on."

"The telephone is very expensive," Ellen reminded him sharply. Important or not, it was a sinful thing to waste good money.

"What?" He sounded taken aback, as indeed he might. "Oh. Well, never mind about that. I'd be grateful if you could get him. Tell him it's his agent."

Ellen sighed, and resigned herself to missing out on the first hymn, "Very well."

She laid down the receiver, and made the long journey down through the back of the house to the stable yard. When she opened the back door the wind swirled and gusted and nearly pulled the doorknob out of her grasp. Bent against this, holding on her good hat, she crossed the cobbles and opened Roddy's front door.

"Roddy!" Her voice, raised, cracked a little.

There was a pause, and then footsteps crossed the floor above her, and Mr Dobbs himself appeared at the head of the stairs, as tall, thought Ellen, as a lamp-post.

"He's not here, Ellen. He's gone to Creagan to get the Sunday papers."

"There's a telephone call for you, Mr Dobbs. The man says he is your agent, and it is very important."

His face lit up. "Oh. Right." And he came helter-skelter down the stairs, so fast that Ellen was obliged to step sideways to avoid being knocked flat. "Thanks, Ellen," he said, as he shot past her.

"He's waiting at the other end of the telephone . . ." she raised her voice to his retreating back ". . . and the Lord himself knows what it's costing him."

But Mr Dobbs was already out of earshot of her grumblings. Ellen made a face. Some people. She pulled her hat down, and followed him at her own pace. In the kitchen, she saw, through the window, the Guthries' van, waiting for her, with Jess Guthrie at the wheel. She was flustered and halfway through the door before she realised that she had forgotten her gloves.

Oliver's telephone call from London lasted for more than half an hour, and by the time he got back to the Stable

House, Roddy had returned from Creagan with all the Sunday papers, was ensconced in his deepest leather armchair in front of a furnace of a fire, and was already looking forward to the first gin and tonic of the day.

He laid down the *Observer*, and looked up over his spectacles as Oliver came bounding up the stairs two at a time.

"Hello," he said. "I thought I'd been deserted."

"I had a phone call." Oliver came to sit in the chair opposite to Roddy, with his hands hanging loose between his bony knees.

Roddy sent him a keen look. He sensed the suppressed, secret excitement. "Good news, I hope."

"Yes. Good. It was my agent. It's all fixed. The new play's moving to London when it's finished the run at Bristol. Same cast, same producer, everything."

"Fantastic." Roddy dropped the paper to the floor, reached up a hand to pull off his spectacles. "My dear boy, that really is the most splendid news."

"There are other goodies in the pipeline as well, but those can wait till later. I mean, they're not actually signed and sealed yet."

"I couldn't be more pleased." Roddy glanced at his watch. "The sun's not over the yardarm yet, but I think this calls – "

But Oliver interrupted him. "There's just one thing. Would you mind if I left Victoria and Thomas with you for a couple of days? I have to go to London. I have to go tomorrow. Just for one night. There's a plane from Inverness about five o'clock in the evening. I wondered, too, if someone would be able to drive me over to catch it."

"But of course. You can leave them here as long as you like. And I'll take you over in the MG."

"It's only for two days. I'll be coming back the next day. And after that I'll pack the others up and we'll make our way back south in the car."

The very idea of them all leaving made Roddy feel miserable. He dreaded being on his own again, not simply because he loved to have young company about the place, but because with Oliver and Victoria and little Thomas gone, he knew that there would no longer be an excuse not to face up to facts. And the facts were cold. Jock was dead. John was going to sell Benchoile. Ties and traditions would be broken for ever. It was the end of a way of life. This was the last house party.

He said, with the vague notion of putting off the evil moment, "You don't have to go. You know you don't have to go."

"You know that we have to. As it is, you've been more than kind and marvellously hospitable, but we can't stay for ever. Anyway, fish and guests stink after three days, and we've been here three already, so tomorrow we're going to start stinking."

"I'll miss you. We all will. Ellen has lost her heart to Thomas. It won't seem the same without you all around."

"You'll still have John."

"John won't stay longer than he has to. He can't. He's got to get back to London."

"Victoria tells me that he's going to sell Benchoile."

Roddy was surprised. "I didn't realise he'd discussed it with Victoria."

"She told me last night."

"Yes. He's going to sell up. He really has no alternative. To be truthful, it's what I expected."

"What will happen to you?"

"It depends who buys the place. If it's a rich American with sporting instincts, perhaps I could get a job as ghillie. I rather see myself touching my cap and collecting massive tips."

"You should get married," said Oliver.

Roddy sent him another sharp look. "You're a fine one to be talking."

Oliver grinned. "I'm different," he said smugly. "I'm a different generation. I'm allowed to have a different set of morals and values."

"You certainly have those."

"Don't you approve?"

"It would make no difference whether I approved or not. I'm too idle a man to take up attitudes about matters which really don't concern me. Perhaps I was too idle to get married, because getting married was expected of me. I never really did anything that was expected of me. Not getting married was just part of the pattern. Like writing books and watching birds and drinking too much. My brother Jock despaired of me."

"I think it's a good way to be," said Oliver. "I suppose I've followed pretty much the same pattern myself."

"Yes," said Roddy, "but in my case I had a golden rule. I never got involved with anybody, because I knew that once I did I was in danger of hurting them."

Oliver looked at him, surprised. "You're talking about Victoria, aren't you?"

"She is very vulnerable."

"She is also intelligent."

"The heart and the head are two separate entities."

"Reason and emotion?"

"If you like."

Oliver said, "I can't be tied."

"You already are," Roddy pointed out. "You have the child."

Oliver reached for his cigarettes. He took one and lit it with a spill kindled from the fire. When it was alight, he tossed the spill on to the flames. He said, "In that case, isn't it a little late to start talking to me like a father?"

"It's never too late to rectify matters."

Across the hearthrug their eyes clashed, and Roddy recognised the coldness in Oliver's pale gaze. When he spoke, it was to change the subject. "Do you know where Victoria is?"

It was a sort of dismissal. Roddy sighed. "I think she took Thomas for a walk."

Oliver stood up. "In that case, I'd better go and find her. Tell her what's happening."

He went, running down the wooden staircase, and slamming the front door shut behind him. His footsteps rang across the cobbles of the stable yard. Roddy was left no wiser as to Oliver's intentions, suspecting that he had done more harm than good, and wishing that he had kept his mouth shut. After a little, he sighed again, hauled himself out of his chair and went to pour himself that longed-for gin and tonic.

Victoria, making her way back through the birchwood, saw Oliver emerge from beneath the stableyard archway, and walk out on to the gravel in front of the house. He was smoking a cigarette. She was about to call out to him, when he caught sight of her and Thomas, and came across the grass to meet them.

Thomas, whose legs had given out on him halfway home, was riding pickaback on Victoria's shoulders. When she saw Oliver coming towards them, Victoria bent down and let Thomas slip to the ground. He ran ahead of her and reached Oliver before she did, butting his father in the legs with his head and hobbling Oliver's knees with his arms.

Oliver did not pick him up, but stood there, penned, waiting until Victoria was within earshot.

"Where have you been?" he asked her.

"Just for a walk. We found another stream, but not as pretty as the waterfall." She reached his side. "What have you been doing?"

"Telephoning," he told her. The walk, the cold air, had brought colour to her cheeks. Her pale hair was blowing and tousled. She had found, somewhere, a clump of yellow aconites, and had picked one or two and put them in the buttonhole of her jacket. Oliver pulled her into his arms and kissed her. She smelled cool and fresh, of apples and the outdoors. Her lips were sweet and clean, her kiss tasted as innocent as clear water.

"Telephoning who?"

"I wasn't telephoning anybody, I was being telephoned."

"Who by?"

"My agent." He let her go, and stooped to disentangle Thomas from his legs. They began to walk towards the house, but Thomas protested, so Victoria went back to lift him up in her arms. When she was alongside Oliver once more, she asked, "What did he say?"

"Good things. *Bent Penny*'s going to London."

She stopped dead. "*Oliver!* But that's *marvellous*."

"And I'm going to London too, tomorrow." Her face dropped. "I'm leaving you and Thomas behind."

"You can't mean it."

He laughed. "Don't look so tragic, you ninny. I'm coming back the next day."

"But why can't we come with you?"

"What's the point of coming to London for one day? Anyway, I can't talk business with you and Thomas under my feet all the time."

"But we can't stay here without you!"

"Why not?"

"I don't want to be left behind."

In a flash, Oliver became irritated. He stopped his good-natured teasing, and said, in some exasperation, "I'm *not* leaving you behind. I'm simply going to London for a night. I'm flying down and I'm flying back. And when I get back, we're packing up and we're getting into the car and we're all going south again. Together. Now, does that make you happy?"

"But what am I going to do without you?"

"Exist, I imagine. It shouldn't be too difficult."

"I just feel it's so awful for Roddy. We dumped ourselves on him in the first place, and now . . ."

"He's fine. He's delighted at the idea of having you and Thomas to himself for a day or two. And as for dumping ourselves on him, he doesn't want us to go. Once we've gone, he'll have to face reality, and he doesn't relish that in the very least."

"That's a horrible thing to say about Roddy."

"OK, it's horrible, but it's true. OK, he's charming and amusing, a character straight from the pages of some old nineteen-thirties comedy. Rattigan, perhaps, at his most fresh-faced. But I doubt if he's ever faced an issue in his life."

"He was in the war. Anybody who went through the war was bound to face issues. That was what it was all about."

"I'm talking about personal issues. Not National Emergencies. You can't hide from a National Emergency by climbing behind a brandy and soda."

"Oh, *Oliver*. I hate it when you're like this. And I still don't want you to go and leave Thomas and me behind."

"Well, I'm going." She did not reply, and he put his arm around her, and bent and kissed the top of her head. "And you are not to sulk about it. And on Tuesday, when I fly back, you can jump into the Volvo and come and meet me. And if you're particularly charming, I shall take you out to dinner in Inverness. And we'll eat haggis and chips and join in the folk dancing. Can you think of anything more riveting?"

"I'd rather you didn't go." But she was beginning to smile.

"I have to. Duty calls. I'm a successful man. Leaving you behind is one of the prices I have to pay for being successful."

"Sometimes I wish you weren't."

He kissed her again. "You know what's wrong with you? You're never happy."

"That's not true."

He relented. "I know it isn't."

"I've been happy here," she told him, and she was suddenly shy. She hoped that Oliver would tell her that he had been happy too. But he did not say anything, and she heaved Thomas's weight from one arm to the other, and together, they walked back to the house.

13

MONDAY

Roddy stood at the top of his staircase and called "Victoria!"

Victoria, who had spent the morning ironing shirts and handkerchiefs for Oliver, sorting out socks and sweaters, and finally packing a suitcase, straightened up from her task, pushed a lock of hair from her face, and went to open the bedroom door.

"I'm here!"

"John's here, and Oliver. Come and join us. We're having a drink."

It was nearly half past twelve, a bright, cold day and the sun was shining. Roddy and Oliver were leaving for the airport after lunch. A quarter of an hour previously, Ellen had appeared to take charge of Thomas and to get him ready for lunch, for lunch today was to be a substantial affair, cooked by Ellen and Jess Guthrie and eaten in the big dining-room at Benchoile. This was Ellen's decision. She had always been of the opinion that no person should set out on a journey, however short, without a good meal inside him, and Oliver was, apparently, no exception. Accordingly, she and Jess had been busy all morning. Appetising smells had wafted through from the big house, and there was a certain sense of occasion in the air, as though something important was happening, like a birthday, or the last day of the holidays.

Above her, in Roddy's sitting-room, Victoria could hear the murmured conversation of the others. She closed the suitcase and snapped shut the locks. She went to the mirror and combed her hair, gave a final glance about the room to make sure that nothing had been forgotten, and then went upstairs to join the rest of the party.

Because of the sunshine and the brightness of the day, she found them gathered, not about the fireside, but at the huge window. Oliver and Roddy sat on the window seat with their backs to the view, and John Dunbeath on a chair that he had pulled back from the desk. When Victoria appeared, Roddy said, "Here she is, come along, we've been waiting for you," and John stood up and moved his chair to one side in order to make space for her. "What'll you have to drink?"

She considered this. "I don't think I really want a drink."

"Oh, come on," said Oliver. He held out a long arm, and drew Victoria to his side. "Don't be prissy. You've been beavering around all morning, being domestic. You deserve a drink."

"Oh, all right."

John said, "What would you like? I'll get it for you."

Still caught in the circle of Oliver's arm, she looked across at him. "A lager, perhaps?" And he smiled, and went through to Roddy's kitchen to collect her a can out of the fridge.

But there was scarcely time to open the can and pour the lager before they were interrupted by the sound of the front door opening, and Ellen's voice from the foot of the stairs, raised to tell them all that lunch was ready, it was on the table, it would spoil if they didn't come immediately.

Roddy said, sotto voce, "Drat the woman," but there was obviously nothing to be done about it, and so, carrying their various glasses, they all got to their feet and made their way downstairs and across the yard to the big house.

They found the dining-room full of sunshine, the big table laid with a white cloth. A roast of beef steamed on the sideboard, dishes of hot vegetables stood on the hotplate, and Thomas was already installed, hungry and bibbed, in an ancient wooden high chair that Jess Guthrie had brought down from the old nursery.

Ellen pottered to and fro on her unsteady legs, telling everybody where they were to sit, complaining that the roast was getting cold, and what was the point of cooking good meat if folks couldn't be on time for their meals?

John said, good-naturedly, "Now come on, Ellen, that's not true. We were off our backsides the moment you hollered up the stairs. Who's going to carve?"

"You," said Roddy instantly, and went to sit down with his back to the window, as far from the sideboard as possible. He had never been any good at carving. Jock had always done the carving.

John sharpened the horn-handled knife with all the élan of a master butcher, and got to work. Ellen took the first plate for Thomas, and herself dealt with it, cutting up the meat and squashing the vegetables and gravy into a mess like brown porridge.

"There he is, the wee man. You eat that up now, pet, and you'll turn into a great big boy."

"Not that we have too many problems," Roddy murmured when Ellen had departed and closed the door behind her, and everybody laughed because this morning Thomas's cheeks appeared to be fatter and rounder than ever.

They had finished their first course and were just beginning on Ellen's apple pie and baked custard, when the telephone started to ring. They all waited, as seemed to be the custom at Benchoile, for somebody else to go and answer it. Finally Roddy said, "Oh, damn."

Victoria took pity on him. "Shall I go?"

"No, don't bother." He took another leisurely mouthful of apple pie, and pushed back his chair and ambled from the room, still grumbling. "What a bloody stupid time to ring up." He had left the dining-room door open, and they could hear his voice from the library. "Benchoile. Roddy Dunbeath here." Then a pause. "Who? What? Yes, of course. Hold on a moment and I'll go and get him." A moment later he reappeared, still holding the table napkin, which he had taken with him.

"Oliver, dear boy, it's for you."

Oliver looked up from his plate. "Me? Who is it?"

"No idea. Some man or other."

He returned to his apple pie, and Oliver pushed back his chair and went to take the call. "I can't think," said Roddy, "why they can't invent some device so that when you sit down to a meal, you can stop the telephone ringing."

"You could always take it off the hook," John suggested mildly.

"Yes, but then I'd forget to put it back again."

Thomas was beginning to be bored with his pudding. Victoria picked up his spoon and began to help him. She said, "You could always just let it ring."

"I'm not strong-minded enough. I can let it ring for just so long, and then I can't bear it for another moment. I always imagine that someone is waiting to tell me something tremendously exciting, and I go cantering off to grab the receiver from the hook, only to find myself voice-to-voice as it were with the Inland Revenue. Or else it's a wrong number."

John said, "If you're a wrong number, then why did you answer the phone?" which was somehow all the funnier, because he didn't often make jokes.

By the time Oliver returned, their meal was over. Roddy had lighted a cigar, and John brought the tray of coffee through from the kitchen. Victoria was peeling an orange for Thomas, because however much he ate, he always liked oranges more than anything. The orange was juicy and the task absorbed her, so that she did not look up when Oliver came back into the room.

"Good news, I hope," she heard Roddy say. The last of the peel fell away, and she broke the orange into sections and handed the first one to Thomas. Oliver did not reply. "Nothing serious?" Roddy now sounded concerned.

Still Oliver said nothing. The silence suddenly caught Victoria's attention. It grew longer, more strained. Even Thomas was stilled by it. He sat, with a piece of orange in his hand, and stared across the table at his father. Victoria's cheeks began to prickle. She realised that they were all looking at her. She looked at Roddy, and then up at Oliver. She saw his face, intensely pale, and his cold, unblinking eyes. She felt the blood drain from her own cheeks, and a reasonless sense of doom, like a sickness, knot her stomach.

She swallowed. "What is it?" Her voice sounded thin and insubstantial.

"Do you know who that was on the telephone?" Oliver asked her.

"I've no idea," but she could not keep her voice from trembling.

"It was Mr Bloody Archer. Ringing up from Hampshire." *But I told her not to ring up. I said I'd write again. I explained about Oliver.* "You wrote to them."

"I . . ." Her mouth was dry, and she swallowed again. "I didn't write to him. I wrote to her."

Oliver advanced to the table, he laid the palms of his hands flat upon its surface, and leaned towards her.

"I told you not to write to her." Each word came out like a hammer blow. "I told you you were not to write to her, nor telephone her, to get in touch with her in any way at all."

"Oliver, I had to . . ."

"How did you know where to write, anyway?"

"I . . . I looked it up in the telephone directory."

"When did you write?"

"On Thursday . . . Friday . . ." She was beginning to be flustered. "I can't remember."

"What was I doing?"

"I . . . I think you were still asleep." It was beginning to sound so underhand, so secretive, that she was impelled to stand up for herself. "I *told* you I wanted to write to her. I couldn't bear her not knowing about Thomas . . . not knowing where he was." Oliver's expression softened not one whit. Victoria realised, with horror, that she was going to cry. She could feel her mouth shaking, the lump grow in her throat, her eyes begin to swim with terrible, shaming tears. In front of them all, she was going to start crying.

"She *knew* where he bloody was."

"No, she *didn't*."

"She knew he was with me. And that's all that bloody matters. He was with me and I am his father. What I do with him, and where I take him, is no concern of anyone else. Least of all, you."

Tears were now running down her face. "Well, I think – " she managed before he interrupted her.

"I never asked you to think. I simply told you to keep your stupid little mouth *shut*."

This was accompanied by Oliver's fist coming down in a massive blow on the dining-room table. Everything on it shivered and bounced. Thomas, who had been stunned into silence by the unfamiliar violence of words that he did not know, but understood only too well, chose this moment to emulate Victoria, and burst into tears. His eyes screwed up, his mouth fell open, the remains of his half-chewed orange dribbled from his mouth down on to his feeder.

"Oh, for God's sake . . ."

"Oh, Oliver, *don't*." She sprang to her feet, her knees trembling, and tried to lift Thomas out of his chair, to comfort him. Thomas clung to her, burying his sticky face into her neck, trying to hide from the shouting. "Don't, in front of Thomas. *Stop!*"

But her anguished appeal was ignored. By now Oliver was past stopping. "You knew why I didn't want you to get in touch with the Archers. Because I guessed that as soon as they knew where we were, I'd be bombarded with maudlin appeals, and when they failed, threats. Which is precisely what has happened. The next thing we know, there'll be some black-coated little bastard on the doorstep delivering a letter from some lawyer or other . . ."

"But you said . . ." She couldn't remember what he had said. Her nose had started to run, and she could scarcely speak for crying. "I . . . I . . ." She hardly knew what she was trying to say. *I'm sorry*, perhaps, but it was just as well that this final abasement was never uttered, because Oliver was in no mood to be placated by anything. Not his weeping son, nor his weeping mistress, nor all the apologies in the world.

"You know what you are? You're a deceitful little bitch."

And with this final broadside, Oliver straightened up from the table, and turned and stalked out of the room. Victoria was left, trapped by her own tears, with the weeping, hysterical child in her arms, with the appalled silence of the other two men, with the shambles of the ruined meal. Worst of all, with humiliation and shame.

Roddy said, "My dear," and got up from the table and came around to her side, and Victoria knew that she must stop crying, but she couldn't stop, or wipe away her tears, or even start looking for a handkerchief, while still burdened with the howling Thomas.

John Dunbeath said, "Here." He was beside her,

lifting Thomas out of her arms and up against his broad shoulder. "Here, come along now, we'll go and find Ellen. She'll maybe have some candy for you to eat." Bearing Thomas with him, he made for the door. "Or a chocolate biscuit. Do you like chocolate biscuits?"

When they had gone, "My dear," said Roddy again.

"I . . . I can't help it . . ." Victoria gasped.

He could bear it no longer. Streaming face, running nose, sobs and all, he pulled her into his arms and held her against him, cradling the back of her head with his gentle hand. After a little, he reached up and took the red-and-white handkerchief from the breast pocket of his aged tweed jacket, and gave it to her, and Victoria was able to blow her nose and wipe her eyes.

After that, things got a little better, and the nightmare scene started to be over.

She went in search of Oliver. There was nothing else to be done. She found him down by the edge of the loch, standing at the end of the jetty, smoking a cigarette. If he heard her coming across the grass, he gave no sign of it, for he never turned round.

She reached the jetty. She said his name. He hesitated for a moment, and then threw his half-smoked cigarette into the sun-dappled water, and turned to face her.

Victoria remembered him saying, *If you so much as pick up a telephone, I'll batter you black and blue*. But she hadn't really believed the threat, because in all the time that she had known him, she had never seen the true violence of Oliver's uncontrolled rage. Now, she knew, she had seen it. She wondered if his wife, Jeannette, had seen it. If that, perhaps, was one of the reasons why his marriage had lasted only for a few months.

"Oliver."

His eyes rested on her face. She knew she looked hideous, still swollen from weeping, but even that didn't matter any longer. Nothing mattered except that the dreadful quarrel, for Thomas's sake, had to be patched up.

She said, "I really am sorry."

He still said nothing. After a little, he gave a long sigh, and then shrugged.

She went on, painfully. "It's difficult for you to understand. I know that. And I don't suppose I understood, either, because I'd never had a child of my own. But after I'd been with Thomas for a bit, I began to realise what it was like. I mean, having a little boy, and loving him." She wasn't doing it right at all. She was making it sound sentimental, and that wasn't what she was trying to be at all. "You get bound up with a child. Involved. As though it were part of you. You begin to feel that if anybody hurt it, or even threatened it, you could kill them."

"Do you imagine," said Oliver, "that Mrs Archer was going to kill me?"

"No. But I did know that she was probably out of her mind with anxiety."

"She always hated me. They both did."

"Perhaps you didn't give them much reason to do anything else?"

"I married their daughter."

"And fathered their grandchild."

"He's my son."

"That's the whole point. Thomas is your son. You've told me over and over that the Archers have no legal claim on him. So how can it hurt you to be a little generous to them? He's all they have left of their daughter. Oh, Oliver, you must try to understand. You're perceptive and clever, you write plays that wring people's hearts. Why can't you come to terms with a situation that should be so close to your own heart?"

"Perhaps I haven't got a heart."

"You've got a heart." She began, tentatively, to smile. "I've heard it beating. Thump thump thump, all through the night."

It worked. His grim expression softened a little, as though the situation had, in its way, a wry humour. It wasn't much, but emboldened by this, Victoria went down the jetty to his side, she put her arms around his waist, beneath his jacket, and pressed her cheek against the front of his rough, thick sweater.

She said, "They don't matter anyway, the Archers. What they do can't make any difference."

His hands rubbed up and down her back, as though he were absently fondling a dog. "Any difference to what?"

"My loving you." It was said. Pride, self-esteem no longer mattered. Loving Oliver was their only talisman, all she had to hold on to. It was the key to the lock that held the two of them, and Thomas, together.

He said, "You must be mad."

He did not apologise for any of the searing remarks and accusations he had thrown at her down the length of the lunch table. She wondered if he would apologise to Roddy and John, and knew that he would not. Simply because he was Oliver Dobbs. But that didn't matter. Victoria had bridged the breach between them. The wound of the hideous scene was still open, and agonising, but perhaps, in time, it would heal. She realised that it was always possible to pick yourself up and start again, however many times you fall.

She said, "Would you mind very much if I was?"

He did not reply. Presently he laid his hands on her shoulders and put her away from him. "I must go," he told her. "It's time I was going, or I'll miss my plane."

They went back to the Stable House and collected his suitcase, a couple of books. When they came out again, they saw Jock's old Daimler parked in front of the house, and Roddy and John standing beside it, waiting.

It seemed that everybody had decided to behave as though nothing had happened. "I thought it would be better to take the big car," Roddy explained. "There's not much room for luggage in the MG."

His tone was quite matter-of-fact, and Victoria felt grateful to him.

"That's great," Oliver opened the back door and heaved his case in, and the books on top of it. "Well," he grinned, quite unrepentant, even perhaps a little amused by the lack of expression on John Dunbeath's face, "I'll say goodbye, John."

"I'll see you again," John told him. He did not hold out a hand. "I'm not leaving till Wednesday."

"That's great. 'Bye, Victoria," he stooped to kiss her cheek.

"Tomorrow," she said. "What time does your plane get in?"

"About seven-thirty."

"I'll be there to meet you."

"See you then."

They got into the car. Roddy started the engine. The Daimler moved away, ponderous and dignified, tyres crunching on the gravel. Down through the rhododendrons, over the cattle grid, through the gate.

They had gone.

He was terribly afraid that now it was all over, now he was alone with her, she would start to cry again. It was not that he was afraid of tears, or would even be embarrassed by them. In fact, he would have almost welcomed them. But he knew, too, that this was not the right time to take her in his arms, to comfort her as Roddy had done.

She was standing with her back to him. She was done with waving goodbye. To John, her erect and slender back seemed immensely courageous. He saw the firm set of her shoulders under the thick sweater, the long silky tail of fair hair, and was reminded of a colt his father had reared, long ago, on the ranch back in Colorado. Once frightened by a clumsy hand, only the most patient and perceptive of handling had finally brought it back to anything approaching trust. But little by little, letting the colt take his own time, John himself had achieved this.

He knew that he had to be very careful. He waited. After a bit, perhaps realising that he was not going to simply melt away and tactfully disappear, Victoria pushed her hair out of her face, and turned to face him. She was not crying. She was smiling. The sort of smile that lights up a face, but does not reach the eyes.

She said, briskly, "Well, that's that."

He said, "They've got a good day for a drive. It'll be very beautiful, going over Struie."

"Yes."

"Don't you think we ought to go for a drive, too?" Victoria's smile froze and became agonised, and he knew that this was what she had been dreading; he was sorry for her and so he was going to be kind to her. He went on, quickly, "I have to go to Creagan, anyway. I have to go to the chemist. I've run out of shaving soap. And I thought the newsagent might have a *Financial Times*. I haven't seen the market prices for three days." This was not true, but it was a face-saver, and as good an excuse as any.

Victoria said, "What about Thomas?"

"We'll leave Thomas here. He's happy with Ellen."

"I haven't taken Thomas to the beach yet. I've always meant to take him."

"You can take him another time. If you don't tell him where you're going, he won't want to come."

She considered this. She said at last, "Well . . . all right. But I must go and tell Ellen that we're going out."

That was good enough. "You'll find them out at the back, on the drying-green. I'll get the car and meet you here in a moment or two."

When he returned, at the wheel of the hired Ford, she was back on the steps by the front door, waiting for him. He knew that in Creagan it would be windswept and cold, and she was wearing no sort of coat, but there was a spare sweater of his own lying on the back seat of the car, and he did not want to put off any time. He drew up beside her, leaned across to open the passenger door, and let Victoria get in beside him. Then, with no more discussion, they were on their way.

He took it slowly. There was no hurry. The more leisurely their passage, the more relaxed he hoped she would become. He said, casually, "How was Thomas?"

"You were right. He and Ellen are perfectly happy. Ellen's taken a chair out into the sun, and she's doing her knitting, and Thomas and Piglet are playing with her clothes pegs." She added, a little wistfully, "They looked very peaceful."

He said, "Thomas isn't your child, is he?"

Victoria, beside him, was very still. She stared ahead at the convolutions of the narrow road. Her hands lay clasped in her lap. She said, "No."

"I don't know why, but I always imagined that he was. I suppose Roddy thought he was, too. At least, he never gave me any reason to suspect that he wasn't. And he looks like you. That's the extraordinary thing. A bit fatter, perhaps, but he really looks like you."

"He isn't my child. But he's Oliver's. Thomas's mother was called Jeannette Archer. Oliver married her, but then the marriage broke up and she was killed in an air crash soon after."

"How do you come into it?"

"I've been in it for years . . ." Her voice began to shake. "I'm terribly sorry, but I think I'm going to start crying again."

"It doesn't matter."

"Don't you mind?" She sounded surprised.

"Why should I mind?" He leaned forward and opened

the cubbyhole on the dashboard, and revealed an enormous box of Kleenex. "See? I'm even prepared."

"Americans always have paper handkerchiefs." She took one out and blew her nose. "Crying's horrible, isn't it? Once you start, it's like a terrible addiction. However many times you stop, you always start again. I don't usually ever cry."

But this brave assertion dissolved, even as she made it, into tears. John waited peacefully, taking no notice, saying nothing. After a little, when the sobs had reduced themselves to chokes and then to sniffs and she had blown her nose, determinedly, once more, he observed, "If a person wants to cry, I never see any reason why they shouldn't. I always cried when I was a kid and being sent back to Fessenden. And my father never tried to stop me nor tell me that it wasn't manly. In fact, he sometimes looked as though he were about to burst into tears himself."

Victoria smiled wanly, but made no comment on this, and John decided to leave it, and nothing more was said until they reached Creagan. The little town lay bathed in cold afternoon sunshine, its streets swept and empty of the modest throngs who would fill it later on in the year as the summer season swelled.

He drew up in front of the chemist. "Do you want to do any shopping?" he asked Victoria.

"No. I'm all right, thank you."

He left her and went into the shop and bought the shaving soap and some razor blades. Next to the chemist was a newsagent, so he went in there and asked for the *Financial Times*, but they didn't have one, so he bought a bag of peppermints instead, and bore these back to the car.

"Here." He tossed them into Victoria's lap. "If you don't like them, we'll give them to Thomas."

"Perhaps Ellen would like them. Old people always like peppermints."

"These are toffees. Ellen can't eat toffees on account of her false teeth. Now, what shall we do?"

"We could go back to Benchoile."

"Is that what you want to do? Don't you want to go for a walk or something? Don't you want to go to the beach?"

"Do you know the way?"

"Sure I know the way, I used to come here when I was knee-high to a bee."

"Haven't you anything else you'd rather do?"

"Not a mortal thing."

The beach at Creagan was divided from the town by the golf links, and there was no access by road to the sands, so John parked the car by the clubhouse. When he switched off the engine, they could hear the whine of the wind. The long pale grasses that flanked the fairways lay flat beneath its blast, and the brightly coloured waterproof jackets of a couple of hardy golfers were filled with it, so that they resembled balloons. John pulled up the zipper of his old leather jacket, and reached for the sweater that lay on the back seat.

It was blue and very thick with a tall polo neck. She pulled it over her head and the tight, ribbed collar dragged her hair. She flipped it free and shook it loose. The cuffs of the sweater covered her hands, the hem reached below her narrow hips.

They got out of the car, and the wind pounced on the open doors and it was a struggle to get them shut. A path, a right-of-way, led down towards the sea across the fairways. Wild thyme grew underfoot, and there were hazards of whin and gorse. Beyond the links lay dunes of coarse grass, "bents" they were called in this part of the world, and there was a little caravan site, and small, ramshackle edifices, which in summer would open their shutters and sell chocolate and fizzy drinks and ice-creams. The dunes ended abruptly in a sloping cliff of sand. The tide was out. Now there was nothing but white beach and the distant sea. Far away, the rollers creamed in, crested with spray. There was not another soul about, not a dog, not a scampering child. Only the wheeling gulls hung overhead screaming their disdain at the world in general.

After the soft, dry sand of the dunes, the beach seemed very flat and firm underfoot. They ran, trying to get warm. As they approached the sea, shallow pools, fed from some mysterious source, reflected the brightness of the sky, and there were immense quantities of shells. Victoria's attention was caught by these. She picked up one and then another, marvelling at their size and unbroken state.

"They're so beautiful. I've never seen shells before that weren't all broken to bits. Why aren't these broken?"

"I suppose because this is a shallow, sandy shore." He joined in her ploy, grateful for any diversion that would take her mind off her woes. He found the skeleton of a starfish, the delicate fossilised claw of a miniature crab.

"What's this?" she asked him.

He inspected it. "A sand gaper. And the blue one is a common mussel."

"And this? It looks exactly like a very small baby's toenail."

"That's called a banded wedge."

"How do you know their names?"

"I used to come and collect shells when I was a boy, and Roddy gave me a book so that I'd learn to identify them."

They walked on in silence, and came at last to the sea. They stood, facing the wind, and watched the breakers pouring in. The waves rose and curled and broke and hissed in over the sand, and the water was clear and clean and the colour of aquamarine.

The shell lay, just out of reach of the ebbing tide. John stooped and picked it up, and placed it, wet and shining, in the palm of Victoria's hand. It was the colour of coral, with a sunburst of raised ribs, semi-spherical in shape, so that if it had still been attached to its twin they would have formed a whole roughly the size of a tennis ball.

"Now there's a prize," he said.

She was open-mouthed. "Whatever is it?"

"That's a queen scallop, and what a size of one."

"I thought you only found shells like that in the West Indies."

"Well, now you know you can find them in Scotland."

She held it away from her, taking enormous pleasure in its shape, the very feel of the shell. She said, "I shall keep it for always. Just for an ornament."

"And a keepsake, perhaps."

Victoria looked at him, and he saw the beginnings of her first smile. "Yes. Perhaps as a keepsake too."

They turned their backs on the sea, and started on the long return journey. The sands stretched for ever, and the dunes seemed very far away. By the time they had reached the steep cliff of sand down which they had tumbled so easily, Victoria was beginning to flag, and John had to take her hand, and pull her, floundering and slipping, to the top. Halfway up, she began to laugh, and when they finally reached the summit, they were both breathless. In wordless agreement, they collapsed, exhausted, into a sheltered hollow, where the sand gave way to a thick, coarse grass, and the tussocks of bents protected them from the worst of the wind.

Here, there even seemed to be a little heat in the sun. John lay back on his elbows, and let its warmth generate through the thick, dark suede of his jacket. Victoria sat forward, her chin on her knees, still gloating over her shell. Her hair had parted at the back of her neck, and his enormous sweater made her look even thinner and frailer than she actually was.

After a bit, she said, "Perhaps I shouldn't keep it. Perhaps I should give it to Thomas."

"Thomas wouldn't appreciate it."

"He would, when he's older."

"You're very fond of Thomas, aren't you? Even though he isn't your child."

Victoria said, "Yes."

"Do you want to talk about it?"

"It's difficult to know where to begin. And you probably wouldn't understand anyway."

"You could try me."

"Well . . ." She took a deep breath. "The Archers are Thomas's grandparents."

"I gathered that."

"And they live in Hampshire. And Oliver was driving back from Bristol, and he passed near Woodbridge – that's where the Archers live . . ."

Slowly, hesitantly, the story unfolded. All the time she was speaking, Victoria kept her back turned to John, and he was forced to listen to the entire saga while staring at the back of her neck. He found this intensely frustrating.

". . . that night you brought me back from the Fairburns' party, and Thomas was crying – that was the evening they turned up."

He remembered that night, the evening before he had flown to Bahrain. The dark windy skies and the little house in the Mews; Victoria with her chin buried in the fur collar of her coat, and her eyes filled with apprehension and anxiety.

". . . and all come away for a little holiday. So we came to Benchoile on account of Oliver knowing Roddy. I told you about that."

"I take it you don't have a job to keep you in London?"

"Oh, yes I do. But I work in a dress shop in Beauchamp

Place, and Sally, the girl I work for, wanted me to take a holiday anyway. So she said I could have a month off, and she's got a temporary girl in to help out till I get back again."

"And are you going back?"

"I don't know."

"Why don't you know?"

"I may just stay with Oliver."

This silenced John. He could not comprehend how any girl could want to stay with that raving egotist. Despite all his original and laudable intentions of keeping a fair and open mind, he found himself becoming slowly more and more incensed.

She was talking again. ". . . I knew how worried Mrs Archer must be, so I said to Oliver that I thought I should write to her, and Oliver was furious because he didn't want them to know where we were. But I did write, although I explained to her about Oliver being so difficult, and I asked her not to get in touch, but I suppose Mr Archer got hold of my letter."

Now that the telling was safely over, Victoria appeared to decide that the time had come to look John in the eye. She turned to face him, her attitude confiding, her weight resting on one hand, her long legs curled up beneath her.

"And it was he who rang up Oliver at lunchtime. So now you see why Oliver was so angry."

"Yes, I suppose I do see. But I still think it was a fairly gruesome scene."

"But you do understand?"

It was obviously important to her that he did. But for John, understanding made things no better. In fact, if anything, a good deal worse, for his most pessimistic suspicions had proved themselves well-founded. It was all in place now, the pieces of the jigsaw slotted together and the pattern clear. A person was selfish. Another person was greedy. Pride came into it, and resentment and even a sort of spite. Nobody came out of it well, and only the innocent suffered. The innocent. A noxious word, but how else to describe Victoria and Thomas?

He thought of Oliver. From the first encounter, there had been antipathy between the two men. Like dogs, they had circled each other, hackles bristling. John had told himself that this antipathy was reasonless, instinctive, and with the inbred good manners of a man staying in another man's house, had fallen over backwards in his efforts not to let it show. But the antipathy was obviously mutual and before long John found himself resenting Oliver's casual treatment of Victoria, his offhand attitude to Roddy, his lack of interest in his child. After a couple of days in Oliver's company he had to admit that he actively disliked him. Now, after the appalling scene over the lunch table, he knew that he detested him.

He said, "If you stay with Oliver, will you marry him?"

"I don't know."

"Do you mean you don't know if you'll marry him, or if he'll marry you?"

"I don't know." A flush crept up into her pale cheeks. "I don't know if he'll marry me. He's funny. He . . ."

All at once, John was filled with a boiling, unaccustomed rage. Brutally, he interrupted her. "Victoria, don't be a fool." She stared at him, her eyes enormous. "I mean that. Don't be a fool. You have a whole, wonderful life in front of you, and you talk about getting married to a guy, and you don't even know if he loves you enough to marry you. Marriage isn't a love affair. It isn't even a honeymoon. It's a job. A long hard job, at which both partners have to work, harder than they've worked at anything in their lives before. If it's a good marriage, it changes, it evolves, but it goes on getting better. I've seen it with my own mother and father. But a bad marriage can dissolve in a welter of resentment and acrimony. I've seen that, too, in my own miserable and disastrous attempt at making another person happy. And it's never one person's fault. It's the sum total of a thousand little irritations, disagreements, idiotic details that in a sound alliance would simply be disregarded, or forgotten in the healing act of making love. Divorce isn't a cure, it's a surgical operation, even if there are no children to consider. And you and Oliver already have a child. You have Thomas."

She said, "I can't go back."

"Sure you can."

"It's all very well for you to talk. Your marriage may have broken up, but you still have your parents, your job. You have Benchoile, too, whatever you decide to do with it. If I don't have Oliver and Thomas, then I don't have anything. Not anything really precious. Not anyone to belong to, not anyone to need me."

"You have yourself."

"Perhaps I'm not enough."

"In that case, you dismally underestimate yourself."

Victoria turned swiftly away from him, and John was presented once more with the back of her head. He realised that he had been shouting at her, and this astonished him, because it was the first time in many months that he had felt sufficiently involved or aroused to shout at anyone. He said, gruffly, "I'm sorry," and when she did not move or speak, he went on, more gently, "It's just that I hate to see someone like you make such a goddamn mess of her life."

She said, sounding sullen as a child, "You forget. It's still my life."

"It's Thomas's too," he reminded her. "And Oliver's." Still she did not move. He put his hand on her arm and pulled her around to face him. With an immense effort she met his eyes. He said, "You have to love Oliver very much. Much more than he loves you. To make it work, I mean."

"I know."

"In that case you're going into it with your eyes open."

"I know," she said again. Gently, she eased herself free of his grasp. "But you see, there was never anyone else. There was never anyone but Oliver."

14

TUESDAY

The wind, he thought, was the same wind that blew in Scotland, but in London it took on a different shape. It sneaked from around corners, it tore the first buds from the trees in the park, and littered the streets with torn scraps of paper. It was not a friend. People pressed against it, their faces agonised, their coats wrapped tight against them. The wind was an enemy, invading the city.

The rain came as the taxi, which had brought him out from Fulham, turned at last into the complexities of Heathrow Airport. It came through tunnels and circled rotaries, a tiny entity on an endless stream of traffic. Lights flashed, reflected in the wet roadways; overhead a jet droned, waiting to land. There was the heavy smell of petrol.

This taxi, in a long queue of taxis, drew in at last under the canopy of the terminal building. Oliver got out, pulled his suitcase after him, and stood at the pavement's edge feeling in his pocket for the fare. The driver, waiting, let his eyes move over his passenger, his passenger's luggage.

"Here." Oliver handed the notes over.

"Sure I've brought you to the right place, mate? This is domestic flights here. Terminal one."

"Yes, that's right."

"Just saw the label on your case. You ought to be over in international flights, terminal three."

"No. This is the one I want." He grinned. "Keep the change."

"Well, it's you who's travelling. You ought to know."

He picked up his case and went in through the glass doors, across the polished expanse of the great building, up the escalator, following the signs that led to domestic departures.

The departure hall was crowded as usual, every seat taken with travellers waiting for their various flights to be called. There was the smell of coffee, and cigarette smoke and humanity. Oliver moved slowly down the room, looking about him, like a man with a rendezvous. He saw the woman with her five exhausting children; a pair of nuns. He saw the man in the tweed overcoat and bowler hat, immersed in his newspaper. His briefcase stood on the floor between his legs. Oliver stopped before him.

"Excuse me."

Startled, the man looked up from his paper. He had a long, pale face, a neat collar, a dark tie. He wore spectacles. A lawyer, thought Oliver. A businessman. He said, "I *am* sorry, but I saw the label on your briefcase. Are you flying to Inverness?"

"Yes," said the man, sounding as though he did not think it was any of Oliver's business.

"On the five-thirty plane?"

"Yes."

"I wonder if you'd be very kind and deliver a letter for me." He reached into his pocket and took out the envelope. "The thing is, I'd arranged to catch this flight, but I'm not going to be able to make it after all, and there's someone meeting me at Inverness."

The man in spectacles continued to look unenthusiastic. He probably thought the envelope contained some sort of an explosive device, and that he and the rest of his fellow passengers were going to be blown to kingdom come whilst in transit over the Pennines.

"This has just all cropped up in the last couple of hours, and I can't telephone her – the girl who's meeting me, I mean – because she's driving to Inverness from Sutherland, and she'll have left by now."

The man in spectacles looked at the envelope and then back at Oliver. Oliver put on his sincere and open expression. The man laid down his newspaper.

"If I do take your letter, how shall I know the young lady?"

"Well, she's young, and she's got long fair hair, and she'll probably be wearing trousers. She's called Victoria Bradshaw." He added, as though it were a little lure, "She's very pretty."

But the other was not to be so easily seduced. "What shall I do if she isn't there?"

"She will be there. I promise you. She'll be there."

The man took the envelope at last, gingerly. "Wouldn't it be better to hand this over to the air hostess?"

"I suppose we could, but you know what they're like, always so busy giving people cups of tea. And anyway, I haven't got time to wait till she turns up, because I've got to get over to the international terminal and catch another plane."

"Very well," said the man at last. Having made the decision, he allowed a small smile to cross his chilly features. "You can leave it with me."

"Thank you," said Oliver. "Thank you very much. I'm really sorry to have bothered you. And I hope you have a good flight."

"The same to you," said the man in spectacles, and went back to his paper.

Oliver picked up his suitcase and turned away. He would go down the stairs and out of this building, and he would walk through the rain, over to terminal three, and check in to the New York flight, and after that he was on his own once more. He was on his way.

He was free. It was over. An interlude, a brief encounter finished. The actors had departed, and the stage lay empty. Like an untouched canvas, it waited for Oliver to inhabit it with his own people, his own private and absorbing world.

You're back then.

That's right.

She's gone, then.

Yes, she's gone.

You can tell. A house has got a funny feeling when the last child goes. You think they're there for ever but they go. And there's nothing much left, really. Except the telly. There's always the telly.

"Oh, excuse me."

He had reached the top of the stairs. He turned and found himself face to face with the man in the bowler hat. It took an instant's mental reorganisation before Oliver even recognised him. He carried his briefcase in one hand, and Oliver's letter in the other.

"I'm sorry, but the young lady I have to give this to, I can't remember what you said she was called. You've written it on the envelope, but your writing's not all that clear. Is it Miss Veronica Bradshaw?"

"No," said Oliver. "It's . . ." he hesitated, having to remember. "It's Victoria."

He supposed there came a time for starting to feel old. Not just mature, or experienced, or any of the other euphemisms. Just old. He was sixty. Jock had died at sixty-nine. If he, Roddy, were to die at sixty-nine, that meant that he had only nine years left to enjoy. Or did it mean that he had nine years to fill in before he was finally released? And if so, then how was he to fill them? He would not have Benchoile to cushion him against the cold winds of the outside world, and he knew – had known for some years – that to all intents and purposes he had out-written himself. There was no longer a readable book inside his head, and scarcely the most banal of articles. His friends, his social life, which had once so satisfyingly filled his time, were fading. His contemporaries had started to die; and delightful women who had once charmed him were becoming grandmothers, unable to cope – as inflation swallowed everything and old servants went into retirement – with house parties and dinner parties and all the endless, pleasant diversions of former days.

Pouring his second drink of the evening, trying to cheer himself up, Roddy Dunbeath told himself that in many ways he was fortunate. He would become old and he would probably be lonely, but at least he would not be penniless. All right, so Benchoile was going to be sold, but Roddy Dunbeath was in a financial position that would allow him to buy, outright, some modest house in which to spend the rest of his days. Where this house was to be, he had not yet decided, but Ellen was another problem which loomed like a shadow at the back of his mind. There could be no question of abandoning Ellen. If none of her many relations could be persuaded to have the cantankerous old thing live with them, then Roddy would have to take her on himself. The very prospect of living in a small house with no one but Ellen Tarbat for company gave him the shivers. He prayed, fervently, that it would never have to happen.

It was eight o'clock in the evening, and he was alone in his house, and it was this very solitude that had brought on his gloomy mood. Oliver was in London, by now – Roddy glanced at his watch – by now probably on his way back to Scotland. Victoria had departed in that immense Volvo to meet him at the airport. Thomas was in the bedroom downstairs, asleep, having been bathed and put to bed by Ellen. John was over in the big house, doing God knew what. The whole business of Benchoile seemed to have got the boy down, for he had been going around all day with a face like a wet weekend and with scarcely a word for anybody. To put the final lid on things, the weather had degenerated dismally with sleet showers and a force eight gale, and the summits of the hills were once more blanketed in snow.

Where, Roddy asked himself, was the spring? On such an evening, in such a mood, it was possible to believe that it would never come again. There would be some freak in the cosmos, the stars would start clashing, earthquakes erupt and the planet Earth be trapped for ever in the grip of eternal winter.

Enough. That was as far as a man's depression could be allowed to go. Supine in his chair, his slippered feet sharing the hearthrug with his old dog, Roddy decided that the time had come to take some positive step to raise his spirits. He looked once more at his watch. He would go over to the big house and take a drink with John. They would then eat dinner together, and later, when Oliver and Victoria returned from Inverness, would all sit around the fire and listen to Oliver's news.

This pleasant prospect stimulated him sufficiently to make the effort of pulling himself up out of his chair. The newspaper that he had been reading some time before slipped from his knees. Outside, the wind howled, and an icy draught came up the stairs and stirred the rugs on the polished floor. The Stable House was usually cosy, but no door or window built by man's hands could keep that northwest wind from penetrating. The room felt chilly. The fire was dying. He took logs from the basket, tossed them on to the dying embers, building up a good blaze that would still be alight when he returned later on in the evening.

He turned off the lamp and said, "Come along, Barney," and the old dog heaved himself up, obviously feeling, as Roddy was, his age. "You're not the only one," he told him, and he turned off the centre light, and together, slowly, they started down the stairs.

Without occupants, the darkened room was still and quiet. The fire flickered. A log cracked and kindled into flame. There came a crack of splitting wood, and a shower of sparks erupted like fireworks, out on to the hearthrug. Unattended, they smouldered. Then a draught snaked in up the stairs, a spark flared for a second, and caught the corner of the abandoned newspaper. Tiny flames began to lick and then grew larger. They played up the leg of Roddy's chairside table, where he kept his books and his cigars and a pile of old magazines. They reached the tindery withies of the old basket where he kept his logs. Soon, the hem of the curtain had started to smoulder.

John Dunbeath sat at the desk in the library, where he had spent most of the afternoon going through his uncle's papers, sorting out farm accounts from personal accounts, arranging neat piles for the attention of Robert McKenzie, for Jock's stockbroker in Edinburgh, for his accountant.

The old man had kept a neat and efficient tally of his affairs, and this task had not been complicated, but tedious and inevitably sad. For there were as well old diaries, dance cards, and faded photographs of people whom John had never known. Regimental groups taken in the Red Fort at Delhi; a snapshot of a party of guns in jungly surroundings gathered for what looked like a tiger shoot; a wedding. Some of the photographs were of Benchoile. He recognised his father as a small boy, and Roddy, a slender stripling, wearing white flannels and looking as though he were about to burst into song, the juvenile lead in some pre-war musical comedy.

The door opened and the present-day Roddy ambled in. John was pleased to see him and to have the excuse to stop working. He pushed his chair back from the desk and held up the photograph.

"Look what I've just found."

Roddy came to inspect it over John's shoulder. "Good God. Inside every fat man there's a thin man struggling to get out. Where did you find that?"

"Oh, put away with some other old papers. What time is it?" He looked at his watch. "A quarter past eight already? I didn't realise it was as late as that."

"Quarter past eight on a vile cold winter's evening." He shivered. "I was nearly blown away just coming across the yard."

"Let's have a drink."

"Splendid idea," said Roddy as though he had not thought of it himself. He headed over to the table where the bottles and glasses had already been set out by Ellen, and John wondered how many private Scotches his uncle had already consumed, and then told himself that it didn't matter anyway, and it was none of his business. He only knew that he felt tired, and the prospect of a restoring drink was all at once very welcome.

He got up and went to build up the fire, and to draw a chair close to the blaze, for Roddy. Roddy brought the drinks over, and handed John his, and then sank into the chair with what sounded like a sigh of relief. John remained standing, and the warmth of the flames crept up his back, and he realised that he was stiff and cold from sitting in the bay of the window.

"Slainte," said Roddy, and they both drank. "When are the others getting back, do you know?"

"No idea," John's dark face was impassive. "Around ten, I guess. Depends on whether the plane's on time or not. This gale might delay them."

"Are you really going back to London tomorrow?"

"Yes, I should. I'll probably be back again, next week or the week after, but we've got this big thing going just now, and I should be around."

"It was good that you were able to come."

"I've liked it. I'm just sorry that it had to end this way. I'd have liked Benchoile to go on."

"Dear boy, nothing can go·on for ever, and we've had a good run for our money."

They started talking about the old days, and as they both relaxed in the warmth, and each other's companionship, the time slipped pleasantly by. They were on to their second drink (or John's second drink and Roddy's fourth) when there came a scuffling sound from outside the door, the door opened, and Ellen advanced into the room. Neither of the men were surprised by this sudden appearance, for Ellen had long since given up knocking on doors. She was looking tired and particularly old. The wind and the bitter cold were bad for her bones, and she had been on her feet most of the day. Her expression showed this. Her mouth was buttoned up. She seemed determined to be put upon.

"I don't know when you two are wanting your dinner, but you can have it any time you like."

"Thank you, Ellen," said Roddy, with a mild sarcasm that was wasted upon her.

"And when the others are getting back from Inverness I do not know, but they'll just have to make do with a bowl of broth."

"That'll be all they want," John assured her, and added, with some idea of placating her, "We'll be in the dining-room in a moment. We're just having a drink."

"So I can see for myself." She hovered for a moment, trying to think of some other fault to find. "Did you check on the little boy before you came across, Roddy?"

"Um?" Roddy frowned. "No, I didn't. Was I meant to?"

"It seems it might have been a sensible thing to do instead of just leaving the mite there, abandoned for the evening."

Roddy became exasperated. "Ellen, I've only just got

over here. Anyway, we leave him happily every evening."

"Oh, well, never you mind. I'll go and look for myself."

She began to shuffle off, but seemed, in truth, so tired, so old, with her stick-like black legs and her trodden shoes that John couldn't bear it. He laid down his drink. "Here, Ellen, don't you worry. I'll go."

"It's no trouble."

"It's no trouble for me either. It'll take me one minute. And when I get back, we'll come and eat dinner, and then you can take yourself off to bed."

"Who said anything about bed?"

"I did. You're looking tired, and it's the best place for you."

"Well, I don't know . . ." Shaking her head, she made for the kitchen, and John started down the long flagged passages that led to the stable yard. Tonight they were as cold as dungeons, eerily lighted by naked bulbs which swung in the draughts. He seemed to be surrounded by looming shadows.

He opened the back door to the outside. The wind snatched at it and nearly blew it out of his hand, and for a second that seemed like for ever, he stood there in the doorway.

For ahead of him, across the cobbles of the yard, every upstairs window of Roddy's house was filled with dancing orange light. Smoke and flames gushed from the roof, and above the wind's fury, he could hear the terrifying sounds of the fire, a roar like a furnace, the splinter and crack of wood, sharp as rifle fire. Even as he stood there, a window exploded into a shatter of glass as its frame disintegrated in the heat. Instantly, flames leapt from the empty void, and John felt the heat of them sear his face.

Thomas.

He was across the yard and had opened the door

before he considered the consequences. The stairs were already alight, and the wind caught the flames and the whole edifice turned into a sort of blast furnace from which he reeled. The smoke was suffocating. He turned from it, and holding his arm up to his face, made his way down the narrow passage and threw open the door of the first bedroom.

"Thomas!" He had no idea where Thomas was sleeping. *"Thomas!"*

This room was empty. The second door. *"Thomas!"*

Now, he was directly under Roddy's sitting-room, and the smoke was blinding; his eyes began to stream and sting, he started to cough.

"Thomas!" His voice was a croak. He plunged on through the smoke and found the other door, the other bedroom.

Here, mercifully, the air was a little clearer.

"Thomas!"

A wail answered him. There was no time to be relieved, to give thanks that the child had not already died from asphyxiation, for it was clear that the charred ceiling of the room was about to give way at any moment. As John scooped Thomas up in his arms, there came a great load of plaster and charred laths, spilling down from above and making a sound like falling rocks. He looked up, and saw the ragged crater of the hole, the inferno beyond. Thomas let out a scream, and John pressed the child's face against his shoulder and stumbled from the room.

He was scarcely through the door before the remainder of the ceiling collapsed, and the floor, the carpet, Thomas's bed, everything was obliterated beneath an avalanche of burning debris.

The London plane, fifteen minutes late on account of headwinds, could be heard long before it was seen. The dark evening was stormy, the cloud ceiling very low, and when the aircraft did appear, it was with great suddenness, breaking through the murk at the end of the runway as it came in to land on the black, puddled tarmac.

Soon after this, the usual small activities began to take place. Trucks and tankers converged on the stationary plane. Steps were wheeled up to its side by two men in black oilskins. Doors opened. An air hostess appeared at the head of the steps. Slowly the passengers began to alight, to walk across the windswept apron towards the terminal building. They struggled with cases and baskets and awkwardly shaped parcels. The wind caught their clothes, they ducked their heads against the rain. One woman's hat blew off.

Victoria, with her hands in the pockets of her coat, stood just inside the plate glass doors and waited. One by one the other people, who had waited with her, claimed their various friends and relations. "There you are, pet. And did you have a good flight?" Affectionate kisses. There were two nuns met by a priest in a black biretta. "I've got a car waiting," he told them matter-of-factly. A woman with far too many children and no husband to help her, a few businessmen with briefcases.

The straggle of passengers thinned. There was still no sign of Oliver. She imagined him still sitting in the aircraft, taking his time, waiting until the first ugly rush was over. Then he would unfold his long legs, reach for his coat, and make his own leisurely way down the aisle. He would probably stop to chat with the air hostess. Victoria found herself smiling wryly, because she knew him so well.

"Excuse me." The voice spoke from just behind her. Startled, she turned. She saw one of the businessmen, with his bowler hat and his stiff collar and his briefcase. "Are you by any chance Miss Victoria Bradshaw?" He held an envelope in his hand.

"Yes, I am."

"I thought you must be. This letter's for you. Your friend asked me to give it to you."

She did not take the letter. "My friend?"

"A young man with a beard, I'm afraid I never caught his name. He asked me to give you this."

"But isn't he on the plane?"

"No, he couldn't come. But I'm sure this will explain everything."

Victoria took her hand from her pocket and took the envelope. She saw Oliver's tightly formed black writing. Miss Victoria Bradshaw.

"But where is he?"

"He just said he couldn't make the flight, and he told me what you looked like and asked me to give you the letter."

"I see. Well, thank you. I . . . I'm sorry you were bothered with it."

"No bother. It was no bother at all," he assured her. "Well, I must be off. My wife's waiting in the car, and she'll wonder what's happened to me." He began to back away, eager to be off. He tipped his bowler hat. "I'll say goodbye."

"Goodbye."

She was alone. Everybody had gone. Only a few official-looking people moved briskly about. A man in overalls wheeled a trolley of luggage. Shocked, confused, Victoria stood there, with Oliver's letter in her hand. She could not think what she was meant to do with it.

On the other side of the arrivals hall, she saw a small refreshment booth. She went across the polished floor and sat on one of the tall stools and asked for a cup of black coffee. A homely woman poured it for her from an urn.

"Do you take sugar?"

"No. No sugar, thank you."

She slit the envelope and took out the letter.

"It's a terrible night, isn't it?"

"Yes it is." She opened her bag and found her purse and paid for the coffee.

"Have you far to go?"

"Yes. I have to drive to Sutherland."

"Oh, my, what a way. Rather you than me."

She unfolded the letter. He had typed it, on his battered old typewriter. She was filled with cold apprehension. With her hand closed around the mug of hot coffee, she began to read.

Fulham
Tuesday
February 24

Victoria,

If I were any other sort of man I should start this letter by telling you that it is a difficult one to write. But I'm not going to say that, because writing is the one thing I have never found difficult, even when it has to be a letter like this one.

I am not coming back to Scotland. I have spent most of the day with my agent, and he is very anxious that I should go to New York where a director called Sol Bernstein is already waiting to sign on the dotted line and to launch *A Man in the Dark* – with, I hope, a tremendous fanfare of trumpets – on Broadway.

So I am going, catching a plane out of Heathrow this evening.

But he can't do this to me.

Oh, yes he can. He has.

I don't know when I shall return. This year, next year, some time, never. Certainly not in the foreseeable future. There is too much at stake for plans to be made. Too much to think about. Too much buzzing around in my head.

I haven't made this decision without thought of you. In fact, I thought about you most of last night. The night is a good time to get things sorted out. It's dark and quiet and the truth comes more clearly. It's easier to see.

And the truth is that I could never stay with you, because I could never stay with any woman. A long time ago, when I left you for the first time, I told you that I'd never loved anybody, and it's still the same way. I suppose what I feel for you is something rather special, but still the only thing that really turns me on is what goes on inside my head and somehow putting all that down on paper.

This decision had nothing to do with what happened when we were at Benchoile. It has nothing to do with the letter that you wrote the Archers, it really has nothing to do with you. The few days we spent together were unforgettable, and you gave me the closest thing to delight that I have ever known. But they were days stolen out of time and now I have to get back to reality.

There are things that you will have to do. You'll have to get Thomas back to the Archers for one, and hand him over once more to their loving care. I still resent their hold over him. I still curl up at the sort of conventional life they will undoubtedly map out for him, but it is obvious that this is just one of those things that I am going to have to accept.

The Volvo is another problem. You probably won't feel like driving it south by yourself. If this is the case, then ask Roddy if he will take it off your hands and perhaps find a buyer for it in Creagan. Tell him I shall be writing to him.

There is also the vexing problem of cash, but I have spoken to my agent and I will put his name and address at the bottom of this letter, so that if you get in touch with him when you get back to London, he will reimburse you and cover any expenses that you may have to incur.

So that's it. I did not mean to finish on such a mundane and mercenary note. I did not mean anything to finish quite this way. But happy endings are things that don't seem to be part of my life. I've never expected them, and in a funny way, I don't suppose I've ever wanted them.

She was crying. Now the words swam and shimmered before her eyes, and she could scarcely read them. Tears fell on the paper and blurred the handwritten signature.

Take care of yourself. I wish I could end by telling you that I loved you. Perhaps I do a little. But it could never begin to be enough, either for you or for me.

Oliver

Victoria folded the letter and put it back into the envelope. She fumbled in her bag and found a handkerchief. It wasn't any good crying. With a two-hour drive ahead of her through the stormy night, she had to stop crying. Otherwise she would drive into a ditch, or a river, or another car, and have to be dragged, mangled, from the wreckage of the Volvo, and then what would happen to Thomas?

After a little the kindly woman behind the bar, unable to ignore the obvious distress of her lonely customer, said, "Are you all right, dear?"

"Yes," lied Victoria.

"Was it bad news?"

"No, not really." She blew her nose again. She tried to smile. "I have to go." She got off the stool.

"Have another cup of coffee. Have a bite to eat."

"No, I'm all right. I'm really all right."

The Volvo stood lonely in the deserted car park. She found the key and got in behind the wheel. She fastened the seat belt. High above, a hidden plane droned, perhaps coming in to land. She thought of being in an aeroplane, going somewhere, anywhere. She thought of landing on some sunbaked airstrip surrounded by palm trees, in a place where nobody knew her, where she could lick her wounds and start again. Like a criminal, searching for a new life, a new identity.

Which was, of course, exactly what Oliver had done, settling his few affairs with a single letter, shedding his responsibilities like an old coat. By now he would be in the transatlantic plane, high over the ocean, Victoria and Thomas already fading into the past, into forgetfulness. Unimportant. Important was what lay ahead. She imagined him, drinking a highball, filled with anticipation for the excitement ahead. A new production. Probably a new play. New York.

Oliver Dobbs.

The only thing that really turns me on is what goes on inside my head.

This was the key to Oliver, his own personal, private key. And Victoria had never come near to understanding the private obsessions of his innermost mind. Perhaps if she had been his intellectual equal, a brilliant bluestocking with a university degree, it might have been different. Perhaps if she had known him longer, or closer; if she had been a stronger personality, able to stand up to his moods. Perhaps if she had not always been so dependent upon him, had been able to give him something in return.

But I gave him myself.

That wasn't enough.

I loved him.

But he never loved you.

I wanted to make a life for him. I wanted to make a life for Thomas.

She was back to Thomas. At the thought of Thomas, the old, ridiculous, protective tenderness took possession of her. For the time being Thomas still needed Victoria. For his sake, she would be efficient, calm, practical. Thomas must be delivered back to his grandparents with as little upheaval as possible. She saw herself calmly packing, buying train tickets. Hiring a taxi, taking him to Woodbridge, finding the Archers' house, ringing the bell. She saw the door opening. . . .

But beyond that her imagination shied. Because once Thomas was gone from her life, then it really was the end. It would be all over. Not simply the reality, but the dream as well.

She started the car, switched on the headlights and the windscreen wipers and moved forward, away from the little airport and out on to the main road.

Two hours later she had reached Creagan, but it was not until she had turned into the single-track road that led to Benchoile that she began to realise that something was wrong. The weather conditions, unpredictable as always, had begun to improve. The wind had dropped slightly, the clouds thinned, and as these were blown to rags across the night sky, the stars were revealed, and a pale new moon rose out of the east.

But it was not starlight that warmed the darkness ahead of her, and stained the sky like the glow from a whole city full of street lamps. It was not starlight that flickered and billowed and sent great storms of smoke up into the wind. She rolled down the window and smelled the reek of bonfires. Bonfires? More likely burning heather. Someone had started to burn heather, and it had got out of control and started a hill fire. But did one burn heather in February? And even if one did, surely the fire would have been extinguished by now.

Suddenly, she was afraid. She put her foot down on the accelerator, and the Volvo surged forward, swinging around the bends of the narrow road. The brightness of the fire seemed to grow no less. She had passed the Guthries' house, she was coming at last to the final bend of the road. Then the house lay ahead of her, the gate and the pine trees, and she knew that it was neither heather nor bonfires that burned, but Benchoile itself.

With a roar of its powerful engine, the Volvo racketed over the cattle grid and up the slope to the sweep in front of the house. The light of flames made all as bright as day. She saw the cars lined up at random, the fire engine, the huge snaking hosepipes. There seemed to be people everywhere, all grimed and red-eyed. A man ran across the beam of her headlights, shouting instructions to a colleague, and she saw, with a shock, that it was Davey Guthrie.

The big house was untouched, although lights blazed from every window. But the Stable House . . . She brought the Volvo to a screeching halt, struggled with her seat belt, the door handle, remembered the handbrake.

Panic, like the worst sort of sickness, threatened to choke her.

Thomas.

The arch to the stable yard was there, but Roddy's house was almost gone. Only the stone gable-end had withstood the onslaught of the flames; it loomed, stark as a ruin, the void where the window had been bright as an eye, with the glow of the conflagration that still raged beyond.

Thomas, in his room, on the ground floor, in his bed. She had to know, but there was no time to ask, no time to wait for answers. She began to walk towards the fire, to run. The smoke was acrid in her nostrils, and the heat was blown towards her on great gusts of wind.

"Thomas!"

"Look out there . . ." a man shouted.

She had nearly reached the archway.

"Victoria!"

She heard the footsteps coming up behind her. Arms came around her, caught her, held her. She struggled to be free.

"Victoria."

It was John Dunbeath. Because she could not hit him with her hands, she kicked backwards at his shins with the heels of her boots. He swung her round to face him.

"Don't you understand?" she shouted into the blur that was John Dunbeath. "It's Thomas."

"Listen, stop . . ." She kicked him again, and he took her by the shoulders and shook her. "Thomas is all *right*. He's all *right*. He's *safe*."

She was still at last. She could hear her own breathing, laboured, like a person on the point of death. When she felt strong enough, she looked up into his face. In the glow of the fire, she saw his dark eyes, red-rimmed and bloodshot, and there was dirt all over his face and down the front of his shirt.

She said, faintly, "He's not in there?"

"No. We got him out. He's fine. He's all right."

Relief made her weak as a kitten. She closed her eyes, afraid that she was either going to be sick or faint. She tried to tell John that her legs had started to feel like cooked spaghetti, but somehow could find neither the words nor the energy to speak them. By then it didn't matter anyway. Because by then John had already picked her up in his arms and was carrying her across the gravel and in through the front door of the big house of Benchoile.

By midnight it was more or less over. The fire was out, the ruin of the Stable House a still-smoking confusion of charred stone and fallen timber. The cars John had managed to rescue, backing them out of the garage on to the grass by the loch while Roddy telephoned the fire brigade. With them disposed of, and the cans of petrol that stood about, fuel for the motor mowers and the chain saws, he had felt a little easier in his mind for the safety of the big house. But even so, the garage roof had been swallowed and destroyed in the conflagration, and all that remained within it had gone as well.

And yet, the main house stood, miraculously unharmed. Within it, in various rooms, the survivors of the household were now bedded down. Thomas had wept, heartbreakingly, not from fear, but because he had lost Piglet. There was no way to tell him that Piglet was no more. Ellen had found him some other toy, a teddy bear that had once belonged to John's father, but at the very sight of this harmless, threadbare creature, Thomas had screamed more loudly than ever, and had finally gone to sleep with his arms wrapped around a wooden engine, the paint scarred and scratched and one of the wheels long since missing.

Ellen had come through it like the tough old thing

she was. Only at the very end had she given way and started to tremble, and John had sat her down and given her a brandy, and Jess Guthrie had helped the old woman to bed. For Jess and Davey had been on the scene almost before Roddy had made his telephone call, and it was Davey who organised the team of fire fighters, and helped the men from Creagan – torn so abruptly from their own firesides – to set up the pumps and go about extinguishing the flames.

As for Victoria . . . As though he were controlling, reining-in a belting horse, John's thoughts came to an abrupt halt. But one indisputable fact stood out. She had returned from Inverness alone, and nobody had had the time nor the inclination to ask her what had happened to Oliver. As far as John was concerned, her sudden reappearance in the midst of chaos, her mindless dash towards the holocaust which was all that remained of Roddy's house, had simply been the unthinkable climax of what had so nearly been a ghastly tragedy, and then he had had no thought in his head but to grab her back from the edge of the fire and carry her to safety.

He had taken her, for want of anywhere better, to his own bedroom, placed her on his own bed. She had opened her eyes and said once more, "Thomas is really safe, isn't he?" and he had time to do no more than reassure her before Jess Guthrie came bustling in to take over with soothing words and hot drinks. Now, presumably, Victoria was sleeping. With luck, she would sleep till the morning. In the morning there would be all the time in the world to talk.

So, it was midnight, and it was over. He stood at the edge of the loch, with his back to the water, staring up at the house. He realised that he was exhausted, drained of emotion and energy, and yet beneath this aching lassitude lay a calmness and a peace that he had not known for years.

Why he felt thus was a mystery. He only knew that

Thomas was alive, and Oliver Dobbs had not come back from London. He sighed with an enormous content as though, single-handed, he had successfully achieved some impossible task.

Around him, the stormy evening was slipping into a peaceful night. The wind had dropped, the clouds thinned to a few sailing shreds, like billows of mist. Above, a sliver of moon hung in the sky, and the dark waters of the loch were touched with the silver of its reflection. A pair of ducks flew over. Mallards, he guessed. For an instant he glimpsed them, silhouetted against the sky, and then they were swallowed into the darkness and their cry faded to an immense silence.

But there came other sounds. The wind in the topmost branches of the pines, the whisper of water nudging against the wooden piles of the old jetty. He looked at the house and saw the comfort of lights in windows. He saw the dark swell of the hills that rose behind it.

His hills. Benchoile hills.

He stood there for a long time, his hands in his pockets, until a fit of the shivers made him realise that he was growing cold. He turned back for a final look at the loch, and then, slowly, made his way up the slope of the lawn and so indoors.

Roddy had not gone to bed. Roddy waited still in the library, slumped in Jock's old armchair by the dying fire. John's heart bled for his uncle. Of all of them, Roddy was the one to suffer most. Not simply because he had lost his house, his clothes, his books and papers, all the personal and cherished possessions of a lifetime, but because he blamed himself for what had happened.

"I should have *thought*," he had said, over and over again, his usual loquacity overwhelmed by the potential tragedy, by the ghastly realisation of what could have happened to Thomas. "I simply never thought."

But he had always piled logs on to his open fireplace,

carelessly trodden out the random sparks on his old hearthrug, never bothered about a fireguard. "One of the last things Jock ever said to me was that I should have a fireguard. But I never did. Put it off. Lazy, procrastinating bastard that I am. Simply put it off."

And then, again, "Supposing Ellen hadn't had the wit to think about the child. Supposing, John, you hadn't gone along then to check . . ." His voice trembled.

"Don't think about it," John had interrupted quickly, because it didn't bear contemplating. "She did have the sense, and I did go. Come to that, it should have occurred to me to go without Ellen's prompting. I'm just as much to blame as you are."

"No, I'm totally to blame. I should have thought . . ."

Now, John stood in the chilling room, looking down at his father's brother and filled with a sympathy and affection that were, for the time being, of little use to Roddy. He was inconsolable.

A log crumbled into the dying fire. The clock showed a quarter past twelve. John said, "Why don't you go to bed? Jess has made beds up for all of us. There's no point in staying down here."

Roddy rubbed a hand over his eyes. "No," he said at last. "I suppose there isn't. But I don't think I could sleep."

"In that case . . ." He did not finish the sentence. He stirred the ashes of the fire, and put on more wood. In a moment the flames began to lick up around the dry bark. Roddy stared at them morosely.

"It's over," John told him firmly. "Don't think about it any more. It's over. And if it helps to lessen your guilt, just remember that you've lost everything you possess."

"That's of small account. Possessions have never mattered."

"Why don't you have a drink?"

"No. I don't want a drink."

John managed not to look surprised. "Do you mind if I do?"

"Help yourself." He poured himself a small brandy and filled the glass up with soda. He sat facing his uncle. He raised his glass. "Slainte."

A spark of wry amusement glimmered in Roddy's eye. "What an old Scotsman you're becoming."

"I've always been one. Or half one, at any rate."

Roddy heaved himself up in the chair. He said, "Oliver didn't come back from London."

"Apparently not."

"Why not, I wonder?"

"I have no idea."

"Do you suppose he's coming?"

"Again, I have no idea. I simply dumped Victoria on my bed, and after that Jess took over. No doubt we'll hear about it tomorrow."

"He's a strange man," mused Roddy. "Clever, of course. Perhaps a little bit too clever." Across the fireside, their eyes met. "Too clever for that little girl."

"Yes, I guess you're right."

"Still, she has the child."

"I have news for you. Thomas is not her child."

Roddy raised his eyebrows. "Really? Now you do surprise me." He shook his head. "The world is full of surprises."

"I have more surprises up my sleeve."

"You do?"

"Do you want to hear about them?"

"What, now?"

"You've already told me you don't want to go to bed. If we're going to sit here for the rest of the night, we might as well talk."

"All right," said Roddy, and composed himself to listen. "Talk."

15

WEDNESDAY

John Dunbeath, bearing a tray laid for breakfast, cautiously opened the kitchen door with the seat of his pants, and made his way across the hall and up the stairs. Outside a breeze, baby sister of last night's gale, stirred the pine trees and disturbed the surface of the loch, but already a cold and brazen sun, rising in a sky of frosty blue, was beginning to penetrate the house. Roddy's old Labrador had already found a bright lozenge of sunshine by the fireplace, and lay there, supine, basking in its frail warmth.

John crossed the landing and, carefully balancing the tray on one hand, knocked at the door of his own room. From within, Victoria's voice called, "Who is it?" and he said, "The floor waiter," and opened the door. "I've brought you your breakfast."

She was still in bed, but sitting up and looking quite alert, as though she had been awake for some time. The curtains had been drawn back, and the first oblique rays of sunshine touched a corner of the chest of drawers and lay like gold on the carpet. He said, "It's going to be a beautiful day," and set the tray, with something of a flourish, on her knees.

She said, "But I don't need breakfast in bed."

"You've got it. How did you sleep?"

"As though I'd been drugged. I was just going to

come down. The thing is, I must have forgotten to wind my watch, and it's stopped, and I've no idea of the time."

"Nearly half past nine."

"You should have woken me before."

"I decided to let you sleep."

She wore a nightdress lent to her by Ellen. It was peach pink crepe de Chine, much hemstitched and embroidered and had, in fact, once belonged to Lucy Dunbeath. Over this, in lieu of a dressing-gown, was wrapped a white Shetland shawl. Her hair, tangled from sleep, lay forward across one shoulder, and there were dark shadows, like bruises, beneath her eyes. She seemed to John, in that moment, intensely frail. As though, if he were to take her into his arms, she would break into pieces, as fragile as china. She looked about her. "This is your room, isn't it? When I woke up I couldn't think where I was. Is it your room?"

"It is. It was the only bed that happened to be made up at the time."

"Where did you sleep?"

"In Uncle Jock's dressing-room."

"And Roddy?"

"In Jock's bedroom. He's still there. We sat up talking till four o'clock in the morning, and he's catching up on his beauty sleep."

"And . . . Thomas?" She sounded as though she could scarcely bring herself to say his name.

John pulled up a chair and settled himself, facing her, with his long legs stretched out in front of him, and his arms folded.

"Thomas is downstairs in the kitchen, being given breakfast by Ellen and Jess. So now, why don't you start eating *your* breakfast before it gets cold?"

Victoria unenthusiastically eyed the boiled egg and the toast and the coffeepot. She said, "I don't actually feel very hungry."

"Just eat it, anyway."

She began, half-heartedly, to take the top off the egg. Then she laid down the spoon again. "John, I don't even know how it happened. I mean, how the fire started."

"None of us do, for sure. We were having a drink in the library before dinner. But Roddy says he made up his fire before he came over. I suppose, as usual, the logs sparked all over the hearthrug, and there wasn't anybody there to put them out. Added to which, there was the hell of a wind blowing. Once it started, the whole room went up like a tinderbox."

"But when did you first realise the house was on fire?"

"Ellen came to tell us supper was ready, and then she started fussing about Thomas being on his own. So I went along to check on him, and found the place blazing away like a bonfire."

She said, faintly, "I can't bear it. What *did* you do?"

He proceeded to tell her, playing down the circumstances as much as possible. He felt that Victoria had enough trouble on her mind as it was, without adding to it by graphic descriptions of the nightmare of Thomas's smoke-filled bedroom, the collapsing ceiling, the flaming crater, and the inferno overhead. He knew that the memory of that moment would return to haunt him, like some ghastly dream, for the rest of his life.

"Was he frightened?"

"Of course he was frightened. It was enough to frighten any man. But we got out all right, through one of the bedroom windows, and then we came back here, and Ellen took Thomas over, and Roddy rang the fire brigade in Creagan, and I went back to get the cars out of the garage before the petrol exploded and we were all blown to kingdom come."

"Did you manage to salvage anything from Roddy's house?"

"Not a thing. It all went. Everything in the world that he owned."

"Poor Roddy."

"Losing his possessions doesn't seem to bother him much. What bugs him is that he feels the fire was his fault. He says he should have been more careful, he should have had a fireguard, he should never have left Thomas alone in the house."

"I can't bear it for him."

"He's all right now, but that's why we sat up talking till four in the morning. And Thomas is all right too, except that he's lost Piglet. He spent last night with an old wooden engine in his arms. And of course, he's lost all his clothes as well. He's still wearing his pyjamas, but this morning some time Jess is going to take him into Creagan and buy him a new outfit."

Victoria said, "I thought he was still there. I mean, when I got back from the airport, and saw the fire. At first I thought it was a bonfire, and then I thought it was someone burning heather, and then I saw it was Roddy's house. And all I could think of was that Thomas was in the middle of it somewhere . . ."

Her voice had begun to shake. "But he wasn't," John said quietly. "He was safe."

Victoria took a deep breath. "I'd been thinking of him," she said and her voice was quite steady again. "All the way back from Inverness. The road seemed to go on for ever, and I was thinking of Thomas all the way."

"Oliver didn't come back from London." He made it, not a question, but a statement of fact.

"No. He . . . he wasn't on the plane."

"Did he call you?"

"No. He sent a letter." With some determination, as if the time had come to put fancies aside, Victoria took up her spoon again and ate a mouthful or two of the boiled egg.

"How did he do that?"

"He gave a letter to one of the passengers. I suppose he told him what I looked like, or something. Anyway, the man delivered it to me. I was still waiting. I still thought Oliver was going to get off the plane."

"What did the letter say?"

She gave up the impossible task of eating breakfast and pushed the tray away from her. She leaned back on her pillows and closed her eyes. "He isn't coming back." She sounded exhausted. "He's going to New York. He's in New York now. He flew out yesterday evening. Some producer's going to put on his play, *A Man in the Dark*, and he's gone out to see about it."

Dreading the answer, it took a certain courage to ask the question, "Is he coming back?"

"I suppose he will one day. This year, next year, some time, never." She opened her eyes. "That's what he said. Anyway, not in the foreseeable future." He waited and she finished, "He's left me, John," as though there could be any doubt still in his mind.

He did not say anything.

She went on, her voice inconsequent, trying to make what she was saying of small importance. "That makes it twice he's left me. It's almost becoming a habit." She tried to smile. "I know you said I was being a fool about Oliver, but this time I really, truly thought it would be different. I thought he would want the things he'd never wanted before. Like maybe buying a house and making a home for Thomas . . . and getting married, too. I thought he wanted the three of us to be together. To be a family."

John watched her face. Perhaps the abrupt disappearance of Oliver Dobbs, the paralysing shock of the fire, had acted as a sort of catharsis. He only knew that the barriers between them, her frigid reserve, were tumbling at last. She was being, at the end of the day, honest with herself, and so had nothing left to shut away from him.

He was filled with a marvellous sort of triumph, and recognised this as a carry-over from his private elation of the previous night.

She said, "Yesterday, on the beach at Creagan, I wouldn't listen to you. But you were right, weren't you? You were right about Oliver."

"I wish I could say 'I wish I weren't.' But truthfully I can't."

"You're not going to say 'I told you so.'"

"I'd never say that in a thousand years."

"You see, the real trouble was that Oliver doesn't need anybody. That's what's wrong with him. He admitted as much in his letter. He told me that the only thing that turns him on is his writing." She managed a wry smile. "And that was a smack in the face. I'd been telling myself it was me."

"So what will you do now?"

Victoria shrugged. "I don't know. I don't know where to start. But Oliver says I have to take Thomas back to the Archers, and I've been trying to think how I'm going to do it. I don't even know where they live, and I certainly don't know what I'm going to say to them when I get there. And I don't want to lose Thomas, either. I don't want to have to say goodbye to him. It's going to be like being torn apart. And there's the business of the car. Oliver said that if I left the Volvo here, perhaps Roddy could sell it. He said that I could drive it south if I wanted to, but I really don't want to, not with Thomas. I suppose I could get a plane or a train from Inverness, but that means . . ."

John found that he could not stand it for another instant. Loudly he interrupted her, "Victoria, I don't want to hear another word."

Halted in mid-sentence, astonished at the roughness of his voice, Victoria stared open-mouthed. "But I have to talk about it. I have to do things . . ."

"No, you don't. You don't have to do anything. I

shall see to it all. I shall arrange to get Thomas back to his grandparents . . ."

". . . but you have enough to think about . . ."

". . . I shall even placate them . . ."

". . . with the fire, and Roddy, and Benchoile . . ."

". . . though, from the sound of things they're going to require some placating. I shall take care of Thomas, and I shall take care of you, but as for Oliver's car, it can rot on a rubbish heap for all I care. And Oliver Dobbs, for all his genius and his sexual prowess and whatever it is that turns him on – can rot as well. And I never want to hear that self-centred son of a bitch's name again. Is that totally understood?"

Victoria considered this. Her face was serious. "You never really liked him, did you?"

"It wasn't meant to show."

"It did, a little. Every now and again."

John grinned. "He was lucky not to get his nose punched in." He looked at his watch, stretched like a cat, and then pulled himself to his feet.

"Where are you going?" she asked him.

"Downstairs to the telephone. I have a million calls to make. So why don't you eat that breakfast now? There's nothing more to worry about."

"Yes, there is. I just thought of it."

"What's that?"

"My shell. My queen cockle. It was on the window-ledge in my bedroom. In Roddy's house."

"We'll find another."

"I liked that one."

He went to open the door. He said, "The sea is full of gifts."

In the kitchen he found Jess Guthrie, peeling potatoes at the sink.

"Jess, where's Davey?"

"He's away up the hill this morning."

"Will you be seeing him?"
"Yes, he'll be down for his dinner at twelve."
"Ask him to come down and have a word with me, would you? This afternoon some time. Say about half past two."
"I'll give him the message," she promised.

If my true love, she were gone
I would surely find another,
Where wild mountain thyme,
Grows around the blooming heather.
Will ye go, lassie, go?

He went into the library, shut the door firmly behind him, built up the fire, sat at his uncle's desk, and settled down to a positive orgy of telephoning.

He rang the office in London. He spoke to his vice-president, a couple of colleagues, and his secretary, Miss Ridgeway.

He rang directory inquiries and was told the Archers' address and telephone number in Woodbridge. He made the call and spoke, at some length, to them.

With this safely behind him, he called the station in Inverness, and booked three seats on the Clansman for the following day.

He rang the lawyers, McKenzie, Leith and Dudgeon. He spoke to Robert McKenzie, and then, later, to the insurance company about the fire damage.

By now it was nearly midday. John did a few swift time-lag calculations, put a call through to his father in Colorado, dragged that good man from his early morning sleep and talked to him for an hour or more.

Finally, at the very end, he rang up Tania Mansell, dialling her London telephone number from memory. But the line was engaged, and after waiting for a little, he rang off. He did not try the number again.

16

THURSDAY

It did not take very long to pack for the simple reason that they had nothing to pack. Everything that Victoria and Thomas had brought to Benchoile with them had been lost in the fire. And so they left bearing only a paper carrier containing Thomas's pyjamas and the old wooden engine, which Ellen said that he could keep.

Goodbyes were brief and brisk, for the true Highlander is neither demonstrative nor sentimental. As well, there was little opportunity for prolonged farewells. No sooner had breakfast been eaten in the kitchen at Benchoile than it was time to be off. Before Thomas had finished munching his toast, John Dunbeath was behaving like a family man with a punctuality complex, rounding them up and insisting that it was time to leave.

For this Victoria was deeply grateful. She even suspected that he was overplaying his role a little. His car was parked and waiting in front of the door, already loaded with his own suitcase, and John himself appeared to have deliberately taken on a new image, for he had abandoned the casual and comfortable clothes in which they were used to seeing him, and appeared at breakfast in the formality of a dark suit and a tie. The different clothes changed him. Not just the way he looked, but his entire manner. He was no longer the amiable, easy-going house guest of the last few days, but a man used to responsibility and authority. A man to be reckoned with. He was in charge, not aggressively, but comfortingly, so that Victoria was left with the good feeling that nothing would go wrong. They would not have a puncture, they would not lose their tickets, there would be porters and reserved seats, and they would not miss the train.

"It's time to go."

Ellen put the last finger of toast into Thomas's mouth, wiped it clean and lifted him from his high chair. He wore tartan dungarees and a blue sweater, chosen for him by Jess Guthrie in the small shop in Creagan that was owned by her sister-in-law, so Jess had got a discount. His new shoes were brown lace-ups, and there was a small blue anorak with red stripes to go on top. Ellen had brushed his red-gold hair flat to his head. She was wanting to kiss him goodbye, but decided not to with everybody watching. Her eyes had a way, these days, of filling with tears at the most inconvenient moments. Running, Ellen called it. "My eyes are starting to run," she would say, blaming the wind or the hay fever. She never cried. At times of great emotion, like anniversaries or weddings or funerals, she would shake a body's hand, but nothing more. So now, "There he is," she said, setting Thomas firmly down on to his feet. "Put your coat on." She picked up the new jacket, and stooped over him to help him with the zipper.

They were all on their feet: Victoria gulping the last mouthful of coffee; Roddy standing, scratching the back of his head, but not looking as disconsolate as she had feared he might. He seemed to have recovered with amazing rapidity from the shock of the fire and losing everything he owned. Indeed he was really being quite organised; had spent most of yesterday with the man from the insurance company, and had already started to make a little nest for himself in the big house, sleeping in his brother's old bedroom and tossing logs as carelessly as ever on to the fire in the library. The library fire was surrounded by a hearth of stone flags and a huge club fender, but still, said Roddy, he would get a proper fireguard. One of those chain curtains. He had seen one advertised. Just as soon as he could find the advertisement, he would order one for Benchoile.

"We must go *now,*" said John, so they all left the kitchen and the remains of breakfast and trooped out, across the hall and through the front door. Outside, it was cold again and frosty, but it was going to be fine. It was goodbye. To the garden, the loch, the hills beyond, sparkling in the crystal clear morning air. It was goodbye to the friendly, peaceful house, goodbye to the sad charred remains of what had once been Roddy's domain. It was goodbye, Victoria knew, to a dream. Or perhaps a nightmare. Only time would give the answer to that one.

"Oh, Roddy." He opened his arms and she went to him, and they hugged. "Come back again," he said. "Come back again and see us all." He kissed her on both cheeks and let her go. Thomas, with the cheerful prospect of a car ride in front of him, had already climbed, independent of anyone, on to the back seat, had taken his wooden engine out of the paper bag, and had started to play with it.

"Goodbye, Ellen."

"It's been nice to know you," said Ellen briskly and stuck out her gnarled, red hand to be shaken.

"You've been so endlessly kind. You and Jess. I can't thank you enough."

"Away with you," said Ellen, brisk and much embarrassed. "Into the car, and don't keep John waiting."

Only John was allowed to kiss her. She had to stand tiptoe in her flat old shoes to receive his kiss, and then she had to fumble up the sleeve of her dress for her handkerchief. "Oh, my, what an edge to that wind," she remarked to no one person in particular. "It fairly makes your eyes run."

"Roddy."

"Goodbye, John." They shook hands, smiling into each other's faces, two men who had come together through a bad time.

"I'll be back some time, but I'll call you and let you know when."

"Any time," said Roddy.

That was all. They got into the car, fastened the safety belts, John started up the engine and they were away. There was scarcely time for Victoria to turn in her seat and wave a last farewell – scarcely time for a final glimpse of the two of them, Roddy and Ellen, standing there on the gravel sweep in front of the house. Roddy was waving, and Ellen was waving too, her white handkerchief a tiny flag. And then they were hidden, gone, lost behind the curving bank of the rhododendrons.

"I hate saying goodbye," said Victoria.

John's eyes were on the road ahead. "Me too," he said. He was driving very fast.

Behind them Thomas rolled his three-wheeled engine up and down the seat. "Meh meh, meh," he intoned to himself.

He played with the engine for most of the day, taking time off to sleep, to look out the windows, to be taken down the corridor at decent, regular intervals, to be given lunch, to be given tea. As the train thundered south, the weather, disobligingly, degenerated. They were no sooner across the border than thick clouds rolled up, obliterating the sky, and soon the rain started to fall. The hills were left behind them, the countryside became flat and incredibly dull, and watching acres of flat, wet plough wheel past the window, Victoria's own spirits sank accordingly.

She discovered that it was all very well being brisk

and sensible about your future when you happened to be eight hundred miles from it, but now, with every moment and every turn of the wheel, it was drawing closer. She felt lamentably unprepared.

It was not just the distant prospect of the remainder of her own life, which would presumably fall into some pattern of its own. As for Oliver . . . she was not thinking about Oliver just now. Later, she told herself, she would find the necessary moral courage. When she was back in her own flat, with her own familiar possessions around her. Possessions helped, whatever anybody said. And friends. She thought of Sally. She would be able to talk to Sally about Oliver. Sally's robust attitudes, her impatience with the vagaries of the opposite sex in general, would swiftly cut the whole disastrous episode down to size.

No, worse was the immediate and dreaded ordeal of having to hand Thomas back to the Archers; of having to say goodbye to him for ever. Victoria could not imagine what she was going to say to his grandparents. Unfortunately, without much difficulty, she could imagine what they might be going to say to Victoria in her role of Oliver's accomplice.

There were other hideous possibilities as well. Suppose Thomas did not want to return to them? Suppose he took one look at the Archers, and burst into tears and had hysterics and clung to Victoria?

He had adjusted so easily to her in two weeks, had been so happy and become so affectionate. She found that she was torn in two opposite directions where Thomas was concerned; one half of her wanting him to need her as much as she needed him, the other shying like a frightened horse at the idea of any sort of a scene.

She looked at Thomas. He was sitting on the opposite side of the first-class carriage, his legs sticking straight out in front of him, his head, tousled by now, leaning against John Dunbeath's arm. John was entertaining him by drawing pictures with a felt-pen on the pink pages of the *Financial Times*. He had drawn a horse, a cow, a house, and now he was drawing a pig.

"He's got a big nose that sticks out in front. That's for snuffling with and finding stuff to eat. And he has a tail with a curl in it." He drew the tail. Thomas's face broke into a smile. He settled down more cosily. "More," he ordered, and plugged his mouth with his thumb.

Victoria closed her eyes and leaned her head against the rain-streaked window of the train. It was sometimes easier not to cry if you didn't keep your eyes open.

It was dark long before they reached Euston, and Thomas had gone to sleep again. When the train stopped, Victoria picked him up in her arms. His head lolled on her shoulder. John carried his suitcase, and the little party stepped out on to the dark platform, into the usual confusion of barging passengers, trolleys, porters, luggage and mail vans. Victoria, weighed down by Thomas's considerable weight, felt overwhelmed, She supposed they must now trudge the length of the platform, wait in a queue for a taxi . . .

But she supposed wrong, and realised that in this supposition she had totally underestimated John Dunbeath. For from the confusion emerged a figure, grey-suited, with a grey uniform cap.

"Good evening, Mr Dunbeath."

"George, you're a wonder. How did you know where we'd be?"

"Had a word with the ticket collector, he said you'd probably be down this end." With no more fuss, he relieved John of his suitcase. John duly relieved Victoria of Thomas. They followed the neat, uniformed figure down the length of the platform.

"Who is he?" asked Victoria, having to run every now and then to keep up with John's long legs.

"He's the office driver. I told my secretary to send him to meet us."

"Has he brought a car?"

"I hope he's brought my car."

He had. Outside the station, they were left waiting for a moment or two while George disappeared into the rainy darkness. In no time he was back, at the wheel of John's Alfa-Romeo. He got out and they got in, Victoria with Thomas still sleeping on her shoulder.

"Thanks a lot, George, that was very good of you. Now, how are you going to get back?"

"I'll pop into the tube, Mr Dunbeath. Very handy."

"Well, thanks again, anyway."

"A pleasure, Mr Dunbeath."

"How nice," said Victoria.

"Nice of him?"

"Yes, nice of him, but nice to be met. Not to have to wait for a taxi, or wait for a bus, or fight your way down the Underground. Just nice to have a friendly face on a station platform."

"It makes all the difference between travelling hopefully and arriving," said John.

She knew what he meant.

The car sped west down the rain-drenched motorway. Three-quarters of an hour later, they had turned off it, and down the side road that led to Woodbridge. Now, there were little fields and hedgerows, and water meadows fringed with willows. Lights shone, here and there, from the windows of small, red-brick houses. They came over a bridge, and a train screamed past beneath them.

John said, "That's lucky."

"What is?"

"Going over a bridge the same time that the train's going under it."

"What else is lucky?" She needed luck.

"Letters crossing. If you write someone a letter, and

he writes you and the letters cross, that's enormously lucky."

"I don't think it's ever happened to me."

"And black cats and picking up pins and new moons."

"There was a new moon the night of the fire."

"Disregard new moons, then."

At last, the lights of the village twinkled ahead of them. They passed the sign, WOODBRIDGE. The road swung around into a curve, and the long, wide main street sloped away before them. The car idled down to a gentle crawl. There were shops and a pub with a lighted sign. A church, set back behind a stone wall.

"We don't know where they live."

"Yes, we do. It's on the right-hand side, and it's red brick, and it has a yellow door, and it's the only one in the street that is three storeys high. There it is."

He drew up at the pavement's edge. Victoria saw the flight of steps that led up to the door from the pavement, the pretty fanlight, the tall lighted windows. She said, "How do you know this is the house?"

He switched off the engine. "Because I rang Mrs Archer, and she told me."

"Did she sound furious?"

"No." He opened his door. "She sounded very nice."

Thomas, disturbed by the sudden cessation of movement, chose this moment to wake up. He yawned, bleary with sleep, rubbed his eyes, gazed about him with the confused expression of a person on whom some terrible trick has been played. He still held the wooden engine.

"You're home," Victoria told him gently. She smoothed down his hair with her hand, with some vague idea of tidying him up.

Thomas blinked. The word "home" apparently meant little to him. He gazed out at the darkness. Then John opened the door and lifted Thomas and his engine up and off Victoria's knee. She reached around into the back of the car, retrieved Thomas's paper-carrier luggage, and followed them.

They stood in front of the yellow front door, and John rang the bell. Almost instantly, as though the person inside had been waiting for them, there was a footstep and the door was flung open. From the bright, warm hallway, light poured out upon the three of them, so that they were caught in its beam, like actors spotlighted upon a stage.

"Good evening," said John, "I'm John Dunbeath."

"Yes, of course." He looked nice. Sixtyish, grey-haired, not tall, nor particularly impressive, but nice. He did not try to snatch Thomas from John's arms. He simply looked at Thomas and said, "Hello, old boy," and then stepped back, and went on, "I think you should all come in."

They did so, and he closed the door behind them. John stooped and set Thomas on his feet.

"I'll just call my wife. I don't think she can have heard the bell . . ."

But she had heard it. From a door at the far end of the narrow hall, she appeared. She had curly white hair and the sort of complexion that would go on being young, even when she was in her eighties. She wore a blue skirt with a cardigan to match and a rose-pink shirt with a bow at the neck. In her hand she carried her spectacles. Victoria imagined her, sitting in some chair, trying to read, or to do a crossword, anything to fill in the time while she waited for them to bring Thomas back to her.

There was a long silence. She and Thomas eyed each other down the length of the hall. Then she began to smile. She leaned forward, her hands on her knees. "And who is this," she asked him, "that Thomas has come home to?"

Victoria was frigid with anxiety, but she need not have had any worries. For Thomas, after an astonished silence, suddenly realised what was happening. Slowly, his rosy face became suffused by an expression of total, incredulous delight. He took a single enormous breath, and let it all come out in the first proper sentence that anyone had ever heard him utter.

"It my *Ganny*!"

He flung himself towards her, and was instantly swept up, lost in her embrace.

It was all very emotional. Mrs Archer laughed, and cried, and then laughed again, and hugged her grandson. Mr Archer took out his handkerchief and blew his nose. From upstairs, alerted by the noise, came running helter-skelter a young girl, round and plump and pretty as a milkmaid, and when Mrs Archer could be persuaded to relinquish Thomas, he was engulfed in yet another pair of loving arms. Finally, he was set down and allowed to go to his grandfather, who had stopped blowing his nose, and who, in his turn, picked him up, and jigged him up and down, in a manly sort of way, which Thomas seemed to find wholly satisfactory.

While all this was happening, Victoria and John could do nothing but stand and watch. Victoria wanted to go, to get away while everyone was still happy and before any possible recriminations could set in, but it was hard to know how to achieve this without appearing rude.

It was Thomas who finally put an end to the great reunion scene. He wriggled himself down from his grandfather's arms, and with deadly determination made for the stairs that led to his nursery, where he remembered leaving a number of delightful toys. His grandparents sensibly let him go, and the little au pair girl went with him. As they disappeared around the bend in the staircase, Victoria took hold of John's sleeve and gave it a tug, but if Mrs Archer noticed this, she showed no sign of it.

"I am sorry, keeping you standing there like that. But it's all just so . . ." She wiped away the last of her happy tears, and blew her nose on a lacy handkerchief. "You must come in and have a drink."

"We really ought to go . . ." Victoria began, but Mrs Archer would have none of it.

"Of course you must stay, for just a moment. Come along in by the fire. Edward, I am sure Mr Dunbeath would like a drink . . ."

There was nothing for it but to follow her, through a door that led into a pleasant, chintz-upholstered sitting-room. A fire flickered pleasantly from an old-fashioned grate, there was a grand piano arrayed with family photographs, there were flowers, beautifully arranged, and the sort of cushions that looked as though nobody ever sat on them.

But it was warm and welcoming and under the influence of Mrs Archer's obvious good intentions, her obvious gratitude, Victoria began to relax a little. The men had gone, presumably, to fetch the drinks, so she and Mrs Archer were to be left alone together for a moment or two. Cautiously Victoria let herself down on to the sofa, and Mrs Archer did not look disappointed about the cushions being squashed.

"Have a cigarette? You don't smoke. You must be tired. You've been travelling all day, And with a little boy, too. And I know how active Thomas can be."

Victoria realised that Mrs Archer was just about as nervous as she was, and her manner was so different from the antagonistic reception that Victoria had anticipated that she felt totally confused.

She said, "He was good. He's always good. He's been good all the time we were away."

"It was you who wrote that kind letter, wasn't it? You're Victoria?"

"Yes."

"It was sweet of you. Very thoughtful."

"Oliver was furious."

"I wanted to apologise about that. I would never have

tried to ring you or get in touch, but my husband read the letter, and he was so incensed by the whole business, that I could do nothing to stop him telephoning Benchoile and having it out with Oliver. Nothing. It isn't very often," she added, her sweet face concerned, "that I don't get my own way, but there was nothing I could do to stop Edward making that call."

"It didn't matter."

"I hope not. You see, Edward never liked Oliver even when he was married to Jeannette. But he is very fond of Thomas. And when Oliver just walked into our house, out of the blue, and stole Thomas, you can imagine the scenes. It had Helga in hysterics, poor girl, as though it could possibly have been her fault. And Edward saying he was going to put the police on to Oliver, and all the time I had no idea where the little boy was. It was a nightmare."

"I do understand."

"Yes. I believe you do." Mrs Archer cleared her throat, "Your . . . your friend, Mr Dunbeath. He rang me up yesterday to say you were bringing Thomas back. He told me, too, that Oliver has gone to America."

"Yes."

"Something about a play?"

Victoria said, "Yes," again.

"Do you suppose he'll come back to this country?"

"Yes, I suppose he will. Some time or other. But I don't think he'll ever bother with Thomas again. I don't mean that he wasn't fond of him, and very good to him, but being a father isn't exactly Oliver's scene."

Their eyes met. Victoria smiled. Mrs Archer said, very gently, "Nor being a husband, my dear."

"No, I suppose not. I really wouldn't know."

"He's a destroyer," said Mrs Archer.

Perhaps no other person could have told her. She knew it was true. She knew something else as well. "He hasn't destroyed me," she told Mrs Archer.

The men returned, Mr Archer bearing a tray with glasses and bottles, and John following with a soda syphon. The conversation turned to day-to-day matters. The weather in Scotland, the weather in Hampshire, the state of the stock market, the variable fluctuation of both dollar and pound. John, without waiting for her to ask for one, quietly handed Victoria a whisky and water. This small service filled her with gratitude. She seemed to spend her time being grateful to him for one reason or other. It occurred to her then that his perception was remarkable, all the more so because he seemed to achieve it with so little fuss. He was, perhaps, the kindest person she had ever known. She had never even heard him say an unkind thing about any person, except to call Oliver Dobbs a son of a bitch, and he hadn't done that until Oliver had taken himself off to America, and there was no point in prevaricating any longer.

Now, she watched him, deep in conversation with the Archers. She saw his heavy, serious face, which could light up so unexpectedly in a smile. The dark, close-cut hair, the intensely dark eyes. He had been travelling all day with a small child, and yet he gave no sign of the sort of exhaustion that Victoria felt. He appeared as fresh and alert as the moment they had set out from Benchoile, and it was this resilience that she so envied and admired, because she knew that it was lacking in herself.

She thought, nothing defeats him. His disastrous marriage had left behind no apparent trace of bitterness. Things will always go right for him, because he likes people, but mostly because people like him.

Even over the telephone, it seemed, this genuine benevolence came through, for how else had he contrived, in the short space of the trunk call he had put through to Mrs Archer yesterday morning, to make everything all right for Victoria, to somehow condone the circumstances of Thomas's abduction, and to pave the way for Mrs Archer's reunion with Thomas?

One thing, she thought, I haven't had time to start taking him for granted. Before she knew what was happening, they would be saying goodbye. He would drive her to London, and leave her at the door of Pendleton Mews. There wouldn't even be the excuse of carrying luggage to invite him in and up the stairs, because she had no luggage to carry. They would just say goodbye. Perhaps he would kiss her. He would say, "Take care now."

That would be the end. John Dunbeath would walk away from her, and be instantly absorbed back into that busy, important life about which Victoria knew nothing. She remembered the anonymous girlfriend who had not been able to come to the Fairburns' party with him. Probably the first thing John would do when he returned to the peaceful familiarity of his own flat would be to dial her number and tell her he was safely back in London. "How about dinner tomorrow night?" he would say, "and I'll give you all my news then." And her voice would float back to him over the line, "Darling, how heavenly." Victoria imagined her a little like Imogen Fairburn, beautiful, sophisticated, and knowing everybody.

"We really mustn't keep you." John's drink was finished. He stood up. "You'll be wanting to go and talk to Thomas before he goes to bed."

The Archers, too, rose to their feet. Victoria jerked back to reality, began to struggle up out of the deep sofa, but John took her empty glass from her, gave her his hand, and helped her.

"I feel," said Mrs Archer, "that we should offer you something to eat."

"No, we really must get back to London. It's been a long day."

They all went out into the hall. Mrs Archer said to Victoria, "Do you want to say goodbye to Thomas before you go?" But she said, "No." And then, because this sounded a little abrupt, she explained, "I mean, it wouldn't do any good, upsetting him again. Not that I think he would be upset, he's obviously so glad to be home, but . . . well, I'd rather just go, I think."

"I believe," said Mrs Archer, "that you've become quite fond of Thomas."

"Yes." They were all looking at her. She wondered if she was going to start blushing. "Yes, I suppose . . ."

"Come along," said John, putting an end to all this by opening the front door. Victoria said goodbye, and was surprised when Mrs Archer leaned forward to kiss her.

"You've looked after him so beautifully. I can't thank you enough. He looks rosy and well, and I'm sure the little experience has done him no harm at all."

"I hope not."

"Perhaps one weekend, when the weather is better, you'd like to come down one Sunday and see him. We could have lunch. You could take him for a walk." She looked at John, including him in this invitation. "You too, Mr Dunbeath."

"That's very kind," said John.

"You're very quiet."

"I'm trying not to cry again."

"You know I don't mind if you do cry."

"In that case, I probably won't. Isn't it extraordinary, if you know you can cry, and nobody is going to become upset or embarrassed about it, then you stop wanting to."

"Did you want to cry about anything in particular?"

"Thomas, I suppose. Thomas in particular."

"Thomas is fine. Thomas is nothing to cry about, except that you're going to miss him. Thomas has got a great home, and he's surrounded by people who love him. And what did you think of that welcome he gave his grandmother?"

"I nearly cried *then*."

"I have to admit to a lump in my throat myself. But you can see him any time you want. Mrs Archer liked you. It isn't goodbye to Thomas. You've got a standing invitation to go and see him."

"They were nice, weren't they?"

"Did you think they wouldn't be?"

"I don't know what I thought." She remembered something. "I didn't say anything to Mrs Archer about the fire."

"I told Mr Archer while we were in the dining-room getting the glasses out of a cupboard. At least, I told him what had happened. I didn't enlarge too much on the possibility of Thomas being frizzled to a cinder."

"Oh *don't.*"

"I have to say things like that every now and then to lay my own private spectre of what might have happened."

"But it didn't happen."

"No. It didn't happen."

They fell silent. The car nosed its way back along the narrow country road. A soft persistent rain blurred everything like mist. The windscreen wipers swung to and fro.

Victoria broke the silence at last. "I suppose," she said, "I could cry for Benchoile."

"What a girl you are for thinking of things to cry about."

"It's just that I so hated leaving it."

John made no comment on this. The car travelled on, swiftly, down the winding road, but they passed the sign of an approaching lay-by, and he began to slow down. Moments later they came to the lay-by itself, and here John drew off the road, pulled on the handbrake and turned off the engine.

The windscreen wipers ceased their demented dance. There was only the whisper of the rain, the ticking of the dashboard clock.

Victoria looked at him. "What are we stopping for?"

He switched on the interior light and turned towards her. "It's all right," he reassured her, "I am not about to ravish you. It's just that I want to talk to you. Ask you some questions. And I want to see your face when you answer them. You see, before we go a step further, I have to be totally and absolutely certain about Oliver Dobbs."

"I thought you never wanted his name mentioned again."

"I didn't. This is the last time."

"Mrs Archer was talking about him. She was very wise. I didn't realise that she would be such a wise person. She said that Oliver was a destroyer."

"What did you say to that?"

"I said that he hadn't destroyed me."

"Is that the truth?"

She hesitated for an instant before replying. Then "Yes," she said. She looked at John and smiled, and it felt as though his heart was turning over. "It is the truth. Perhaps I've always known it was the truth, but I wouldn't admit it, even to myself. I suppose everybody has to have one great traumatic love affair in his life, and Oliver was mine."

"What about when he comes back from America?"

"Somehow, I don't think he'll ever come back . . ." She thought about this, and then went on, in tones of the greatest conviction, "And even if he did, I wouldn't want to see him."

"Because he hurt you, or because you've stopped loving him?"

"I think I stopped loving him when we were at Benchoile. I can't tell you the exact moment. It just happened gradually. Now . . ." She made a vague gesture with her hands. ". . . I don't think I even like him any more."

"That makes two of us," said John, "and with Oliver

Dobbs disposed of, we can now go on to talk of other things. Just before I stopped the car, you said that you supposed that if you needed something to cry about, you could cry about Benchoile. And I think that this is as good a time as any to tell you that you don't have to. You'll be able to go back there, any time, and see them all, because I'm not going to sell it. At least not just yet."

"But . . . you said . . ."

"I've changed my mind."

"Oh . . ." She looked as though she were going to burst into tears, but she didn't do this. She said "Oh, *John*," and then she began to laugh, and finally she flung her arms around his neck and kissed him.

He was immensely gratified, but as well taken totally unawares by her spontaneous delight. He had known that she would be pleased, but scarcely expected this throttling embrace.

"Hey, you'll strangle me!" But she took no heed.

"You're not going to sell it! Oh, you marvellous man! You're going to keep Benchoile."

He put his arms around her and pulled her close. She felt small-boned and fragile, and her fair hair was soft against his cheek, and she rattled on, excited as a child. "You said it wasn't viable, it wasn't practical," she drew away from him but he still kept his arms about her. "Without your Uncle Jock to run the place, you said that Benchoile would fall to pieces."

"Like I said, I changed my mind. I'm going to hang on to it, anyway for a year, till we see how things work out."

"What made you change your mind?"

"I don't know." He shook his head, a man still confused by the reasons for his sudden volte-face. "Perhaps it was the fire. Perhaps a man doesn't realise how much something means to him until he's in danger of losing it. That night, I had visions of the whole place going up. You weren't there, but it was only by the grace of God that the big house wasn't burnt to the ground with everything else. Late that night, I went out into the garden, and just stood there, and looked at it. And it was still standing, with the hills behind it, and I don't think I've ever been so grateful for anything in all my life."

"But who's going to run it?"

"Roddy and Davey Guthrie between them, and we're going to get another man in to help."

"Roddy?"

"Yes, Roddy. It was you who pointed out that Roddy is more informed and more interested in the land than any of us. He knows more about Benchoile than I could learn in a hundred years. The only reason that he's never become more actively involved before is because he's idle, and because there was always Jock there to do the thinking for him. I have a feeling that without Jock, and with a real job to do, Roddy has a good chance of laying off the booze and astonishing us all."

"Where will he live?"

"In the big house with Ellen. You see, all my problems have been solved by one inspired decision. They'll squabble like crazy, as they always have. But the big house is large enough to contain the two of them, without one murdering the other." He thought about this. "At least," he added, "I devoutly hope so."

"You really think it will work?"

"I told you, I'm going to give it a year. But, yes, I think it will work. And what is more, my father thinks so too."

"How do you know what your father thinks? He's in Colorado."

"I called him yesterday morning, we had a long talk about it all."

Victoria could only marvel. "What a morning you had on the telephone!"

"I'm used to it. In my office I'm on the phone most of the day."

"Even so," said Victoria, "I'd never think of calling someone up in Colorado."

"You should try it some time."

So, at least, for a little longer, Benchoile would go on. And perhaps John was right, and Roddy would take on a new lease of life. He was, after all, only sixty. Perhaps he would turn into a tremendously keen outdoorsman, felling trees and climbing hills, losing weight and generally becoming tanned and fit. The image was not particularly convincing, but there was no denying that it had distinct possibilities. And, living in the big house, perhaps he would be persuaded to enliven his social life a little. Throw small dinner parties, and have people to stay. Ellen would take the dust covers off the furniture in the drawing-room, and rehang the curtains. Someone would light a fire in the fireplace, and people in evening dress would dispose themselves about the room while Roddy played the piano to them, and sang his old songs.

She said, "I know it will work. It has to work."

"So. With Benchoile and Oliver Dobbs safely out of the way, we can now get on to much more important things."

"Like what?"

"Like you and me." Victoria's expression became wary, but before she could start protesting, he went firmly on. "I thought it might be an idea for us to start over, from the beginning. It seems to me that from the moment we first met, we set out on the wrong foot, and it's only now, after all this time, and so much happening, that we've finally fallen into step. And the first thing to be rectified is that I've never got around to taking you out for dinner. So I thought that when we get back to London, we might go out somewhere. If you want we can go straight there, and eat. Or you'd maybe want to wash up first and change your clothes, so I could take you to your flat, and then come around and pick you up later. Or we can both go straight to my flat and have a drink, and then go out to dinner from there. The permutations, as you will realise, are endless. The only constant is that I want to be with you. I don't want to say goodbye. Does that make sense?"

"John, I don't want you to be sorry for me. And you don't have to go on being kind."

"In fact," he told her, "I'm not being kind, I'm being utterly selfish, because it's what I want more than anything else in the world. I always knew I'd fall in love again one day. I didn't think that it would happen just this way. I didn't even think that it would happen so soon. But what I don't want is for you to get tangled up in a new relationship until you've had time to take a deep breath and look around and generally get used to the idea."

I don't want to say goodbye.

She thought, if this were a movie, it's where they'd start playing the really soupy theme music. Or there'd be an explosion of stars, or shots of sun shining down through branches laden with apple blossoms. None of these things was happening. There was just the car, and the darkness beyond, and the man, with whom already she seemed to have come so far.

She said, thoughtfully, "You know, I don't think I ever met any person as nice as you."

"Well, that'll do for a start," he told her. They watched each other, and she began to smile, and he took her face between his hands, and bent his dark head and kissed her smiling mouth. When he had finished kissing her, he put her gently from him, turned back to the driving wheel, switched on the ignition, started up the powerful engine. The car moved forward. Soon they came to the junction that marked the end of the quiet country road and the beginning of the motorway. The car came through a tunnel and then swept up the curved ramp. They waited to filter into the three lanes of cars which poured east.

Victoria said, "When we were with the Archers, I suddenly realised that I didn't want to say goodbye to you. But I never imagined that you wouldn't want to say goodbye to me."

A gap appeared in the traffic. Smoothly John slipped the Alfa-Romeo into gear; the engine changed tune, and the car swept forward.

He said, "Perhaps not wanting to say goodbye is just another word for loving."

The wide, fast road curved ahead of them, leading to London.

BOOK TWO

The Empty House

Rosamunde Pilcher

1

It was three o'clock on a Monday afternoon in July, sunny and warm, the hay-scented air cooled by a sea breeze which blew in from the north. From the top of the hill, where the road wound up and over the shoulder of Carn Edvor, the land sloped down to distant cliffs; farmland, ribboned with yellow gorse, broken by outcrops of granite, and patchworked into dozens of small fields. Like a quilt, thought Virginia, and saw the pasture fields as scraps of green velvet, the greenish gold of new-cut hay as shining satin, the pinkish gold of standing corn as something soft and furry, to be stroked and touched.

It was very quiet. But when she closed her eyes the sounds of the summer afternoon obtruded, singling themselves out, one by one, for her attention. The humming of the wind, soft in her ears, stirred the bracken. A car climbed the long hill from Porthkerris, changed gear, came on up the road. From farther away came that pleasant summer-sound, the bee-murmur of combine harvesters. She opened her eyes and counted three, all minimised by distance to toy-size, scarlet and tiny as the models that Nicholas pushed around his nursery carpet.

The approaching car appeared over the crest of the hill, driven very slowly, its occupants, including the driver, staring from open windows at the marvellous view. Their faces were red with sunburn, spectacles glinted, arms bulged in sleeveless blouses, the car seemed packed with humanity. As it passed the lay-by where Virginia had left her own car, one of the women in the back looked up and saw her watching them from the hillside. For a startling second their eyes met, and then the car had gone, around the next corner and away to Land's End.

Virginia looked at her watch. A quarter past three. She sighed and stood up, dusted grass and bracken fronds from the seat of her white jeans, walked back down the hill to her car. The leather seat was griddle-hot with sunshine. She turned the car and started back towards Porthkerris, her mind filled with random images. Of Nicholas and Cara, incarcerated in the alien London nursery, taken to Kensington Gardens each day by Nanny; to the Zoo and the Costume Museum and suitable films by their grandmother. It would be hot in London, stuffy and airless. She wondered if they had cut Nicholas's hair. She wondered if she should buy him a model combine harvester and send it to him with some suitable, informative, maternal letter.

> Today I saw three of these working in the fields at Lanyon, and I thought of you and thought you would like a model so that you could see how it worked.

A letter for Lady Keile to read approvingly aloud because Nicholas, every inch a male, saw no reason in puzzling out his mother's writing if his grandmother was ready and willing to read it aloud to him. She thought of the other letter, the one from her heart.

> My darling child, without you and Cara I am without reason, aimless. I drive around in the car because I can think of nothing else to do, and the car takes me to places that I used to know, and I watch and wonder who it is who

drives the monster combine, turning out the hay bales, square and strong as neatly tied parcels.

The old farmhouses with their great barns and outbuildings were strung along the five miles of coast like uncut stones on a rugged necklace, so that there was no telling where the fields of Penfolda finished and those of the next farm started. And so distant were the combines that it was impossible to guess at the identity of the men who drove them, or the tiny figures who walked behind, forking the bales into rough stooks to stand and dry in the midsummer sun.

She was not even sure that he still lived here, that he still farmed Penfolda, and yet could not imagine him existing anywhere else in the world. She let her mind's eye, like the lens of some great camera, zoom down on to the busy scene. The figures sprang into focus, huge and clear, and he was there, high at the wheel of the combine harvester, shirt-sleeves rolled back from brown forearms, his hair tousled by the wind. And because there was danger in moving in so close, Virginia swiftly presented him with a wife, pictured her walking across the fields with a basket, flasks of tea, and perhaps a fruit cake to eat, and she wore a pink cotton dress and a blue apron and her long bare legs were brown.

Mrs Eustace Philips. Mr and Mrs Eustace Philips of Penfolda.

The car nosed over the crest of the hill, and the bay and the white beaches and the distant headlands spread out before her, and far below, spilling down to around the blue goblet of the harbour, were the clustered houses and the Norman church tower of Porthkerris.

Wheal House, where the Lingards lived, and with whom Virginia was staying, lay on the far side of Porthkerris. If she had been a stranger, new to the district and visiting it for the first time, she would have followed the main road which led right down into the town and out the other side, and consequently become hopelessly ensnared in crawling traffic and hordes of aimless sightseers who spilled off the narrow pavements, or stood about at strategic corners, sucking ice-creams, choosing postcards and gazing in shop windows filled with brass piskies and pottery mermaids and other horrors considered suitable as souvenirs.

But, because she was not a stranger, Virginia turned off the road long before the houses started and took the narrow, high-hedged lane that wound up and over the hill which stood at the back of the town. It was the long way home, by no means a short cut, but eventually emerged out on the main road again, through a tunnel of wild rhododendrons and not fifty yards from the main entrance to Wheal House.

There was a white-barred gate and a rough drive that ran up between hedges of pink-flowered escallonia. The house was neo-Georgian, pleasingly proportioned, with a pedimented porch over the front door. The drive swept up between shaven green lawns and flower-beds heavy with the scent of wallflowers, and as Virginia parked the car in the shade of the house, there was a sharp cacophony of barking, and Dora, Alice Lingard's old spaniel, emerged from the open front door where she had been lying, for coolness, on the polished floor of the hall.

Virginia stopped to pat her and speak to her and then went indoors, taking off her sunglasses because after the bright day outside, the house seemed pitch dark.

Across the hall the garden doors stood open to the patio, which, facing south and trapping all the sun, was a favourite spot of Alice's in all but really wintry weather. Today, because of the heat, she had unrolled the split cane awnings, and the bright canvas chairs and the low tables, already set out with tea things, were narrowly striped by the shadow patterns which they cast.

On the table in the middle of the hall lay the afternoon's mail. Two letters for Virginia, both with London postmarks. She laid down her handbag and her glasses and picked them up. One from Lady Keile and one from . . . Cara. The italic letters, which she learned at school, were painfully formed, dearly familiar.

Mrs A. Keile,
c/o Mrs Lingard,
Wheal House,
Porthkerris,
Cornwall.

No mistakes, no misspellings. Virginia wondered if she had managed by herself or whether Nanny had had to help. With the letters in her hand she went on across the hall and out to where her hostess sat, reclining gracefully on a long chair, with some sewing in her lap. She was making a cushion cover, stitching silk cord around the edge of the coral velvet square, and the colour lay in her lap like some huge fallen rose petal.

She looked up. "There you are! I was wondering what had happened to you. I thought perhaps you'd got stuck in a traffic jam."

Alice Lingard was a tall, dark woman in her late thirties, her firmly-built figure belied by long and slender arms and legs. She was what Virginia always thought of as a middle-aged friend, not middle-aged in the strictest sense of the word, but belonging to that generation which lay halfway between Virginia and Virginia's mother. She was, in fact, a lifelong family friend, and years ago had been a small bridesmaid at Virginia's mother's wedding.

She herself had married, eighteen years or so ago, Tom Lingard, then a young man on the verge of taking over the small family business of Lingard Sons which specialised in the manufacture of heavy engineering machinery in the nearby town of Fourbourne. Under Tom's chairmanship the firm had expanded and prospered, and after a series of successful take-over bids now controlled interests which spread from Bristol to St Just, and included mining rights, a small shipping business and the sale of agricultural machinery.

They had never had children, but Alice had diverted her natural domestic talents to her house and garden, and over the years had transformed what had once been a fairly unimaginative establishment into an enchanting house and a garden which was constantly being photographed and written about by the Garden Editors of the glossier magazines. Ten years ago, when Virginia and her mother had come to Cornwall to spend Easter with the Lingards, the work had only just started. This time, having not visited Wheal House during the intervening years, Virginia had scarcely recognised the place. Everything had been subtly altered, straight lines curved, outlines and boundaries magically removed. Trees had grown up, casting long shadows on smooth lawns which seemed to spread as far as the eye could see. The old orchard had been transformed into a wild garden tangled with all the sweetest of old-fashioned roses, and where once had drilled rows of runner beans and raspberry canes, now stood magnolias, creamy petalled, and heady-scented azaleas taller than a man could reach.

But, domestically, the patio was Alice's most successful project, neither house nor garden, but with the combined charm of both. Geraniums spilled from terrace pots, and up a trellised wall she had started to train a dark purple-flowered clematis. She had lately decided that she would also grow a vine, and was currently picking the brains of both friends and reference books, to decide on the best way to set about doing this. Her energies appeared to be endless.

Virginia pulled up a chair and dropped into it, surprised to find how hot and tired she felt. She shucked off her sandals and propped up her bare feet on to a handy stool. "I didn't go to Porthkerris."

"You didn't? But I thought you'd gone to the post office."

"I only wanted some stamps. I can buy them another time. There were so many people and so many buses and so much crushed and sweating humanity that I got claustrophobia and never stopped. Just went on driving."

"I can lend you stamps," said Alice. "Let me pour you some tea." She laid down her sewing and sat up to reach for the teapot. Steam rose from the delicate cup, fragrant, refreshing.

"Milk or lemon?"

"Lemon would be delicious."

"So much more refreshing, I think, on a hot day." She handed Virginia the cup and lay back again. "Where did you drive?"

"Um? . . . oh, the other way . . ."

"Land's End?"

"Not so far. I only got as far as Lanyon. I parked the car in a lay-by and climbed the hill for a bit and sat in the bracken and looked at the view."

"So beautiful," said Alice, threading her needle.

"They're cutting hay on the farms."

"Yes, they would be."

"It never changes, does it? Lanyon, I mean. No new houses, no new roads, no shops, no caravan parks." She took a mouthful of scalding hot Lapsang Souchong and then, with care, laid the cup and saucer down on the paved floor beside her chair. "Alice, does Eustace Philips still farm Penfolda?"

Alice stopped sewing, and put up a hand to take off her dark glasses and stare at Virginia. There was a puzzled frown between her dark brows.

"What do you know about Eustace Philips? How do you know him?"

"Alice, your memory is appalling. It was you yourself who took me out there, you and Tom, for an enormous barbecue on the cliffs at Penfolda. There must have been at least thirty people and I don't know who organised it, but we cooked sausages over a fire and drank beer out of a barrel. Oh, surely you remember, and then Mrs Philips gave us tea in her kitchen!"

"Now you remind me, of course I do. It was bitterly cold but quite beautiful and we watched the moon rise from behind Boscovey Head. I do remember. Now, who was it who threw that party? It certainly wasn't Eustace, he was always too busy milking cows. It must have been the Barnets – he was a sculptor and had a studio for a couple of years in Porthkerris before he went back to London. His wife wove baskets or belts or something, terribly folksy, and they had a lot of children who never wore shoes. They were always thinking up the most original parties. It must have been the Barnets . . . How extraordinary! I hadn't thought about them in years. And we all went out to Penfolda." But here her memory let her down. She looked at Virginia blankly. "Or did we? Who went to that party?"

"Mother didn't come. She said it wasn't up her street . . ."

"How right she was."

"But you and I and Tom went."

"Of course. Bundled up in sweaters and socks. I'm not sure I didn't wear a fur coat. But we were talking about Eustace. How old were you, Virginia? Seventeen? Fancy your remembering Eustace Philips after all these years."

"You haven't answered my question. Is he still at Penfolda?"

"As the farm belonged to his father, and *his* father, and as far as I know *his* father before that, do you really think it likely that Eustace would up sticks and depart?"

"I suppose not. It's just that they were cutting hay this afternoon and I wondered if it was he who drove one of the combines. Do you ever see him, Alice?"

"Hardly ever. Not because we don't want to, understand me, but he's a hard-working farmer, and Tom's so busy being a tycoon, that their paths don't often cross. Except sometimes they meet at the hare shoot, or the Boxing Day meet . . . you know the sort of thing."

Virginia picked up her teacup and saucer, and observed, minutely, the rose painted upon its side.

"He's married," she said.

"You say that as though you were stating an irrefutable fact."

"Aren't I?"

"No, you're not. He never married. Heaven knows why. I always thought he was so attractive in a sunburned, D. H. Lawrence-ish sort of way. There must have been a number of languishing ladies in Lanyon, but he resisted the lot. He must like it that way."

Eustace's wife, so swiftly imagined, as swiftly died, a wraith blown to nothing by the cold wind of reality. Instead, Virginia saw the Penfolda kitchen, cheerless and untidy, with the remains of the last meal abandoned on the table, dishes in the sink, an ashtray filled with cigarette stubs.

"Who looks after him?"

"I don't know. His mother died a couple of years ago I believe . . . I don't know what he does. Perhaps he's got a sexy housekeeper, or a domesticated mistress? I really don't know."

And couldn't care less, her tone implied. She had finished sewing on the silk cord, now gave a couple of neat firm stitches and then broke the thread with a little tug. "There, that's done. Isn't it a divine colour?

But it's really too hot to sew." She laid it aside. "Oh dear, I suppose I must go and see what we'll have for dinner. What would you say to a delicious fresh lobster?"

"I'd say 'pleased to see you'."

Alice stood up, unfolding her long height to tower over Virginia. "Did you see your letters?"

"Yes, they're here."

Alice stooped to pick up the tray. "I'll leave you," she said, "to read them in peace."

Keeping the best to the last, Virginia opened her mother-in-law's letter first. The envelope was dark blue, lined with navy-blue tissue. The writing-paper was thick, the address blackly embossed at its head.

32 Welton Gardens, S.W.8.

My dear Virginia,

I hope you are enjoying this wonderful weather, quite a heatwave and into the nineties yesterday. I expect you are swimming in Alice's pool, such a joy not having to drive to the beach every time you want to swim. The children are both well and send their love. Nanny takes them into the park every day and they take their tea with them and eat it there. I took Cara to Harrods this morning to buy some new dresses, she is getting so tall and was quite out of her old ones. One is blue with appliquéd flowers, the other pink with a little smocking. I think you would approve! Tomorrow they are going to tea with the Manning-Prestons. Nanny is looking forward to a good gossip with their Nanny, and Susan is just the right age for Cara. It would be nice for them to be friends. My regards to Alice, and let me know when you decide to come back to London, but we are managing beautifully, and don't want you to cut short your holiday at all for any reason. You really were due for one.

Affectionately,

Dorothea Keile

She read the letter twice, torn by conflicting emotions. Double meanings sprang at her from between the meticulously-penned, well-turned sentences. She saw her children in the park, the baked London grass turned yellow in the heat, trodden and tired, and fouled by dogs. She saw the white-hot morning sky high above the roof-tops and the little girl being fitted into dresses that she would neither like nor want, but would be too polite to reject. She saw the Manning-Prestons' tall, terraced house, with the paved garden at the back where Mrs Manning-Preston held her famous cocktail parties, and where Cara and Susan would be sent to play while the Nannies talked about knitting patterns and what a terror Nanny Brigg's little charge was going to be. And she saw Cara standing silent, petrified with shyness, and Susan Manning-Preston treating her with contempt because Cara wore spectacles and Susan thought she was a ninny.

And "we are managing beautifully". The statement seemed to Virginia completely ambiguous. Who was "we"? Nanny and the grandmother? Or did it include the children, Virginia's children? Did they let Cara sleep with the old teddy that Nanny swore was unhygienic? Did they remember always to leave the light on so that Nicholas could get himself to the bathroom in the middle of the night? And were they ever left alone, disorganised, dirty, untidy, to play secret, pointless games in small corners of the garden, with perhaps a nut or a leaf, and all the imaginings that were contained within their small, clever, bewildering brains?

She found that her hands were shaking. She was a fool

to get into this state. Nanny had looked after the children since they were born, she knew all their idiosyncrasies and nobody could cope with Nicholas's sudden rages better than she.

(But should he have such rages? At six, shouldn't he have grown out of them? What frustration sparks them off?)

And Nanny was gentle with Cara. She made dolls' clothes and knitted scarves and sweaters for the teddies out of left-over bits of wool. And she let Cara wheel her doll's perambulator into the park; over the crossing by the Albert Memorial, they went. (But did she read to Cara, the books that Cara loved? *The Borrowers* and *The Railway Children* and every word of *The Secret Garden*.) Did she love the children, or simply possess them?

These were all familiar questions which, lately, had been raising themselves with ever-increasing frequency within the confines of Virginia's own head. But never answered. Knowing that she was evading a vital issue, she would shelve her own anxiety, always with some excuse to herself. I can't think about it now, I'm too tired. Perhaps in a couple of years when Nicholas goes away to prep school, perhaps then I'll tell my mother-in-law that I don't need Nanny any longer; I'll say to Nanny it's time to go, to find another new baby to look after. And perhaps just now I'm too emotional, I wouldn't be good for the children; they're better with Nanny: after all, she's been looking after children for forty years.

Like a familiar sedative the well-worn excuses came pat, blunting Virginia's uneasy conscience. She put the blue letter back into its expensive envelope and turned, in relief, to the second one. But the relief was short-lived. Cara had borrowed her grandmother's writing-paper, but the sentences this time were neither meticulously penned nor well-turned. The ink was blotched and the lines ran down the side of the paper as though the words were tumbling hopelessly downhill.

Darling Mother,

I hope you are having a good time. I hope it is nise wether. It is hot in London. I have to go and have tea with Susan Maning Preston. I dont no what we will play. Last night Nicholas screemed and Granny had to give him a pil. He went all red. One of my dolls eyes has come out and I cant find it. Please will you rite to me soon and tell me when we are going back to Kirkton.

With love from Cara

P.S. Dont forget to rite.

She folded the letter and put it away. Across the garden, across the lawns, the blue of Alice's swimming-pool glimmered like a jewel. The cooling air was filled with bird-song and the scent of flowers. From inside the house she could hear Alice's voice talking to Mrs Jilkes, the cook, doubtless about the lobster which they were going to eat for dinner.

She felt helpless, totally inadequate. She thought of asking Alice to have the children here, and in the next instant knew that it was impossible. Alice's house was not designed for children, her life did not cater for their inclusion. She would be irritated beyond words by Cara forgetting to change her gumboots, or by Nicholas kicking his football into the treasured flower-borders, or drawing "pictures" on the wallpaper. For without Nanny, he would doubtless be impossible because he was always twice as naughty without her to keep an eye on him.

Without Nanny. Those were the operative words. On her own. She had to have them on her own.

And yet the very thought filled her with dread. What would she do with them? Where would they go? Like feelers her thoughts probed around, searching for ideas. A hotel? But hotels here would be filled to the brim with summer visitors and terribly expensive. Besides, Nicholas in a hotel would be as nerve-racking as Nicholas at Wheal House. She thought of hiring a caravan, or camping with them on the beach, like the summer migration of hippies, who lit fires of driftwood and slept curled up on the chilly sand.

Of course, there was always Kirkton. Some time, she would have to go back. But all her instincts shied away from the thought of returning to Scotland, to the house where she had lived with Anthony, the place where her children had been born, the only place they thought of as home. Thinking of Kirkton, she saw tree shadows flickering on pale walls, the cold northern light reflected on the white ceilings, the sound of her own feet going up the uncarpeted, polished stairway. She thought of clear autumn evenings when the first skeins of geese flew over, and the park, in front of the house, sweeping down to the banks of the deep, swift-flowing river . . .

No. Not yet. Cara would have to wait. Later, perhaps, they would go back to Kirkton. Not yet. Behind her a door slammed, and she was jerked back to reality by the arrival of Tom Lingard, back from work. She heard him call Alice, then drop his briefcase on the hall table, and come out to the patio in search of his wife.

"Hello, Virginia." He bent and dropped a kiss on the top of her head. "All alone? Where's Alice?"

"Interviewing a lobster in the kitchen."

"Letters from the children? All well? Well done, that's great . . ." One of Tom's idiosyncrasies was that he never bothered to wait for an answer to any of his questions. Virginia sometimes wondered if this was the secret of his outstanding success. "What have you been doing all day? Lying in the sun? That's the job. How about coming and having a swim with me now? The exercise'll do you good after all this lazing about. We'll get Alice to come too . . ." He went, spring-footed and bursting with energy, back into the house and down the passage towards the kitchen, bellowing for his wife. And Virginia, grateful for directions, stood up and collected her mail and went indoors, obediently, and upstairs to her bedroom to change into a bikini.

2

The solicitors were called Smart, Chirgwin and Williams. At least, those were the names on the brass plate by the door, a plate which had been polished so long and so hard that the letters had lost their sharpness and were quite difficult to read. There was a brass knocker on the door, too, and a brass doorknob, as smooth and shining as the plate, and when Virginia turned the knob and opened the door, she stepped into a narrow hall of polished brown linoleum and shining cream paint and it occurred to her that some hard-working woman was using up an awful lot of elbow grease.

There was a glass window, like an old-fashioned ticket-office with INQUIRIES written over it, and a bell to press. Virginia pressed the bell and the window flew up.

"Yes?"

Startled, Virginia told the face behind the window that she wanted to see Mr Williams.

"Have you got an appointment?"

"Yes. It's Mrs Keile."

"Just a moment, please."

The window slammed down and the face withdrew. Presently a door opened and the face reappeared, along with a well-upholstered body and a pair of legs that went straight down into sturdy lace-up shoes.

"If you'd like to come this way, Mrs Keile."

The building which housed the solicitors' office stood

at the top of the hill which led out of Porthkerris, but even so Virginia was taken unawares by the marvellous view which leapt at her as soon as she walked into the room. Mr Williams's desk stood in the middle of the carpet and Mr Williams was, even now, getting to his feet behind it. But, beyond Mr Williams, a great picture window framed, like some lovely painting, the whole jumbled, charming panorama of the old part of the town. Roofs of houses, faded slate and whitewashed chimneys, tumbled without pattern or order down the hill. Here a blue door, there a yellow window; here a window-sill bright with geraniums, a line of washing gay as flags, or the leaves of some unsuspected and normally unseen tree. Beyond the roofs and far below them was the harbour, at full tide and sparkling with sunshine. Boats rocked at anchor and a white sail sped out beyond the shelter of the harbour wall, heading for the ruler line of the horizon where the two blues met. The air was clamorous with the sound of gulls, the sky patterned with their great gliding wings and as Virginia stood there, the church bells from the Norman tower struck up a simple carillon and clock chimes rang out eleven o'clock.

"Good morning," said Mr Williams, and Virginia realised that he had already said this twice. She tore her attention from the view and tried to focus it on him.

"Oh, good morning. I'm Mrs Keile, I . . ." But it was impossible. "How *can* you work in a room with a view like that?"

"That's why I sit with my back to it . . ."

"It's breathtaking."

"Yes, and quite unique. We're often asked by artists if they can paint the harbour from this window. You can see the whole structure of the town, and the colours are always different, always beautiful. Except, of course, on a rainy day. Now – " his manner changed abruptly as though anxious to get down to work and to waste no more time " – what can I do for you?" He drew a chair forward for her.

Trying to stop looking out of the window and to concentrate on the matter in hand, Virginia sat down. "Well I've maybe come to quite the wrong person, but you see I can't find an estate agent anywhere in the town. And I looked in the local paper for a house to rent, but there didn't seem to be one. And then I saw your name in the telephone book, and I thought perhaps you might be able to help me."

"Help you find a house?" Mr Williams was young, very dark, his eyes frankly interested in the attractive woman who faced him across his desk.

"Just to rent . . ."

"For how long?"

"A month . . . my children go back to school the first week in September."

"I see. Well, we don't actually *deal* in this sort of thing, but I could ask Miss Leddra if there's anything that she could suggest. But of course this is the high season, and the town is already packed to the gunwales with visitors. Even if you do find something, I'm afraid you'll have to pay a fairly steep rent."

"I don't mind."

"Well, just a moment . . ."

He left her and went out, and Virginia heard him speaking to the woman who had let her in. She got up and went back to the window, and opened it wide and laughed as a furious gull flew crossly off the sill where he had been perching. The wind off the sea was cool and fresh. A pleasure boat packed with passengers started off across the harbour and suddenly Virginia longed to be on board, irresponsible, sun-burned, wearing a hat with KISS ME written on it and screaming with laughter as the first waves sent the boat rocking.

Mr Williams came back. "Can you wait a moment? Miss Leddra's making a few inquiries . . ."

"Yes, of course." She returned to her chair.

"Are you staying in Porthkerris?" Mr Williams asked conversationally.

"Yes. I'm staying with friends. The Lingards up at Wheal House."

His previous manner had been neither off-hand nor familiar, but all at once he was almost deferential.

"Oh yes, of course. What a charming place that is."

"Yes. Alice has made it lovely."

"Have you been there before?"

"Yes. Ten years ago. But I haven't been since."

"Are your children with you?"

"No. They're in London, with their grandmother. But I want to get them down here with me, if I can."

"Is London your home?"

"No. It's just that my mother-in-law lives in London." Mr Williams waited. "My home . . . that is, we live in Scotland."

He looked delighted . . . Virginia could not think why it should delight him that she lived in Scotland. "But how splendid! What part?"

"In Perthshire."

"The most beautiful. My wife and I spent a holiday there last summer. The peace of it all, and the empty roads and the quiet. How could you bear to come away?"

Virginia had opened her mouth to tell him when the discussion was mercifully interrupted by the arrival of Miss Leddra, bearing a sheaf of papers.

"Here it is, Mr Williams. Bosithick. And the letter from Mr Kernow saying that if we could find a tenant for August he'd be willing to rent. But only to a *suitable* tenant, Mr Williams. He's very firm about that point."

Mr Williams took the papers and smiled at Virginia over the top of them.

"Are you a suitable tenant, Mrs Keile?"

"It depends. On what you're offering me, doesn't it?"

"Well, it's not actually in Porthkerris . . . thank you, Miss Leddra . . . but not too far away . . . out at Lanyon actually . . ."

"Lanyon!"

She must have sounded appalled, for Mr Williams sprang at once to Lanyon's defence. "But it's a most charming spot, quite the most beautiful bit of coastline left anywhere."

"I didn't mean that I didn't like it. I was just surprised."

"Were you? Why?"

He was too sharp, like a beady-eyed bird. "No reason, really. Tell me about the house."

He told her. It was an old cottage, neither distinguished nor beautiful, but with a small claim to fame in that a famous writer had once lived and worked there during the nineteen-twenties.

Virginia said, "Which?"

"I beg your pardon?"

"Which famous writer?"

"Oh, I'm sorry. Aubrey Crane. Didn't you know that he spent some years in this part of the world?"

Virginia did not. But Aubrey Crane had been one of the many authors of whom Virginia's mother did not approve. She remembered her mother's chill expression, lips pursed, whenever his books were mentioned; remembered them being returned swiftly to the library before the young Virginia could get her eyes on them. For some reason this seemed to make the cottage called Bosithick even more desirable. "Go on," said Virginia.

Mr Williams went on. Despite its age Bosithick had been modernised to a certain degree – there was now a bathroom and a lavatory and an electric cooker.

"Who does it belong to?" Virginia asked.

"Mr Kernow is the nephew of the old lady who used to own the house. She left it to him, but he lives in Plymouth so he uses it just for holidays. He and his family intended coming down for the summer, but his wife fell ill and can't make the trip. As we are Mr Kernow's solicitors, he put the matter in our hands, with the instructions that, if we did let the house, it must be to a tenant who can be trusted to take care of it."

"How big is it?"

Mr Williams perused his papers. "Let's see, a kitchen, a sitting-room, a downstairs bathroom, and a hall, and three rooms upstairs."

"Is there a garden?"

"Not really."

"How far is it from the road?"

"About a hundred yards down a farm lane, as far as I can remember."

"And could I have it right away?"

"I can see no objection. But you must see it first."

"Yes, of course . . . when can I see it?"

"Today? Tomorrow?"

"Tomorrow morning."

"I'll take you out myself."

"Thank you, Mr Williams." Virginia stood up and made for the door, and he had to make a little rush to get there and open it before she did.

"There's just one thing, Mrs Keile."

"What's that?"

"You haven't asked what the rent is."

She smiled. "No I haven't, have I? Goodbye Mr Williams."

Virginia said nothing to Alice and Tom. She did not want to have to put into words what was, at best, only a vague idea. She did not want to be drawn into an argument, to be persuaded either that the children were best left in London with their grandmother or that Alice could disregard the possible destruction that they might perpetrate at Wheal House and would insist on having them there. When Virginia had found somewhere for

them all to live, she would present Alice with what she had done as a *fait accompli*. And then Alice would maybe help her take the biggest hurdle of all, which was to persuade the grandmother to let the children come to Cornwall without Nanny. At the very prospect of this ordeal, Virginia's imagination turned and ran, but there were other and smaller obstacles to be overcome first, and these she was determined to do by herself.

Alice was a perfect hostess. When Virginia told her that she would be out for the morning it never occurred to Alice to quiz her as to what she intended doing. She only said, "Will you be in for lunch?"

"I don't think so . . . Better say not . . ."

"I'll see you at tea-time, then. We'll have a swim together afterwards."

"Heaven," said Virginia. She kissed Alice and went out, got into her car and drove down the hill into Porthkerris. She parked the car near the station and walked to the solicitors' office to pick up Mr Williams.

"Mrs Keile, I couldn't be more sorry, but I'm not going to be able to come out with you this morning to Bosithick. An old client is coming down from Truro and I must be here to see her; I do hope you understand! But here are the keys of the house, and I've drawn a fairly detailed map of how to find it . . . I don't think you could go wrong. Do you mind going on your own, or would you like to take Miss Leddra with you?"

Virginia imagined the daunting presence of the formidable Miss Leddra and assured Mr Williams that she'd manage perfectly on her own. She was given a ring of large keys, each with a wooden label. Front Door, Coal Shed, Tower Room. "You'll need to watch out for the lane," Mr Williams told her, as they went together towards the door. "It's fairly bumpy and although there's no room to turn by the gate of Bosithick itself, you can manage easily if you carry on down the lane; you'll come to an old farmyard and you can turn the car there. Now, you're sure you'll be all right . . . I couldn't be more sorry about this, but I'll be here, of course, waiting to hear what you think of the place. Oh, and Mrs Keile . . . it's been empty for some months. Try not to be influenced if it feels a little dingy. Just throw open a few windows and imagine it with a nice cheerful fire."

Slightly discouraged by these parting remarks, Virginia went back to her car. The keys of the unknown house weighed heavy as lead in her handbag. All at once, she longed for company, and even considered, for a mad moment, returning to Wheal House to make a true confession to Alice and persuade her to come out to Lanyon and lend a little moral support. But that was ridiculous. It was just a little cottage, to be viewed, and either rented or rejected. Any fool . . . even Virginia . . . could surely do that.

The weather was still beautiful and the traffic still appalling. She crawled, one of the long queue of cars, down into the depths of town and out the other side. At the top of the hill where the roads forked, the traffic thinned a little and she was able to put on some speed and pass a line of dawdling cars. As she went up and over the moor and the sea dropped and spread beneath her, her spirits rose. The road wound like a grey ribbon through the bracken-covered hillside; to her left towered the great outcrop of Carn Edvor stained purple with heather, and on her right the country swept away down to the sea, the familiar patchwork of fields and farms that she had sat and watched only two days before.

She had been told by Mr Williams to look out for a clump of wind-leaning hawthorns by the side of the road. Beyond this was a steep corner and then the narrow farm track which led down towards the sea. Virginia came upon it and turned the car down into it, no more than a stony lane high-hedged with brambles. She went into bottom gear and edged cautiously downhill, attempting to avoid bumps and potholes and trying not to think about the damage that the prickly gorse bushes were inflicting on the paintwork of her car.

There was no sign of any house, until she turned a steep corner and was instantly upon it. A stone wall, and beyond, a gable and a slated roof. She stopped the car in the lane, reached for her handbag and got out. There was a cool, salty wind blowing in from the sea, and the smell of gorse. She went to open the gate, but the hinges were broken and it had to be lifted before she could edge through. A path of sorts led down towards a flight of stone steps and so to the house, and Virginia saw that it was long and low with gables to the north and the south, and at the north end, looking out over the sea, had been added an extra room with a square tower above it. The tower imparted an oddly sanctified look to the house which Virginia found chilling. There was no garden to speak of, but at the south end a patch of unmown grass blew in the wind and two leaning poles supported what had once been a washing-line.

She went down the steps and along a dank pathway that led along the side of the house towards the front door. This had once been painted dark red and was scarred with splitting sun blisters. Virginia took out the key and put it in the keyhole and turned the doorknob and the key together and the door instantly, silently, swung inwards. She saw a tiny flight of stairs, a worn rug on bare boards, smelled damp and . . . mice? She swallowed nervously. She hated mice, but now that she had come so far there was nothing for it but to go up the two worn steps and tread gingerly over the threshold.

It did not take long to go over the old part of the house, to glance in at the tiny kitchen with its inadequate cooker and stained sink; the sitting-room cluttered with ill-matching chairs. An electric fire sat in the cavern of the huge old fireplace, like a savage animal at the mouth of its lair. There were curtains of flimsy cotton hanging at the windows, fly-blown and dejected, and a dresser packed with cups and plates and dishes in every sort of size and shape and state of dilapidation.

Without hope, Virginia went upstairs. The bedrooms were dim with tiny windows and unsuitable, looming pieces of furniture. She returned to the top of the stairs, and so up another pair of steps, to a closed door. She opened this, and after the gloom of the rest of the house, the blast of bright, northern light by which she was immediately assailed, was dazzling. Stunned by it, she stepped blindly into an astonishing room; small, completely square, windowed on three walls, it stood high above the sea like the bridge of a ship, with a view of the coastline that must have extended for fifteen miles.

A window seat with a faded cover ran along the north side of this room. There was a scrubbed table, and an old braided rug and in the centre of the floor, like a decorative well-head, the wrought-iron banister of a spiral staircase which led directly down to the room beneath, the "Hall" of Mr Williams's prospectus.

Cautiously Virginia descended, to a room dominated by an enormous *art nouveau* fireplace. Off this was the bathroom; and then another door, and she was back where she'd started, in the dark and depressing sitting-room.

It was an extraordinary, a terrible house. It sat around her, waiting for her to make some decision, contemptuous of her faintness of heart. To give herself time, she went back up to the tower room, sat on the window seat and opened her bag to find a cigarette. Her last. She would have to buy some more. She lit it and looked at the bare scrubbed table, and the faded colours of the rug on the floor, and knew that this had been Aubrey Crane's study, the workroom where he had wrestled out the lusty love stories that Virginia had never been encouraged to read. She saw him, bearded and knickerbockered, his conventional appearance belying the passions of his rebellious heart. Perhaps in summertime, he would have flung wide these windows, to catch all the scents and sounds of the countryside, the roar of the sea, the whistle of the wind. But in winter it would be bitterly cold, and he would have to wrap himself in blankets, and write painfully with chilblained fingers mittened in knitted wool . . .

Somewhere in the room a fly droned, blundering against the window-pane. Virginia leaned her forehead on the cool glass of the window and stared sightless at the view and started one of the interminable ding-dong arguments she had been having with herself for years.

I can't come here.

Why not?

I hate it. It's spooky and frightening. It's got a horrible atmosphere.

That's just your imagination.

It's an impossible house. I could never bring the children here. They've never lived in such a place. Anyway, there's nowhere for them to play.

There's the whole world for them to play in. The fields and the cliffs and the sea.

But looking after them . . . the washing and the ironing, and the cooking. And there's no refrigerator, and how would I heat the water?

I thought that all that mattered was getting the children to yourself, away from London.

They're better in London, with Nanny, than living in a house like this.

That wasn't what you thought yesterday.

I can't bring them here. I wouldn't know where to begin. Not on my own like that.

Then what are you going to do?

I don't know. Talk to Alice, perhaps I should have

talked to her before now. She hasn't children of her own, but she'll understand. Maybe she'll know about some other little house. She'll understand. She'll help. She has to help.

So much, said her own cool and scathing voice, *for all those strong resolutions.*

Angrily, Virginia stubbed out the half-smoked cigarette, ground it under her heel and got up and went downstairs and took out the keys and locked the door behind her. She went back up the path to the gate, stepped through and shut it. The house watched her, the small bedroom windows like derisive eyes. She tore herself from their gaze and got back into the safety of her car. It was a quarter past twelve. She needed cigarettes and she was not expected back at Wheal House for lunch, so, when she had turned the car, and was driving back on to the main road again, she took not the road to Porthkerris, but the other way, and she drove the short mile to Lanyon village, up the narrow main street, and finally came to a halt in the cobbled square that was flanked on one side by the porch of the square-towered church and on the other by a small whitewashed pub called The Mermaid's Arms.

Because of the fine weather, there were tables and chairs set up outside the pub, along with brightly coloured sun-umbrellas and tubs of orange nasturtiums. A man and a woman in holiday clothes sat and drank their beer, their little boy played with a puppy. As Virginia approached, they looked up to smile good morning, and she smiled back and went past them in through the door, instinctively ducking her head beneath the blackened lintel.

Inside it was dark-panelled, low-ceilinged, dimly illuminated by tiny windows veiled in lace curtains; there was a pleasant smell, cool and musty. A few figures, scarcely visible in the gloom, sat along the wall, or around small wobbly tables, and behind the bar, framed by rows of hanging beer-mugs, the barman, in shirt-sleeves and a checkered pullover, was polishing glasses with a dishcloth.

". . . I don't know 'ow it is, William," he was saying to a customer who sat at the other end of the bar, perched disconsolately on a tall stool, with a long cigarette ash and half a pint of bitter, ". . . but you put the litter bins up and nobody puts nothing into them . . ."

"Ur . . ." said William, nodding in sad agreement and sprinkling cigarette ash into the beer.

"Stuff blows all over the road, and the County Council don't even come and empty them. Ugly old things they are, too, we'd be better without them. Managed all right without them before, we did . . ." He finished polishing the glass, set it down with a thump and turned to attend to Virginia.

"Yes, madam?"

He was very Cornish, in voice, in looks, in colouring. A red and wind-burned face, blue eyes, black hair.

Virginia asked for cigarettes.

"Only got packets of twenty. That all right?" He turned to take them from the shelf and slit the wrapper with a practised thumbnail. "Lovely day, isn't it? On holiday, are you?"

"Yes." It was years since she had been into a pub. In Scotland women were never taken into pubs. She had forgotten the atmosphere, the snug companionship. She said, "Do you have any Coke?"

He looked surprised. "Yes, I've got Coke. Keep it for the children. Want some, do you?"

"Please."

He reached for a bottle, opened it neatly, poured it into a glass and pushed it across the counter towards her.

"I was just saying to William, here, that road to Porthkerris is a disgrace – " Virginia pulled up a stool and settled down to listen. " – All that rubbish lying around. Visitors don't seem to know what to do with their litter. You'd think coming to a lovely part like this they'd have the sense they was born with and take all them old bits of paper home with them, in the car, not leave them lying around on the roadside. They talk about conservation and ecology, but, my God . . ."

He was off on what was obviously his favourite hobby-horse, judging by the well-timed grunts of assent that came from all corners of the room. Virginia lit a cigarette. Outside, in the sunny square, a car drew up, the engine stopped, a door slammed. She heard a man's voice say good morning, and then footsteps came through the doorway and into the bar behind her.

". . . I wrote to the MP about it, said who was going to get the place cleaned up, he said it was the responsibility of the County Council, but I said . . ." Over Virginia's head he caught sight of the new customer. "'Allo, there! You're a stranger."

"Still at the litter bins, Joe?"

"You know me, boy, worry a subject to death, like a terrier killing a rat. What'll you have?"

"A pint of bitter."

Joe turned to draw the beer, and the newcomer moved in to stand between Virginia and lugubrious William, and she had recognised his voice at once, as soon as he spoke, just as she had known his footfall, stepping in over the flagged threshold of The Mermaid's Arms.

She took a mouthful of Coke, laid down the glass. All at once her cigarette tasted bitter; she stubbed it out and turned her head to look at him, and she saw the blue shirt, with the sleeves rolled back from his brown forearms, and the eyes very blue and the short, rough, brown hair cut like a pelt, close to the shape of his head. And because there was nothing else to be done she said, "Hello, Eustace."

Startled, his head swung round and his expression was that of a man who had suddenly been hit in the stomach, bemused and incapable. She said, quickly, "It really is me," and his smile came, incredulous, rueful, as though he knew he had been made to look a fool.

"Virginia."

She said again, stupidly, "Hello."

"What in the name of heaven are you doing here?"

She was aware that every ear in the place was waiting for her to reply. She made it very light and casual. "Buying cigarettes. Having a drink."

"I didn't mean that. I mean in Cornwall. Here, in Lanyon."

"I'm on holiday. Staying with the Lingards in Porthkerris."

"How long have you been here?"

"About a week . . ."

"And what are you doing out here?"

But before she had time to tell him, the barman had pushed Eustace's tankard of beer across the counter, and Eustace was diverted by trying to find the right money in his trouser pocket.

"Old friends, are you?" asked Joe, looking at Virginia with new interest, and she said, "Yes, I suppose you could say that."

"I haven't seen her for ten years," Eustace told him, pushing the coins across the counter. He looked at Virginia's glass. "What are you drinking?"

"Coke."

"Bring it outside, we may as well sit in the sun."

She followed him, aware of the unblinking stares which followed them; the insatiable curiosity. Outside in the sunshine he put their glasses down on to a wooden table and they settled, side by side on a bench, with the sun on their heads and their backs against the whitewashed wall of the pub.

"You don't mind being brought out here, do you? Otherwise we couldn't say a word without it being received and transmitted all over the county within half an hour."

"I'd rather be outside."

Half turned towards her, he sat so close that Virginia could see the rough, weather-beaten texture of his skin, the network of tiny lines around his eyes, the first frosting of white in that thick brown hair. She thought, *I'm with him again.*

He said, "Tell me."

"Tell you what?"

"What happened to you." And then quickly, "I know you got married."

"Yes. Almost at once."

"Well, that would have put paid to the London Season you were dreading so much."

"Yes, it did."

"And the coming-out dance."

"I had a wedding instead."

"Mrs Anthony Keile. I saw the announcement in the paper." Virginia said nothing. "Where do you live now?"

"In Scotland. There's a house in Scotland . . ."

"And children?"

"Yes. Two. A boy and a girl."

"How old are they?" He was really interested, and she remembered how the Cornish loved children, how Mrs Jilkes was for ever going dewy-eyed over some lovely little great-nephew or niece.

"The girl's eight and the boy's six."

"Are they with you now?"

"No. They're in London. With their grandmother."

"And your husband? Is he down? What's he doing this morning? Playing golf?"

She stared at him, accepting for the first time the fact that personal tragedy is just that. Personal. Your own existence could fall to pieces but that did not mean that the rest of the world necessarily knew about it, or even bothered. There was no reason for Eustace to know.

She laid her hands on the edge of the table, aligning

them as though their arrangement were of the utmost importance. She said, "Anthony's dead." Her hands seemed all at once insubstantial, almost transparent, the wrists too thin, the long almond-shaped nails, painted coral pink, as fragile as petals. She wished suddenly, fervently, that they were not like that, but strong and brown and capable, with dirt engrained, and fingernails worn from gardening and peeling potatoes and scraping carrots. She could feel Eustace's eyes upon her. She could not bear him to be sorry for her.

He said, "What happened?"

"He was killed in a car accident. He was drowned."

"*Drowned?*"

"We have this river, you see, at Kirkton . . . that's where we live in Scotland. The river runs between the house and the road, you have to go over the bridge. And he was coming home and he skidded, or misjudged the turn, and the car went through the wooden railings and into the river. We'd had a lot of rain, a wet month, and the river was in spate and the car went to the bottom. A diver had to go down . . . with a cable. And the police eventually winched it out . . ." Her voice trailed off.

He said gently, "When?"

"Three months ago."

"Not long."

"No. But there was so much to do, so much to see to. I don't know what's happened to the time. And then I caught this bug – a sort of flu, and I couldn't throw it off, so my mother-in-law said that she'd have the children in London and I came down here to stay with Alice."

"When are you going away again?"

"I don't know."

He was silent. After a little he picked up his glass and drained his beer. As he set it down he said, "Have you got a car here?"

"Yes." She pointed. "The blue Triumph."

"Then finish that drink and we'll go back to Penfolda."

Virginia turned her head and stared at him. "Well, what's so extraordinary about that? It's dinner-time. There are pasties in the oven. Do you want to come back and eat one with me?"

". . . Yes."

"Then come. I've got my Land-Rover. You can follow me."

"All right."

He stood up. "Come along, then."

3

She had been to Penfolda once before, only once, and then in the cool half-light of a spring evening ten years before.

"We've been invited to a party," Alice had announced over lunch that day.

Virginia's mother was immediately intrigued. She was immensely social and with a seventeen-year-old daughter to launch into society one only had to mention a party to capture her attention.

"How very nice! Where? Who with?"

Alice laughed at her. Alice was one of the few people who could laugh at Rowena Parsons and get away with it, but then Alice had known her for years.

"Don't get too excited. It's not really your sort of thing."

"My dear Alice, I don't know what you mean. Explain!"

"Well, it's a couple called Barnet. Amos and Fenella Barnet. You may have heard of him. He's a sculptor, very modern, very *avant-garde*. They've taken one of the old studios in Porthkerris, and they have a great number of rather unconventional children."

Without waiting to hear more Virginia said, "Why don't we go?" They sounded exactly the sort of people she was always longing to meet.

Mrs Parsons allowed a small frown to show between her beautifully aligned eyebrows. "Is the party in the studio?" she inquired, obviously suspecting doctored drinks and doped cigarettes.

"No, it's out at Lanyon at a farm called Penfolda, some sort of a barbecue on the cliffs. A camp fire and fried sausages . . ." Alice saw that Virginia was longing to go. ". . . I think it might be rather fun."

"I think it sounds terrible," said Mrs Parsons.

"I didn't think you'd want to come. But Tom and I might go, and we'll take Virginia with us."

Mrs Parsons turned her cool gaze upon her daughter. "Do you *want* to go to a barbecue?"

Virginia shrugged. "It might be fun." She had learned, long ago, that it never paid to be too enthusiastic about anything.

"Very well," said her mother, helping herself to lemon pudding. "If it's your idea of an amusing evening and Alice and Tom don't mind taking you along . . . but for heaven's sake wear something warm. It's bound to be freezing. Far too cold, one would have thought, for a picnic."

She was right. It was cold. A clear turquoise evening with the shoulder of Carn Edvor silhouetted black against the western sky and a chill inland wind to nip the air. Driving up the hill out of Porthkerris, Virginia looked back and saw the lights of the town twinkling far below, the ink-black waters of the harbour brimming with shimmering reflections. Across the bay, from the distant headland, the lighthouse sent its warning signal. A flash. A pause. A flash. A longer pause. Be careful. There's danger.

The evening ahead seemed full of possibilities. Suddenly excited, Virginia turned and leaned forward, resting her chin on crossed arms on the back of Alice's seat. The unpremeditated gesture was clumsy and spontaneous, a reflection of natural high spirits that were normally battened firmly down under the influence of a domineering mother.

"Alice, where is this place we're going?"
"Penfolda. It's a farm, just this side of Lanyon."
"Who lives there?"
"Mrs Philips. She's a widow. And her son Eustace."
"What does he do?"
"He farms, silly. I told you it was a farm."
"Are they friends of the Barnets?"
"I suppose they must be. A lot of artists live out around this part of the world. Though I've no idea how they could ever have met."
Tom said, "Probably at The Mermaid's."
"What's The Mermaid's?" Virginia asked.
"The Mermaid's Arms, the pub in Lanyon. On a Saturday night all the world and his wife go there for a drink and a get-together."
"Who else will be at the party?"
"Our guess is probably as good as yours."
"Haven't you *any* idea?"
"Well . . ." Alice did her best. ". . . Artists and writers and poets and hippies and drop-outs and farmers and perhaps one or two rather boring and conventional people like us."
Virginia gave her a hug. "You're not boring or conventional. You're super."
"You may not think we're quite so super at the end of the evening. You may hate it, so grit your teeth and reserve your judgment."
Virginia sat back, in the darkness of the car, hugging herself. *I shan't hate it*.
There were headlights like fireflies, coming from all directions, converging on Penfolda. From the road the farmhouse could be seen to be blazing with light. They joined the queue of assorted vehicles which bumped and groaned their way down a narrow, broken lane and eventually were directed into a farmyard which had been turned temporarily into a car park. The air was full of voices and laughter as friends greeted friends, and

already a steady trickle of people were making their way over a stone wall and down over the pasture fields towards the cliffs. Some were wrapped in rugs, some carried old-fashioned lanterns, some – Virginia was glad all over again that her mother had not come – a clanking bottle or two.

Someone said, "Tom! What are you doing here?", and Tom and Alice dropped back to wait for their friends, and Virginia went on, loving the feeling of being alone. All about her the soft, dark air smelled of peat and sea-wrack and wood-smoke. The sky was not yet empty of light and the sea was of so dark a blue that it was almost black. She went through a gap in a wall and saw, below her, at the bottom of the field, the golden flames of the fire, already ringed with lanterns and the shapes and shadows of about thirty people. As she came closer, faces sprang suddenly into focus, illuminated in firelight, laughing and talking, everybody knowing everybody. There was a barrel of beer, propped on a wooden stand, from which brimming glasses were being continually filled, and there was the smell of potatoes cooking and burning fat, and somebody had brought a guitar and begun to play and gradually a few people gathered about him and raised uncertain voices in song.

There is a ship
And she sails the sea,
She's loaded deep
As deep can be.
But not as deep
As the love I'm in . . .

A young man, running to pass Virginia, stumbled in the dusk and bumped into her. "Sorry." He grabbed her arm, as much to steady himself as her. He held his lantern high, the light in her face. "Who are you?"

"Virginia."

"Virginia who?"

"Virginia Parsons." He had long hair and a band around his forehead and looked like an Apache.

"I thought it was a new face. Are you on your own?"

"N . . . no. I've come with Alice and Tom . . . but . . ." She looked back. "I've lost them . . . they're coming . . . somewhere . . ."

"I'm Dominic Barnet . . ."

"Oh . . . it's your party . . ."

"No, my father's, really. At least he's paid for the barrel of beer which makes it his party and my mother bought the sausages. Come on . . . let's get something to drink," and he grabbed her arm with an even firmer grip and marched her down into the seething, noisy firelit circle of activity. "Hey, Dad . . . here's someone who hasn't got a drink . . ."

A huge bearded figure, medieval in the strange light, straightened up from the tap of the barrel. "Well, here's one for her," he said, and Virginia found herself holding an enormous mug of beer. "And here's a sausage." The young man whisked one neatly off a passing tray and handed it to her, impaled on a stick. Virginia took that too, and was just about to embark upon some polite social conversation when Dominic saw another familiar face across the circle of firelight, yelled "Mariana!" or some such name, and was away, leaving Virginia once more alone.

She searched in the darkness for the Lingards but could not find them. But everyone else was sitting, so she sat too, with the enormous beer-mug in one hand and the sausage, still too hot to eat, in the other. The firelight scorched her face and the wind was cold on her back and blew her hair all over her face. She took a mouthful of beer. She had never drunk beer before and immediately wanted to sneeze. She did so, enormously, and from behind her an amused voice said, "Bless you."

Virginia recovered from the sneeze and said, "Thank you," and looked up to see who had blessed her, and saw a large young man in corduroys and rubber boots and a massive Norwegian sweater. He was grinning down at her and the firelight turned his brown face to the colour of copper.

She said, "It was the beer that made me sneeze."

He squatted beside her, took the mug gently from her hand and laid it on the ground between them. "You might sneeze again and then you'd spill it all and that would be a waste."

"Yes."

"You have to be a friend of the Barnets."

"Why do you say that?"

"I haven't seen you before."

"No, I'm not. I came with the Lingards."

"Alice and Tom? Are they here?"

"Yes, somewhere."

He sounded so pleased that the Lingards were here that Virginia fully expected him to go, then and there, in search of them, but instead he settled himself more comfortably on the grass beside her, and seemed quite happy to remain silent, simply watching in some amusement, the rest of the party. Virginia ate her sausage, and when she had finished and he still had said nothing, she decided that she would try again.

"Are you a friend of the Barnets?"

"Um . . ." His attention interrupted, he turned to look at her, his eyes a clear and unwinking blue. "Sorry?"

"I wondered if you were a friend of the Barnets, that's all."

He laughed. "I'd better be. These are my fields they're desecrating."

"Then you must be Eustace Philips."

He considered this. "Yes," he said at last. "I suppose I must be."

Soon after that he was called away . . . some of his

Guernseys had wandered in from a neighbouring field and a batty girl who had drunk too much wine thought that she was being attacked by a bull and had thrown a pretty fit of hysterics. So Eustace went to put the matter to rights, and Virginia was presently claimed by Alice and Tom, and although she spent the rest of the evening watching out for him, she did not see Eustace Philips again.

The party, however, was a wild and memorable success. Near midnight, with the beer finished, and the bottles going round, and the food all eaten and the fire piled with driftwood until the flames sprang twenty feet high or more, Alice suggested gently that perhaps it might be a good idea if they went home.

"Your mother will be sitting up thinking you've either been raped or fallen into the sea. And Tom's got to be at the office at nine in the morning and it really is getting bitterly cold. What do you say? Have you had enough? Have you had fun?"

"Such fun," said Virginia, reluctant to leave.

But it was time to go. They walked in silence away from the firelight and the noise, up the slopes of the fields towards the farmhouse.

Now, only one light burned from a downstairs window, but a full moon, white as a plate, sailed high in the sky, filling all the night with silver light. As they came over the wall into the farmyard, a door in the house opened, yellow light spilled out over the cobbles, and a voice called out across the darkness, "Tom! Alice! Come and have a cup of tea or coffee – something to warm you up before you go home."

"Hello, Eustace." Tom went towards the house. "We thought you'd gone to bed."

"I'm not staying down on the cliffs till dawn, that's for certain. Would you like a drink?"

"I'd like a whisky," said Tom.

"And I'd like tea," said Alice. "What a good idea!

We're frozen. Are you sure it's not too much trouble?"

"My mother's still up, she'd like to see you. She's got the kettle on . . ."

They all went into the house, into a low-ceilinged, panelled hall, with a flagged slate floor covered with bright rugs. The beams of the roof scarcely cleared the top of Eustace Philips's head.

Alice was unbuttoning her coat. "Eustace, have you met Virginia? She's staying with us at Wheal House."

"Yes, of course – we said hello," but he scarcely looked at her. "Come into the kitchen, it's the warmest place in the house. Mother, here are the Lingards. Alice wants a cup of tea. And Tom wants whisky and . . ." He looked down at Virginia. "What do you want?"

"I'd like tea."

Alice and Mrs Philips at once busied themselves, Mrs Philips with the teapot and the kettle, and Alice taking cups and saucers down from the shelves of the painted dresser. As they did this they discussed the Barnets' party, laughing about the girl who thought the cow was a bull, and the two men settled themselves at the scrubbed kitchen table with tumblers and a soda siphon and a bottle of Scotch.

Virginia sat too, wedged into the broad window seat at the head of the table and listening to, without actually hearing, the pleasant blur of voices. She found that she was very sleepy, dazed by the warmth and comfort of the Penfolda kitchen after the bitter cold of the outdoors, and slightly fuzzy from the unaccustomed draught beer.

Sunk into the folds of her coat, hands deep in its pockets, she looked about her and decided that never had she been in a room so welcoming, so secure. There were beams in the ceiling, with old iron hooks for smoking hams, and deep window-sills crammed with flowering geraniums. There was a huge stove where the kettle simmered, and a cane chair with a cat curled in its seat, and there was a grain merchant's calendar and curtains of checked cotton and the warm smell of baking bread.

Mrs Philips was small as her son was large, grey-haired, very neat. She looked as though she had never stopped working from the day she was born and would have it no other way, and as she and Alice moved about the kitchen, deft and quick, gossiping gently about the unconventional Barnets, Virginia watched her and wished that she could have had a mother just like that. Calm and good-humoured with a great comforting kitchen and a kettle always on the boil for a cup of tea.

The tea made, the two women finally joined the others around the table. Mrs Philips poured a cup for Virginia and handed it to her, and Virginia sat up, pulling her hands out of her pockets and took it, remembering to say "Thank you."

Mrs Philips laughed. "You're sleepy," she said.

"I know," said Virginia. They were all looking at her, but she stirred her tea and would not look up because she did not want to have to meet that blue and disconcerting gaze.

But eventually it was time to go. With their coats on again, they stood, crowded in the little hallway. The Lingards and Mrs Philips were already at the open front door when Eustace spoke from behind Virginia.

"Goodbye," he said.

"Oh." Confused, she turned. "Goodbye." She began to put out her hand, but perhaps he did not see it, for he did not take it. "Thank you for letting me come."

He looked amused. "It was a pleasure. You'll have to come back again, another time."

And all the way home, she hugged his words close as though they were a marvellous present that he had given her. But she never came back to Penfolda.

Until today, ten years later, and a July afternoon of piercing beauty. Roadside ditches brimmed with ragged robin and bright yellow coltsfoot, the gorse was aflame and the bracken of the cliff-tops lay emerald against a summer sea the colour of hyacinths.

So engrossed had she been in her business of the day, collecting keys, and finding the cottage at Bosithick, and considering such practical questions as cookers and fridges and bedclothes and china, that all the heaven-sent morning had somehow gone unnoticed. But now it was part of what had suddenly happened and Virginia remembered long ago, how the lighthouse had flashed out over the dark sea, and she had been, for no apparent reason, suddenly excited and warm with a marvellous anticipation.

But you're not seventeen any longer. You're a woman, twenty-seven years old and independent, with two children and a car and a house in Scotland. Life doesn't hold those sort of surprises any longer. Everything is different. Nothing ever stays the same.

At the top of the lane which led down to Penfolda was a wooden platform for the milk churns, and the way sloped steep and winding between high stone walls. Hawthorns leaned distorted by the winter winds, and as Virginia followed the back of Eustace's Land-Rover around the corner of the house, two collies appeared, black and white, barking and raising a din that sent the brown Leghorn hens squawking and scuttling for shelter.

Eustace had parked his Land-Rover in the shade of the barn and was already out of it, toeing the dogs gently out of the way. Virginia put her car behind his and got out as well, and the collies instantly made for her, barking and leaping about and trying to put their front paws on her knees and stretching up to lick her face.

"Get down . . . get down, you devils!"

"I don't mind . . ." She fondled their slim heads, their thick coats. "What are their names?"

"Beaker and Ben. That's Beaker and this is Ben . . . shut up, you, boy! They do this every time . . ."

His manner was robust and cheerful as though during the course of the short drive he had decided that this was the best attitude to adopt if the rest of the day was not to become a sort of wake for Anthony Keile. And Virginia, who did not in the least want this to happen, gratefully took her cue from him. The dogs' noisy welcome helped to break the ice, and it was in an entirely natural and easy fashion that they all went up the cobbled path together, and into the house.

She saw the beams, the flagged floor, the rugs. Unchanged.

"I remember this."

There was a smell of hot pasties, mouth-watering. He went in through the kitchen door, leaving Virginia to follow behind, and across to the stove, whisking an oven cloth off a rack as he passed, and crouching to open the oven.

"They aren't burnt, are they?" she asked anxiously. Fragrant smoky smells issued out.

"No, just right."

He closed the oven door and stood up.

She said, "Did you make them?"

"Me? You must be joking."

"Who did?"

"Mrs Thomas, my housekeeper . . . Like a drink, would you?" He went to open a fridge, to take a can of beer from the inside of the door.

"No, thank you."

He smiled. "I haven't got any Coke."

"I don't want a drink."

As they spoke, Virginia looked about her, terrified that anything in this marvellous room should have been altered, that Eustace might have changed something, moved the furniture, painted the walls. But it was just as she remembered. The scrubbed table pulled into the bay of the window, the geraniums on the window-sills, the dresser packed with bright china. After all these years it remained the epitome of everything a proper kitchen should be, the heart of the house.

When they had taken over Kirkton and were doing it up, cellar to attic, she had tried to get a kitchen like the Penfolda one. Somewhere comfortable and warm where the family would congregate, and drink tea and gossip round the scrubbed table.

"Who wants to go into a kitchen?" Anthony had asked, not understanding at all.

"Everybody. A farmhouse kitchen's like a living-room."

"Well, I'm not going to live in any kitchen, I'll tell you that."

And he ordered stainless steel fitments and bright Formica worktops and a black-and-white chequered floor that showed every mark and was the devil to keep clean.

Now Virginia leaned against the table and said with deep satisfaction, "I was afraid it would have changed, but it's just the same."

"Why should it have changed?"

"No reason. I was just afraid. Things do change. Eustace, Alice told me that your mother had died . . . I'm sorry."

"Yes. Two years ago. She had a fall. Got pneumonia." He chucked the empty can neatly into a rubbish bin and turned to survey her, propping his length against the edge of the sink. "And how about your own mother?"

His voice held no expression; she could detect no undertones of sarcasm or dislike.

"She died, Eustace. She became very ill a couple of years after Anthony and I were married. It was dreadful, because she was ill for so long. And it was difficult, because she was in London and I was at Kirkton . . . I couldn't be with her all the time."

"And I suppose you were all the family she had?"

"Yes. That was part of the trouble. I used to visit her as often as I could, but in the end we had to bring her up to Scotland, and eventually she went into a nursing home in Relkirk, and she died there."

"That's bad."

"Yes. And she was so young. It's a funny thing when your mother dies. You never really grow up till that happens." She amended this. "At least, I suppose that's how some people feel. You were grown up long before then."

"I don't know about that," said Eustace. "But I know what you mean."

"Anyway, it was all over years ago. Don't let's talk about miserable things. Tell me about you, and Mrs Thomas. Do you know, Alice Lingard said you'd either have a domesticated mistress or a sexy housekeeper? I can't wait to meet her."

"Well, you'll have to. She's gone to Penzance to see her sister."

"Does she live at Penfolda?"

"She has the cottage at the other end of the house. This used to be three cottages, you know, in the old days, before my grandfather bought the place. Three families lived here and farmed a few acres. Probably had half a dozen cows for milking and sent their sons down the tin mines to keep the wolf from the door."

"Two days ago," said Virginia, "I drove out to Lanyon and sat on the hill, and there were combine harvesters out, and men haymaking. I thought one of them was probably you."

"Probably was."

She said, "I thought you'd be married."

"I'm not."

"I know. Alice Lingard said that you weren't."

After he had finished his beer, he took knives and forks from a drawer and began to lay the table but Virginia stopped him. "It's too nice to be indoors. Couldn't we eat the pasties in the garden?"

Eustace looked amazed, but said, "All right," and

found her a basket for the knives and forks and plates and the salt and pepper and glasses, and he eased the piping hot pasties out of the oven on to a great flowered china dish, and they went out of a side door into the sunshine and the untidy little farmhouse garden. The grass needed cutting and the flower-beds were brimming with cheerful cottage flowers, and there was a washing-line, flapping with bright white sheets and pillow-cases.

Eustace had no garden furniture so they sat on the grass, tall with daisies and plantains, with the dishes of their picnic spread about them.

The pasties were enormous, and Virginia had only eaten half of hers, and was defeated by the remainder, by the time that Eustace, propped on an elbow, had consumed the whole length of his.

She said, "I can't eat any more," and gave him the rest of hers, which he took and placidly demolished. He said, through a mouthful of pastry and potato: "If I weren't so hungry, I'd make you eat it, fatten you up a bit."

"I don't want to be fat."

"But you're much too thin. You were always small enough, but now you look as though a puff of wind would blow you away. And you've cut your hair. It used to be long, right down your back, flowing about in the wind." He put out a hand and circled her wrist with his thumb and forefinger. "There's nothing of you."

"Perhaps it was the flu."

"I thought you'd be enormous after all these years of eating porridge and herrings and haggis."

"You mean, that's what people eat in Scotland."

"It's what I've been told." He let go of her wrist and peacefully finished the pasty, and then began to collect the plates and the basket and carry everything indoors. Virginia made movements as though to help, but he told her to stay where she was, so she did this, lying back in the grass and staring at the straight grey roof of the barn, and the seagulls perched there, and the scudding shapes of small, white fine-weather clouds, blown from the sea across the incredibly blue sky.

Eustace returned, carrying cigarettes and green eating apples and a Thermos of tea. Virginia lay where she was, and he tossed her an apple and she caught it, and he sat beside her again, unscrewing the cap of the Thermos.

"Tell me about Scotland."

Virginia turned the apple, cool and smooth, in her hands.

"What shall I tell you?"

"What did your husband do?"

"How do you mean?"

"Didn't he have a job?"

"Not exactly. Not a nine-to-five job. But he'd been left this estate . . ."

"Kirkton?"

". . . Yes, Kirkton . . . by an uncle. A great big house and about a thousand acres of land, and after we'd got the house in order, that seemed to take up most of his time. He grew trees, and farmed in a rather gentlemanly way . . . I mean, he had a grieve – a bailiff you'd call him – who lived in the farmhouse. Mr McGregor. It was he who really did most of the work, but Anthony was always occupied. I mean – " she finished feebly " – he seemed to be able to fill in his days."

Shooting five days a week in the season, fishing and playing golf. Driving north for the stalking, taking off for St Moritz for a couple of months every winter. It was no good trying to explain a man like Anthony Keile to a man like Eustace Philips. They belonged to different worlds.

"And what about Kirkton now?"

"I told you, the grieve looks after it."

"And the house?"

"It's empty. At least, the furniture's all there, but there's nobody living in it."

"Are you going back to this empty house?"

"I suppose so. Some time."

"What about the children?"

"They're in London, with Anthony's mother."

"Why aren't they with you?" asked Eustace, sounding not critical, merely curious, as though he simply wished to know.

"It just seemed a good idea, my coming away on my own. Alice Lingard wrote and asked me to come, and it seemed a good idea, that's all."

"Why didn't you bring the children too?"

"Oh, I don't know . . ." Even to herself her own voice sounded elaborately casual, unconvincing. "Alice doesn't have any children and her house isn't geared for them . . . I mean, everything's rather special and rare and breakable. You know how it is."

"In fact, I don't, but go on."

"Anyway, Lady Keile likes having them with her . . ."

"Lady Keile?"

"Anthony's mother. And Nanny likes going there because she used to work for Lady Keile. She was Anthony's own nanny when he was a little boy."

"But I thought the children were quite big."

"Cara's eight and Nicholas is six."

"But why do they have to have a nanny? Why can't you look after them?"

Over the years Virginia had asked herself that question time without number, and had come up with no sort of an answer, but for Eustace to voice it, unasked, out of the blue, filled her with a perverse resentment.

"What do you mean?"

"Just what I say."

"I do look after them. I mean, I see a lot of them . . ."

"If they've just lost their father, surely the one person they need to be with is their mother, not a grandmother and an old inherited nanny. They'll think everybody's deserting them."

"They won't think anything of the sort."

"If you're so sure, why are you getting so hot under the collar?"

"Because I don't like you interfering, airing your opinions about something you know nothing about."

"I know about you."

"What about me?"

"I know your infinite capacity for being pushed around."

"And who pushes me around?"

"I wouldn't know for sure." She realised with some astonishment that, in a cold way, he was becoming as angry as she. "But at a rough guess I would say your mother-in-law. Perhaps she took over where your own mother left off!"

"Don't you dare to speak about my mother like that."

"But it's true, isn't it?"

"No, it's not true."

"Then get your children down here. It's inhuman leaving them in London for the summer holidays, in weather like this, when they should be running wild by the sea and in the fields. Take your finger out, ring up your mother-in-law and tell her to put them on a train. And if Alice Lingard doesn't want them at Wheal House, because she's afraid of the ornaments getting broken, then take them to a pub, or rent a cottage . . ."

"That's exactly what I intend doing, and I didn't need you to tell me."

"Then you'd better start looking for one."

"I already have."

He was momentarily silenced, and she thought with satisfaction: That took the wind out of his sails.

But only momentarily. "Have you found anything?"

"I looked at one house this morning but it was impossible."

"Where?"

"Here. In Lanyon." He waited for her to tell him. "It was called Bosithick," she added ungraciously.

"Bosithick!" He appeared delighted. "But that's a marvellous house."

"It's a terrible house."

"Terrible?" He could not believe his ears. "You do mean the cottage up the hill where Aubrey Crane used to live? The one that the Kernows inherited from his old aunt."

"That's the one, and it's creepy and quite impossible."

"What does creepy mean? Haunted?"

"I don't know. Just creepy."

"If it's haunted by the ghost of Aubrey Crane you might have quite an amusing time. My mother remembered him, said he was a dear man. And very fond of children," he added with what seemed to Virginia a classic example of a *non sequitur*.

"I don't care what sort of a man he was, I'm not going to take the house."

"Why not?"

"Because I'm not."

"Give me three good reasons . . ."

Virginia lost her patience. "Oh, for heaven's sake . . ." She made as if to get to her feet, but Eustace, with unexpected speed for such a large man, caught her wrist in his hand and pulled her back on to the grass. She looked angrily into his eyes and saw them cold as blue stones.

"Three good reasons," he said again.

She looked down at his hand on her arm. He made no effort to move it and she said, "There's no fridge."

"I'll lend you a meat-safe. Reason number two."

"I told you. It's got a spooky atmosphere. The children have never lived anywhere like that. They'd be frightened."

"Not unless they're as hen-brained as their mother. Now, number three."

Desperately she tried to think up some good, watertight reason, something that would convince Eustace of her nameless horror of the odd little house on the hill. But all she came out with was a string of petty excuses, each sounding more feeble than the last. "It's too small, and it's dirty, and where would I wash the children's things, and I don't even know if there's an iron for the ironing or a lawn-mower to cut the grass. And there's no garden, just a sort of washing-green place, and inside all the furniture is so depressing and . . ."

He interrupted her. "These aren't reasons, Virginia, and you know they're not. They're just a lot of bloody excuses."

"Bloody excuses for *what*?"

"For not having a show-down with your mother-in-law or the old nanny or possibly both. For making a scene and asserting yourself and bringing your own children up the way you want them to go."

Fury at him caught in her throat, a great lump that rendered her speechless. She felt the blood surge to her cheeks, she began to tremble, but although he must have seen all this, he went calmly on, saying all the terrible things that the voice in the back of her head had been saying for years, but to which she had never had the moral courage to pay any attention.

"I don't think you can give a damn for your children. You don't want to be bothered with them. Someone else has always done the washing and the ironing and you're not going to start now. You're too bloody idle to take them for picnics and read them books and put them to bed. It's really nothing to do with Bosithick. Whatever house you found, you'd be sure to find something wrong with it. Any excuse would do provided you never have to admit to yourself that you can't be bloody bothered to take care of your own children."

Before the last word was out of his mouth, she was on her feet, tearing her arm free of his grip.

"It's not true! It's none of it true! I do want them! I've been wanting them ever since I got here . . .!"

"Then get them here, you little fool . . ." He was on his feet too, and they were shouting at each other across three feet of grass as though it were a desert.

"That's what I'm going to do. That's just exactly what I'm going to do."

"I'll believe that when you do it!"

She turned and fled and was into her car before she remembered her handbag, still lying on the kitchen table. By now in floods of tears, she was out of the car and running into the house to retrieve it before Eustace reached her again. Then back to the car and turning it furiously, dangerously in the narrow confines of the farmyard, then back up the lane, with a roar of the engine and a great spattering of loose gravel from the back wheels.

"Virginia!"

Through tears, through the driving mirror she saw him standing far behind her. She jammed her foot on the accelerator and swung out on to the main road without bothering to wait and see if anything was coming. By good chance there wasn't, but she didn't slow down all the way back to Porthkerris, down into the town and up the other side, parking the car on the double yellow lines outside the solicitors' office and leaving it there while she ran inside.

This time she did not ring the bell, nor wait for Miss Leddra, but went, like the wind, through the outer office to fling open wide the door of Mr Williams's room, where Mr Williams was rudely interrupted in the course of interviewing an autocratic old lady from Truro about the seventh set of alterations to her will.

Both Mr Williams and the old lady, silenced by astonishment, stared, open-mouthed. Mr Williams, recovering first, began to scramble to his feet. "Mrs Keile!" But before he could say another word Virginia had flung the keys of Bosithick on to his desk and said, "I'll take it. I'll take it right away. And as soon's I've got my children, I'm moving in!"

4

Alice said, "I'm sorry, Virginia, but I think you're making the most terrible mistake. What's more, it's a classic mistake and one so many people make when they suddenly find themselves alone in the world. You're acting on impulse, you haven't really thought about this at all . . ."

"I have thought about it."

"But the children are fine, you know they are, settled and happy with Nanny and your mother-in-law. The life they're leading is simply an extension of life at Kirkton, all the things they know and that helps them to feel secure. Their father's dead, and nothing's ever going to be the same for them again. But if there have to be changes, at least let them happen slowly, gradually; let Cara and Nicholas have time to get used to them."

"They're my children."

"But you've never looked after them. You've never had them on your own, except the odd times when Nanny could be persuaded to take a holiday. They'll exhaust you, and honestly, Virginia, at the moment I don't think you're physically capable of doing it. After all, that's why you came here, to recuperate from that loathsome flu, and generally have a little peace and quiet, give yourself time to get over the bad things that have been happening. Don't deprive yourself of that. You're going to need all your resources when you do eventually go back to Kirkton and start picking up the threads and learning to live without Anthony."

"I'm not going to Kirkton. I'm going to Bosithick. I've already paid the first week's rent."

Alice's expression stopped being patient and became exasperated.

"But it's so ridiculous! Look, if you feel so strongly about having the children down here, then have them by all means, they can stay here, but for heaven's sake let Nanny come too."

Only yesterday the idea could have been tempting. But now Virginia never even let herself consider it.

"I've made up my mind."

"But why didn't you *tell* me? Why didn't you discuss it with me?"

"I don't know. It was just something I had to do on my own."

"And where *is* Bosithick?"

"It's on the Lanyon road . . . You can't see it from the road, but it's got a sort of tower . . ."

"The place where Aubrey Crane lived? But, Virginia, it's ghastly. There's nothing there but moor and wind and cliffs. You'll be totally isolated!"

Virginia tried to turn it into a joke. "You'll have to come and see me. Make sure the children and I aren't driving each other slowly insane."

But Alice did not laugh, and Virginia, seeing her frown and the disapproving set of her mouth, was suddenly, astonishingly reminded of her own mother. It was as though Alice was no longer Virginia's contemporary, her friend, but had swung back a generation and from that lofty height was telling the young Virginia that she was being a fool. But perhaps, after all, this was not so strange. She had known Rowena Parsons long before Virginia was born, and the fact that she had no children of her own to contend with meant that her attitudes and opinions remained rigidly unchanged.

She said at last, "It isn't that I want to interfere, you know that. But I've known you all your life, and I can't stand to one side and watch you do this insane thing."

"What's so insane about having your children on holiday with you?"

"It's not just that, Virginia, and you know it. If you take them away from Lady Keile and Nanny without their approval, which I doubt very much you'll get, there's going to be one devil of a row."

Virginia felt sick at the thought of it. "Yes, I know."

"Nanny will probably take the most terrible umbrage and give in her notice."

"I know . . ."

"Your mother-in-law will do everything she can to stop you."

"I know that too."

Alice stared at her, as though she were staring at a stranger. Then suddenly, she shrugged and laughed, in a hopeless sort of way. "I don't understand. What made you suddenly so determined?"

Virginia had said nothing about her encounter with Eustace Philips and had no intention of doing so.

"Nothing. Nothing in particular."

"It must be the sea air," said Alice. "Extraordinary what it does for people." She picked a fallen newspaper off the floor, began folding it meticulously. "When are you going to London?"

"Tomorrow."

"And Lady Keile?"

"I'll phone her tonight. And Alice, I am sorry. And thank you for being so kind."

"I haven't been kind, I've been critical and disapproving. But somehow, I always think of you as someone young and helpless. I feel responsible for you."

"I'm twenty-seven. And I'm not helpless. And I'm responsible for myself."

* * *

Nanny answered the telephone. "Yes?"
"Nanny?"
"Yes."
"It's Mrs Keile."
"Oh, hello! Do you want to speak to Lady Keile?"
"Is she there?"
"Just a moment and I'll get her."
"Nanny."
"Yes."
"How are the children?"
"Oh, they're very well. Having a lovely time. Just gone to bed." (This was slipped in quickly in case Virginia should ask to speak to them.)
"Is it hot?"
"Oh, yes. Lovely. Perfect weather. Hold on and I'll tell Lady Keile you're there."
There were the sounds of Nanny putting down the receiver, her footsteps going across the hall, her distant voice. "Lady Keile!"
Virginia waited. *If I was a woman who was taking to drink I would have one in my hand, right now. A great tall tumbler of dark-coloured whisky*. But she wasn't and her stomach lay heavy with impending doom.
More footsteps, sharp, neat, unmistakable. The receiver was lifted once more.
"Virginia."
"Yes, it's me."
The situation was hideously complicated by the fact that Virginia had never known what to call her mother-in-law. "Call me Mother," she had said kindly, as soon as Virginia and Anthony were married, but somehow this was impossible. And "Lady Keile" was worse. Virginia had compromised by only corresponding by postcard or telegram, and always calling her "you".
"How nice to hear you, dear. How are you feeling?"
"I'm very well . . ."
"And the weather? I believe you're having a heatwave."

"Yes, it's unbelievable. Look . . ."

"How is Alice?"

"She's very well, too . . ."

"And the darling children, they've been swimming today – the Turners have got a delicious pool in their garden, and invited Cara and Nicholas over for the afternoon. What a pity they're in bed; why didn't you call earlier?"

Virginia said, "I've got something to tell you."

"Yes?"

She closed her hand around the receiver until her knuckles ached. "I've been able to find a little cottage, quite near here. It's near the sea, and I thought it would be nice for the children if they came down and we spent the rest of the holidays together."

She paused, waiting for comment but there was only silence.

"The thing is, the weather is so beautiful and I feel so guilty enjoying it all on my own . . . and it would be good for them to have some sea air before we all have to go back to Scotland and they have to go back to school."

Lady Keile said, "A cottage? But I thought you were staying with Alice Lingard?"

"Yes, I am. I have been. I'm calling from Wheal House now. But I've taken this cottage."

"I don't understand."

"I want the children to come down and spend the rest of the holidays with me. I'll come up tomorrow in the train to fetch them."

"But what sort of a cottage?"

"Just a cottage. A holiday cottage . . ."

"Well, if that's what you want – " Virginia began to breathe a sigh of relief. " – But it seems hard luck on Nanny. It's not often she gets the chance of being in London and seeing all her own friends." The relief swiftly died. Virginia went back into the attack again.

"Nanny doesn't have to come."

Lady Keile was confused. "I'm sorry, the line's not very clear. I thought you said Nanny didn't have to come."

"She doesn't. I can look after the children. There's not room for her anyway. I mean there isn't a bedroom for her, or a nursery . . . and it's terribly isolated, and she'd hate it."

"You mean you intend taking the children *away* from Nanny?"

"Yes."

"But she'll be most terribly upset."

"Yes, I'm afraid she will, but . . ."

"Virginia . . ." Lady Keile's voice was upset, distressed. "Virginia, we can't talk about this over the telephone."

Virginia imagined Nanny on the upstairs landing, listening to the one-sided conversation.

"We don't need to. I'm coming up to London tomorrow. I'll be with you about five o'clock. We can talk about it then."

"I think," said Lady Keile, "that that would be best."

And she rang off.

The next morning Virginia drove to Penzance, left her car in the station park and caught the train to London. It was another hot, cloudless morning and she had not had time to reserve a seat, and, despite the fact that she managed to get hold of a porter and tip him handsomely, he could only find her an empty corner in a carriage that was already uncomfortably full. Her fellow passengers were going home at the end of their annual holidays, grumpy and disconsolate at the thought of returning to work, and resentful at leaving the sea and the beaches on such a perfect day.

There was a family, a father and mother and two children. The baby slept damply in its mother's arms, but as the sun climbed higher into the unwinking sky and the train rattled northwards through the shimmering heat of a midsummer noon, the elder child became more and more fractious, whining, grizzling, never still, and grinding his dirty sandalled feet on to Virginia's every time he wanted to look out of the window. At one point, in order to keep the child quiet, his father bought him an orangeade, but no sooner was the bottle opened than the train lurched and the entire contents went all over the front of Virginia's dress.

The child was promptly slapped by his distracted mother and roared. The baby woke up and added his wails to his brother's. The father said, "Now look what you've done," and gave the child a shake for good measure, and Virginia, trying to mop herself up with face tissues, protested that it didn't matter, it couldn't be helped, it didn't matter at all.

After a good deal of screaming the child subsided into hiccuping sobs. A bottle was produced from somewhere and stuffed into the baby's mouth. It sucked for a bit, and then stopped sucking, struggled into a sitting position and was sick.

And Virginia lit a cigarette and looked firmly out of the window and prayed, "Don't let Cara and Nicholas ever be like that. Don't let them ever be like that on a railway journey, otherwise I shall go stark, staring mad."

London was airless and stuffy, the great cavern of Paddington Station hideous with noise and aimless, hurrying crowds. As soon as she was off the train Virginia, carrying her suitcase, and filthy and crumpled in her stained, sticky dress, walked the length of the platform to the booking-office and, like a secret agent making sure of his escape route, bought tickets and reserved three seats on the Riviera for the following morning. Only then did she return to the taxi rank, wait in the long queue, and finally capture a cab to take her home.

"Thirty-two Melton Gardens, please. Kensington."

"OK. 'Op in."

They went down by Sussex Gardens, across the park. The brown grass was littered with picnicking families, children in scanty clothes, couples entwined beneath the shade of trees. In Brompton Road there were window-boxes bright with flowers, shop windows filled with clothes "For Cruising", the first of the rush-hour crowds was being sucked, a steady stream of humanity, down Knightsbridge Underground.

The cab turned into the network of quiet squares that lay behind Kensington High Street, edged down narrow roads lined with parked cars, and finally turned the corner into Melton Gardens.

"It's the house by the pillar-box."

The taxi stopped. Virginia got out, put her case on the pavement, opened her bag for the fare. The driver said, "Thanks very much," and snapped up his flag, and Virginia picked up her case and turned towards the house and, as she did so, the black-painted door opened and her mother-in-law waited to let her in.

She was tall, slim, immensely good-looking. Even on this breathless day she looked cool and uncrushed, not a wrinkle in her linen dress, not a hair out of place.

Virginia went up the steps towards her.

"How clever of you to know I was here."

"I was looking out of the drawing-room window. I saw the taxi."

Her expression was friendly, smiling, but quite implacable, like the matron of a lunatic asylum come to admit a new patient. They kissed, touching cheeks.

"Did you have a terrible journey?" She closed the door behind them. The cool, pale-coloured hall smelled of beeswax and roses. At the far end steps led down to the glass side door, and beyond it could be seen the garden, the chestnut tree, the children's swing.

"Yes, it was ghastly. I feel filthy and a revolting child spilled orange juice all over me." The house was silent. "Where are the children?"

Lady Keile began to lead the way upstairs to the drawing-room. "They're out with Nanny. I thought perhaps it would be better. They won't be long, not more than half an hour. That should give us time to get this all thrashed out."

Treading behind her, Virginia said nothing. Lady Keile reached the top of the stairs, crossed the small landing and went in through the drawing-room door and Virginia followed her, and, despite her anxiety of mind, was struck, as always, by the timeless beauty of the room, the perfect proportions of the long windows which faced out over the street, open today, the fine net curtains stirring. There were long mirrors, filling the room with reflected light, and these gave back images of highly polished antique furniture, tall cabinets of blue-and-white Meissen plates, and the flowers with which Lady Keile had always surrounded herself.

They faced each other across the pale, fitted carpet. Lady Keile said, "We may as well be comfortable," and lowered herself, straight as a ramrod, into a formal, wide-lapped French chair.

Virginia sat too, on the very edge of the sofa, and tried not to feel like a domestic servant being interviewed for a job. She said, "There really isn't anything to thrash out, you know."

"I thought I must have misunderstood you on the telephone last night."

"No, you didn't misunderstand me. I decided two days ago that I wanted the children with me. I decided it was ridiculous, me being in Cornwall and them in London, specially during the summer holidays. So I went to a solicitor and I found this little house. And I've paid the rent and I've got the keys. I can move in right away."

"Does Alice Lingard know about this?"

"Of course. And she offered to have the children at

Wheal House, but by then I'd committed myself and couldn't go back."

"But Virginia, you *surely* can't mean that you want them without Nanny?"

"Yes, I do."

"But you'll never manage."

"I shall have to try."

"What you mean is that you want the children to yourself."

"Yes."

"Are you sure you aren't being a little . . . selfish?"

"*Selfish?*"

"Yes, selfish. You're not thinking of the children, are you? Only yourself."

"Perhaps I am thinking of myself, but I'm thinking of the children too."

"You can't be if you intend taking them away from Nanny."

"Have you spoken to her?"

"I had to, of course. She had to have some idea of what I understood you wanted to do. But I hoped I would be able to change your mind."

"What did she say?"

"She didn't say very much. But I could tell that she was very upset."

"Yes, I'm sure."

"You must think of Nanny, Virginia. Those children are her life. You must consider her."

"With the best will in the world I don't see that she comes into this."

"Of course she comes into it. She comes into everything that we do. Why, she's family, she's been part of the family for years, ever since Anthony was a tiny boy . . . and the way she's looked after those babies of yours, she's devoted herself, given her life to them. And you say she doesn't come into this."

"She wasn't my nanny," said Virginia. "She didn't

look after me when I was a little girl. You can't expect me to feel quite the same about her as you do."

"You really mean to say you feel no sort of loyalty towards her? After letting her bring up your children? After virtually living with her for eight years at Kirkton? I must say you fooled me. I always thought there was a very happy atmosphere between you."

"If there was a happy atmosphere it was because of me. It was because I gave in to Nanny over every little thing, just to keep the peace. Because if she didn't get her own way, she would go into a sulk that would last for days, and I simply couldn't bear it."

"I always imagined you were the mistress of your own home."

"Well, you were wrong. I wasn't. And even if I'd plucked up the courage to have a row with Nanny, and asked her to leave, Anthony would never have heard of it. He thought the sun rose and fell on her head."

At the mention of her son's name Lady Keile had gone a little pale. Her shoulders were consciously straight, her clasped hands tightened in her lap. She said, icily, "And I suppose now that no longer has to be considered."

Virginia was instantly repentant. "I didn't mean that. You know I didn't mean that. But I'm left now. I'm on my own. The children are all I have. Perhaps I'm being selfish, but I need them. I need them so badly with me. I've missed them so much since I've been away."

Outside, across the street, a car drew up, a man began to argue, a woman answered him in anger, her voice shrill with annoyance. As though the noise were more than she could stand, Lady Keile stood up and went over to close the window.

She said, "I shall miss them too."

If we had ever been close, thought Virginia, I could go now and put my arms around her and give her the comfort she is longing for. But it was not possible.

Affection had existed between them, and respect. But never love, never familiarity.

"Yes, I'm sure you will. You've been so wonderfully good to them, and to me. And I'm sorry."

Her mother-in-law turned from the window, brisk again, emotion controlled. "I think," she said, making for the bell-pull which hung at the side of the fireplace, "that it would be a good idea if we were to have a cup of tea."

The children returned at half past five. The front door opened and shut and their voices rose from the hall. Virginia laid down her teacup and sat quite still. Lady Keile waited until the footsteps had passed the landing outside the drawing-room door and were on their way upstairs to the nursery. Then she got up and went across the drawing-room and opened the door.

"Cara. Nicholas."

"Hello, Granny."

"There is someone here to see you."

"Who?"

"A lovely surprise. Come and see."

Much later, after the children had gone upstairs for their bath and supper, after Virginia herself had bathed and changed into a clean cool silk dress, and before the gong rang for dinner, she went upstairs to the nursery to see Nanny.

She found her alone, tidying away the children's supper things and straightening the room before she settled to her nightly session with the television.

Not that the room needed straightening, but Nanny could not relax until every cushion was plump and straight on the sofa, every toy put away, and the children's dirty clothes discarded, and clean ones set out for the following morning. She had always been like this, revelling in the orderly pattern of her own rigid routine. And she had always looked the same, a neat spare woman, over sixty now, but with scarcely a trace of grey in her dark hair which she wore drawn back and fastened in a bun. She appeared to be ageless, the type that would continue, unchanging, until she was an old woman when she would suddenly become senile and die.

She looked up as Virginia came into the room, and then hastily away again.

"Hello, Nanny."

"Good evening."

Her manner was frigid. Virginia shut the door and went to sit on the arm of the sofa. There was only one way to deal with Nanny in a mood and that was to jump right in off the deep end. "I'm sorry about this, Nanny."

"I don't know what you mean, I'm sure."

"I mean about my taking the children away. We're going back to Cornwall tomorrow morning. I've got seats on the train." Nanny folded the checked tablecloth, corner to corner into perfect squares. "Lady Keile said she'd spoken to you."

"She certainly mentioned something about some hare-brained scheme . . . but it was hard to believe that my ears weren't playing me tricks."

"Are you cross because I'm taking them, or because you're not coming too?"

"Who's cross? Nobody's cross, I'm sure . . ."

"Then you think it's a good idea?"

"No, that I do not. But what I think doesn't seem to matter any more, one way or the other."

She opened a drawer in the table and laid the cloth away, and shut the drawer with a little slam which instantly betrayed her scarcely-banked rage. But her face remained cool, her mouth primly set.

"You know that what you think matters. You've done so much for the children. You mustn't think I'm not grateful. But they're not babies any longer."

"And what is that meant to convey, if I might ask?"

"Just that I can look after them now."

Nanny turned from the table. For the first time, her eyes met Virginia's. And as they watched each other, Virginia saw the slow, angry flush spread up Nanny's neck, up her face, up to her hairline.

She said, "Are you giving me my notice?"

"No, that's not what I intended at all. But perhaps, now we've started to discuss it, it would be the best thing. For your sake as much as anyone else's. Perhaps it would be better for you."

"And why would it be better for me? All my life I've given to this family, why, I had Anthony to look after from the beginning, and there was no reason why I should come up to Scotland and take care of your babies, I never wanted to go, to leave London, but Lady Keile asked me, and because it was the family, I went, a real sacrifice I made, and this is all the thanks I get . . ."

"Nanny – " Virginia interrupted gently when Nanny paused for a breath " – it would be better for you because of this. For that very reason. Wouldn't it be better to make a clean break, and maybe have a new baby to take care of, a new little family? You know how you always said a nursery wasn't a nursery without a little baby, and Nicholas is six now . . ."

"I never thought I'd live to see the day . . ."

"And if you don't want to do that, then why not speak to Lady Keile? You could maybe make some arrangement with her. You get on so well together, and you like being in London, with all your friends . . ."

"I don't need you to give me any suggestions, thank you very much . . . given up the best years of my life . . . bringing up your children . . . never expected any thanks . . . never would have happened if poor Anthony . . . if Anthony had been alive . . ."

It went on and on, and Virginia sat and listened, letting the invective pour over her. She told herself that this was the least she could do. It was over, it was done, and she was free. Nothing else mattered. To wait, politely, for Nanny to finish was no more than a salute of respect, a tribute paid by the victor to the vanquished after a bloodthirsty but honourable battle.

Afterwards, she went to say good night to the children. Nicholas was already asleep, but Cara was still deep in her book. When her mother came into the room, she looked up slowly, dragging her eyes away from the printed page. Virginia sat on the edge of her bed.

"What are you reading now?"

Cara showed her. "It's *The Treasure Seekers*."

"Oh I remember that. Where did you find it?"

"In the nursery bookcase."

Carefully, she marked the place in her book with a cross-stitched marker she had made herself, closed it and put it down on her bedside table. "Have you been talking to Nanny?"

"Yes."

"She's been funny all day."

"Has she, Cara?"

"Is something wrong?"

It was hard to be so perceptive, so sensitive to atmosphere when you were only eight years old. Especially when you were shy and not very pretty and had to wear round steel spectacles that made you look like a little owl.

"No, nothing's wrong. Just different. And new."

"What do you mean?"

"Well, I'm going back to Cornwall tomorrow morning in the train, and I'm going to take you and Nicholas with me. Will you like that?"

"You mean . . ." Cara's face lit up. "We're going to stay with Aunt Alice?"

"No, we're going to stay in a house on our own. A funny little house called Bosithick. And we're going to have to do all the housekeeping ourselves and the cooking . . ."

"Isn't Nanny coming?"

"No. Nanny's staying here."

There was a long silence. Virginia said, "Do . . . you mind?"

"No, I don't mind. But I expect she will. That's why she's been so funny."

"It's not easy for Nanny. You and Nicholas have been her babies ever since you were born. But somehow I think you're growing out of Nanny now, like you grow out of coats and dresses . . . You're both old enough to look after yourselves."

"You mean, Nanny's not going to live with us any more?"

"No, she's not."

"Where will she live?"

"She'll maybe go and find another little new baby to take care of. Or she may stay here with Granny."

"She likes being in London," said Cara. "She told me so. She likes it much better than Scotland."

"Well, there you are!"

Cara considered this for a moment. Then she said, "When are we going to Cornwall?"

"I told you. Tomorrow on the train."

"When will we leave?" She liked everything cut and dried.

"About half past nine. We'll get a taxi to the station."

"And when are we going back to Kirkton?"

"I expect when the holidays are over. When you have to go back to school." Cara remained silent. It was impossible to tell what she was thinking. Virginia said, "It's time to go to sleep now . . . we've got a long day tomorrow," and she leaned forward and gently unhooked Cara's spectacles and kissed her good night.

But as she went towards the door, Cara spoke again. "Mummy."

Virginia turned. "Yes."

"You came."

Virginia frowned, not understanding.

"You came," said Cara again. "I said to write to me, but you came instead."

Virginia remembered the letter from Cara, the catalyst that had started everything off. She smiled. "Yes," she said. "I came. It seemed better." And she went out of the room, and downstairs to endure the ordeal of a silent dinner in the company of Lady Keile.

5

Virginia awoke slowly, to a quite unaccustomed mood of achievement. She felt purposeful and strong, two such alien sensations that it was worth lying for a little, quietly, to savour them. Pillowed in Lady Keile's incomparably comfortable spare bed, lapped in hemstitched linen and cloudy blankets, she watched the early sunshine of another perfect summer morning seep in long strands of gold through the leafy branches of the chestnut tree. The bad things were over, the dreaded hurdles somehow cleared, and in a couple of hours she and the children would be on their way. She told herself that after last night she would never be afraid to tackle anything, no problem was insurmountable, no problem too knotty. She let her imagination move cautiously forward to the weeks ahead, to the pitfalls of coping with Cara and Nicholas single-handed, the discomfort and inconvenience of the little house she had so recklessly rented for them, and still her good spirits remained undismayed. She had turned a corner. From now on everything was going to be different.

It was half past seven. She got up, revelling in the fine weather, the sound of bird-song, the pleasant, distant hum of traffic. She bathed and dressed and packed and stripped her bed and went downstairs.

Nanny and the children always had breakfast in the nursery and Lady Keile had hers on a tray in her bedroom, but this was a perfectly ordered household and

Virginia found that coffee had been set out for her on the dining-room hotplate, and a single place laid at the head of the polished table.

She drank two cups of scalding black coffee and ate toast and marmalade. Then she took the key from the table to the hall and let herself out of the front door into the quiet morning streets and walked down to the small old-fashioned grocer's patronised by Lady Keile. There she laid in sufficient provisions to start them off when they eventually got back to Bosithick. Bread and butter and bacon and eggs and coffee and cocoa, and baked beans (which she knew Nicholas adored, but Nanny had never approved of) and tomato soup and chocolate biscuits. Milk and vegetables they would have to find when they got down there, meat and fish could come later. She paid for all this, and the grocer packed it for her in a stout cardboard carton and she walked back to Melton Gardens with her weighty load carried before her in both arms.

She found the children and Lady Keile downstairs; no sign of Nanny. But the small suitcases, doubtless perfectly packed, were lined up in the hall, and Virginia dumped the carton of groceries down beside them.

"Hello, Mummy!"

"Hello." She kissed them both. They were clean and tidy, ready for their journey, Cara in a blue cotton dress and Nicholas in shorts and a striped shirt, his dark hair lately flattened by a hairbrush. "What have you been doing?" he wanted to know.

"I've been buying some groceries. We probably won't have time to go shopping when we get to Penzance; it would be terrible if we didn't have anything to eat."

"I didn't know till this morning when Cara told me. I didn't know till I woke up that we were going in the train."

"I'm sorry. You were asleep last night when I came in to tell you and I didn't want to disturb you."

"I wish you had. I didn't know until *breakfast*." He was very resentful.

Smiling at him, Virginia looked up at her mother-in-law. Lady Keile was drawn and pale. Otherwise she looked, as always, perfectly groomed, quite in charge of the situation. Virginia wondered if she had slept at all.

"You should telephone for a taxi," said Lady Keile. "You don't want to risk missing the train. It's always best to be on the early side. There's a number by the telephone."

Wishing that she had thought of this herself Virginia went to do as she was told. The clock in the hall struck a quarter past nine. In ten minutes' time the taxi was there and they were ready to leave.

"But we have to say goodbye to Nanny!" said Cara.

Virginia said, "Yes, of course. Where is Nanny?"

"She's in the nursery." Cara started for the stairs, but Virginia said, "No."

Cara turned and stared, shocked by the unaccustomed tone of her mother's voice.

"But we *have* to say goodbye."

"Of course. Nanny will come down and see you off. I'll go up now and tell her we're just on our way. You get everything together."

She found Nanny determinedly occupied in some entirely unnecessary task.

"Nanny, we're just going."

"Oh, yes."

"The children want to say goodbye."

Silence.

Last night Virginia had been sorry for her, had, in a funny way, respected her. But now all she wanted to do was take Nanny by her shoulders and shake her till her stupid head fell off. "Nanny, this is ridiculous. You can't let it end this way. Come downstairs and say goodbye to them."

It was the first direct order she had ever given to

Nanny. The first, she thought, and the last. Like Cara, Nanny was obviously shaken. For a moment she stalled, her mouth worked, she seemed to be trying to think up some excuse. Virginia caught her eye and held it. Nanny tried to stare her out, but was defeated, her eyes slid away. It was the final triumph.

"Very well, madam," said Nanny and followed Virginia back down to the hall, where the children rushed at her in the most gratifying way, hugged her and kissed her as though she were the only person in the world they loved, and then, with this demonstration of affection safely over, ran down the steps and across the pavement and into the waiting taxi.

"Goodbye," said Virginia to her mother-in-law. There was nothing more to be said. They kissed once more, leaning cheeks, kissing the air. "And goodbye, Nanny." But Nanny was already on her way up to the nursery again, fumbling for her handkerchief and blowing her nose. Only her legs were visible, treading upstairs, and the next moment she had reached the turn of the landing and disappeared.

She need have had no fear about her children's behaviour. The novelty of the train journey did not excite, but silenced them. They had not often been taken on holiday, and never to the seaside, and when they travelled to London to stay with their grandmother had been bundled into the night train already dressed in their pyjamas and had slept the journey away.

Now, they stared from the window at the racing countryside as though they had neither of them ever seen fields or farms or cows or towns before. After a little, when the charm of this wore off, Nicholas opened the present Virginia had bought for him at Paddington and smiled with satisfaction when he saw the little red tractor.

He said, "It's like the Kirkton one. Mr McGregor had a Massey Ferguson just like this." He spun the wheels and made tractor noises in the back of his throat, running the toy up and down the prickly British Rail upholstery.

But Cara did not even open her comic. It lay folded on her lap, and she continued to stare out of the window, her bulging forehead leaning against the glass, her eyes intent behind her spectacles, missing nothing.

At half past twelve they went for lunch and this was another adventure, lurching down the corridor, rushing through the scary connections before the carriages came apart. The dining-car they found enthralling, the tables and the little lights, the indulgent waiter and the grown-upness of being handed a menu.

"And what would madam like?" the waiter asked, and Cara went pink with embarrassed giggles when she realised that he was speaking to her, and had to be helped to order tomato soup and fried fish, and to decide the world-shaking problem of whether she would eat a white ice-cream or a pink.

Watching their faces Virginia thought: Because it's new and exciting to them, it's new and exciting for me. The most trivial, ordinary occurrences will become special because I shall see them through Cara's eyes. And if Nicholas asks me questions that I can't answer, I shall have to go and look them up and I shall become informed and knowledgeable and a brilliant conversationalist.

The idea was funny. She laughed suddenly, and Cara stared and then laughed back, not knowing what the joke was, but delighted to be sharing it with her mother.

"When did you first come on this train down to Cornwall?" Cara asked.

"When I was seventeen. Ten years ago."

"Didn't you come when you were a little girl my age?"

"No, I didn't. I used to go to an aunt in Sussex."

Now, it was afternoon and they had the compartment to themselves. Nicholas, charmed by the adventure of the corridor, had elected to stay out there, and could be seen straddle-legged, trying to adjust his small weight to the rocking of the train.

"Tell me."

"What? About Sussex?"

"No. About coming to Cornwall."

"Well, we just came. My mother and I, to stay with Alice and Tom Lingard. I'd just left school, and Alice wrote to invite us, and my mother thought it would be nice to have a holiday."

"Was it a summer holiday?"

"No. It was Easter. Springtime. All the daffodils were out and the railway cuttings were thick with primroses."

"Was it hot?"

"Not really. But sunny, and much warmer than Scotland. In Scotland we never really have a proper spring, do we? One day it's winter and the next day all the leaves are out on the trees and it's summertime. At least that's the way it's always seemed to me. In Cornwall the spring is quite a long season . . . that's why they're able to grow all the lovely flowers and send them to Covent Garden to be sold."

"Did you swim?"

"No. The sea would have been icy."

"But in Aunt Alice's pool?"

"She didn't have a pool in those days."

"Will we swim in Aunt Alice's pool?"

"Sure to."

"Will we swim in the sea?"

"Yes, we'll find a lovely beach and swim there."

"I . . . I'm not very good at swimming."

"It's easier in the sea than in ordinary water. The salt helps you to float."

"But don't the waves splash into your face?"

"A little. But that's part of the fun."

Cara considered this. She did not like getting her face wet. Without her spectacles things became blurred and she couldn't swim with her spectacles on.

"What else did you do?"

"Oh, we used to go out in the car, and go shopping. And if it was warm we used to sit in the garden, and Alice used to have friends to tea, and people for dinner. And sometimes I used to go for walks. There are lovely walks there. Up to the hill behind the house, or down into Porthkerris. The streets are all steep and narrow, so narrow you could scarcely get a car down them. And there were lots of little stray cats, and the harbour, with fishing boats and old men sitting around enjoying the sunshine. And sometimes the tide was in and all the boats were bobbing about in the deep blue water, and sometimes it was out, and there'd be nothing but gold sand, and all the boats would be leaning on their sides."

"Didn't they fall over?"

"I don't think so."

"Why?"

"I haven't any idea," said Virginia.

There had been a special day, an April day of wind and sunshine. On that day the tide was high, Virginia could remember the salt smell of it, mixed with the evocative sea-going smells of tar and fresh paint.

Within the shelter of the quay the water swelled smooth and glassy, clear and deep. But beyond the harbour it was rough, the dark ocean flecked with white horses and, out across the bay, the great seas creamed against the rocks at the foot of the lighthouse, sending up spouts of white spray almost as high as the lighthouse itself.

It was a week since the night of the barbecue at Lanyon, and for once Virginia was on her own. Alice had driven to Penzance to attend some committee meeting, Tom Lingard was in Plymouth, Mrs Jilkes, the cook, had her afternoon off and had departed, in a considerable hat to visit her cousin's wife, and Mrs Parsons was keeping her weekly appointment with the hairdresser.

"You'll have to amuse yourself," she told Virginia over lunch.

"I'll be all right."

"What will you do?"

"I don't know. Something."

In the empty house, with the empty afternoon lying, like a gift, before her, she had considered a number of possibilities. But the marvellous day was too beautiful to be wasted, and she had gone out and started walking, and her feet had taken her down the narrow path that led to the cliffs, and then along the cliff path, and down to the white sickle of the beach. In the summer this would be crowded with coloured tents and ice-cream stalls and noisy holidaymakers with beach balls and umbrellas, but in April the visitors had not started to arrive, and the sand lay clean, washed by the winter storms, and her footsteps left a line of prints, neat and precise as little stitches.

At the far end, a lane leaned uphill and she was soon lost in a maze of narrow streets that wound between ancient, sun-bleached houses. She came upon flights of stone steps and unsuspected alleys and followed them down until all at once she turned a corner out at the very edge of the harbour. In a dazzle of sunshine she saw the bright-painted boats, the peacock-green water. Gulls screamed and wheeled overhead, their great wings like white sails against the blue, and everywhere there was activity and bustle, a regular spring-cleaning going on. Shop-fronts were being whitewashed, windows polished, ropes coiled, decks scrubbed, nets mended.

At the edge of the quay a hopeful vendor had set up his ice-cream barrow, shiny white, and lettered seductively "Fred Hoskings, Cornish Ice-cream, The Best Home-made" and Virginia suddenly longed for one, and wished she had brought some money. To sit in the sunshine on such a day and lick an ice-cream seemed, all at once, the height of luxury. The more she thought about it the more desirable it seemed, and she even went through all her pockets in the hope of finding some forgotten coin, but there was nothing there. Not so much as a halfpenny.

She sat on a bollard and gazed disconsolately down on to the deck of a fishing boat where a young boy in a salt-stained smock was brewing up tea on a spirit lamp. She was trying not to think about the ice-cream when, like the answer to a prayer, a voice spoke from behind her.

"Hello."

Virginia looked around over her shoulder, pushing her long dark hair out of her face, and saw him standing there, braced against the wind, with a package under his arm, and wearing a blue polo-necked sweater that made him look like a sailor.

She stood up. "Hello."

"I thought it was you," said Eustace Philips, "but I couldn't be sure. What are you doing here?"

"Nothing. I mean, I just came for a walk, and I stopped to look at the boats."

"It's a lovely day."

"Yes."

His blue eyes gleamed, amused. "Where's Alice Lingard?"

"She's gone to Penzance . . . she's on a committee . . ."

"So you're all alone?"

"Yes." She was wearing worn blue sneakers, blue jeans and a white cable-stitch sweater, and felt miserably convinced that her naiveté was painfully obvious not only in her clothes but her lack of small-talk as well.

She looked at his package. "What are *you* doing here?"

"I came in to pick up a new rick cover. The wind last night blew the old one to ribbons."

"I expect you're going back now."

"Not immediately. How about you?"

"I'm not doing anything. Just exploring, I suppose."

"Don't you know the town?"

"I've never got this far before."

"Come along then, I'll show you the rest of it."

They began to walk back along the quay, in no hurry, their slow paces matched. He caught sight of the ice-cream barrow and stopped to talk.

"Hello, Fred."

The ice-cream man, resplendent in a white starched coat like a cricket umpire, turned and saw him. A smile spread across features browned and wizened as a walnut.

"'Allo, Eustace. 'Ow are you?"

"Fine. How's yourself?"

"Oh, keeping not too bad. Don't often see you down 'ere. 'Ow are things out at Lanyon?"

"All right. Working hard." Eustace ducked his head at the barrow. "You're early out. There's nobody here yet to buy ice-creams."

"Oh well, early bird catches the worm I always say."

Eustace looked at Virginia. "Do you want an ice-cream?"

She could not think of any person who had offered her, so instantly, exactly what she wanted most.

"I'd love one, but I haven't any money."

Eustace grinned. "The biggest you've got," he said to Fred, and reached his hand into the back pocket of his trousers.

He took her the length of the wharf, up cobbled streets at whose existence she had never even guessed, through small, surprising squares, where the houses had yellow doors and window-boxes, past little courtyards filled with washing-lines and flights of stone steps where the cats lay and sunned themselves and attended to their ablutions. They came out at last on to a northern beach which lay with its face to the wind, and the long combers rolled in jade green with the sun behind them, and the air was misted with blown spume.

"When I was a boy," Eustace told her, raising his voice above the wind, "I used to come here with a surf-board. A little wooden one my uncle made me, with a face painted on the curve. But now they have these Malibu surf-boards, made of fibreglass they are and they surf all year round, winter and summer."

"Isn't it cold?"

"They wear wet suits."

They came to a sea wall, curved against the wind with a wooden bench built into its angle and here Eustace, apparently deciding that they had walked far enough, settled himself, his back to the wall and his face to the sun and his long legs stretched in front of him.

Virginia, consuming the last of the mammoth ice-cream, sat beside him. He watched her, and when she had demolished the final mouthful and was wiping her fingers on the knees of her jeans he said, "Did you enjoy it?"

His face was serious but his eyes laughed at her. She didn't mind. "It was delicious. The best. You should have had one too."

"I'm too big and too old to go walking round the streets licking an ice-cream."

"I shall never be too big or too old."

"How old are you?"

"Seventeen, nearly eighteen."

"Have you left school?"

"Yes, last summer."

"What are you doing now?"

"Nothing."

"Are you going to university?"

She was flattered that he should imagine she was so clever. "Goodness, no."

"What are you going to do, then?"

Virginia wished that he had not asked.

"Well, eventually, I suppose, next winter I'll learn how to cook or do shorthand and typing or something gruesome like that. But you see my mother has this bee in her bonnet about being in London for the summer and going to all the parties and meeting all the right people and generally having a social whirl."

"I believe," said Eustace, "it's called 'Doing the Season'."

His tone of voice made it very clear that he thought as little of the idea as she did.

"Oh, don't. It gives me the shivers."

"It's hard to believe, in this day and age, that anybody bothers any more."

"I know, it's fantastic. But they do. And my mother's one of them. She's already met some of the other mothers and had ghastly tea parties with them. She's even booked a date for a dance, but I'm going to try my hardest to talk her out of that one. Can you think of anything worse than having a coming-out dance?"

"No, I can't, but then I'm not a sweet seventeen-year-old." Virginia made a face at him. "If you feel so strongly about it why don't you dig in your toes, tell your mother you'd rather have the price of a return ticket to Australia or something?"

"I already have. At least I've tried. But you don't know my mother. She never listens to anything I say, she just says that it's so *important* to meet all the right people, and be asked to all the right parties and be seen in all the right places."

"You could try getting your father on your side."

"I haven't got a father. At least I never see him; they were divorced when I was a baby."

"I see." He added, without much heart: "Well, cheer up – who knows – you might enjoy it."

"I shall hate every moment of it."

"How do you know?"

"Because I'm useless at parties, and I get tongue-tied with strangers, and I can never think of anything to say to young men."

"You're thinking of plenty to say to me," Eustace pointed out.

"But you're different."

"How am I different?"

"Well, you're older. I mean you're not young." Eustace began to laugh and Virginia was embarrassed. "I mean you're not really young, like twenty-one or twenty-two." He was still laughing. She frowned. "How old *are* you?"

"Twenty-eight," he told her. "Twenty-nine next birthday."

"You are lucky. I wish I was twenty-eight."

"If you were," said Eustace, "you probably wouldn't be here now."

All at once it turned dark and cold. Virginia shivered, and looked up and saw that the sun had disappeared behind a large grey cloud, the vanguard of a bank of dirty weather which was blowing in from the west.

"That's it," said Eustace. "We've had the best of the day. It'll be raining by this evening." He looked at his watch. "It's nearly four o'clock, time I made for home. How are you getting back?"

"Walking, I suppose."

"Do you want a ride?"

"Have you got a car?"

"I've got a Land-Rover, parked round by the church."

"Won't I be taking you out of your way?"

"No. I can go back to Lanyon over the moor."

"Well, if you're certain . . ."

Driving back to Wheal House, Virginia fell silent. But it was a natural, companionable silence, comfortable as an old shoe, and had nothing to do with being shy or unable to think of anything to say. She could not remember when she had felt so at ease with a person – and certainly never with a man whom she had known such a short time. The Land-Rover was an old one, the seats worn and dusty and there were stray scraps of straw lying about the floor and a faint smell of farmyard manure. Virginia did not find this in the least offensive – rather, she liked it because it was part of Penfolda. She realised that she wanted, above all things, to go back there. To see the farm and the fields in daylight, to inspect the stock and be shown around, perhaps to be allowed to see the rest of the farmhouse and be asked to tea in that enviable kitchen. To be accepted.

They came up the hill out of the town, where the houses of the old residential area had all been turned into hotels, with gardens bulldozed into car parks, and glassed-in porches. There were sun-rooms and palm trees, dismal against the grey sky, and municipal flower-beds planted with straight rows of daffodils.

High above the sea, the road levelled out. Eustace changed into top gear and said, "When are you going back to London?"

"I don't know. In about a week."

"Do you want to come out to Penfolda again?"

This was the second time that day that he had offered her what she craved most. She wondered if he were psychic.

"Yes, I'd love to."

"My mother was very taken with you. Not often she sees a new face. It would be nice for her if you'd come and have a cup of tea with her."

"I'd like to come."

"How would you get out to Lanyon?" asked Eustace, his eyes on the road ahead.

"I could borrow Alice's car. I'm sure if I asked her she'd let me borrow it. I'd be very careful."

"Can you drive?"

"Of course. Otherwise I wouldn't borrow the car." She smiled at him. Not because it was meant to be a joke, but because all at once she felt so good.

"Well, I'll tell you," said Eustace in his deliberate way. "I'll have a word with my mother, find out which day suits her best, give you a ring on the telephone. How would that be?"

She imagined waiting for the call, having it come, hearing his voice over the wire. She almost hugged herself with pleasure.

"It would be all right."

"What's the number?"

"Porthkerris three two five."

"I'll remember that."

They had reached home. He turned into the white gates of Wheal House and roared up the drive between the hedges of escallonia.

"There you are!" He stopped with a great jerk of brakes and a splattering of gravel. "Home safely, just in time for tea."

"Thank you so much."

He leaned on the wheel, smiling at her. "That's all right."

"I mean, for everything. The ice-cream and everything."

"You're welcome." He reached across and opened the door for her. Virginia jumped down on to the gravel, and as she did so, the front door opened and Mrs Parsons emerged, wearing a little suit of raspberry-red wool, and a white silk shirt, tied like a stock at the neck.

"Virginia!"

Virginia swung around. Her mother came across the gravel towards them, immaculate as always, but her hair, short and dark, blew casually in the wind and had obviously not been attended to that afternoon.

"Mother!"

"Where have you been?" The smile was friendly and interested.

"I thought you were at the hairdresser."

"The girl who usually does me is in bed with a cold. They offered me another girl of course, but, as she's the one who usually spends her days sweeping hair off the floor, I declined with thanks." Still smiling, she looked beyond Virginia to where Eustace waited. "And who is your friend?"

"Oh. It's Eustace Philips . . ."

But now Eustace had decided to get out of the car. He jumped down on to the gravel and came around the front of the Land-Rover to be introduced. And, hating herself, Virginia saw him through her mother's eyes: the wide powerful shoulders beneath the sailor's sweater, the sun-burned face, the strong, calloused hands.

Mrs Parsons came forward graciously. "How do you do."

"Hello," said Eustace, meeting her eyes with an unblinking blue gaze. Her hand was halfway out to shake his, but Eustace either didn't see this or chose to ignore it. Mrs Parsons's hand dropped back to her side. Her manner became, subtly, a fraction more cool.

"Where did Virginia meet *you*?" The question was harmless, even playful.

Eustace leaned against the Land-Rover and crossed his arms. "I live out at Lanyon; farm Penfolda . . ."

"Oh, of course, the barbecue. Yes, I heard all about it. And how nice that you met up again today."

"By chance," said Eustace, firmly.

"But that makes it even nicer!" She smiled. "We're just going to have tea, Mr Philips. Won't you join us?"

Eustace shook his head. His eyes never left her face. "I've got seventy cows waiting to be milked. I'd better be getting back . . ."

"Oh, of course. I wouldn't want to keep you from

your work." Her tone was that of the lady of the house dismissing the gardener, but she continued to smile.

"I wouldn't let you," said Eustace, and went to get back into the car.

"Goodbye, Virginia."

"Oh. Goodbye," said Virginia faintly. "And thank you for bringing me home."

"I'll ring you up some time."

"Yes, do that."

He gave a final salute with his head, then started the engine, put the Land-Rover into gear, and without a backward glance, shot away, down the drive and out of sight, leaving Virginia and her mother standing, staring after him, in a cloud of dust.

"Well!" said Mrs Parsons, laughing, but obviously nettled.

Virginia said nothing. There did not seem to be anything to say.

"What a very basic young man! I must say, staying down here, one does meet all types. What's he going to ring you up about?"

The tone of her voice implied that Eustace Philips was something of a joke, a joke that she and Virginia shared.

"He thought perhaps I might go out to Lanyon and have tea with his mother."

"Isn't that marvellous? Pure *Cold Comfort Farm*." It began, very lightly, to rain. Mrs Parsons glanced at the lowering sky and shivered. "What are we doing, standing out here in the wind? Come along, tea's waiting . . ."

Virginia thought nothing of the shiver, but the next morning her mother complained of feeling unwell, she had a cold, she said, an upset stomach, she would stay indoors. As the weather was horrible nobody questioned this, and Alice laid and lit a cheerful fire in the drawing-room, and by this Mrs Parsons reclined on the sofa, a light mohair rug over her knees.

"I shall be perfectly all right," she told Virginia, "and you and Alice must just go off and not bother about me at all."

"What do you mean, we must just go off! Where is there to go off to?"

"To Falmouth. To lunch at Pendrane." Virginia stared blankly. "Oh, darling, don't look so gormless, Mrs Menheniot asked us ages ago. She wanted to show us the garden."

"Nobody ever told me," said Virginia, who did not want to go. It would take all day to get to Falmouth and back again and have lunch and see the boring garden. She wanted to stay here and sit by the telephone and wait for Eustace to ring.

"Well, I'm telling you now. You'll have to change. You can't go out for lunch dressed in jeans. Why not wear that pretty blue shirt I bought for you? Or the tartan kilt? I'm sure Mrs Menheniot would be amused by your kilt."

If she had been any other sort of a mother Virginia would have asked her to listen for the telephone, to take a message. But her mother did not like Eustace. She thought him ill-mannered and uncouth, and her smiling reference to *Cold Comfort Farm* had put the official stamp of disapproval upon him. Since his departure his name had not been mentioned, and although, during dinner last night, Virginia had tried more than once to tell Alice and Tom about her chance encounter, her mother had always firmly overridden the conversation, interrupting if necessary, and steering it into more suitable channels. While she changed, Virginia debated what to do.

Eventually, dressed in the kilt and a canary yellow sweater, with her dark hair brushed clean and shining, she went along to the kitchen to find Mrs Jilkes. Mrs Jilkes was a new friend. One wet afternoon she had taught Virginia to make scones, at the same time regaling her with a great deal of gratuitous information concerning the health and longevity of Mrs Jilkes's numerous relations.

"'Allo, Virginia."

She was rolling pastry. Virginia took a scrap and began, absently, to eat it.

"Now, don't go eating that! You'll fill yourself up, won't have no room for your lunch."

"I wish I didn't have to go. Mrs Jilkes, if a phone call comes through for me, would you take a message?"

Mrs Jilkes looked coy, rolling her eyes. "Expecting a phone call are you? Some young man, is it?"

Virginia blushed. "Well, all right, yes. But you will listen, won't you?"

"Don't you worry, my love. Now, there's Mrs Lingard calling . . . time you was off. And I'll keep an eye on your mother, and give her a little lunch on a tray."

They did not return home until half past five. Alice went at once to the drawing-room, to inquire for Rowena Parsons's health, and to tell her all that they had done and seen. Virginia had made for the stairs, but the instant the drawing-room door was safely closed, turned and sprinted down the kitchen passage.

"Mrs Jilkes!"

"Back again, are you?"

"Was there a phone call?"

"Yes, two or three, but your mother answered them."

"Mother?"

"Yes, she had the phone switched through to the drawing-room. You'll have to ask her if there are any messages."

Virginia went out of the kitchen, and back down the passage, across the hall and into the drawing-room. Across Alice Lingard's head, her eyes met and held her mother's cool gaze. Then Mrs Parsons smiled.

"Darling! I've been hearing all about it. Was it fun?"

"It was all right." She waited, giving her mother the

chance to tell her that the telephone call had come through.

"All right? No more? I believe Mrs Menheniot's nephew was there?"

". . . Yes."

Already the image of the chinless young man was so blurred that she could scarcely remember his face. Perhaps Eustace would ring tomorrow. He couldn't have phoned today. Virginia knew her mother. Knew that, however much she disapproved, Mrs Parsons would be meticulous about such social obligations as passing on telephone messages. Mothers were like that. They had to be. Because if they didn't live by the code of behaviour which they preached, then they lost all right to their children's trust. And without trust there could be no affection. And without affection, nothing.

The next day it rained. All morning, Virginia sat by the fire in the hall, pretending to read a book, and flying to answer the telephone each time it rang. It was never for her; it was never Eustace.

After lunch her mother asked her to go down to the chemist in Porthkerris to pick up a prescription. Virginia said she didn't want to go.

". . . It's pouring with rain."

"A little rain won't hurt you. Besides, the exercise will do you good. You've been sitting indoors all day, reading that silly book."

"It's not a silly book . . ."

"Well, anyway, reading. Put on some wellingtons and a raincoat and you won't even notice the rain . . ."

It was no good arguing. Virginia made a resigned face and went to find her raincoat. Trudging down the road towards the town, the pavements dank and grey between the dripping trees, she tried to face up to the unthinkable possibility that Eustace was never going to ring her.

He had said that he would, certainly, but it all seemed to depend on what his mother said, when she would be free, when Virginia would be able to borrow the car and drive herself out to Lanyon.

Perhaps Mrs Philips had changed her mind. Perhaps she had said, "Oh Eustace, I haven't got time for tea parties . . . what were you thinking of, saying she could come out here?"

Perhaps, having met Virginia's mother, Eustace had changed his own mind about Virginia. They said that if you wanted to know what sort of a wife a girl was going to turn into, you looked at her mother. Perhaps Eustace had looked and decided that he did not like what he saw. She remembered the challenge in his unblinking blue eyes, and that final bitter exchange.

I wouldn't want to keep you from your work.

I wouldn't let you.

Perhaps he had forgotten to telephone. Perhaps he had had second thoughts. Or perhaps – and this was chilling – Virginia had misconstrued his friendliness, unburdened all her problems, and so aroused his sympathy. Perhaps that was all it was. That he was sorry for her.

But he said he would telephone. He said he would.

She collected the prescription and started home once more. It was still raining. Across the street from the chemist stood a call-box. It was empty. It would all be so simple. It wouldn't take a moment to look up his number, to dial. She had her purse in her pocket, with coins to pay for the call. *It's Virginia,* she would say, and make a joke of it, teasing him. *I thought you were going to ring me up!*

She almost crossed the road. At the edge of the pavement she hesitated, trying to pluck up the courage to take the initiative in a situation which was beyond her.

She imagined the conversation.

"Eustace?"

"Yes."

"This is Virginia."

"Virginia?"

"Virginia Parsons."

"Oh, yes. Virginia Parsons. What do you want?"

But at this point her courage turned on its heels and fled, and Virginia never crossed the road to the telephone box, but carried on up the hill with the rain in her face and her mother's pills deep in the pocket of her waterproof coat.

As she came in through the front door of Wheal House she heard the telephone ringing, but by the time she had got her wellingtons off the ringing had stopped, and by the time she burst into the drawing-room, her mother was just putting down the receiver.

She raised her eyebrows at her breathless daughter.

"Whatever's wrong?"

"I . . . I thought it might be for me."

"No. A wrong number. Did you get my pills, darling?"

"Yes," said Virginia dully.

"Sweet of you. And the walk has done you good. I can tell. Your cheeks are quite pink again."

The next day Mrs Parsons announced out of the blue that they must return to London. Alice was astonished. "But, Rowena, I thought you were going to stay at least another week."

"Darling, we'd love to, but you know, we do have a very busy summer to put in, and a lot of arrangements and organisation to be seen to. I don't think we can sit here enjoying ourselves for another week. Much as I would adore to."

"Well, anyway, stay over the weekend."

Yes, stay over the weekend, Virginia prayed. *Please, please, please stay over the weekend.*

But it wasn't any use. "Oh, adore to, but we must go . . . Friday at the latest I'm afraid. I'll have to see about booking seats on the train."

"Well, it seems a shame, but if you really mean it . . ."

"Yes, darling, I really do mean it."

Let him remember. Let him phone. There wouldn't be time to go out to Penfolda but at least I could say goodbye, I'd know that he'd meant it . . . perhaps I could say I'd write to him, perhaps I could give him my address.

"Darling, I wish you'd get on with your packing. Don't leave anything behind, it would be such a bore for poor Alice to have to parcel it up. Have you put your raincoat in?"

This evening. He'll ring this evening. He'll say, I am sorry but I've been away; I've been so busy I haven't had a moment; I've been ill.

"Virginia! Come and write your name in the visitors' book! There, under mine. Oh, Alice, my dear, what a wonderful holiday you've given us. Sheer delight. We've both adored it, haven't we, Virginia? Can't bear to go."

They went. Alice drove them to the station, saw them into their first-class carriage, the corner seats reserved, the porter being deferential because of Mrs Parsons's expensive luggage.

"You'll come again soon," said Alice as Virginia leaned out of the window to kiss her.

"Yes."

"We've loved having you . . ."

It was the last chance. *Tell Eustace I had to go. Tell him goodbye for me.* The whistle shrilled, the train began to move. *Ring him up when you get back.*

"Goodbye, Virginia."

Send him my love. Tell him I love him.

By Truro her misery had become so obvious with sniffs and sobs and brimming tears that her mother could ignore them no longer.

"Oh, darling." She put down her newspaper. "Whatever is the matter?"

"Nothing . . ." Virginia stood at the window swollen-faced, unseeing.

"But it has to be something." She put out a hand and rested it, gently, on Virginia's knee. "Was it that young man?"

"Which young man?"

"The young man in the Land-Rover, Eustace Philips? Did you break your heart over him?" Virginia, weeping, could make no reply. Her mother went on, reassuring, gentle. "I wouldn't be too unhappy. It's probably the first time you've been hurt by a man, but I assure you it won't be the last. They're selfish creatures, you know."

"Eustace wasn't like that."

"Wasn't he?"

"He was kind. He was the only man I've ever really liked." She blew her nose lustily and gazed at her mother. "You didn't like him, did you?"

Mrs Parsons was momentarily taken aback by such unusual directness. "Well . . . let's say I've never been very fond of his.type."

"You mean, you didn't like him being a farmer?"

"I never said that."

"No, but that's what you mean. You only like chinless weeds like Mrs Menheniot's nephew."

"I never met Mrs Menheniot's nephew."

"No. But you would have liked him."

Mrs Parsons did not reply to this at once. But after a little she said, "Forget him, Virginia. Every girl has to have one unhappy love affair before she finally meets the right man and settles down and gets married. And this summer's going to be such fun for us both. It would be a pity to spoil it, yearning for something that probably never even existed."

"Yes," said Virginia and wiped her eyes and put her sodden handkerchief away in her pocket.

"That's a good girl. Now, no more tears." And, satisfied that she had poured oil on troubled waters, Mrs Parsons sat back in her seat and picked up the newspaper again. But presently, disquieted, disturbed by something, she lowered the paper and saw that Virginia was watching her, unblinking, an expression in her dark eyes that her mother had never seen before.

"What is it?"

Virginia said, "He said he'd phone. He promised he'd telephone me."

"Well?"

"Did he? You didn't like him, I know. Did you take the call and never tell me?"

Her mother never hesitated. "Darling! What an accusation. Of course not. You surely didn't think. . . ?"

"No," said Virginia dully as the last flicker of hope died. "No, I never thought." And she turned to lean her forehead against the smeared glass of the train window, and the rocketing countryside, together with everything else that had happened, streamed away, for ever, into the past.

That was April. In May Virginia met up again with an old schoolfriend, who invited her down to the country for the weekend.

"It's my birthday, darling, too super, Mummy says I can ask anyone I like, you'll probably have to sleep in the attic, but you won't mind, will you? We're such a madly disorganised family."

Virginia, taking all this with a pinch of salt, accepted the invitation. "How do I get there?"

"Well, you *could* catch a train, and someone *could* meet you, but that's so dreadfully boring. I tell you what, my cousin's probably coming, he's got a car, he'll maybe give me a lift. I'll speak to him and see if he's got room for you. You'll probably have to squeeze in with the luggage or sit on the gear lever, but anything's better than fighting the crowds at Waterloo . . ."

Rather surprisingly, she duly arranged this. The car was a dark blue Mercedes coupé, and once Virginia's luggage had been crammed into the over-loaded boot, she was invited to squash herself into the front seat, between the girlfriend and the cousin. The cousin was tall and fair, with long legs and a grey suit and hair that curled in ducks' tails from beneath the brim of his forward-tilted brown trilby hat.

His name was Anthony Keile.

6

Travel-worn and tired, and with all the problems of Bosithick still to be faced, Virginia got out of the train at Penzance, took a lungful of cool sea air, and was thankful to be back. The tide was low, the air strong with the smell of seaweed. Across the bay, St Michael's Mount stood gold in the evening sun, and the wet sands were streaked with blue, where small streams and shallow pools of sea-water gave back the colour of the sky.

Miraculously, here was a porter. As they followed him and his barrow out of the station Nicholas said, "Is this where we're going to stay?"

"No, we've got to drive over to Lanyon."

"How are we going to drive?"

"I told you, I left my car here."

"How do you know it hasn't been stolen?"

"Because I can see it, waiting for us."

It took some time to pack all their belongings into the boot of the Triumph. But in the end it was all piled in, crowned by the cardboard crate of groceries, and Virginia tipped the porter and they got in, all three of them in the front seat, with Cara in the middle, and the door on Nicholas's side firmly locked.

She had put down the hood and then tied a scarf around her head, but the wind blew Cara's hair forward all over her face.

"How long will it take us to get there?"

"Not long, about half an hour."

"What does the house look like?"

"Why don't you wait and see?"

At the top of the hill she stopped the car, and they looked back to see the view, the lovely curve of Mount's Bay, still and blue, enclosed in the warmth of the day that was over. And all about them were little fields, and ditches blue with wild scabious, and they went on and dropped into a miniature valley filled with ancient oak trees, and a stream ran beneath a bridge, and there was an old mill and a village, and then the road twined up on to the moor again, and all at once the straight bright horizon of the Atlantic lay before them, glittering to the westward in a dazzle of sun.

"I thought the sea was behind us," said Nicholas. "Is that another sea?"

"I suppose it is."

"Is that our sea? Is that the one we're going to use?"

"I expect so."

"Is there a beach?"

"I haven't had time to look. There are certainly a lot of steep cliffs."

"I want a beach. With sand. I want you to buy me a bucket and spade."

"All in good time," said Virginia. "How about taking things one at a time?"

"I want to buy a bucket and spade *tomorrow*."

They joined the main road and turned east, running parallel to the coast. They left Lanyon village behind them and the road which led to Penfolda, and they climbed the hill and came to the clump of leaning hawthorns which marked the turning to Bosithick.

"Here we are!"

"But there's no house."

"You'll see."

Bumped and jarred, the car and its occupants lurched down the lane. From beneath them came sinister banging sounds, the great gorse bushes closed in at either side, and Cara, anxious for their provisions, reached back a hand to hang on to the grocery carton. They swung around the last corner with a final lurch, ran up on to the grass bank at a frightening angle, and stopped with a jerk. Virginia put on the handbrake, turned off the engine. And the children sat in the car and stared at the house.

In Penzance there had been no wind, the air was milky and breathlessly warm. Here, there was a faint whining, a coolness. The broken washing-line stirred in the breeze and the long grass on the top of the stone hedge lay flattened like a fur coat, stroked by a hand.

And there was something else. Something was wrong. For a moment Virginia stared, trying to think what it was. And then Cara told her. "There's smoke in the chimney," said Cara.

Virginia shivered, a frisson of unease, like a trickle of cold water, ran down her spine. It was as though they had caught the house unawares, they had not been expected by the nameless, unimagined beings who normally occupied it.

Cara felt her disquiet. "Is anything wrong?"

"No, of course not." She sounded more robust than she felt. "I was just surprised. Let's go and investigate."

They got out of the car, leaving the cases and groceries behind. Virginia manhandled the gate open and stood aside for the children to go through while she felt in her bag for the ring of keys.

They went ahead of her, Nicholas running, to investigate what lay around the far corner of the house, but Cara trod cautiously as though trespassing, avoiding an old rag, a broken flower-pot, her hands held fastidiously, anxious not to be asked to touch anything.

Together, they opened the front door. As it swung inwards Cara said, "Do you suppose it's gipsies?"

"What's gipsies?"

"Who've lit the fire."

"Let's look . . ." The smell of mice and damp had gone. Instead the house felt fresh and warm, and when they stepped into the living-room they found it bright with firelight. The whole aspect of the house was changed by this, it was sullen and depressing no longer . . . on the contrary, quite cheerful. The hideous electric fire had somehow been disposed of, and a tall rush basket stood by the hearth, piled with a good supply of logs.

What with the fire and the last of the afternoon sun filtering in through the west window, the room was very warm. Virginia went to open a window, and saw, through the open kitchen door, the bowl set on the table, piled with brown eggs, the white enamel milk pan. She went into the kitchen and stood in the middle of the floor and stared. Someone had been in and cleaned the place up, the sink was shining and the curtains laundered.

Cara stole in behind her, still cautious. "It's like fairies," she said.

"It's not fairies," said Virginia, smiling. "It's Alice."

"Aunt Alice Lingard?"

"Yes, isn't she a dear? She pretended to be so disapproving about us coming to Bosithick and then she goes and does a thing like this. But that's just like Alice. She's very kind. We'll have to go tomorrow and thank her. I'd ring up, only we haven't got a telephone."

"I hate the telephone anyway. And I want to go and see her. I want to see the swimming-pool."

"If you take your bathing-suit you can have a swim."

Cara stood staring up at her mother. Virginia thought she was still thinking about swimming and was surprised when she said, "How did she get in?"

"Who?"

"Aunt Alice. We've got the keys."

"Oh. Well. I expect she got a spare key from Mr Williams. Something like that. Now what are we going to do first?"

Nicholas appeared at the door. "I'm going to look all over the house and then I want some tea. I'm starving!"

"Take Cara with you."

"I want to stay with *you*."

"No." Virginia gave her a gentle push. "You go and tell me what you think of the rest of the house. Tell me if you don't think it the funniest house you've ever seen in your life. And I'll put the kettle on and we'll boil some eggs, and after that we'll bring all the stuff in from the car and see about unpacking and making the beds."

"Aren't the beds even made?"

"No, we've got to do it all. We're really on our own now."

Somehow, by the end of the evening they had managed to attain a semblance of order, but finding the switch for the hot-water tank and the cupboard where the sheets were kept, and trying to decide who was going to sleep in which bed, all took a very long time. For supper Nicholas wanted baked beans on toast, but they couldn't find a toaster and the grill on the cooker was fiercely temperamental, so he had baked beans on bread instead.

"We need washing-up stuff and a mop, and tea and coffee . . ." Virginia searched for a piece of paper and a pencil and started, frantically, to make a list.

Cara chimed in, ". . . And soap for the bathroom and stuff to clean the bath with, because it's got a *horrid* dirty mark."

"And a bucket and spade," said Nicholas.

"And we'll have to get a fridge," said Cara. "We haven't got anywhere to keep our food and it'll all grow a blue beard if we let it just lie about."

Virginia said, "Perhaps we could borrow a meat-safe," and then remembered who had offered to lend her one, and frowned down at her shopping list and hastily changed the subject.

When the little water tank finally heated up, they had baths in the gimcrack bathroom, Nicholas and Cara going in together, and then Virginia swiftly before the water went cold. In dressing-gowns, by firelight, they made cocoa . . .

"There isn't even a television."

"Or a wireless."

"Or a clock," said Nicholas cheerfully.

Virginia smiled and looked at her watch. "If you really want to know, it's ten past nine."

"Ten past nine! We should be in bed ages ago."

"It doesn't matter," she told them.

"Doesn't *matter*? Nanny would be furious!"

Virginia leaned back in her chair, stretched out her legs and wriggled her bare toes at the heat of the fire. "I know," she said.

After they were in bed, after she had kissed them, and left the door open on the landing and showed them how the light worked, she left them, and went down the narrow passage and up the two steps that led to the Tower Room.

It was cold. She sat by the window and looked out across the still, shadowed fields, and saw that the peaceful sea had turned pearly in the dusk, and the sky in the afterglow of sunset was streaked in long scarves of coral. Clouds were gathered in the west. They lay, piled beyond the horizon, threaded with shafts of gold and pink light, but gradually even these last shreds of light filtered away, and the clouds turned black, and in the east a little new moon, like an eyelash, floated up into the sky.

One by one lights started to twinkle out across the soft darkness, along the whole length of the coast, from farmhouses, and cottages and barns. Here, a window burned square and yellow. There a light bobbed across a rick yard. A pair of headlights tunnelled up a lane, and headed out on to the main road towards Lanyon, and

Virginia wondered if it was Eustace Philips, making for Lanyon and The Mermaid's Arms, and she wondered if he would come and see how they were getting along, or whether he would be taciturn and sulky and wait for Virginia to produce some sort of an olive branch. She told herself that it would be worth doing even this, if it were only for the satisfaction of seeing his face when he realised how well she and Cara and Nicholas were managing for themselves.

But next day it was different.

In the night the wind had got up, and the dark clouds which last evening had lain banked on the horizon, were blown inland, bringing with them a dark and drenching rain. The sound of gutters trickling and dripping, the rattle of raindrops against the glass of the window-pane were the sounds which woke Virginia up. Her bedroom was so gloomy that she had to turn on the lamp before she could read her watch. Eight o'clock.

She got out of bed and went and shut the window. The floor-boards beneath her feet were quite wet. The rain curtained everything, and she could see no more than a few yards. It was like being in a ship, marooned in a sea of rain. She hoped the children would not wake up for hours.

She dressed in trousers and her thickest jersey and went downstairs and found that the rain had come down the chimney and effectively put out the fire, and the room felt damp and chilly. There were matches, but no firelighters; wood, but no kindling. She pulled on a raincoat and went out into the rain and across to the sagging garden shed, and found a hatchet, blunt with age and misuse. On the stone front doorstep, and at considerable personal danger to herself, she chopped a log into kindling, then took some paper which had been wrapped in with their groceries, and kindled a little fire. The sticks snapped and crackled, the smoke, after one or two surly billows into the room, ran sweetly up the chimney. She piled on logs and left the fire to burn.

Cara appeared when she was cooking breakfast.

"Mummy!"

"Hello, my love." She bent to kiss her. Cara wore sky blue shorts, a yellow tee shirt, an inadequate little cardigan. "Are you warm enough?"

"No," said Cara. Her fine, straight hair was bunched into a slide, her spectacles were crooked. Virginia straightened them. "Go and put on some more clothes, then. Breakfast isn't ready yet."

"But there isn't anything else. In my suitcase, I mean. Nanny didn't pack anything else."

"I don't believe it!" They gazed at each other. "You mean no jeans or raincoats or gumboots."

Cara shook her head. "I suppose she thought it was going to be hot."

"Yes, I suppose she did," said Virginia mildly, mentally cursing Nanny. "But you'd have thought she knew enough about packing to put a raincoat in."

"Well, we've sort of got raincoats, but not proper ones."

She looked so worried that Virginia smiled. "Don't worry."

"What shall we do?"

"We'll have to go and buy you both some clothes."

"Today?"

"Why not? We can't do anything else in weather like this."

"How about seeing Aunt Alice and swimming in her pool?"

"We'll keep that for a finer day. She won't mind. She'll understand."

They drove through the downpour to Penzance. At the top of the hill the mist was thick and grey, swirling in the wind, parting momentarily to allow a glimpse of the road ahead, and then closing in once more so that Virginia could scarcely see the end of the car bonnet.

Penzance was awash with rain, traffic and disconsolate holidaymakers, prevented by the weather from their usual daily ploy of sitting on the promenade or the beach. They clogged the pavements, stood in shop doorways, aimlessly surged round the counters of shops, looking for something to buy. Behind the steamy windows of cafés and ice-cream shops they could be seen, packed in at little tables, slowly sipping, licking, munching; spinning it out, making it last, so as to postpone the inevitable moment when they had to go out into the rain again.

Virginia drove around for ten minutes before she found a place to leave the car. In the rain they searched the choked streets until they came to a shop where fishermen's oilskins were for sale, and huge thigh-length rubber boots and lanterns and rope, and they went in and she bought jeans for Cara and Nicholas, and dark blue Guernseys, and black oilskins and sou'westers which obliterated the children like candle-snuffers. The children put on the new oilskins and the sou'westers, then and there, but the rest of the clothes were tied up in a brown paper parcel. Virginia took the parcel and paid the bill, and with the children, stiff as robots in their new coats, blinded by the brims of the hats, she went out into the street again.

It still poured. "Let's go home now," said Cara.

"Well, while we're here, we may as well get some fish or some meat or a chicken. And we haven't any potatoes or carrots or peas. There may be a supermarket."

"I want a bucket and spade," said Nicholas.

Virginia pretended not to hear. They found the supermarket, and joined the herd-like crowds, queuing and choosing, waiting and paying, packing the parcels into carriers, lugging them out of the shop.

The gutters gurgled, water streamed from drainpipes.

"Cara, can you really carry that?"

"Yes . . ." said Cara, dragged down to one side by the weight of the carrier.

"Give half of it to Nicholas."

"I want a bucket and spade," said Nicholas.

But Virginia had run out of money. She was about to tell him that he would have to wait until the next shopping expedition, but he turned up his face under the brim of the sou'wester, and his mouth was mutinous, but his eyes huge and beginning to fill with tears. "I want a bucket and spade."

"Well, we'll buy you one. But first I'll have to find a bank and cash a cheque and get more money."

The tears, as if by magic, vanished. "I saw a bank!"

They found the bank, filled with queuing customers. The children made their way to a leather bench and sat, exhausted, like two little old people, their chins sunk into their chests, and their legs stuck out in front of them, regardless of whom they might trip up. Virginia waited in a queue, then produced her bank card and wrote her cheque.

"On holiday?" asked the young cashier. Virginia wondered how he could still be good-tempered at the end of such a morning.

"Yes."

"It'll clear up by tomorrow, you'll see."

"I hope so."

The red bucket and the blue spade were their final purchases. Laden, they walked the long way back to the car, and for some reason it was all uphill. Nicholas, banging the bucket with the spade as though it were a drum, trailed behind. More than once Virginia had to turn and wait for him, exhort him to get a move on. Finally, she lost her patience. "Oh, Nicholas, *do* hurry," and a passing woman heard the suppressed irritation in her voice, and glanced back, her face full of disapproval at such a disagreeable and short-tempered mother.

And that was after only one morning.

It still rained. They came at last to the car, and loaded the boot with parcels, and pulled off their dripping raincoats and stuffed them into the boot, and then scrambled into the car and slammed the door, thankful beyond words to be at last sitting down and out of the rain.

"Now," said Nicholas, still banging the bucket with the spade, "do you know what I want?"

Virginia looked at her watch. It was nearly one o'clock. "Something to eat?" she guessed.

What I would like would be to go back to Wheal House and know that Mrs Jilkes had lunch ready and waiting, and there would be a cheerful fire in the drawing-room, and lots of new magazines and newspapers and nothing to do for the rest of the afternoon except read them.

"Yes, that. But something else as well."

"I don't know."

"You've got to guess. I'll give you three guesses."

"Well." She thought. "You want to go to the loo?"

"No. At least not yet."

"You want . . . a drink of water?"

"No."

"Give in."

"I want to go to a beach this afternoon and dig. With my new bucket and spade."

The young man in the bank proved to be quite correct in his weather forecast. That evening, the wind swung around to the north, and the shredded clouds were sent bowling away, over the moors. At first small patches of sky appeared, and then these grew larger and brighter and at last the evening sun broke through, to set, triumphantly, in a welter of glorious pinks and reds.

"Red Sky At Night, Shepherd's Delight," said Cara as they went to bed. "That means it's going to be a lovely day tomorrow."

It was.

* * *

"I want to go to the beach today and dig with my bucket and spade," said Nicholas.

"You will," Virginia told him firmly. "But first we have to go and see Aunt Alice Lingard, otherwise she'll think we're the rudest, most ungrateful people she's ever known."

"Why?" said Nicholas.

"Because she got the house all ready for us and we haven't even said thank you . . . finish up your egg, Nicholas, it's getting all cold."

"I wish I could have cornflakes."

"We'll buy cornflakes," said Virginia, and Cara got the pencil and the shopping list and they wrote Cornflakes underneath Steel Wool, Peanut Butter and Caster Sugar, Splits, Jellies, Soap Powder and Cheese. Virginia had never done so much shopping in her life.

She sent them off to play while she did the breakfast dishes and went upstairs to make the beds. The children's room was awash with clothes. Virginia had always imagined they were neat and tidy, but realised now that it had simply been Nanny, who moved along behind them, picking up and putting away everything that they dropped. She gathered up the clothes, not knowing if they were dirty or clean, took a sock from the top of the chest of drawers, and carefully did not touch a crumpled paper bag with two sticky sweets in the corner.

.There was also a big pigskin folder of photographs. This belonged to Cara, and had been packed by Nanny, with what intention Virginia could only guess. One side of the folder was taken up with a selection of small photographs, many of which had been taken by Cara herself, and arranged with more affection than artistry. The front of the house, rather crooked; the dogs, the farm men on the tractor; an aerial view of Kirkton, and a picture postcard or two. On the other side was an impressive studio portrait of Anthony, a head and shoulders, all lighting and angles, so that his hair looked white-blond, and his jaw very square and determined. The photographer's impression was of a strong man, but Virginia knew the narrowed eyes, and the weak, handsome mouth. And she saw the striped collar of the Turnbull and Asser shirt, the discreetly patterned silk of the Italian tie, and she remembered how clothes had mattered to Anthony; just as his car was important, and the furnishings of his house and his manner of living. Virginia had always imagined that these were subsidiary considerations, and took their shape from the character of the individual. But with Anthony Keile it was the other way round, and he had invariably given the highest priority to the smallest details, as though realising that they were the props behind his image, and without them his inadequate personality would crumble.

Carrying the armful of clothes, she went downstairs and washed them in the tiny sink. When she took these outside to peg them crookedly on to the knotted clothes-line, she found only Nicholas, alone, playing with his red tractor and a few pebbles and bits of grass. He wore his new navy-blue Guernsey and was already scarlet in the face with heat, but Virginia knew better than to suggest that it might be a good idea if he took the sweater off.

"What are you playing?"

"Nothing much."

"Is the grass straw?"

"Sort of."

Virginia pegged out the last pair of pants. "Where's Cara?"

"She's inside."

"Reading, I expect," said Virginia and went in to find her. But Cara was not reading; she was in the Tower Room, sitting by the window staring sightlessly out across the fields to the sea. When Virginia appeared at the door, she turned her head slowly, bemused, unrecognising.

"Cara . . ."

Her eyes behind the spectacles came into focus. She smiled. "Hello. Is it time to go . . .?"

"I'm ready when you are." She sat beside Cara. "What are you doing? Thinking, or looking at the view?"

"Both, really."

"What were you thinking about?"

"I was really wondering how long we were going to stay here . . ."

"Oh – I suppose about a month. I've taken it for a month."

"But we'll have to go back to Scotland, won't we? We'll have to go back to Kirkton."

"Yes, we'll have to go back. There's your school for one thing." She waited. "Don't you want to go?"

"Isn't Nanny coming with us?"

"I shouldn't think so."

"It'll be funny, won't it, Kirkton, without Daddy or Nanny? It's so big for just the three of us. I think that's why I like this house. It's just the right size."

"I thought perhaps you wouldn't like it."

"I love it. And I love this room. I've never seen a room like it, with the stairs going down in the middle of the floor and all the windows and the sky." She was obviously not bothered by spooky sensations. "Why isn't there any furniture, though?"

"I think it was built as a study, a workroom. There was a man who lived here, about fifty years ago. He wrote books and he was very famous."

"What did he look like?"

"I don't know. I suppose he had a beard, and perhaps he was rather untidy and forgot to do up his sock suspenders, and buttoned his suit all wrong. Writers are often very absent-minded."

"What was his name?"

"Aubrey Crane."

"I'm sure he was nice," said Cara, "to have made such

a pretty room. You can just sit and see everything that happens."

"Yes," said Virginia, and together they gazed out at the patchwork fields, where peaceful cows grazed, and the grass was emerald green after the rain, and stone walls and leaning gateposts were tangled with brambles which, in just a month or two, would be sweet and heavy with black fruit. Away to the west a tractor hummed. She turned her head, pressing her forehead against the window and saw the patch of scarlet, bright as a pillar-box, and the man sitting up behind the wheel, wearing a shirt as blue as the sky.

"Who's that?" asked Cara.

"That's Eustace Philips."

"Do you know him?"

"Yes. He farms Penfolda."

"Are these all his fields?"

"I expect so."

"When did you know him?"

"A long time ago."

"Does he know you're here?"

"Yes, I think so."

"I expect he'll come for a drink or something."

Virginia smiled. "Yes, perhaps he will. Now come and comb your hair and get ready. We're going to see Alice Lingard."

"Shall I put in my bathing things? Can we swim in her pool?"

"That's a good idea."

"I wish we had a swimming-pool."

"What, here? There wouldn't be room in the garden."

"No, not here. At Kirkton."

"Well, we could," said Virginia, without thinking. "If you really wanted one. But do let's go, otherwise it'll be lunchtime, and we shall have done nothing but sit here and talk."

But when they got to Wheal House, they found only Mrs Jilkes at home. Virginia had rung the bell but only as a formality, immediately opening the door and stepping into the hall with the children at her heels. She waited for the dog to start barking, for Alice's voice to say "Who is it?" and Alice to appear through the drawing-room door. But she was met only by silence, broken by the slow ticking of the grandfather clock which stood by the fireplace.

"Alice?"

Somewhere a door opened and shut. And then Mrs Jilkes came up the kitchen passage, like a ship in full sail with her starched white apron. "Who is it?" She sounded quite cross until she saw Virginia standing there with the children beside her.

Then she smiled. "Oh, Mrs Keile, you did surprise me, I couldn't think who you were, standing there. And these are your children. My, aren't they lovely? Aren't you lovely?" she inquired conversationally of Cara, who had never been asked such a question before. She wondered if she would say "no" because she knew that she wasn't lovely, but she was too shy to say anything. She simply stared at Mrs Jilkes.

"Cara, isn't it? And Nicholas. Brought your swimming things, too, I can see. Going to go and have a dip in the pond?" She turned back to Virginia. "Mrs Lingard's not here."

"Oh dear."

"Been away she has, ever since you went. Mr Lingard had to go to some big dinner in London, so Mrs Lingard suddenly decided she'd go too. Said she hadn't been up for a bit. She'll be home this evening, though."

Virginia worked this out. "You mean, she's been away since Thursday?"

"Thursday afternoon she went."

"But . . . Bosithick . . . A fire had been lighted when we got there, and it was all clean and there were eggs and milk waiting for us . . . I thought it was Mrs Lingard."

Mrs Jilkes looked coy.

"No. But I'll tell you who it was, though."

"Who was it?"

"It was Eustace Philips."

"Eustace?"

"Well, don't sound so shocked, it's not as though he's done anything wrong."

"But how do you know it was Eustace?"

"Because he telephoned me," Mrs Jilkes said, importantly. "Least, he telephoned Mrs Lingard, but her being in London I spoke to him instead. And he said was anybody doing anything about you coming back to Bosithick with those children, and I said I didn't know, and told him Mrs Lingard was away, and he said, 'Well, never mind, I'll look after it,' and that was it. Make a good job, did he?"

"You mean he came in and did all that *house-cleaning*?"

"Oh no. Eustace wouldn't know one end of a duster from the other. That would have been Mrs Thomas. She'd scrub the flags off the floor if you'd give her half a chance."

Cara put her hand into Virginia's. "Is that the man on the tractor we saw this morning?"

"Yes," said Virginia, distracted.

"But won't he think we're terribly rude? We haven't said thank you."

"No, I know. We'll have to go this afternoon. When we get back, we'll go down to Penfolda and explain."

Nicholas was furious. "But you said I could dig on the beach with my bucket and spade!"

Mrs Jilkes knew a rebellious voice when she heard one. She stooped towards Nicholas, hands on her knees, her face close to his, her voice seductive.

"Why don't you go and have a lovely swim? And when you come out you and your Mummy and your sister can come and eat shepherd's pie, in the kitchen with Mrs Jilkes . . ."

"Oh, but Mrs Jilkes . . ."

"*No.*" Mrs Jilkes shook her head at Virginia's interruption. "It's no trouble. All waiting to be eaten it is. And I was just beginning to think that the house was somehow empty, and me rattling around in it like a pea in a drum." She beamed at Cara. "You'd like to do that, wouldn't you, my lovely?"

She was so kind that Cara's icy shyness thawed. She said, "Yes, please."

That warm Sunday afternoon they walked across the fields to Penfolda, across the stubble fields where, only a week ago, Virginia had watched the harvesters at work; across the grassy meadows, going from field to field by stiles made of granite steps laid across the open ditches. As they approached the farm, they saw the Dutch barns, the gates, the concrete cattle court, the milking parlours. Cautiously opening and shutting the gates behind them they crossed the court and came out in the old cobbled farmyard. There was the sound of scrubbing, wet bristles on stone, and Virginia went to an open door of what looked like stables, with looseboxes, and found a man, who was not Eustace, cleaning the place out. He wore a faded navy-blue beret on the back of his curly grey head, and old-fashioned dungarees with braces.

He saw her and stopped sweeping. Virginia said, "I'm sorry, I'm looking for Mr Philips . . ."

"'E's around somewhere . . . up at the back of the house . . ."

"We'll see if we can find him."

They went through a gate, and along a path that led between the farmhouse and the tangled little garden where she and Eustace had shared the pasty. A tabby cat sat on the doorstep in a warm patch of sun. Cara squatted to pet it and Virginia knocked on the door. There were footsteps and the door opened, and a little round woman stood there, cosy as an armchair, upholstered in a black dress and loose-covered with a print apron. From behind her, from the kitchen, came a good smell, the memory of a hearty Sunday dinner.

"Yes?"

"I'm Virginia Keile . . . from Bosithick . . ."

"Oh *yes* . . ."

A smile creased the rosy face, pushing up her cheeks into two little bunches.

"You must be Mrs Thomas."

"That's right . . . and these your children, are they?"

"Yes. Cara and Nicholas. We feel so bad because we never came down to thank you. For cleaning the house I mean, and leaving the eggs and the milk and the firewood and everything."

"Oh, that wasn't me. I just cleaned the place up a bit, opened a few windows. It was Eustace who got the logs there, took up a load on the back of the tractor . . . left the milk and the eggs at the same time. We thought you wouldn't have had time to do much before you went to London . . . dismal it is coming home to a dirty house; couldn't let you do that."

"We'd have come before, but we thought it was Mrs Lingard . . ."

"Want to see Eustace, do you? He's up in the vegetable garden at the back, digging me a bucket of potatoes." She smiled down at Cara. "Do you like the little pussy cat?"

"Yes, she's sweet."

"She's got kittens in the barn. Do you want to go and see them?"

"Will she mind?"

"She won't mind. Come along, Mrs Thomas will show you where to find them."

She made for the barn, with the children at her heels; not a backward glance did they spare for their mother, so intent were they on seeing the kittens. Left alone,

Virginia went up the garden path, through a wicket gate, arched in ivy. Eustace's blue shirt could be glimpsed beyond the pea-vines, and she made her way towards this and found him forking up a drill of potatoes. Round and white and smooth as sea pebbles, they were, caked in earth the same colour and consistency as rich, dark chocolate cake.

"Eustace."

He looked over his shoulder and saw her. She waited for him to smile, but he did not. She wondered if he had taken offence. He straightened up, leaning on the handle of the spade.

"Hello," he said, as though it were a surprise to see her there.

"I've come to say thank you. And I'm sorry."

He shifted the spade from one hand to another. "What have you got to be sorry for?"

"I didn't realise it was you who'd brought the wood and lit the fire and everything. I thought it was Alice Lingard. That's why we haven't been down before."

"Oh, that," said Eustace and she wondered if there was something else she should be sorry about.

"It was terribly kind. The milk and the eggs and everything. It just made all the difference." She stopped, terrified of sounding insincere. "But how did you get into the house?"

Eustace drove the prongs of the fork into the ground, and started towards her. "There's a key here. When my mother was first married, she used to go over sometimes, do a bit of work for old Mr Crane. His wife was ailing, my mother used to clean the place up. He gave her a key to hang on the dresser and it's been there ever since."

He reached her side, and stood, looking down at her, then he suddenly smiled, his blue eyes crinkled with amusement and she knew that her fears were unjustified, and that he bore no grudge. He said, "So you decided to take the house after all."

Ruefully, Virginia said, "Yes."

"I felt badly, saying those things, and you so upset about everything. I lost my temper, but I shouldn't have."

"You were right. It was all I needed to make me make up my own mind."

"That's why I brought up the logs and stuff . . . I thought it was the least I could do. You'll be wanting more milk . . ."

"Could you let us have it every day?"

"If someone comes and fetches it."

"I could, or one of the children. I hadn't realised, but over the fields and the stiles it's no distance at all."

They had begun to walk back towards the gate.

"Are your children here?"

"They've gone with Mrs Thomas to see some kittens."

Eustace laughed. "They'll fall in love with them, so be warned. That little tabby got caught by a Siamese up the road, and you've never seen such pretty kittens." He opened the gate for Virginia to go through. "Blue eyes they've got and . . ."

He stopped, watching over her head as Cara and Nicholas came, slowly, carefully, out of the barn, their cupped hands held cradled to their chests, their heads bent in adoration. "What did I tell you?" said Eustace and shut the gate behind them.

The children came up the slope of the lawn, ankle deep, knee deep, in plantains and great white daisies. And all at once Virginia saw them with fresh eyes, with Eustace's eyes, as though she were seeing them for the first time. The fair head and the dark, the blue eyes and the brown. And the sun blinked on to Cara's spectacles so that they flashed like the headlights of a little car, and their new jeans, bought too big, slipped down over their hips and Nicholas's shirt-tail hung out over his firm, round little bottom.

A love-like pain caught at Virginia's throat, unshed tears prickled at the back of her eyes. They were so defenceless, so vulnerable, and for some reason it mattered so much that they should make a good impression on Eustace.

Nicholas caught sight of her. "Look what we've got, Mummy; Mrs Thomas said that we could bring them out."

"Yes," said Cara, "and they're tiny and they've got their eyes . . ." She saw Eustace, behind her mother, and stopped dead, where she was standing, her face closed up, her eyes watching him from behind her glasses.

But Nicholas came on . . . "Look, Mummy you've got to look. It's all furry and it's got tiny claws. But I don't know if it's a boy or girl. Mrs Thomas says she can't tell." He looked up and saw Eustace and smiled engagingly into his face. "They've stopped sucking their mother, Mrs Thomas says, she was getting too thin, and she's put a little saucer of milk out for them, and they lap and their tongues are tiny," he told Eustace.

Eustace put out a long brown finger and scratched the top of the kitten's head. Virginia said, "Nicholas, this is Mr Philips, you're meant to say how do you do."

"How do you do. Mrs Thomas said that if we wanted one we could have one but we had to ask you, but you wouldn't mind, would you, Mummy? It's so little and it could sleep on my bed and I'd look after it."

Virginia found herself coming out with all the classic arguments produced by the parents of children, in the same situation as herself. *Too young to be taken from its mother yet. Still needs her to keep him warm. Only at Bosithick for the holidays, and think how he'd hate the train journey back to Scotland.*

Eustace had put down the bucket of potatoes and now went over to where Cara stood, clutching her kitten. Virginia, in agony for her, saw Eustace squat to Cara's height, loosen her fingers gently with his own. "You don't want to hold him too tight, otherwise he won't be able to breathe."

"I'm frightened of dropping him."

"You won't drop him. He wants to look out and see what's happening in the world. He's never seen sun as bright as that." He smiled at the kitten, at Cara. After a little, slowly, she smiled back, and you forgot the ugly spectacles and the bumpy forehead and the straight hair, and saw only the marvellous sweetness of her expression.

After a little he sent them to put the kittens back, and telling Virginia to stay outside in the sunshine, went into the house with the potatoes for Mrs Thomas, only to emerge a moment or so later with a packet of cigarettes and a bar of chocolate. They lay where they had lain before, in the long grass, and were joined there by the children.

He gave them the chocolate but talked to them like adults. What have you been doing? What did you do yesterday in all that rain? Have you been swimming yet?

They told him, voices chiming against each other, Cara, her shyness over, as eager to impart information as Nicholas.

"We bought raincoats, and we got *drenched*. And Mummy had to go to the bank to get more money, and Nicholas got a bucket and spade."

"But I haven't been to the beach to dig yet!"

"And we swam this morning at Mrs Lingard's. We swam in her pool. But we haven't swum in the sea yet."

Eustace raised his eyebrows. "You haven't swum in the sea and you haven't been to a beach? That's all wrong!"

"Mummy says there hasn't been time . . ."

"But she promised me," Nicholas, reminded of his grievance, became indignant. "She said today I could dig with the spade, but I've not been near one grain of sand."

Virginia began to laugh at him, and he became, naturally, angrier than ever. "Well, it's true, and it's what I want more than anything."

"Well," said Eustace, "if you want it more than anything, what are we doing sitting around here talking our heads off!"

Nicholas stared at Eustace, his eyes narrowed suspiciously. "You mean go to the beach?"

"Why not?"

"Now?" Nicholas could not believe his ears.

"Is there anything else you'd rather do?"

"No. Nothing. Nothing else." He sprang to his feet. "Where shall we go? Shall we go to Porthkerris?"

"No, we don't want to go there – nasty crowded place. We'll go to our own private beach, the one that nobody knows about, that belongs to Penfolda and Bosithick."

Virginia was astonished. "I didn't know we had one. I thought there was nothing but cliffs."

By now Eustace was also on his feet. "I'll show you . . . come along, we'll take the Land-Rover."

"My bucket and spade's at our house."

"We'll pick them up on the way."

"And our swimming things," said Cara.

"Those too."

He went into the house to fetch his own things, shouted a message to Mrs Thomas, led the way through the gate and back across the farmyard. He whistled and the dogs, barking, came rushing around the side of the barn, knowing that the whistle meant a walk, smells, rabbits, maybe a swim. Everybody, including the dogs, clambered into the Land-Rover, and Cara, her shyness now quite forgotten, screamed with delight, as they lurched out of the cobbled farmyard, and went bumping and bouncing up the lane towards the main road.

"Is it far?" she asked Eustace.

"No distance at all."

"What's the beach called?"

"Jack Carley's cove. And it's not a place for babies, only for big children who can look after themselves and climb down the cliff."

They assured him hastily that they came into this category and Virginia watched Nicholas's face, and saw the joyful satisfaction upon it at being indulged, at last, in the one thing he had been wanting to do for a whole day. And what was more, doing it instantly. Not told maybe, or tomorrow, or to wait or to be patient. And she knew exactly how he felt for long ago Eustace had done the very same, performed the same miracle for the young Virginia; had bought her the ice-cream she had been yearning for, and then, out of the blue, asked her to come back to Penfolda.

7

They left the Land-Rover in the deserted farmyard below Bosithick and started to walk down towards the sea. At first, crossing the fields, they went in a bunch, four abreast, Eustace taking Nicholas by the hand because he was inclined to lag. But then the fields gave way to brambles and bracken and they fell into single file with Eustace leading the way; over crumbling stone walls and across a stream, where rushes grew shoulder high to a small person. Then over another wall, and the path disappeared beneath a jungle of green bracken. Through this they pushed their way, gorse bushes pressing in at either side. The ground all at once slid steeply away from beneath their feet, and the path zig-zagged down through the undergrowth, down to the very lip of the curving cliff. And beyond, space. Blue air. Soaring, screaming gulls, and the distant creaming of the sea.

At this point the coast seemed to fling itself out into a jagged headland, composed of great granite outcrops. Between these the turf was smooth and very green, stained with patches of purple-belled heather, and the path wound down between these outcrops and as they followed its convolutions, a little cove, sheltered and enclosed, gradually revealed itself, far below. The sea was deep and still, purple over the rocks and jade green over the sand. The beach was tiny, and backed by the remains of an old sea wall. Beyond this the land sloped up to the green wedge of the cliff, down which trickled, in a series of small waterfalls, a fresh-water stream. And above the sea wall, tucked snug against the foot of the cliff, stood the remains of a cottage; derelict, windows broken, slates torn from the roof.

They stood in a row, the four of them, buffeted by the gentle wind, looking down. It was a disturbing sensation. Virginia wondered if the children might suffer from vertigo, but neither of them seemed in the least disturbed by the dizzy emptiness of the great height.

"There's a house," said Cara.

"That was where Jack Carley lived."

"Where does he live now?"

"With the angels, I reckon."

"Did you know him?"

"Yes, I knew him. He was an old man when I was a boy. Didn't like people coming down here. Not any old people. Had a great barking dog and he used to chase them away."

"But he let you come?"

"Oh, yes, he let me come." He grinned down at Nicholas. "Do you want me to carry you, or can you manage?"

Nicholas peered out and over. The path trickled down the face of the cliff and so out of sight. Nicholas remained undismayed.

"No. I don't want to be carried, thank you. But I'd like it better if you went first."

In fact, the dogs went first, unafraid, sure-footed as goats. The humans followed at a more prudent speed, but Virginia found that the path was not as dangerous as it appeared. After the dry spell the ground was hard and firm underfoot, and in steep places, steps had been cut, shored up with driftwood or fashioned roughly out of cement.

Much sooner than she had expected they were all safely down. Above them, the cliff loomed, dark and cold in the shadow, but when they jumped down on to the beach they came out of the shade and into the sunshine, and the sand was warm, and there was the smell of tar from the little house, and no sound but the gulls and the creaming sea, and the splash of the stream.

There was an air of unreality about the little cove, as though they had somehow strayed out of time and space. The air was still, the sun burning hot, the sand white and the green water clear as glass. The children stripped off their clothes, and took Nicholas's new bucket and spade and went at once to the water's edge, where they began to dig a sandcastle, moated and turreted with bucket-shaped towers.

"If the tide comes in it'll wash the whole castle away," said Cara.

"No, it won't, because we're going to make a great huge moat and then the water will go into that."

"If the tide comes in higher than the castle, it's going to wash it away. Like King Canute."

Nicholas considered this. "Well, it won't for ages."

It was the sort of day that they would remember for the rest of their lives. Virginia imagined them, middle-aged, reminiscing, nostalgic.

There was a little cove and a ruined cottage and not another soul but us. And there were two dogs and we had to climb down a suicidal path.

Who took us?

Eustace Philips.

But who was he?

I can't remember . . . he must have been a farmer, some sort of a neighbour.

And they would argue over details.

There was a stream.

No, it was a waterfall.

There was a stream running down the middle of the beach. I can remember it quite clearly. And we dammed it with a sandbank.

But there was a waterfall too. And I had a new spade.

When the tide was high, they all swam, and the water was clear and salty and green and very cold. Virginia had forgotten her cap and her dark hair lay sleek to her head, and her shadow moved across the pebbled sea-bed like some strange new variety of fish. Holding Cara, she floated, drifting between the sea and the sky, with her eyes dazzled by water and sunshine; and the air was cleft with screaming gulls, and always the gentle murmur of breaking waves.

She became very cold. The children showed no signs of chill, however, so she left them with Eustace, and came out of the water, and went to sit on the dry sand, above the high-water mark.

She sat on the sand because they had brought no rug, no super-sized bath-towels. And no comb or lipstick, or biscuits or knitting, and no Thermos of tea, and no extra cardigan. And no plum cake or chocolate biscuits, and no money for the donkey rides or the man with the ice-cream.

She was joined at last by Cara, teeth chattering. Virginia wrapped her in a towel and began gently to dry her. "You'll soon be swimming at this rate."

Cara said, "What time is it?"

Her mother squinted up at the sun. "I suppose, nearly five . . . I don't know."

"We haven't had tea yet."

"No, nor we have. And I don't suppose we will either."

"Not have any *tea*?"

"It doesn't matter for once. We'll have supper later on."

Cara made a face, but raised no objections. Nicholas, however, was vociferous in his complaints when he realised that Virginia had brought nothing for him to eat.

"But I'm hungry."

"I'm sorry."

"Nanny always had shivery bites and you haven't got anything."

"I know. I forgot. We were in such a hurry and I never thought of biscuits."

"Well, what am I going to eat?"

Eustace caught the tail end of this conversation as he came, dripping, up the beach. "What's this?" He stopped to pick up a towel.

"I'm very hungry and Mummy hasn't brought anything to eat."

"Too bad," said Eustace unsympathetically.

Nicholas sent him a long, measured look, and turned away, headed in a sulky silence back to his digging, but Eustace caught him by an arm and pulled him gently back and held him against his knees, rubbing at him absently with the towel, rather as though he were fondling one of the dogs.

Virginia said, placatingly, "Anyway, we'll have to go soon, I expect."

"Why?" asked Eustace.

"I thought you had all those cows to milk."

"Bert's doing them."

"Bert?"

"He was at Penfolda today, cleaning out the loose-boxes."

"Oh, yes."

"He used to work for my father, he's retired now, but he comes along every alternate Sunday, gives me a hand. He likes to do it, and Mrs Thomas feeds him a good dinner, and it means I have a few hours to myself."

Nicholas became irritated by the pointless small-talk. He reared around in Eustace's hands, turned up a furious face towards him. "I am *hungry*."

"So am I," said Cara, wistful if not so vehement.

"Well, listen," said Eustace.

They listened. And heard, over the sound of the sea

and the gulls, another sound. The soft drumming of an engine, putt-putt-putt, all the time coming closer.

"What is it?"

"You watch and see."

The sound grew louder. Presently around the point they saw approaching a small open boat, white with a blue stripe, riding the waves with a scud of white spray. A stocky figure stood at its stern. Putt-putt, it swung round into the shelter of the cove, and the engine idled down to a steady throb . . .

They all stared. "There you are!" said Eustace, smug as a conjuror who has brought off a difficult trick.

"Who is it?"asked Virginia.

"That's Tommy Bassett from Porthkerris. Come to pick up his lobster pots."

"But he won't have any biscuits," said Nicholas, who would never be diverted from the matter in hand.

"No. But he might have something else. Shall I go and see?"

"All right." But they sounded doubtful.

He put Nicholas aside and went back down the sand and into the sea, diving through the eye of a peacock-coloured wave, and swimming, with a strong and steady crawl, far out to where the boat bobbed. The lobster pots were already being hauled aboard. The fisherman emptied one and dropped it back, and then saw Eustace coming, and stood, watching.

"Hello there, boy!" His voice carried across the water.

They saw Eustace catch the gunwales with his hands, hang there for a moment, and then with a heave pull himself clean out of the water and into the rocking boat.

"What a long way to swim," said Cara.

Nicholas said, "I hope he isn't going to bring back a lobster."

"Why not?"

"Lobsters have got claws."

In the boat, some discussion seemed to be taking place. But at last Eustace stood up, and they saw that he was carrying some sort of bundle. He let himself overboard and started back, swimming more slowly this time, hampered as he was by his mysterious burden. This proved to be, of all things, a string shopping-bag, but it contained, wet and dripping, a dozen gleaming mackerel.

Nicholas opened his mouth to say, "I don't like fish," but caught Eustace's eye, and closed his mouth and said nothing instead.

"I thought he might have a few," Eustace told them. "He usually puts a line out when he's coming out to the pots." He smiled down at Cara. "Ever eaten mackerel, have you?"

"I don't think so. But," said Cara, "fancy giving you the string bag." To her, this seemed far more amazing than the gift of the mackerel. "Doesn't he want it back again?"

"He didn't say he did."

"Shall we have to take them back to Bosithick?"

"What would we do that for? . . . No, we cook them here . . . come on, you can come and help."

And he collected six or seven big stones, round and smooth, and built them into a ring, and he took matches, and a scrap of an old cigarette packet, and some chips of driftwood and straw, and he kindled a fire and sent the children off to find more wood and soon they had a regular bonfire going. And when the wood ash was deep and grey and burned red when you blew on it, he laid the fish there, in a row, and there was a sizzling and a spitting and presently a most delicious smell.

"But we haven't got knives and forks," said Cara.

"Fingers were made before forks."

"But it'll be hot."

She and Nicholas squatted by the fireside, hair on end, naked except for their bathing pants and a coating of sand. They looked like savages, and perfectly content.

Cara watched Eustace's clever hands. "Have you done this before?"

"What, whittled a stick?"

"No, had a fire, and cooked fish."

"Many times. This is the only way to cook mackerel, and eat it, fresh out of the sea."

"Did you use to do this when you were a boy?"

"Yes."

"Was the old man alive then? Jack Carley."

"Yes. He used to come out and sit on the beach and join in the party. Bring a bottle of rum with him and a smelly old pipe and sit there and tell us yarns so hair-raising we could never be quite sure if they were true."

"What sort of yarns?"

"Oh, adventures . . . he'd been all over the world, done everything. Been a cook in a tanker, a lumberjack, built roads and railways, worked in the mines. He was a tin miner, see. A tinner. Went off to Chile, worked there for five years or more, came home a rich man, but all his money was gone within the twelve months, and he was off again."

"But he came back."

"Yes, he came back. Back to Jack Carley's cove." Cara shivered. "You cold?"

"Nanny calls it a ghost going over your grave."

"Put on a sweater then, and that'll keep the ghosts away, and then it'll be time to eat our tea."

And seeing him with her children, Virginia thought of Anthony who had missed so much because he had never wanted to have anything to do with them. If Cara had been pretty, perhaps he would have paid attention to her . . . Cara who longed for attention and love and thought her father the most wonderful being in the world. But she was plain and shy and wore spectacles, and he never endeavoured to hide the fact that he was ashamed of her. And Nicholas . . . with

Nicholas it might have been different. When he was old enough, Anthony would have taught him to shoot and play golf and fish, they would have become friends and gone about together. But now Anthony was dead, and none of this would happen and she felt sorry because they would never now remember swimming with him, they would never crouch with him round a camp fire, listening to his stories and watching his clever hands whittle wooden skewers to be used instead of forks.

The sun slipped down out of the sky, shone directly in upon them, and the sea was turned to a liquid dazzle. It would soon be evening and then it would be dark. And Jack Carley had lived here, just as Aubrey Crane had lived at Bosithick. You didn't see them. You didn't hear them. But you knew that they were still around.

It was disturbing, this awareness of the past, but somehow elemental, and so not really frightening. And it was not possible to live in this part of the world as a nervous or a timid person, for, beneath the beauty it was a savage land, and danger lurked everywhere. In the sea, deep and treacherous, with its undertows and unsuspected currents. In the cliffs and caves, so swiftly cut off and submerged by racing tides. Even the quiet fields down which they had walked this afternoon concealed unthought-of horrors; abandoned mine workings, deep pits and shafts, black as wells, lay hidden beneath the bracken. And scraps of fur and feather, and little bleached bones bore witness to the foxes who built their lairs in earthy hollows under the gorse.

And after nightfall the owl set up his predatory hooting, and the badger emerged to tunnel and scavenge. Not for him the thrill of the hunt. He was just as content to push the lid off a dustbin in the middle of the night, causing such a clatter as to waken the farmer's wife in a cold sweat of fright.

"Mummy. It's cooked." Cara's voice broke across her

thoughts. She looked up and saw Cara holding a stick aloft, a fragment of fish impaled dangerously upon its point. "Come and get it *quickly* before it falls off!" Her voice was agonised, and Virginia got to her feet, dusting the sand off the seat of her bathing-suit, and went down to join in the picnic.

In the afterglow of the setting sun, with the offshore wind cool on their faces, they climbed slowly home. After the swim the children were sleepy and silent. Nicholas was not too proud to accept a piggy-back from Eustace, and Virginia carried the wet bathing things and towels in the string bag which had been used for the mackerel, and helped Cara along with the other hand. They were all sandy, salty, tousled, weary, and the path was steep and the climb, up through the bracken and the treacherous undergrowth, exhausting. But at last they reached the fields at the top, and after that the going was easy. Behind them the sea, luminous in the half-light, reflected all the colours of the sky, and ahead was Bosithick, cradled in the curve of the hill, with the road behind it flickering, every now and then, with the searchlight glare of a passing car.

Some of Eustace's cows had strayed through a gap in the hedge into the top field. In the dusk they loomed, brown and white, and made pleasant munching sounds, raising their heads to watch as the small procession walked by.

Nicholas said, leaning forward to speak into Eustace's ear, "Are you going to come back with us?"

He smiled. "Time I was getting home."

"We would like you to stay for supper."

"You've had your supper," Eustace told him.

"I thought that was tea."

"Don't tell me you've got room for more food."

Nicholas yawned. "No, maybe not."

Virginia said, "I'll make you cocoa, and you can drink it in bed."

"Yes," said Nicholas. "But it would be nice if Eustace would come and talk to us while we had our baths . . ."

Cara chimed in. "Yes, and then Mummy could get our cocoa ready, and you could talk to us."

"I'll do more than that," said Eustace. "I'll scrub the sand off your backs."

They giggled in a high-pitched fashion as though this were very funny, and as soon as they were indoors raced for the bathroom to fight over the taps. Ominous splashing sounds came from beyond the door, and Eustace, rolling up his sleeves, moved in to break it up. Virginia heard him saying, "Quiet now, you'll sink the ship if you don't watch out."

Leaving him to it, she carried the fishy string bag out to the kitchen and emptied the bathing things and the sand-encrusted towels into the sink, and rinsed them out and wrung them, and carried them out into the dark garden, and, by feel, found the clothes-line and pegged them out, leaving them to billow and flap like ghosts in the darkness.

Back in the kitchen, she poured milk into a saucepan, put it on to heat, stood watching it, leaning against the cooker, yawning a little. She put up a hand to her eyes, and found that her face was rough with sand, so she took the little mirror out of her handbag, and a comb, and propped the mirror on one of the shelves of the dresser and tried to do something about her hair, but it was stiff and dry with salt, and full of sand. She thought that if there had been a shower, she would have washed it, but the idea of putting it under a tap was somehow all too difficult, too complicated. In the inadequate light her reflection gazed back at her from the round mirror, and there were freckles across the bridge of her nose, but her eyes were shadowed, dark as two holes in her face.

The milk rose in the pan. She made the two mugs of cocoa, put them on a tray, started upstairs with them. She saw that the bathroom was empty, a trail of damp towels and footprints led upstairs. She heard voices and came along the passage, and their bedroom door stood open.

They were inside and they did not see her. She stood and watched them. Eustace sat, with his back to her, on Cara's bed, and the children were perched on Nicholas's bed. All three heads together, Eustace was being given a guided tour of Cara's photographs.

"And this is Daddy. The big one here. He's terribly good-looking, don't you think? . . ." This was Cara, as chatty now as she could be with someone with whom she was completely at ease. "And this is our house in Scotland, that's my bedroom, and that's Nicholas's bedroom, and that's the nursery up at the top . . ."

"That's my bedroom!"

"I said it was that bedroom, silly. And this is Nanny's room, and that's Mummy's room, but you can't see the rooms at the back because they're round at the back. And this is an aerial view . . ."

"A man took it in an aeroplane . . ."

"And that's all the park and the river. And that's the walled garden."

"And that's Mr McGregor on his tractor, and that's Bob and that's Fergie."

Eustace was beginning to lose the thread. ". . . Hold on now, who are Bob and Fergie?"

"Well, Bob helps Mr McGregor and Fergie helps the gardener. Fergie plays the bagpipes and do you know who taught him? His uncle. And do you know what his uncle is called? Muncle." Nicholas triumphantly produced the answer.

Eustace said, "Uncle Muncle."

"And this is Daddy skiing at St Moritz, and that's all of us at a grouse shoot – at least, we went to the picnic bit, we didn't go up the hill. And that's the bit of the river where we sometimes swim, but it's not always very safe, and the stones hurt your feet. But Mummy says we can have a swimming-pool, she says when we go back to Kirkton, we can have a swimming-pool, just like Aunt Alice Lingard's . . ."

"And that's Daddy's car, it's a great big Jaguar. It's a . . ." Nicholas faltered. "It was a great big Jaguar." He finished bravely, "Green."

Virginia said, "Here's your cocoa."

"Oh Mummy, we were showing Eustace all the photographs of Kirkton . . ."

"Yes, I heard."

"That was very nice," said Eustace. "Now I know all about Scotland."

He stood up, as though to get out of Virginia's way, and went to put the photograph frame back on to the chest of drawers.

The children climbed into bed. "You'll have to come and see us. You'll have to come and stay. Won't he, Mummy? He can sleep in the spare room, can't he?"

"Maybe," said Virginia. "But Eustace is a busy man."

"That's it," said Eustace. "Busy. Always got plenty to do. Well . . ." He moved towards the open door. "I'll say good night."

"Oh, good night, Eustace. And thank you for taking us to that lovely place."

"Don't dream about Jack Carley."

"Even if I do I shan't be frightened."

"That's the way. Good night, Nicholas."

"Good night. I'll see you in the morning."

Virginia said to him, "Don't go. I'll be down in a moment."

He said, "I'll wait downstairs."

The cocoa was duly consumed, between yawns. Their eyes drooped. At last they lay down and Virginia kissed them good night. But when she kissed Nicholas he did a surprising thing. Most undemonstrative of children, he put his arms around her neck and held her cheek down against his own.

She said, gently, "What is it?"

"It was a nice place, wasn't it?"

"You mean the little beach?"

"No. The house where Eustace lives."

"Penfolda."

"Will we go back?"

"Sure to."

"I loved that little kitten."

"I know you did."

"Eustace is downstairs."

"Yes."

"I shall hear you talking." His voice was filled with satisfaction. "I shall hear you go talk, talk, talk."

"Will that be cosy?"

"I think so," said Nicholas.

They were near to sleep, but still she stayed with them, moving quickly about the room, picking up stray clothes and folding them and putting them, neat as Nanny, across the seats of the two rickety cane chairs. This done, she went to close the window a little, for the night air was growing chill, to draw the skimpy curtains. The room, by the meagre light of the bedside lamp was all at once enclosed, safe, soft with shadows, the only sound the ticking of Cara's clock and the breathing of the children.

She was filled, in that moment, with love. For her children; for this strange little house; for the man, downstairs, who waited for her. And aware, too, of a marvellous sense of completion, of rightness. It will be the first time, she thought, that Eustace and I have been alone, with all the time in the world. Just the two of us. She would light the fire for company and draw the curtains and make him a jug of coffee. If they wished, they could talk all night. They could be together.

Cara and Nicholas were sleeping. She turned off the light and went downstairs to unexpected and surprising darkness. For an incredulous moment she thought that

Eustace had changed his mind and already gone, but then she saw that he stood by the window, smoking, watching the very last of the light fade from the sky. A little of this light was reflected upon his face, but when he heard her footstep he turned, and she could see no expression on his face, only shadows.

She said, "I thought you'd gone."

"No. I'm still here."

The darkness disturbed her. She reached for the lamp on the table and switched it on. Yellow light was thrown, like a pool, between them. She waited for him to speak, but when he said nothing, simply stood there, smoking, she began to fill the silence with words.

"I . . . I don't know about supper. Do you want something to eat? I don't even know what time it is."

"I'm all right."

"I could make you some coffee . . ."

"You haven't got a can of beer?"

She made a helpless gesture. "I haven't, Eustace. I'm sorry. I never bought any. I never drink it." That sounded priggish, as though she disapproved of beer. "I mean, I just don't like the taste." She smiled, trying to turn it into a joke.

"It doesn't matter."

The smile collapsed. Virginia swallowed. "Are you sure you wouldn't like coffee?"

"No, thank you." He began to look about for somewhere to stub out his cigarette. She found him a saucer and put it on the table, and he demolished the stub as though he had a personal, vicious grudge against it.

"I must go."

"But . . ."

He turned towards her, waiting for her to finish. She lost her nerve. "Yes. It's been a good day. It was kind of you to give up your day for us and show us the cove and . . . everything." Her voice sounded high-pitched and formal as though she were opening a sale of work. "The children loved it."

"They're good children."

"Yes. I . . ."

"When are you going back to Scotland?"

The abruptness of the question, the coldness of his voice, were shocking. She was suddenly cold, a shiver of apprehension trickling down her spine like a stream of icy water.

"I . . . I'm not sure." She took hold of the back of one of the wooden chairs, leaning against it as if for support. "Why do you ask?"

"You're going to go back."

It was a statement, not a question. Faced with it, Virginia's natural diffidence leapt to the worst conclusion. Eustace expected her to go, even wanted her to go. She heard herself telling him, with marvellous lightness, "Well, some time, of course. After all, it's my home. The children's home."

"I hadn't realised until this evening that it was such a considerable property . . ."

"Oh, you mean, Cara's photographs . . ."

"But then, you have plenty of people to help you run it."

"I don't run it, Eustace."

"Then you should. Learn something about farming. You'd be surprised how much there is to it. You should take an interest, start up something new. An Aberdeen Angus herd. Did your husband ever think of doing that? You can sell a good bull at the Perth sales for sixty, seventy thousand pounds."

It was like a conversation in a nightmare, mad and pointless. She said, "Can you?" but her mouth was dry and the words scarcely made any sound at all.

"Of course. And who knows, one day you may have built up something really great to hand on to that boy of yours."

"Yes."

He said again, "I must go." The trace of a smile crossed his features. "It was a good day."

But Virginia remembered a better one, that other day she had spent with Eustace, the spring afternoon of sun and wind when he had bought her an ice-cream and finally driven her home. And he had promised to telephone her, and then forgotten, or perhaps he had changed his mind. She realised that she had been waiting, all afternoon, for him to tell her what really happened. She had been expecting him to bring up the subject, perhaps as a story for the children to share, or as a scrap of harmless nostalgia to be remembered, over the years, by two old friends. But he had said nothing. And now she would never know.

"Yes." She let go of the chair and straightened up, folding her arms across her chest as though she were trying to stay warm. "A special day. The kind that people never forget."

He moved towards her, around the edge of the table, and Virginia turned away from him and went to open the door. Cool air, smelling sweet and damp, flooded in from a night arched in a sapphire sky, bright with stars. Out of the darkness a curlew sent up its long mournful cry.

He was beside her. "Good night, Virginia."

"Good night, Eustace."

And then he was going down the steps, away from her, over the wall and down the field towards the old farmyard where he had left his car. The dusk swallowed him. She closed the door and locked it and went back to the kitchen and took the children's cocoa mugs and washed them, slowly and carefully. She heard his Land-Rover go grinding up past the gate, up the lane towards the main road, heard the sound of the engine die away into the quiet night, but she never looked up from what she was doing. When the mugs were dry, the tea towel folded and there was nothing more to do, she found that she was exhausted. She turned off the lights and went slowly upstairs and undressed and climbed into bed. Her body lay slack, but the inside of her head behaved as though she had been living on black coffee for a week.

He doesn't love you.

I never thought he did.

But you were beginning to think so. After today.

Then I was wrong. We have no future together. He made that very clear.

What did you imagine was going to happen?

I imagined that he would be able to talk about what happened ten years ago.

Nothing happened. And why should he remember?

Because I did. Because Eustace was the most important person, the most important thing that ever happened to me.

You didn't remember. You married Anthony Keile.

They were married in London, in July; Virginia in a cream satin dress with a six-foot train and a veil that had belonged to Lady Keile's grandmother, and Anthony in a grey frock-coat and an immaculately cut pair of sponge-bag trousers. They emerged from St Michael's, Chester Square, with bells jangling, sun shining, and a small retinue of beribboned bridesmaids, extorting *oohs* and *aahs* of admiration from the thin crowd of inquisitive women who had realised that there was a wedding going on, and hung about to see what turned up when the doors were opened.

The excitement, the champagne, the pleasures of being loved and congratulated and kissed kept Virginia going until it was time to go upstairs and change. Her mother was there, ubiquitous, efficient, to unzip the clinging satin and unpin the borrowed tiara and the filmy veil.

"Oh, my dear, it all went off so beautifully, and you really did look enchanting, even though perhaps I shouldn't say anything so conceited about my own child . . . Darling, you're shivering, you're surely not cold?"

"No. I'm not cold."

"Change your shoes, then, and I'll help you on with your dress."

It was rose pink, with a tiny petalled hat to match, a charming useless ensemble that she would never wear again. She imagined coming back from her honeymoon, still wearing paper silk and pink petals, a little crushed by now, and going brown at the edges. (But of course they couldn't go brown, they weren't real, they were pretence petals . . .)

"And your suitcase is in the boot of Anthony's car, such a good idea taking a taxi round to the flat and picking the car up there, then you have none of this terrible horse-play with kippers and old shoes."

A roar, a galloping of feet, came from the passage outside the bedroom. Anthony's voice was raised in a comic sound like a hunting horn. "There! He sounds as though he's ready." She kissed Virginia briskly. "Have a good time, my darling."

The door burst open, and Anthony stood there, wearing the suit that he had chosen to go away in, and with a large sunhat on the top of his head. He was considerably drunk.

"Here she is! We're off to the South of France, my love, which is why I am wearing this hat."

Mrs Parsons, laughing indulgently, removed it, smoothed his hair with her long fingers, straightened his tie. She might have been the bride, not Virginia, who stood and watched this little ceremony with a face that held no expression whatsoever. Anthony held out a hand to her. "Come on," he said. "Time we went."

The hired car, awash in confetti, took them back to the Parsons' flat, where Anthony's car was waiting for them. The plan had been that they should get straight into his car and drive to the airport, but Virginia had a latch-key in her purse, and instead, they let themselves in and went into the kitchen, and she tied an apron around the pink silk dress, and Anthony sat on the table and watched while she brewed him up a jug of black coffee.

For their honeymoon they had been lent a villa in Antibes. By their second day Anthony had met an old friend; by the end of the first week, he knew everyone in the place. Virginia told herself that this was what she had expected, was what she wanted. Anthony's gregarious instincts were part of his charm, and one of the things that had attracted her to him in the first place. Besides, after one day it became very obvious that they were going to find it hard to think of things to say to each other. Conversation at meals was inclined to be distinctly sticky. She realised then, that they had never been alone together before now.

There was a couple, called Janey and Hugh Rouse; he was a writer and they had rented a house at Cap Ferrat. Janey was older than Virginia and Virginia liked her, and found her easy to talk to. Once, sitting on the terrace at the Rouses' house, waiting for the men to come up from the rocks, Janey had said, "How long have you known Anthony, honey?" She had lived, as a child, in the States, and although she did not speak with an American accent, her speech was spattered with words and phrases which instantly gave her origins away.

"Not very long. I met him in May."

"Love at first sight, hm?"

"I don't know. I suppose so."

"How old are you?"

"Eighteen."

"That's awfully young to settle down. Not that I can see that Anthony settling down too much for a few years yet."

"He'll have to," Virginia told her. "You see, we're going to live in Scotland. Anthony's been left this estate, Kirkton . . . it used to belong to an uncle who was a bachelor. And we're going to go and live there."

"You mean, you think Anthony will spend all his time tramping around in a tweed suit with mud on his boots?"

"Not exactly. But I can't believe that living in Scotland is going to be quite the same as living in London."

"It won't," said Janey, who had been there. "But don't expect the simple life, or you'll be disappointed."

But Virginia did expect the simple life. She had never seen Kirkton, never been to Scotland for that matter, but she had once spent an Easter holiday with a schoolfriend who lived in Northumberland and somehow she imagined that Scotland would be rather like that, and that Kirkton would be a low-ceilinged, rambling, stone farmhouse, with flagged floors, and worn Turkey carpets, and a dining-room with a great log fire and hunting prints on the walls.

Instead, she was presented with a tall, square, elegantly proportioned Adam house, with sash windows full of reflected sunshine, and a flight of stone stairs which led, from the carriage sweep, up to the front door.

Beyond the gravel was grass, and then a ha-ha wall, and then the park, landscaped with giant beeches, sloping down to the distant silver curve of the river.

Overwhelmed, silent, Virginia had followed Anthony up the steps and through the door. The house was empty, old-fashioned and unfurnished. Between them they were going to do it up. To Virginia the task seemed daunting, but when she said as much Anthony overrode her.

"We'll get Philip Sayer on to it, he's this interior decorator my mother got to do the house in London for her. Otherwise we'll make the most ghastly mistakes and the place will be a mess."

Virginia privately thought she preferred her own ghastly mistakes to somebody else's impeccable taste – it was more homely; but she said nothing.

"And this is the drawing-room, and then the library beyond. And the dining-room, and there are kitchens and stuff downstairs."

The room soared and echoed, the icy prisms of crystal chandeliers glinted, descending from ornately decorated ceilings. There was panelling and marvellous cornices over the tall windows. There was dust and a distinct feeling of chill.

They mounted to the first floor up a curved stairway, airy and elegant, and their steps echoed on the polished treads and through the empty house. Upstairs, there were bedrooms, each with its own bathroom, dressing-rooms, linen rooms, housemaid's cupboards, even a boudoir.

"What would I do with a boudoir?" Virginia wanted to know.

"You can come and boud in it, and if you don't know what that means, it's French for sulk. Oh, come on, take that horrified expression off your face and look as though you're enjoying yourself."

"It's just so big."

"You talk as though it were Buckingham Palace."

"I've never been in such a big house. I certainly never thought I would live in one."

"Well, you're going to, so you'd better get used to it."

Eventually they were outside again, standing by the car, staring up at the elegant front elevation, regularly spaced with windows. Virginia put her hands deep in the pockets of her coat and said, "Where's the garden?"

"What do you mean?"

"I mean flower-beds and stuff. Flowers. You know. A garden."

But the garden was a half-mile away, enclosed by a wall. They drove there and went inside and found a gardener and rows of fruit and vegetables like soldiers, waiting to be picked off.

"This is the garden," said Anthony.

"Oh," said Virginia.

"What's that meant to mean?"

"Nothing. Just oh."

The interior decorator duly arrived. Hard on his heels came vans and lorries, builders, plasterers, painters, men with carpets, men with curtains, men in pantechnicons which spilled out furniture like cornucopias, endlessly, as though they would never run out.

Virginia let it all happen. "Yes," she would say, agreeing to whatever shade of velvet Philip Sayer was suggesting. Or "Yes" when he thought of Victorian brass bedsteads in the spare room, and thick white crochet bedcovers. "Terribly Osborne, my dear, you know, Victorian Country Life."

The only time that she had raised her voice with an independent idea was over the kitchen. She wanted it like the one she remembered, the marvellous room at Penfolda with its air of stability, the suggestion in the air of good things cooking, the cat in the chair and the geraniums crowded on the window-sill.

"A farmhouse kitchen! That's what I want. A farmhouse kitchen's like a living-room."

"Well, I'm not going to live in any kitchen, I'll tell you that."

And she had let Anthony have his way because, after all, it was not her house, and it was not her money which paid for the stainless steel sinks, and the black-and-white floor and the patent self-cleaning cooking unit with eye-level grill, and a spit for broiling chickens.

It was finished and Virginia was pregnant.

"How marvellous for Nanny!" said Lady Keile.

"Why?"

"Well, darling, she's in London, doing temporary work, but she's longing, but longing for a new baby. Of course she won't be all that keen on leaving London, but she's bound to make friends, you know what this nannies' network's like, better than the English Speaking Union I always say. And that top floor is *meant* to be a nursery, you can tell by the gate at the top of the stairs, and the bars on the windows. Gorgeously sunny. I think pale blue, don't you? For carpets, I mean, and then French chintz curtains . . ."

Virginia tried to stand up for herself. To say, *No. I will look after my own baby*. But she was so sick carrying Cara, so weak and unwell, that by the time she once again felt strong enough to cope with the situation and stand on her own two feet, the nursery had been decorated and Nanny was there, established, rigid, immovable.

I'll let her stay. Just until the baby's born and I'm on my feet again. She can stay for a month or two, and then I'll tell her that she can go back to London because I want to look after my baby for myself.

But by then, there were further complications. Virginia's mother, in London, complained of pains and tiredness; she thought she was losing weight. Virginia at once went south to see her, and after that, her loyalties were torn between her baby in Scotland and her mother in London. Travelling up and down in the train it became very clear that it would be madness to get rid of Nanny until Mrs Parsons had recovered. But of course, she didn't recover and, by the time the whole ghastly nightmare was over, Nicholas had arrived and, with two babies in the nursery, Nanny was dug in for good.

At Kirkton they were surrounded, within a radius of ten miles or so, by a number of entertaining neighbours. Young couples with time and money to spare, some with young children like the Keiles's, all with interests which matched Anthony's.

For appearances' sake, he put in a certain amount of time on the farm, talking to McGregor, the grieve, finding out what McGregor thought should be done, and then telling McGregor to do it. The rest of the day was his own, and he used it to the full, doing exactly what he wanted. Scotland is a country geared to the pleasures of menfolk, and there was always shooting to be got, grouse in the summer, and partridges and pheasants in the autumn and winter. There were rivers to be fished and golf courses and a social life which was even gayer than the one he had left behind in London.

Virginia did not fish or play golf and Anthony would not have invited her to join him even if she had wanted to. He preferred the company of his men friends, and she was expected to be present only when they had been invited specifically as a couple. To a dinner or a dance, or perhaps to lunch before a point-to-point, when she would go through agonies trying to decide what to put on, and inevitably turn up in what everybody had been wearing last year.

She was still shy. And she didn't drink so there seemed no artificial way of getting over this terrible defect. The men, Anthony's friends, obviously thought her a bore. And their wives, though kind and friendly, terrified her with their private jokes and their incomprehensible references to places and persons and events known only to them. They were like a lot of girls who had all been to the same school.

Once, driving home after a dinner party, they quarrelled. Virginia had not meant to quarrel but she was tired and unhappy, and Anthony was more than a little drunk. He always seemed to drink too much at parties, almost as though it were a social grace that was expected of him. This evening it made him aggressive and bad-tempered.

"Well, did you enjoy yourself?"

"Not particularly."

"You certainly didn't look as though you did."

"I was tired."

"You're always tired. And yet you never seem to do a thing."

"Perhaps that's why I'm tired."
"And what does that mean?"
"Oh, nothing."
"It has to mean something."
"All right, it means that I get bored and lonely."
"That's not my fault."
"Isn't it? You're never there . . . sometimes you're not in the house all day. You have lunch at the club in Relkirk . . . I never see you."
"OK. Me and about a hundred other chaps. What do you suppose their wives do? Sit and mope?"
"I've wondered what they do with their time. You tell me."
"Well, they get around, that's what. They see each other, take the children to Pony Club meets, play bridge; I suppose, garden."
"I can't play bridge," said Virginia, "and the children don't want to ride ponies, and I would garden only there isn't a garden at Kirkton, just a four-walled prison for flowers, and a bad-tempered gardener who won't let me so much as cut a bunch of gladioli without asking him first."
"Oh, for heaven's sake . . ."
She said, "I watch other people. Ordinary couples, sometimes on Saturdays in Relkirk. Doing the shopping together in the rain or the sunshine, and children with them, sucking ice-creams, and they put all the parcels into shabby little cars and drive home, and they look so happy and cosy, all together."
"Oh, God. You can't want that."
"I want not to be lonely."
"Loneliness is a state of mind. Only you can do anything about that."
"Weren't you ever lonely, Anthony?"
"No."
"Then you didn't marry me for company. And you didn't marry me for my startling conversation."

"No." Coldly agreeing, his profile was stony.

"Then why?"

"You were pretty. You had a certain fawn-like charm. You were very charming. My mother thought you were very charming. She thought your mother was very charming. She thought the whole bloody arrangement was charming."

"But you didn't marry me because your mother told you to."

"No. But you see, I had to marry somebody, and you turned up at such a singularly opportune time."

"I don't understand."

He did not reply to this. For a little he drove in silence, perhaps prompted by some shred of decency not to tell her the truth, now or ever. But Virginia, having come so far, made the mistake of pressing him. "Anthony, I don't understand," and he lost his temper and told her.

"Because I was left Kirkton on condition that I was married when I took it over. Uncle Arthur thought I would never settle down, would break the place up if I moved in as a bachelor . . . I don't know what he thought, but he was determined that if I lived at Kirkton I'd do it as a family man."

"So that's why!"

Anthony frowned. "Are you hurt?"

"I don't think so. Should I be?"

He fumbled for her hand with his own . . . the car swerved slightly as his fingers closed over hers. He said, "It's all right. It may be no better, but it's certainly no worse than other marriages. Sometimes it's a good thing to be frank and clear the air. It's better to know where we both stand."

She said, "Do you ever regret it? Marrying me, I mean."

"No. I don't regret it. I'm just sorry that it had to happen when we were both so young."

One day she found herself in the house alone. Quite

alone. It was Saturday, and afternoon. Mr McGregor, the grieve, had gone to Relkirk, taking Mrs McGregor with him. Anthony was playing golf, and Nanny and the children were out for a walk. An empty house and nothing to do. No washing to be done, no cake to be baked, no ironing, no garden to weed. Virginia walked through it, going from room to room, as though she were a stranger who had paid to see around, and her footsteps echoed on the polished staircase, and there was the tick of the clock, and everywhere order, neatness. This was what Anthony loved. This was what he had created. This was why he had married her. She ended up in the hall, opened the front door and went down the steps on to the gravel, thinking that she would maybe spy Nanny and the children in the distance; she would go to meet them, run and snatch Cara up in her arms, hug her and hold her, if only to prove that she really existed, that she was not a dream-child that Virginia had conceived, like some frustrated spinster, out of her own imagination.

But there was no sign of Nanny and, after a little, she went back up the steps and so indoors again, because there did not seem to be anywhere else to go.

There was a pretty girl, called Liz, married to a young lawyer. He worked in Edinburgh, but they lived only a mile or two from Kirkton, in an old, converted Presbyterian manse, with a wild garden, that was filled with daffodils in the spring, and a paddock for the ponies.

She had young children, dogs, a cat, and a parrot in a cage, but – perhaps because she missed her husband who was in Edinburgh all week, or perhaps because she was simply a girl who enjoyed people – her house was always full. Other mothers' children lolloped about on the ponies, crowded the dining-room table at tea-time, played rounders on the lawn. If she didn't have whole families staying with her, then she had whole families for the day, feeding them on huge roasts of beef, and steak-and-kidney pies, marvellous old-fashioned puddings, and home-made ice-creams. Her drinks cupboard, which must have taken a frightening beating from the hordes who passed through her hospitable doorway, was always open, always at hand for any guest in need of a little liquid refreshment.

"Help yourself," she would call through the open door, while she knocked up a three-course dinner for ten unexpected guests. "There's ice in the fridge if the ice-bucket's empty."

Anthony, naturally enough, adored her, flirted cheerfully and openly with her, put on a great show of jealousy when the weekends came around and her husband was home.

"Get that bloody man out of the house," he would tell Liz, and she would go into gales of delighted laughter, as would everybody else who was listening. Virginia smiled, and over their heads met the eye of Liz's husband. He was a quiet young man, and though he stood there, with a glass in his hand, smiling, it was almost impossible to tell what he was thinking.

"You'll have to watch out for that husband of yours," one of the other wives said to Virginia. But she only said, "I have been, for years," and changed the subject, or turned to speak to somebody else.

One Tuesday, Anthony called her from the club in Relkirk. "Virginia. Look, I've got embroiled in a poker game, God knows when I'll be home. But don't wait, I'll get a bite to eat here. See you later."

"All right. Don't lose too much money."

"I shall win," he told her. "I shall buy you a mink coat."

"That's just what I need."

He arrived home, after midnight, stumbling up the stairs. She heard him moving about in his dressing-room, dropping things, opening and shutting drawers, swearing at some cuff-link or button.

After a little, she heard him getting into bed, and the light beyond the open door went out, and there was only darkness. And she wondered if he had chosen to sleep in his dressing-room out of consideration to Virginia, or whether there was some other, more sinister reason.

She soon knew. The society in which they moved, the narrow clique, was too small for secrets. "Virginia darling, I told you to watch out for that naughty man of yours."

"What's he done now?"

"You are marvellous, the way you never get ruffled. You obviously know all about it."

"All about what?"

"Darling, the intimate dinner party that he had with Liz."

". . . Oh, yes, of course. Last Tuesday."

"He is an old devil. I suppose he thought none of us would find out. But then Midge and Johnny Gray suddenly decided on the spur of the moment to go up to the Strathtorrie Arms for dinner, you know, there's a new manager now, and it's all frightfully dark and chic and you can get a very good dinner. Anyway, off they went, and of course there were Anthony and Liz, all snugged up in a corner. And you knew all the time!"

"Yes."

"And you don't mind?"

"No."

That was the terrible thing. She didn't mind. She was apathetic, bored by Anthony and the outrageous schoolboy charm that had, as far as Virginia was concerned, long since worn itself to shreds. And this was not the first affair. It had happened before and it would doubtless happen again, but still, it was daunting to look down the years ahead and see herself tied for ever to this tedious Peter Pan. A man so unperceptive that he could gaily embark on a clandestine involvement, and yet conduct the whole affair on what was virtually his own front doorstep.

She thought about divorce, but knew that she would never divorce Anthony, not simply because of the children, but because she was Virginia, and she could no more embark, voluntarily, upon such a course than she could have flown to the moon.

She was not happy, but what would be the good of broadcasting her failure, her disillusion, to the rest of the world? Anthony did not love her, had never loved her. But then she had never loved him. If he had married Virginia to get his hands on Kirkton, then she had married Anthony on the rebound, in an emotional state of extreme unhappiness, and in a desperate bid to avoid the London Season that her mother had planned for her, culminating in the final nightmare of a coming-out dance.

She was not happy, but, to all intents and purposes, she had everything. A lovely house, a handsome husband, and the children. The children were worth everything. For them she would shore up her crumbling marriage, and for them she would create a world of security that they would never know again.

Anthony had been with Liz that night he was killed. He had called in at the Old Manse for a drink on his way back from Relkirk and was invited to stay for supper.

He rang Virginia.

"Liz has got the Cannons staying. She wants me to eat here and make up a four for bridge. I'll be home some time. Don't wait up."

Liz's cupboard with the whisky bottle stood open, as always. And as always Anthony helped himself liberally and with a generous hand. It was two o'clock before he started home, a black and starless night of pouring rain. It had been raining for days and the river was in spate. Afterwards the police came with tape measures and bits of chalk, and they measured the skid marks, and hung over the broken rail of the bridge and stared down into the muddy, swirling waters. And Virginia stood with them, in the drenching rain, and watched the divers go down, and there was a kindly sergeant who kept urging her to go back to the house, but she wouldn't go because, for some reason, she had to be there, because he had been her husband and the father of her children.

And she remembered what he had said, that night he told her about Kirkton. *I'm just sorry that it had to happen when we were both so young.*

8

The quiet night moved slowly past, the seconds, the minutes, the hours, measured by the ticking of Virginia's wristwatch which she had put on the table by her bed. Now, she reached out for it and saw that it was nearly three o'clock in the morning. She got out of bed, wrapped herself in the quilt and went to sit on the floor by the open window. It was the hour before dawn, dark and very still. She could hear, a mile or more away, the gentle movement, like breathing, of the sea. She could hear the soft shufflings and munchings of the Guernseys, grazing two or three fields distant; she could hear rustlings and whisperings and creepings from hedgerow and burrow, and the hooting of a night owl.

She found that she was devilled by the memory of Liz. Liz had come to Anthony's funeral wearing a face of grief and guilt so naked that instinctively one had turned away from it, not wanting to witness such pain. Soon afterwards her husband had taken her to the South of France for a holiday and Virginia had not seen her again.

But now she knew that she must go back to Scotland and soon, if it was only to square things up with Liz. To convince Liz that no blame could ever be laid at her door, to make – as far as was humanly possible – friends with her again. She thought of returning to Kirkton and this time her imagination did not turn and run but took the journey quietly and without horror. Off the road it went, and down over the bridge and the river, and up the drive between the lush meadows of the park. It came to the curving sweep in front of the house, and went up the steps and in through the front door, and now there was no longer the old familiar sensation of loneliness, of being trapped. But simply a sadness that the lives of the people who had lived in this beautiful house had achieved no lasting cohesion, but had unravelled like a length of badly spun yarn, and finally shredded away.

She would sell the house. Somewhere, some time, her subconscious had made the decision and now presented it to her conscious mind as a *fait accompli*. How much this phenomenon had to do with Eustace, Virginia could not at the moment comprehend. Later on, no doubt, it would all work itself out. For now the relief was enormous, like the shedding of a load carried too long, and she felt grateful, as though another person had stepped in and made the decision for her.

She would sell Kirkton. Buy another house, a little house . . . somewhere. Again, later on, it would all work itself out. She would make a new home, new friends, create a garden, buy a puppy, a kitten, a canary in a cage. Find schools for the children, fill the holidays with pleasures she had previously been too diffident to attempt. She would learn to ski; they would go on skiing holidays together. She would build kites and mend bicycles, let Cara read all the books she ever wanted, and go to Nicholas's sports days wearing the right sort of hat, and achieve marvellous things like winning the egg-and-spoon race.

And it would happen because she would make it happen. There was no more Eustace, no more dreams, but other good things were constant. Like pride, and resolution, and the children. The children. And she smiled, knowing that, like the arrow on the compass forever pointing north, whatever she did and however she behaved, she was always left, facing squarely in their direction.

She was beginning to be cold. The first lightening of dawn was beginning to creep up into the sky. She got up off the floor, took a sleeping-pill and a glass of water and climbed back into bed. When she opened her eyes again the sun, high in the sky, was shining full in her face, and from downstairs came a terrible racket, a banging at the front door and a voice calling her name.

"Virginia! It's me. Alice! Wake up, or are you all dead?"

Dazed with shock and sleep, Virginia stumbled out of bed, across the floor, and hung out of the window. "Alice! Stop making such a din. The children are asleep."

Alice, foreshortened, turned up an astonished face. Her voice dropped to an exaggerated stage-whisper. "I'd begun to think you'd all passed out. It's past ten. Come down and let me in!"

Yawning, incapable, Virginia groped for her dressing-gown, pushed her feet into slippers and went downstairs, pausing at the open door of the children's room on the way. To her surprise they were still asleep, undisturbed by Alice's shouting. She thought, we must have been late last night. We must have been much later than I realised.

She unlocked the door, to let in a flood of sunshine and Alice. Alice wore a crisp blue linen dress, a silk scarf over her head. As usual she was bright-skinned, clear-eyed, maddeningly awake.

"Do you usually wake up at this hour?"

"No, but – " Virginia swallowed a yawn " – I couldn't get to sleep last night. Eventually I took a pill. It must have knocked me out."

"And the children?"

"I didn't give them a pill, but they're still asleep. We were late, we were out all day." She yawned again, forced her eyes open. "How about some coffee?"

Alice looked amused. "You certainly look as though you'll need some. I tell you what. I'll make it, you go and get yourself woken up, and put some clothes on. It's no good talking to you when you're in this state." She laid her handbag on the table in a purposeful way. "I must say, this really isn't too bad a little house, is it? And here's the kitchen. A little poky, perhaps, but perfectly adequate . . ."

Virginia ran a bath, got into it and washed her hair. Afterwards, she went upstairs, wrapped in a towel, and took clean clothes from the drawer, and a cotton dress, as yet unworn, from the wardrobe. She pushed her feet into sandals, combed her sleek wet hair into place, and feeling clean and strangely hungry, went back downstairs to Alice.

She found her thoroughly organised, the kettle on the gas, the jug ready with the coffee, mugs laid out on the table.

"Oh, there you are . . . we're just about ready . . . I thought we'd have proper coffee; I get so fed up with this wishy-washy stuff, don't you?"

Virginia sat on the edge of the table. "When did you get back from London?"

"Last night."

"How was it? Did you have fun?"

"Yes, but I didn't come here to talk about London."

"In that case, what brought you here at ten o'clock on a Monday morning?"

"Curiosity," said Alice. "Sheer, undiluted curiosity."

"About me?"

"About Eustace Philips!"

Virginia said, "I don't understand."

"Mrs Jilkes told me. I was scarcely in through the front door when I was hearing all about it. She said that Eustace had telephoned her while I was away to ask if anybody was getting Bosithick ready for you and the children. And she said I was in London, and he said not to bother, he'd see to it."

"Yes, that's right . . . and he did too . . ."

"But Virginia . . . You talked about Eustace, but you never told me that you'd met him again."

"Didn't I?" Virginia frowned. "No, I didn't, did I?"

"But when did you meet him?"

"That day I came out to see the cottage. Do you remember? I said I wouldn't be back for lunch. And I went to the pub in Lanyon to buy cigarettes and I met him there."

"But why didn't you say anything about it? Was there any particular reason that you didn't want me to know?"

"No." She tried to remember. "But I suppose I just didn't want to talk about him." She smiled. "It wasn't as though it had been such a friendly reunion. In fact, we had the most terrible row . . ."

"But did you *mean* to meet him again?"

"No. It just happened."

"And he remembered you? After all this time? But he'd only ever seen you that once at the barbecue."

"No," said Virginia. "I did see him again."

"*When?*"

"About a week after the barbecue. I met him in Porthkerris. We spent the afternoon together and he drove me back to Wheal House. You didn't see him because you were out that day. But my mother was there. She knew about it."

"But why was it all kept such a secret?"

"It wasn't a secret, Alice. It was just that my mother didn't like Eustace. I must say, he didn't make much of an effort to impress her, and he was rude and the Land-Rover was covered with bits of straw and mud and manure . . . not my mother's cup of tea at all. She treated the whole incident as though it were a sort of joke, but I knew that he had made her angry, and that she didn't like him."

"But you could have talked to me about him. After all, it was I who introduced you to Eustace."

"I tried, but every time I started, my mother somehow

broke into the conversation or changed the subject or interrupted in some way. And . . . you mustn't forget this, Alice . . . you were her friend, not mine. I was just the little girl, out of the nursery. I never imagined for a moment that you'd take my side against hers."

"Was it a question of taking sides?"

"It would have been. You know what a snob she was."

"Oh, yes, of course, but it was harmless."

"No, Alice, it wasn't harmless. It was terribly dangerous. It affected everything she did. It deformed her."

"Virginia!" Alice was shocked.

"That's why we suddenly went back to London. You see, she knew, she guessed right away, that I was in love with Eustace."

The kettle boiled. Alice lifted it, and filled the coffee jug, and the kitchen was suffused with a delicious fresh smell. Alice drew a spoon gently across the surface of the coffee.

"And were you?" she asked at last. "In love with Eustace?"

"Of course I was. Wouldn't you have been at seventeen?"

"But you married Anthony Keile."

"Yes."

"Did you love him?"

"I . . . I married him."

"Were you happy?"

"I was lonely . . ."

"But, Virginia, I always thought . . . I mean, your mother always said . . . I thought you were so happy," Alice finished, hopeless with confusion.

"No. But it wasn't all Anthony's fault. It was my fault, too."

"Did Lady Keile know this?"

"No." Nor did she know the circumstances of

Anthony's death. Nor did she know about Liz. Nor was she ever going to. "Why should she know? She used to come and stay with us, but never for more than a week at a time. It wasn't difficult to foster the illusion of an idyllically happy marriage. It was the least we could do for her . . ."

"I'm surprised Nanny never said anything."

"Nanny never saw anything she didn't want to see. And to her, Anthony was perfection."

"It can't have been easy."

"No, but like I said, it wasn't all Anthony's fault."

"And Eustace?"

"Alice, I was seventeen; a little girl, waiting for someone to come and buy her an ice-cream."

"But not now . . ." said Alice.

"No. Now I'm twenty-seven and the mother of two children. And I'm not waiting for ice-creams any longer."

"You mean, he has nothing to give you."

"And he needs nothing from me. He's self-sufficient. He has his own life. He has Penfolda."

"Have you discussed this with him?"

"Oh, Alice . . ."

"You obviously haven't. So how can you be so certain?"

"Because all those years ago, he said he'd phone me. He said that he wanted me to come out to Penfolda for tea or something, to meet his mother again. And I was going to borrow your car and drive myself out here. But you see, he never telephoned. I waited, but he never telephoned. And before there was time to find out why, or do anything about it, I'd been whisked back to London by my mother."

Alice said, "And how do you *know* he never telephoned?" She was beginning to sound impatient.

"Because he never did."

"Perhaps your mother took the call."

"I asked her. And she said there'd never been any telephone call."

"But, Virginia, she was perfectly capable of taking a call and never telling you about it. Specially if she didn't like the young man. Surely you realised that."

Her voice was brisk and practical. Virginia stared, scarcely able to believe her ears. That Alice should say such things about Rowena Parsons – Alice of all people, her mother's oldest friend. Alice, coming out with a dark truth that Virginia had never had the courage to find out for herself. She remembered her mother's face, smiling across the railway carriage, the laughing protest. *Darling! What an accusation. Of course not. You surely didn't think . . .*

And Virginia had believed her. She said at last, helplessly, "I thought she was telling me the truth. I didn't think she was capable of lying."

"Let's say she was a determined person. And you were her only child. She always had great ambitions for you."

"You knew this. You knew this about her and yet she was still your friend."

"Friends aren't people you particularly like for any special reason. You just like people because they're your friends."

"But if she was lying, then Eustace must have thought that I didn't want to see him again. All these years he's been thinking I simply let him down."

"But he wrote you a letter," said Alice.

"A *letter*?"

"Oh, Virginia, don't be so dense. That letter that came for you. The day before you went back to London." Virginia continued to stare blankly. "I know there was a letter. It came by the afternoon post, and it was on the table in the hall and I thought 'How nice' because you didn't get many letters. And then I went off to do something or other and when I came back the letter had gone. I presumed you'd taken it."

A letter. Virginia saw the letter. Imagined the envelope as white, the writing very black, addressed to her. Miss Virginia Parsons. Lying unattended and vulnerable upon that round table that still stood in the centre of the hall at Wheal House. She saw her mother come out of the drawing-room, perhaps on her way upstairs, pause to inspect the afternoon's mail. She was wearing the raspberry-red suit with the white silk shirt, and when she put out her hand to pick up the letter, her nails were painted the same raspberry-red, and her heavy gold charm bracelet made a jingling sound, like bells.

She saw her frown at the writing, the black masculine writing, inspect the postmark, hesitate for perhaps a second, and then slip the envelope into the pocket of her jacket and carry on with what she was doing, unperturbed, as though nothing had happened.

She said, "Alice, I never got that letter."

"But it was there!"

"Don't you see? Mother must have taken it. Destroyed it. She would, you know. She would say, 'It's all for Virginia's sake. For Virginia's own good.'"

Illusions were gone for ever, the veil torn away. She could look back with a cool, objective regard and see her mother the way she had really been, not merely snobbish and determined, but devious too. In some odd way, this was a relief. It had taken some effort, all these years, to sustain the legend of an irreproachable parent, even though Virginia had been deceiving nobody but herself. Now, remembered, she seemed much more human.

Alice was looking upset, as though already regretting any mention of the letter.

"Perhaps it wasn't from Eustace."

"It was."

"How do you know?"

"Because if it had been from anyone else, then she would have given it back to me, with some excuse or other about opening it by mistake."

"But we don't know what was in the letter."

Virginia got off the table. "No. But I'm going to find out. Now. Will you stay here till the children wake up? Will you tell them I shan't be long?"

"But where are you going?"

"To see Eustace, of course," said Virginia, from the door.

"But you haven't drunk your coffee. I made you coffee and you haven't even drunk it. And what are you going to say to him? And how are you going to explain?"

But Virginia had already gone. Alice was speaking to an empty room, an open, swinging door. With an exclamation of exasperation, she put down her coffee-cup and went to the door as though to call Virginia back, but Virginia was already out of earshot, running like a child through the tall summer grass, across the fields in the direction of Penfolda.

She took the field path because it would have taken too long to get into the car and turn it and drive back along the main road. And time was too precious to be wasted. They had already lost ten years, and there was not another moment to spare.

She was running, through a joyous morning of honey-scents and white daisies and tall grass that whipped at her bare legs. The sea was a dark, purplish blue, striped with ribbons of turquoise, and the horizon was blurred in a haze that promised great heat. She was running, long-legged, taking the steps of the stiles two at a time, and the ditches of the stubble fields brimmed with red poppies and the air was filled with the petals of yellow gorse flowers, blown to confusion, like confetti, by the sea-wind.

She came across the last field, and Penfolda lay ahead of her, the house and the long barns, and the little garden, wall-enclosed from the wind. She went over the last stile that led into the vegetable garden, and down the path and through the gate, and she saw that the cat and her half-Siamese kittens lay in the sun on the doorstep, and the front door stood open and she went indoors and called Eustace, and the house was dark after the brightness of the day outside.

"Who's that?"

It was Mrs Thomas, carrying a duster, peering over the banister.

"It's me. Virginia. Virginia Keile. I'm looking for Eustace."

"He's just coming in from milking . . ."

"Oh, thank you." Without bothering to wait and explain, she went back out of doors, and started across the lawn, making for the cattle court and the milking parlour. But at that moment he appeared, coming through the gate that opened into the far side of the garden. He was in shirt-sleeves, aproned, wearing rubber boots and carrying a polished aluminium pail of milk. Virginia stopped dead. He closed the latch of the gate behind him and looked up and saw her.

She had meant to be very sensible. To say, calmly and quietly, "I want to ask you about the letter you wrote me." But it didn't happen like that at all. For everything was said in that long moment, while they stood and looked at each other, and then Eustace set down his bucket and started towards her, and she ran down the slope of the grass and into his arms, and she was laughing, her face pressed into the front of his shirt, and he was saying, "It's all right. It's all right," just as though she were crying, not laughing. And Virginia said, "I love you," and then she burst into tears.

He said, "Of course I telephoned. Three or four times. But you were never there. It was always your mother and each time I felt more of a fool and each time she said that she'd tell you I'd called and that you'd ring me back. And I thought maybe you'd changed your mind. I thought perhaps you'd decided you had better things to do than come and have tea with someone like me and my old mother. I thought maybe your mother had talked you round. She didn't lose any love on me, not from the first moment she set eyes on me. But you knew that, didn't you?"

"Yes, I knew. And I wondered. Once, I nearly rang you up. I thought perhaps you'd forgotten . . . and then I lost my nerve. And then, out of the blue, my mother said we had to go back to London and after that, there wasn't any time. And in the train, I asked her, straight out, if you'd ever called and she said never. And I believed her. That was the terrible thing, I always believed her. I should have known. It was my fault, I should have known. Oh, Eustace, why was I such a ninny?"

They had come indoors, ostensibly to find a clean handkerchief for Virginia, and for no particular reason had stayed there, ending up, inevitably, in the kitchen, sitting at the scrubbed table, with the air filled with the smell of baking saffron bread, and the only sound to disturb them the slow ticking of the old-fashioned pendulum clock.

"You weren't a ninny," said Eustace. "You were seventeen. That was another of the things that bothered me. It would have been easy to persuade you, push you around, before you'd even had time to grow up and make up your own mind about things. That's what I said in the letter. When you never rang me back, I thought maybe you'd got cold feet. So I said that if you wanted to wait a couple of years, I'd be ready to wait too, see how we felt about things then." He grinned, ruefully. "It took some writing, I can tell you. I'd never said such things to a girl before, nor have since."

"And you thought I'd never even bothered to reply?"

"I didn't know what to think . . . And then, the next thing, I saw in the paper that you were getting married."

"Eustace, if I'd got the letter, I wouldn't have gone back to London. I'd have refused."

"You couldn't refuse, you were under age."

"I'd have had hysterics, then. A nervous breakdown. Made the most ghastly scenes. Made myself ill."

"You'd still have gone."

She knew that he was right. "But I'd have known you were there, waiting. And I would never have married Anthony. I would never have gone to Scotland. I would never have wasted all these years."

Eustace raised his eyebrows. "Wasted? They weren't wasted. What about Cara and Nicholas?"

Virginia's eyes stung with sudden tears. She said, "Now it's all too complicated."

He put his arms around her, kissed the tears away, pushed her hair back off her face. He said, "Things happen the way they're meant to. There's a pattern and a shape to everything. You look back and see it all. Nothing happens without a reason. Nothing is impossible, like meeting again, walking into The Mermaid's Arms and seeing you sitting there, just as though you'd never been away. Like a miracle."

"You didn't behave as though it were a miracle. In no time at all you were bawling at me."

"I was scared of getting hurt a second time. I was scared that I'd been mistaken about you, that all the things that were so important to your mother had become important to you, too."

"I told you. They were never important."

He took her hand in his. "After the picnic yesterday, I thought it was going to be all right. After being with you and Cara and Nicholas, and swimming and cooking the fish, and you all seeming to enjoy it so much, I thought then, coming up the cliff, that it was like being back where we started. And I thought I would be able to talk about that time, when you went back to London and I was left not knowing what had happened, and we never saw each other again. I thought we could have talked about it, perhaps made a new beginning."

"But I was thinking the same, you stupid man, and all you did was to tell me to go back to Scotland and learn how to be a farmer. I want to be a farmer's wife, but I don't want to be a farmer. And I wouldn't know one end of an Aberdeen Angus herd from the other."

Eustace grinned again, faintly sheepish. "I told you, it was those photographs of Cara's. We'd seemed so close all day, and all at once I realised that we weren't close, we belonged to different worlds. We always have done, Virginia. A place like Kirkton and a little farm like Penfolda, well, you just don't talk about them in the same breath. And suddenly it seemed insane to imagine that I could ask you to leave all that, give it all up, just for the sake of being with me. Because that's all I've got to offer."

"And that's what I want. That's all I've ever wanted. Kirkton was Anthony's house. Without him to keep it going, it has no life at all. Anyway, I'm going to sell it. I decided last night. I shall have to go back, of course, break the news to everybody, put the whole thing in the lawyer's hands . . ."

"Have you thought about the children?"

"I never stop thinking about them. And they'll understand."

"It's their home."

"Penfolda's going to be their home." She smiled at the thought, and Eustace took her shoulders between his big hands and leaned forward to kiss her open, smiling mouth. "A new home and a new father," she finished when she had got her breath back.

But Eustace did not seem to be listening to her. "Talk of the devil," he said.

And Virginia heard the children, coming across the garden, talking, their voices high-pitched.

"Look, there are the kittens. Look, they're in the sun, and they haven't drunk their milk."

"Oh, leave them, Nicholas. They're having a sleep."

"This one isn't sleeping. It's got its eyes open. Look. Its eyes are open."

"I wonder where Mummy is? Mummy!"

"In here," called Eustace.

"Mummy, Aunt Alice Lingard wants to know if you're ever coming home again." Cara appeared at the kitchen door, her spectacles crooked, her hair hanging out of its slide. "She gave us some bacon and eggs, but we've been waiting and waiting and she says Mrs Jilkes will think that she's been in a car accident, and died . . ."

"Yes," said Nicholas, appearing, hard on her heels, with a kitten spread-eagled by pin-like claws across the front of his sweater. "And we didn't wake up till ten past ten when Aunt Alice came up to see us, and we very nearly didn't have any breakfast at all, we very nearly just waited until lunch-time . . . but I was . . . so hungry . . ."

His voice trailed away. He had realised that nobody was talking but him. His mother and Eustace were simply sitting, watching him, and Cara was staring at her mother as though she had never seen her before. Nicholas was disconcerted. "Well, what's wrong? Why isn't anybody talking?"

"We're waiting for you to stop," said Virginia.

"Why?"

Virginia looked at Eustace. Eustace leaned forward to draw Cara towards him. Very gently, seriously, he set her spectacles straight. Then Nicholas saw that he was smiling.

"We've got something to tell you," said Eustace.

BOOK THREE

The End of Summer

Rosamunde Pilcher

1

All summer long the weather had been heavy and clouded, the warmth of the sun blanketed by sea fogs which had continually rolled in from the Pacific. But by September, as so often happens in California, the fogs retreated, far out into the ocean, where they lay along the edge of the horizon, sullen as a long bruise.

Inland, beyond the coastal range, farmlands, heavy with crops, with bursting fruit, and corn and artichokes, and orange pumpkins, simmered in the sunshine. Small wooden townships dozed, skewered by the heat, grey and dusty as specimen moths. The plains, rich and fertile, stretched east to the foothills of the Sierra Nevada, and through it all arrowed the great freeway of the Camino Real, north to San Francisco, and south to Los Angeles, crammed and glittering with the hot steel of a million cars.

Through the summer months, the beach had been deserted, for Reef Point was the end of the line and seldom patronised by the casual day-tripper. For one thing, the road was unsurfaced, unsafe, and uninviting. For another, the little resort of La Carmella, with its charming tree-shaded streets, exclusive country club and spotless motels, lay just over the point, and anyone with sense and a few dollars to spare, stayed put right there. Only if you were adventurous, or broke, or surfing mad, did you risk the last mile and come slipping and scrambling over the dirt track that led down to this great, empty, storm-washed bay.

But now, with the fine hot weather and the clean rolling breakers pouring up on to the beach, the place flowered with people. Cars of all sorts came tumbling down the hill, to park in the shade beneath the cedars, and disgorge picnickers, campers, surfers and whole families of hippies, newly wearied of San Francisco, and heading south for New Mexico and the sun, like so many migrating birds. And the weekends brought the university students up from Santa Barbara in their old convertibles and their flower-stickered Volkswagens, all packed with girls and crates of canned beer, and hung about with the big brightly-coloured Malibu surf boards. They set up little camps all over the beach and the air was full of their voices and laughter, and the smell of sun oil.

And so, after weeks and months of being virtually on our own, we were surrounded by people and every sort of activity. My father was hard at work, trying to write a script to a deadline, and in an impossible frame of mind. Unnoticed by him, I moved out on to the beach, taking sustenance with me (hamburgers and Coca-Cola), a book to read, a large bath-towel for comfort and Rusty for company.

Rusty was a dog. My dog. A brown woolly thing of indeterminate breed, but great intelligence. When we first moved to the cabin, back in the spring, we hadn't got a dog, and Rusty, spying us, had decided to remedy this. Accordingly he hung around. I chased him off, shooed him away, Father threw old boots at him, still he returned, unrepentant and bearing no malice at all, to sit a yard or two from the back porch, smiling and thumping away with his tail. One hot morning, taking pity on him, I gave him a bowl of cool water to drink. He lapped it clean, then sat down and smiled and started thumping again. The next day, I gave him an old ham bone, which he took politely, removed, buried, and was back again in five minutes. Smiling. Thump, thump, went the tail.

My father came out of the house and threw a boot at him, but without much enthusiasm. It was simply a half-hearted show of force. Rusty knew this and moved in a little nearer.

I said to my father, "Who do you suppose he belongs to?"

"God knows."

"He seems to think he belongs to us."

"You're wrong," said my father. "He thinks we belong to him."

"He's not fierce or anything and he doesn't smell."

He looked up from the magazine he was trying to read. "Are you trying to say you want to keep the bloody thing?"

"It's just that I don't see . . . I don't see how we're going to get rid of him."

"Short of shooting him."

"Oh don't."

"He'll have fleas. Bring fleas into the house."

"I'll buy him a flea collar." Father watched me over his spectacles. I could see he was beginning to laugh. I said, "Please. Why not? He'll be company for me while you're away."

Father said, "All right," so I put on some shoes, then and there, and whistled up the dog, and walked over the hill into La Carmella where there is a very fancy vet's, and there I waited in a little room filled with pampered poodles and Siamese cats, and their various owners, and at last I was let in, and the vet looked at Rusty and pronounced him fit, and gave him an injection, and told me where I could buy a flea collar. So I paid the vet and went out and bought the flea collar, and we walked home again. We came into the house, and Father was still reading his magazine, and the dog came politely in, and after standing around a little, waiting to be asked to sit down, he sat, on the old rug in front of the empty fireplace.

My father said, "What's his name?" and I said, "Rusty," because I'd once had a dog-nightdress-case called Rusty and it was the first name that came into my head.

There was no question of his fitting into the family, because it seemed that he had always belonged. Wherever I went, Rusty came too. He loved the beach, and was forever digging up splendid treasures and bringing them home for us to admire. Old bits of flotsam, plastic detergent bottles, long dangling strips of seaweed. And sometimes things that he had obviously not dug up. A new sneaker, a bright bath-towel, and once a punctured beach-ball, which my father had to replace once I had run its small and weeping owner to earth. He liked to swim too, and always insisted on accompanying me, although I could swim much faster and farther than he could, and he was always tagging behind. You'd have thought he'd have got discouraged, but he never did.

We had been swimming that day, a Sunday. Father, the deadline met, had driven down to Los Angeles to deliver the script in person, and Rusty and I had kept each other company, in and out of the sea all afternoon, gathering shells, playing with an old stick of driftwood. But now it was getting cooler and I had put some clothes on again, and we sat, side by side, the setting sun gold and blinding in our eyes, watching the surfers.

They had been at it all day, but it seemed that they would never tire. Kneeling on their boards, they paddled out to sea, through the breakers to the smooth green water beyond. There they waited, patient, perched on the skyline like so many cormorants, waiting for the swell to gather, to form and finally break. They chose a wave, stood as the water curved up and crested and showed white at its edge, and as it curled over and thundered in, so the surfers came too, riding across the wave, a poem of balance, arrogant with the confidence of youth; riding the wave until it swept up on to the sand, and then stepping casually off, and gathering up the board, and back into the sea again, for the surfer's creed is that there is always a bigger and a better comber, just around the corner, and now the sun was setting and it would soon be dark, and there was not a moment to be lost.

One boy in particular had caught my eye. He was blond, crew cut, very brown, his skinny knee-length shorts the same bright blue as his surf board. He was a wonderful surfer, with a style and a dash that made all the others look clumsy amateurs. But now, as I watched, he seemed to decide to call it a day, for he rode in on a final wave, beached himself neatly, stepped off the board, and with a final long look at the rose-washed evening sea, turned and picked up the surf board and began to walk in up the sand.

I looked away. He came close beside me, and then went on a few yards to where a pile of neatly folded clothes had been waiting. He dropped the surf board and picked up a faded college sweatshirt from the top of the pile. I glanced his way again, and as his face came out of the opening at the top of the sweatshirt, he looked straight at me. Firmly, I met his eye.

He seemed amused. He said, "Hi."

"Hello."

He settled the sweatshirt down over his hips. He said, "Want a cigarette?"

"All right."

He stooped and took a packet of Luckys and a lighter out of a pocket and came over the sand to where I was sitting. He flipped a cigarette up for me and took one himself and lit them both, and then let himself down beside me, stretching full length and leaning back on his elbows. His legs and his neck and his hair were all lightly dusted with sand, and he had blue eyes and that clean, well-scrubbed look still to be seen on the campuses of American universities.

He said, "You've been sitting there all afternoon. When you weren't swimming."

"I know."

"Why didn't you join us?"

"I haven't got a surf board."

"You could get one."

"No money."

"Then borrow one."

"There's no one I know to borrow one from."

The young man frowned. "You're British, aren't you?"

"Yes."

"You visiting?"

"No, I live here."

"In Reef Point?"

"Yes." I jerked my head, indicating the line of faded clapboard cabins visible just over the curve of the sand dunes.

"How d'you come to live here?"

"We rented the cabin."

"Who's we?"

"My father and I."

"How long have you been here?"

"Since spring."

"But you're not staying over the winter."

It was a statement of fact more than a question. Nobody stayed in Reef Point over the winter. The houses weren't built to withstand the storms, the access road became impassable, the telephone lines blew down, the electricity failed.

"I think so. Unless we decide to move on."

He frowned. "Are you hippies, or something?"

Knowing how I looked at the time, I kindly did not blame him for asking this question.

"No. But my father writes film scripts and stuff for

TV. But he hates Los Angeles so much he refuses to live there, so . . . we rented this cabin."

He seemed intrigued. "And what do you do?"

I took up a handful of sand, let it run away, coarse and grey through my fingers.

"Nothing much. Buy food and empty the garbage can and try to keep the sand swept out of the house."

"Is that your dog?"

"Yes."

"What's his name?"

"Rusty."

"Rusty. Hey, Rusty, fella!" Rusty acknowledged his advances with a nod that would have done credit to Royalty and then continued to gaze out to sea. To make up for his lack of manners I said, "Are you from Santa Barbara?"

"Uh-huh." But the young man did not want to talk about himself. "How long have you lived in the States? You still have a terribly terribly British accent."

I smiled politely at a joke heard many times before. "Since I was fourteen. Seven years."

"In California?"

"All over. New York. Chicago. San Francisco."

"Is your father American?"

"No. He just likes it here. He came in the first place because he wrote a novel, and it was bought by a film company and he came to Hollywood to write the script."

"No kidding? Have I heard of him? What's his name?"

"Rufus Marsh."

"You mean, *Tall as the Morning*?" I nodded. "Boy, I read that cover to cover, when I was still in high school. I got all my sex education out of that book." He looked at me with new interest, and I thought that this was how it always was. They were friendly and quite kind, but never interested until I mentioned *Tall as the Morning*. I suppose it had something to do with the way I look, because my eyes are pale as sixpences, and my lashes are quite colourless, and my face doesn't go brown but gets splashed and splattered with hundreds of enormous freckles. Besides that, I am too tall for a girl, and the bones in my face all show. "He must be quite a guy."

A new expression had come into his face, puzzled, and crossed with questions that he was obviously going to be too polite to ask.

If you are Rufus Marsh's daughter, how come you're sitting on this god-forsaken beach in the backwoods of California wearing patched jeans and a man's shirt that should have been relegated to the ragbag decades ago, and you haven't even got enough dollars raked together to buy yourself a surf board?

He said, following with laughable predictability the line of my own reflections, "What kind of a man is he, anyway? I mean, apart from being a father."

"I don't know." I could never describe him, even to myself. I took another handful of sand, trickled it into a miniature mountain, stubbed my cigarette out on its apex, forming a little crater, a tiny volcano, with a cigarette stub as its smoking core. A man who must always be on the move. A man who makes friends easily and loses them the next day. A quarrelsome, argumentative man, talented to the point of genius, but utterly baffled by the small problems of day-to-day living. A man who can charm and infuriate. A paradox of a man.

I said again, "I don't know," and turned to look at the boy beside me. He was nice. "I'd ask you home for a beer, and then you could meet him and see for yourself. But he's in Los Angeles just now, won't be home until tomorrow morning."

He considered this, scratching thoughtfully at the back of his head and dislodging a small storm of sand.

"Tell you what," he said, "I'm coming back next weekend if the weather holds."

I smiled. "Are you?"
"I'll look out for you."
"All right."
"I'll bring a spare board. You can surf."
I said, "You don't need to bribe me."
He pretended to be offended. "Whaddya mean, bribe?"
"I'll take you up to meet him next weekend. He likes new faces around the place."
"I wasn't bribing. Honest."
I relented. Besides, I wanted to surf. I said, "I know."
He grinned and stubbed out the cigarette. The sun, sinking towards the edge of the sea, was taking shape and colour – an orange pumpkin of a sun. He sat up, screwing his eyes against its glare, yawned slightly and stretched. He said, "I must go," and stood up and then hesitated for a moment, standing over me. His shadow seemed to stretch for ever. "Goodbye then."
"'Bye."
"Next Sunday."
"OK."
"That's a date. Don't forget."
"I won't."
He turned and moved off, stopping to collect the rest of his gear, and turning to sketch a final salute before walking away, the length of the beach, to where the old sand-buried cedars marked the track that led up to the road.
I watched him go, and realised that I didn't even know his name. And, worse, he hadn't bothered to ask mine. I was simply Rufus Marsh's daughter. But still, next Sunday, if the weather held, he would maybe be back. If the weather held. That was always something to look forward to.

2

It was because of Sam Carter that we were living at Reef Point. Sam was my father's agent in Los Angeles, and it was in sheer desperation that he eventually offered to find somewhere cheap for us to live, because Los Angeles and my father were so acutely antipathetic that not one sellable word was he able to write while we lived there, and Sam was in danger of losing both valuable clients and money.

"There's this place at Reef Point," Sam had said. "It's a one-horse set-up, but real peaceful . . . end of the world type peace," he added, conjuring up visions of a sort of Gauguin paradise.

And so we had taken a lease on the cabin, and packed all our worldly possessions, which were sadly small, into Father's old beat-up Dodge, and driven here, leaving the smog and ratrace of Los Angeles behind us, and excited as children by the first smell of the sea.

And at first, it had been exciting. After the city it was magic to wake to nothing but the sound of sea birds and the endless thunder of the surf. It was good, in the early mornings, to walk out on to sand, to watch the sun rise over the hills, to hang out a line of washing, and watch it billow and fill with the sea wind, white as new sails.

Our housekeeping was necessarily simple – I have never been much of a housekeeper anyway, and at Reef Point there was only one small shop – a drugstore, but back in Scotland my grandmother would have called it a Jenny a' Thing, for it sold everything from gun licences to house frocks, from frozen foods to packets of Kleenex. It was run by Bill and Myrtle, in a half-hearted, time-consuming sort of way, for they always seemed to be clean out of fresh vegetables, fruit, chickens and eggs, which were the sort of things I wanted to buy. However, over the summer we became quite fond of tinned chilli con carne and frozen pizza pie, and all the various species of ice-cream that Myrtle obviously adored, for she was enormously fat, her great hips and thighs bulging in blue jeans, and her ham-like arms fully exposed by the girlish sleeveless blouses she chose to wear with them.

But now, after six months of Reef Point, I was getting restless. This fine Indian summer weather would last – how long? Another month, perhaps. And then the storms would start in earnest, the darkness fall earlier, the rains would come and the mud and the wind. The cabin had no sort of central heating, only the enormous fireplace in the draughty living-room, which burned driftwood at a terrifying pace. I thought of homely buckets of coal with longing, but there was no coal. Every time I came up off the beach, I lugged a spar or branch of driftwood with me, like some pioneer woman, and added it to the pile by the back porch. It was assuming vast dimensions, but I knew that once we started needing fires, it would take no time to get through the lot.

The cabin lay just back off the beach, a small rise of sand dune its only shelter from the sea winds. It was built of wood, faded to a silvery grey, and stood up on piers, so that a couple of steps led up to the front and back porches. Inside, there was a big living-room, with picture windows facing over the ocean; a tiny, narrow kitchen; a bathroom – with no bath, but a shower – and two bedrooms, one large "master" bedroom where my father slept, and a smaller one, with a bunk, perhaps intended for a small child or an unimportant elderly relative, which was mine. It was furnished in the faintly depressing manner of summer cabins, in that all the furniture had obviously been thrown out of other, and larger, houses. Father's bed was a vast brass monstrosity, missing knobs, and with a set of springs that squeaked every time he turned over. And in my room hung an ornate gilt mirror which looked as though it had started life in a Victorian bordello, and gave me back a reflection of a drowned woman covered with black spots.

The sitting-room was not much better – the old armchairs sagged, their worn patches disguised with crocheted Afghans, the hearthrug had a hole in it, and the other chairs were stuffed horsehair with the horsehair fighting a winning battle to get out. There was only one table, and Father had taken over one end of this as a desk, so that we were forced to take our meals, cramped and with elbows jammed in, at the other end. The best thing in the house was the window seat, which took up the whole width of the room, was padded with foam and warm rugs and cushions, and was inviting as an old nursery sofa, if you wanted to curl up and read, or watch the sunset, or simply think.

But it was a lonely place. At night the wind nudged and whined through the gaps around the window, and the rooms were filled with strange rustlings and creakings, for all the world like a ship at sea. When my father was there, none of this mattered, but when I was left alone, my imagination, inspired by the tales of everyday violence, culled from the columns of the local newspapers, really got to work. The cabin itself was a fragile thing, none of the locks on the doors or windows would have deterred a determined intruder, and now, with the summer over, and the occupants of the other cabins packed up and returned to their various homes, it was completely isolated. Even Myrtle and Bill were a good quarter of a mile away, and the telephone was a party line, and not always very efficient. One way and another, the possibilities didn't bear thinking about.

I never spoke to my father about these fears – he had, after all, a job of work to do, but he was essentially a perceptive man, and I am sure knew that I was capable of working myself up into a state of jitters, and this was one of the reasons that he let me keep Rusty.

That evening, after the day on the crowded beach, the cheerful sunshine, and my encounter with the young student from Santa Barbara, the cabin seemed doubly deserted.

The sun had slid down over the edge of the sea, an evening breeze was stirring, and soon it would be dark, so, for company, I lit a fire, recklessly piling on the driftwood; and, for comfort, took a hot shower, washed my hair, and then, wrapped in a towel, went into my room for a pair of clean jeans and an old white sweater which had belonged to my father until I mistakenly shrank it.

Underneath the bordello mirror was a varnished chest of drawers which had to do duty as a dressing-table. On it, for lack of anywhere else, I had put my photographs. There were a lot of them and they took up a lot of space, and most of the time I didn't even look at them very much, but this evening was different, and as I combed the snarls out of my long wet hair I studied them, one by one, as though they belonged to a person I scarcely knew, were of places that I had never seen.

There was my mother, a formal portrait, framed in silver. Mother with her shoulders bare and diamonds in her ears, and her hair newly done by Elizabeth Arden. I loved the picture, but it was not as I remembered her. This was better, an enlarged snapshot on a picnic, wearing her tartan skirt, and sitting waist deep in heather, and laughing as though something ridiculous were about to happen. And then there was the collection

– more of a montage – with which I had filled both sides of a big leather folding frame. Elvie – the old white house, set against a fold of larch and pine, the hill rising behind it, the glimmer of the loch at the end of the lawn, the jetty, and the baulky old dinghy we had used when we fished for trout. And my grandmother, at the open french windows, the inevitable pair of secateurs ready in her hand. And a coloured postcard of Elvie Loch that I had bought in the Thrumbo post office. And another picnic, with my parents together, our old car in the background, and a fat liver-and-white spaniel sitting at my mother's feet.

And there were the photographs of my cousin Sinclair. Dozens of them. Sinclair with his first trout, Sinclair dressed in his kilt, headed for some outing or other. Sinclair in a white shirt, captain of his prep school cricket team. Sinclair skiing; at the wheel of his car; wearing a paper top hat at some New Year's Eve party and looking a little drunk. (In this photograph he had his arm around a pretty, dark girl, but I had arranged the pictures so that she didn't show.)

Sinclair was the child of my mother's brother, Aylwyn. Aylwyn had married – far too young, everybody said – a girl called Silvia. The family disapproval of his choice unhappily proved well-founded, for, as soon as she had borne her young husband a baby son, she upped and left the pair of them, and went off to live with a man who sold real estate in the Balearic Islands. After the initial shock had worn off, everybody agreed that it was the best thing that could have happened, specially for Sinclair, who was handed over to his grandmother, and brought up at Elvie under the happiest of circumstances. He had always seemed, to me, to have the best of everything.

His father, my Uncle Aylwyn, I had no recollection of at all. When I was very small, he had gone to Canada, presumably returning every now and then to visit his mother and his child, but never at Elvie when we were there. My only concern with him was the possibility of his sending me a Red Indian headdress. Over the years, I must have made the suggestion a hundred times, but nothing ever came of it.

And so Sinclair was, virtually, my grandmother's child. And I could not remember a time when I hadn't been more or less in love with him. Six years older than I, he had been the mentor of my childhood, enormously wise and endlessly brave. He had taught me to tie a hook on a line, to swing upside-down on his trapeze, to bowl a cricket ball. Together we had swum and sledged, lit illegal bonfires, built a tree house, and played pirates in the leaky old boat.

When I first came to America, I wrote to him regularly, but eventually became discouraged by his lack of response. Soon our correspondence dwindled to Christmas cards, or a scribbled note on a birthday, and it was from my grandmother that I got news of him, and from her too that I had received the photograph of the New Year party.

After my mother died, as if Sinclair on her hands was not enough, she had offered to give me a home as well.

"Rufus, why not leave the child with me?" This was just after the funeral, back at Elvie, with grief put away and the future to be discussed in her usual practical fashion. I was not meant to be listening, but I was there, on the stairs, and their voices came clearly from beyond the closed library door.

"Because one child on your hands is more than sufficient."

"But I would love to have Jane . . . and she would be company for me as well."

"Isn't that a little selfish?"

"I don't think so. And, Rufus, it is her life you should think about now, her future . . ."

My father said a single very rude word. I was horrified, not at the word, but because he had said it to her. I wondered if he was a little drunk . . .

Ignoring this, in her usual ladylike fashion, my grandmother went on, but her voice was buttoned down, the way it always got when she began to be angry.

"You've just told me that you're going to America to write the film script of your book. You can't drag a fourteen-year-old all the way to Hollywood."

"Why not?"

"What about her schooling?"

"There are schools in America."

"It would be so easy for me to have her here. Just until you've settled, found yourself a place to live."

My father pushed back his chair with a scrape. I heard his feet, pacing the floor.

"And then," he said, "I send for her and you put her on the next plane?"

"Of course."

"It won't work, you know."

"Why shouldn't it work?"

"Because if I leave Jane here with you for any length of time, Elvie would become her home and she'd never want to leave it again. You know she'd rather be at Elvie than anywhere else in the world."

"Then for her sake . . ."

"For her sake, I'm taking her with me."

There was a long silence. Then my grandmother spoke again. "That isn't the only reason is it, Rufus?"

He hesitated, as though he wished not to offend her. "No," he said at last.

"With all considerations, I still think you're making a mistake."

"If I am, it's my own. Just as she's my own child and I'm holding on to her."

I had heard enough. I sprang up and ran helter-skelter up the dark staircase. In my room, face down across my bed, I burst into miserable tears, because I was leaving Elvie, because I would never see Sinclair again, and because the two people I loved most in all the world had been fighting over me.

I wrote, of course, and my grandmother replied, and Elvie with all its sounds and smells was contained in her letters. And then, after a year or two had passed, "Why don't you come back to Scotland?" she wrote. "Just for a little holiday, a month or so. We all miss you dreadfully and there is such a lot for you to see. I made a new rose border in the walled garden, and Sinclair will be up for August . . . he has a little flat in Earls Court, and gave me lunch last time I was up in town. If there is any difficulty about the fare you know you only have to say, and I shall get Mr Bembridge at the travel agent's to send you your return ticket. Talk it over with your father."

The thought of Elvie, in August, with Sinclair, was almost irresistible, but I could not talk it over with my father, because I had overheard that angry discussion in the library and I did not think that he would let me go.

Besides, it seemed that there was never the time nor the opportunity to make the journey home. It was as though we had become nomads – we arrived in a place, we settled, and then it was time to go somewhere else. Sometimes we were rich, more often broke. My father, without my mother's restraining hand, spent money like water. We lived in Hollywood mansions, in motels, in Fifth Avenue apartments, in crummy lodging houses. As the years went by, it seemed as if we had spent our whole lives travelling America, and that we should never settle down anywhere again, and the memory of Elvie faded and became unreal, as though the waters of Elvie Loch had risen and engulfed the whole place, and I had to remind myself forcibly that it was still there, peopled by living beings who were part of me, and whom I loved, and not drowned and lost for ever, blurred and dimly seen through the deep waters of some terrible natural disaster.

At my ankles, Rusty whined. Startled, I looked down and for a moment, so far away had I been, I couldn't think who he was or what he was doing. And then, like a home-movie that has stuck in the middle, there was a click in the machinery, and everyday life moved on again, and I realised that my hair was nearly dry, that Rusty was hungry and wanted his dinner, and what was more, so did I. So I laid down my comb, and pushed Elvie out of my mind, and went to throw more wood on the fire, and then inspect the icebox for something that we could eat.

It was nearly nine o'clock when I heard the car come down the hill, over the track that led from La Carmella. I heard it because it came, as all cars necessarily do, in bottom gear, and because I was alone, and all my perceptions were subconsciously sharpened to catch the smallest unfamiliar sound.

I was reading a book, and in the act of turning over a page, but I froze still and pricked my ears. Rusty sensed this, and sat up immediately, very quiet, as though he did not wish to disturb anything. Together, we listened. A log slid down in the fire, the surf distantly boomed. The car came on down the hill.

I thought . . . *Myrtle and Bill. They've been to a movie, in La Carmella*. But the car didn't stop at the drugstore. It came on, still grinding along in low gear, passed the cedars where the picnickers parked their cars, on along the lonely road that could lead only to me.

My father? But he wasn't due back until tomorrow night. The young man I had met today, returning for a glass of beer? A vagrant? An escaped convict? A sex maniac . . . ?

I sprang up, dropping my book on the hearthrug,

and fled to check the snibs on the doors. They were both locked. But the cabin had no curtains, anyone could look in and see me, and I wouldn't be able to see them. In a frenzy of fear, I dashed to turn off all the lights, but the fire still burned bright, and filled the living-room with flickering light . . . it played up the walls and over the furniture, giving the old chairs a brooding, pouncing look.

The approaching headlights probed the darkness outside. Now, I could see the car coming, gently, bumping over the dried ruts of the road. It passed the last empty cabin next to ours, and coasted gently to a halt right alongside our back porch. And it wasn't my father.

I whispered Rusty to my side, for the comfort of holding his flea collar and feeling the warmth of his furry brown coat. Growls and mutters went on in the back of his throat but he didn't bark. Together we heard the engine of the car being killed, then the door opened and slammed shut. Silence for a moment. Then steps came softly over the sandy ground that lay between the back porch and the road, and the next instant there was a knocking at the door.

I let out a sort of gasp and it was too much for Rusty who tore from my grip and ran, barking his head off, to get at whatever waited outside.

"Rusty!" I went after him, but he went on and on barking. "Rusty, don't do it . . . Rusty!"

I caught him by the flea collar and dragged him back from the door, but he went on barking, and it occurred to me that he sounded so large and so fierce that this was possibly the best thing that could have happened.

I pulled myself together, gave him a shake which finally silenced him, and then straightened up. My shadow, thrown by the firelight, danced against the locked door.

I swallowed, took a deep breath and said in a voice as firm and clear as I could make it:

"Who is it?"

A man spoke. "I'm sorry to disturb you, but I'm looking for Mr Marsh's house."

A friend of Father's? Or just a trick to get in? I hesitated.

He spoke again.

"Is this where Rufus Marsh lives?"

"Yes it is."

"Is he at home?"

Another trick?

"Why?" I said.

"Well, I was told I might find him here." I was still trying to decide what to do when he added, in quite a different voice, "Is that Jane?"

There is nothing more disarming than having a stranger know your name. Besides, there was something about his voice . . . even blurred as it was through the tightly closed door . . . something . . .

I said, "Yes."

"Is your father there?"

"No, he's in Los Angeles. Who are you?"

"Well, my name's David Stewart . . . I . . . look, it's rather difficult to talk through the door . . ."

But, before the word was out of his mouth, I had undone the snib, lifted the latch and opened it for him. And I did that apparently crazy thing because of the way he had said his own name. Stewart. Americans invariably find it difficult to pronounce . . . Stoowart, they call it. But he had said Stewart the way my grandmother said it, so he wasn't an American, he came from home. And, with a name like that, he probably came from Scotland.

I suppose I had imagined that I should immediately recognise him, but in fact I had never seen him before in my life. He stood before me, with the headlights of his car still bright behind him, and only firelight to show me his face. He wore horn-rimmed spectacles and he was tall . . . taller than I was. We stared at each other, he startled by my swift change of policy, and I suddenly engulfed by a great wave of pure fury. Nothing makes me so angry as being frightened, and I had been scared half crazy.

"What do you want to come sneaking up like that for, in the middle of the night . . ." Even to myself my voice sounded shrill and not entirely in control.

He answered, reasonably enough, "It's only nine o'clock, and I didn't mean to sneak up."

"You could have phoned and let me know you were coming."

"I couldn't find any number in the book." He had made no move to come in. Rusty was still glowering away in the background. "And I had no idea you'd be on your own or I'd have waited."

My rage was subsiding, and I felt a little ashamed of my outburst. "Well . . . now you're here, you'd better come in." I backed off and reached for the switch. The room sprang into cold, bright, electric light.

But he still hesitated. "Don't you want any credentials . . . you know, credit card? passport?"

I looked at him sharply, thought I detected a gleam of amusement behind the glasses, wondered what he found so damn funny. "If you'd lived out here as long as I have, you wouldn't open the door to any creepy prowler either."

"Well, before the creepy prowler comes in, perhaps he'd better go and turn off the car lights. I left them on so that I could see my way."

Without waiting for the snappy answer which I would have loved to be able to deliver, he went back outside. I left the door open and went back to the fire and put on another log, and found that my hands were shaking and my heart thumping like a drum. I straightened the hearthrug, kicked Rusty's bone under the chair and was lighting myself a cigarette when he came back into the cabin, shutting the back porch door behind him.

I turned to face him. He was dark, with the pale skin and black hair that a good many Highlanders possess, thin and rather scholarly looking in an angular and uncoordinated way. He wore a smooth tweed suit, worn slightly at elbows and knees and buttonholes, a brown-and-white checked shirt, and a dark green tie, and he looked as though he might be a schoolmaster or a professor of some obscure science. There was no guessing at his age. He could have been anything between thirty and fifty.

He said, "How do you feel now?"

"I'm all right," but my hand was still shaking and he saw it.

"It wouldn't do you any harm to have a little drink."

"I don't know if there's anything in the house."

"Where could we look?"

"Under the window seat?"

He went over and opened the cupboard, groped around a bit, and came out with fluff all over the sleeve of his coat and a quarter of a bottle of Haig in his hand.

"The very thing. Now all we need is a glass."

I went into the kitchen and came back with two and a jug of water, and the ice-tray out of the refrigerator, and watched while he poured the drinks. They looked suspiciously dark. I said, "I don't like whisky, much."

"Think of it as medicine." He handed it to me.

"I don't want to get plastered."

"On that, you won't."

It made sense. The whisky tasted smoky and was marvellously warming. Comforted by it, embarrassed at having been such a ninny, I smiled tentatively at him.

He grinned back. "Why don't we sit down?"

So we sat, me on the hearthrug, and he on the edge of Father's big chair, his hands loose between his knees, and the drink on the floor between his feet. He said, "Out of interest, what made you suddenly open the door?"

"It was the way you said your name. Stewart. You come from Scotland, don't you?"

"Yes."

"Whereabouts?"

"Caple Bridge."

"But that's near Elvie."

"I know. You see, I'm with Ramsay McKenzie and King . . ."

"My grandmother's lawyers."

"That's right."

"But I don't remember you."

"I didn't join the firm until five years ago."

There was a coldness around my heart, but I made myself ask: "There's nothing . . . wrong?"

"Nothing wrong." His voice was very reassuring.

"Then why have you come?"

"It's a question," said David Stewart, "of a number of unanswered letters."

3

After a little I said, "I don't understand."

"Four, to be exact. Three from Mrs Bailey herself and one from me, written on her behalf."

"Written who to?" It was not a time to worry about my grammar.

"Your father."

"When?"

"During the course of the last two months."

"Did you send the letters here? I mean, we move around so much."

"You had written to your grandmother yourself, giving her this address."

This was true. I always let her know when we moved. I threw my half-smoked cigarette into the fire, and tried to get used to this extraordinary situation. My father, for all his faults, was a most un-secret man . . . if anything, he erred in the opposite direction, loudly fuming and complaining for days on end if anything annoyed or disturbed him. But I had heard nothing about any letters.

He prompted me. "You haven't seen any letters?"

"No. But that's not surprising because Father always collects the mail himself, every day, from the drug-store."

"Perhaps he never opened them?"

But this, too, was out of character. Father always opened letters. He didn't necessarily read them, but there was always the happy possibility that the envelope might contain a cheque.

I said, "No, he wouldn't do that." I swallowed the nervous lump in my throat and pushed my hair back off my face. "What were they about? Or perhaps you don't know."

"Yes, of course I know." He could sound very dry, and it wasn't difficult to imagine him ensconced behind an old-fashioned desk, clearing his throat along with his emotions, and dealing crisply with all the incomprehensible pitfalls of wills, affidavits, sales, leases and orders to view. "It's just that your grandmother wants you to come back to Scotland . . . pay a visit . . ."

I said, "I know she does – she's always talking about it in her letters."

He raised an eyebrow. "Don't you want to come?"

"Yes . . . of course I do . . ."

I thought of Father, remembered that long-ago overheard conversation. "I don't know . . . I mean, I can't just make up my mind like that . . ."

"Is there any reason why you shouldn't come?"

"Well, of course there is . . . my father . . ."

"You mean, there's no one to keep house for him?"

"No I don't mean that at all." He waited for me to enlarge on this statement, perhaps to tell him what I did mean. I didn't want to meet his eye, and turned away from him to stare into the fire. I had an uncomfortable suspicion that my face wore an expression which could be described as sheepish.

He said, "You know, there was never any bad feeling about the fact that your father brought you over to America . . ."

"She wanted me to stay at Elvie."

"You know that, then?"

"Yes, I heard them quarrelling. They never quarrelled usually. I think they got on very well. But there was a terrible row over me."

"But that was seven years ago. Now, surely, between us, we can make some arrangements."

I made the most obvious excuse. "But it's so expensive . . ."

"Mrs Bailey, of course, will stand you the fare." (I imagined, ruefully, Father's reaction to this.) "You don't need to be away for more than a month." He said again, "Don't you want to come?"

His manner disarmed me. "Yes, of course I do . . ."

"Then why this lack of enthusiasm?"

"I don't want to upset my father. And he obviously doesn't want me to come, or he'd have answered those letters you spoke about."

"Yes, the letters. I wonder where they would be."

I indicated the table behind him, the pile of manuscript and reference books, old files, envelopes and regrettably unpaid bills. "Over there, I suppose."

"I wonder why he never told you about them."

I said nothing, but thought that I knew. In a way, he resented Elvie and the fact that it meant so much to me. He was, perhaps, a little jealous of my mother's family. He was afraid of losing me.

I said, "I've no idea."

"Well, when are you expecting him back from Los Angeles?"

I said, "I don't think you should see him. It would only make him miserable, because even if he agreed to my going, I couldn't leave him alone, here."

"But surely we could arrange something . . ."

"No, we couldn't. He has to have someone to look after him. He's the most impractical person in the world . . . he'd never buy any food, or gas for the car, and if I left him, I'd just be worried sick about him all the time."

"Jane . . . you do have to think about yourself . . ."

"Some other time I'll come. Tell my grandmother some other time."

In silence he considered this. He finished his drink, and then set down the empty glass. "Well, let's leave it like this. I'm driving back to Los Angeles tomorrow morning, about eleven. I have a seat booked for you on the plane to New York, Tuesday morning. There's no reason on earth why you shouldn't sleep on this, and if you change your mind . . ."

"I won't."

He ignored this. "If you change your mind, there's nothing to stop you coming with me." He stood up, looming over me. "And I still think that you should."

I don't like being loomed over, so I stood up too.

"You seemed very sure that I would come with you."

"I hoped that you would."

"You think I'm just making excuses, don't you?"

"Not entirely."

"I feel very guilty that you've travelled so far for nothing."

"I was in New York, on business. And I've enjoyed meeting you, and only sorry that I missed your father." He held out his hand. "Goodbye, Jane." After a second's hesitation, I put mine into it. Americans aren't much good at shaking hands and one gets out of the habit. "And I'll send your love to your grandmother."

"Yes, and Sinclair."

"Sinclair?"

"You see him, don't you? When he comes to Elvie?"

"Yes. Yes, of course I do. And I'll certainly give him your love."

I said, "Tell him to write," and then bent to make a fuss of Rusty, because my eyes were filled with tears, and I didn't want David Stewart to see.

When he had gone, I went back into the cabin, and over to the table where my father kept all his papers. After a little I found, one by one, the four unanswered letters, all opened, and obviously read. I didn't read them. My finer instincts prevailed – and anyway I already knew what they contained – so I simply replaced them, buried as before.

I went to kneel on the window seat, to open the window and hang out. It was very dark, the ocean inky, the air cold, but my terrors had evaporated. I thought of Elvie, and longed to be there. I thought of geese flying the winter skies, and the smell of peat burning in the fireplace in the hall. I thought of the loch, brilliant blue and calm as a mirror, or grey and lashed into white waves by northern gales. I wanted to be there, suddenly, so badly that it was a physical ache.

And I was angry with my father. I didn't want to leave him, but surely he could have discussed the matter with me, given me the chance to make my own decision. I was twenty-one, no longer a child, and resented what I considered an unbearably selfish and old-fashioned attitude.

Just wait till he gets back, I promised myself. Wait till I face him with those letters. I'll just tell him . . . I'll . . .

But my anger was short-lived. I could never stay angry for long. Cooled by the night air, perhaps, it simmered away and died, and I was left, feeling strangely flat. Nothing, after all, had changed. I would stay with him because I loved him, because he wanted me, because he needed me. There was no possible alternative. And I would not confront him with the letters, because to be found out would embarrass and demean him, and it was important, if we were to have any sort of a future together, that he should always be bigger and stronger and wiser than I was.

I was engaged in scrubbing the kitchen floor the next morning, when I heard the unmistakable grinding of the old Dodge as it came over the hill and down the track to Reef Point. I hastily swiped at the last square foot or so of cracked brown linoleum, then got up off my knees, wrang out the floor cloth, emptied the dirty water down the drain, and went out through the back porch door to meet my father, wiping my hands on the old striped apron as I went.

It was a gorgeous day: the sun hot, the sky blue and scudding with bright white clouds, the sparkling morning filled with wind and the crash of high-tide rollers pouring up on to the beach. I had already done a line of washing and now it strained and flapped at the rope, and I ducked beneath this and went out on to the road as the car came bumping and lurching over the ruts towards me.

I saw at once that my father was not alone. Because of the fine weather, he had put the hood down, and beside him, unmistakable head of red hair a-blow in the breeze, sat Linda Lansing. When she saw me she hung over the side of the car to wave, and her white poodle, sitting on her knee, hung out too, and went into a paroxysm of barking as though I had no right to be there.

Rusty, who had been out on the beach having a good game with an old bit of basket, heard the poodle, and came at once to my rescue, galloping around the corner of the cabin in full cry, snarling and barking, and making little dashes at the Dodge with his teeth bared, unable to wait for the happy moment when he could sink them into the poodle's neck. My father swore, Linda screamed and hugged the poodle, the poodle yapped, and I had to take Rusty by his flea collar and haul him indoors and order him to shut up and behave, before there was the slightest chance of any sort of human conversation.

I left Rusty sulking and went back out again. My father was out of the car. "Hello, cutie." He came around to give me a hug and a kiss. It was like being hugged by a gorilla and his beard scraped my cheek. "Everything all right?"

"Yes, fine," I turned from his embrace. "Hi, Linda."

"Hi, honey."

"Sorry about the dog." I went to open the door for

her. She wore full make-up, false eyelashes, a pale blue jump suit and gold ballet slippers. The poodle had a pink collar, studded with rhinestones.

"That's OK. Mitzi's highly-strung I guess. Something to do with being so highly-bred." She put up her face, lips bunched, to receive my kiss. I gave her one and the poodle started yapping again.

"For God's sake," said my father, "keep that bloody dog quiet," whereupon Linda tipped it unceremoniously out of the car and climbed out after it.

Linda Lansing was an actress. Twenty years or so ago she had turned up in Hollywood as a starlet, which meant a prodigious personal publicity campaign followed by a string of undistinguished movies, in which she usually played some sort of a gipsy or peasant girl, wearing an off-the-shoulder drawstring blouse, dark red lips and brooding expression, very sulky. But, inevitably, this type of movie, along with her style of acting, went out of fashion, and Linda went with them. Astutely, for she was never stupid, she swiftly married. "My husband comes before my career," read the captions beneath their wedding photographs, and for some time she disappeared from the Hollywood scene altogether. But lately, having divorced her third husband, and not yet having buttonholed the fourth, she had started to appear again, in small parts and on television. To a young generation of viewers, she was a new face, and, with clever direction, revealed an entirely unsuspected flair for comedy.

We had met her at one of those dreary Sunday brunch pool parties which were so much part of the Los Angeles scene. My father had latched on to her at once, as being the only woman in the place worth talking to. I like her as well. She has a vulgar sense of humour, a deep plummy voice and a surprising ability to laugh at herself.

My father is attractive to women, but has always handled his liaisons with an admirable discretion. I knew that he had embarked on an affair with Linda, but I had hardly expected that he would bring her back to Reef Point with him.

I decided to play it very cool. "Well, this is a surprise. What are you doing in this neck of the woods?"

"Oh, you know how it is, honey, when your father starts twisting your arm. And just smell that sea air." She took a great lungful, coughed slightly, and turned back to the car to extricate her handbag. It was then that I saw the lavish luggage piled on the back seat. Three cases, a wardrobe-bag, a beauty box, a mink coat in a plastic bag, and Mitzi's dog basket, complete with pink rubber bone. I gaped at its quantity, but before I could say anything, my father had elbowed me out of the way and already lifted out two of the cases.

"Well, don't stand there with your mouth open," he said. "Bring something in."

And with that he headed for the cabin. Linda, after one look at my expression, tactfully decided that Mitzi needed a run on the beach and disappeared. I started after my father, and then thought better of it, went back for the dog basket, and started off again.

I found him in the living-room, having put the two suitcases down in the middle of the floor, thrown his long-peaked cap on to a chair, and unloaded some bundles of old letters and papers out of his pocket on to the table. The room, which I had only just cleaned and tidied, became immediately disordered, impermanent, frantic. My father could do this to any place simply by walking into it. Now, he went over to the window to lean out and check on the view, and get a good lungful of sea air. Over his massive shoulder I could see the distant figure of Linda, skittering about with the poodle at the sea's edge. Rusty, still sulking on the window seat, did not even thump his tail.

My father turned, reaching in his shirt pocket for his cigarettes. He appeared delighted with himself. "Well," he said, "aren't you going to ask how everything went?" He lit the cigarette, and then looked up, and frowned, flicking the lighted match out of the window behind him. "What are you standing holding the dog basket for? Put the bloody thing down."

I didn't. I said, "What's going on?"

"What do you mean?"

I realised that all this hearty good cheer was part of a big bluster.

"You know very well what I mean. Linda."

"What about Linda? You like her, don't you?"

"Of course I like her, but that's hardly the point. What's she doing here?"

"I've asked her to stay."

"With all that luggage? How long for, for heaven's sake?"

"Well . . ." he gestured vaguely with his hand. "For as long as she wants."

"Isn't she working?"

"Oh, she's chucked all that." He went prowling off to the kitchen in search of a can of beer. I heard the refrigerator opening and shutting. "She gets just about as sick of L.A. as we did. So I thought why not?" He appeared again at the kitchen door with the open beer can in his hand. "The suggestion was hardly out of my mouth, when she found someone to rent her house, along with the maid, and she was packed and ready." He frowned again. "Jane, have you conceived some sort of an affection for that dog basket?"

I continued to ignore him. "For how long?" I insisted grimly.

"Well, as long as we do. I don't know. For the winter maybe."

I said, "There isn't room."

"Of course there's room. And whose house is this anyway?" He drained the beer can, tossed it neatly across the kitchen into the trash can, and went out to bring in the next load of luggage. This time he carried the cases into his bedroom. I put down Mitzi's dog basket and followed him. What with the bed and the suitcases and the two of us, there wasn't much room.

I said, "Where's she going to sleep?"

"Well, where do you think she's going to sleep?" He sat on the monstrous bed, and the springs complained bitterly. "Right here."

I could think of nothing to say. I simply stared at him. This had never, ever happened before. I wondered if he had gone out of his mind.

Something in my face must have got through to him then, for he suddenly looked contrite and took my hands.

"Janey, don't look like that. You're not a kid any more, I don't have to pretend to you. You like Linda, I wouldn't have brought her back if I didn't know you liked her. And she'll be company for you, I won't have to leave you alone so much. Oh, come on, take that dismal face off and go and make a pot of coffee."

I pulled my hands free. I said, "I haven't got time."

"What do you mean?"

"I . . . I have to go and pack."

I went out of his room, and into my own, and I pulled my suitcase out from under the bed, and put it on the bed and opened it, and started to pack, like people do in films, opening drawers one by one and emptying them into the suitcase.

From the open door behind me my father spoke.

"What do you think you're doing?" I turned to look at him, my hands full of shirts and belts and scarves and handkerchiefs. I said, "I'm going."

"Where?"

"Back to Scotland."

He took a single step into the room, and jerked me round to face him. I went on quickly, not letting him say a word. "You had four letters," I told him. "Three from my grandmother and one from the solicitors. You opened them and you read them and you never told me, because you didn't want me to go back. You didn't even discuss them with me."

His grip on my arm never loosened, but I thought his face lost a little of its colour.

"How did you know about those letters?"

I told him about David Stewart. "He told me everything," I finished. "Not that I needed to be told," I added recklessly, "because I knew it all anyway."

"And just what exactly did you know?"

"That you never wanted me to stay at Elvie after Mother died. That you wouldn't ever want me to go back." He watched me, puzzled. "I was *listening*," I shouted at him, as though he had suddenly gone deaf. "I was in the hall, listening, and I heard everything that you and my grandmother said to each other."

"And you never said a word?"

"What good would it have done?"

He sat carefully on the edge of my bed, so as not to disturb my packing. "Did you want to be left behind?"

His obtuseness infuriated me. "No, of course I didn't, I've loved being with you, I wouldn't have had it any other way, but that was all seven years ago, and now I'm an adult, and you had no right to hide away those letters and not say anything to me."

"Do you want to go back so badly?"

"Yes, I do. I love Elvie, you know how much it means to me." I picked up a hairbrush, my photographs, jammed them down the sides of the case. "I . . . I wasn't going to say anything about the letters. I thought it would make you miserable, and I couldn't go anyway, because you hadn't anyone to look after you. But now, it's different."

"All right, so it's different, and you're going. I'm not going to stop you. But how are you going to get there?"

"David Stewart's leaving La Carmella at eleven. If I hurry I can catch him. He has a seat booked for me on the New York plane tomorrow morning."

"And when are you coming back?"

"Oh, I don't know. Some time I suppose." I pushed in a book, Anne Morrow Lindbergh's *Gift from the Sea*, which I can never be without, and my Simon and Garfunkel LP. I shut down the lid of the case, and everything bulged out and it wouldn't close, so I opened it again, and flattened things frantically, and still it wouldn't work, and in the end it was my father who did it for me, by sheer brute force, holding down the lid of the case, and forcing the locks to snib.

Over the closed suitcase, I met his eye. I said, "I wouldn't be going if Linda hadn't come . . ." My voice trailed away. I took my raincoat from the hook on the back of the door, and put it on over my shirt and jeans.

My father said, "You're still wearing your apron."

It was the sort of thing that once we would have laughed at. Now, in deathly silence I reached round and untied it, and tore it off, and dropped it across the bed.

I said, "If I take the car, and leave it at the motel, could you or Linda pick it up?"

"Sure," said my father . . . and then, "Wait . . ." and he disappeared into his room again, only to return with a fistful of money, five-dollar bills, ten-dollar, one-dollar, all dirty and ragged as a bundle of old newspapers. "Here," he said, and shoved them into the pocket of my raincoat, "you'd better take this. You might need it."

I said, "But you . . ." but at that moment Linda and Mitzi chose to return from the beach, Mitzi shedding sand all over the floor, and Linda delighted with her short commune with nature.

"Oh, those waves, I've never seen anything like them. They must be ten feet high." She noticed then, my suitcase, my raincoat, my presumably miserable face. "Jane, what are you doing?"

"I'm going away."

"Where, for heaven's sakes?"

"To Scotland."

"I hope not because of me."

"Partly. But only because it means that there's someone to look after Father."

She looked a little disconcerted, as though looking after Father had been the last thing she expected to do, but she gamely covered up and made the best of it. "Well, that's fun for you. When're you going?"

"Today. Now. I'm taking the Dodge over to La Carmella . . ." I had already started to back away, because the situation was becoming more than I could bear. My father picked up my case and came after me. "And I hope you have a good winter. And that there aren't too many storms. And there are eggs and canned tuna fish in the icebox . . ."

I went backwards down the porch steps, was out of the house, turned, and ducked under the line of washing (would Linda have the sense to bring it in?), and I got in behind the wheel of the car and my father heaved the suitcase in on to the back seat.

"Jane – " but I was incapable of saying goodbye. I was actually moving, on my way, when I remembered Rusty. By then it was too late. He had heard me, heard the car door, heard the engine start up, and he was out of the house and after me like a shot, barking indignantly, racing alongside me, his ears flat against his head, and in imminent danger of almost certain death.

It was the last straw. I stopped the car. My father with a great bellow of "Rusty!" came after the dog. Rusty stood on his back legs and scratched and scrabbled with his claws on the car door, and I leaned over and tried to push him off and said, "Oh, Rusty, don't. Get down. I can't take you. I can't take you with me."

Father, actually running, had caught up with us. He swept Rusty up into his arms and stood looking down at me. Rusty's eyes were hurt and reproachful, but my father had an expression on his face which I had never seen before and did not wholly understand. But I knew in that moment I didn't want to say goodbye to either of them, and I burst into tears.

"You will look after Rusty, won't you?" I bawled, my mouth going square. "Shut him up so that he can't follow the car. And don't let him get run over. And he only likes Red Heart dog food, not the other kind. And don't leave him alone on the beach, someone might steal him." I groped for a handkerchief. As usual I hadn't got one, and as usual, my father took one out of his pocket, and silently handed it to me. I blew my nose, and then I put up my arms, and pulled him down so that I could kiss him, and Rusty too, and I said goodbye and Father said, "Goodbye, my Pooch," which he hasn't called me since I was six, and bawling harder than ever, and hardly able to see a thing, I never looked back, but I knew that they stood there, and that they watched until I was over the ridge and out of sight.

It was a quarter to eleven when I walked into the reception office of the motel and the man behind the desk looked at my blurred and tear-stained face without interest, as though weeping females came in and out all day long.

I said, "Has Mr David Stewart left yet?"

"No, he's still around. Got a phone bill to settle up."

"What number's his room?"

He glanced at a board. "Thirty-two." His eyes ran over my raincoat, my jeans, my stained sneakers, and his hand reached for the phone. "You want to see him?"

"Yes, please."

"I'll call him . . . tell him you're coming. What's your name?"

"Jane Marsh."

He ducked his head in the direction of the door, sending me on my way. "Number thirty-two," he said.

I set off blindly, down a covered path which led alongside a large, very blue swimming-pool. Two women lay in long chairs and their children swam and screamed and fought over a rubber ring. Before I had got halfway, David Stewart was coming to meet me. When I saw him I started to run, and much to the interest of the two women, and also to my own surprise, I ran straight into his arms, and he caught me and gave me a reassuring sort of hug, and then held me off and said, "What's wrong?"

"Nothing's wrong." But I had started to cry again. "I'm coming with you."

"Why?"

"I've changed my mind, that's all."

"Why?"

I hadn't meant to tell him, but it all started spilling out. "Father's got a friend, and she's come from Los Angeles . . . and she's . . . she said . . ."

He took a look at the two goggling women, said, "Come along," and led me back to the privacy of his room, pushed me inside, and shut the door behind us.

"Now," he said.

I blew my nose and made a real effort to pull myself together.

"It's just that he has someone to look after him. So I can come with you."

"Did you tell him about the letters?"

"Yes."

"And doesn't he mind your coming?"

"No. He said OK."

David was quiet. I looked at him and saw that he had turned his head, was now regarding me thoughtfully from the corner of his right eye. I found out later that this was a habit picked up over the years on account of his bad eyesight and the fact that he had to wear glasses, but at the moment it was both disconcerting and uncomfortable; like being nailed to the wall.

I said miserably, "Don't you want me to come with you?"

"It's not that. It's just that I don't know you well enough to know if you're telling the truth."

I was too unhappy to be offended. "I never lie," I said, and then amended this. "And when I do I go all shifty and blush. And Father did say it was all right." And to prove this I put my hand in my raincoat pocket and pulled out the dirty bundle of dollars. Some of the bills fell, like old leaves, to the carpet. "He gave me some money to spend."

David stooped and picked them up and handed them back to me. "I still think, Jane, I should make a point of seeing him before we fly off. We could . . ."

"I couldn't say goodbye again."

His face lost its severity. He touched my arm. "Stay here then. I won't be more than fifteen minutes."

"You promise?"

"I promise."

He went, and I wandered around the room he had occupied, and read a bit of a newspaper, and looked out of the open door, and then went into the bathroom and washed my face and my hands, and combed my hair and found a rubber band and fastened it back. I went out and sat by the pool and waited for him, and when he returned and had loaded our luggage, I got into the car beside him, and we drove out and on to the highway and south to Los Angeles. We stayed the night in a motel near the airport, and the next day we flew to New York, and the next night, to London, and it was not until we were halfway out over the Atlantic that I remembered the young boy who had been coming, next Sunday, to take me surfing.

4

I had lived for most of my life in London, but returning was like coming to a city I had never seen before, so changed was it. The airport buildings, the approach roads, the skyline, the great towering blocks of flats, the mass of traffic . . . all this had happened in the last seven years. In the taxi I sat wedged in a corner with my case at my feet, and it was foggy so that the street lights still burned, and damply cold in a way that I had forgotten.

I had not slept in the plane and was dizzy with fatigue; nauseated by unlikely meals presented to me at what was, according to my watch, which I had kept at California time, two o'clock in the morning. My body, my head, my eyes ached with travelling, my teeth felt gritty, and my clothes as though I had been wearing them for ever.

There were billboards, flyovers, rows of houses, and London enclosed us. The taxi turned off at some traffic lights, nosed its way down a quiet crescent, lined with parked cars, and stopped in front of a terrace of tall, early Victorian houses.

I watched them dully and wondered what I was meant to do now. David leaned across me and opened the door and said, "This is where we get out."

"Uh?" I looked at him and wondered how any man, who had shared the – to me – soul-destroying experience of flying, non-stop, halfway round the world, could continue to look clean, relaxed and in charge of the situation. But I fell obediently out of the taxi and stood on the pavement, blinking like an owl and yawning, while he paid the driver off, collected our suitcases, and led the way down a flight of basement steps. The railings which enclosed them were shiny black, the little paved area was clean and swept, and there was a wooden tub full of geraniums . . . a little sooty, but still bright and gay. He took out a key, the yellow door swung inwards, and I followed him blindly into the flat.

It was white-painted, smelled of country houses, the floor was scattered with Persian rugs, there were chintz covers on the sofa and armchairs, small, old, polished pieces of furniture, a Venetian mirror over the fireplace. I saw books and a pile of magazines, a glass-fronted cabinet filled with Dresden, small patches of hand-worked tapestry . . . and, beyond the windows on the far side of the room, a miniature sunken patio garden, with a plane tree, ringed by a wooden seat, and a small statue set into the recess of the faded brick wall.

I stood, yawning. He went to open a window, and I said, "Is this your flat?"

"No, it's my mother's, but I use it when I come to London."

I looked around vaguely. "Where is your mother?" It sounded as though I expected her to be hiding under the sofa, but he didn't smile.

"She's in the South of France, on holiday. Come on now, take off your coat, and get comfortable. I'll go and make a cup of tea."

He disappeared through a door. I heard the sound of a tap turned on, a kettle being filled. A cup of tea. The very words were comforting and homely. A cup of tea. I thought of elocution lessons. How Now Brown Cow How Would You Like A Cup Of Tea. I fumbled with the buttons of my raincoat, and eventually got them undone, pulled the coat off and draped it across what looked like a Chippendale chair. I let myself down on to the sofa. It had leaf-green velvet cushions and I took one and pulled it into position and put my head down, but I think I was asleep before I actually had time to get my feet up off the floor. I certainly don't remember doing this.

When I awoke, the light had changed. A long beam of sunshine, dancing with dust, lay like a spotlight across my line of vision. I moved, and knuckled the sleep from my eyes, and looked again, and there was a rug over me, warm and light.

In the fireplace, a fire flickered. I looked at it for some time before I realised that it was an electric one with sham logs and coal and flames. It seemed, at that moment, infinitely cosy. I turned my head slightly and saw David, deep in an armchair, awash in papers and briefcases. He was wearing different clothes – a blue shirt, a cream-coloured sweater with a V-neck. I wondered in a detached sort of way if he was one of those people who never needed to sleep. He had heard my stirrings and was watching me.

I said, "What day is it?"

He was amused. "Wednesday."

"Where are we?"

"London."

"No, I mean whereabouts?"

"Kensington."

I said, "We used to live in Melbury Road. Is that far?"

"No. Quite near."

After a little, "What time is it?"

"Nearly five."

"When do we go to Scotland?"

"Tonight. We've got sleepers booked on the Royal Highlander."

With an enormous effort I sat up, and yawned and tried to wipe sleep out of my system and hair out of my face. I said, "I suppose I couldn't possibly have a bath?"

"Of course you can," he said.

So I had a bath, boiling water that wouldn't lather properly and handfuls of his mother's bath salts which he kindly said I could use. When I had bathed I got my suitcase, and found some clean clothes and put them on, and jammed all the dirty ones back in the case, and somehow got the case shut again, and went back into the sitting-room, and found that he had made tea, and that there was hot buttered toast and a plate of chocolate biscuits – the proper kind, not chocolate flavoured cookies which you get in America, but plain biscuits covered with real chocolate.

I said, "Are these your mother's?"

"No. I went out and bought them while you were asleep. There's a little shop around the corner, very handy when you run out of things."

"Has your mother lived here always?"

"Not at all, only a year or so. She used to have a house in Hampshire, but it got too big for her and the garden was a worry . . . it's not easy to get help. So she sold it, and kept a few of her favourite things and moved here."

So that explained the country house atmosphere. I looked out at the little patio and said, "And she has got a garden."

"Yes, a small one. But she can manage that herself."

I took another piece of toast and tried to imagine my grandmother in such a situation. But it was not possible. Grandmother would never be defeated by the size of her house or the amount she had to do, or the difficulties of getting and keeping cooks and gardeners. Indeed, Mrs Lumley had been with her ever since I could remember, standing on her swollen legs at the kitchen table, and rolling out pastry. And Will, the gardener, had a little cottage and an allotment of his own, where he grew potatoes and carrots and enormous mop-headed chrysanthemums.

"So you didn't ever live in this flat?"

"No, but I stay with her when I come to London."

"Is that often?"

"Fairly."

"Do you ever see Sinclair?"

"Yes."

"What does he do?"

"He works for an advertising agency. I would have thought you knew that."

It occurred to me that I could ring him up. After all, he lived in London, it would take only moments to look up his number. I thought of doing this, and then decided against it. I was not entirely sure of Sinclair's reaction, and did not wish David Stewart to witness my possible discomfiture.

I said, "Has he got a girlfriend?"

"Heaps, I should think."

"No, you know what I mean. Anyone very special."

"Jane, I really wouldn't know."

I licked hot butter, thoughtfully, from the ends of my fingers.

I said, "Do you suppose he'll come up to Elvie when I'm there?"

"Bound to."

"And his father? Is Uncle Aylwyn still in Canada?"

David Stewart pushed his glasses up his nose with a long, brown finger. He said, "Aylwyn Bailey died, about three months ago."

I stared. "Now I never knew *that*. Oh, poor Granny. Was she very upset?"

"Yes, she was . . ."

"And the funeral and everything . . ."

"In Canada. He'd been ill for some time. He never managed to get home."

"So Sinclair never saw him again."

"No."

I digested this information, and felt sad. I thought of my own father, infuriating as he was, and knew that not for anything would I have missed a single moment of the time we had spent together, and I felt sadder than ever for Sinclair. And then I remembered that in the old days it had been I who envied him, for, while I merely spent holidays at Elvie, it was Sinclair's home. And as for missing a father's companionship, the place had always been teeming with men, for as well as Will the gardener – whom we loved – there was Gibson the keeper, a dour man but wise in all respects; and Gibson's two sons, Hamish and George, who were about Sinclair's age and included him in all their pursuits, both legal and otherwise. And so he had been taught to shoot and cast a fly, play cricket and climb trees, and one way and another had a good deal more time and attention lavished on him than most boys of his age. No, all things considered, Sinclair had missed very little.

We caught the Royal Highlander at Euston, and it seemed that I spent half the night getting out of bed to look out of the window and gloat over the fact that the train was tearing northwards, and nothing, save a disastrous act of God, could stop it. In Edinburgh I was wakened by a female voice, sounding like Maggie Smith being Miss Jean Brodie, saying "Edinburgh Waverley. This is Edinburgh Waverley," and I knew that I was in Scotland, and I got up and put my raincoat on over my nightdress and sat on the cover of the washbasin and watched as the lights of Edinburgh slid away, and waited for the bridge, when the train, suddenly making an entirely different sound, plunged out and over the Forth, and the river lay miles below us, a gleam of dark water, touched with the riding lights of miniature craft.

I got back into bed, and dozed until we reached

Relkirk, when I got up again, and opened the window, and the air poured in, cold and edged with the smell of peat and pine. We were on the edge of the Highlands. It was only a quarter past five, but I dressed and spent the last part of the journey with my cheek pressed against the dark, rain-spattered glass. To begin with I could see little, but by the time we had ground our way over the pass, and started in on the long run down the gentle gradient that finally leads to Thrumbo, the day was beginning to lighten. There was no sign of the sun, simply an imperceptible fading from darkness. Clouds were thick, grey and soft over the tops of the hills, but as we ran down into the valley, they thinned and shredded away to nothing and the great wide sweep of the glen lay before us, golden brown and tranquil in the early morning light.

There was a thump on my door and the attendant looked in.

"The gentleman's wanting to know if you're awake. We'll be in to Thrumbo in ten minutes or so. Will I take your case?"

He removed it, and the door shut behind him and I turned back to the window, because now the countryside was becoming closely familiar and I didn't want to miss a thing. I had walked on that bit of road, ridden a Highland pony in that field, had been taken to tea in that white cottage. And then there was the bridge which marked the boundaries of the village, and the filling station, and the refined hotel that was always filled with elderly residents, and where you could never buy a drink.

The door opened again, and David Stewart stood there, filling the doorway.

"Good morning."

"Hi."

"How did you sleep?"

"OK."

Now the train was slowing, braking. We moved past the signal box, under the bridge. I slid off the top of the washbasin, and followed him out into the corridor, and over his shoulder watched the sign saying Thrumbo sail triumphantly past, and then the train stopped and we were there.

He had left his car in a garage, so he abandoned me to wait in the station yard while he went to fetch it. I sat there on my suitcase, in the deserted, slowly waking village, and watched as lights came on, one by one, and chimneys smoked, and a man came wobbling down the street on a bicycle. And then I heard, far above me, a honking and a chattering and it became louder and passed clear overhead but I couldn't see the formations of wild geese, because they were flying above the cloud.

Elvie Loch lay about two miles beyond the village of Thrumbo, a wild expanse of water looped to the north by the main road to Inverness and enclosed, on the opposite shore, by the great bastions of the Cairngorms. Elvie itself was very nearly an island, shaped like a mushroom and joined to the mainland by its stalk, a narrow spit of land that was no more than a causeway between reed-filled marshes, nesting-place for hundreds of birds.

For many years the land had belonged to the church, and indeed there were still the ruins of a little chapel, roofless now and deserted, although the small graveyard surrounding it was still kept neat and tidy, the yews tightly clipped, the grass mown smooth as velvet, and, in spring, gay with the tossing heads of wild daffodils.

The house where my grandmother lived had been the manse for this little church. Over the years, however, it had outstripped its original modest bounds, as wings were added and extra rooms to accommodate, one supposed, large Victorian families. From the back, from the approach road, it appeared tall and forbidding, the windows to the north being small and sparse in order to conserve warmth in the bitter winters, and the front door was snug and unimpressive, and usually tightly closed. This fortress-like impression was enhanced by the two high garden walls, which, like arms, reached from the house to east and west, and against which even my grandmother had been unable to coax a climber to grow.

But, from the other side, the aspect of Elvie was entirely different. The old white house, protected and enclosed and facing due south, blinked and drowsed in the sunlight. Windows and doors stood open to the fresh air, and the garden sloped down to a shallow ha-ha, dividing it from a narrow field where a neighbouring farmer grazed his cattle. The field dipped to the water's edge, and the lap of small waves on shingle, and the gentle lowing and munching of cattle were so constant a part of Elvie that after a little you stopped hearing them. It was only when you'd been away, and returned, that you became aware of them all over again.

David Stewart's car was a surprise, a dark blue TR4, and unexpectedly racy for such a solid-seeming citizen. We packed in our cases, and headed out of Thrumbo, and I sat forward on my seat and churned with excitement. Familiar landmarks appeared, and flew away behind us. The garage, the sweet shop, and the McGregors' farm, and then we were out in open country. The road swept up through fields of golden stubble, the hedges were spattered scarlet with the hips of wild roses, and there had been frost already, for trees were touched with the gold and red of the first autumn colours.

And then we swung around the last corner and the loch stretched away to our right, grey in the grey morning, and the mountains on the far side were lost in cloud. And, not half a mile away, stood Elvie itself, the house hidden by trees and the roofless church looking romantically desolate. Excitement made me speechless and, with a rare understanding, David Stewart offered no sort of comment. We had come a long way together, so far indeed that it was hard to comprehend, but it was in silence that we finally turned off by the roadside cottage, and the car wound down through the high hedges, over the causeway between the marshes, and up under the copper beeches, to come to a halt at the front door.

I was out of the car in an instant, running across the gravel, but my grandmother was quicker than I. The door opened and she appeared, and we met, our arms tight around each other, and she kept saying my name, and she smelled of the scented sachets she keeps with her clothes, and I told myself that nothing had changed.

5

A reunion after so many years is always confusion. We said things like, "Oh, you're really here . . ." and "I never thought I'd make it . . ." and "Did you have a good journey . . ." and "Everything's just the same," and we held each other off, and laughed at our idiocies, and hugged again.

Next the dogs added to the turmoil, boiling out of the house, barking around our feet, demanding attention. They were liver-and-white spaniels, new to me, and yet familiar too, because there had always been liver-and-white spaniels at Elvie, and these were no doubt descended from the ones I remembered. And no sooner had I started to greet the dogs than we were joined by Mrs Lumley, who had heard the din and was unable to resist the temptation to be in on the homecoming. She was fatter than ever in her green overall, and she appeared out of the house smiling from ear to ear, to be kissed, to tell me I'd grown awful tall and that I'd got more freckles than ever and that she was making a really big breakfast.

Behind me David was quietly unloading my suitcase, and now my grandmother went to greet him.

"David, you must be tired out." Rather to my surprise she gave him a kiss. "Thank you for bringing her safely back."

"You got my wire."

"Of course I did. I've been up since seven. You'll

come in and have breakfast with us, won't you? We're expecting you."

But he excused himself, saying that his housekeeper would be expecting him, that he must get home and change and then get to the office.

"Well, then, come back for dinner tonight. Yes, I insist. About half past seven. We want to hear all about everything."

He allowed himself to be persuaded, and we looked at each other, smiling. It occurred to me, with some surprise, that I had only met him four days ago, and yet now, when it was time to say goodbye, I felt that I was leaving an old friend, someone I had known all my life. He had been given a difficult job to do, and he had done it tactfully and with good humour, and as far as I knew, had offended nobody.

"Oh, David . . ."

He hastily forestalled my garbled thanks.

"I'll see you this evening, Jane," and he backed away, and got into his car, and slammed the door, and we watched him turn and drive away, under the beeches, down the road and so around the corner and out of sight.

"Such a nice man," said my grandmother thoughtfully. "Don't you think so?"

"Yes," I said, "sweet," and dived to prevent Mrs Lumley picking up my case, and carried it into the house myself, and Grandmother and the dogs came behind me, and the door was shut and David Stewart was, for the moment, forgotten.

I was assailed by the smell of peat smoke from the hall fire, the smell of roses from the big bowl of pink blooms on the chest by the clock. One of the dogs was panting for attention, tail wagging and all excitement, and I stopped to scratch his ears and was just going to tell them about Rusty, when my grandmother said, "I've got a surprise for you, Jane," and I straightened and looked up and saw a man coming down the stairs towards me, silhouetted against the light of the staircase window. For an instant I was dazzled by this light, and then he said, "Hello Jane," and I realised that it was my cousin Sinclair.

I could only gape, while Grandmother and Mrs Lumley stood, delighted by the success of the surprise they had planned. He had reached my side, and taken my shoulders between his hands and stooped to kiss me before I found breath to say weakly, "But I thought you were in London."

"Well I'm not. I'm here."

"But how . . . ? Why . . . ?"

"I've got a few days' leave."

For me? Had he taken them so that he could be at Elvie for my return? The possibility was both flattering and exciting, but before I could say anything more, my grandmother started organising us.

"Well, there's no point in our standing around here . . . Sinclair, perhaps you'd carry Jane's case up to her room, and then when you've washed your hands, dear, you'd better come down and have some breakfast. You'll be tired out after that journey."

"I'm not tired." And indeed I wasn't. I felt vital and wide awake and ready for anything. Sinclair picked up my case, and went upstairs two at a time, and I followed his long legs as though I had wings on my heels.

My bedroom, looking out over the garden and the loch, was inhumanly neat and polished but otherwise unchanged. Still, the white-painted bed stood, pushed in the bay of the window which was where I always preferred to sleep. And there was a pin cushion on the dressing-table and lavender bags in the wardrobe and the blue rug, covering the worn patch of carpet.

While I shed my coat and washed my hands, Sinclair went and dumped himself on my bed, sadly creasing the starched white cover, and watched me. In the seven years that had passed he had changed, of course, but the differences I saw in him were almost too subtle to be pin-pointed. He was thinner, certainly, there were fine lines round his mouth and at the corners of his eyes, but that was all. He was very good looking, with dark brows and lashes and deep blue eyes, which slanted tantalisingly up at the corners. His nose was straight and his mouth curved and full, with a lower lip which, when he was young, could look very sulky. His hair was thick and straight, and he wore it long, tapered down the back of his neck on to his collar, and used as I was to the hair fashions of Reef Point, either crew cut (surfers) or shoulder length (hippies), I thought the effect was very attractive. He wore that morning a blue shirt with a cotton handkerchief knotted in the open neck and a pair of washed-out cord trousers hitched round his waist with a belt of plaited wool.

I said, fishing for confirmation of what I hoped was true, "Are you really on leave?"

"Of course," he said shortly, confirming nothing.

I resigned myself to never knowing. "You're with an advertising firm?"

"Yes. Strutt and Seward. P.A. to the Managing Director."

"Is that a good job?"

"It includes an expense account."

"You mean boozy lunches with prospective clients."

"It doesn't have to be a boozy lunch. If the prospective client is pretty, it's just as likely to be an intimate candle-lit supper."

A twinge of jealousy had to be firmly battened down. I was at the dressing-table now, combing out the long heavy tassel of my hair, and he said, without any change of expression, "I'd forgotten how long it was. You used to wear it in plaits. It's like silk."

"Every now and then I swear I'm going to get it cut off, but I never get round to it." I finished my hair and laid down the comb and went to join him on the bed, kneeling to open the window and hang out.

"Delicious smell," I told him. "All damp and autumny."

"Doesn't California smell damp and autumny?"

"Most of the time it smells of petrol." I thought of Reef Point. "When it isn't smelling of gum trees and the Pacific."

"And how is life with the Redskins?"

I shot him a sharp look, daring him to start being offensive, and he relented. "Honestly Jane, I was terrified you'd come back chewing gum and slung with cameras, and say 'Gee, Sin' every time you addressed a remark in my direction."

"You're out of date, brother," I told him.

"Protesting, then, you know, with a picket saying, 'Make Love Not War'." He said this in a fake American accent which I found as tedious as being kidded in California about my terribly terribly British voice.

I told him so and added, "I promise you that when I start protesting, you will be the first to know."

He acknowledged this with a wicked gleam. "How's your father?"

"He's grown a beard and he looks like Hemingway."

"I can imagine." A pair of mallards flew down out of the sky, came in to land on the water, with that little scud of white foam, just as they touched down. We watched them and then Sinclair yawned and stretched and gave me a brotherly slap and said it was time for breakfast, so we got up off the bed and closed the window again and went downstairs.

I found that I was ravenous. There was bacon, and eggs and Cooper's marmalade and hot floury rolls which I remembered were called baps, and while I ate, Sinclair and my grandmother talked, in a desultory fashion – breakfast chat concerning news in the local paper, the result of a flower show, a letter that my grandmother had received from an elderly cousin who had gone to live in a place called Mortar.

"What the hell's he gone to live there for?"

"Well, it's cheap of course, and warm. The poor old thing always suffered dreadfully from rheumatics."

"And how does he propose passing his days? Rowing sightseers around Grand Harbour?"

I realised that they were talking about Malta. Mortar; Malta. I was more Americanised than I had thought.

My grandmother poured coffee. I watched her and worked out that she must now be in her seventies, but she still looked exactly as I had always remembered her. She was tall, dignified and very good looking, her white hair always immaculate, her eyes, deep set beneath finely arched eyebrows, a bright and piercing blue. (At the moment their effect was charmingly youthful, but I knew that she could register a world of disapproval with a single lift of those eyebrows, accompanied by a chilling blue stare.) Her clothes were ageless too, and entirely becoming. Soft heathery tweed skirts and cashmere sweaters or cardigans. In the day-time she wore constantly her pearls, and a pair of coral earrings, shaped like tear drops. In the evenings a modest diamond or two was likely to spark from her dark velvets, for she was sufficiently old-fashioned to change each evening for dinner, even if it was Sunday and we ate nothing more exciting than scrambled eggs.

And as she sat ensconced at the head of her table, I thought that she had had more than her share of tragedy. Her husband had died, and then she had lost her daughter and now her son, the elusive Aylwyn, who had chosen to live and die in Canada. Sinclair and I were all she had left. And Elvie. But her back remained straight and her manner brisk, and I was thankful that she would never become one of those mournful old ladies, perpetually remembering the old days. She was too interested, too active, too intelligent.

Indestructible, I told myself comfortably. That's what she is. Indestructible.

After breakfast Sinclair and I made a ritual tour of the island, missing nothing. We went out through the gate that leads into the graveyard. There we did the rounds of all the old headstones, and peered in through the window-gaps of the ruined church, and then climbed the wall into the field, and went down past the eyes of curious cattle, to the edge of the loch. We disturbed a pair of mallard ducks and had a competition skimming flat stones, seeing who could throw them the farthest. Sinclair won. We walked the length of the jetty to look at the leaky old boat that was such a devil to row, and our footsteps echoed out over the sagging planking.

"One day," I said, "this is going to collapse."

"No point in getting it mended if it's never used."

We went on, around the edge of the water, under the spreading beech where we had built our tree house, and then up through the birch spinney, ringed about by quietly falling leaves, and so back to the house by way of a cluster of outbuildings – abandoned piggeries and henhouses, and stables, and an old coach house which had long since been put to use as a garage.

"Come and see my car," said Sinclair.

We struggled with bolts and the big, old-fashioned door, and it swung creakily back to reveal, alongside my grandmother's large and dignified Daimler, a dark yellow Lotus Elan, black hooded, low to the ground and infinitely lethal.

I said, "How long have you had that?"

"Oh, about six months." He got in behind the driving wheel, and backed it out, the engine purring like an angry tiger, and showed me, like a small boy with a new toy, the car's varied accomplishments: the electrically operated windows; the neat device which worked the hood; the automatic burglar alarm; the headlight covers, which opened and shut like monstrous eyelids.

"How fast does it go?" I inquired nervously.

He shrugged. "Hundred and twenty, hundred and thirty?"

"Not with me in it, you don't."

"Wait until you're invited, my chicken-hearted child."

"You couldn't go sixty on the roads up here without coming off them altogether." He got out of the car.

"Aren't you going to put it away?"

"No." He glanced at his watch. "I've got a date to shoot pigeons." I knew I was home. In Scotland men perpetually go and shoot things regardless of any plans their womenfolk may have made for them.

I said, "When'll you be back?"

"Probably for tea." He grinned down at me. "Tell you what, after tea, I'll walk you up to call on the Gibsons. They can't wait to see you and I promised I would."

"All right. Let's do that."

We went back to the house, Sinclair to change and collect all his shooting clobber, and me to go up to my room and unpack.

As I went in through the door the air struck chill and I shivered and realised that already I was missing the Californian sunshine and American central heating. Elvie was thick-walled and south-facing. Open fires burned constantly and there were always gallons of hot water, but the bedrooms were inclined to be decidedly parky. I laid my clothes in the empty drawers and came to the conclusion that although they were Mild-Wash, Drip-Dry and Perma-Pressed, they were not warm. For Scotland I should have to buy some new ones. Perhaps – happy thought – my grandmother would buy them for me.

With this in mind I went downstairs to find her, and met her coming out of the kitchen wearing rubber boots and an ancient raincoat and carrying a basket.

She said, "I was just coming to look for you. Where's Sinclair?"

"Gone pigeon shooting."

"Oh, yes, he said he'd be out for lunch. Come and help me pick sprouts."

Our progress was held up for a moment while I found boots and an old coat and then we set out once more into the quiet morning, only this time we made for the walled garden. Will, the gardener, was there already. He looked up as we came in, stopped digging and came treading cannily over the newly-turned earth to shake me, muddily, by the hand.

"Eh," he said, "itsh a long time since you were lasht at Elvie." He did not always speak very clearly, as he only wore his teeth on Sundays. "And hoo is life in America?"

I told him a little about life in America, and he asked after my father, and I asked after Mrs Will, who appeared to be ailing, as always, and then he went back to his digging and my grandmother and I went off to pick sprouts.

When we had filled the basket, we went back towards the house, but the morning was so fresh and quiet that Grandmother said she didn't want to go back indoors just yet, so we went around and into the garden, and sat on a white-painted, iron seat, looking out over the garden and the water, to the mountains beyond. The herbaceous border was filled with dahlias and zinnias and purple Michaelmas daisies, and the pearly grass was scattered with the dark red leaves of a Canadian maple.

She said, "I always think autumn is a perfect time. Some people think it's sad, but it's really much too beautiful to be sad."

I quoted,

> September has come, it is hers,
> Whose vitality leaps in the autumn.

"Who wrote that?"

"Louis MacNeice. Does your vitality leap?"

"Well, it might have done twenty years ago." We laughed and she pressed my hand. "Oh, Jane, what a delight to have you back again."

"You wrote so often and I would have come before . . . but it really wasn't possible."

"No, of course not, I quite see that. And it was selfish of me to keep insisting."

"And those . . . letters you wrote to my father. I didn't know anything about them, or I'd have made him reply."

"He was always a very stubborn man." She shot me a glance, very sharp and blue. "He didn't want you to come?"

"I'd made up my mind. He became resigned. Besides, with David Stewart there, waiting to bring me, he could scarcely raise too many objections."

"I was afraid you wouldn't be able to leave him."

"No." I reached down and picked up a maple leaf and started shredding it between my fingers. "No. He has a friend staying with him."

Again that sideways glance. "A friend?"

I looked up ruefully. She had always been high-principled, but never a prude. I said, "Linda Lansing. She's an actress. And his current girlfriend."

After a little, "I see," said my grandmother.

"No, I don't think you probably do. But I like her, and she'll look after him . . . anyway, until I get home again."

"I can't think," said my grandmother, "why he didn't marry again."

"Perhaps because he didn't stay in any one place long enough for the banns to be called?"

"But it's selfish. It hasn't given you a chance to get away, come back and see us all, or even to have some sort of a career."

"A career is one thing I have never wanted."

"But nowadays every girl should be able to support herself."

I said that I was very happy being supported by my father, and my grandmother said I was as stubborn as he was and hadn't I ever wanted to do some sort of a job?

I thought hard, but could only remember being eight years old and wanting to join a circus and help wash the camels. I did not think my grandmother would appreciate this, so I said, "Not really."

"Oh, my poor Jane."

I rose like a bird to my father's defence. "Not poor. Not poor anything. I don't feel I've missed a thing." But I added, to soften this, "Except Elvie. I did miss Elvie. And you. And everything." She made no comment on this. I dropped the shredded leaf, and stooped to pick up another. I said, intent on it, "David Stewart told me about Uncle Aylwyn. I didn't say anything to Sinclair . . . but . . . I was sorry . . . I mean, his being so far away and everything."

"Yes." Her voice was expressionless. "But then, that's what he chose . . . to live in Canada, and finally, to die there. You see, Elvie never meant very much to Aylwyn. He was essentially a restless person. He needed, more than anything, the company of a lot of different people. He liked variety in everything he did. And Elvie was never the best place for that."

"It's strange . . . a man being bored in Scotland . . . it's so essentially a man's ambience."

"Yes, but you see he didn't like shooting and he never wanted to fish, he was bored by it. He liked horses and racing. He was a great racing man."

I realised, with some surprise, that this was the first time we had spoken about my Uncle Aylwyn. It was not exactly that the subject had been avoided; just that, before, I had been totally incurious. But now I realised it was unnatural how little I knew about him . . . I did not even know how he had looked, for my grandmother, unlike most women of her generation, was not one for family photographs. Any that she had were neatly filed away in albums, not standing about, silver-framed, on top of the grand piano.

I said, "What sort of a person was he? What did he look like?"

"Look like? He looked like Sinclair does now. And he was very charming . . . he would walk into a room and you could see all the women perk up, and start smiling and being very attractive. It was quite amusing to watch."

I was on the point of asking about Silvia, but she forestalled me by glancing at her watch, and turning businesslike again.

"Now, I must go and give these sprouts to Mrs Lumley or she won't get them in time for lunch. Thank you for helping me pick them. And I've enjoyed our little talk."

Sinclair, true to his word, was home for tea. Afterwards, we put on coats and whistled up the dogs and set off to call on the Gibsons.

They lived in a small keeper's cottage, tucked into a fold of the hill which rose to the north of Elvie, so that we had to walk off the island, and cross the main road, and follow a track which wound up between grass and heather, crossing and re-crossing a tumbling burn which passed under the road by means of a culvert and emptied itself into Elvie Loch. It had travelled from deep and high in the mountains, and the glen down which it ran, and the hills on either side, were all part of my grandmother's estate.

In the old days, there had been shooting parties, with schoolchildren as beaters, and hill ponies to carry elderly gentlemen up to their butts, but now the moor was let off to a syndicate of local businessmen, who enjoyed walking the moor during two or three Saturdays in

August but appeared just as well content to bring their families picnicking, or to fish the waters of the burn.

As we approached the cottage, there was a cacophony of barking from the kennels, and, disturbed by the noise, the figure of Mrs Gibson presently appeared through the open door. Sinclair waved and called, "Hello there!" and Mrs Gibson waved back, and then disappeared hastily back inside again.

"Gone to put the kettle on?" I suggested.

"Or warn Gibson to put his teeth in."

"That's not at all kind."

"No. But likely."

There was an old Land-Rover parked by the side of the house with half a dozen white Leghorn hens pecking round its wheels and a line of breeze-stiffened washing. As we came up to the door, Mrs Gibson came out once more, having removed her apron. She wore a blouse with a cameo brooch at the collar and was beaming from ear to ear.

"Oh, Miss Jane, I'd have known you anywhere. I was speaking to Will, and he said you hadna' changed at a'. And Mr Sinclair . . . I didn't know you were up."

"Taken a few days' leave."

"Come away in then, Gibson's just taking his tea."

"I hope we've not come at a bad time . . ." Sinclair stood aside and waited for me to go ahead of him. I ducked my head cannily at the door, and went into the kitchen, where a fire burned redly in the grate and Gibson was heaving himself to his feet from behind a table laden with scones, cakes, butter and jam, tea and milk, and a comb of honey. There was also a strong smell of haddock.

"Oh, Gibson, we *are* disturbing you . . ."

"Not at all, not at all . . ." He put out his hand and I took it, and it felt dry and gnarled as old tree bark. Without his inevitable tweed hat he looked strange and unfamiliar, as vulnerable as a policeman without his helmet, his bald head protected by only a few wisps of white hair. And I realised that, of all my friends at Elvie, he was the only one who had truly aged. His eyes were pale and rimmed with white. He was thinner, more stooped, his voice had lost its manly depth.

"Aye, we haird you were on your way home." He turned as Sinclair followed us into the hot, crowded little room. "An' you, too, Sinclair."

"Hello, Gibson."

Mrs Gibson bustled in behind him, organising us all. "He's just having his tea, Sinclair, but you can just sit down for a wee while, Gibson willna' mind. Now, you sit here, Jane, near the fire where it's nice and warm . . ." I sat, so close to the heat I thought I would roast ". . . would you like a cup of tea?"

"Yes I'd love one."

"And a wee bit to eat." She made for the scullery, laying a hand on her husband's shoulder as she passed behind him, and pressing him back on to his chair. "Sit down, dearie, and finish your haddock, Jane won't mind . . ."

"Yes, please finish it."

But Gibson said that he had had enough, and Mrs Gibson whisked away his plate as though it were indecent, and went off to fill her kettle. Sinclair pulled a chair out from the other side of the table, and sat down, facing Gibson across the electro-plated cake stand. He took out his cigarettes and gave the old keeper one and took one for himself, and then leaned across to light it.

"How've you been?" he asked.

"Oh, no' so bad . . . it's been a braw, dry summer. I hear you were after the pigeons today – how did you get on?"

They talked, and listening to their conversation and seeing them thus, the young strong man, and the old one, it was hard to remember that once Gibson had been the only man the boy Sinclair really respected.

Mrs Gibson bustled back with two clean cups – her best, I realised – and set them on the table, and poured tea, and offered us scones, iced "fancies" and short-bread, all of which we tactfully refused. Then she settled herself down on the opposite side of the fireplace and we gossiped cosily, and once more I was asked for news of my father, and gave it, and then I asked after her sons, and was told that Hamish was in the army, but George had managed to get into Aberdeen University where he was reading Law.

I was very impressed. "But that's wonderful. I never knew he was as clever as that!"

"He was always a very hard-working boy . . . a great one for the books."

"So neither Hamish nor George will follow their father."

"Och, it's not the same for the young ones. They don't want to spend their lives on the hill in all weathers . . . it's too quiet for them. And mind, you can't blame them. It's no life for a young man these days, and while we managed to bring them up all right, there's not the money in it these days. Not when they can earn three times as much with a job in a city, or a factory, or an office."

"Does Gibson mind?"

"No." She looked at him fondly, but he was too involved with Sinclair to notice her glance. "No, he was always anxious that they should do what they wanted, and do well for themselves. He encouraged Geordie all the way . . . and mind," added Mrs Gibson, unconsciously quoting Barrie, "there's nothing like a good education."

"Haven't you got pictures of them? I'd love to see how they look."

She was delighted at being asked. "I have them by my bed. I'll go and fetch them . . ."

She bustled off, and I heard her footsteps, heavy-treaded, up the little staircase, and across the floor of the room above. Behind me, Gibson was saying, "Mind, there's nothing wrong with the old butts . . . when they were built, they were built to last . . . they're just a wee bit overgrown."

"And the birds?"

"Aye, there are ony number of birds. Mind, I got a couple of vixen and their cubs during the spring."

"What about cows?"

"I've kept them awa'. And the heather's great, it was well burnt at the beginning of the season . . ."

"You're not finding it too much for you?"

"Och, I'm fit enough yet."

"My grandmother said you had a week or two in bed last winter."

"That was just a touch of the flu. The doctor gave me a bottle and I was richt as rain . . . you don't need to listen to what the women say . . ."

Mrs Gibson, returning with the photographs, picked this up.

"What's that about women?"

"You're just a lot of auld hens," her husband told her. "Fussing over a wee bit flu . . ."

"Ach, it wisna' so wee . . . and whit a time I had to keep him in bed," she added for Sinclair's benefit. She handed the photographs over for me to study, and warmed to the subject. "And I'm not so sure it was just flu . . . I wanted him to have an X-ray, but he wouldn't hear of it."

"You should, Gibson."

"Ach, I havna' time to be going to Inverness for all that caper . . ." and, as if bored by the subject of his health and wishing to change the subject, he shifted his chair in my direction in order to peer over my shoulder at the photographs of his sons: Hamish, a solid-looking corporal in the Camerons, and George, formally posed in a photographer's salon. "Geordie's at the University, did Mrs Gibson tell you? In his third year now, and he'll end up a lawyer. Do you mind the time he helped you build yon tree house?"

"It's still standing, too. It hasn't blown down yet."

"Onything Geordie did, he always did well. He's a great lad."

We stayed to gossip a little longer, and then Sinclair pushed back his chair and said that it was time to go. The Gibsons came out to see us off, and the dogs, hearing voices again, started up their barking, so we all went over to the kennels to talk to them. There were two, both bitches, one gold and the other black. The one had a soft, creamy coat, and an endearing expression, with dark tip-tilted eyes.

I said, "She looks like Sophia Loren."

"Oh, aye," said Gibson. "She's bonnie. She's on season just now, so I'm taking her over to Braemar tomorrow. There's a man there with a good dog. I thought maybe we'd see if we could get a litter of pups."

Sinclair raised his eyebrows. "You're going tomorrow? What time?"

"I'll be leaving around the back end of nine."

"What's the weather forecast? What sort of a day is it going to be?"

"We should have a bit of a wind tonight, blow all this murk away. It's a good forecast for the week-end."

Sinclair turned to smile at me. "What do you say?"

I had been playing with the dog and scarcely listening to all this. "Uh?"

"Gibson's going to Braemar tomorrow morning. We could get a lift, walk back home through the Lairig Ghru . . ." He turned back to Gibson. "Could you get up to Rothiemurchus in the evening and meet us?"

"Oh aye, I could do that. About what time would that be?"

Sinclair considered. "About six? We should be in by

then." He looked at me again. "What do you say, Jane?"

I had never walked the Lairig Ghru. In the old days, every summer, it had been done by someone from Elvie, and I always longed to go, but was never included in the party because my legs were not considered sufficiently long. But now . . .

I looked up at the sky. The cloud of the morning had never cleared and was now turning, as the day died, to a fine mist. "Is it really going to be a good day?"

"Oh, aye, and verra warm."

Gibson's opinion was enough. "I'd like to do it. More than anything."

"Well that's settled. Nine o'clock at the house then?"

"I'll be there," promised Gibson, and we thanked them for the tea and left them, walking down the hill and across the wet road, and so to Elvie. The dank air hung with moisture and beneath the copper beeches it was very dark. I was suddenly depressed. I had wanted nothing to change . . . had wanted Elvie to be exactly as I remembered it, but seeing Gibson, so aged, had brought me up with a jolt. He had been ill, he said. One day he would die. And the thought of death, in that chill, in-between hour, made me shiver.

Sinclair said, "Cold?"

"I'm all right. It's been a long day."

"Are you sure you want to go tomorrow? It's a hell of a walk."

"Yes, of course." I yawned. "We'll have to get Mrs Lumley to give us a picnic."

We came out from under the beeches and the forbidding north aspect of the house reared before us, silhouetted against the lowering sky. A single light burned, shining yellow across the blue dusk. And I decided that before dinner I would have a hot bath, and then I would not feel cold and depressed any longer.

6

I was right. Lapped in silky Scottish water, I dozed. It was still early, so I found a hot-water bottle in the bathroom cupboard and filled it from the tap and went to bed for an hour, lying in the darkness with the curtains undrawn and listening to the endless honking and gabbling of the wild geese.

After this, I dressed again, and with a vague idea of making my first night home something of an occasion, took trouble to pile up my hair and to use every sort of artifice on my eyes. Then I took down my only formal garment, a gold-and-black caftan in heavy silk, all embroidered and frogged in gold, which my father had found in an obscure Chinese shop in a back street of San Francisco and had been unable to resist.

It made me look very regal. I fixed on my earrings, splashed some scent around and went downstairs. I was early, but I wanted to be early. As I lay in bed, I had made a small plan and wanted the place to myself.

My grandmother's drawing-room, made ready for the evening, had an impact as visually charming as a stage set. The velvet curtains had been closed against the darkness, the cushions plumped, magazines straightened, and the fire made up. The room was softly lit by a pair of lamps, and flamelight was reflected in brass fender and coal scuttle, and from lovingly polished wooden surfaces all over the room. There were flowers everywhere, and boxes filled with cigarettes, and the small table which did duty as a bar was neatly lined up with bottles and glasses, an ice-bucket and a small dish of nuts.

Over on the other side of the room, flanking the fireplace, was a highly decorated bombé cabinet, with glass-fronted bookshelves on top, and three deep, heavy drawers beneath. I went over to this, and pushing a small table out of the way, knelt to open the bottom drawer. One of the handles had broken and the drawer was very heavy, and I was struggling with it when I heard the door open again and someone came in. Feeling foiled, I swore to myself, but there wasn't time to get to my feet before a voice said, from just behind me, "Good evening."

It was David Stewart. I looked up over my shoulder, and found him standing over me, looking unexpectedly romantic in a dark blue dinner jacket.

I was too surprised to be polite. "I'd completely forgotten you were coming for dinner."

"I'm afraid I'm a little early. There didn't seem to be anyone around, so I let myself in. What are you doing? Looking for an earring, or playing bears?"

"Neither. I'm trying to get this drawer open."

"What for?"

"It used to be full of photograph albums. Judging from the weight, I should guess it still is."

"Let me have a go."

I moved obediently aside, and watched while he doubled up on his long legs, took hold of the two handles, and gently eased the drawer open.

"It looks so easy," I said, "when someone else does it."

"Are these what you are looking for?"

"That's right." There were three of them, old, bulging albums, weighing a ton.

"Did you intend indulging in a long, nostalgic session? With this lot it should take you the rest of the evening."

"No, of course not. But I want to find a picture of Sinclair's father . . . I thought perhaps there'd be a wedding group."

There was a small silence. Then, "Why this sudden desire to find a photograph of Aylwyn Bailey?"

"Well, it seems ridiculous, but I've never seen one. I mean, Grandmother never had any standing around. I don't think there's even one in her room . . . I don't remember it. It's funny, isn't it?"

"Not necessarily. Not when you know her."

I decided to take him into my confidence. "We were talking about him today. She said that he looked like Sinclair, and that he was very charming. She said that he only had to walk into a room for all the women to start falling about in heaps. I never paid him much heed when I was little . . . he was simply Sinclair's father-in-Canada. But . . . I don't know . . . I suddenly got all curious."

I lifted out the first book, and opened it, but it was dated only ten years ago, so I went down to the bottom of the drawer, and took out the last one. It was a handsome album, bound in leather, and all the photographs – faded now and inclined to be sepia coloured – had been entered with geometrical precision and labelled in white ink.

I leafed through the pages. Shooting parties and picnics, and groups, and studio portraits, complete with painted backdrops and potted palms. A girl in presentation feathers, and a black-stockinged child (my mother) dressed as a gipsy.

And then a wedding group. "This is it." My grandmother, stately in what looked like a velvet turban and a very long dress. My mother, smiling gaily as though determined to look as though she were enjoying herself. My father, young and slim, clean-shaven and wearing his suffering expression. Probably his collar was too tight. An unknown child being a bridesmaid, and finally, the bride and groom: Silvia and Aylwyn, their young faces round and curiously untouched by any sort of experience. Silvia with a little, painted, dark-red mouth and Aylwyn smiling in a private way at the camera, his tip-tilted eyes suggesting that the whole business was the most enchanting joke.

"Well?" said David at last.

"Grandmother was right . . . he's exactly like Sinclair . . . it's just that his hair's shorter and cut differently, and perhaps he's not quite so tall. And Silvia – " I didn't like Silvia " – Silvia left him after they'd only been married about a year. Did you know that?"

"Yes, I knew."

"That's why Sinclair was always at Elvie. What are you doing?"

He was feeling around in the back of the drawer. "Here are some more," he said, and brought out a pile of heavily mounted photographs which had been put away at the back and out of sight.

"What are they?" I laid down the book I had been holding.

He turned them over in his hand. "Yet another wedding. At a guess, I'd say your grandmother's."

Aylwyn was forgotten. "Oh, let me see."

We were back now into the years of the First World War, hobble skirts and enormous hats. The group was posed around on chairs, like Royalty; high collars and cut-away coats, and expressions on faces of enormous solemnity. My grandmother as a young bride was large-bosomed, and draped in lace, her new husband scarcely older than she was, with that same amused, merry expression which even his sombre clothes and considerable moustache could do nothing to quench.

I said, "Here, he looks fun."

"I think he probably was."

"And who's this? The old fellow in whiskers and a kilt?"

David looked over my shoulder. "Probably the bridegroom's father. Isn't he splendid?"

"Who was he?"

"I believe a great character – called himself Bailey of Cairneyhall – they were an old family around here, and legend has it that he used to give himself tremendous airs and graces, despite the fact that he didn't have a ha'penny to bless himself with."

"And my grandmother's father?"

"That impressive-looking gentleman, I imagine. Now, he was a very different kettle of fish. A stockbroker in Edinburgh. He made a lot of money and died a rich man. And your grandmother," he added in lawyer-like tones, "was his only child."

"You mean . . . she was an heiress."

"You could say that."

I looked at the picture again, the solemn, unfamiliar faces who were my ancestors, the people who had made me, with all my faults and my small talents, and had given me my face and my freckles, and my fair Nordic hair.

"I never even heard of Cairneyhall."

"You wouldn't. It became so derelict and ramshackle it eventually had to be pulled down."

"So my grandmother never lived there?"

"I think for a year or two she did, probably in the greatest possible discomfort. But when her husband died, she moved to this part of the world, bought Elvie, and brought her children up here."

"So . . ." I stopped. I realised that, without ever having thought very much about it, I had always taken it for granted that my grandmother was if not exactly "richly left", then certainly well provided for. But it seemed now that this was not so. Elvie, and everything in it, had come from her own inheritance, belonged solely to her. And it had no connection whatsoever with her marriage to Aylwyn's father.

David was watching me. "So?" he prompted gently.

"Nothing." I was embarrassed. The whole question of money makes me feel uncomfortable, a trait I have inherited from my father, and I hastily changed the subject. "How do you know so much about them all, anyway?"

"Because I look after the family affairs."

"I see."

He closed the photograph album. "Perhaps we'd better put them all away . . ."

"Yes, of course. And, David . . . I don't want Grandmother to know I've been asking all these questions."

"I won't say a word."

We put the books and the photographs back where we had found them, and closed the drawer. I moved the table back into its place, then went to take the guard from in front of the fire, and find a cigarette, and light it with a spill. As I straightened, I found David watching me. He said, out of the blue, "You're looking very beautiful. Scotland obviously agrees with you."

I said, "Thank you," which is what nicely raised American girls are taught to say when paid a compliment. (English girls say things like, "Oh, I don't, I look a mess", or "How can you say you like this dress? It's ghastly", which I am assured can be very off-putting.)

And then, because I felt suddenly shy and needed a diversion, I suggested that I should fix him a drink, and he said that in Scotland one didn't fix drinks, one poured them.

"Not martinis," I insisted. "You can't pour a martini until you've fixed it. It stands to reason."

"You have a point. Do you want a martini?"

I was doubtful. "Do you know how to make one?"

"I like to think so."

"My father says only two men in Britain can make a martini, and he's one of them."

"Then I must be the other." He went over to the

table and busied himself amongst the bottles and ice and twists of lemon peel. He said, "What have you been doing today?"

I told him, right up to the hot bath and the session on my bed, and then I said, "And tomorrow you couldn't guess what we've planned."

"No, I couldn't. Tell me."

"Sinclair and I are going to walk the Lairig Ghru."

He was gratifyingly impressed. "Are you *really*?"

"Yes, really. Gibson's going to drive us over to Braemar and then meet us at Rothiemurchus in the evening."

"What sort of day is it going to be?"

"Gibson says fine. He says all this murk's going to blow away and it'll be 'verra hot'." I watched him, liking his brown hands, and his dark neat head, and the wide shoulders beneath the soft blue velvet. I said, on an impulse, "You should come too . . ."

He came across the room, carrying the two pale golden, icy drinks. "I'd like to more than anything, but I'm busy all day tomorrow."

I took the glass and said, "Perhaps another time."

"Yes, perhaps."

We smiled, raised glasses, drank. The martini was delicious, cold and heady as fire. I said, "I'll write and tell my father I've met the other martini-fixer," and then I remembered something. "David, I simply have to get some clothes . . ."

He took the abrupt change of subject in his stride. "What sort of clothes?"

"Scottish clothes, sweaters and things. I've got that money my father gave me, but it's all in dollar bills. Do you think you could get them changed for me?"

"Yes, of course, but where do you intend doing your shopping? Caple Bridge isn't exactly the fashion centre of the north."

"I don't want anything fashionable, I just want something warm."

"In that case I suppose it would be all right. When do you want to do this shopping?"

"Saturday?"

"Can you drive your grandmother's car?"

"I can drive it, but I'm not allowed to. I haven't got a British licence . . . but it doesn't matter, I'll catch the bus . . ."

"All right. Then come to the office – I'll tell you how to find it – and I'll give you your money, and then when you've fixed yourself up with woollies, and if you haven't anything better to do, I'll give you lunch."

"Will you?" I had not expected this, and I was delighted. "Where?"

He scratched thoughtfully at the back of his neck. "There's not really much choice. Either the Crimond Arms, or my house, and my housekeeper doesn't come in on a Saturday."

I said, "I can cook. You buy something and I'll cook it. Anyway I'd like to see where you live."

"It's not very exciting."

But I found that I was mildly excited, all the same. I have always thought that you don't know a man until you have seen his home, his books, his pictures, the way he fixes his furniture. David, all that time in California, and while we were travelling home together, had been sweet and kind, but had shown me only the correct and businesslike side of his character. But now he had helped me find the photograph I wanted, and answered, with great patience, all my questions, and finally asked me out to lunch. I realised that there was a great deal more to him than I had first thought, and it was enormously gratifying to imagine that perhaps he felt the same way about me.

By the end of dinner I was overcome once more by fatigue, or jet lag or whatever you like to call it, and using my energetic day tomorrow as an excuse, I said good night to the others, and went to bed where I immediately fell sound asleep.

I awoke, some time later, to the sound of the wind that Gibson had promised us, nudging at the house, whistling under my door, whipping up the waters of the loch into small waves which broke and splashed against the shingle. And, above the sounds of the night, I heard voices.

I reached for my watch, saw that it was not yet midnight, and listened again. The voices became clearer and I realised then that they belonged to my grandmother and Sinclair, and that they were out on the lawn below my room, doubtless taking the dogs for a turn around the garden before locking the house up for the night.

". . . thought he'd aged a lot." That was Sinclair.

"Yes, but what can one do?"

"Pension him off. Get another man."

"But where would they go? It's not as though either of the boys were married, with a home to give them. Besides, he's been here for nearly fifty years . . . as long as I have. I couldn't get rid of him just because he's getting old. Anyway, he'd be dead in two months without a job of work to do."

I realised, uncomfortably, that they were talking about Gibson.

"But he's not able to do this particular job any longer."

"Now, what grounds have you got for saying that?"

"It's obvious. He's past it."

"As far as I'm concerned, he's still perfectly adequate. It's not as though he were expected to run a lot of highly-powered shoots. The syndicate is – "

Sinclair interrupted her. "That's another thing. It's utterly impractical letting off a superb moor like this to one or two local businessmen from Caple Bridge. What they pay you doesn't even begin to cover Gibson's keep."

"The one or two local businessmen, Sinclair, happen to be my friends."

"That's beside the point. As far as I can see, we seem to be running some sort of charitable institution."

There was a pause, and then, coldly, my grandmother corrected him. "I seem to be running some sort of charitable institution."

The iciness of her voice would have silenced me, but Sinclair seemed impervious to it, and I wondered how much of his courage was the Dutch variety, bolstered by post-prandial brandies.

"In that case," he said, "I suggest that you stop. Now. Pension Gibson off and sell the moor, or at least let it to a syndicate that is able to afford to pay a reasonable rent . . ."

"I have told you already . . ."

Their voices faded. They were walking away, still deeply in discussion; they went round the corner of the house, and I could hear them no longer. I found that I was lying rigid in my bed, miserable at having been forced to hear what was obviously not intended for my ears. The thought of them quarrelling made me sick, but worse was what they quarrelled about.

Gibson. I thought of him as he used to be, strong and tireless, and a mine of countryman's lore and wisdom. I remembered him, endlessly patient, teaching Sinclair to shoot and fish, answering questions, letting us tag along at his heels like a pair of puppies. And Mrs Gibson, who had spoiled and petted us, bought us sweets and fed us scones hot from her oven, dripping with the strong yellow butter that she churned herself.

It was impossible to reconcile the past with the present – the Gibson I remembered and the old man I had seen today. And harder still to realise that it was my cousin Sinclair who spoke so glibly of getting rid of Gibson, as if he were a smelly old dog, and the time had come at last to have him painlessly put down.

7

I awoke again, drawn from sleep by some subconscious alarm. I knew it was daylight. I stirred and opened my eyes, and a man was standing at the foot of my bed, watching me, cold-eyed. I let out a gasp of fright, and sat up with my heart pounding, but it was only Sinclair, come to wake me.

"It's eight o'clock," he said. "We have to leave at nine."

I sat rubbing the sleep out of my eyes, giving myself time to let the panic run out of my veins. "You gave me the most dreadful fright."

"Sorry, I didn't mean to . . . I was just going to wake you up . . ."

I looked up again, and this time saw no menace, simply the familiar figure of my cousin, arms crossed on the end of my bed, tip-tilted eyes dancing with amusement. He wore a faded kilt and a big ribbed pullover, with a scarf knotted at the neck. He looked clean and brushed, and smelt deliciously of the after-shave he had slapped on his face.

I scrambled into a kneeling position and hung out of the open window to inspect the day. It was perfect, bright, clean, cold, the sky cloudless. I said, in wonder, "Gibson was right."

"Of course he was right. He always is. Did you hear the wind in the night? And there's been a frost, soon all the trees will be turning."

The loch, blue with reflected sky, was flecked with small scuds of white foam, and the mountains opposite were no longer veiled in mist, but clear and sparkling, bruised with great sweeps of purple heather, and in the morning's crystal air, I could trace every rock and crack and corrie that led to their swelling summits.

It was impossible not to be elated by such a day. The uncertainties of the night had gone with the darkness. I had heard what was not intended for my ears. But in the clear light of morning, it seemed perfectly possible that I had been mistaken, had misunderstood. After all, I had not heard the beginning of the discussion, nor the end . . . and it was wrong to make any sort of a judgment when I was in possession of only half the facts.

Relief at having so easily shed my private worries made me suddenly enormously happy. I jumped off the bed, and went, in my nightdress, to find some clothes, and Sinclair, his mission successfully accomplished, went downstairs to start his breakfast.

We ate it in the kitchen, warm and snug by the Aga. Mrs Lumley had fried sausages and I ate four, and drank two enormous cups of coffee, and then I went and found an old rucksack, and we packed it with lunch: sandwiches and chocolate, apples and cheese.

"Do you want a Thermos?" Mrs Lumley wanted to know.

"No," said Sinclair, still filling himself with toast and marmalade. "Put in a couple of plastic mugs, though, and then we can drink out of the river."

There was the hooting of a car horn from outside, and presently Gibson emerged through the back door. He wore his sagging greenish tweeds, the knickerbockers enormous around his skinny calves. On his head was the old tweed hat.

"Are you ready?" he asked, obviously not expecting that we would be.

But we were. We gathered up waterproof anoraks and the rucksack of rations, bade goodbye to Mrs Lumley, and went out into that glorious morning. The air was icy inside my nose, cut deep into my lungs, made me feel as though I could jump over the house.

"But aren't we lucky?" I crowed. "It's the most perfect day."

And Gibson said, "It's all right," which, being a Scotsman, was the most enthusiastic comment he could muster.

We piled into the Land-Rover. There was room for the three of us in the front, but Gibson's dog looked nervous and in need of company, so I chose to sit in the back with her. To begin with, she whined and was restless and worried, but after a little became used to the lurching of the car and settled down to sleep, with her soft, velvety head across my shoe.

Gibson took the road to Braemar by way of Tomintoul, driving south over the mountains and running down into the gold and sunlit valley of the Dee at about eleven o'clock. The river was in spate, deep and clear as brown glass, winding through fields and farmland and great stands of tall Scots pine. We came to Braemar, and drove through it, and out the other side, and on for another three miles or so until we came to the bridge that crosses the river and leads the way to Mar Lodge.

There we stopped and all got out, the dog was given a little run, and Gibson went to fetch the key of the forestry gates. Then we all went into the bar, and Sinclair and Gibson had beer, and I was given a glass of cider.

"How much farther?" I wanted to know.

"Another four miles or so," Gibson told me. "But the road is verra rough, maybe you'd be better in the front with us."

So I abandoned the dog, and went and sat in the front between the two men, and the road was scarcely a road at all, simply a bulldozed track, deeply rutted, and used by the Forestry Commission. Every now and then we would pass a team of foresters, working with huge chain saws and tractors. We waved, and they waved back, and sometimes had to back their great lorries off the track so that we could pass. The air was filled with the piney smell of trees, and when at last we came to the little lodge, which is used for climbers and weekend expeditions, and got out of the Land-Rover, stiff and aching from the ride, there was the most immense quiet. The forests, the moor and the mountains were all about us, and only a distant trickle of water, and the soughing of the pines far above us, broke the silence.

"I'll meet you at Loch Morlich," said Gibson. "Do you think you can make it by six o'clock?"

"If we don't, wait for us. And if we're not in by dark, get a call through to the Mountain Rescue." Sinclair grinned. "We'll stay on the path, so it should be perfectly easy to find us."

"Don't go turning your ankle over," Gibson warned me. "And have a good day."

We said that we would. We watched him get back into the car, and turn and drive off the way we had come. The sound of his engine died away into the immensity of the morning. I looked up at the sky, and thought, not for the first time, that Scotland seems to have more than its fair ration of sky . . . it sweeps and soars and appears to reach to infinity. A pair of curlews flew over and in the distance I could hear the baa-ing of sheep. Sinclair smiled down at me. He said, "Shall we go?"

We walked, and Sinclair led the way, and I followed him up a path that ran alongside a burn set deep in rushes. We came to a solitary sheep farm, set about with wooden pens, and a dog came out to bark at us, and we passed the farm, and went on, and the dog retired to its kennel, and silence fell again. There were, every now and then, small patches of colour, harebells blowing, and huge purple thistles, and the dark stain of heather, humming with bees. The sun climbed up into the sky, and we peeled off our sweaters and tied them around our waists, and the path leaned upwards against the hill, and we climbed through trees and Sinclair, ahead of me, started to whistle under his breath. I remembered the tune: "Mairi's Wedding"; we had sung it as children, after tea in the drawing-room, with Grandmother playing the accompaniment on the piano.

Step we gaily, on we go,
Heel for heel and toe for toe,
Arm in arm and row on row
All for Mairi's wedding.

We came to a bridge and a waterfall, and the waterfall was not brown, but green, the colour of Chinese jade, plunging twenty feet or more into a cauldron of pale rock. We stood on the bridge and watched it, an arc of water bright as a jewel, translucent and shot with sunlight, curving down to the boiling pool, and ringed by a miniature rainbow. I had never seen anything so lovely. Over the roar of the water I said, "Why is it that colour? Why isn't it brown?" and Sinclair told me that it was because the water here dropped fresh from the limestone peaks, and so had not become stained with peat. And we stayed for a little, until he said that we had no time to waste, and must be on our way.

For encouragement, we sang again, each vying with the other at remembering words. We sang "The Road to the Isles", and "Westering Home", and "Come Along", which is the best marching song of all, and then our path began to climb, leading up and over the shoulder of a great mountain, and we stopped singing because we needed all our breath. The ground was thick with old heather roots and very boggy, and with every step dark mud oozed on either side of my shoes. My legs started to ache, and my back; I found that I was short of breath, and, although I would set myself the goal of this summit, and then the next, it seemed there was always another, waiting beyond. It was very disheartening.

And then, just as I was giving up hope of ever getting anywhere, there appeared, ahead of us, a black tooth of a mountain, jagged tip piercing the blue of the sky, and sheer face dropping a thousand feet or more to the foot of a narrow brown valley.

I stopped and pointed. "Sinclair, what's that?"

"The Devil's Peak." He had a map. We sat, and he opened it and flattened it against the wind and identified the surrounding peaks. Ben Vrottan and Cairn Toul, Ben Macdui, and the long ridge that led to Cairngorm.

"And this valley?"

"Glen Dee."

"And the little burn?"

"The little burn, as you call it, is the mighty Dee itself, in its early stages, of course." And indeed it was ludicrous to identify this modest stream with the majestic river we had seen earlier on in the morning.

We ate some chocolate and started off again, mercifully downhill, and now we had joined the long path that leads to the Lairig Ghru itself. It wound ahead of us, a scribble of white through the brown grass, climbing gently to a distant point on the horizon where the mountains and the sky seemed to meet. We walked, and the Devil's Peak towered ahead of us and over us, and then fell behind. We walked and were alone – really alone. There were no rabbits, no hares, no deer, no grouse. No eagles. Nothing broke the silence. No living creature stirred. There was only the sound of our own footsteps, and Sinclair's whistling.

Plenty herring, plenty meal,
Plenty peat to fill her creel
Plenty bonnie bairns as weel
That's the toast for Mairi.

Presently a house came into view, a stone bothy tucked into the foot of the hill on the opposite shore of the river.

"What's that?" I asked.

"It's a refuge hut, for climbers or walkers to use in bad weather."

"What sort of time are we making?"

"Good time."

After a little, "I'm hungry," I told him.

He grinned back at me over his shoulder.

"When we reach the hut," he promised, "we'll eat."

Later we lay supine, cushioned in blowing grass, Sinclair with his head pillowed on his sweater, me with my head pillowed on his stomach. I stared up at the empty blue sky and thought that to be with a cousin was a strange thing – at times we were as close as brother and sister, but at others there was an unease between us. I told myself that it was to do with no longer being children . . . with the fact that I found Sinclair enormously attractive, and yet this could not wholly explain an instinctive restraint, as though, somewhere in the back of my mind, a bell was warning danger.

A fly, a midge, some sort of a bug landed on my face, and I brushed it away. It landed again. I said, "Darn it."

"Darn what?" came, sleepily, from Sinclair.

"A fly."

"Where?"

"My nose."

His hand came down to brush away the fly. It rested against the curve of my jaw and stayed there, his fingers cupping my chin.

He said, "If we go to sleep we'll wake to find Gibson and the entire mountain rescue team come thundering through the pass to find us."

"We won't go to sleep."

"How can you be so sure?"

I did not reply, I could not speak about my inner tensions, the tightening of my stomach at the touch of his hand . . . the fact was that I did not know if this tightening was caused by sex or – fear? It seemed an extraordinary word to use in connection with Sinclair, but now the conversation that I had heard last night came surfacing up out of my subconscious, and I worried at it again, like a dog with an old and unsavoury bone. I told myself that I should have made a point of seeing my grandmother before coming out this morning. One look at her face, and I would have known the true lie of the land. But she had not appeared before we left, and if she was sleeping then I did not want to disturb her.

I shifted uncomfortably, and Sinclair said, "What's the matter? You're as tense as a string of wire. You must have a secret worry, some sort of a guilt complex."

"What would I have to be guilty about?"

"You tell me. Leaving Poppa perhaps?"

"Father? You must be joking."

"You mean you were quite happy, shaking the dust of Reef Point, California, off your pretty heels?"

"Not at all. But Father, at the moment, is more than well provided for, and not in the least worthy of a guilt complex."

"Then it must be something else." The ball of his thumb moved lightly over my cheek. "I know, it's the love-lorn lawyer."

"The *what*?" Now, my amazement was genuine.

"The lawyer. You know, old pawky-Rankeillour himself."

"Quoting Robert Louis Stevenson will get you nowhere . . . and I still don't know what you're talking about." But of course I did.

"David Stewart, my love. Do you know, he couldn't keep his eyes off you last night? He watched you all through dinner, with a lusty glint to his eye. I must say, you were a fairly toothsome spectacle. Where did you get that Eastern-looking outfit?"

"In San Francisco, and you're being ridiculous."

"Not ridiculous at all . . . honestly, it stuck out a mile. How do you fancy the idea of being an old man's darling?"

"Sinclair, he's not old."

"I suppose about thirty-five. But so dependable, my dear." His voice took on the honeyed tones of some desiccated dowager. "And such a nice boy."

"You're being bitchy."

"So I am." And, without any change of expression, he went on, "When are you going back to America?"

I was taken off-guard. "Why?"

"Just want to know."

"A month?"

"As soon as that? I'd hoped you'd stay. Abandon Father and put down your roots in your ain countree."

"I like my father too much to abandon him. And, anyway, what would I do?"

"Take a job?"

"You sound like Grandmother. And I couldn't take a job because I'm not qualified to do anything."

"You could be a secretary."

"No, I couldn't. Every time I try to type it always comes out red."

He said, "You could get married."

"I don't know anyone."

"You know me," said Sinclair.

His thumb, stroking my cheek, was suddenly still. After a little I sat up, and turned to look down at him. His eyes were bluer than the sky, but their clean gaze gave nothing away.

"What did you say?"

"I said 'you know me'." His hand moved, and took hold of my wrist, ringing it easily with his fingers.

"You can't be serious."

"Can't I? All right, then let's pretend I am. What would you say?"

"Well, in the first place, it would be practically incest."

"Rubbish."

"And why me?" I warmed to my subject. "You know perfectly well that you've always thought me as plain as a pikestaff, you were forever telling me so . . ."

"Not now. You're not plain now. You've turned into a gorgeous Viking . . ."

". . . and I haven't a single talent. I can't even arrange flowers."

"Why on earth should I want you to arrange flowers?"

"And anyway, I can't believe you haven't got strings of eager females, scattered all over the country, just pining away for love of you and dreaming of the day when you'll ask them to be Mrs Sinclair Bailey."

"Maybe so," said Sinclair with maddening complacency. "But I don't want them."

I considered the idea, and despite myself, found it intriguing.

"Where would we live?"

"In London of course."

"I don't want to live in London."

"You're mad. It's the only place to live. Everything happens there."

"I like the country."

"We'll go to the country at weekends – that's what I do anyway – go and stay with friends . . ."

"And do what?"

"Potter around. Sail, maybe. Go racing."

I pricked up my ears. "Racing?"

"Haven't you ever been to a race meeting? It's the most exciting thing on earth." He sat up, leaning back on his elbows, so that his eyes were on a level with mine. "Am I persuading you?"

I said, "There is a small consideration that you haven't mentioned yet."

"And what is that?"

"Love."

"Love?" He smiled. "But Janey, surely we love each other. We always have done."

"But that's different."

"How different?"

"I can't explain if you don't already know."

"Try."

I sat in a troubled silence. I knew that in a way he was right. I had always loved him. As a child he had been the most important person in my life. But I was not entirely sure about the man he had become. Anxious that he should not read all this in my face, I looked down and began to tug at the tough grass, pulling out tufts by the roots, and then letting them loose, to be blown away by the wind.

I said at last, "I suppose because we've both changed. You have become a different person. And I am, virtually, an American . . ."

"Oh Janey . . ."

"No, it's true. I've been brought up there, educated there . . . the fact that I have a British passport can't alter any of that. Or the way I feel about things."

"You're talking in circles. You know that, don't you?"

"Perhaps I am. But don't forget that this whole conversation is hypothetical anyway . . . we're arguing around an assumption . . ."

He took a deep breath as if to continue the argument and then seemed to change his mind and let it all out again on a laugh. "We could sit here all day, couldn't we, and 'tire the sun with talking'."

"Shouldn't we go?"

"Yes, we've another ten miles, at least, to cover. But we've come a long way, and for your information, that remark is meant to be ambiguous."

I smiled. He put his hand around my neck and pulled my face towards his and kissed my open, smiling mouth.

I had been half-expecting this, but still not prepared for my own panicky reaction. I had to make myself be still in his arms, wait for him to finish, and when at last he drew away, I stayed for a moment where I was, and then slowly began to gather in our rucksack the paper that had wrapped the sandwiches, the red plastic drinking mugs. All at once our solitude was frightening, and I saw the two of us, tiny as ants, the only living creatures in this vast and deserted landscape, and wondered if Sinclair had brought me today with the intention of starting his extraordinary discussion, or whether the idea of marrying was just a whim, blown up out of nothing by the wind.

I said, "Sinclair, we must go. We really must go."

His eyes were thoughtful. But he only smiled and said, "Yes," and stood up, took the rucksack from me, and turned to lead the way, on up the path towards the distant pass.

We were home by dark. The last few miles I had walked blindly, simply putting one foot in front of the other, not daring to stop, for if I had, I should never have got going again. When at last we came round the final curve of the track, and, through the trees, saw the bridge and the gate, and Gibson and the Land-Rover, waiting on the road beyond, I could scarcely believe we had actually made it. Aching in every muscle, I came up the last few yards, climbed the gate, and fell into the car, but when I tried to light a cigarette, I found that my hands were shaking.

We drove home through the blue dusk. To the east a tiny new moon, pale and fine as an eyelash, hung low in the sky. Our headlights probed the road ahead, a rabbit skittered for cover, the eyes of a roaming dog glittered like twin beads, and were gone. Across me the two men talked, but I slumped, silent in an exhaustion which was not entirely physical.

That night I was awakened by the ringing of the telephone. Its shrilling cut across my dreams and pulled me out of sleep like a hooked fish. I had no idea of the time, but, turning my head, saw that the moon hung over the loch, its reflection touching the black water with small brushstrokes of silver.

The ringing continued. Dazed, I stumbled out of bed, across my room, and out on to the dark landing. The telephone was downstairs, in the library, but there was an extension upstairs as well, along a passage that led to the old nurseries, and it was for this that I made.

Some time during my half-conscious progress the ringing must have stopped, but I was too sleepy to register this, so that when I reached the telephone and picked up the receiver, a voice was already speaking. A female voice, unknown to me, but pleasantly pitched, and attractive. ". . . of course I'm certain. I saw the doctor this afternoon and he says there's no doubt at all. Look, I think we should talk about this . . . I'd like to see you anyway, but I can't get away . . ."

Listening dopily, I supposed that the telephone lines had become crossed. The girl on the Caple Bridge exchange had made a mistake, or gone to sleep, or something. This call was not for us. I was about to speak, when a man's voice interrupted, and all at once I was wide awake, and clearly conscious.

"Is it really so urgent, Tessa? Can't it wait?"

Sinclair. On the other line.

"Of course it's urgent . . . we haven't any time to waste . . ." and then, less calmly, as though hysteria was not very far below the surface, "Sinclair, I'm having a baby . . ."

I put down the receiver gently, quietly. The instrument made a tiny click and the voices were extinguished.

I stood in the darkness, shivering, and then turned and made my way back to the landing and hung over the banister to listen. The stairs and the hall yawned below me, black as a well, but, from beyond the closed library door, came the unmistakable murmur of Sinclair's voice.

My feet were icy. Crawling with cold I made my way back to my room, and gently closed the door and got back into bed. Presently I heard the single ring of the telephone and knew that the call was finished, and soon after that, Sinclair came quietly upstairs. He went into his room, and there were soft sounds as he moved about, opened and shut drawers, then he came out again, and went down once more. The front door opened and closed, and moments after I heard the tiger hum of the Lotus as it drove off, down the lane, and on to the main road and away.

I found that I was trembling, as I had not done since I was a child, waking from a nightmare, and convinced there were ghosts hiding in my wardrobe.

8

Next morning, when I went downstairs, I found my grandmother already at the breakfast table. As I bent to kiss her, she said, "Sinclair's gone to London."

"How do you know?"

"He left a letter in the hall . . ." She sorted it out from the rest of her opened mail, and handed it to me. He had used the thick writing paper with *Elvie* engraved at its head, and his writing was strong and black and full of his personality.

> Terribly sorry, have to go south for a day or two. Should be home Monday night or Tuesday morning. Take care of yourselves while I'm away, and don't get into any sort of trouble.
>
> Much love
>
> Sinclair.

That was all. I laid down the letter, and my grandmother said, "The telephone rang last night at about half past midnight. Did you hear it?"

I went to pour coffee, thankful for a reason not to meet her eyes.

"Yes, I did."

"I was going to answer it, but I was fairly sure it would be for Sinclair, so I let it ring."

"Yes . . ." I brought the full cup back to the table. "Does . . . does he often do this?"

"Oh, every now and then." She sorted out some bills. It occurred to me that she seemed as anxious as I to keep herself occupied. "He leads such a full life, and then this job he has seems to make tremendous demands on his time . . . not like being in an office from nine till five."

"No, I suppose not." The coffee was hot and strong, and helped to loose the knot of tension at the back of my neck. Encouraged by this, I said, "Perhaps it's a girlfriend."

My grandmother shot me a sharp, blue glance. But she only said, "Yes, perhaps."

I leaned my elbows on the table, and tried to sound casual. "I should think he has about a hundred. He's still the best-looking thing on two legs I've ever seen. Does he ever bring them home? Have you ever met any of them . . . ?"

"Oh, sometimes when I've been in London . . . you know, he brings them for dinner, or we go to the theatre or something."

"Did you ever think he'd marry one of them?"

"You can never be sure, can you?" Her voice was cool, almost disinterested. "His life in London is so different from the one he leads when he comes up here. Elvie's sort of a rest-cure as far as Sinclair's concerned . . . he simply potters. I think he's quite glad to get away from late nights and expense-account lunches."

"So there wasn't ever anyone in particular? One you specially liked?"

My grandmother laid down her letters. "Yes, there was." She took off her spectacles, and sat, looking out of the window, across the garden to where the loch sparkled blue in the sunshine of another perfect autumn day. "He met her in Switzerland, skiing. I think they saw a lot of each other when she got back to London."

I said, "Skiing? Did you send me a photograph?"

"Did I? Oh, yes, it was New Year at Zermatt. That

was where they met. I think she was taking part in some championship or other, you know these international races they have . . ."

"She must be very good."

"Oh, she is. She's quite famous . . ."

"Did you ever meet her?"

"Yes, Sinclair brought her for lunch at the Connaught when I was in town during the summer. She was a charming girl."

I took a piece of toast and started to butter it. "What's she called?"

"Tessa Faraday . . . You've probably heard of her."

I had heard of her, but not in the way my grandmother meant. I looked at the toast I was buttering, and suddenly felt that if I ate it, I should be sick.

After breakfast, I went back upstairs, took up my double folder of family photographs, and drew out the one of Sinclair that my grandmother had sent to me, and that I had arranged in my montage, so that only Sinclair showed, and his companion was hidden.

But now, I was interested only in her. I saw a small, slim girl, dark-eyed, laughing, with hair caught back from her face by a ribbon, and thick gold rings in her ears. She wore a velvet trouser-suit, banded with some sort of embroidery, and she stood in the curve of Sinclair's arm, the two of them wound and tangled by yards of festive paper streamers. She looked gay and vital, very happy, and, remembering the careful voice on the telephone last night, I was suddenly frightened for her.

The fact that Sinclair had gone so promptly south – presumably to see her – should have reassured me, but somehow it did not. His departure had been too swift and businesslike, unencumbered by any personal consideration of either my grandmother or myself. Reluctantly I was reminded of his attitude towards Gibson, when he and my grandmother had discussed the old keeper's possible retirement, and I realised that, subconsciously, I had been making excuses for Sinclair.

But now it was different, and I was forced to be honest with myself. The word "ruthless" sprang to mind. Where ordinary people were concerned he could be entirely ruthless, and, torn as I was by anxiety for this unknown girl, I could only hope that he could also be compassionate.

From the hall my grandmother called me. "Jane!"

I hastily pushed the picture back in the frame, set it down on the dressing-table, and went back out on to the landing.

"Yes."

"What are you doing today?"

I went down to the half-landing and sat on the stairs, and talked to her from there. "I'm going shopping. I have to buy some sweaters, otherwise I'll die of cold."

"Where did you plan to go?"

"Caple Bridge."

"Darling, you can't buy anything in Caple Bridge."

"I'm sure I can buy a sweater . . ."

"I have to go to Inverness for a hospital board meeting . . . why don't I take you with me in the car?"

"Because David Stewart has some money for me. He changed the dollars Father gave me. And he said he'd give me lunch."

"Oh, how kind . . . but how will you get to Caple Bridge?"

"I'll jump on a bus. Mrs Lumley says there's one every hour at the end of the road."

"Well, if you're sure," but she still sounded doubtful. Standing there, with one hand on the newel post, she took off her glasses, and looked me over carefully from beneath her finely arched brows. "You look tired, Jane. Yesterday was really too much for you after all that travelling."

"No, it wasn't. I loved it."

"I should have made Sinclair wait a day or two . . ."

"But then we might have missed the lovely weather."

"Yes. Perhaps. But I noticed you didn't eat anything for breakfast."

"I never do. Honestly."

"Well, you must make sure David gives you a proper lunch . . ." She turned away and then thought of something else, and turned back. "Oh, and Jane . . . if you are shopping, why not let me stand you a new raincoat? You should have something really warm to wear."

Despite everything, I grinned. I loved it when she ran so true to form. I said wickedly, "But what's wrong with the one I've got?"

"If you must know, it makes you look like a tinker."

"In all the ten years I've been wearing it, I've never had that said to me before."

She sighed. "You get more like your father every day," she said, and without smiling at my feeble joke, went off to her desk and wrote me a cheque which would have bought me a fur-lined, floor-length, sable-hooded raincoat, if that was what I happened to be wanting.

I waited, in brilliant sunshine, at the end of the road for the bus that would take me to Caple Bridge. I could not remember a day so bright or fresh or full of colour. It had rained a little during the night, so that everything shone newly-washed, and the damp roads reflected back the blue of the sky. The hedges were full of scarlet hips, bracken was gold, and turning leaves every colour from deep crimson to butter yellow. The air, sweeping down from the north, was cold and sweet as iced wine, with a bite to it suggesting that already, much farther north, the first snow of the winter had already fallen.

The bus came around the corner, stopped for me and I got in. It was packed with country people, heading for

Caple Bridge for their weekly shopping session, and the only seat I could find was next to a fat woman with a basket on her knee. She wore a blue felt hat, and was so enormous there was only room for half of me on the seat, and every time the bus turned a corner, I was in deadly danger of being thrown off altogether.

It was five miles to Caple Bridge, and I knew the road as well as I knew Elvie itself. I had walked it, ridden on my bicycle, watched the landmarks fly by from the window of my grandmother's car. I knew the names of the people who lived in the wayside cottages . . . Mrs Dargie and Mrs Thomson, and Mrs Willie McCrae. And here was the house with the bad-tempered dog, and there the field where the flock of white goats grazed.

We came to the river, ran alongside it for half a mile or so and then the road swept into a deep S-bend in order to cross the river by means of a narrow humpbacked bridge. Up to now, nothing had apparently changed in all the years I had been away, but as the bus ground cautiously over the crest of the bridge I saw, ahead of us, a roadworks and traffic lights, and realised that considerable excavations were taking place in order to eliminate a dangerous curve.

There were signs and warnings everywhere. Hedges had been bulldozed away, leaving great scars of raw earth in their wake; men were working with picks and shovels, enormous earth removers growled away like prehistoric monsters, and over it all hung the clear and delicious smell of hot tar.

The lights were against us. We waited, engines running, and then the light went from red to green, and the bus rolled on, down the narrow track between the warning signals, and back on to the road. The woman next to me began to shift about, checking the contents of her basket, looking up at the luggage rack.

I said, "Do you want something?"

"Did I put my umbrella up there?"

I stood up and delved for the umbrella, and gave it to her, also a large cardboard box of eggs, and a bundle of shaggy asters, inexpertly wrapped in newspaper. By the time all this had been collected and delivered, we had reached our destination. The bus made a huge turn around the town hall, rolled into the market square and came to a final halt.

Because I had no baskets or encumbrances, I was one of the first out. My grandmother had told me the whereabouts of the lawyers' office, and from where I stood, I could see the square stone building she had described, directly opposite me, across the cobbled marketplace.

Waiting for the passing traffic, I crossed over and went in through the door, and read the indicator board in the hall and saw that Mr D. Stewart could be found in room No. 3 and that he was IN. I went up a dark staircase, nicely decorated in sludge green and mud brown, passed beneath a stained-glass window that let in no light at all, and finally knocked on a door.

He said, "Come in."

I went in and was delighted to find that his office, at least, was light, bright, and had a carpet. The window looked out over the busy market square, there was a jug of Michaelmas daisies on the marble mantelpiece, and somehow he had managed to create an ambience of cheerful business. He wore, I suppose because it was a Saturday, a sporty-looking checked shirt, and a tweed jacket, and when he looked up and smiled a welcome for me the doom-like weight that had lain in the pit of my stomach all morning was suddenly not so doom-like after all.

He stood up, and I said, "It's a gorgeous morning."

"Isn't it? Too good to be working."

"Do you always work on a Saturday?"

"Sometimes . . . depends how much there is to be done. You can get a surprising amount achieved when other people aren't ringing you up on the telephone all the time." He opened a drawer in his desk. "I changed the money for you at the current exchange rate . . . I made a note . . ."

"Don't bother about that."

"You should bother, Jane; your Scottish blood should make certain that I haven't diddled you out of a single bawbee."

"Well, if you have you can count it as personal commission." I held out my hand and he gave me a bundle of notes and some loose change. "Now you'll really be able to join the big spenders, though what you're going to find to spend it on in Caple Bridge is beyond me."

I stuffed the money in the pocket of my tinker's raincoat.

"That's what my grandmother said. She wanted to take me to Inverness, but I said I was having lunch with you."

"Do you like steaks?"

"I haven't had a steak since Father stood me dinner on my birthday. At Reef Point we lived on cold pizzas."

"How long will you be?"

"Half an hour . . ."

He looked astonished. "Is that all?"

"I loathe shopping at the best of times. Nothing ever fits, and when it does I always hate it . . . I shall come back wearing a lot of unsuitable clothes and probably in the worst of tempers."

"I shall say they're charming, and coax you back into a good mood, then." He glanced at his watch. "Half an hour . . . say, twelve? Here?"

"That's fine."

I went out again with a pocket full of money and searched for somewhere to spend it. There were butchers' shops, and grocers, and game merchants, and a gunsmith's and a garage. Eventually, between the inevitable Italian ice-cream parlour that exists in most small

Scottish towns, and the post office, I ran Isabel McKenzie Modes to earth. Or more accurately, Isabel MODES McKenzie. I went in, through a glassed door, modestly draped in net, and found myself in a small room lined with shelves of unhopeful-looking clothes. There was a glass counter filled with underclothes in peach and beige, and here and there were tastefully draped, sad, string-coloured pullovers.

My heart sank, but before I could escape, a curtain opened at the back of the shop and I was joined by a small, mouse-like woman, wearing a jersey suit two sizes too big for her, and a huge Cairngorm brooch.

"Good morning." I guessed that she had started life in Edinburgh and I wondered if she were Isabel Modes McKenzie in person, and if so, what had brought her to Caple Bridge. Perhaps she had been told that the garment trade was brisker here.

"Oh . . . good morning. I – I wanted a sweater."

As soon as I said the word I knew I had made my first mistake.

"We have some very nice *jairseys*. Did you want it in wool or bouclé?"

I said I wanted it in wool.

"And what size would it be?"

I said I supposed a sort of medium size.

She began to pull out shelves, and soon I was picking my way through sweaters in old rose, moss green and dead-leaf brown.

"H – haven't you any other colours?"

"What other colour did you have in mind?"

"Well, navy-blue?"

"Oh, there's very little navy being worn this year." I wondered where she got her information. Perhaps she had a hot line to Paris.

"Now, this is a charming shade . . ."

It was petrol blue, a colour that I am convinced goes with nothing and nobody.

"I really wanted something plainer . . . you know, warm and thick . . . perhaps a polo neck . . . ?"

"Oh no, we haven't any polo necks . . . polo necks aren't being . . ."

I broke in rudely, but I was getting desperate.

"It doesn't matter then, I'll leave the sweater . . . the jersey . . . Perhaps you've got some skirts?"

It started all over again. "Did you want it in tartan, or a tweed . . . ?"

"A tweed, I suppose . . ."

"And what is your waist measurement?"

Beginning to sound terse, I told her. There was more searching, this time through an unhopeful-looking rack. She brought out two, and laid them, with a grand gesture, before me. One was unspeakable. The other not quite so hideous, in a brown-and-white herringbone. Feebly I agreed to try it on, was squeezed into a space as small as a cupboard, closed in by yet another curtain and left to get on with it. With some difficulty I struggled out of the clothes I was wearing, and pulled on the skirt. The tweed prickled, and caught at my stockings as though it had been woven from thistles. I did up the waist hooks and the zip and looked at myself in the long mirror. The effect was startling. The tweed zig-zagged around me like an op-art picture, my hips had become elephantine, and the waistband dug into my meagre flesh like a wire-cutter.

Isabel Modes McKenzie coughed discreetly and whisked back the curtain, like a conjuror.

"Oh, you're lovely in that," she said. "You suit tweed."

"Don't you think it's . . . well, a little bit long?"

"Skirts are longer this season you know . . ."

"Yes, but this one nearly covers my knees . . ."

"Well, if you wanted, I could take it up a fraction . . . it's very good looking . . . there's nothing so good looking as a nice tweed . . ."

To get away, I might have bought it . . . but I took another look in the mirror, and was strong-minded.

"No. No, I'm afraid it really won't do . . . it's not what I wanted." I undid the zipper and tore it off before she could talk me into buying the dreadful thing, and she took it back, sadly, averting her eyes discreetly from my petticoat.

"Perhaps you'd like to try the tartan, the ancient colours are so soft . . ."

"No . . ." I pulled on my old, American drip-dry, un-warm skirt and it felt like a friend. "No, I think I'll leave it . . . it was just an idea . . . thank you so much."

I pulled on my raincoat, picked up my bag, and together, in sidling fashion, we made for the net-curtained door. She reached it first and opened it for me, reluctantly, as though letting a prized animal out of a trap.

"Perhaps if you were passing another day . . ."

"Yes . . . maybe . . ."

"I shall be getting my new stock next week."

Straight from Dior, no doubt. "Thank you . . . I am sorry . . . good morning."

Out and away, and into the blessed open air, I turned and walked off as fast as I could. I passed the gunsmith's, and then, on an inspiration, turned round and walked back and went in, and bought, in two minutes flat, a large navy-blue sweater originally intended for a young man. Relieved beyond words that my morning had not been a total failure, and clasping the sturdily wrapped parcel, I returned to David.

While he stacked papers and locked up filing cabinets, I sat on his desk and told him the saga of my disastrous shopping expedition. Spiced by his comments (he could do an Edinburgh accent to perfection) the story grew in its telling, and in the end I laughed so much that my ribs ached. We collected ourselves at last; David stuffed a pile of files into a bulging briefcase, gave a last look round, and then closed the door on his office and we went down the dingy stairs and out into the sunlit, crowded street.

He lived only a hundred yards or so from the centre of the little town, and we walked this short distance together. David's old briefcase slapped and banged against his long legs and every now and then we had to separate in order to avoid a parked perambulator or a pair of gossiping women. His house, when we came to it, was one of a row – identical, small, two-storey stone houses, each set in its own plot of ground, fronted by a modest garden, and with a gravel path leading from gate to front door. David's differed from his neighbours only in that he had added a garage, built into the space between his house and the next, with a concrete driveway connecting it to the street. And he had painted his front door a bright, sunny yellow.

He opened the gate and I followed him down the path and waited while he unlocked the door. He stood aside and waited for me to go in ahead of him. There was a narrow hallway with a staircase rising out of it, doors to right and left, and a kitchen visible through the open door at the back. It should have been very ordinary, and yet he – or somebody – had made it charming with close carpeting and leafy wallpaper, and groups of precisely arranged sporting prints.

He took my parcel and my raincoat from me, and dumped them, and his briefcase, on the chair in the hall, and then led me into a long sitting-room, with windows at either end. And it was only then that I appreciated the unique position of the unpretentious little house, for the windows to the south had been enlarged into a deep bay, and this looked out over a long narrow garden, sloping gently down towards the river.

The room itself was full of promise. Shelves of books, a stack of records, magazines on the low table in front of the fireplace. There were cushiony-looking armchairs and a little sofa, an old-fashioned cabinet filled with Meissen china, and over the mantelpiece . . . I went to look . . .

"A Ben Nicholson?" He nodded. "But not an original."

"Yes, it is. My mother gave it to me for my twenty-first."

"This reminds me of your mother's flat in London . . . it's got the same sort of feeling . . ."

"Probably because it was furnished more or less from the same house. And of course she helped me choose the curtains and the wallpaper and stuff."

Secretly glad that it was his mother, and no one else, I went over to the window. "Who would have thought you'd have a garden like this?" There was a little terrace, with a wooden table and chairs, and then a lawn, scattered now with fallen leaves, and flower-beds still filled with late roses, and clumps of purple Michaelmas daisies. There was a birdbath and an old, leaning apple tree. "Do you do the gardening yourself?"

"You could hardly call it gardening . . . as you can see, it's not very big."

"But having the river and everything . . ."

"That's what decided me when I bought the house. I tell all my friends that I have fishing on the Caple, and they're all enormously impressed. I don't tell them that it's only ten yards . . ."

There was a clutter of photographs and snapshots arranged on the top of the bookcase, and I was irresistibly drawn to them. "Is this your mother? And your father? And you?" About twelve years old with an engaging grin. "Is this you?"

"Yes, it is."

"You didn't wear glasses then."

"I didn't wear glasses till I was sixteen."

"What happened?"

"I had an accident. It was a paper chase, at school, and the boy in front of me let a branch of a tree snap back into my eye. It wasn't his fault, it could have happened to anyone. But I partly lost the sight of the eye, and I've worn glasses ever since."

"Oh, what bad luck!"

"Not really. I can do most things I want . . . except play tennis."

"Why can't you play tennis?"

"I don't quite know. But if I can see the ball I can't hit it, and if I can hit it, I can't see it. It doesn't make for much of a game."

We went through to the kitchen, which was as small as a galley in a yacht and so tidy that I felt ashamed at the memory of my own inadequacies. He peered into the oven where he had left some potatoes baking, and then found a frying-pan, and butter, and took a bloodstained parcel from the fridge and unfolded it to reveal a couple of inch-thick Aberdeen Angus steaks.

"Will you cook them, or shall I?" he asked.

"You cook them . . . I'll lay the table or something." I opened the door that led on to the terrace, baking in the unseasonable heat. "Can't we have lunch here? It's like being in the Mediterranean."

"If you want."

"It's blissful . . . shall we use this table?"

Talking, getting in his way, having to ask where everything was, I eventually got the table laid. While I did this, he had tossed a salad, unwrapped a crisp French loaf and taken small dishes of frosty cold butter from the refrigerator. With all this completed and the steaks gently sizzling in the pan, he poured two glasses of sherry and we went out to sit in the sunshine.

He shucked off his jacket, and leaned back, long legs stretched before him, and turned up his face to the heat.

"Tell me about yesterday," he said suddenly.

"Yesterday?"

"You walked the Lairig Ghru – " he cocked an eye at me " – or didn't you?"

"Oh. Yes, we did."

"What was it like?"

I tried to think what it had been like, and found I could remember nothing save the extraordinary discussion I had had with Sinclair after lunch.

"It was . . . all right. Marvellous, really."

"You don't sound very enthusiastic."

"Well, it was . . . marvellous." I couldn't think of any other word.

"But exhausting, perhaps."

"Yes. I was tired."

"How long did it take?"

Again, I could hardly remember. "Well, we were back by dark. Gibson met us at Loch Morlich . . ."

"Umm." He seemed to consider this. "And what's cousin Sinclair doing today?"

I stooped and picked up a piece of gravel and began to toss it, catching it on the back of my hand as though I were playing jacks. "He's gone to London."

"To London? I thought he was on leave."

"Yes, he is." I dropped the stone, bent to pick up another. "But he had a phone call last night . . . I don't know what about . . . we found a note when we came down for breakfast this morning."

"Did he drive?"

I remembered the tiger roar of the Lotus, splitting the still darkness. "Yes, he took the car." I dropped the second stone. "He'll be back in a day or so. Monday evening, perhaps, he said." I did not want to talk about Sinclair. I was afraid of David asking questions, and clumsily, tried to change the subject. "Do you really fish from the bottom of your garden? I shouldn't think there'd be room to cast . . . and you'd get all tied up in your apple tree . . ."

And so the conversation veered to fishing, and we talked about this, and I told him about the Clearwater river in Idaho where my father once took me for a holiday.

". . . it runs with salmon . . . you can practically lift them out with a bent pin . . ."

"You like America, don't you?"

"Yes. Yes, I do." He was silent, supine in the sunshine, and encouraged by his silence, I warmed to the subject, and the dilemma in which, inevitably, I found myself. "It's funny belonging to two countries, you never seem to quite fit into either. When I was in California I used to wish I were at Elvie. But now I'm at Elvie . . ."

"You wish you were back in California."

"Not exactly. But there are things I miss."

"Such as?"

"Well, specific things. My father, of course. And Rusty. And the sound of the Pacific, late at night, when the rollers come pouring up on to the beach."

"And what about the unspecific things?"

"That's more complicated." I tried to decide what I really missed. "Ice water. And the Bell Telephone Company. And San Francisco. And central heating. And the garden centres where you can go and buy plants and stuff and everything smells of orange blossom." I turned towards David, and found that he was watching me. Our eyes met, and he smiled. I said, "But there are good things over here too."

"Tell me about them."

"Post offices. You can buy anything in a country post office – even stamps. And the way the weather is never the same, two days running. It's so much more exciting.

And afternoon tea, with scones and biscuits and soggy gingerbread . . ."

"Are you reminding me in your subtle way that it's time to eat those steaks?"

"Not consciously I wasn't."

"Well, if we don't eat them now, they're not going to be eatable. Come along."

It was a perfect meal, eaten under perfect circumstances. He even opened a bottle of wine, rough and red, the exact complement to steaks and French bread, and we finished with cheese and biscuits and a bowl of fresh fruit, topped with a cluster of white grapes. I found that I was ravenous and ate enormously, wiping my plate clean with a thick white crust, and going on to peel an orange so juicy that it dripped from the ends of my fingers. When he had completely finished, David went inside to make coffee.

"Shall we have it outside?" he asked through the open door.

"Yes, let's, down by the river." I went in to join him, to run my sticky hands under a tap.

He said, "You'll find a rug in the chest in the hall. You take it down and settle yourself and I'll bring the coffee."

"What about the dishes?"

"Leave them . . . it's too good a day to waste slaving over a hot sink."

It was comfortably like the sort of remark my father would make. I went and found the rug, and took it back outside, and went down to the sloping lawn and spread the rug on the sunlit grass, only a few yards from the edge of the river. After the long dry summer, the Caple was running low, and there was a bank of pebbles, like a miniature beach, between the grass and the deep brown water.

The apple tree was loaded with fruit, windfalls lay at its feet. I went to shake it, and a few more tumbled to the grass, making soft plopping noises. Beneath the tree it was shady and cool and smelled pleasantly musty, like old lofts. I leaned against its trunk, and watched the sunlit river through a lace-work of branches. It was very peaceful.

Soothed by this, comforted by good food and easy company, I felt my spirits rise, and told myself briskly that this was a suitable moment to start being sensible about all my half-acknowledged fears. What was the point of letting them churn around at the back of my mind, nagging like a bad tooth, and giving me a perpetual stomach ache?

I would be realistic about Sinclair. There was no reason to suppose that he wouldn't accept responsibility for the baby that Tessa Faraday was going to have. When he returned to Elvie on Monday, he would probably tell us that he was going to be married, and Grandmother would be delighted (hadn't she thought the girl was charming?) and I would be delighted too, and need never say a word about the telephone call I had overheard.

And as for Gibson, he *was* getting old, there was no denying it, and perhaps it would be better for all concerned if he were to be retired. But if he did have to go, then Grandmother and Sinclair between them could surely find him a little cottage, perhaps with a garden, where he could grow vegetables, and have a few hens, and so keep himself happy and occupied.

And as for myself . . . This was not so easy to shrug off. I wished I knew why, yesterday, he had brought up the question of our getting married. Perhaps it had been simply an amusing idea to pass the half-hour after our picnic lunch. As such, I would have been prepared to accept it, but his kiss had been neither cousinly, nor light-hearted . . . just to remember it made me uncomfortable, and it was because of this that I felt so utterly confused. Perhaps he had done it deliberately, to upset me. He had always been a wicked tease. Perhaps he simply wanted to gauge my reactions . . .

"Jane."

"Um?" I turned and saw David Stewart watching me from the sunlight beyond the broken shadow of the tree. Behind him, I saw the coffee tray, set down by the rug, and I realised that he had spoken my name before, but that I had not heard. He dipped his head under the low branches and came to stand in front of me, putting up a hand to prop himself against the tree.

He said, "Is anything wrong?"

"Why do you ask that?"

"You look a little worried. You also look very pale."

"I'm always pale."

"And always worried?"

"I didn't say I was worried."

"Did . . . anything happen yesterday?"

"What do you mean?"

"Just that I noticed you weren't very anxious to talk about it."

"Nothing happened . . ." I wished I could walk off and leave him, but his arm was over my shoulder, and I couldn't get away without deliberately ducking beneath it. He turned his head to watch me from the corner of his eye, and beneath this familiar, disconcerting regard, I felt my face and neck grow warm.

"You once told me," he said pleasantly, "that when you lie, you blush. Something is wrong . . ."

"No, it isn't. And anyway, it's nothing . . ."

"If you wanted to tell me, you would, wouldn't you? Perhaps I could help."

I thought of the girl in London, and Gibson . . . and myself, and all my fears came flooding up again. "Nobody can help," I told him. "Nobody can do anything."

He left it at that. We went back into the sunlight, and I found that I was cold, my skin crawled with goose-flesh.

I sat on the warm rug and drank coffee, and David gave me a cigarette to keep the midges away. After a little, I lay down, my head on a cushion, my body spread to the sun. I was tired and the wine had made me drowsy. I closed my eyes, and the river noises took over, and presently I was asleep.

I awoke about an hour later. David lay a yard or so from me, propped on one elbow and reading the paper. I stretched and yawned, and he looked up, and I said, "This is the second time this has happened."

"What has happened?"

"I've woken, and found you there."

"I was going to wake you in a moment anyway. Wake you up and take you home."

"What time is it?"

"Half past three."

I eyed him drowsily. "Will you come back for tea at Elvie? Grandmother would love to see you."

"I would, but I have to go and see an old boy who lives out in the back of beyond. Every now and then he starts fretting about his will, and I have to go and reassure him."

"It's rather like Scottish weather, isn't it?"

"What do you mean by that?"

"One week you're in New York, doing goodness-knows-what. The next you're trailing up some remote glen to set an old man's mind at rest. Do you like being a country lawyer?"

"Yes, as a matter of fact, I do."

"You fit in so well. I mean . . . as though you'd been here all your life. And your house and everything . . . and the garden. It all goes together as though someone had matched you up."

"You match too," said David.

I longed for him to enlarge on this, and for a moment thought he was going to, but he seemed to change his mind, and instead got up, collected the coffee things and his paper and carried them back up to the house. When he returned I was still lying there, watching the river, and he stood over me, put his hands under my shoulders and pulled me to my feet. I turned and found myself in the circle of his arms, and I said, "I've done this before, too."

"Only then," said David, "your face was all swollen and blotched with crying, and today . . ."

"What about today . . ."

He laughed then. "Today you've collected about six dozen more freckles. And a lot of old apple leaves and grass in your hair."

He drove me home. The hood of his car was down, and my hair blew all over my face, and David found an old silk scarf in the cupboard on the dashboard and gave it to me, and I tied it over my head.

When we came to the roadworks, the lights were red, so we waited, the engine of the car idling, and watched the approaching traffic filing towards us down the single-line track.

"I can't help feeling," said David, "that instead of straightening out this bit of road, it would have been better to demolish the bridge and build a new one . . . or even to do something about that hellish corner on the other side."

"But the bridge is so pretty . . ."

"It's dangerous, Jane."

"But everyone knows about it, and takes it about one mile an hour."

"Not everyone knows about it," he corrected me drily. "In summer every other driver is a visitor."

The lights turned green and we moved forward, past a huge sign saying RAMP. A funny thought occurred to me. "David, you've broken the law."

"Why?"

"The notice said Ramp. And you didn't."

There was a long silence, and I thought, Oh, God,

which is what I think when I've said something funny and the other person doesn't think it is.

"I don't know how to," he said at last.

"You mean you've never been taught?"

"My mother was a poor widow. She couldn't afford lessons."

"But everyone ought to be able to ramp, it's one of the social graces."

"Well," said David, easing his car over the hump-backed bridge, "for your sake, I'll make a point of learning," and with that he put down his foot, and with the wind roaring about my ears, he drove me back to Elvie.

Later, I showed my grandmother my single purchase, the navy-blue sweater I had bought in the gunsmith's.

"I think," she said, "you were very clever to find anything at all in Caple Bridge. And it certainly looks very warm," she added kindly, eyeing the shapeless garment. "What will you wear it with?"

"Pants . . . anything. I really wanted a skirt, but I couldn't find anything."

"What sort of a skirt?"

"Something warm . . . perhaps next time you go to Inverness . . ."

"What about a kilt?" said my grandmother.

I had not thought of this. It seemed a splendid idea. Kilts are the cosiest things in the world, and the colours are always mouth-melting. "Where could I buy a kilt?"

"Oh, my dear, you don't need to buy one, the house is full of them. Sinclair's worn kilts since he could walk and not one has ever been thrown away."

I had forgotten the happy fact that a kilt, unlike a bicycle, is sexless. "But that's a marvellous idea! Why didn't we think of it before? I'll go and look right away. Where are they? In the attic?"

"Not at all. They're in Sinclair's room, in the cupboard on top of his wardrobe. I packed them all away in mothballs, but if you do want one, we can hang it out to air, and get rid of the smell, and it'll be as good as new."

Not wanting to waste a moment, I went in search of a kilt. Sinclair's room, for the moment vacant of its owner, had been cleaned and swept, and was immaculately tidy. I remembered this inherent neatness had always been strong in his character. As a boy he could not stand disorder, and never had to have his clothes folded, or his toys put away.

I took up a chair and went across to his cupboard. This had been built into the alcove at the side of the fireplace, and the space above the top of the wardrobe was put to use as extra cupboard space for suitcases and out-of-season clothes. I stood on the chair and opened the doors, and saw a neat stack of books, some motoring magazines, a squash racket, a pair of swimming flippers. There was a strong smell of camphor coming from a huge dress box, all laced up with string, and I reached up to lift this down. It was heavy and awkward, and as I struggled with it, my elbow caught the pile of books, and dislodged them. Encumbered as I was, there was nothing I could do to stop them falling, and I simply stood on the chair and listened to them crashing, in terrible disorder, to the floor.

I swore, took a firmer grip of my burden, lifted it down, laid it on the bed, and stooped to retrieve the books. They were mostly textbooks, a Thesaurus, *Le Petite Larousse*, a life of Michelangelo, and, at the bottom . . .

It was thick and heavy, bound in scarlet leather, the cover emblazoned with a private coat-of-arms, the title tooled in gold letters on the crimson spine, *A History of the Earth and Animated Nature*, Volumes I and II.

I knew that book. I was six years old again, and my father had brought it back to Elvie after one of his spasmodic forays into Mr McFee's second-hand bookshop in Caple Bridge. Mr McFee had died a long time ago, and the shop was now a tobacconist's, but in those days my father had spent many happy hours discoursing with Mr McFee, a cheerful eccentric with no tiresome prejudices about dirt or dust, and browsing through endless shelves of musty volumes.

He had found Goldsmith's *Animated Nature* by chance, and brought it home in triumph, for not only was it a rare volume, but it had been privately bound by some previous noble owner, and was, in itself, a thing of beauty. Delighted with it, wanting to share his pleasure, the first thing my father did was to bring it up to the nursery to show to Sinclair and myself. My reaction was probably disappointing. I stroked the pretty leather, looked at one or two pictures of Asian elephants, and then returned to my jigsaw puzzle.

But with Sinclair it was different. Sinclair loved everything about it, the old printing, the thick pages, the aquatints, the detail of the tiny drawings. He loved the smell, and the marbled endpapers, and the very weight of the big old book.

The addition of such a prize to my father's collection seemed to merit some sort of ceremony. Accordingly, he went off to fetch one of his own Ex Libris labels, a woodcut, with his initial wound about with much decorative plant life, and solemnly affixed it to the marbled endpaper of Goldsmith's *Animated Nature*. Sinclair and I watched this operation in total silence, and when it was done I heaved a sigh of satisfaction, because it had been accomplished so neatly, and because it proved, beyond any shadow of doubt, that the book now belonged to my father.

It was then taken downstairs and left on a table in the drawing-room, along with some magazines and daily newspapers, where it could be admired, and handled, and perused in passing. It was not spoken of again until two or three days later when my father realised that it had disappeared.

No one was particularly concerned, Goldsmith's *Animated Nature* had simply been moved. Someone had borrowed it, perhaps, forgotten to put it back. But no one had. My father began to ask questions, and drew nothing but blanks. My grandmother searched diligently, but the book did not come to light.

Sinclair and I were then involved. Had we seen the book? But of course we hadn't, and said so, and our innocence was never questioned. My mother started to say, "Perhaps a burglar . . ." but my grandmother pooh-poohed this. What burglar would turn a blind eye to the Georgian silver and make off with only an old book? She insisted that Goldsmith's *Animated Nature* was simply mislaid. It would turn up. Like any nine-day wonder the mysterious affair died a natural death, but the book was never found.

Until now. In Sinclair's cupboard, neatly filed away with some other possessions for which he did not have a regular use. And it was as beautiful as ever, the red leather smooth and soft to touch, the lettering bright and gold. Standing with it, heavy as lead in my hands, I remembered Father's Ex Libris, and I lifted the front cover of the book, and saw that the marble endpaper and the Ex Libris had been removed altogether, delicately and finely, close to the spine, probably with a razor blade. And on the white fly-leaf which lay below was written in Sinclair's firm, black, twelve-year-old writing:

Sinclair Bailey,
Elvie.
THIS IS HIS BOOK.

9

The beautiful, fine weather went on. On the Monday afternoon, my grandmother, armed with a spade and a pair of gardening gloves, went out to plant bulbs. I offered to help her, but she declined. If I was there, we would only talk, she said, and nothing would get done. She would be quicker on her own. Thus rejected, I whistled up the dogs and set off for a walk. I don't much like gardening anyway.

I went for miles and was out for two hours or more. By the time I returned, the brightness of the day was beginning to fade, and it was turning cold. A few clouds had appeared over the tops of the mountains, blown from the north, and a drift of mist lay over the loch. From the walled garden, where Will was stoking a bonfire, plumed a long feather of blue smoke, and the air was filled with the smell of burning rubbish. With my hands deep in my pockets, and my head full of thoughts of tea by the fire, I crossed the causeway and came up the road beneath the copper beeches. One of the dogs began to bark, and I looked up, and saw, parked in front of the house, the dark yellow Lotus Elan.

Sinclair was back. I looked at my watch. Five o'clock. He was early. I went on, across the grass, ankle-deep in fallen leaves, on to the gravel. As I passed the car, I trailed my hand across one glossy bumper, as if to reassure myself that it was really there. I went into the warm, peat-smelling hall, waited for the dogs, and then shut the door behind me.

I heard the murmur of voices from the drawing-room. The dogs went to drink from their bowl and then collapsed in front of the hall fire. I unbuckled the belt of my raincoat, and pulled it off, toed off my muddied shoes, smoothed my hair down with my hands. I crossed the hall and opened the door. I said, "Hello Sinclair."

They had been sitting on either side of the fire, with a low tea-table between them. But now Sinclair got up and came across the room to greet me.

"Janey . . . where have you been?" He kissed me.

"For a walk."

"It's nearly dark, we thought you'd got lost."

I looked up at him. I had thought that he would be noticeably different. Quieter; tired, perhaps, from his long drive. More thoughtful, weighed down with new responsibilities. But it was obvious that I had thought wrong. If anything, he looked happier, younger and more light-hearted than ever. There was a glitter to him that evening – a shine of excitement, like a child on Christmas Eve.

He took my hands. "And you're as cold as ice. Come on over by the fire and get warm. I've kindly left you one piece of toast, but I'm sure if you want some more Mrs Lumley will make it."

"No, that's fine." I pulled up a low leather stool and sat between them, and my grandmother poured my tea. "Where did you go?" she asked, and I told her. "Have the dogs had a drink? Were they wet and muddy? Did you dry them?" I assured her that they had, they weren't, and I hadn't needed to. "We didn't go anywhere wet, and I picked up all the heather off their coats before we got home." She handed me the cup and I folded my cold hands round it, and looked at Sinclair.

"How was London?"

"Hot and stuffy." He grinned, his eyes glinting with amusement. "Full of exhausted businessmen in winter suits."

"Did you . . . achieve what you went to do?"

"That sounds very pompous. Achieve. Where did you learn a long word like that?"

"Well, did you?"

"Yes, of course I did, I wouldn't be here otherwise."

"When – when did you leave London?"

"Early this morning . . . about six o'clock . . . Grandmother, is there any more tea in that pot?"

She lifted the teapot, took off the lid to look. "Not really. I'll go and make some more."

"Get Mrs Lumley . . ."

"No, her feet are hurting, I'll make it. I want to talk to her about dinner anyway, we'll need to put another pheasant in the casserole."

When she had gone, "Delicious, pheasant casserole," said Sinclair, and he took my wrist in his fingers, ringing it, like a bracelet, with his fingers. His touch was cool and light. He said, "I want to talk to you."

This was it. "What about?"

"Not here, I want you all to myself. I thought after tea we'd go out in the car. Up to the top of Bengairn and watch the moon rise. Will you come?"

If he wanted to tell me privately about Tessa, I supposed that the inside of the Lotus Elan was as good a place as any. I said, "All right."

Driving in the Lotus was, for me, a new experience. Lashed low into the seat by the band of my seat belt, I felt as if I was on my way to the moon, and the speed with which Sinclair took off did nothing to dispel this impression. We roared up the lane, paused for a moment at the main road, and then streamed out and on to it, the needle of the speedometer climbing to seventy in a matter of seconds, and fields and hedges and familiar landmarks flying up and falling away in dizzying succession.

I said, "Do you always drive so fast?"

"Darling, this isn't fast."

I left it at that. In no time it seemed, we were at the humpbacked bridge, slowed slightly, and then swept over it – leaving my stomach suspended somewhere two feet over my head – and poured down towards the roadworks. The lights were green, and Sinclair accelerated, so that we were through the obstruction and well beyond before they changed back to red.

We came to Caple Bridge and the thirty-mile limit. In deference to the local police constable, and much to my relief, he changed down, and idled the Lotus through the town at the regulation speed, but once the last house had dropped behind, we were off again. Now, there was no traffic. The road, smoothly cambered, curved ahead of us, and the car leapt forward, like a horse given its head.

We came to our turning, the small side road that led to the south, climbing in a succession of steep bends, up to and over the summit of Bengairn. Fields and the farmland dropped below us; with a roar of tyres we crossed the cattle grid, and were now on the moor, the blown grass patched with heather, and populated only by mildly interested flocks of black-faced sheep. The cold air, blown through the open window, smelled of peat, and there was mist ahead of us, but before we had driven into this, Sinclair turned the Lotus into a lay-by, and switched off the engine.

The view spread before us, the valley quiet beneath a sky of pale turquoise, more green than blue, and washed, in the east, with the pink of sunset. Far below, Elvie Loch lay still and bright as a jewel, and the Caple was a winding silver ribbon. It was very quiet; only the wind nudging at the car, and the cry of curlews.

Beside me, Sinclair undid his seat belt, and then, when I did not move to follow his example, leaned over to undo mine. I turned then, to look at him, and without saying anything, he took my face between his gloved hands and kissed me. After a little, I pushed him gently away. I said, "You wanted to talk to me, remember?"

He smiled, not in the least put out, and heaved himself around in order to reach a pocket. "I've got something for you . . ." He took out a small box and opened it, and it seemed that all the sky was reflected in the star-sparkle of diamonds.

I felt as though I was rolling, somersaulting, topsy-turvy down a long, steep bank. I came out of it reeling and stupid. When I could speak, I could only say, "But Sinclair, that's not for *me*."

"Of course it is. Here . . ." He took out the ring, tossed the little box casually on to the shelf on the dashboard, and before I could stop him had taken my left hand and thrust the ring deep on to my finger. I tried to pull away, but he held on to my hand, and closed it, clenched round the ring, so that the diamonds bit into my flesh and hurt.

"But it *can't* be for me . . ."

"Just for you. Only for you."

"Sinclair, we have to talk."

"That's why I brought you here."

"No, not about this. About Tessa Faraday."

If I had thought this would shock him, I was mistaken. "What do you know about Tessa Faraday?" He sounded indulgent, not in the least upset.

"I know that she's going to have a baby. Your baby."

"And how did you find that out?"

"Because the night she rang up, I heard the telephone and I went to answer it, on the upstairs extension. But you'd answered it already, and I heard her . . . telling you . . ."

"So it was you?" He sounded quite relieved as though some small dilemma had been solved. "I thought I heard the other line cut off. How very tactful of you not to listen to the end of the conversation."

"But what are you going to do about it?"

"Do? Nothing."

"But that girl is having your baby."

"Darling Janey, we don't know that it is my baby."

"But it *could* be yours."

"Oh, yes, it could be. But that doesn't mean that it is. And I am not taking the responsibility for another man's carelessness."

I thought of Tessa Faraday and the image I had built up of her. The gay and pretty girl, held, laughing, in the curve of Sinclair's arm. The successful, dedicated skier, with her own chosen world at her feet. The young woman, approved and admired, lunching at the Connaught with my grandmother. "Such a charming girl," my grandmother had said, and she was seldom mistaken about people. None of this had anything to do with the impression that Sinclair was trying to give me.

I said, carefully, "Did you tell her that?"

"In so many words, yes."

"What did she say?"

He shrugged slightly. "She said if that was how I felt, she would make other arrangements."

"And you left it at that?"

"Yes. We left it at that. Don't be too naive, Jane, she's been around, she's a sensible girl." All this time, he had not loosened his grip on my arm, but now he let it go, and I was able to unfold and stretch my cramped fingers, and he took hold of the ring between his forefinger and thumb, and turned it a little, to and fro, as though he were screwing it on. "Anyway," he said, "I told her that I was going to marry you."

"You told her *what*?"

"Oh, darling, do listen. I told her I was going to marry you . . ."

"But you had no right to do that . . . you haven't even asked me."

"Of course I've asked you. What did you think we were discussing the other day? What did you think I was doing?"

"Play-acting."

"Well – I wasn't. And, what's more, you know I wasn't."

"You're not in love with me."

"But I love you." He made it sound entirely reasonable. "And being with you, and having you back at Elvie, is the best thing that's ever happened to me. There's such a freshness about you, Janey. One moment you're as naive as a child, and the next, you come out with something so astonishingly wise. And you make me laugh; and I find you deliciously attractive. And you know me almost better than I know myself. Isn't all that better than simply being in love?"

I said, "But if you marry someone, it's for ever."

"Well?"

"You must have been in love with Tessa Faraday, and now you don't want anything more to do with her . . ."

"Janey, that was entirely different."

"How different? I don't see how it's so different."

"Tessa's attractive and gay and very easy to be with, and I enjoyed her company enormously . . . but for a lifetime . . . no."

"She's going to have that child for the rest of her life."

"I've already told you, it almost certainly isn't mine."

It was obvious that from that angle he considered himself invulnerable. I tried another tack. "Supposing, Sinclair, just supposing, that I didn't want to marry you. Like I said the other day, we're first cousins . . ."

"It's happened before . . ."

"We're too close . . . I wouldn't want to risk it."

"I love you," said Sinclair. It was the first time anyone had ever said that to me. I had often imagined it happening in secret teenage daydreams. But never like this.

"But . . . but I don't love you . . ."

He smiled. "You don't sound very sure."

"But I am. Quite sure."

"Not even enough to . . . help me?"

"Oh, Sinclair, you don't need help."

"But that's where you're wrong. I do. If you don't marry me, then my world will come crashing in little pieces around my ears."

It was a lover-like statement, and yet I did not believe it was said with love.

"You mean that literally, don't you?"

"How perceptive you can be, Janey. Yes, I do."

"Why?"

He was suddenly impatient, dropping my hand as though he were bored with it, turning for diversion to search for a cigarette. There were some in his coat pocket. He took one, and lit it from the lighter on the dashboard. "Oh, because," he said at last.

After a little, "Because?" I prompted him.

He took a deep breath. "Because I'm over my ears in debt. Because I have either to find the money to pay it, or the security to borrow, and I haven't got either. And if it all comes out, which it's in deadly danger of doing, then I have every certainty that my managing director will send for me and reluctantly inform me that he can do very nicely without my services, thank you."

"You mean, you'll lose your job?"

"Not only perceptive, but also quick on the uptake."

"But . . . how did you get into debt?"

"How do you think? Backing horses, playing blackjack . . ."

It sounded very harmless. "But how much for?"

He told me. I couldn't believe anyone could have so much money, let alone owe it. "You must be out of your mind. You mean, just playing cards . . ."

"Oh, for heaven's sake, Jane, you can lose that much in some gambling clubs in London in a single evening. And it's taken me the best part of two years."

It took me a moment or two to accept the fact that any man could be such a fool. I had always thought my father was completely unrealistic about money, but this . . .

"Couldn't Grandmother help you? Lend you the money?"

"She's helped me before . . . without obvious enthusiasm, I may add."

"You mean, this isn't the first time."

"No, it isn't the first time, and you can take off that shocked, pie-faced expression. Besides, our grandmother doesn't have that much money lying around. She belongs to a generation that believes in tying up her capital, and hers is all in trusts and investments and land."

Land. I said, casually, "How about selling some land, then? The . . . moor, for instance?"

Sinclair sent me a sideways glance, full of reluctant respect. "I'd already thought of that. I'd even lined up a group of Americans more than anxious to buy the moor, or if they couldn't do that, then to take it yearly at a substantial rent. To be honest, Janey, that's why I took this bit of leave, to come north and put the idea to her. But of course, she won't think of it . . . though what possible good it can be to her as it is, is more than I can imagine."

"It's rented out already . . ."

"For peanuts. The rent that little syndicate pays her scarcely covers the cost of Gibson's cartridges."

"And Gibson?"

"Oh, to hell with Gibson. He's past it anyway, it's time he was pensioned off."

We fell silent once more. Sinclair sat smoking, and I, beside him, tried frantically to sort out a confusion of thoughts. I found that what astonished me was not his soulless attitude – I had already suspected this – nor the fact that he had got himself into such a mess; but simply that he had been so frank with me. Either he had given up all idea of our getting married, and so had nothing to lose, or else his conceit of himself was without bounds.

I was beginning to be angry. I lose my temper slowly and seldom, but once I do I become quite incoherent. Knowing this, and anxious for it not to happen, I deliberately battened down my finer feelings, and concentrated on staying cool and practical.

"I don't really see why it should be my grandmother's decision any more than yours. After all, Elvie will belong to you one day. If you want to sell off great chunks of it now, I should think that that would be your concern."

"What makes you say that Elvie will belong to me?"

"Of course it will. You're her grandson. There isn't anyone else."

"You talk as though it were entailed, as though it had come down through generations, from father to son. But it isn't. It hasn't. It belongs to our grandmother, and if she chooses, she can leave it to a cats' home."

"But why not you?"

"Because, my darling, I am my father's son."

"And what is that meant to mean?"

"It means that I am a no-good, a ne'er-do-well, a black sheep. A true Bailey, if you like." I stared at him blankly, and suddenly he laughed and it was not a pleasant sound. "Didn't anyone ever tell you, little innocent Jane, about your Uncle Aylwyn? Didn't your father tell you?"

I shook my head.

"I was told when I was eighteen . . . as a sort of unwanted birthday present. You see, Aylwyn Bailey was not merely dishonest, but incompetent as well.

Five of those years he spent in Canada, he spent in jail. For fraud and embezzlement and God knows what else. Didn't it ever occur to you that the whole set-up was a little unnatural? No visits. Very few letters. And not a single photograph in the whole of the house?"

It was suddenly so obvious that I wondered why I had never realised the truth for myself. And I thought of the conversation I had had with my grandmother, only days ago, and the tiny glimpses she had let me have of her only son. *He chose to live in Canada, and finally to die there. Elvie never meant very much to Aylwyn . . . He looked like Sinclair. And he was very charming.*

I said, stupidly, "But why did he never come back?"

"I suppose he was a sort of remittance man . . . probably our grandmother imagined that I would be better off without his influence." He pressed the button that lowered his window, and tossed away the half-smoked cigarette. "But the way things turned out, I don't suppose it made any difference, one way or the other. I've simply inherited the family disease." He smiled at me. "And what can't be cured must be endured."

"You mean everyone else has to do the enduring."

"Oh, come, it's not easy for me either. You know, Janey, it's odd that you should bring that up – about Elvie eventually coming to me – because the other night, when we were discussing selling the moor and what to do about Gibson, that was my final ace, the one I'd kept tucked up my sleeve. 'Elvie will be mine one day. Sooner or later it will be mine. So why shouldn't I decide now what is to be done with it?'" He turned to me and smiled . . . his charming, disarming smile. "And do you know what our grandmother said?"

"No."

"She said, 'But Sinclair, that's where you are mistaken. Elvie means nothing to you except as a source of income. You've made a life for yourself in London and you would never want to live here. Elvie will go .o Jane.'"

And so this was how I came into it. This was the final piece of the jigsaw and now the picture was complete.

"So that's why you want to marry me. To get your hands on Elvie."

"It sounds a little bald put that way . . ."

"*Bald!*"

". . . but I suppose you could say that that was the rough idea. On top of all the other reasons I have already given you. Which are real and true and entirely sincere."

It was his use of those words which finally tipped my temper over the bounds of control, like a boulder sent rolling down a hill.

"Real and true and sincere. Sinclair, you don't even know the meaning of those words, and how you can use them, in the same breath . . . as telling me all this . . ."

"You mean about my father?"

"No, I don't mean about your father. I don't give a damn about your father and neither should you. And I don't give a damn about Elvie. I don't even want Elvie, and if Grandmother leaves it to me, I shall refuse it, burn it down, give it away, rather than let you get your greedy hands on it."

"That's not very charitable."

"I don't mean it to be charitable. You don't merit charity. You're obsessed by possessions, you always have been. You always had to *have* things . . . and if you didn't have them, you simply took them. Electric trains, and boats, and cricket bats and guns when you were small. And now fancy cars, and flats in London and money and money and more money. You'd never be satisfied. Even if I did everything you wanted me to, married you and handed Elvie over, lock, stock and barrel, that wouldn't be enough . . ."

"You're being unrealistic."

"I don't call it that. That's not what it's called. It's simply a question of getting your priorities right and knowing that people matter more than things."

"People?"

"Yes, people. You know, human beings, with feelings and emotions and all the things you seem to have forgotten about, if you ever knew they existed. People like our grandmother, and Gibson, and that girl Tessa, having your baby . . . and don't start telling me that it isn't your child, because I know, and what is more, you know damn well that it is. They've served their purpose and they're expendable, and so you simply push them overboard."

"Not you," said Sinclair. "I'm not pushing you. I'm taking you with me."

"Oh, no you're not." The ring was too tight. I dragged it off, bruising my knuckle, and just managed to resist throwing it in his face. I reached for the little jeweller's box, jammed the ring back into the velvet, snapped the box shut, and tossed it back on to the shelf. "You were right when you said we loved each other. We did, and I always thought you were the most wonderful person in the world. But you've turned out to be not only despicable, but stupid as well. You must be out of your mind to imagine that I would simply play along with you as though nothing had happened. You must think that I am the most terrible fool."

To my horror I heard my voice start to shake. I flung myself away from him, and sat trembling, longing to be out in the open, or in some enormous room where I could scream and throw things around and generally indulge in a fit of hysterics. But I wasn't. I was pinned into the tiny space of Sinclair's car, and there was scarcely room in it for our seething emotions, let alone us.

Beside me, I heard him sigh. He said, "Who would

have thought you'd return from America with such a set of lofty principles."

"It has nothing to do with America. It's just the way I am and the way I'll always be." I could feel my mouth go down, my eyes fill with tears. "And now I want to go home."

It wasn't any good. Despite my efforts, I started to cry in earnest. I searched for a handkerchief, but of course couldn't find one, and eventually had to accept Sinclair's which, silently, he handed me.

I wiped my eyes and blew my nose, and for some ridiculous reason this mundane action broke the tension between us. He took a couple of cigarettes from his pocket and lit them both and gave me one. Life went on. I noticed that while we talked the light had faded. The moon, not new any more, but still curved and delicate, was rising in the east, but its clarity was blurred by the mist which had dropped from the top of the mountain, and now enveloped us.

I blew my nose again. I said, "What will you do?"

"God knows."

"Perhaps if we spoke to David Stewart."

"No."

"Or my father. He may not be very practical, but he's very wise. We could call him . . ."

"No."

"But, Sinclair . . ."

"You were right," he said. "It's time to go home." He put out a hand to switch on the ignition. The engine purred into life, drowning all other sounds. "But we'll stop off for a drink in Caple Bridge on the way. I think we both need one – I certainly do, and it'll give your face time to recover before Grandmother sees it."

"What's wrong with my face?"

"It's all puffy and swollen. Just like when you had the measles. It makes you look like a little girl again."

10

The serious business of drinking in Scotland is, like going to funerals, a purely male prerogative. Females of any sort are not welcomed in the public bars, and if a man should make the mistake of taking his wife or girlfriend into a pub, he is expected to do his entertaining in some dim parlour, well out of sight and sound of the rest of his roistering cronies.

The Crimond Arms in Caple Bridge was no exception to this rule. We were shown that evening into a chill and unwelcoming room, papered in orange, furnished with cane chairs and tables, and decorated with flights of plaster ducks and the occasional vase of dusty plastic flowers. There was a gas fire, unlit, some large brewery ashtrays, and an upright piano which, on inspection, proved to be firmly locked. We were defied to enjoy ourselves.

Depressed and chilled by the room, by nameless fears for Sinclair, by everything that had happened, I sat alone, waiting for him. He came at last, bearing a small pale sherry for me, and a large dark whisky for himself. He said at once, "Why haven't you lit the fire?"

Thinking of the locked piano and the general air of disapproving unwelcome, I said, "I didn't think I'd be allowed to."

"You're ridiculous," said Sinclair, and took a match and knelt to light the gas fire. There was a small explosion, a strong smell, and a blaze of little flames, and a ray of heat impinged upon a minute area around my knees.

"Is that better?"

It wasn't, for my chill seeped from deep inside me, and couldn't be warmed away, but I said that it was. Satisfied, he sat himself in a little cane chair which stood across the fancy hearthrug, found a cigarette and lit it, and raised his whisky glass in my general direction.

"I looks towards you," he said.

It was an old joke, and as such, recognisable as a flag of truce. I was meant to say, "And I raises my glass," but I didn't because I was not sure if I could ever be friends with him again.

After that, he did not speak again. I finished my sherry, put down my empty glass, and seeing that he was only halfway through his, said that I would go and find a Ladies', with the idea of checking on my general appearance before facing up to my grandmother. Sinclair said that he would wait, so I went out and stumbled down a passage and up a flight of stairs and found the Ladies', which was no more welcoming or prepossessing than the dismal room downstairs. I looked in the mirror and was met by a dejected reflection, my face blotchy and swollen, and my mascara smudged. I washed my hands and face in cold water, and found a comb in my pocket and smoothed the tangles out of my hair, and all the time felt as though I were dressing a dead body, like those macabre stories about American morticians.

All this took some time, and when I went back downstairs again, I found the cheerless room empty, but heard, from behind the door which led into the bar proper, the sound of Sinclair's voice, talking to the barman, and guessed that he had grabbed the opportunity of buying himself the other half and drinking it under more congenial circumstances.

Not wanting to hang around, I went out to the car to wait for him. It had begun to rain, and the marketplace was wet and black as a lake, shimmering with the orange reflections of the street lights. I sat huddled and cold, lacking even the energy to find and light a cigarette, and presently I saw the door of the Crimond Arms open. Sinclair's silhouette showed black for a moment, and then the door fell shut, and he came across the wetness towards me.

He was carrying a newspaper.

He got into the Lotus, behind the wheel, slammed the door, and simply sat there, breathing. There was a smell of whisky, and I found myself wondering just how many whiskies he had found time to drink while I was upstairs washing my face. After a little, when he still made no move to start the car, I said, "Is anything wrong?"

He did not reply. He simply sat, looking down, his profile pale, his lashes lying dark and thick against the bones of his cheek.

I was suddenly concerned. "Sinclair."

He handed me the paper. I saw that it was the local evening news, which he had, presumably, picked up off the bar. By the light of the street lamps, I read the headlines which told of a bus accident; there was a photograph of a newly-elected town councillor, a column on some Thrumbo girl who had made good in New Zealand . . .

And then I found it, an inch of type, down in the bottom corner.

> DEATH OF WELL-KNOWN SKIER
> The body of Miss Tessa Faraday was found yesterday morning in her home at Crawley Court, London, S.W.1. Miss Faraday, who was 22, was the winner of the Ladies' Ski Championship held last winter . . .

The print danced and swam and was lost. I closed my eyes, as though to shut the horror away, but the darkness only made it worse and I knew that there could be no escape from the inside of my own head. *She said she would make other arrangements*, Sinclair had told me. *She's been around. She's a sensible girl.*

I said, stupidly, "But she's killed herself . . ."

I opened my eyes. He had not moved. I heard my own voice, saying, "Did you know what the other arrangements were going to be?"

He said, dully, "I thought she meant she'd get rid of it."

I was suddenly very wise. I knew. I said, "She wouldn't have been afraid of having the baby. She wasn't that sort of a girl. She killed herself because she knew you didn't love her any longer. You were going to marry someone else."

He suddenly rounded on me savagely in a storm of rage. "Shut up, and don't say anything about her, do you hear? Don't speak about her, talk about her, say one single, solitary word. You don't know anything about her, so don't pretend to. You don't understand, and you could never be expected to."

And with that, he switched on the ignition, let off the brake, and with a great swish of wet tyres on wet cobbles, swung the Lotus round, across the square, and in the direction of the street that led out into the country, and so to Elvie.

He was drunk, or frightened, or heartbroken, or shocked. Or perhaps all of these things. There was no thought now of rules or regulations or even simple native caution. Sinclair was escaping, hounded by a thousand devils, and speed was his only defence.

We roared through the narrow streets of the little town, and rocketed out into the dark country beyond. Reality became nothing but the road ahead, the white lines and cat's-eyes at its centre pouring headlong towards us so that they were all blurred into a single entity. I had never before been really physically frightened, but now I found my teeth were clenched until they ached, and my foot pressed down so hard upon an imaginary brake that I was in real danger of dislocating my spine. We came around the last corner, and the way lay clear to the roadworks. The light was green, and in order to get through before it changed colour, he gave the Lotus more power, and we surged forward, faster than ever. I found myself praying, *Let the light go red. Now. Please let the light go red.*

And then, with only fifty yards or so to go, the miracle happened, and the light did go red. Sinclair started to brake, and I knew in that moment what I should do. To the tearing of tyres the Lotus finally jarred to a stop, and, shaking all over, I opened the door on my side, and got out.

He said, "What are you doing?"

I stood in the rain and the darkness, caught like a moth in the beam of slowly approaching headlights, as the traffic from the other direction moved towards us.

"I'm frightened," I told him.

He said, quite kindly, "Get back in. You'll get wet."

"I'll walk."

"But it's four miles . . ."

"I want to walk."

"Janey . . ." He leaned across as though to pull me back into the car, but I stepped back out of his reach.

"Why?" he asked.

"I told you, I'm frightened. And the light's gone green again . . . you must go or you'll hold everybody up."

To add conviction to my words, a small van, drawn in behind Sinclair, blew its horn. It made a rude and impudent noise, the sort of noise which, in other times, and other places, would have made us laugh.

He said at last, "All right." He took hold of the door-handle to pull it shut, and then hesitated.

"You were right about one thing, Janey," he said.

"What was that?"

"That baby of Tessa's. It *was* mine."

I began to cry. Tears mingled with the rain on my face and I could do nothing to stop them, could think of nothing to say, no way of helping him. Then the door slammed shut between us, and the next moment he was gone, the car moving away from me through the obstructions and the flashing lights, faster and faster towards the bridge.

Like a nightmare, for no reason, I found that my head was full of music jangling like a barrel organ, and it was Sinclair's tune, and now that it was too late, I wished that I had gone with him.

Step we gaily, on we go,
Heel for heel and toe for toe,
Arm in arm and row on row . . .

He had reached the bridge now, and the Lotus took its soaring humpback like a steeplechaser. The tail-light disappeared over the edge of the curve and the next moment the still night was torn with the scream of brakes, of tyres skidding on wet tarmac. And then the crunch of shattered metal, a spatter of broken glass. I began to run, as useless as a person in a dream, stumbling and splashing through the puddles, surrounded by flashing lights and great red cat's-eyes spelling out DANGER, but before I had got within a hundred yards of the bridge, there came the soft thud of an explosion, and, before my eyes, the whole night flowered into the rosy glow of flamelight.

It was not until after Sinclair's funeral that I had the chance to talk to my grandmother. Before that, any sort of conversation had been impossible. We were both shocked and instinctively shied away from the mention of his name, as though even to talk about him would open the flood-gates of our carefully controlled grief.

To add to this, there was so much to do, so much to arrange and so many people to see. Especially so many people to see. Old friends, like the Gibsons, and Will the gardener, the minister, and Jamie Drysdale, the Thrumbo joiner, transformed by sober clothes and a suitable expression of pious gloom, into an undertaker. There were interviews with the police, and telephone calls from the press. There were flowers, and letters, dozens of letters. We started to reply to them, but finally gave up, leaving them to pile up on the brass tray in the hall.

My grandmother, belonging to a generation that is not afraid of the idea of death, and so is undistressed by its trappings, had insisted on a proper, old-fashioned funeral, and had come through it without visible tremor, even when Hamish Gibson, on leave from his regiment, played "The Flowers of the Forest" on his pipes. She had sung the hymns in church, stood, for half an hour or more, shaking hands; remembered to thank even those who had performed the most humble tasks.

But now she was tired. Mrs Lumley, exhausted with emotion and standing, had returned to her room to put up her swollen feet, so after I had lit the drawing-room fire, I settled my grandmother beside it, and went into the kitchen to make a cup of tea.

Standing against the warmth of the Aga, waiting for the kettle to boil, I stared absently out of the window at the grey world beyond. It was October now, the afternoon cold and quite motionless. Not a breath of wind stirred the last few remaining leaves from the trees. The loch, reflecting the grey sky, was still as a sheet of silver, the hills beyond bloomed softly, like plums. Tomorrow, perhaps, or the day after, they would be frosted with the first snows – it was cold enough for that – and we would be into winter.

The kettle boiled, so I made the tea, and carried it back to the drawing-room, and the chink of teacups and the crackle of the fire were comforting, as small things always are in the face of tragedy.

My grandmother was knitting a child's woollen hat in scarlet and white, destined, I knew, for the church Christmas bazaar. Thinking that she wanted to be quiet, I had set down my empty teacup, lit a cigarette and was reading the paper, half-lost in a review of a new play, when she suddenly spoke.

"I've been feeling very guilty, Jane. I should have told you about Aylwyn, that day when we were sitting out in the garden, and you started to ask me about him. I was on the verge of doing so, and then something made me change my mind. It was very stupid of me."

I had lowered the paper, and now folded it. Her needles clicked gently on, she had not looked up from her knitting.

I said, "Sinclair told me . . ."

"Did he? I thought perhaps he would. It mattered very much to Sinclair. It would be important to him that you should know. Were you very shocked?"

"Why should I be shocked?"

"For a number of reasons. Because he was dishonest. Because he went to prison. Because I tried to hide it from you all."

"It was probably better hidden. It would have done us no good to know. Nor him."

"I always thought perhaps your father would have told you."

"No."

"That was good of him . . . he knew how fond you were of Sinclair."

I put the newspaper down and lowered myself on to the hearthrug – a good place for confidences. "But why was Aylwyn *like* that? Why wasn't he like you?"

"He was a Bailey," said my grandmother simply. "And a feckless lot they've always been, but with all the charm in the world. Not a penny to bless themselves with, and less idea of earning money or holding on to it than the man in the moon."

"Was your husband like that?"

"Oh, yes." She smiled to herself as though remembering a long-ago joke. "Do you know the first thing that happened after we were married? My father paid off all his debts. But it didn't take him long to acquire some new ones."

"Did you love him?"

"Madly. But I very soon learned that I'd married an irresponsible boy without the slightest intention of reforming."

"But you were happy."

"He died so soon after we were married, I didn't have time to be anything else. But I realised then that I was on my own, and I decided that it would be better for my children if I made an entirely new start, away from the Baileys. So I bought Elvie, and I brought my children here. I thought everything would be different. But you know, environment doesn't entirely cancel out heredity, whatever child psychologists may say. I told you about Aylwyn. I watched him grow up, and turn into his father all over again, and there wasn't a thing I could do to stop him. He grew up and he went to London and he got a job, but in no time at all he was in a financial mess. I helped him, of course, over and over again, but the day inevitably came when I couldn't help. He'd manipulated some shares, or taken some sort of fraudulent action, and the head of his firm said, quite rightly, that it was a matter for the police. But in the end I persuaded him otherwise, and he agreed to say nothing, provided Aylwyn gave his word never to practise in the City of London again. So that's why he went to Canada. But of course, the whole business simply repeated itself, and that time poor Aylwyn wasn't so lucky. It would have been different, you know, Jane, if he'd married a sensible girl with her feet on the ground, and strength of character that would have kept Aylwyn's feet there, too. But Silvia was as feather-headed as he was, they were just a pair of children. Heaven knows why she decided to marry him in the first place, perhaps she thought he had money; one can hardly believe that she was in love, leaving Aylwyn and the baby the way she did."

"Why didn't Aylwyn ever come back from Canada?"

"Because of Sinclair. Sometimes, the image of a father can be better than . . . the father himself. Sinclair is . . ." she corrected herself, with scarcely a tremor to her voice, "Sinclair was another Bailey. It's astonishing how a single bad trait will go right down through generations of the same family."

"You mean, all that gambling and stuff."

"Sinclair did talk to you, didn't he?"

"A little."

"There was no need for it, you know. He had a good job and a good salary, but he simply couldn't resist the thrill. And the fact that we don't understand it should never make us unsympathetic, although I sometimes think it was all Sinclair lived for."

"But he loved coming to Elvie."

"Only now and again. He didn't feel about it as your mother did . . . or you. In fact –" she turned her needles and started in on another row " – I decided some time ago, that it would be a good idea if Elvie should belong to you one day. Would you welcome that?"

"I . . . I don't know . . ."

"That was the real reason I was so anxious for your father to let you come home, and bombarded him with letters which the wretch refused to answer. I wanted to talk to you about Elvie."

I said, "It's a wonderful idea, but I'm scared of owning things . . . I don't think I'd want to be tied down by all the responsibilities of a place like Elvie. And I wouldn't be free to get up and go the way I'd want to."

"That sounds very chicken-hearted, and also a little

like your father talking. If he'd been more realistic about possessions, he might have put down a few roots by now, and a good thing too. Don't you want roots, Jane? Don't you want to get married and have a family?"

I looked into the fire and thought of many things. Of Sinclair and my father . . . and David. And I thought of all the world I had seen, and the vast tracts of it which I hoped very much that one day I would see. And I thought of children at Elvie, my children, being brought up in this perfect place, and doing all the things that Sinclair and I had done . . .

I said at last, "I don't know what I want. And that's the truth."

"I didn't think you did. And today, when neither of us is in a frame of mind to be sensible about anything, is not the best time to discuss it. But you should think about it, Jane. Weigh up the pros and cons. There's all the time in the world to discuss it together."

A log broke, and fell into the smouldering embers of the fire. I got up to put on another, and while I was on my feet, stooped to pick up the tea tray, and carry it out to the kitchen, but as I reached the door, and stood, juggling with the tray and the door-handle, my grandmother spoke again.

"Jane."

"Yes."

Still holding the tray, I turned to face her. She had stopped knitting and now she took off her glasses, and I saw the blueness of her eyes, set deep in the pallor of her face. I had never seen her look so pale. I had never seen her look so old.

"Jane . . . do you remember, we were talking the other day, about Sinclair's friend, Tessa Faraday?"

My fingers closed over the handles of the tray and my knuckles showed white. I knew what was coming and prayed that it wouldn't.

"Yes."

"I saw in the paper that she had died. Something about an overdose of barbiturates. Did you see that?"

"Yes, I did."

"You never said anything."

"No, I know."

"Was it . . . had it anything to do with Sinclair?"

Across the room, our eyes met and held. I would have given my soul at that moment to be able, convincingly, to lie. But I was incompetent, and my grandmother knew me very well. I hadn't a hope in hell of getting away with it.

I said, "Yes, it had." And then, "She was going to have his baby."

My grandmother's eyes filled with tears, and it was the only time I ever saw her cry.

11

David came the next afternoon. My grandmother was writing letters, and I had retreated to the garden and was sweeping up leaves, having once been told that physical toil is the best form of therapy for mental distress. I had made a small pile, and was about to transfer it to a handy wheelbarrow, when the french windows opened, and David came out to join me. I straightened to watch him cross the grass, all tall lankiness and wind-ruffled hair, and wondered in that moment how we would have got through the last few days without him. He had done everything, seen to everything, arranged everything, even finding time to put through a person-to-person call to my father, and tell him personally of Sinclair's death. And I knew that, whatever happened to the two of us, I should never cease being grateful to him.

He took the last bit of the bank in a single stride and was at my side. "Jane, what are you going to do with that little handful of leaves?"

"Put them into the barrow," I said, and did. They fluttered around, and most of them blew out again.

He said, "If you can lay your hands on a couple of bits of wood, you'll speed the process up considerably. I've brought you a letter . . ."

He took it out of his capacious pocket and I saw that it was from my father.

"How did you get this?"

"It was enclosed in one he wrote to me. He asked me to give it to you."

We abandoned the wheelbarrow and the broom, went down the garden, jumping the ha-ha into the field, and so on to the old jetty, where we settled ourselves, in some danger, side by side on the rotting boards, and I opened the letter and read it aloud to David.

> My darling Jane,
>
> I was so very sorry to hear about Sinclair and your involvement in his death, but glad that you were able to be with your grandmother, and no doubt of the greatest possible comfort to her.
>
> I feel guilty – and have been, ever since you went away – that I let you return to Elvie without putting you in the picture as regards your Uncle Aylwyn. But somehow, with one thing and another and the dramatic fashion in which you departed, the opportunity never presented itself. I did, however, mention it to David Stewart, and he promised to keep an eye on you and the general situation . . .

I said, "But you never told me."

"It wasn't my business."

"But you knew."

"Of course I knew."

"And you knew about Sinclair as well?"

"I knew that he was getting through a hell of a lot of your grandmother's money."

"There's worse to come, David."

"What do you mean by that?"

"Sinclair died owing the most terrible amount."

"I was afraid that would happen. How did you know about this?"

"Because he told me. He told me lots of things." I went back to the letter.

> The reason that I was never over-anxious for you to return to Elvie was not so much what your Uncle had been, but what I was pretty sure your cousin Sinclair had become. After your mother died, your grandmother suggested that I should leave you with her, and indeed, this would have seemed to be the obvious answer. But there was the question of Sinclair. I knew how fond you were of him and how much he meant to you, and I was pretty sure that if you continued to see so much of him, the day would come when you would either have your heart broken, or your illusions shattered. Either process was bound to be painful, if not disastrous, and so instead, I kept you with me and brought you to America.

David interrupted. "I wonder what made him so sure about Sinclair."

I thought of the book, of Goldsmith's *Animated Nature*, and for a moment considered telling David the whole story. And then I decided against it. The book was no more. The day after Sinclair was killed, I retrieved it from his cupboard, took it downstairs and shovelled it into the boiler, where I watched it burn. Now, there was no trace left of it. Out of loyalty to Sinclair, it was best forgotten.

"I don't know . . . I suppose, instinct. He was always a very perceptive person, and impossible to fool." I went on reading:

> This was also the reason I was so tardy in replying to your grandmother's requests that you should return to Elvie. It would have been different if Sinclair were married, but I knew he wasn't and was devilled with apprehensions.

I expect you will want to stay at Elvie for a bit, but business here has been fairly brisk. Sam Carter is doing great stuff for me, so I am in the money as the saying goes, and could even afford to buy you a ticket back to sunny California whenever you say the word. I miss you very much, and so does Rusty. Mitzi the poodle is small compensation for your absence, though Linda is determined that when the time is ripe and the moon in the right quarter, Mitzi and Rusty will fall madly in love and get themselves a family, but it is my considered opinion that the issue of such a union simply does not bear thinking about.

Linda is well, adores Reef Point and what she calls the simple life, and has started, surprisingly, to paint. I don't know if my instincts are right or not, but I have a feeling that she may be very good. Who knows, she may yet be able to support me in the style to which I would like to be accustomed. Which is more than I could ever say for you.

My love, darling child,
from your father.

In silence I folded the letter, and put it back into its envelope, and so into the pocket of my coat. After a little, I said, slowly, "It sounds to me as though he's trying to talk her into marrying him. Or maybe she's trying to talk him into marrying her. I'm not sure which."

"Perhaps they're trying to talk each other. Would you like that to happen?"

"Yes, I think I would. Then I wouldn't feel responsible for him any longer. I'd be free."

The word had a disappointingly empty ring to it. It was very cold out on the jetty and suddenly I shivered, and David put an arm around me and drew me close into the warm circle of his arm, so that I was warmed by his warmth, my head supported by his solid tweed-clad shoulder.

"In that case," he said, "perhaps this is as good a time as any to start talking you into marrying a half-blind country lawyer who's adored you since the first moment he set eyes on you."

I said, "You wouldn't need to talk very hard."

His arm tightened and I felt his lips brush against the top of my head. "You wouldn't mind living in Scotland?"

"No. Provided you acquire yourself plenty of clients in New York, and California, and perhaps even farther afield, and promise faithfully to take me with you whenever you go to see them."

"That shouldn't be too difficult."

"And it would be nice if I could have a dog."

"Of course you shall . . . not another Rusty, of course, he has to be unique. But perhaps one with the same interesting ancestry and equal intelligence and charm."

I turned in his arms, and buried my face in his chest. I thought for a dreadful moment that I was going to cry, but that was ridiculous, people didn't cry when they were happy, only in books. I said, "I love you," and David held me very close, and I did cry after all, but it didn't matter.

We sat there, wrapped around in David's coat, making unrealistic plans, like being married in the Reef Point Mission, and having Isabel Modes McKenzie knit me a wedding dress – which inevitably dissolved into laughter. So we abandoned them and made others, and so preoccupied were we that we did not notice the light fade, and the evening air grow chill. We were finally disturbed by my grandmother, opening the window and calling out to tell us that tea was ready, so we stood up, cramped and cold, and started back to the house.

The garden was bloomed with dusk and thick with shadows. We had not spoken again of Sinclair but all at once I felt him everywhere, not the man, but the boy I remembered. He ran, soft-footed, across the grass, and from the shadows beneath the trees came the soft scuffle of fallen leaves. And I wondered if Elvie would ever be free of him, and this made me sad, for whatever happened, and whoever lived there, I did not want it to be a haunted place.

David, going ahead of me, had stopped to collect my broom and the wheelbarrow and stow them, out of harm's way, under the maple. Now, he waited, his tall figure silhouetted against the lights of the house.

"What is it, Jane?"

I told him. "Ghosts."

"There aren't any," he said, and I looked again, and saw that he was right. Only sky and water, and the wind stirring the leaves. No ghosts. I went on and he took my hand in his, and together we went in to tea.